MORE STORIES TO REMEMBER

VOLUME II

MORE STORIES TO REMEMBER

SELECTED BY

Thomas B. Costain and John Beecroft

ILLUSTRATIONS BY FREDERICK E. BANBERY

Doubleday & Company, Inc., Garden City, New York

BOOKS BY THOMAS B. COSTAIN

The Three Edwards: *The Pageant of England*
Below the Salt
Stories to Remember [*with John Beecroft*]
The Tontine
The Mississippi Bubble
The White and the Gold: *The French Regime in Canada*
The Silver Chalice
The Magnificent Century: *The Pageant of England*
Son of a Hundred Kings
The Conquerors: *The Pageant of England*
High Towers
The Moneyman
The Black Rose
Ride with Me
Joshua: A Biography [*with Rogers MacVeagh*]
For My Great Folly

BOOKS BY JOHN BEECROFT

Plain and Fancy Cats
The Gentleman from Indianapolis
Stories to Remember [*with Thomas B. Costain*]
A Treasury of Great Mysteries [*with Howard Haycraft*]
The Best Stories of W. Somerset Maugham
Kipling: *A Selection of His Stories and Poems*
Mr. Maugham Himself
The Modern Reader

44360

CONTENTS

VOLUME I

VOLUME II

MORE STORIES TO REMEMBER

VOLUME II

GOOD MORNING, MISS DOVE

FRANCES GRAY PATTON

LIBERTY HILL was a small freshwater town—not a hill, really, but just a modest rise in the land—where the streets were named for trees and heroes, and a sense of life's continuity ran in the air. It was like a hundred American towns, smug and cozy, and it put its special stamp upon its own. People born and raised there—high and low, rich and poor—were neighbors in an irrevocable way, because their imaginations had been nursed on the same sights and sounds and legends and early ordeals. They had played in the same sunny fields and cooled off after the heat of their games in the same shade. They had grown up hearing the same courthouse clock tell the hours and the quarters in a tone as timeless as time itself. They had all, for the space of a whole generation, been exposed at a tender and malleable age to the impartial justice, the adamantine regulations, and the gray, calm, neutral eyes of the same teacher—the terrible Miss Dove.

This community of experience was absorbed, of course, into the stream of consciousness. It was so settled, so accustomed, that it seemed a manifestation of natural law. Like the dew on the grass or the return of morning light (that recurrent miracle that passes for a commonplace) it excited no wonder. But if the light had failed to return, if the voice of the clock had fallen silent—even in the night when its sound was muffled by dreams—then people would have heard the silence and noticed the darkness. So when, without warning, the tenor of Miss Dove's existence was interrupted, and she was seen, at an hour when she should have graced the geography room at Cedar Grove School, being borne down the sidewalks in the direction of the hospital—then Liberty Hill caught its breath, and looked beneath the surface of its life and fastened its hand upon its heart.

The Wednesday upon which Miss Dove took sick began in an ordinary way. It was mid-April. The weather was mild. The sun rose at five-twenty-five, two minutes earlier than it had risen on Tuesday—which was precisely what Miss Dove had predicted the afternoon before when, shining a flashlight on a plaster-of-Paris globe, she had demonstrated to the sixth grade the reason for the lengthening of the vernal days. During the night a flock of robins had returned from their southern winter resort (Miss Dove had told the first grade this was the week for the robins) and now they were busy pulling innocent angle-worms from new-spaded garden plots, looking spruce and pompous and complacent—as if they knew they were expected and thought the worm-rich earth had been loosened expressly for their benefit. At seven, households stirred. Families, groggy from dreams, fought among themselves for the bathroom. Lost socks were hunted, ears were scrubbed, hair was combed, milk was spilt and the air was rent with squeals and remonstrances and the resumption of those domestic hostilities which, in general, keep personal identity alive. At seven minutes past eight—punctual as the sun and, unlike the sun, not varying with the seasons—Miss Dove descended the front steps of her house on Oakwood Street. At her gate she paused for a moment. She looked at three fat robins in her pansy border—not severely but strictly, as she might have looked at children to see how they were occupied; she observed, with a slight frown, a dandelion blooming out of place on her lawn; she lifted a critical gaze to the sky and, seeing that it was quite clean, gave a nod of approval. Then she opened her gate—it was an old gate made of wrought-iron in a Victorian pattern of hearts and ferns but it did not squeak because Miss Dove kept its hinges oiled—and began her morning walk to Cedar Grove Elementary School.

Jincey Baker saw her from an upstairs window. Jincey was eating breakfast in bed, not because she was ill or lazy but because she was going to have a baby any time now and she was young and beautiful and her husband liked to pamper her.

"There she goes, Tommy!" Jincey cried on that note of delight with which she often singularized the trivial or accustomed. "Right on the dot!" She patted her stomach. "I wish little Whosit—the slow-poke—would copy Miss Dove and develop a sense of time!"

Tommy (Dr. Thomas Baker, surgeon) laughed. "It would be a strain, though, to have a baby like the terrible Miss Dove. Imagine burping it!"

"Do you suppose *she* ever was a baby?" Jincey said.

"No," Thomas replied flatly. "She simply emerged from her house one day—fully formed like Venus on the half-shell."

"With her hat on?" said Jincey.

"Of course," said Thomas.

"And her mousey hair in a little bun behind?"

"I'm not sure," said Thomas. "You see, I have a unique distinction. I'm the only man in Liberty Hill who's ever seen the terrible Miss Dove with her hair down."

"Tommy!" Jincey clapped her hands. "You kept it from me!"

"Oh, I have my reticence," Thomas said darkly. "And that is a solemn memory."

"Tell me now," demanded Jincey.

"I'll save it for a long winter evening when we can't get a baby sitter," Thomas said. "I have to tear myself away now 'from your chaste nunnery'.

She has already passed which means I'm late for rounds. I'll be home for lunch unless some rash fool bursts an appendix."

"Stop at the Burnhams' and pick up the bathinet they're lending us," said Jincey.

"Sure. And if anything happens—if you have the slightest twinge—don't dally. The hospital's alerted for you." He bent and pressed his cheek against her soft, sweet-smelling red hair. "Don't worry, darling."

"I'm not worried," Jincey said. "Are you?"

"Of course not," Thomas said with more than necessary emphasis. He straightened up, squared his shoulders, and assumed a professional nonchalance. "It's a normal physiological process."

He ran downstairs whistling an optimistic tune from *Oklahoma* and thinking with remorse of all the prospective fathers he had privately jeered at. Those wan creatures with their stubble cheeks and dying-calf eyes, pacing the halls, needing a drink—they were his brothers now! "If she's all right— if the child's recognizably human—" he promised Something, "—I vow I'll—" But what bargain could he make? He was a young man of exemplary habits. He had no major vice—not even a grandiose sense of sin—to sacrifice in propitiation of the gods.

At nine minutes past eight Miss Dove crossed LaFayette Avenue. Old Mr. Porter, who had been her father's friend, saw her from his flag-stone terrace where he was taking his preprandial constitutional. He checked his watch by her. At eighty-two, Mr. Porter was an epicure of time. He relished it, unseasoned, for its own essential flavor.

A few minutes later, from the window of a dining room facing on Maple Street, Polly Burnham saw Miss Dove go by. "Finish your oatmeal, Davie-dear," she said to her nine-year-old son. "Miss Dove has passed. You don't want to be tardy."

"Oh, puke," said Davie-dear. "The oatmeal stinks!"

Polly flushed but held her peace. Her husband, the Reverend Alexander Burnham, was aware of a curious tingling sensation in the palm of his right hand and a nearly irrepressible longing to bring that palm down, wham, in a series of blows upon a plump portion of his son's anatomy. He rose. "If you'll excuse me," he said to his wife, "I must go over my notes for the vestry meeting." He scuttled off to his study, marveling at his self-restraint.

Both the elder Burnhams knew that in gently-nurtured children, rough language was a healthy sign—a sign of growth and toughening of the ego. They knew, furthermore, that David, because he resembled one of Raphael's cherubs and was a minister's son, had more need than most for toughness. Parents must bow to the wind and pretend not to notice. All the books said that.

At eight-twenty, Miss Dove crossed to the corner of Maple and Grant, where Cedar Grove School sat—redbrick, stolid, with only one cedar left to soften its ugliness, for its grove had been chopped down long before in the interests of level playgrounds. Bill Holloway, the traffic cop on duty, saw her. "She looked as natural as nature," he reported later in a tone of wonder. "I tipped my cap and said: 'Good morning, Miss Dove' and she says, genteel like always, 'Good morning, William.'"

By eight-thirty, some two hundred and fifty children, ranging in age from six to twelve, were safely inside the school building. In various home-rooms they gauged, with the uncanny shrewdness of innocence, the various moods of various teachers. How far dared they go today?

But as the morning progressed and the classes went, in turn, to spend forty-five minutes in the geography room with Miss Dove, they dropped their restless speculation.

For Miss Dove had no moods. Miss Dove was a certainty. She would be today what she had been yesterday and would be tomorrow. And so, within limits, would they. Single file they would enter her room. Each child would pause on the threshold as its mother and father had paused, more than likely, and would say—just as the policeman had said—in distinct, formal accents: "Good morning, Miss Dove." And Miss Dove would look directly at each of them, fixing her eyes directly upon theirs, and reply: "Good morning, Jessamine," or "Margaret," or "Samuel." (Never "Sam," never "Peggy," never "Jess." She eschewed familiarity as she wished others to eschew it.) They would go to their appointed desks. Miss Dove would ascend to hers. The lesson would begin.

There was no need to waste time in preliminary admonitions. Miss Dove's rules were as fixed as the signs of the zodiac. And they were known. Miss Dove rehearsed them at the beginning of each school year, stating them as calmly and dispassionately as if she were describing the atmospheric effects of the Gulf Stream. The penalties for infractions of the rules were also known. If a child introduced a foreign object—a pencil, let us say, or a wad of paper, or a lock of hair—into his mouth, he was required to wash out his mouth with the yellow laundry soap that lay on the drainboard of the sink in the corner by the sand table. If his posture was incorrect he had to go and sit for a while upon a stool without a back-rest. If a page in his notebook was untidy, he had to copy it over. If he emitted an uncovered cough, he was expected to rise immediately and fling open a window, no matter how cold the weather, so that a blast of fresh air could protect his fellows from the contamination of his germs. And if he felt obliged to disturb the class routine by leaving the room for a drink of water (Miss Dove loftily ignored any other necessity) he did so to an accompaniment of dead silence. Miss Dove would look at him—that was all—following his departure and greeting his return with her perfectly expressionless gaze and the whole class would sit idle and motionless, until he was back in the fold again. It was easier—even if one had eaten salt fish for breakfast—to remain and suffer.

Of course, there were flagrant offenses that were dealt with in private. Sometimes profanity sullied the air of the geography room. Sometimes, though rarely, open rebellion was displayed. In those instances, the delinquent was detained, minus the comfort of his comrades, in awful seclusion with Miss Dove. What happened between them was never fully known. (Did she threaten him with legal prosecution? Did she beat him with her long map-pointer?) The culprit, himself, was unlikely to be communicative on the subject or, if he were, to overdo the business with a tale that revolved to an incredible degree around his own heroism. Afterward, as was duly noted, his classroom attitude was subdued and chastened.

Miss Dove had no rule relating to prevarication. A child's word was taken at face value. If it happened to be false—well, that was the child's problem. A lie, unattacked and undistorted by defense, remained a lie and was apt to be recognized as such by its author.

Occasionally a group of progressive mothers would contemplate organized revolt. "She's been teaching too long," they would cry. "Her pedagogy hasn't changed since we were in Cedar Grove. She rules the children through fear!" They would turn to the boldest one among themselves. "*You* go," they would say. "You go talk to her!"

The bold one would go, but somehow she never did much talking. For there in the geography room, she would begin to feel—though she wore her handsomest tweeds and perhaps a gardenia for courage—that she was about ten years old and her petticoat was showing. Her throat would tickle. She would wonder desperately if she had a clean handkerchief in her bag. She would also feel thirsty. Without firing a shot in the cause of freedom she would retreat ingloriously from the field of battle.

And on that unassaulted field—in that room where no leeway was given to the personality, where a thing was black or white, right or wrong, polite or rude, simply because Miss Dove said it was, there was a curiously soothing quality. The children left it refreshed and restored, ready for fray or frolic. For within its walls they enjoyed what was allowed them nowhere else—a complete suspension of will.

On this particular Wednesday the first-graders, to whom Miss Dove gave a survey course in the flora and fauna of the Earth, drew pictures of robins. They drew them in crayon on eight-by-eleven sheets of manila paper. They did not draw them from memory. They copied the bird Miss Dove had drawn for them on the blackboard. (She knew exactly how a robin looked and saw no sense in permitting her pupils to rely upon their own random observations.) They left an inch-wide margin, measuring it with a ruler, around each picture. (Miss Dove believed in margins—except for error!) All the first grade's robins would look alike. Which was as it should be. Which was true of robins everywhere. Miss Dove was concerned with facts, not with artistic impressions.

She divided the second grade into activity groups. One group cut scenic photographs from old magazines and pasted them in a scrapbook. Another modeled clay caribou for the sand table. Still another drew a colored mural on the rear blackboard. The groups did not talk among themselves, asking questions and pooling advice. They had no need to. Miss Dove had told them what to do.

The third grade recited the states of the Union. It was Miss Dove's experience that the eight-year-old mind learned best by rote.

At a quarter past eleven the fourth grade filed in. This grade was studying

economic geography—the natural resources of different regions and their manifold uses in civilized life—and on Monday was to take a proficiency test prepared by the state Board of Education. Each year in April all grammar-grade students—students in the fourth, fifth and sixth grades—were so examined. Regarding these tests, Miss Dove's sentiments were mixed. She resented them as an intrusion upon her privacy and as an implication that her efficiency was open to question. But she recognized in them, grudgingly, a certain practice-value to the children.

For in every life—once, if not oftener—there was a proficiency test. A time came when one was put to the proof. One stood alone. He was what he was. He knew what he knew. He did what he could. And he had no source of strength outside himself. Certainly, such a time had come to Miss Dove.

And on a plane more human than sublime, Miss Dove's vanity had always been flattered by the results of the test. Cedar Grove led the state in geography.

"You may utilize this period for review, children," she said. "Open your books to page ninety-three. Memorize the agricultural products of the Argentine pampas."

At that moment Miss Dove was first aware of a pain in her back. The pain was small in area but it was acute. It thrust like a knife into her spine. It was so intense, so unfamiliar, and so unexpected that she hardly believed in it. It descended along her right thigh. Miss Dove counted ten. The pain was easier. It was gone. It had been only a threat.

Tension, she thought. Anxiety about the proficiency tests. She was displeased with herself. She despised women who had backaches. *I must tranquilize my mind,* she told herself. *I will think of the Alps. White. Clean. Lofty. Rising above Lake Lucerne. The lake is blue; it reflects the evening star.* So she concentrated her thoughts upon mountains and water that she had never seen. And after a while she was sure she had imagined that stab of agony in her spine.

She slipped a rubber band from a sheaf of fifth grade essay papers. She took a red pencil and began to correct them. But part of her mind stayed with the class that was present. She knew, for instance, when Vicky Evans, who was disposed to day-dreams, tired of her book and started gazing out the window. "Come back, Victoria," she said.

She heard when David Burnham sighed and muttered something exceedingly improper under his breath. "Hell and damn," David said.

"You will remain after class, David," Miss Dove said without glancing up from the fifth grade papers.

"Yes, Miss Dove," said David.

At noon an electric buzzer, operated from a switch in the principal's office, shrilled through Cedar Grove School. It was the signal for lunch and "big recess." In almost every room children slammed their books shut, shuffled their feet, sloshed their paint-water, and made a mass lunge toward food and freedom. Different teachers reacted according to their different temperaments. The art teacher, for instance, was a full-blown, husky girl who had been a college hockey star as well as an esthetics major. She made a flying leap and reached the door ahead of her class. "Clean your paint brushes!" she yelled. "Police up your desks!" Her thick, wiry hair stood out around her face and—so the enchanted children claimed—was heard to crackle. "It's nothing to me if you starve!" The music teacher began to play the piano. "Softly, softly!" she begged in her sweet, tinkly voice. "Trippingly on our toes! Let's all be elves and fairies!" The literature teacher was not sorry to be interrupted; she had been reading aloud from *Hiawatha,* a work she considered unworthy of her critical talents. She shrugged, not caring what the children did so long as they went away, and began a letter to her fiance who was pursuing his doctorate at Purdue. "Lover," she wrote, "I am sinking in an intellectual quagmire."

But in the geography room there was no disorder. Forty-three children sat quietly in their places. They did not look up. Their posture was superb. Their brows were puckered in thought as they read on of wheat and beef and leather. From this room they were not to be becked or called by mechanical noises. Here they acknowledged one sole authority which, in due time, would speak.

"Attention, please," said Miss Dove in the serene voice of one who expects to be obeyed.

Forty-three children folded their hands on their desks and raised limpid eyes to her face.

"Close your books, please," said Miss Dove.

Forty-three books were closed, not slammed, in the respectful manner due to books.

"The class will rise," said Miss Dove.

The class rose. So did its teacher. The pain returned. It nibbled at a vertebra like some small rodent with sharp, burrowing teeth. But it was bearable, as most things are in moments sustained by duty.

Miss Dove continued standing there on her raised platform as she did at the end of every class period. (To sit down would be to show weakness. And no teacher, Miss Dove was convinced, could afford to show weakness if she wished her pupils to show strength.) On the desk before her, like an orb and scepter, were her map-pointer and her globe. On the wall behind her, like a tapestry depicting far-flung dominions, hung the map of the world.

"The class is dismissed," said Miss Dove.

Forty-two children, one by one—without scrambling or pushing—filed out into the hall. David Burnham remained standing in the aisle.

For an instant Miss Dove was tempted to let David go with the others—to excuse him with a reprimand or, at least, to defer his punishment until the next day. If she could rest during the whole lunch hour, sitting perfectly still and even (though the notion was unorthodox) putting her head down upon her desk— But no. David's character was in her keeping.

Miss Dove understood, quite as well as David's parents did, the child's motivation. (She had taught other ministers' sons.) But unlike them she did not care whether David loved or hated her. She cared only that he conform to the rules.

She had pondered the new psychology which held that in the depths of human nature lay wild-animal instincts of greed, anger, idleness, and discourtesy. She could credit that theory. She had no rosy concept of human nature. But what did the theory prove? The thing that distinguished a man from a brute—a gentleman from a savage—was not instinct but performance.

David knew she had heard his naughty oath. He had meant her to hear it. In vulgar parlance, he had "asked for it" and he had a right to "get it."

Miss Dove looked at David. Her gaze was not contemptuous. Not impressed. She saw no hero in the aisle and no monster, either. She saw a nine-year-old boy who had gone a little further than he now wished he had.

And what did David see as he looked at Miss Dove? How did any of Miss Dove's pupils, past or present, see her? Offhand, that would seem an easy question. There was nothing elusive about Miss Dove's appearance and it had, moreover, remained much the same for more than thirty-five years. When she had begun to teach geography her figure had been spare and angular and it was still so. Her hair was more shadowy than it had once been but, twisted into a meagre little old-maid's-knot, it had never had a chance to show much color. Her thin, unpainted mouth bore no sign of those universal emotions—humor, for instance, and love, and uncertainty—that mark most mouths in the course of time. Her pale, bleached-out complexion never flushed with emotion—a slight pinkness at the tip of her pointed nose was the only visible indication that ordinary human blood ran through her veins. She wore round-toed black shoes with low, rubber-tapped heels that did not clatter when she walked. Her dress, of some dull-surfaced dark material, was close cousin to the one in which she had made her pedagogical debut: It had the same long sleeves, the same high neck, and the same white linen handkerchief (or one very like) fluted into a fan and pinned to its left bosom. (The handerchief was not for use—Miss Dove did not cough or sneeze in public—nor was it for ornament. It was a caution to its owner's pupils that it behooved each of them to possess a clean handkerchief, too.) All in all, in bearing and clothing and bony structure, Miss Dove suggested that classic portrait of the eternal teacher that small fry, generation after generation, draw upon fences and sidewalks with nubbins of purloined chalk; a grown-up stranger, catching his first glimpse of her, might be inclined to laugh with a kind of relief, as if he'd seen some old, haunting ogress of his childhood turned into a harmless joke. And then Miss Dove would look at him and all the comedy would ebb from his mind. Her large eyes were quite naked (for she had retained perfect vision) and gray like a flat, calm sea on a cloudy day. They were shrewd and unillusioned; and when one stood exposed to their scrutiny feeling uncomfortably that they penetrated veil upon veil of one's private life and perceived, without astonishment, many hidden—and often unlovely—truths in the deep recesses of one's nature, it was impossible to see anything about Miss Dove as ridiculous. Even the elevated position of her desk—a position deplored by modern educators who seek to introduce equality into the teacher-student relation—was right and proper. The dais of aloof authority suited her as a little hill near Ratisbon suited Napoleon Bonaparte.

But there was more to Miss Dove. There was something that defies analysis. She had an extra quality as compelling as personal charm (which she did *not* have and would have scorned to cultivate) that captured the imagination. She gave off a sort of effulgence of awe and terror. But the terror did not paralyze. It was terror that caused children to flex their moral muscles and to dream of enduring, without a whimper, prolonged ordeals of privation and fatigue. Sometimes, if their ideal of courage was high, it caused them even to dare Miss Dove's disapproval.

The little ones, the six-year-olds, whose geographical primer was entitled "At Home with Birds and Beasts," often pictured Miss Dove in the guise of some magnificent creature, furred or feathered. She was a huge black grizzly reared on its hind legs to block a mountain pass; she was a camel—bigger than other camels—leading a caravan across the desert; she was a Golden Eagle on a crag in Scotland. Later, when they had progressed to the intellectual sophistication of the fourth, the fifth, or the sixth and final grade of Cedar Grove School they were likely to cast her in the image of symbol. (One fanciful child had likened her to the Pharos watching little skiffs in the harbor of Alexandria.) But David Burnham was not fanciful; he was scared. Had he been pressed, at the moment, to describe Miss Dove, he would have said: "She looks like a teacher."

Miss Dove would have been gratified. A teacher was what she was and what she wished to be.

She had been under twenty when she had begun to teach—a reserved, hesitant girl whose deep romantic impulses had not yet caught fire. A girl who had felt calamity in one swift blow before she had felt more than a tentative "fluttering up toward joy." She had embraced her profession with the singleness of purpose that she might, under other circumstances, have bestowed upon matrimony, or foreign travel, or carving in stone.

Miss Dove's first youth had been a small-town American idyl. She was the eldest of three daughters in the first family of Liberty Hill. Her father, Alphonzo, was president of the bank—a witty, bookish man, more amiable than provident. Her mother was a fragile woman who smelled of violets and had the kind of gentle beauty that "trembles over children sleeping." Her two little sisters were like their mother. Miss Dove was like herself.

Though she was not so pretty as her mother and sisters, she was not entirely without a claim to vanity. Her figure was too spare for fashion, her expression too self-contained, but her carriage was superb and she had a cloud of soft, blowy hair, the color of sunshine sifting through pale brown leaves. She wore it gathered back, tied with a school-girl ribbon, long after she was old enough to pin it up. (Her father, whose special pet she was, had liked to see it hanging loose and in that innocent period of history a girl could cater to a parent's whim without the fear of being thought morbid.) She had, also, that innate appreciation of excellence which occurs, *sui generis*, in the morally elect.

The whole family admired her but it was her father who—having enjoyed the advantages of travel and being, in a dilettante way, a connoisseur of human nature—perceived most clearly the special quality of his daughter. It was a quality that should not be tampered with. It was like the delicate glaze that distinguishes fine porcelain from ordinary ware; like the bouquet of a vintage wine; like the star in the heart of a sapphire. Accordingly, he assumed responsibility for her early education. He taught her languages and the geography of the earth, ancient and modern. He introduced her to the genre of rare travel books which he collected at great expense. He read the poets with her—taking care to delete such passages as might offend her ear. He taught her to play chess and to dance and to ride (there was no girl in town who could sit a horse the way Miss Dove could), and he taught her to think well of herself. Above all, Mr. Dove delighted in expounding those sentiments of lofty principle and honor that he truly worshipped (though sometimes from afar!) and that his first-born child understood so well.

When she was eighteen she was sent off to school for a year of finishing. The school was a good one, built of gray stone turreted like a castle and set among spacious lawns overlooking a river. Once a week there was a party to which select young gentlemen were invited. At one of those functions, Miss Dove met a Princeton graduate student who was interested in archeology. He was taken with her and she, within ladylike bounds, with him. She allowed him to call upon her. They sat on a marble bench under a willow tree reading *The Last Days of Pompeii* and discoursing at intervals upon the glory of Greece and the grandeur of Rome.

In 1916, the summer she was nineteen, she "came out." She was presented to the simple, old-fashioned society of Liberty Hill in a simple, old-fashioned way. Her mother gave a tea to which the settled ladies of the town were invited. In a white dress—a charming dress of imported muslin and lace insertion—and with her hair still down, Miss Dove stood in the parlor and was introduced, in a new role, to her mother's friends. She was no longer a child with a child's privileges and limitations. She was a young lady, a social entity in her own right. She was the grownup daughter of the house.

No, she was not pretty. She was still far too thin. Her nose was too pointed. Her eyes were too large for her face. But she had a look of elegance. Her bones were small. Her features were carven. Her complexion, though it wanted brilliance, had transparency. Her floating hair, like autumn water, caught the light. And she had another look—a young girl's "threshold look" —that could pierce the heart. She was poised, motionless for a moment in time, waiting for a sign from Life. Any time now, a poet might have said (if indeed, there had been a poet in that parlor), some inner leaven might begin to work in Miss Dove, the miraculous bloom and sheen of a girl's full springtime might flow through and over her and she might become anything at all. Whatever she did become was certain to be remarkable.

That evening her mother retired early. Miss Dove sat on in the parlor with her father. He had just received from his London book-dealer an exceedingly fine edition of Marco Polo's *Travels*. He took it to a table under a lamp. Miss Dove went to the piano. She began to play a Viennese waltz that her father liked. The room was full of roses and through the open window came the honey-rich scent of leaves and new-cut grass. Life seemed to stretch ahead in a succession of summer days. It would bear her smoothly, decorously, like the music of the waltz, to further and further realms of felicity. To balls, to horse-shows, to foreign cities. To—love?

In the bosom of her dress she had stuck a letter from the young archeologist. In it he asked leave to visit her in Liberty Hill. "Perhaps," he wrote, "our friendship begun under such happy auspices, will ripen into something warmer."

And then something—a deepening quiet in the room behind her or the sound of a barely audible sigh—made her whirl around on the piano stool. Her father was slumped forward. His cheek rested upon his open book, on a page describing the great wall of China. One arm lay flung out on the table, palm up, as if in a gesture of apology. Without a cry of farewell he had embarked upon the most mysterious journey that the soul of man can undertake.

Miss Dove did not take to her bed with a bromide as her dainty mother did, or weep, like her little sisters, in the arms of every matronly caller. Her grief was a walking paralysis. Yet she could have borne that grief. She could have borne, as well, her unexpected poverty (Mr. Dove had left his family only an annuity from a small trust fund), but there was a worse thing to bear. He had not left them a good name. Mr. Alphonzo Dove had lifted money from the bank.

Mr. Porter, her father's successor at the bank, told Miss Dove that on the evening after the funeral. He was obliged to tell someone in the family. He chose the eldest daughter whose numb composure he mistook for phlegm.

Miss Dove was sitting with him in the parlor when he told her. The room, she thought, was unchanged in a cruel, callous way. There were still roses in the vases and a beeswax luster on the furniture. But there was no music in the air and drawn blinds held the fragrance of the garden at bay. And Miss Dove's dress was black.

"Your father," said Mr. Porter, phrasing the matter delicately, "borrowed money without first observing the conventional forms."

Miss Dove's world began to whirl round and round, spinning itself into a dark, narrowing funnel.

"He *stole?*" she said.

Mr. Porter was shocked by the brutal word. Was the girl a monster? "Your father was my friend," he said.

"How much did he steal?" asked Miss Dove.

"He *borrowed* four or five thousand," Mr. Porter said. "In driblets here and there. No more than he could have hoped to return."

"Oh," said Miss Dove. To a pampered girl who had never had a defined allowance, the sum was astronomical.

"I want to manage this discreetly," Mr. Porter told her. "But I'm responsible to our depositors."

Miss Dove said nothing.

"Of course," he said, "the banking business is Caesar's wife." His glance, casual but appraising, went over the parlor. It touched the books behind the thirteen octagonal panes of the old highboy. "A valuable library," he said. It skimmed the wide floor-boards that showed at the edge of the French rug. "A solid house," he said.

Miss Dove nodded. "A house built on sand," her heart whispered.

After Mr. Porter had gone she stood staring at the travel books. They seemed to mock her. It was for them that her father had ruined her life. She lay down, inert and hopeless, upon the horsehair sofa. She closed her eyes.

It was broad day when she opened them again. Slivers of sun slid between the closed slats of the blinds and were filtered through the Brussels lace curtains, and in Miss Dove's mind was the calm clarity of morning. A plan as clear and detailed as a well-drawn map unfolded before her. And that plan —that map of destiny—was illumined by a hard but happy truth. Nobody, not even her adored father, could ruin her life. Only she could do that. And she did not intend to.

She arose, bathed and dressed. Some impulse made her take her abundant hair in her two hands and twist it, so tightly that the skin was strained at her temples, into a knot. She walked downtown. When Mr. Porter arrived at his office he found her waiting for him. She looked so small and young in her mourning dress—so like a half-fledged blackbird—that she made his throat ache.

"Mr. Porter," she said, "I shall pay my father's debt." She looked directly at him, as if defying him to contradict her. "All I ask is time."

"My dear child—" said Mr. Porter. He took her gloved hand in his. Miss Dove withdrew it.

"We will keep the house and the books," she said. "I shall secure a teaching position."

"You would ornament any profession," Mr. Porter said. "But what are you prepared to teach?"

"I know a good deal about the world," she said.

Mr. Porter made a benevolent clucking noise with his teeth. "I can scarcely imagine a young lady who knows less," he said gallantly.

The young Miss Dove's nose pinkened at the tip. She did not enjoy being patronized. "About the *earth*," she said. "I have read my father's books. I shall teach geography."

The banker drummed his fingers. Though he was not a man who relished the prospect of turning widows and children into the cold, still he was far from rash with the stuff of commerce. But he saw something in the eyes of this redoubtable maiden that reassured him as to the safety of his money. "Suppose I make you a personal loan," he suggested. "I can reimburse the bank immediately, before there's any scandal. You can reimburse me at your leisure. Without interest."

"I am not asking favors," said Miss Dove.

"We can call this a favor to your father," he said. "He did more than one for me." For an instant he fancied he saw a bright film—a little dew of filial affection, perhaps—glaze the eyes of Miss Dove.

"Thank you," she said. "I accept your offer."

"Your father's only fault," Mr. Porter said with a catch in his voice, "was optimism. Remember that."

But some uncompromising accuracy within Miss Dove told her that she must recognize a fact for what it was. "He broke a rule," she said.

Mr. Porter escorted her to the door. He watched her thoughtfully as she walked away—back rigid, head high, glancing neither to the right nor the left. He went to the telephone and called the Superintendent of Schools.

The banker's recommendation did Miss Dove's project no harm, of course, and then the times were in her favor. Liberty Hill had long been affably incurious as to the world beyond its environs, but by 1916 the war in Europe had begun to trouble its composure. Vaguely, it felt that a vast portion of the earth that it had been wont to dismiss with the indifferent term "abroad" had become closer and more significant. It would be a splendid move—a modern, progressive move—thought the Superintendent of Schools, to secure a specialist in geography for the elementary grades. Besides, his wife was a third cousin to Mrs. Dove.

The rest of that summer, while generals mapped their strategies in France, Miss Dove mapped hers in her bed-chamber. To represent a classroom she laid her father's chessboard—an exquisite board of ebony inlaid with mother-of-pearl—on a table by the north window. The squares were desks. The ivory men were children. For hours on end, moving them about the board, speaking to them in unequivocal terms, she did what might be called "practice teaching." To the last detail she planned her procedure. The greeting to each class, as it entered the room ("Good morning, Pawn," she said in a low, uninflected voice. "Good morning, Castle. Good morning, Knight."), the ceremony of its dismissal, the rules and penalties and forms were all settled upon. The presentation of her subject matter was carefully considered. And just as carefully, she considered how to impart the new and terrible knowledge that had come to her—life was not easy. Life did not excuse mistakes. Life demanded all the disciplined courage and more, that one could bring to it.

So, as she talked to the little carven figures on the board, she introduced moral value into factual matter. By slight variations of tone, compressions of the lips, or nods of approval, she made it plain that to her certain forces of nature, beasts of the jungle, and formations of the land were more worthy than others. She was partial to the yak which was "a useful animal"; she admired the domestic habits of bears and the cleanliness of cat creatures. Of ostriches who kicked, wolves who howled, monkeys who swung by their tails and chattered incessantly, she spoke with asperity. (The camel she gave his due. "He is not a pretty beast, either in looks or disposition," she told her class, "but he can go many days without water.") She did not entirely approve of volcanoes: their action, she implied, was disruptive like the tantrum of a child. Rivers that overflowed their banks were rather silly. The grandeur of mountain ranges and the fertility of valleys she spoke of with respect. Her tone, when she described a plateau, was almost affectionate.

It was a game, of course—an absorbing game in which she forgot despair. But it was as serious as death—or life. It was the last game she ever played.

She had written the young archeologist that her bereavement would prevent her receiving him. If he had disregarded her letter—if he had come post-haste to Liberty Hill, stomped up the stairs to the bedroom, stormed the fortress, scattered the chessmen, clasped the young preceptress in his arms and loosened her bound hair—well, who knows? But he wrote Miss Dove a beautiful letter of condolence and kept his distance. He was not a Lochinvar.

In September Miss Dove exchanged her chessmen for pupils of flesh and blood. As she stood on the dais in the geography room, wearing her black mourning dress, her white handkerchief, and her small, tight, lustreless bun of hair, she looked very pale. But her pallor was that of purpose. She knew exactly how to proceed.

She kept her father's name clear of obloquy. She repaid Mr. Porter's loan, though that look twenty years. She saw that her sisters were suitably educated. She supplied her mother, through a long period of failing health, with every possible comfort and care and finally buried her with circumstance befitting a Dove of Liberty Hill.

In the accomplishment of these ends Miss Dove had denied herself much. She had ignored fashion. (Hair styles came and went—the spit curls, the overblown ear-puffs, the boyish bob, the page-boy, and the pony-tail. Flesh-colored georgette blouses were all the rage, knee-high skirts, empire waists, the New Look—she scarcely noticed them). She had dismissed her dreams of travel. She had renounced her youth. Persons of Mr. Porter's vintage who had seen her riding a blooded bay mare or standing in white beside her mother, winced at their recollections.

But Miss Dove did not wince. Fortitude—that quality of which her dear, weak father had spoken so often and so admiringly—sustained her and she discovered that responsibility was the native climate of her soul. She liked utilizing her strength to its utmost limits. She liked making and keeping rules. And just as a teacher with a genuine love for poetry will awaken that passion in her pupils, so Miss Dove imbued her charges with her philosophy. By her insistence upon even margins and correct posture and punctuality and industriousness, she told them, in effect, that though life was not easy, neither was it puzzling. You learned its unalterable laws. You respected them. You became equal to your task. Thus, you controlled your destiny.

Now, gazing at David Burnham she realized that she had gazed at him long enough. His mouth was beginning to tremble. She wished to rein his spirit, not to break it. With her map-pointer she gestured to the sink. "Very well, David," she said.

David went to the sink. He tore off a piece of paper towel, rubbed it on the bar of yellow soap, and scoured his mouth. He returned to the aisle.

"You may be seated," Miss Dove said. "Open your notebook to a blank page, please."

Miss Dove walked to the blackboard. Each step cost her an effort. It was as if her right leg had forgotten how to move of itself and had to be consciously directed. She took a stick of chalk and wrote a sentence on the board in her neat, round, legible hand. The chalk did not squeak. Chalk under Miss Dove's command never squeaked. She held it properly.

"Nothing is achieved by swearing," Miss Dove's sentence read. "Twenty times."

Twenty times was exactly right; when David had finished, the cafeteria would still be open. The supply of choice items on the menu—hot dogs and eskimo pies—would be exhausted, but he could nourish himself upon such less popular dishes as fish-loaf and tapioca pudding. It was Miss Dove's observation that whereas the punishment of a boy's palate had a salutary effect upon his behavior, the punishment of his stomach to the point of growling hunger often roused the brute in him.

She started back to her desk. She reached it just as pain gripped her in earnest. There was a crushing weight upon the lower part of her spine. A searing sensation flashed all the way down her right leg. A wave of giddiness swept over her.

She lowered herself into her chair. The pain lifted. But in its place was something more frightening than pain. In her leg, Miss Dove realized, there was no feeling at all. She pinched it to make sure. She tried to move it. It did not move.

For the first time since that evening in the shuttered parlor with Mr. Porter, panic seized her. She must do something. But what? She could send David for aid from other teachers but her heart sank as she imagined those women fluttering over her, exclaiming, witnessing the humiliation of her weakness. She wished, above all, to behave with circumspection and aplomb.

"David," she said. Her voice was hoarse.

David looked up from his penance. He saw Miss Dove's face pasty-white— with anger, he presumed. He saw her hand gripping the map-pointer. He gulped. "Yes, Miss Dove," he said.

"Is your father likely to be at home?" she asked.

This was worse, thought David, infinitely worse than anything he'd feared. She meant not to beat him herself but to have his father do it, in her presence! He wished devoutly that he'd been content with a namby-pamby "heck" or "darn." He said nothing.

"Your father. Does he come home for lunch?" said Miss Dove.

Wildly David considered replying that his father had gone to New York or was in bed with pneumonia. But habit was strong. *He told the truth.*

"Yes, Miss Dove. Daddy's home," he said.

"I am indisposed, David," said Miss Dove. "I— Will you go and tell your father? Ask him to call young Dr. Hurley."

David could scarcely believe his luck. "Do I need a permission slip from the office?" he asked.

"No," said Miss Dove. "My permission is sufficient. Mention this to no one. And, David—" her tone came close to pleading, "do not loiter. *Run!*"

David ran.

Miss Dove noticed, with objective surprise, that she was trembling. Then, as she had before in times of transient trouble, she turned her mind to her work, which was eternal in character. She felt steady.

She stared critically at the second grade's mural. It was a jaunty effort, covering half the blackboard. It showed an expanse of snow, a row of igloos, a man, a dog and a reindeer (all approximately equal in size) and, in the background, the northern lights spreading a fan of garish colors—purple, green, orange, and pink. Across the white field of snow—lest anyone entertain a doubt—was written in large red script: The Artic. Reginald Smith had written that; Miss Dove knew his sprawling hand. Tomorrow she would call his attention to his error in spelling and have him write the word divided into its syllables—"arc-tic"—three times in his notebook.

But suppose she were not here tomorrow? Suppose—the palms of her hands grew clammy—she were never here again. Rubbish! That was arrant nonsense. Except when the school itself had been closed because of blizzards or epidemics or a burst boiler, she had always been here. She was not entirely proof against the ills of the flesh, but she managed to suffer them at convenient times. Miss Dove had her colds during the Christmas holidays. She had summer complaint in the *summer*.

The pain had been mechanical, she decided. A kink in a muscle. A sudden movement of a joint held stiff too long. And the numbness? But why should numbness be alarming? Feet went to sleep and woke again. Soon young Dr. Hurley would arrive. He would prescribe a tonic and a heating-pad. He would warn her, in the coarse, jesting way that she would accept from nobody else, that the ideal of perfectionism was repugnant to God and man—that she ought to kick up her heels, raise merry hell, go on a three days' spree!

Dr. Hurley was seventy-two. It was to distinguish him from his doctor-father who had delivered her and had been dead now for a quarter-century that Miss Dove called him "young." In his actual youth he had been a radical —doubting the efficacy of the calomel purge and scoffing at the theory that the blood grew thick in winter—but, to the general astonishment, he had not killed his patients. And the years had mellowed him. Beneath his bluster he was, Miss Dove felt, a sound man. She trusted him.

"A penny for your thoughts, Miss Dove!"

Lorraine Ellwood, the music teacher, stood in the doorway. She was a wispy blonde of thirty-four who had begun to fade without knowing it in the crumply way of a hothouse rosebud. She wore bangs and an Alice-blue dress with a dirndl skirt that had come from a sub-deb shop. She was fond of saying that she felt like a big sister to her pupils and although her devotion to them was sincere—Miss Dove granted her that—she could not control them because she lived on their level. She had, Miss Dove thought, more soul than sense.

"Mona Leckford's engagement is out of the bag," she chirped. "We're cutting a cake in her honor in the rest-room. Won't you join us?"

Miss Dove indicated the essay papers. "Thank you, Miss Ellwood," she said. (She remembered her colleague as an infant in a go-cart, but while on duty she did not use first names). "Unfortunately, I am busy."

"All work and no play—" Lorraine began and let her voice trail off without finishing the proverb.

"Be so kind as to convey my felicitations to Miss Leckford," said Miss Dove.

"We'll miss you," said the music teacher as she turned away. Her little feet went down the hall, pitty-pat, like the feet of a dainty child.

Suppose, Miss Dove thought, letting her mind return to its hideous speculations, the doctor didn't pooh-pooh her complaint. If she were really ill, if her strange bodily sensations declared the close of her career as the buzzer had declared the close of the morning's work—*what kind of teacher would take her place in the geography room?*

Would it be a soft little person like Lorraine Ellwood? A person who did not guess that children must be marshaled and trained for life as green soldiers are trained in field manoeuvres for the reality of battle? A person who lived in a never-never land where discipline was a singing-game?

Would it be a brash hearty girl like the art teacher? Someone who encouraged self expression? (Miss Dove had seen paintings done in the art class —great, free, brilliant blobs of color running into the margins, and had shuddered to imagine maps executed with such techniques!) Someone who shouted for order and grew red in the face?

Or worst of all—oh, too bad to think of!—would another Mona Leckford sit here on this dais, slumping, stifling yawns behind a hand? A languid woman, Miss Dove thought with contempt. A teacher *whose heart was not in her work!*

Suddenly the room seemed thronged with figures. They folded their hands and waited for Miss Dove to direct them.

She leaned forward.

Let happen what may, she promised silently to the phantom company, *I shall return!*

There was a sound of footsteps—rapid, solid, masculine—in the hall. The Reverend Alexander Burnham hurried into the room. With him was Dr. Thomas Baker. David brought up the rear.

"Davie said you needed help, Miss Dove," said Alexander. "So I brought Tommy."

"Young Dr. Hurley is my physician," said Miss Dove. Her tone implied that to ask for a seasoned medical man and to be offered instead, the services of Thomas Baker, was like being sent a troop of Boy Scouts when one had requested aid from the militia.

"Davie told us that," Thomas said quickly, remembering the importance Miss Dove had always attached to the delivery of "a straight message." He felt protective toward David and, illogically, toward himself. The familiar room was casting its spell upon him. The mural on one blackboard, the map on the other, the clay caribou on the sand table, the cactus plants on the window sill and, above all, the dry odor of chalk and boy that permeated the air (chalk smells the same forever and so do little boys, he thought with a sense of discovery)—all these belied the passage of time. He was eight years old, or eleven, or twelve at the most. He was facing the terrible Miss Dove who had accurately surmised, through some clairvoyance of her own, that he had a live garter snake in his trousers pocket. "Dr. Hurley is ill with a recurrence of his bronchitis."

"The immoderate use of tobacco," Miss Dove said. She glanced at David who was guilty, she suspected, of smoking in the boys' basement.

David slid into his seat and resumed his copy-work.

"Quite likely. At any rate, he's *hors de combat*," said Thomas. (He was surprised and somewhat elated at the formality of his own language.) "I happened to be at Sandy's when David came."

"Tommy's had excellent training, you know," said Alexander.

"I know," said Miss Dove. Of course she knew. It was she who had begun his training. It was she who, day after unremitting day, had drilled into him respect for industry, desire for exactitude, and the civilizing grace of inhibition. "Only—" Only what? Only that for all his six-foot stature, his degrees, and his accomplishments, he was still, to her, the boy who had wiggled his ears whenever her back was turned.

Thomas understood Miss Dove's hesitation. He remained near the doorway, standing firmly upon etiquette. "Perhaps Miss Dove would prefer someone riper," he said.

But Miss Dove was not prepared to wound an old pupil's professional pride. Besides, she needed advice.

"I shall be glad of your opinion, Doctor," she said. With succinctness and clarity, as though she were listing the chief products of the Great Lakes region, she described the symptoms of her malaise.

Thomas nodded. He strode across the floor. He mounted the low, raised platform (and as he did, he had the feeling that he took the final and necessary step up from childhood to the plateau of adult authority); with the tip of his finger he touched a spot in the teacher's rigid back.

Sharply, Miss Dove drew in her breath.

"That's all," Thomas said. "Was it bad?"

"Yes," said Miss Dove.

"I was afraid it would be," Thomas said. "And your leg? There's a complete absence of sensation?"

"My limb has gone to sleep," Miss Dove said. "As soon as I move about—"

"But that's what we can't allow," said Thomas.

"Can't—what?" Miss Dove inquired. It had been a long time since anyone had proposed to impose his will upon her.

"Can't allow you to move about," said Thomas.

"And pray who are we?" Miss Dove asked with acidity. She glanced at Alexander Burnham. Her glance was a challenge.

Alexander fiddled with his clerical collar. "This isn't my province," he said. "Tommy's the doctor."

"Lindbergh's 'we,'" said Thomas. "Me. I—that is."

"What is your diagnosis?" asked Miss Dove.

"I haven't one yet," Thomas told her. "I'll have to get you to the hospital. Right away."

"Is that necessary?" Miss Dove demurred. "Young Dr. Hurley—"

"It is quite necessary," Thomas said. "Right away."

"Next week, perhaps," said Miss Dove. By next week Dr. Hurley's bronchial tubes would doubtless be clear and his comfortable skill at her command. "At present I am very busy. I am reviewing my grammar grades for the state proficiency tests. They will be given on Monday."

"Right away," said Thomas. His voice was flat. In it was the unyielding tone she had heard in her own when her patience was tried and she meant to brook no more nonsense.

"But the fifth grade is weak on the winds and the tides," she said.

" 'There is a tide in the affairs of men—' " said Thomas. "Frankly, Miss Dove, the decision is not yours. Medicine is *my* theatre of command."

"Yes, Thomas," Miss Dove said meekly.

"Shall I call an ambulance?" asked Alexander.

"No! Please!" begged Miss Dove. With horror she imagined a siren shrieking down the street. She saw herself supine on a stretcher emerging from the portals of Cedar Grove School. "Not an ambulance!"

"I know," said Thomas. And he did know. In his instant of power he was granted perception. "Sandy and I could carry you to my car. That won't be so comfortable, of course—"

"It will be quieter," said Miss Dove. "More discreet."

"Very well then," Thomas said briskly. He wished to seize, before it changed, Miss Dove's submissive mood. "Now, Sandy—"

"My hat, please," said Miss Dove. "My gloves and my bag. They are in the closet."

"I'll fetch them," said Alexander. But with his hand on the china knob of the closet door he trembled. He was about to penetrate an awful mystery. How often, especially when his conscience had been heavy, he had looked at that closet door and looked away! No one, to his knowledge—no one except the terrible Miss Dove—had ever seen behind it. Speculation had been rife, of course, and everyone had agreed that the closet was an eerie place festooned with cobwebs and containing strange instruments of torture. There were rumors of blood stains on the floor. One lad with a ghoulish literary bent (he had later become a successful playwright) had claimed to know for a certainty that the skeleton of a boy was propped, grinning, against the wall. The children didn't really believe in those Gothic fancies, of course, any more than they believed in other dreadful rumors—that ghosts walked on Friday nights, for instance; that they, themselves, would some day lie in the graveyard; or that Miss Dove chastised miscreants with her map-pointer. They clung to them because they gilded dull routine with danger. Alexander opened the door.

The shallow, white-washed closet was uncluttered. From a peg beside the door hung a turkey-feather duster. On the floor were a pair of rubber gaiters and standing in the corner was no fleshless cadaver but a furled umbrella. From a shelf Alexander took Miss Dove's hat—black, small, straight-brimmed, a hat and nothing more—her long gold hatpin, her gray gloves, and her handbag. He backed out of the closet shutting the door quickly lest his son David should see inside and suffer disillusion.

Miss Dove drew the gloves over her long, elegant fingers. In one hand she took her hat, in the other, her pin.

Alexander averted his eyes. (It had been the consensus of his classmates that the teacher secured her hat by driving that pin straight through her cranium.) His gaze met Thomas' and asked a question.

Thomas answered with a shrug. His expression was grave.

Miss Dove's hat sat, level and steady, upon her head. She looped the strap of her bag over her arm.

"I await your convenience, gentlemen," she said.

"If you'll lean forward—this way," Thomas said, helping her to her feet, "and support yourself on the desk— Now, Sandy!"

The two men joined their four hands, making the sort of chair that children make at play. They lowered it behind Miss Dove.

"Sit down," said Thomas. "Put your arms around our necks."

All this while David had bent over his notebook, intent on escaping notice. But when he heard the doctor's strange command and realized to whom it was addressed, he looked up. His marrow was chilled.

His father and Dr. Baker had lifted Miss Dove into the air. She was sitting between them, on their hands, with her bony arms (and how, David wondered, could they endure the touch?) hugging their necks. Her feet dangled down.

"You may go, David," she said.

"Yes, Miss Dove," said David.

Alexander regarded his son. "Were you kept in because of your conduct?"

"Yes, sir," said David.

Alexander glanced at the board. His face darkened the way—David remembered—it had darkened at breakfast. "Have you finished your twenty copies?"

"I've done fifteen," said David.

"Do the other five," said Alexander. "Do five extra for good measure."

Miss Dove stiffened. This was the typical parental error. To indulge a child in his folly, gloss over his faults and then, in an outraged moment, to punish him excessively.

"David has been diligent," she said. "He was interrupted to run an errand at my request."

"He has to learn—" David's father began.

"It is I who deal with him here," said Miss Dove. "To borrow Thomas' words, this classroom is *my* theatre of command. David may go."

"Yes, Miss Dove," said Alexander. He and Thomas carried their proud passenger into the hall.

Left alone, David began to weep. He wept because, being a child of sensibility, he appreciated the austere beauty of justice and was moved when a tyrant came to his defense. He wept because he sensed that the world was subject to change and because to be left to his own undirected devices made him feel forlorn. He hated himself for crying. He hated his tender nature. It was his dream to become a big-league pitcher or a space-rocket pilot like the heroes on the ready-to-eat cereal boxes—who were *never* pictured in tears!

"Hell and damn!" he said aloud to the echoing room.

But the fine-flavored oath had lost its tonic property. It caused him to feel no bigger, no tougher, no less deserted. Why, he thought, shocked at the heresy to boyhood, the teacher was right! Nothing *was* achieved by swearing.

Down the central corridor of Cedar Grove School Miss Dove was borne aloft. The big front door was open to the brilliant day; the corridor was dim by contrast, like the tunneled passage in a dream. The pictures on the walls—those reproductions in sepia of Galahad petting his horse, of Washington kneeling in the snow, and of the peasant girl enraptured by her lark, all of which had been chosen for moral inspiration—looked blurred and shadowy and downright silly. The drinking fountain, a fixture of which Miss Dove severely disapproved (she regarded it as an open invitation, like a poolroom, to laxness and rowdy behavior) had an aspect of pathos. From the teachers' rest-room on the second floor came Lorraine Ellwood's thin, true voice singing "Always" in honor of Mona Leckford; it sounded wistful and unreal—the ghost of a song. Yes, everything was very strange. And strangest of all was the fact that Miss Dove, herself, should move without the exercise of volition through territory where her presence had stood for law.

"Spine straight, Miss Dove," Thomas warned her. "Don't wobble about." Miss Dove could scarcely believe her ears.

"It is not my custom to wobble," she said.

They approached the door. Beyond lay the schoolyard—a piece of the large, uncloistered world—harsh with the glare of publicity. What would the children do when they saw her? Would they stare? Would they gape? (Miss Dove abhorred a hang-jawed child!) Would they giggle? She did not know. She only knew that children in the mass were unpredictable.

But she must face them, and face them down. She thought of the Spartan boy smiling while the fox gnawed his vitals (though he had been *wrong* to steal the fox in the first place—she had always reminded her pupils of that);

she thought of Marie Antoinette on her way to the guillotine. Then, as if she were recalling another figure from history, she saw the young girl she, herself, had been. She saw that girl lifting her head above dismay; twisting her pale, bright hair—the symbol of everything easy and debonair—into a hard knot; bending above a chessboard by a northern window. *I am predictable*, she thought.

Alexander Burnham glanced up at her briefly. His brown eyes, remarkably like David's, were full of concern. "You'll be all right, Miss Dove," he said.

"I am always all right," said Miss Dove.

Mercifully, although she was prepared to carry it off with éclat, Miss Dove was not obliged to run the gauntlet of her pupils. A soft-ball game and two or three vendettas had drawn the student body to the playground behind the school. On the front lawn only a flock of robins and one child, hidden among the boughs of the namesake cedar, observed Miss Dove's departure.

The robins cocked their yellow eyes and continued pecking for worms.

The invisible child was Vicky Evans, the dreamer. She had climbed the tree for solitude. She was thinking up a story. And just as the elements of literature—an explorer lost among the mountains of the moon, a ruined castle, an enchanted princess—had begun to emanate from her mind, she saw something stranger than fiction. She saw two tall men carrying a woman between them. The woman was Miss Dove. There was no mistaking, even from a distance and through the gloom of the cedar, the prim black hat and the handkerchief-flower on the bodice of the dark dress.

In her first surprise Vicky felt only a mild shock of the ineffable wonder that all children feel when events go topsy-turvy. It was the way she might have felt if she'd heard a white rabbit talking to himself or seen a baby turning into a pig. But as she watched the group move down the cement path through the schoolyard, she was seized by horror. Miss Dove was being abducted! She had been "drugged into submission"—that was why she did not scream!

The fact that Vicky recognized both the "abductors"—that Mr. Burnham was the rector of her church and Dr. Baker the surgeon who had removed her grandmother's gall-bladder—did nothing to allay her fears. (She had learned from comic books that wolves employ many disguises other than the fleece of lambs.) Swinging from limb down to limb, like one of those arboreal monkeys Miss Dove disliked, she dropped to the grass. She raced across the lawn, scattering robins.

She plunged through the doorway and ran, with mounting terror, down the cavernous hall of the school. Her voice froze in her throat. When she saw five or six teachers descending the stairway, looking gay and sentimental, she began to howl.

"Vicky, darling!" cried Miss Ellwood, rushing ahead of her companions. "Are you hurt, dear?"

Vicky shook her head. Between howls she made a burbling, unsuccessful attempt at articulation.

"Something's frightened her," Mona Leckford said, with an air of perspicacity.

"Steady in the boat there, Evans!" boomed the art teacher.

"Kidnappers!" Vicky managed to gasp. "They've snatched Miss Dove!"

The music teacher sat down upon the bottom step and pulled Vicky into her lap. "Sweetheart," she said, "you've been making up stories—nice little let's-pretend stories that belong in books and you're all mixed up. But we mustn't confuse let's-pretend with really-so, must we?"

"They snatched her!" Vicky sobbed. "I saw them!"

"Classic hysteria," said Mona Leckford who dipped widely, if not deeply, into the literature of abnormal psychology. She peered at Vicky. For the first time in her brief teaching career she found a child fascinating.

"It's her vivid imagination," said Lorraine. "Now, Vicky-Wicky, let's think hard! You didn't *see* them. You just—"

Then David Burnham came out of the geography room and told what had happened.

Miss Dove was not transferred to the doctor's automobile. Thomas decided against that for fear of jolting his patient. He discussed his decision, beneath and across Miss Dove, with Alexander.

"It's five blocks to the hospital," he said. "Can you make it, Sandy?"

"If you can," Alexander replied. He sounded offended, as though he considered the question a reflection upon his age (he was a few years the senior of Thomas) or upon the staying power of the clergy.

"Good man," said Thomas.

"What of Miss Dove's comfort?"

"Oh, she'll be okay so long as she keeps her spine rigid," Thomas assured him. "And that's an old habit of hers."

Miss Dove found it odd to hear herself spoken of in the third person as if she were absent or deaf. Odder yet, it was agreeable. For the fact that she was not consulted put her anxieties—for a brief interlude at least—at a certain remove. Like any pupil in the geography room she had now to think only of her present duty and that duty was defined. *She was to keep her spine rigid.*

Back down the route she had taken in the morning she rode between her bearers. Along Maple through a shower of winged, coral-colored seeds some of which settled on her hat; up Oakwood, across LaFayette, past her own house to Elm where, half a block further on, the hospital was situated.

The noonday hush was on Liberty Hill but Miss Dove's progress did not go unnoticed. Polly Burnham was on her porch, awaiting her husband's return. She started forward when she saw him; he warned her off with a shake of his head. He walked very slowly, she observed, keeping careful step with Thomas. She telephoned Jincey Baker.

Jincey called her sister and her mother-in-law. Within five minutes a score of persons stood, half-eager and half-afraid, at front windows. And when they beheld the awaited spectacle they felt betrayed as people feel when they first glimpse the outrageous fact that their parents are not immune to change but have been touched, as by frost in the night, with an intimation of mortality. If Miss Dove's strength could crumble, what of their own? The shape of bones showed through the buxom face of nature—

Law, embodied in the muscular bulk of Patrolman Holloway, was cruising the streets in a police car. The car drew close to the curb.

"Has there been an accident, Doc? Is she bad off?" Holloway asked. He was abjectly devoted to Miss Dove who had once shown him consequence when that was what he needed. He pronounced "she" as with a capital letter, like the pronoun of deity.

"I have the immediate situation under control, Bill," Thomas said. "Scoot over to the hospital and tell them I want a private room. Say I'm not asking for it—I'm *telling* them!"

"Yes, sir." With siren wailing, the car sped off at sixty miles an hour.

Jincey Baker was in her front yard. She wore a full yellow smock. The sun gave an extra gloss to her hair. Her complexion had the glowing delicacy that blesses some women in the terminal weeks of pregnancy and there was a sprinkling of freckles—a touching, left-over grace of childhood—on the bridge of her exquisite nose. She looked like Spring.

After nearly a year of marriage, Thomas was not hardened to his wife's beauty. For an instant the world rocked and he was oblivious of all else. He nearly stumbled.

But Miss Dove was not dazed. She noted only that the girl seemed to have outgrown the flighty butterfly airs that had made her first youth absurd.

"How d'y'do, Virginia," she said.

"How d'y'do, Miss Dove," said Jincey. She looked at her husband. "Can I help, Tommy?"

"No," Thomas said. He rapped out the negative, wishing to cut clear of the tenderness that threatened to unman him. "Just look after yourself. Don't do anything foolish."

Silently, Miss Dove approved the doctor's admonition to his wife. His tone had been unnecessarily brusque, perhaps—but what better advice could a man give Virginia (who had been one of the volatile Webbs) than a warning against impulsive behavior?

It had been nearly a year before—the very first day of the preceding June, to be exact—when Miss Dove had talked alone with Jincey in the geography room, had been interrupted by Thomas, and had been reasonably sure, when she'd seen the two young people go off together, of how the next chapter of their lives would read.

That first of June had been graduation day at Cedar Grove Elementary School. The exercises had not deviated from tradition. On the platform of the school auditorium forty white-clad children of the outgoing sixth grade, all with rapt, dedicated faces, had presented a tableau of propriety. (At least thirty-nine of them had. Sterling Baker, a boy remarkable for pinkness and aplomb, had attempted, by practicing Morse code with his mobile ears, to provide comic relief for the transcendent solemnity of the occasion. But, with a single exception, the audience had ignored Sterling. Only his elder brother, Dr. Thomas Baker—the sole visiting adult male in attendance—had suffered a brief fit of coughing.) "Trees" had been recited with much flutter of the hands to denote nesting robins, much walling of the eyes to denote piety, by Fae Patricia Rigsbee, a bisque doll of a girl. Finally, the Citizenship Cup had been awarded to Lester Knight, Jr.; thrusting his lower jaw forward almost to the angle of dislocation, Lester had declared that to him the trophy "rep-er-esented just one more challenge!"

At last the graduates left the stage. Preceded by the principal and most of the faculty, they marched single file down the center aisle of the auditorium. Their voices, raised in the school's song of farewell, had a sweetness independent of pitch or harmony.

> "Dear old Cedar Grove, to thee-ee-eee
> We pledge love and loyaltee-ee-eee—"

sang the graduates and proceeded to vow, off-key, that whatever temptations might beset them "upon life's stormy sea" (i.e., junior high school) they would cling to the ideals of their first alma mater. Every mother who heard them (even the rare candid one who considered her own darling's eligibility for promotion a minor miracle) grew damp in the eye.

Miss Dove was acquainted with the sensibility of the female parent. On thirty-odd successive Commencement Days, just at this point in the ceremonies, she had been aware of an increased humidity in the emotional atmosphere. And, since she had taught most of the mothers present and knew their individual quirks, she could—if pressed—have told what each of them thought in her heart or whispered to her neighbor.

"They will become the men and women of tomorrow," murmured Lester Knight, Junior's mother. Like her son, she had a gift for appropriate platitude.

Mrs. Rigsbee, sandwiched between Mrs. Knight and her own young sister, Jincey Webb, suppressed a sneer. "What does anyone expect them to become? Yaks?" she inquired behind her hand of Jincey. It was obvious to Mrs. Rigsbee that except for some foul element of favoritism her Fae Patricia would have received the cup.

Jincey shrugged. *What dull, provincial lives these women lead,* she thought. *Never tasting glory or despair. Moving about in their little orbits from market to P. T. A. to country club to market. Merely motorized vegetables.* She raised her lovely eyes to the ceiling. *At least I have suffered. I have lived!*

At the tail end of the line, separated by three paces from the last singing child, came Miss Dove. She walked with her usual measured tread. She wore her usual dark dress. She looked precisely as she had always looked. But she knew that the mothers, regarding her through a haze of emotion, saw her with a difference. Ordinarily—try as they might to disguise the fact by poking fun at her sharp nose, her impassive countenance, and the tight little ball of hair at the nape of her rigid neck—they were afraid of her. "The terrible Miss Dove," they had called her in their childhood and still called her; and their title for her derived less from her dogmatic insistence upon the less dramatic virtues than from the suspicion that she knew all about them. She could put her finger on the snively, ignoble spots in their natures as unerringly, they felt, as she could touch with her long map-pointer the capital of Bolivia or the source of the Danube. But on this June morning most of them forgot that. Rich and charitable in successful maternity they glimpsed infinite pathos in the spinster's life.

She was no longer the terror who had stalked through their school days—who had made them wash out their mouths when they'd chewed their pigtails or used inelegant language; who had forced them, through dread of her silent contempt, to sit still until the bell rang, no matter how badly they needed to go to the bathroom; who had known, though she hadn't stooped to question their word, when they were fibbing. She was not even the cold-blooded monster who had, later, remained unsoftened by their own children's infantile graces—by Sistie's bashfulness and Bubbie's imperfect articulation, and the adorable way Jackie Boy stomped his foot, like a regular little man, when his will was crossed. She was Woman Bereft.

For the sixth-graders were leaving her. Each one irreplaceable and differing from all other children as star differed from star, they were marching straight out of her life as sixth-graders had marched, June after June, year after cruel year. They would never return.

"Poor Miss Dove!" the mothers sighed in silent unison and Miss Dove heard them with that inward ear, sensitive to vibrations of the mass mind, that is the genius—though scarcely the bliss—of the true teacher. "Poor childless, chickless, figless Miss Dove!" The sentiment drew them together into one warm, yeasty lump of compassion. Forgiving the miscarriage of the Cup, Mrs. Rigsbee reached for Mrs. Knight's hand and squeezed it. Very tenderly she laid her other hand over Jincey's.

Jincey withdrew her fingers. She lifted her head in a delicate, fastidious way as if to hold it aloof from banality. On her pale face was the languid hauteur that is natural to a young beauty whom tragedy has touched.

Miss Dove, though she was attempting to notice nothing, noticed Jincey. It would have been difficult not to see the slightest motion of the girl's head with its red-gold hair that seemed to give off sparks like a cat's fur stroked in the dark. Miss Dove noticed, as well, that Thomas Baker noticed and that his eyes appeared dazed as if they were staring into an open fire.

Miss Dove was not pleased. She was cognizant of the details of Jincey Webb's disappointment. She could imagine (though she could *not* imagine allowing herself to wander into such a predicament) that to be publicly jilted was galling to the self-esteem. But she gave short shrift to the wan weeds of melancholy. If Virginia—for Miss Dove believed in calling people as well as facts by their full names—would stop mooning about in an atmosphere of broken orange-blossoms, play-acting and walling her eyes much as her silly niece, Fae Patricia, walled hers, then she might reap some benefit from experience and enjoy a fuller, saner life.

As for Thomas Baker—surely a qualified surgeon, accustomed to the stern realities of health and sickness, could keep his mind from meandering in the maze of a girl's red hair. Surely he must realize—as Miss Dove realized—that those distracting tresses had done Virginia harm. If her mother had kept them braided, the nonsense of beauty and glamor would never have begun. (Miss Dove reflected complacently upon her own hair—washed once a week, brushed night and morning, and screwed into a sensible bun out of folly's way.) And if Thomas wished to contemplate something other than his profession he might well consider the flippant attitude—that sad family failing!—that his young brother had just displayed upon the rostrum.

But disdain as she might the marvelous hair and the bemused, half-drowning look in the doctor's eyes, Miss Dove was not oppressed by them as she was by her consciousness of the sticky emotion that oozed toward her from the assembled matrons. Her place in society was one, Miss Dove believed, to excite envy. That other women should presume to pity her—and especially that soft species of women who leaned upon the protection of men and who, with the advent of maternity, lost the power of reason and replaced it with a vague, yearning sort of mawkishness that they held sacred and called instinct —seemed to her fantastic. She was not tempted to laugh, for a sense of humor was not her defense against impudence. That touted faculty she regarded, indeed, as morally vestigial and, like the tonsils, apt to breed trouble. She looked through air as clear as glass upon the human scene; in it she saw much that was right, much that was wrong, and nothing that was funny. No. Laughter was not her style. She was inclined, however, for one outraged instant, to come to a full stop in the aisle. To stand there, revolving slowly like a weathercock on a windless day, sweeping her sympathizers with a gelid gaze that would leave them little doubt as to her opinion of mothers.

Naturally, however, the sedate Miss Dove did not yield to that impulse. She continued her stately progress as rear guard of the graduates. The position was not—as the lachrymose mothers thought—one of loneliness or rejection. It was a position of her own choosing. Seven years before a disconcerting thing had happened at a Cedar Grove graduation. The last child in the line —a little girl known as Jincey whose angelic brow and pellucid hair had moved most people to poetry—had whipped a water-pistol from the depths of her frilly bodice and had shot the boy preceding her in the seat of his trousers. Other guns had appeared as if by prearranged signal. The graduates had broken ranks. They had rioted through the building, leaping desks, drenching flowery-bonneted bystanders with the ammunition of their side-arms and singing, instead of the school's inspiring anthem, a rowdy ballad known as Pistol-Packing Mama! Since that unhappy day, Miss Dove had deemed it prudent to let the children know that the eyes of decorum were upon them, aft as well as fore.

Now, nineteen and wretched, Jincey herself recalled that occasion. She smiled, remembering the surge of daring, the intoxicated leap toward freedom. And she remembered as well, the disciplined years that had, paradoxically, given her the heady moment of bravado. Miss Dove did not evoke her pity. Jincey saw her as the symbol of a bygone era when life had been unchancey and as plain as a map on a wall. She remembered how the teacher had stood, stiff as a yardstick, behind her desk; with her long fingers she had touched the globe of the earth, turning it slowly to illustrate its predictable diurnal revolution. And, recollecting, Jincey experienced again an old, comfortable conviction that if you obeyed the law—if you sneezed in your handkerchief and raised your hand for permission to speak and kept your margins neat—that globe and all it represented was certain to be your oyster.

For the first time in weeks it occurred to Jincey that a broken heart was cumbersome baggage.

Miss Dove followed the class into the hall. The mothers arose. They fanned themselves with their programs. "It was the end of something," they said mournfully, "but think—now we'll have our families all to ourselves, all day, all summer!" Then, staring suddenly down a tunnel of ninety hot, unbroken days of intensive maternity, they added, as if to bolster their optimism, "Poor, dear Miss Dove!"

"It's nice to see you here, Jincey. It will mean so much to Little Fae," Mrs. Knight said. "That green dress with your hair—" Her glance was caressing as behooved a glance cast by a fruitful married woman upon a slip of a girl whose hopes were blighted, but it was patronizing, too. Lester, Senior, was no Romeo, the glance said. He didn't own a yacht. His Adam's apple was prominent, he snored, and his jokes were ancient. But he had *been* there when he'd said he would—waiting at the altar!

"She came to please me. She's a cutie-pie," Mrs. Rigsbee said, giving her sister an affectionate spank. "We're driving out to the club for lunch. Afterwards you can get a swim and a sunbath, Jince. I put your things in the car."

Jincey felt smothered by tact and solicitude. And to be called "a cutie-pie" was more than she could bear. "I believe I won't. Thanks all the same," she said. She added, and the resolve, and the words that clothed it were simultaneous, "I want to go see Miss Dove."

Before her sister could argue she escaped and went her way.

"Hi, Ellen. Hi, Jane," said Dr. Thomas Baker to Mesdames Knight and Rigsbee. "This makes me feel my age and more. You two girls here *in parentis* and me *in loco!*"

"Wasn't it sad?" said Mrs. Knight. "I bawled at the song. And poor Miss Dove!"

"*Poor?*" Thomas demanded. "She scared me stiff the way she always did. I sat there sweating—perspiring I mean—and wondering if I had a clean handkerchief." He took a handkerchief from his pocket—it was quite clean—and mopped his brow. "No. She'll always be 'the terrible' to me and nothing more!"

"But she's old, Tommy," pleaded Mrs. Rigsbee. "And lonely. Year after year other people's children leave her forever!"

Thomas thought he could endure with equanimity a lifetime minus the company of the affected Fae Patricia, the pompous Lester, Junior, his own ebullient sibling, Sterling, or any other twelve-year-old. But he did not voice his unorthodox sentiment. He was, after all, a young physician with his way to make. "Wasn't little Jincey with you?" he asked, employing an elaborately casual tone. "I hadn't seen her since she was Fae's age, but I spotted that fire-engine hair."

"She *was* here. It's the first time I've been able to drag her out since—" Mrs. Rigsbee finished with a wave of her hand. "She went off to speak to Miss Dove."

"A palpable error," Thomas said. "She could have waited and spoken to *me*." He raised his left eyebrow in the cocksure, maddening, irresistible manner of the skittish bachelor who doesn't underestimate his value. He drifted with the crowd to the door.

Back in the classroom—her castle, as it were—Miss Dove sat at her desk on the dais and closed her eyes. Below her, five rows of lesser desks stood tenantless. The blackboards were washed clean of drawings of isthmuses and peninsulas. The sand tables were shrouded in oilcloth. But Miss Dove was not closing her eyes against the sadness of these things. She was trying to visualize clearly the twoscore children who had left her. For six years she had pruned and polished and molded them and had sought to blow into their clay the breath of purpose. Now they had passed beyond the scope of her influence, beyond the aid of her stricture or approval. She did not wish them back. She wished only to believe that they would do well without her. But she had to wait and see. Miss Dove was like an author whose book was on the press, like a cook whose cake was in the oven, like a flight instructor whose cadet had departed on a lonely mission in the sky. For weal or woe her job was done.

But as the author ponders the merits of that poetic passage in his third chapter, as the cook wishes she had flavored her batter with almond instead of vanilla, as the instructor wonders about forced landings, so Miss Dove tormented herself with questions. She thought first of Fae Patricia. The child was tractable and honest but she had given herself a great many airs today as she'd recited Kilmer's poem. *Did I teach her enough humility? Enough common sense to withstand the adulation of a fatuous mother and many fatuous men?* Miss Dove thought, with a pang, of Fae's aunt, Jincey Webb.

Jincey had been a likely child. Not intellectual or original, but thoroughly nice—cheerful, obliging, and amenable to suggestion. Though she had been subject to animal spirits (witness the "pistol-packing" episode) she had recognized the beauty of discipline. Her notebooks had been jewels of neatness, things of sheer delight. And her posture had been superb—spine straight, head erect, feet planted on the floor. And then, within a few years of her leaving Cedar Grove, something had happened to the girl. Everything about her—her complexion, her figure, her direct brown eyes and, most demonstrably, her hair—had taken on a kind of burnished symmetry that had dazzled the beholder. Worse, it had dazzled Jincey. At the State University she had been elected—by acclaim—the "Sweetheart of Sigma Chi." She had won a talent show and had gone to New York where she got a small job singing TV commercials for a shampoo product—though her voice was slight and indifferent in quality. Soon her engagement had been announced. She was to marry the scion of a wealthy family. She would have a Mediterranean honeymoon aboard a private yacht. She would live, when she returned, in a penthouse—a twelve room cottage with a terrace and a lily pool built in the sky above Manhattan.

She had come home for the wedding. She had wanted it in the little stone church where she'd been christened with all her old friends there to bless her.

But the wedding had been a mirage. Two days after Jincey had arrived home her fiance had eloped with a night-club entertainer. He had not apprised Jincey of his intention. She had heard of it, as a *fait accompli*, on a radio gossip program.

Miss Dove had not been greatly astonished by the turn of events. She had seen a photograph of the defaulting groom and had noted a shiftiness in his eye and an over-fullness, indicative of petulance, about his mouth. What *had* astonished her had been Jincey's behavior. The girl had not conducted herself with the poise that should have distinguished an alumnus of Cedar Grove. She had wept and wilted. She had secluded herself in her sister's house where she had allowed close friends to dab her forehead with *eau de cologne*. She had not—though Miss Dove would have phrased the matter with more urbanity—had the guts to spit in the eye of circumstance!

Was there something more I could have done, Miss Dove asked herself now, *before the girl was twelve?*

She sighed and considered the case of Sterling Baker. It was odd and discouraging how an idiosyncrasy could run like a warped thread through a whole family. Sterling was the youngest of four brothers. Thomas, Andrew, Randolph, and Sterling—Miss Dove had taught them all. They all had cleft chins. They all had fine muscular control—they could wiggle their ears; they could raise one eyebrow without so much as twitching its mate. They were all quick to learn and respond to ethical values. None of them knew how to lie. But try as she had, Miss Dove had never been able to cure them of their love of clowning. And of course she'd got no help from their mother. "Oh, they'll be serious soon enough," that fat, amiable woman was reported to have said. "Leave them to fate and the terrible Miss Dove!"

Recalling Mrs. Baker's remark, Miss Dove pursed her mouth as though she held pins in it.

There was a hesitant step at the open doorway. Jincey Webb stood on the threshold. "Good morning, Miss Dove," she said. Her voice was that of a well-instructed child. It made her unchildish beauty seem fancy dress put on for a masquerade.

"Good morning, Virginia," said Miss Dove.

Jincey advanced into the room. Her shoes were thin green shells supported by thin, high heels. Her green frock made a sound reminiscent of wind in grass. Her hair shook off a peculiarly unacademic fragrance. Jincey went straight to the third seat in the third row of desks.

"This was my place," she said.

"Will you sit there now, Virginia?" Miss Dove said politely.

Jincey took her seat. "The room is different, empty," she said.

Miss Dove was not adept at small talk.

Jincey made another try. "Like life," she said.

Miss Dove said nothing.

"It doesn't smell the same, either," Jincey said. "Remember the boys' corduroy pants—dirty and sort of cheesy at the end of the week? And wet sneakers?"

Miss Dove maintained her silence. To discuss odors, especially in reference to persons or clothing, she considered coarse.

"Is that the same map?" Jincey asked. She pointed to the large map of the world that hung, rolled up for the summer, above the blackboard behind Miss Dove. "Is China still orange?"

"It is a new map," Miss Dove said. "China is purple."

"I liked the old map," Jincey said. "I liked the old world."

"Cartography is a fluid art," said Miss Dove.

With the flat of her hand Jincey pushed her hair back from her forehead. She had done that in moments of perplexity long ago. "Oh, Miss Dove," she said, and her voice shook, "tell me what to do!"

Miss Dove was not at a loss. She told Jincey in three short words. "Do your duty," she said.

Jincey's eyes filled with tears. "But what is your duty when your world has ended?"

"You are nineteen, I believe," said Miss Dove. Her statement was devoid of sarcasm. Miss Dove had been nineteen when her own world had ended and begun. And now she could remember without pain or longing the old lost world. It was a charming memory, like a fairy tale read to a sleepy child. But the new world was real. Whether she was happy in it she did not ask herself. She was strong. She was useful. She was Miss Dove.

"This is how it was," Jincey said. She told Miss Dove all that had happened to her. None of it was wicked. All of it, as Miss Dove had surmised, was a chronicle of vanity and innocence. She told of meeting Michael, the villain of the piece, at the Stork Club. "He spoke to the waiter in French," she said, "and wore a cummerbund."

She told of the places he had taken her to dine. "Did you ever drink champagne, Miss Dove?" she asked.

"No," said Miss Dove.

"It tastes like cider," Jincey said, "but its effect is different." She told of the compliments Michael had paid her. She told of his proposal. ("You are my rainbow's end," he had said.) She was on the verge of describing the sensations she had experienced when he'd clasped her in his arms, but at that point Miss Dove halted her.

"Reticence, Virginia, is the *sine qua non* of gentility," Miss Dove said.

Then Jincey told of the evening in her sister's house when the devastating news had come over the radio. "Everything went black," she said. Tears gushed down her cheeks. She looked very appealing, not very pretty, and about ten years old. "Next day I had a telegram. It said, 'Gorgeous, only you can understand.'"

"Could you?" asked Miss Dove.

"No," Jincey sobbed. "I still can't. Can you?"

"Certainly," said Miss Dove. "Have you a handkerchief, Virginia?"

"I forgot," said Jincey.

From a box on her desk, Miss Dove took a piece of facial tissue. Like a queen stepping down from her throne to distribute largess to the poor, she stepped down from her dais and gave the tissue to Jincey. She returned to her desk.

Jincey wiped her eyes. She blew her nose. "What must I do—exactly?" she asked. She folded her hands and waited to be told.

Of course Miss Dove knew the answer. Jincey's problem, like most problems, was uncomplicated when viewed objectively. And yet, she hesitated. To tell an adult exactly what steps to take toward his salvation was apt to weaken him. It deprived him of his inalienable right to trial and error which was tonic to the character. But today Jincey laid the claims of childhood upon her. She was sitting in her old place. And she had forgotten her handkerchief.

"Very well," Miss Dove said quietly. "First, you must return to your sister's house. You must enter your bedroom, fall upon your knees, and give thanks to your Heavenly Father."

"Thanks!" Jincey gasped. "For what?"

"For preserving you from a fate worse than death," Miss Dove said. The expression, uttered in her precise, calm accents, sounded neither trite nor melodramatic.

"Than death?" Jincey echoed.

"Than death," Miss Dove repeated flatly. "It is evident that the young man to whom you had given your affection discovered that his feelings for you had altered."

Jincey nodded, dumb with misery.

"He had, however, an honorable avenue of escape. He could have requested you to release him from his commitment."

Jincey began to cry again.

"He did not choose to take that honorable avenue," Miss Dove said. "Why?"

"I don't know," said Jincey.

"Then I will tell you," said Miss Dove. Her tone was bland and informative. She might have been explaining the difference between longitude and latitude. "It was because he was a cad, a coward and a person of low principles."

"Oh!" cried Jincey. She sounded shocked, as if she were hearing blasphemy. But slowly over her face spread an expression of exquisite relief. "I thought there must be something wrong with *me!*"

"Your fault lay in a rashness of judgment," said Miss Dove. "His lay in dishonor." She paused to let the distinction sink into the girl's consciousness. "And then," she went on more briskly, "after you have expressed gratitude to the Power that kept you from a disastrous alliance, you must consider your duty to your neighbor and yourself. You must find a useful occupation."

"Do you think I could teach?" asked Jincey.

"Decidedly not," said Miss Dove. "But there are other spheres of service."

"I might be a nurse."

"You might," Miss Dove agreed. Nurses were disciplined. They wore uniforms. Their shoes had low, solid heels. And their hair! Miss Dove thought approvingly of Jincey's hair tucked into a net and crowned with a starched white cap.

"I might enter a nursing order," Jincey said dreamily, "and become a nun." She laid her hand, in a graceful gesture of renunciation, upon her bosom.

"What's this about nunneries?" Thomas Baker demanded from the doorway. He sounded alarmed and breathless, like a doctor who hopes he's arrived in time to countermand a wrong prescription.

"Good morning, Thomas," said Miss Dove.

"Good morning, Miss Dove," said Thomas. He came into the room, a tall, lean young man with a humorous mouth, a steady eye and a stubborn chin. "Why, Jincey!" he exclaimed, affecting surprise at her presence. "Holy mackerel, kitten, you're all grown up!" His tone implied that fact to be felicitous and arranged primarily for his benefit.

"So are you," said Jincey.

"Naturally," said Thomas. He was twenty-nine. He had fought in a war and studied medicine and was on the staff of the local hospital. Of course he was grown up. "But it's rather odd of *you*. Though extremely becoming."

"Thank you," said Jincey. "It's nice you approve."

"The last time I saw her was before I went east to med school," Thomas told Miss Dove. "I was being separated from the Navy and she from Cedar Grove. She shot my brother Randy in the—"

"Virginia cannot enjoy being reminded of that," said Miss Dove.

"It was very reprehensible," Thomas said. "You must be relieved, Miss Dove, to be finished with us Bakers. Sterling was mamma's last black lamb."

"Sterling has many sterling qualities," Miss Dove said with no intention of making a pun. "Except for his levity—"

"Levity is a handicap," Thomas said. "I'm a martyr to it. I often think it's what's kept me single. I'm going fine with a girl, you know. Everything's leading up to Lohengrin. And then—just at the throbbing, tender moment —I can't resist a wisecrack!"

Jincey laughed. Her laughter was sweet bells in tune. She tossed her head. The dazed expression passed over Thomas' eyes.

"Sterling's behavior during the graduation was inexcusable," said Miss Dove.

"He was giving me the SOS with ear jerks while Fae was reciting 'Trees,'" said Thomas. "I taught him to do that."

"It was rude," said Miss Dove.

"I'll speak to my mother when she returns from Boston," Thomas said. "She knows how to deal with smart guys."

"I dare say," said Miss Dove.

Jincey wrinkled her shapely nose. "Does this room smell different to you, Tommy?"

Thomas took a step toward her. He inhaled deeply. "And much better," he said.

Jincey laughed again.

Miss Dove deplored what seemed to be transpiring before her eyes. Jincey's new found purpose was not yet proof against blandishment. In the Webbs the vein of romance ran as close to the skin as did the vein of comedy in the Bakers.

"I expect the hospital keeps you busy, Thomas," she said.

"Yes. It calls me now." He glanced at Jincey. "My car's out back. If I could drop you off somewhere—"

"Fine," said Jincey. She rose. "Good-by, Miss Dove. And thank you. I'll remember." (But it struck Miss Dove that she'd forgotten a good deal already.) "I'll think about the nursing career. Maybe Tommy can advise me."

"I'll advise her very carefully," Thomas said with the utmost gravity. And suddenly, just before he left with Jincey, he gave Miss Dove a smile of such ineffable sweetness as she had never seen before. She remembered a metaphor, read somewhere long ago and scarcely thought of since, that spoke of life—or was it love?—as "honey on the tongue."

Miss Dove put on her hat without benefit of mirror. She closed the windows and drew the green shades down over the glass. In the dim, watery light the room looked mysterious, like a room in a dream. For an instant Miss Dove had a fleeting vision of children—familiar children and yet new—stirring in the shadows. All the end-of-the-year fatigue fell away from her. She felt elated and greedy for the future. It was a curious sensation. Perhaps it was what people meant by happiness.

I am fifty-four, she thought. *I won't have to retire until sixty-seven.* She paused, calculating. (A different kind of woman would have counted on her fingers.) If they didn't tarry—and recalling the smile and the laughter, she didn't expect they *would* tarry—then she could take the first child straight through to graduation.

The child would need her. Jincey would be a doting, dandling mother. She would rock her children to sleep and kiss their bruises and call them by baby-talk names like Punkin and Buttons and Boo. And Thomas, as a father, would cut a sorry figure indeed. Fancy a father who was a "martyr to levity." A father who "couldn't resist a wisecrack!"

And yet, Miss Dove reflected, possibly all that, along with shiny hair and silly shoes and pretty smells (for Jincey's agreeable scent still hung on the air), was part of a plan designed by an Authority she did not question. For if everyone lived upon Miss Dove's own lofty plane—if everyone perceived

with perfect clarity the hard, serious truths of human life—then there would
be no parents and no children. There would be only teachers.

In this magnanimous mood Miss Dove left her classroom. In the foyer
of the building, under the picture of Galahad and his horse, the art teacher
had set up a trestle table and was serving refreshments to the graduates and
their guests. Miss Dove moved among the mothers, greeting them graciously.
As she approached Mrs. Knight she saw that lady slap a slice of coconut
cake out of the hand of her illustrious son.

"Lester, Junior, you pig!" Mrs. Knight sputtered between clenched teeth.
"You're going to be sick, sick, sick, and serve you right!"

"Good morning, Mrs. Knight," said Miss Dove. "I'm sure you are proud
of Lester."

Mrs. Knight wheeled around. With her foot she shoved the cake, which
had fallen to the floor, beneath the overhang of the crepe-paper tablecloth.
As she gazed up into the teacher's serene, cloudless, omniscient eyes—as she
imagined a summer uncluttered with the care and feeding of children—pity
was the least of her emotions.

But she managed to compose her features. She put her arm around Lester,
Junior's shoulders. "All that he is he owes to you, Miss Dove," she said.

Miss Dove inclined her head in acknowledgment of the tribute. "It is my
rule," she said, "to regard my each success simply as one more challenge."

And now, from the elevation of the crisscrossed hands of Burnham and
Baker, Miss Dove looked down at Virginia and saw that she—against the
odds of soft hair and eyes, pretty bodily proportions and a heart very quickly
made glad—had attained, no less than Lester, Junior, the condition of being
"a challenge." In the gauzy April light she stood there in her husband's garden—still beautiful and still, perhaps, a trifle too conscious of her beauty,
but with all her folly fallen away. She carried her unborn child high, as the
country saying is, and she carried it with pride. In her face was the steady
glow of vocation. Maternity, Miss Dove felt, was a humbler career than
teaching—a talent rather than a craft, drawing more from instinct than from
intelligence. But it was abundantly clear that it was this girl's—this woman's
—ordained sphere of usefulness, that she had found it and that she would
give it her energies without reserve. That was success; Miss Dove respected
it. It gave her the same stab of esthetic satisfaction that she had often felt
when some hitherto graceless child had shown understanding or had made a
map with meticulous care (preventing the colors of different nations from
running into one another), or had told the truth when the truth was to his
immediate disadvantage.

When they came in view of Miss Dove's own house—a large white house,
with fluted columns and a cut-glass fanlight, that had long since been con-
verted into apartments—Miss Dove suggested stopping while she gathered together a few conveniences.

"No," said Thomas.

"I'll attend to them later," the minister said.

"I am afraid that is an office for a lady," said Miss Dove.

Alexander blushed. "Most certainly," he said. The notion of invading Miss Dove's virginal boudoir, of touching her comb, her toothbrush, and her various articles of intimate apparel, caused his nerves to quiver. "Polly will get them."

"We're almost there," said Thomas as he and his companion turned into Elm Street.

"If I may be permitted to indulge my curiosity," said Miss Dove with a touch of hauteur, "how long must I expect to be hospitalized? Overnight?"

"Longer than that," said Thomas.

"This is Wednesday," said Miss Dove. "I should like to be in school by Monday at the latest." She could give the children no factual aid on their tests, but she could aid them intangibly merely by being there. In her sedative presence they would be unlikely to be rattled.

"Not next Monday," said Thomas. "A week from then maybe. Or a month. It all depends."

"Oh," said Miss Dove.

In the front bedroom of the bungalow that abutted the hospital grounds John Wesley Evans had just arisen from his couch. Wes, as he was known generally, was a man of charm and unfortunate habits. He was recovering from a spree of considerable scope so—and what could be more natural?—he poured himself a little "hair of the dog." He took his glass to the window and raised it in a salute to a new day and a new start. Light kindled in the liquor. Fire, he thought, in the heart of a rare jewel. He was smiling, somewhat fatuously, at his pretty conceit when he saw Miss Dove.

The sight unnerved him. Several times before he had been subject to alcoholic fancies, but those had taken vague, fumey shapes suggesting snakes and legendary beasts. He had never seen anything like this.

"Come here, Pearl," he implored his wife who was entering the room to bring him a raw egg masked in Worcestershire sauce. "Quick!"

Pearl hurried to his side. "Why, it's Miss Dove," she cried. "Your terrible Miss Dove!"

"You see her, too?" Wes said. His forehead was damp with the sweat of relief. "But what else do you see? Who's got her?"

"Tommy and Sandy," Pearl said. "She must be sick."

"She must be more than sick," said Wes. The teacher's face—a tragic mask, he thought, put on for death—moved him deeply. He differed in many salient respects from Miss Dove, but he admired her. What she stood for—certitude, principle, authority—was what Wes yearned to stand for. Often it was the appalling consciousness of the gulf between the ideal and the reality that sent him to the bottle.

" 'The time you won your town the race
'They chaired you through the market place—' " he quoted softly.

"What say, darling?" his wife said in an anxious tone.

"Housman," he said. He set his glass down, untasted. "I'm through with *that*, forever!"

"Of course you are," Pearl said as she had said countless times. She did not know what passed through his mind (after all, she had been raised in another town), but she knew that something had touched a liberating spring in his nature. For weeks now—oh, for months with any luck—she could bask in the halcyon weather of her husband's sobriety. "Can you swallow an egg?"

Absently, Wes swallowed the egg.

He continued to stare out the window. He could now see only Miss Dove's back—the prim feet visible beneath the decent skirt, the uncompromising neck, the shape of the hat as stiff and uncoquettish as a mortar-board. But upon his mind her pale set face was stamped. The nose was supercilious. The brow was lofty and calm. The eyes met with recognition, he was sure, with composure and cold disdain, the eyes of mankind's uncouth and dusty foe.

However, as had happened before, his poetic temperament deceived him. Miss Dove was not thinking of death. She was thinking of the proficiency tests.

But the hospital, like the theatre or the schoolroom, is a world contained in itself, turning on its own axis. In its atmosphere is some hypnotic or amnesiac quality before which ordinary life recedes. Even Miss Dove, with her high resistance to foreign influences, was affected by the spell. She approved of the hospital. Of its formality, its regard for order, and its implacable determination to seem exactly what it was. The faint pervading odors of ether, lysol, and formaldehyde did not offend her; they were germane to the place as the odors of chalk, floor-oil, and children were germane to a school building. She admired the way the nurses walked—briskly, without switching—with their starched skirts making a clean, rustling sound. She admired the way they did their hair (they wore it tucked into nets and topped by stiff caps that were only by accident more ornamental than her own black hat) and the way they all had fluted handkerchiefs peeping out from their breast pockets, and the way they stood at attention and said "Sir" in the presence of doctors. She admired—though with initial reluctance—the authority exercised over herself.

She did not, of course, quite abandon her self-determination; she relinquished it into temporary safekeeping along with two possessions of value that she carried in her purse. One was a mother-of-pearl cardcase containing a dozen visiting cards upon which her name (plain MISS DOVE without amplification) was engraved in chaste block letters. The other was a large, heavy-lidded gold watch that had been her father's. In this place she had no need to prove her identity (it was posted on the outside of her door) nor to measure the passage of time. She lay becalmed in the present.

When Mr. Spivey, the principal of Cedar Grove School, called to express his concern for her health and to say he was assuming personal responsibility for her classes (he would be up at the bat pinch-hitting for her, he said, for he was an idealist who thought of life as a major sport) he found her curiously at ease. Not once did she fix him with the dead-sea gaze that had so often made him feel naive in faculty meetings. Even when she touched upon the preparation for the coming tests—upon the fifth grade's confusion about the winds and the tides, for instance—she seemed neither tense nor haughty. Next day, with a catch in his voice, he told his teaching staff: "The old quarterback is resting on her oars!"

(Like many men who employ athletic metaphor, Mr. Spivey leaned to the potpourri.)

The hospital, forewarned by Holloway, had been ready for Miss Dove. It was small by contemporary standards but big for Liberty Hill and so new that its vanity was still intact. When word came that the town's perfectionist was bound thither, everyone, from the superintendent down, rose to the challenge.

The double entrance doors were flung wide. Against one of them stood the superintendent himself. (He had been, Miss Dove recalled, a boy who organized his time.) Against the other stood William Holloway. They stood at attention as if awaiting a visit of state. As she passed between them Miss Dove bowed graciously, once to the right and once to the left.

Inside the lobby, near the door, was a bed made up with linen that shone like snow against the moss-green walls. Beside it stood a thin, black-haired nurse.

So gently that she felt only a twinge, Miss Dove was deposited upon the bed. She looked up at solicitous faces. It was a new sensation for her who was accustomed to look down at faces from an eminence.

"I secured a special in case you wanted one," the superintendent said. "A 'practical' was the most I could do for day duty, but Mrs. Green is one of our best."

"I try to be," the nurse said, drawing a blanket over Miss Dove's knees. "Do you remember me? I was Billie Jean McVay."

"Yes," said Miss Dove. She remembered Billie Jean very well. A sloe-eyed child who had been languorous at seven and who, at twelve, had troubled the air of the school with a suggestion—almost an aroma—of sex precociously in the ascendant. "I remember you, Mrs. Green."

"Of course, I'm older now," Billie Jean said as if she'd read her patient's thoughts.

Alexander took his leave and Thomas, after a hurried consultation with the nurse, did likewise. There was an emergency case for him, the superintendent told him. The Knight boy—Lester, Junior—had been admitted half an hour before with abdominal pain and a high white count. His mother was with him, in worse shape than Lester.

"I dare say," said Miss Dove. She could imagine how Jane Knight would behave under threat of a son's appendicitis. (Jane had been a Simpson. All Simpsons were flighty and likely to go to pieces on examinations.)

Thomas, who was also acquainted with the Simpson strain, laughed shortly. But immediately he sobered. He felt himself projected into the future and had a vision of Jincey distraught beside a suffering child—running her lovely fingers through her lovely hair and praying God to let the doctor come. "I'll see you later, Miss Dove," he said. He walked rapidly away without a backward glance.

Miss Dove did not feel abandoned. Thomas, she knew, had put her problems into the proper pigeonhole of his mind, much as she did with the problems of the third grade when the fourth grade trooped in.

"I'll take you up now," said Billie Jean. The bed was on rollers. Grasping it by the footboard she propelled it down the hall to the elevator.

Miss Dove had traversed that hall before but as a visitor, under her own power, and in an upright position. Now, with the power gone and the position changed, that hall, like the hall of Cedar Grove School, seemed different and longer.

The nurse's skirts made a whispering noise—like water among reeds, she thought—the light had an aqueous quality, and she, herself, seemed to be drifting in a boat. The fancy produced in her a rhythmic peacefulness, as of lapping waves, and the rhythm became a recollection. She remembered a parody in verse that one of her less reverent pupils had composed back in the '30s.

Geoffrey Lyons the parodist had been. (A fat boy with a sullen, and even stupid-looking countenance that had a disconcerting way of lighting up suddenly, for no discernible reason.) He had taken for his model some lines from the Arthurian legends—those elegiac lines describing the "lily maid," the fair and lovable Elaine. "Miss Dove the grim, Miss Dove the terrible," Geoffrey had written. "Miss Dove the Gorgon's Head of Cedar Grove!"

Some tattle-tale prig had left the verses on Miss Dove's desk hoping, no doubt, to anger the teacher and make trouble for the poet. But the prig had failed on both counts. Miss Dove's concept of honor would not have allowed her to be affected by an anonymous communication. Besides, she would have stooped to anger with a twelve-year-old boy no more than she would have raised her voice or bribed her class to good behavior or reduced learning to the level of entertainment. When, twenty years later, Geoffrey had become a playwright of distinction, she had been mildly elated and not particularly surprised.

At Geoffrey's invitation she had condescended to be his guest at his first play's opening night. He had sent her an orchid and a round-trip ticket on the plane to New York. And Miss Dove, though she hadn't flown before, had felt entirely comfortable as the huge airliner bore her above a terrain with whose contours she was, academically speaking, familiar. (She took the precaution to sit far front where she could, if it seemed expedient, advise the pilot in matters of navigation.) She had been comfortable in the theatre, too. Geoffrey's play, dealing as it did with the problems of three marines who were stranded upon a tropic isle among a number of hibiscus-clad female natives, struck her as lacking a certain elevation of tone, but it did not embarrass her. Nothing embarrassed Miss Dove. After the show she boarded the one-o'clock plane for home so as to avoid being late for school next morning.

Later, when school was over, she had written a letter. "My dear Geoffrey," she wrote in her discreet, legible script, "As your former teacher, I am gratified by your worldly success. But in the same capacity I am obliged to recommend to you the cultivation of felicity in language. With more than three hundred thousand words at your disposal in any unabridged dictionary, is it necessary to permit your characters the use of expressions that are frequently inelegant, often profane, and (unless I misinterpret their meaning) occasionally improper?" Before she made her signature she hesitated. An odd light—something very like a twinkle—appeared in her eyes for a moment. She signed herself "The T. Miss D."

Gossip columns reported that when Geoffrey read the letter, sitting with a bunch of his cronies at Toots Shor's, he wept aloud and implored God to make him a better man. But Miss Dove had never credited that story. She'd thought it unlikely that any of her "old children"—even those who dabbled in the creative arts—could so far forsake the principles of dignity and restraint.

Now, in her illusory floating state, as Geoffrey's audacious lines recurred to her, she suddenly perceived a connection beyond the metrical between herself and the lady from Astolot. Elaine had floated, too. Elaine had floated upon a bier. Is this bed—? Am I—?

The unfinished question was preposterous. She lifted a hand as if to banish it into limbo.

"Are you feeling ill, Miss Dove?" asked Billie Jean.

"I was thinking of Lord Tennyson," said Miss Dove.

"Oh," said Billie Jean. "That's nice." She was not at home with the Victorian poets but she felt safe in the choice of her adjective. Whoever or whatever Miss Dove thought of was bound to be nice.

The room into which Miss Dove was wheeled was a small, blue room. Its window, giving upon budding treetops and gabled roofs, was like a big framed picture that dwarfed the wall.

"Now we'll take off our clothes and then we'll feel more comfy," said Billie Jean. She spoke in a humoring tone with steel behind it. It was clear that she intended to assume command.

"The pronoun 'we' is misleading," said Miss Dove. "Unless you propose to take *your* clothes off."

Billie Jean tittered nervously, but refused to be intimidated.

She undressed Miss Dove. ("You're not to try and help," she said. "Dr. Baker doesn't wish you to exert yourself.") She removed Miss Dove's outer garments, her camisole and chemise and petticoat and her old-fashioned boned stays. She gave her a bath.

"I made my ablutions this morning," demurred Miss Dove.

"It's routine," Billie Jean said, lathering her patient's flat, immaculate stomach.

"Very well, Mrs. Green," said Miss Dove. She could not, in conscience, oppose routine.

"Now here's something to make our skin soft and sweet. *Your* skin," Billie Jean said. She smoothed a few drops of emollient lotion over Miss Dove's neck and shoulders. "Know what I think of when I put this on my patients? The little can of talcum you gave me for Christmas in the third grade."

"The second grade," said Miss Dove. Her Christmas gifts had long been standardized. Talcum was for second-grade girls. Girls in the third grade got celluloid thimbles.

"Mine had a picture of lilacs on the tin," the nurse said. She eased Miss Dove's arms into the sleeves of a cambric bed-shirt.

"Yes," said Miss Dove.

"I was some kind of proud," said Billie Jean. She pulled the bed-clothes up. "And when you gave it to me you said something I never forgot. You said: 'This is to use *after* you wash your neck.' "

"I intended no reflection upon you," Miss Dove said quickly. "That is what I say to all the little girls."

"I didn't take it personal," Billie Jean assured her. "But it's funny what kids remember. I can hear you say that like it was ten minutes ago!" She emptied the bathwater down the lavatory drain and hung the washcloth and towel (neatly, Miss Dove observed, with the corners pulled out straight) on a rod. She returned, still talking, to the bedside. "You know how some girls can't pass a cosmetic counter without they spray themselves with free cologne? Well, I couldn't bring myself to do that. I'd feel dirty. Everybody thinks it's so queer!"

"Our standards are our own," said Miss Dove. She was, she discovered, fatigued. She wished that hospital regulations enjoined silence upon nurses—that they were required to raise their hands for permission to speak.

But it was Miss Dove's lips that were closed. Billie Jean stuck a thermometer between them.

"It's not that I don't care for perfume," she mused on after a minute of grateful silence during which she had counted her patient's pulse. "I guess every normal girl does. Take my baby—my little Ava. She's going on five and she's crazy about my Elizabeth Arden's 'Blue Grass.' " She withdrew the thermometer. "But I tell her every single time she begs for it—I say: 'First, you go wash yourself good!' "

"*Well,*" murmured Miss Dove.

Billie Jean, mistaking the monosyllabic correction for an exclamation of interest, nodded. "That's exactly what I tell her!" She read the thermometer and jotted down a figure on a small pad.

"What is my temperature?" asked Miss Dove.

"That's confidential information for the doctors," said Billie Jean. Apologetically, she patted Miss Dove's hand. "Even if I told you, you wouldn't know what it meant. It's in centigrade."

Miss Dove did not defend herself against the girl's bland assumption of her ignorance. "My question was indiscreet," she said.

"Oh, no! Not indiscreet!" Billie Jean protested. "All patients ask. But you know rules."

"Yes. I know rules," said Miss Dove.

"That 'Blue Grass,'" Billie Jean said, as if eager to return to a safe subject. "Bill Holloway gave it to me. He said it smelled refined." She blushed shyly. "He's going to give me something else. A ring."

"An engagement ring?" asked Miss Dove.

Billie Jean nodded. "I feel like a dream walking! I've been a widow for five lonely years and now—"

Miss Dove made an inarticulate sound of sympathy. Billie Jean, she knew, had gone west to work in a factory. She had been married there to a Mr. Green who had met with some sort of untimely—and, perhaps, unseemly—demise, the details of which had never been clarified in Liberty Hill. At any rate, Billie Jean had returned with a new name and a new baby and had become a practical nurse.

"And now," sighed Billie Jean, "I'm the happiest girl in the world!"

"But your life is full as it is," said Miss Dove. "You have your child and your work."

"A woman's life," said Billie Jean, "is never too full for a man!"

Miss Dove said nothing.

"Bill has you on a pedestal," Billie Jean went on. "He says you're his idea of 'genteel.'"

"I value William Holloway's opinion," said Miss Dove.

She voiced no idle politeness. She did value his opinion as she valued her own. That fact would have startled the society of Liberty Hill in which Miss Dove was considered—not entirely without reason—to be something of a snob. But such snobbery as she had was not of the common variety that flies, like a homing pigeon, to money or prestige. She was a moral snob. And so, in his way, was William.

Anything could be taught, of course—fine points of deportment as well as the names of the tributaries of the Nile. By six years of drill and example— forty-five minutes a day, Monday through Friday, September through May— Miss Dove had brought many a child to conform to a code that ran counter to his inclinations. But now and then—oh, a dozen times, perhaps, in the course of her teaching career—she had met a child in whom the ethical instinct, microcosmic but fully-formed, was as innate as original sin. It was an almost mystical thing, that gift for goodness—and rarer than mathematical genius or perfect pitch. Hardened as she was to surprises, Miss Dove never recognized it without a sudden leap of the pulse. She had recognized it in William.

All the signs had been against the boy. He came from a home—if one could call it a home—that might euphemistically have been described as "underprivileged." He was an orphan who lived with his grandmother, a woman of unsavory repute, in a leaky shack near the gas-works. On his first day at school he had been barefoot. There had been scabs on his toes. His hair had been matted and over one pasty cheek had been the brownish stain of a fading bruise. He had held an elbow crooked as if to ward off a blow.

Mothers, entering their pretty six-year-olds in Cedar Grove School, had gasped. One, a Mrs. Holmes, had begged Miss Dove to keep her son on the other side of the room from William.

"I believe in democracy," she had said, "but I don't want Charlie to catch anything!"

"My seating arrangement is alphabetical," Miss Dove had told her coldly. But privately her heart had sunk.

It was wearisome enough to deal with raw but scrubbed first-graders from decent families. An unwashed child from the criminal fringe of town posed a problem indeed.

And then William surprised her.

All the rules of manners and procedure that Miss Dove persuaded ("bullied," her critics said) the other children to accept, William took to his bosom. When he greeted Miss Dove at the door he did so in the accents of dedication. At her "attention please" he sat up straight and showed the proud poker-face of a soldier presenting arms. He began to wash. Like a badge of honor he wore a clean handkerchief protruding from his breast pocket.

Miss Dove gave him Saturday jobs raking leaves or mowing grass. He performed these jobs well and later, on her recommendation, he procured a paper route. He was the best paper boy in town. He was never late and he always laid the paper, folded, on the doorstep instead of twisting it and tossing it on the roof. ("What is worth doing is worth doing well," Miss Dove had said and William had taken her literally.)

Shortly before he finished the sixth grade Miss Dove had put beside his name in an old leather-bound ledger a single letter that was her mark of unqualified approval.

The ledger in which Miss Dove made that mark was no ordinary roll-book containing a record of pupils' attendance and statutory misconduct. It was a book as sacrosanct as that golden one in which Abou Ben Adhem's angel wrote in the lily-like room. No human eye except Miss Dove's (and that eye, there were many to say, was something more or less than human) ever perused its pages. In it were inscribed the names of all the children who had passed, during Miss Dove's incumbency there, through the final grade of Cedar Grove School. In it each child was given a single letter of the alphabet indicating what Miss Dove considered the basic trait of its character. (Miss Dove generally thought of children as "its" instead of "he's" and "she's.") She could have guessed that trait, with fair accuracy, the day any child first came into the geography room frightened or boisterous or homesick for its mother. But, in charity, she deferred her judgment. Unpromising as any lump of humanity might be, there was always the possibility that half a dozen years of thumping and molding might work it into respectable shape. Not until Miss Dove was nearly done with a child, until it was about to escape forever from her supervision, was she willing to call its character established.

The commonest letter in the ledger was T for Tractable. That letter was appropriate for the rank and file of Miss Dove's pupils—youngsters not born for Who's Who but amenable to reason and capable, under wise leadership, of becoming decent citizens. There were a number of W's for Willing given to those children who showed more than the usual desire to be improved. There were some A's for Awkward and a sprinkling of B's—a really bad mark —which stood for Babyish and was given most frequently to the kind of pouting little girl who would become, in the future, a fattish middle-aged woman who wore frilly bathing suits that showed her stomach and wept when the cook failed to come. O's for Original went to unregulated children who formed ideas of their own without consulting Miss Dove, who decorated their maps with pictures of Viking ships off the coast of Denmark, or were disposed to argue points of philosophy. (O's were not signs of Miss Dove's esteem; she gave them regretfully. She had given one to Geoffrey Lyons.) But beside William Holloway's name she placed the symbol that she might, without undue complacency or spurious modesty, have placed beside her own. It was an S. It stood for Satisfactory.

And yet, highly as she had regarded him, she had known far less of him outside the geography room than she had known of most of the children. For though it was her custom to pay pastoral calls at the residences of her pupils, she had never called upon William's grandmother. In his case, she had felt a separation of school and home to be eminently desirable.

So she never saw the squalid little house on the alley until William had been for years beyond her care. And then it wore a pitiful dignity. Upon its door was a sheaf of carnations. It was a house made significant for a day by death.

In a larger world than that of Cedar Grove, beset by temptations and not sustained by the classic simplicity of inflexible rights and wrongs, William had not done well. He had played truant. He had hung around pool-rooms. Once he had been haled into juvenile court for shooting crap. And yet Miss Dove had not lost faith in him. The thing that set him apart from the generality—a congenital sensitivity to virtue—was, she believed, enduring. As a diamond dissolved in the crucible hardened again into its pristine crystalline shape, so William, with any modicum of luck, would return to his S. She would have liked to help ensure that luck. But what could she do? She was a teacher, not a probation officer.

One day, when William was seventeen and had quit school, Miss Dove heard that his grandmother was dead. She had died under sordid circumstances. In a free-for-all fight over the rights to a debouchment of coins from a slot machine, someone had split her skull with a beer-bottle. She was to be buried late that afternoon.

After school Miss Dove put on her hat and gloves and set out for the house of bereavement. On the listing lean-to porch were a few neighbors. Miss Dove bowed distantly to them. She walked straight to the door.

Inside, wearing an ill-fitting, evidently borrowed dark suit, stood William. He was a tall fellow now—thin, but with powerful shoulders—and Miss Dove thought she had never seen a more perplexed distress than that which marked his face. (It was like a bruise—the bruise he had worn on his first day at school.) She extended her hand.

"May I offer my expressions of sympathy?" she asked.

William took her hand. He straightened his shoulders. "Thank you, Miss Dove," he said. "Would you like to come in and see Grandma?"

There was little Miss Dove would have liked less, but she followed William into the front room. There the remains of the disreputable Mrs. Holloway reposed in a cheap coffin. In death, Miss Dove was certain, the old woman had achieved an aspect of decency that she had not achieved in life.

"She did the best she could," said William. "She didn't—" he gave Miss Dove a glance of reverence. "She didn't have my opportunities."

"Her troubles are over," said Miss Dove.

"I hope so," said William. "Some say they're not."

Miss Dove rode with William to the cemetery, sitting erect in the undertaker's limousine. But when the obsequies were over she bade him farewell. "I will walk home," she explained. "I wish the exercise." Then she looked William full in the face and said in a clear tone that could be heard by all the lesser mourners, "I shall follow your career with interest."

She went off, leaving him to decide in that loneliness which is the true climate of decision, whether to respect his life or throw it away.

As it turned out, William was sensible. He joined the army. After three years, honorably discharged and seventy pounds heavier, he returned to Liberty Hill. Using his G. I. educational allowance for living expenses, he completed his high-school education. Then, with a sound understanding of himself, he entered the field of law enforcement.

Each morning when Miss Dove saw him at the intersection of Grant and Maple—spruce and solid, lifting his great, white-gloved hand to halt traffic or beckon children across the street—she experienced a moment of stern exhilaration. There was a man whose mind and muscles functioned in harmony. A man in love with his work. For him, she knew, a policeman's lot was a very happy one.

Of his domestic lot, which he planned to cast with Billie Jean's, Miss Dove was less certain. And yet, she remembered, Billie Jean *did* wash her neck before applying scent. That was a straw in the wind.

"I've tired you," Billie Jean said ruefully. "I always go yak-yak when I'm nervous. You see, Bill thinking so much of you and you being the terri—well, being who you are—I got flustered."

"That was natural," said Miss Dove.

"A nurse has got no business being natural," said Billie Jean, rebuking herself. "A nurse should think of her patient."

Quiet reigned in the room. Miss Dove relaxed. Some thread that had always stretched taut, holding her fast to responsibility, seemed to have snapped clean through. She closed her eyes and let her mind bob up and down like a cork on the surface of a pond. She thought of pleasant, far-off things. Of a golden afternoon when she had sat on a campus lawn with the young archeologist, watching cloud shadows move over the grass and talking of the buried cities of antiquity. Of her mother arranging roses in a silver bowl. Of her little sisters wishing on the first star. Of her father reading

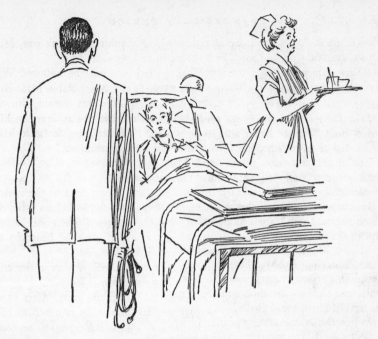

aloud by the fire. And often, as those images thinned out like smoke, she did not think at all.

Billie Jean fed her soup from a spoon. A technician drew blood from her finger-tip and carried it away in a test-tube. She scarcely noticed.

Through the window floated the blithe and quarrelsome voices of children released from school. They floated from an alien sphere, from a point remote in time.

An interne came into the room. He was a short young man with a crew-cut, bright pink cheeks, and the gloss of appalling youth. In his white coat and trousers he reminded Miss Dove of a sixth-grader dressed up for the graduation exercises of Cedar Grove Elementary School. The stethoscope around his neck, his horn-rimmed glasses, and his deep bass voice all seemed assumed like poor theatrical disguises that did not succeed in lending credibility to a role.

Billie Jean, as she leapt to her feet, stood at attention, and registered deference, appeared to be play-acting, too. "Here's Dr. Temple, Miss Dove," she said.

"Oh?" said Miss Dove, sounding unconvinced.

"I am Dr. Baker's house officer," the interne announced from somewhere low in his visceral cavity.

Not knowing what a house officer was, Miss Dove reserved comment.

"I hope you're fairly comfortable," he said. "I believe you're complaining of pain in the low dorsal region and of extended numbness in the right leg?"

"I am comfortable, thank you," said Miss Dove. She added: "And I did *not* complain."

"We use the word in a medical sense," said Dr. Temple. "I'll do a physical now before I take your history."

"You?" said Miss Dove.

"A superficial one," he assured her. "The fine points I'll leave for Dr. Baker."

Miss Dove sought words for protest. It had been strange enough to take orders from Thomas Baker and to be washed by Billie Jean; to lie here at the mercy of an owlish child with a false voice was ridiculous.

But Billie Jean had unbuttoned Miss Dove's bed-shirt. The doctor's stethoscope was cupped against her chest. Submission was the better part of dignity.

Lights were flashed in her eyes, up her nose, and down her throat. Her blood pressure was tested. She was prodded in the ribs, in the solar plexus, and in the abdomen.

"The belly muscles are remarkably firm," the young man said. His tone was so admiring that Miss Dove forgave him his indelicacy of diction. Coarseness, like an occupational disease, seemed to derive from the practice of medicine, and should—she supposed—be deplored rather than condemned. Even young Dr. Hurley said "belly."

When the examination was over Billie Jean retired from the room.

"Now we'll take your history," said Dr. Temple.

The questions he asked were personal, Miss Dove thought, to the point of irrelevance. However, she answered them.

She had been born in 1896. Her mother had been nineteen and her father thirty-eight. So far as she knew there had been no untoward circumstances attending her birth. "Naturally, my mother did not describe her confinement," she said.

Yes, she had siblings. Two sisters much younger than she. They lived three states away now, with growing families of their own. No. She had never been jealous of them.

Jealous of Flora and Lucy! Those timorous creatures who echoed their husbands' opinions and jumped on chairs when they saw mice!

She had had the usual juvenile diseases.

She was five when she had measles. She lay in the big, canopied four-poster in the company room with all her dolls to keep her company. Her mother sat by the window and sewed little doll dresses and told her fairy tales. Every evening her father brought her a new present. He brought her a music box that played Sur le Pont d'Avignon, a silver ring enameled with forget-me-nots, a string of coral beads, and a canary in a cage. He brought her a globe of the Earth.

He set the globe on a table and showed her the different seas and rivers and continents and countries. "This is France," he said. "Artists live there and the people speak differently from us. They say 'ma petite fille' for 'my little girl.' This is Switzerland where the mountains are covered with snow all year long. The mountains are called the Alps. And beyond the Alps lies Italy. See—it is shaped like a boot."

"Where is *here?*" she asked.

"Here is here," he said, showing her. "Here is home. But some day, when you're bigger, you and I will make the grand tour. We'll make a grander tour than anybody. We'll get on a boat and go down the Atlantic Ocean—" he traced the course with a finger "—and around the Horn, and up the Pacific. We'll visit China and eat bird's-nest soup. We'll go to India and see the fakirs—magic men—throw ropes into the air and climb up them."

"Can I climb?" she asked.

"No," he said. "If you did I'd be lonesome on the ground. We'll ride camels across the desert. We'll go to Venice where the streets are made of water and people go shopping in boats—gondolas they're called—instead of carriages."

The place-names filled her with enchantment. But what opened a real vista in her mind was the fact that the world was round. She had thought it was flat and four-cornered like the top of a candy box. If you walked far enough you would come to the edge and be in danger of falling off. She drifted into slumber on a new, slowly spinning sense of wonder.

No, she told Dr. Temple, she did not suffer from headaches. She had no allergies. She was not often afflicted with respiratory infections. Her family tree revealed no epilepsy, night-blindness, eczema, or melancholy.

"What about your emotional life?" he asked.

"I beg your pardon?" said Miss Dove.

The doctor blushed which made him appear more immature than ever. "Well—love, you know. And feelings of frustration. Inadequacy."

"I have never felt inadequate."

"The question was routine," he assured her. "Suppose we call your emotional life satisfactory?"

"That will be correct," said Miss Dove.

"Are you subject to fantasy?"

For a moment Miss Dove was not sure. Should she mention the floating sensation in the hospital corridor? Or the phantom children she had almost seen more than once in the empty geography room?

"Within reason," she said at last.

Dr. Temple did not press the matter.

"Thank you, Miss Dove," he said. "Dr. Baker will be in later, of course. And if there's anything I can do—" He smiled in an engaging, unprofessional way. "You and I are really old friends," he said. "In a manner of speaking, I've known you all my life."

"You have known *me?*" Miss Dove said. She scanned his face. It was vaguely familiar, but only vaguely.

"I'm Adams Temple," he told her. "My mother was a Liberty Hill girl."

"Angela Adams, of course," said Miss Dove. He had the same brown eyes, myopic and speculative, and the same conformation of the forehead—bulging over each eyebrow as if small, stubby horns were about to sprout through the bone. He had the same *enfant terrible* expression. "I should have known."

"Well, it's been a long time. Mother's family moved to Kansas when she was fourteen. But she remembers you."

"I remember her," Miss Dove said without marked enthusiasm. "She had an inquiring mind."

Angela Adams—who had received in the Judgment Book a C for Contentious—had taught Miss Dove, indirectly, valuable lessons in the technique of classroom management. Her name being what it was, she had sat on the front seat of the first row and had shown a tendency to lean forward with her elbow on her desk and her chin cupped in her palm instead of sitting erect with her hands folded. In the show-offy way in which most children enjoy turning cartwheels or somersaults, Angela had enjoyed mental gymnastics. "Why" and "how" were her favorite words—tiresome words to a very young instructress who was striving for a reputation for infallibility—and when Angela uttered them she was apt to look smug as if she thought: "*This* time I'll trip the teacher!"

Once, had she had the humility to leave well enough alone, she might have done just that.

Miss Dove had been reading aloud from a book on the dietary habits of undomesticated animals. "Bears like honey," she read. "They are also fond of red ants which have a flavor similar to that of pickles."

Angela had waved her hand. "How does he know, Miss Dove?" she had demanded. "How does the author know what ants taste like?"

The thirty-nine other children in the room had fixed their trusting eyes upon Miss Dove, waiting for her answer. Then Angela, herself, saved the day. Brash with the imminence of victory, she had pushed her advantage too far.

"Did he eat an ant to see?" she had asked sarcastically. "Or did a bear tell him?"

The class had giggled. Ordinarily, Miss Dove frowned upon laughter, but this time it fell like music on her ear. She directed upon Angela her steady, solemn, scrutinizing gaze.

The child blushed. She folded her hands.

"Never *pretend* to be silly, Angela," Miss Dove said at last. She waited until a hush settled upon the room. Then she continued to read from the book: "The giraffe is a vegetarian. His long neck enables him to nibble the leaves of trees."

"She used to tell us stories about you," Dr. Temple said in the happy, nostalgic manner of a boy who is fond of his mother. "She said you reminded her of Mary Poppins."

"Mary Who?"

"Poppins. A magic English nanny in a fairy story. As soon as she walked into a nursery all babies stopped yelling and all buttons flew into the right buttonholes. According to Mother you had that effect, morally speaking, on a roomful of boisterous brats."

"It was not magic," said Miss Dove.

"Maybe character is a kind of magic," he said. "Mother said, too, that my Latin teacher in high school was like you. She kept us on our toes. Right now I could conjugate any verb, regular or irregular, you cared to give me."

Miss Dove did not care to give him a verb. "I am honored by the comparison," she said.

"Of course, she was more narrow-minded than you," he went on.

(And by what rule, pray, have you measured the breadth of my mind? Miss Dove asked silently.)

"It came from a surfeit of dead grammar, I guess. Do you know what she said to me when I left for college?"

"No," said Miss Dove.

Dr. Temple grinned reminiscently. "She said: 'Good-by, Adams. Don't get any new ideas!'"

Miss Dove saw nothing funny in the Latin teacher's advice. She thought it shrewd and cogent and particularly sound for the son of Angela. "And did you?" she asked.

Dr. Temple laughed. "Very few," he admitted. "You know, there *aren't* many!"

With a nod he was gone. And it dawned upon Miss Dove that for all his volubility he had told her nothing of her physical condition. She said as much to her nurse.

"He's not in charge," said Billie Jean. "You're Dr. Baker's private patient."

"Then what is it—" Miss Dove began and her mouth went dry, "—what is it Dr. Baker suspects?"

Billie Jean shook her head. "He will tell you what you need to know."

"I see no occasion for mystery," said Miss Dove.

"Don't try to see," said Billie Jean. "Let *us* do the thinking!"

Let us do the thinking! Us! Billie Jean McVay whose expression when she'd looked at a little boy had been that of a gourmand surveying the cherry on top of a butterscotch sundae; Thomas Baker, the erstwhile clown, wit, wag, and ear-wiggler; and the complacent rosebud son of Angela Adams! Oh, no. *Miss Dove* did the thinking. It was the habit of a lifetime—the teacher's burden accepted long ago and never sloughed off for an instant! The modern fad of urging the young to "reason things out" she considered pedagogical laziness. Moreover, it encouraged agnosticism. In the geography room *she* drew the conclusions. She doled them out to her pupils who received them whole, without analysis, and wrote them down between even margins in their notebooks.

But this was not the geography room.

Billie Jean knitted the toe of an enormous Argyle sock. Now and then, as if to tease her patient's mind away from the exploration of unprofitable channels, she quoted some artless pearl that had dropped from the milky lips of her little Ava.

Mrs. Lester Knight, Senior, stuck her head in at the door to report the condition of Lester, Junior. (Maternal fatuity had persuaded her that Miss Dove would be aching for such news.) "Tommy got his appendix just in time," she declared. "They were sizzling!"

Mr. Spivey came with his messages from the school. He delivered them in a bluff, hearty voice, resonant with spurious optimism.

Alexander Burnham came with the things he'd promised to bring. He stayed only a few minutes, confining his conversation to small, safe topics far removed from illness. A pair of robins were nesting in the ivy over the church door. Geoffrey Lyons, en route from New York to Hollywood, was stopping overnight with his brother. Jincey Baker was preserving her status quo and becoming rather impatient.

"He's a wonderful man," Billie Jean said when the minister had gone. "He believes in giving folks a second chance."

"Yes," said Miss Dove, "he is an ornament to his cloth."

But she was not concerned with Alexander's virtues. She was waiting for Thomas Baker.

Thomas did not appear until after supper. By that time, Billie Jean had been relieved by the night nurse, a dour, middle-aged woman who was not a native of Liberty Hill. She had been trained (as she made known immediately) to be a ward supervisor. At present she was resting between positions and had taken Miss Dove's case as a favor to the superintendent of the hospital.

"I am interested in the *theory* of nursing," she said.

"I see," said Miss Dove without pretending to be impressed. The mental keenness of the new nurse was probably greater than that of Billie Jean, she reflected, but her manual skill was less and she lacked humility. Routine duties of the bedside—the smoothing of pillows, the fetching of pans, and the counting of pulses—she regarded as unworthy of her talents, much as Mona Leckford regarded the teaching of Longfellow's poems to the fifth grade.

Thomas breezed into the room. He was dressed all in green. Green trousers and short-sleeved blouse and a green, turban-like cap on his head. Miss Dove was startled. Had he, she wondered, been acting in a pageant to celebrate the arrival of Spring?

"This is the latest fashion for operating-room wear," said Thomas. "It's easy on the eyes. Did you think I'd forgotten you?"

"No," said Miss Dove. She never fancied herself forgotten.

"I've been busy since I left you," Thomas said. "Dull, run-of-the-mine stuff that consumes time. First the Knight boy, of course—"

"Lester eats imprudently and too much," said Miss Dove. "Mrs. Knight informed me that his affected part was in danger of rupture."

Thomas laughed. "It was inflamed but not dramatic," he said. "Of course I told Jane it was sizzling. Give her something to brag about at the bridge table."

"I trust Lester's convalescence will be unimpeded," said Miss Dove.

"He's hungry already," said Thomas. "We'll have him up tomorrow." He gave Miss Dove's hand a perfunctory pat. "I just dropped by to see that you were being well treated."

But Miss Dove did not intend to let him escape so easily.

"I should like to ask a few questions concerning my own state of health," she said.

"Why, certainly," Thomas said, assuming the transparent disguise of candor that Miss Dove had come to recognize. "But I'm not sure I can answer them. Dr. Temple—did you know, by the way, that he's Angela Adams' son?"

"Yes," Miss Dove said indifferently, rejecting that decoy.

Dr. Temple's findings had all been negative, Thomas told her, which was good. Her blood pressure—systolic and dystolic—was ideal. Refraction of the eyes normal. Heart function unimpaired. No palpable abdominal masses.

"What is your guess?" asked Miss Dove.

"I don't guess," said Thomas. "Tomorrow we will do exhaustive tests. By Friday I should be able to speak with some degree of conviction. Until then—" He moved away. At the door he paused and turned to her. "Until then," he said, and his tone, though casual, carried an undertone of command, "I shall expect you, Miss Dove, to assume the virtue of docility."

"Yes, doctor," said Miss Dove. She closed her eyes and surrendered to the inevitable. Nothing had ever taxed her powers as did that passive act of resignation.

The weather changed in the night. Next day—Thursday—was raw and wet. At Cedar Grove School the children were restless. Mr. Spivey called a special assembly.

"As we're all sorry to know," he said, standing on the podium, "Miss Dove is in the hospital. But we're going right on with our geography work. We're not planning to let her down. I will take her place!"

A gust of giggles swept the air in the auditorium. The vision of Mr. Spivey with his bald, glittering head, his big Adam's apple, and his toothy grin sitting at Miss Dove's desk struck the student body as irresistibly comical.

"In other words," the principal shouted above the laughter, "we're all members of one team! Our quarterback has been injured in scrimmage, and I'm going to sub for her. I want to call the same plays she would call. But I don't know those plays as well as you do. So whenever I'm offside I want you to tell me. Okay?"

"Okay!" the audience responded.

"And we're all in there pitching together?"

"Sure!" Several boys spat on their hands and delivered imaginary round-house curves.

Later, incongruously throned in the geography room, he found the children as good as their promise.

At eight-forty-five the first grade filed in. Mr. Spivey, though a bachelor, was a family man at heart and like many such men—especially those who are amply built—he was charmed by littleness. The first-graders were his pets. He liked to give them lolly-pops, to join in their round games at recess, and to feel that they loved him. Generally, when they greeted him, their faces broke into merry smiles. Today, they kept their distance and forced him to keep his.

The first to enter the room was a lisping, pinafored girl known to all and sundry as Sister Abernathy. She blushed when she addressed the principal, but her face remained expressionless. "Good morning, Mithter Thpivey," she said.

"Good morning, Sister."

Sister shook her head. "Mith Dove callth me Annabel," she said. "And firtht you have to make me do my mannerth again becauthe I lithped."

Mr. Spivey cleared his throat. "Pronounce my name correctly," he said in a gruff voice. He felt like an ass. He twinkled at Sister.

She did not return his twinkle. "Good morning, Mi-sss-ter S-spivey," she said.

With the remainder of the class—excusing a couple of slips when he called Raymond "Buddy" and Susan "Peaches,"—he did moderately well.

Buddy—or Raymond—raised his hand. "Congratulations," he said.

"Thank you," said Mr. Spivey.

"You're welcome," said Raymond. He folded his hands upon his desk.

The others did likewise. They all sat there, perfectly silent, with their hands—as Mr. Spivey told Miss Ellwood later—closed together like the wings of sitting ducks, and their wide eyes fixed on him.

"What do I do now, Raymond?" he said at last.

"You say 'Attention, please. The lesson will begin,'" said Raymond.

Step by step, grade by grade, Mr. Spivey was helped through the day.

Acting on the principle that requires a captain to be the last man to leave a ship, Mr. Spivey made it his rule to remain in the building for a full hour after school was dismissed. Today, he was surprised that the music teacher, Miss Ellwood, had stayed too. He met her in the hall. She wore a red rain-cape of transparent plastic. Its hood cast a glow upon her complexion. Attached to the zippers on her rubber boots were tiny silver bells that tinkled when she walked.

"Some third grade moppets were making a dish-garden for Miss Dove," she explained. "I stayed to help them. You know what store she sets on neatness."

"That was awfully nice of you," said Mr. Spivey.

"She taught *me*," said Lorraine. Her blue eyes were misty. "Back in the dark ages."

Mr. Spivey understood that her reference to the far past of her childhood was intended to elicit from him a gallant contradiction. But à deux with a woman he was a bashful man.

"I took her classes and I feel I've been through a wringer," he said.

"I'll bet you do!" cried Lorraine. She laughed. A single tear shook out of one eye and was impaled, like a dewdrop, on the end of a lash.

"Such regimentation I've never seen," he declared. "And the queer thing is—the kids like it!"

"Yes. Deep down they do," said Lorraine. With a dainty handkerchief that smelled of lily-of-the-valley she dabbed her eye. "She was a fabulous teacher! I mean she *is!*"

The spectacle of this gentle creature—all tenderness and femininity—weeping for an old tartar was infinitely touching to Mr. Spivey. "You're right to say '*is,*'" he said. "We must be positive and optimistic. I know Tom Baker is gravely concerned but—'no game is ever over 'til the final whistle blows!'"

"Life can be so sad," said Lorraine. "There she was reviewing the fourth grade for the proficiency tests! And with no warning—"

"I still don't approve of her didactic methods," said Mr. Spivey. "I believe in being pals with children. In classroom democracy."

"Oh, so do I!" said Lorraine.

"I don't approve of them," he went on musingly, "but I'll have to admit, they *work!* I figure it this way: Miss Dove is sincere. And kids are fair. You can't fool 'em. When they see somebody doing a sincere job, they know it. And they play ball!"

"It's so *big* of you to understand that," said Lorraine.

"I strive for tolerance," said Mr. Spivey. Then he suggested that Miss Ellwood let him drive her home. On the way they might stop at the Grill and Fountain for a cup of coffee. He would like to discuss with her a paper he was writing on the problems of extracurricular activities in the elementary school.

"Oh, Mr. Spivey, that would be super!" cried Lorraine.

Thomas Baker once again brought Jincey her breakfast. He tried to maintain his usual bantering manner but his humor was forced and distrait.

"Are you worried about me or Miss Dove?" asked Jincey.

"Both," said Thomas. "But I have to stop worrying about you." He took her hand in his. "I have to shut you right out of my mind."

"Can you?"

"Yes." He gave her a level look. "I am Miss Dove's doctor."

Jincey wanted to cry. She was not in the least alarmed about herself. She was, in fact, one of those fortunate women in whom pregnancy induces a euphoric illusion of immunity to mischance. But she had counted on having her husband with her during labor much as she might have counted on having him at a dinner party.

"Well," she said, "I have a doctor too. Sam Tillet will probably be relieved not to have you messing 'round."

"I'll speak to Sam," said Thomas.

"I'll speak to him, myself," said Jincey. "In my interesting condition I'm still capable of using a telephone! Look, Tommy. Seriously, this is what I'll do. I'll move over to your mother's house today. Then you won't need to give me a thought. Tomorrow, if I'm still navigating, I'll enter the hospital for the duration."

"That's a very smart idea," Thomas said, beaming upon his wife. She was ten years younger than he. He had married her for love—light-hearted love evoked by such charm as her coloring, the music in her laughter, and the exquisite balance of her flesh and bone—so that her gift for rationality, which he'd discovered after marriage, he thought of as a bonus he'd had no right to expect.

"I never was as stupid as I looked," said Jincey. She tossed her head. Loose tendrils of her tumbled hair glittered like delicate copper wires in the lamplight.

"Your hair's a halo," said Thomas.

"Miss Dove never thought so. She considered it Satan's own device to make me vain and divert little boys from their lessons!" Jincey laughed. "And she was so right! Once, I remember—" The gaiety went out of her voice and left it low and gentle and full of wood-pigeon notes; she crossed her arms as if to warm her recollection against her breast—"she took it in her hand and pulled it back and tied it with a little old piece of grocery string!"

Thomas had seen the teacher deal just so with other little girls. He stood in the doorway of the bedroom trying to visualize how Jincey must have looked—mortified or indignant?—for his wife's childhood, now that she was about to lose it finally and forever in the childhood of another, had begun to beguile his imagination. But Jincey's memory was not his to share because, though he had been, in a way, its hero, he had been so in absentia. And, really, it was not Jincey's either. It was more Miss Dove's.

The episode Jincey recalled had occurred in the geography room during World War Two. Miss Dove had been waiting for the sixth grade to file in when suddenly she had had the feeling of not being alone. Someone or something was moving about the room. Over there, near the sand table, it paused and looked at her. But even when the presence glided along the wall behind her; even when she heard—or almost heard—a new stick of chalk squeaking on the blackboard, Miss Dove did not turn around. She knew, of course, that nobody was there. Her nerves were playing tricks on her again. Miss Dove did not believe in nerves.

Through the open door she watched the sixth graders come out of the music room down the hall. They came out with a rush, as if for two minutes of freedom between classroom and classroom they were borne along upon some mass exhilaration. They always left the music room in that fashion but today they managed to be noisier than usual. It was the season, she supposed. The day was warm and the children were restless as the weather. There was a sharp sound as of someone being spanked with a book; there was a voice saying, "Double dare, Randy!"; there was a breathless giggling.

But as they approached Miss Dove's room they pulled their excitement in like proud but well-broken ponies. They greeted her politely and went to their places. At a nod from her they took their seats.

Jincey Webb, Miss Dove noticed without enthusiasm, had a permanent wave. Yesterday her carrot-colored mane had been neatly braided and pulled back from her serious freckled face. Now it hung to her shoulders, a bushy mop of undulations and frizz. It hung on her mind, too; that was plain to see. Jincey's expression was one of utter and enviable complacency. It seemed doubtful that a long lifetime of repeated triumphs could again offer her an achievement so sublime with self-satisfaction.

Randy Baker wiggled his ears at Jincey. Miss Dove looked at him. His eyes grew round with innocence. His ears grew very still.

Miss Dove kept looking at him, but she had stopped seeing him. Instead, she was seeing his brother Thomas, who had sat there at Randy's desk years before, with the same film of specious virtue over the mischief in his eyes. And then she saw Thomas on a raft in the Pacific. She did not see him as they had described him in the papers—skin and bones and haggard young face overgrown with a rough, wild beard. The Thomas she saw looked like Randy. He had braces on his teeth and a dimple in his chin. And he was all alone in the dismal gray mountains of the sea.

A wave of giddiness swept over her, but she did not sit down. It was nothing. It had happened to her off and on all year, and it had always passed.

"Open your notebooks, class," she said.

It was Tuesday and Tuesday was note-book day in the geography room. Miss Dove had so ordained it when she had first assumed control there and she had never toyed with the notion of changing Tuesday's function. She was not a woman to toy with notions. On that day each week her pupils inscribed on ruled pages such verbal matter as their teacher believed suitable to their stage of development. The first grade, for example, might write— copying from the board—"The yak is a very useful animal" and, later, the more complicated sentence about the camel. The third grade made lists of the states in a prescribed order, they began with Maine and went down the Atlantic coastline to Florida and then, moving over to Alabama, up to Michigan, and so on. The sixth graders, who were being prepared by degrees for the inescapable perils of independent thinking that would beset them soon, copied a statement of fact that contained an aphorism and enlarged upon it in their own words. Miss Dove had a goodly store of these geographical maxims. "The trade winds maintain a steady course" she would often write, or "Above the fiftieth parallel life requires hardihood," or "Gibraltar is proof against the erosion of the waters." She was about to choose from one of these when a boy on the back row choked on a clandestine peppermint, sputtered, bulged his eyes, turned purple in the face and was obliged to leave the room for water.

Miss Dove watched him go, but her mind watched two small boys who had long since departed from Cedar Grove.

She had come on those lads at the drinking fountain. (They'd had no business at the fountain; it was their library period. But the librarian was lax.) They had been discussing her.

"I bet Miss Dove could lick Joe Louis," one of them had said.

"Who? That old stick?" the other one had jeered. "I could beat her with my little finger!"

He had glanced up to see Miss Dove looking down at him. She had looked at him for a long time. Her gray eyes were expressionless. The tip of her long nose was pink, but no pinker than normal. At last she had spoken.

"Thomas Baker," she had said in the tone of one making a pure observation, "you talk too much, don't you?"

"Yes, ma'am," Thomas had said in a tiny voice. He had gone off without getting any water. For a long time afterwards he sweated when he thought of the incident. He could not know that Miss Dove remembered too. But she did.

Ever since Pearl Harbor Miss Dove had been troubled. She lived quite alone, for her sisters were married by then and her mother was dead, and one evening while she was correcting papers she sensed, with that uncanny extra-perception of the teacher, that something had intruded upon her solitude. She looked quickly about her sitting-room. A curtain rustled in a puff of breeze; her grandmother's whatnot cast a grotesque shadow on the polished floor; a finger of lamplight picked out a gold title on one of her father's old brown travel books. There was nothing else. But the red correction pencil shook in her fingers; for a moment her throat constricted in a spasm of desolate, unaccountable grief and a conviction of her own unworthiness. Miss Dove had never before felt unworthy in all her life.

After that the thing happened frequently, until at last she saw who the intruders were. They were the children she had taught long ago.

War had scattered those children. There was a girl—a vain, silly little piece she had been—who was a nurse on Corregidor. At least, when last heard of she had been on Corregidor. One of the boys was dead in Tunisia. Others were on the Anzio beachhead, or in the jungles of New Guinea, or in the flak-brightened sky over Germany. But they came back to Miss Dove. She saw them as they had been at seven, at ten, at twelve. Only they had a beauty she had not seen in them then. They lifted their faces like starry morning flowers. Their limbs quivered with the unreasoned joy of childhood. And then, as Miss Dove looked at them, they grew still. Their faces paled. They clasped their little hands. They faded and were gone.

The child who came oftenest was Thomas Baker. The town paper had been full of Thomas. His ship had been bombed, his officers killed, and Thomas had taken over. A hundred men owed their lives to his presence of mind. For days he had floated on a raft with no food and only the water in his canteen. When they picked him up his tongue had protruded from his mouth, black and swollen with thirst. That was what got Miss Dove—he had run out of water.

The Thomas who came to stand before her now was a sturdy boy in knickers. He held his chin at a cocky angle, but the dimple in it trembled. He ran the tip of his tongue over his lips.

But the children came only at night. When daylight returned Miss Dove could believe she had been the victim of waking dreams. She would eat her customary boiled egg and her whole-wheat toast; she would take a vitamin pill with her orange-juice; she would walk forth at her usual pace and assume her usual role of unshakable authority. The children at the school would seem to have little in common with those graceful and evanescent figures that haunted her. And no intruders dared invade the geography room. Or they hadn't until today.

The boy who had choked returned. Another boy, in the row by the window, cleared his throat. One in the middle row followed suit. Soon the whole room was dotted with the sound, a rough "h-hrmph" like frogs in a marsh. Miss Dove knew what the sound meant. It was the school's traditional signal—a kind of dare. She had heard other teachers speak of it in exasperation. It was the first time it had occurred in her room.

Slowly Randy Baker raised his hand. The sounds stopped. Silence like a caught breath hung on the room. Miss Dove could see beads of sweat on Randy's brow. His open palm was damp and gleaming.

"Yes, Randolph?" she said.

Randy stood up. Miss Dove's pupils always stood when they addressed her. He smoothed his plump stomach with his hand. "I got a letter from Tommy yestiddy," he said.

"*Received*, Randolph," said Miss Dove. "You received a letter from your brother *yesterday*. That was nice."

"Yes, Miss Dove," said Randy. He hesitated. Clearly, he was floundering. "He sent me a dollar he won playing poker in the convalescent hospital."

"I am sorry to hear that Thomas gambles," said Miss Dove, "but we are all very proud of his war record. If you have nothing more interesting to tell us you may take your seat, Randolph."

"H-hr-rmph!" went the boy behind Randy.

"He's been decorated," said Randy, "for bravery beyond the call of duty." The high words seemed to inspirit him. "He sent a message to the class."

"Did you bring the letter?" asked Miss Dove. "If so, you may read that part aloud."

Randy took an air-mail envelope from his hip pocket.

The class stirred. The ghost of a titter rippled the air.

"Attention, please," said Miss Dove.

Randy opened the letter. The paper was smudged and crumpled. Obviously, it had suffered many readings in many hands. Randy cleared his throat. The sound he made was not a link in the chain signal. Miss Dove could tell the difference. "It's sort of long," Randy demurred hopefully.

"We can spare the time," she said.

Randy began to read. His voice was high and clear; it had the girlish sweetness that comes just before the breaking point.

"The funny thing about the world," Randy read, "is that it looks just like you think it does. When they flew me back to Cal. in a hospital plane I looked down and, heck, kid, I might as well have been looking at those diagrams on the geography board back in dear (ha, ha!) ole Cedar Grove. I spotted a peninsula. A body of water almost entirely surrounded by land. I saw some atolls too. And they really are made in rings like doughnuts with palm trees sprouting out of the cake part and blue water in the hole in the middle. The water is the color of that blue chalk I swiped once and drew a picture of Miss Dove on the sidewalk with. Remember?"

He swallowed hard.

"Proceed, Randolph," said Miss Dove.

"You want to know if I was scared when the little yellow insects from—" Randy blushed but went on—"from hell"—in his embarrassment he brought out the word with unnecessary force—"dive-bombed us. The answer is, you bet. But it came to me in a flash that I wasn't much scareder than I was that time ole lady Dove caught me bragging about how I could beat her up at the drinking fountain. 'I didn't run that time,' I told myself, 'so I won't run now.' Besides there wasn't much place to run to."

The class laughed nervously.

"And later," Randy read on doggedly, "when I was bobbing up and down like Crusoe on my raft, what do you guess I thought about? It wasn't any pin-up girl. It was Miss Dove. I thought about the fishy stare she used to give us when we needed a drink of water. So to make my supply hold out I played I was back in the geography room. And even after the water was gone I kept playing. I'd think, 'The bell is bound to ring in a few minutes. You can last a little longer.' It took the same kinds of guts in the Pacific it did in school. Tell that to the guys in Cedar Grove." Randy stopped abruptly.

"Hr-hrmph!" went someone.

"Is that the end?" asked Miss Dove.

Randy looked directly at her. For a fleeting moment she thought he was going to say yes. If he did, that would be that.

Randy shook his head. "No, Miss Dove," he said. "There's a little more." His face turned the color of a ripe tomato. "He says here"—Randy gulped— "he says"—Randy took a deep breath—"he says: 'Give the terrible Miss Dove a kiss for me!'"

Miss Dove came down from her platform. She inclined her head with her cheek turned in Randy's direction.

"Well, Randolph," said Miss Dove, "I am waiting."

There was an electric stillness that was followed, as the full meaning of her words penetrated the children's consciousness, by a gasp. Randy folded the letter and put it back into his pocket. Then he began to walk toward the teacher. He walked with the deliberate stoicism of a martyr going to the chopping block. He did not come any closer than he had to. He leaned forward stiffly from the waist and placed his puckered lips against her cheek. His kiss resounded, a small explosion in the room.

"Thank you, Randolph," said Miss Dove. "You may give Thomas my regards." She straightened up and faced the class. To her surprise, nobody was grinning.

Jincey Webb spoke. She did not raise her hand for permission. She just spoke out.

"It's like a medal," Jincey said softly. "It's like he pinned a medal on Miss Dove."

For a moment a lamp seemed to burn behind her face. Then over the light swept a shadow. It was as if Jincey had glimpsed some universal beauty —of sorrow, perhaps, or of nobility—too poignant for her youth to bear. She began to cry. She flopped her head down on her desk with her red hair falling forward and spreading out like a crinkly fan.

All the other girls wept with her. All the boys stared sternly into space.

For the first time in her teaching career Miss Dove was at a loss. She wanted to make a speech. She wanted to say something beautiful and grateful about what life really meant to her, about the overwhelming generosity of children. But the words would not come.

Then she saw that what she had to thank her class for was not generosity at all. It was something much better than that and much harder to come by. It was justice.

And as she realized that, she realized also that she was neglecting her duty. The first duty of a teacher was to preserve order.

She fished a piece of string out of a receptacle on her desk. She walked down the aisle to Jincey Webb. She took Jincey's hair, that marvel of art and nature, and bunched it in her hand. She tied it securely at the nape of Jincey's neck with the little bit of grocery string.

"Now it will be out of your way," she said.

At the sound of her voice, cool, precise, and usual, the children rallied.

They sat erect. They blew their noses with clean handkerchiefs. They folded their hands on their desks.

"Pens in position, class," she said.

A transient mist stung her eyes. Through it, as through a prism, the children glowed. Freckles, cowlicks, pinafores, and polo shirts seemed bathed in a rainbow iridescence. Her love flowed out to those children—to those with their pen points poised above their paper and to those in the far places she had once helped them locate on the map. It did not flow tenderly like a coddling mother's love. It flowed on a fierce rush of hope and pride, the way an old general's heart might follow his men into battle.

She went to the blackboard and picked up a piece of chalk. "Above the fiftieth parallel—" wrote the terrible Miss Dove.

The Thursday Bridge Club was as select and small as a bridge club could be. It was composed of four young matrons who took it seriously. But today, at Mrs. Reese's house, the play was erratic.

"If you hadn't finessed the ten we'd have made our contract," Mrs. Reese said testily to her partner, Mrs. Knight. "The board was good."

"I can't keep my mind on the game," Mrs. Knight said. "I've been through too much. Lester, Junior's, narrow squeak and Miss Dove paralyzed!"

"Is that what it is? Paralysis?"

"She can't move her leg. A rose by any other name—"

"Tommy hasn't arrived at a diagnosis," said Mrs. Briggs who, as Jincey Baker's sister, presumed to a knowledgeable air.

"What does he think?"

"Tommy's a clam," Mrs. Briggs said just airily enough to convey the impression that she, alone, was in the surgeon's confidence. "But he's deeply concerned. He told Jince this morning that she'd have to manage having the baby with no help from him!"

"The poor child! If there's ever a time a woman needs her husband—" Mrs. Evans sighed sentimentally. Her own husband, John Wesley, had been conspicuously drunk throughout her hours of discomfort preceding Victoria's birth. But he had stayed at her bedside looking like a stricken deer, matching her groans with his, and protesting his devotion in flowery phrases as heartfelt as they were maudlin.

"Jince has plenty of spunk," Mrs. Briggs said. "She knows her duty as a doctor's wife."

"Besides, Sam Tillet is an excellent obstetrician," said Mrs. Reese.

"I saw her yesterday," Mrs. Knight said, trying to sound modest. "Miss Dove, I mean."

"You weren't supposed to," said Mrs. Briggs. "Tommy's discouraging visitors."

"I just wanted to reassure her about Lester, Junior. You know when they opened him up his appendix were sizzling."

But the club had heard all it cared to hear about Lester, Junior.

"Appendix *was*. Not *were*," said Mrs. Briggs. "How did she look?"

"Like herself," Mrs. Knight replied. "Only—well, different in a way I can't explain. Gentler. Like an old lion with its teeth pulled."

"Dear Lord!" Mrs. Reese said. "It breaks my heart to think of the terrible Miss Dove being *gentle!*"

"We saw her on her way to the hospital," said Mrs. Evans. "Tom and Sandy were carrying her. She was sitting on their hands just like it was nothing out of the way at all. Not batting an eye."

"Miss Dove has never batted an eye," Mrs. Knight declared on a note of almost familial pride.

"Wes knew something serious had happened. He acted like he'd seen a ghost," Mrs. Evans said. Not being a born Liberty Hillian, she thought her husband's reactions vastly more important than the teacher's illness. "He'd been under the weather, you know—"

Her companions nodded. They had all observed Mr. Evans' antics at a recent country club dance.

"—and he was about to take a morning pick-me-up. But he didn't. He swallowed an egg instead."

"Maybe that will prove the turning point of his life," said Mrs. Reese. Her sarcasm was lost upon Mrs. Evans.

"I have faith that it will," declared Mrs. Evans in whom faith died hard. "He said he was through forever." Her face was suffused with hope and happiness. "God moves in a mysterious way!"

This was too much for Mrs. Knight. "I don't believe for an instant that God was thinking of Wes Evans' habits," she said, "when He struck down Miss Dove!"

"Oh, no! I didn't mean that exactly!" Mrs. Evans cried. "I'm dreadfully sorry about Miss Dove. You must all have been devoted to her."

"If we were we didn't know it," said Mrs. Reese. "She turned us to stone."

"Remember the poem Geoff wrote?"

"Remember the clean handkerchiefs and the margins?"

"The laundry soap?"

"Remember in the first grade how she told us about the camel who was 'not a pretty beast' but who could go 'many days without water'?" said Mrs. Briggs. "And how she stared at us 'til we knew she meant we weren't to hang around the drinking fountain?"

"Can anybody bound Russia?" asked Mrs. Knight.

"No. Not now," said Mrs. Reese.

The three women were drawn backward in time. They returned to a safe charted world where colors were paint-box bright, boundaries stayed the same, and all the ideas they could conceivably use were handed down to them, complete with punctuation, from a raised dais.

"I was counting on her to break Snookie of chewing her hair the way she broke me," Mrs. Briggs said almost petulantly. Then she began to cry. So did Mrs. Knight and Mrs. Reese.

They sat there at a bridge table in a pretty living room—three plumpish, prosperous women, with pearls on their ear lobes—and wept for their childhood. Mrs. Evans looked on in silent sympathy. After a moment, she managed to squeeze out a tear of her own.

Mrs. Briggs fumbled in the pocket of her purple gabardine suit. "Damn!" she said. "I haven't got a handkerchief!"

"Take mine," said Mrs. Evans.

"What would Miss Dove think of this?" Mrs. Briggs sniffled. "At my age—having to borrow a hanky!"

"And saying a great big D!" added Mrs. Knight.

Mrs. Reese rose abruptly. "We'll have to pull ourselves together, girls. Life must go on!" She went out to the kitchen to fetch hot coffee and patty shells filled with creamed chicken and—since the club was dieting—a dish of crystallized ginger in lieu of a heavy sweet.

The local Rotarians had convened for their weekly luncheon meeting. Alexander Burnham had said grace. The shrimp cocktails had been served. Suddenly Mr. Porter, who was a founder and president-emeritus of the club, and who saw no reason to address the chair before he took the floor, struck his knife against his cocktail bowl. He struck so hard that a blob of red sauce leapt out, as if in fright, and landed upon the white tablecloth.

"Boys," said Mr. Porter, rising to his full height, which was imposing in spite of the stoop of age, "it is my considered opinion, after a lifetime's observation, that a good businessman's heart is not in his chest, but in his wallet."

This remark was greeted with polite laughter.

But Mr. Porter had not meant to be witty. He beetled his brows, craned his long, gaunt old neck and looked severely at his audience. He lifted his water goblet.

"Before I proceed," he said in a voice that creaked with emotion, "let me propose a toast. To the terrible Miss Dove!"

The Rotarians drank. They set their goblets down. They applauded. Then, on a common impulse, they squirmed in their chairs. They planted their feet firmly upon the carpet. They straightened their backs. A few of them folded their hands.

In the hospital, undergoing those tests that Thomas Baker had called exhaustive and that were, she discovered, certainly exhausting, Miss Dove did not imagine that her plight created any stir of feeling in Liberty Hill. She considered herself a private person, moving in a private orbit. That this orbit, this small, limited range of endeavor, should be multiplied into a series of rings—ever-widening as time went on, like those rings that originate from a pebble cast into a still pond, had never occurred to her.

She did not undervalue her talents. She knew she was a good teacher of elementary geography. She knew she had a gift for molding the clay of children's minds and laying upon them a hard protective glaze of discipline. But that was all in her job. If she did not forget her pupils after she was through with them, that was only because she was, by an accident of nature, a person of retentive memory. She remembered them without illusion—fancying that they hadn't altered much for better or worse; and so, she presumed, they remembered her. To believe that wholesome fear would some day be transmuted into affection would have struck her as nonsense. That was a pathetic fallacy embraced by mothers, not teachers!

And even if she had not scorned that sentimental dream she would hardly have indulged in it today. Today was here and now. In this hospital. With this pain. Miss Dove's joints were tapped with a small hammer. Her spine was pierced by a needle. In her bed she was rolled from strange place to strange place. Steel plates were clasped to her head and her brain waves recorded. All the bones in her body were X-rayed.

Thomas was in constant attendance. He promised to be with her through all her tests unless some emergency arose too complicated for the interne to handle.

"And Adams Temple is a good boy. He can handle most things," he said. "I'll be sorry to see him go."

"He is not staying?"

"No. He's only temporary. He finished med school at Christmas and starts a Hopkins internship in July," Thomas told her. "He's helping us out in the meantime. I gather his mother wanted him to get acquainted with Liberty Hill."

"His mother had an inquiring mind," said Miss Dove.

Thomas laughed. "I know what you mean. Adams gets a bit above himself at times." He turned to Billie Jean. "And now, Mrs. Green, the percussion hammer please."

Thomas' attitude altered subtly. It became aloof in a way that gave Miss Dove confidence. His whole attention was directed upon his investigation. His eyes had a penetrating look. He was gentle. He was deft. But he did not apologize when he was obliged to hurt her. Only once—just after the first spinal puncture—did she see him wince with compassion.

(All the Bakers shrank from causing pain, Miss Dove remembered. It was a family trait. Through the haze of her own pain she seemed to see those boys again—Thomas, Charles, Randolph, and Sterling! They were all the same size. All about ten or twelve years old and as alike as four paper dolls cut from one folded sheet of paper. They all wore red sweaters—it was the same sweater, of course, passed down from first to last—and brown corduroy pants with leather patches on the knees. They all had candid eyes and unexpected fits of shyness that came from sympathy.)

But as if he guessed her thoughts, Thomas gave her a strict, impersonal look. And as the day wore on she ceased to think of him as one of the Baker boys. She ceased to think of herself as a teacher. He was a doctor. She was a patient. Her will hung suspended in his.

With a sense of mingled triumph and distress, Thomas perceived all this. He had taken a high hand with Miss Dove because he had felt that no other hand would do. He had won the struggle for ascendancy. But his victory was not very sweet.

The results of the examinations were far from encouraging. Each test drew Thomas closer to the diagnosis he dreaded. But he remained methodical and open to persuasion. He reserved his conclusion. He had learned how to do that in laboratories and dissecting rooms. He had learned it in the Navy. He had learned it even earlier in the geography room at Cedar Grove School.

How he had fought against that lesson! How he had longed to be important enough to give orders to Miss Dove.

Once, he remembered, he had snitched a piece of blue chalk and had drawn her caricature on the cement walk that led to the school. It had been, in his opinion and that of his friends, a work of genius done in heroic proportions and embellished with time-honored details of humor. Miss Dove had been depicted as nine feet tall. She had been smoking a cigar and holding in one upraised hand a large bottle marked WHISKEY. Hidden in the shrubbery, Thomas had waited to see what the original would do when she saw the portrait.

At last she had come out of the building. She had seen the picture. She had given it a cool, appraising glance and had walked across it as if it did not exist.

And suddenly, watching her retreating back—the hat, the neck, the ball of hair, and the stick-like ankles beneath the dark skirt—the boy had been aghast. He had glimpsed a haughty loneliness that had struck him somehow—though he wouldn't have used that word—as being universal. For the first time in his life he had experienced empathy, the least comfortable of human emotions.

Heavy rain had fallen that night. Next morning only a faint blue stain remained on the pavement. But for some time thereafter Thomas had avoided the front walk to the school.

With all that in mind, he found the mild, obedient face of the woman on the bed almost more than he could bear.

But after the final X-rays, when he was helping Billie Jean guide the patient's bed back to her room, an incident occurred to show him that Miss Dove was still Miss Dove.

Lester Knight, Junior, having accomplished the rapid recovery of which callow youth is capable, was making full use of a wheel chair. He had escaped from the children's ward and was speeding along the corridors, careening around corners, and whooping with mirth at the alarm he occasioned to pedestrians.

Thomas started for him but jumped back when Lester, drunk with freedom, aimed the chair in his direction.

"Lester," Miss Dove said quietly. Her tone was level and calm and perfectly usual.

Lester braked his chair. His eyes bulged.

Miss Dove gave him a long gelid look. "You may return to your room," she said.

"Yes, Miss Dove," said Lester. His voice squeaked.

A pursuing nurse with cap askew and expression irate, seized him, chair and all, and rolled him away.

"I hope she smacks his jaws," said Billie Jean.

"Ah, Miss Dove!" said Thomas. He bent over her. Had it not been for her eyes—the eyes that had quenched the spirits of Lester, Junior—he might have saluted her as his little brother had once done for him.

At the door of her room he left her.

"Tomorrow afternoon we'll talk," he said. "Until then I want you to put all this business out of your mind."

He hurried away.

"We won't worry about tomorrow, will we?" said Billie Jean. "Oh, my! Here we are in a greenhouse."

The room was banked with hothouse flowers. On the bureau, the table, and even in corners on the floor they bloomed.

"There are too many," said Miss Dove. "Restraint is the better part of beauty. I will keep the white azalea. Later I can set it outdoors in a sheltered place. Please dispose of the others."

"Yes, Miss Dove," said Billie Jean. She looked as disappointed as a child.

"There must be less fortunate patients who would enjoy them," said Miss Dove.

Billie Jean brightened. The prospect of walking through the wards playing Lady Bountiful to "the less fortunate" was to her taste. After she had completed the last of her errands she sat down and took out her fountain pen.

"I saved the cards," she said. "And I borrowed some stationery. If you'd like me to write the thank-you notes I'd be glad to."

"That would be obliging," said Miss Dove. The notion of using Billie Jean as a social secretary had novelty. The notion of keeping her quiet had charm.

"Will you dictate them?"

"No," said Miss Dove. "Use your discretion, Mrs. Green. Only avoid the fulsome."

The room was restful. The dwarf azalea plant was very pure in color and line against the blue wall. There was no sound except for the Spring rain murmuring against the window and for Billie Jean breathing hard (like a child taking a proficiency test) in the throes of literary composition.

"I've finished," Billie Jean said after a while. "I said the same thing to everybody." She handed a sheet of paper to Miss Dove. "Is it all right?"

Miss Dove perused the sample.

"Dear Mr. Porter," it read, "at the request of Miss Dove I am advising you that she is thrilled by your florial offering. The sympathy of friends brings sunshine to shut-ins. Cordially yours, Billie Jean Green, R.P.N."

Miss Dove, being totally unendowed with humor, had no inclination to laugh. Her inclination, arising from established editorial habit, was to pick the letter to pieces—to point out its errors in tone and spelling. But something in Billie Jean's face—a look of vanity as innocent as the flowers of Spring—deterred her.

"What does R.P.N. stand for?" she asked.

"Registered Practical Nurse," said Billie Jean. "How is the letter?"

"It is very—" Miss Dove sought a word that would carry truth without a wound—"very genteel."

The word was perfect. "Oh," said Billie Jean, "I'll tell Bill!"

"You may, Mrs. Green," Miss Dove said.

Billie Jean brought a damp cloth and washed her patient's face. She did it gently. She was a good nurse, Miss Dove reflected—more gifted in providing kindness and creature comfort than in verbal expression. She was a woman who had found her sphere.

"You know, Miss Dove," Billie Jean blurted out suddenly, "I'm not really Mrs. Green!"

Miss Dove said nothing.

"I took the name for little Ava's sake," said Billie Jean.

Miss Dove still remained silent.

"I was way out there in Detroit!" Billie Jean continued. Her tone was pleading.

"Virtue knows no geography," said Miss Dove.

"I was on the night-shift," said Billie Jean. "It got me all mixed up. I'd never been anywhere before. Mamma was always careful with me—she never let me go on high school hay rides or anywhere much except church socials. I wasn't very mature!"

"No," agreed Miss Dove.

"All the fellows wanted to take me out. I guess it went to my head. There was this one fellow—I didn't know he was married—that was wonderful to me. I—I gave him too much. In other words—"

"You need not elaborate," said Miss Dove.

"He was so good looking and big," said Billie Jean. "And I was so homesick. You know how it is!"

"I do *not* know how it is," said Miss Dove. "But I know that right is right and wrong is wrong."

"That's what Bill says. Those very words," said Billie Jean. "So little Ava came way out in Detroit." (She seemed to imply that the infant had been clever to manage being born in that outlandish place.) "I could have left her for adoption. There was an agency wanted her. And there was this old childless couple—the lady was over forty—that offered me three thousand dollars! But—well, she was mine. She was like home-folks. And how did I know other folks would raise her right?"

"A child is a responsibility," said Miss Dove.

"So I brought her home and told that tale about my husband being killed. Mamma said she'd keep Ava while I worked. I talked to Reverend Burnham and Dr. Hurley. They got me into the practical nursing course. So here I am!"

Miss Dove sighed. She was not astonished. She knew that in the great world, both in and out of literature, such things happened. Even in the smaller world of Liberty Hill they were, though scarcely commonplace, by no means unheard of. And after half a biblical lifetime in a public school she was immunized to astonishment.

Her sigh was for William Holloway.

"And why," she said, "did you confide in me, Mrs.—?"

"Billie Jean," the nurse said. "It was because you said that about the letter. I'm not as genteel as you think and I couldn't deceive you."

"Deceit is a tangled web," said Miss Dove.

"I had to tell Bill too," Billie Jean said. "He's like you. A person you tell the truth to."

"Ah!" said Miss Dove.

"He was cut up," Billie Jean said. "He was furious. He didn't date me for a week. And then he said he'd marry me anyhow but if he ever caught me doing anything unrespectable—even looking fresh at a fellow or smoking in public—he'd"—she paused dramatically—"he'd *take his belt to me!*"

Somehow Miss Dove felt sanguine as to William's domestic future. He was one of those elect who had the gift of authority and the nerve to use it. And Billie Jean was born to love a master.

As she fed Miss Dove her evening meal (asparagus soup and apricot whip) the nurse was silent. Her expression was subdued, but not uncheerful. She was brooding, no doubt, upon Patrolman Holloway's strong right arm. At last she said: "I guess I'm one of those that have to learn the hard way."

"We all are, Billie Jean," said Miss Dove.

When the night nurse arrived she went about her duties more efficiently than before. She maintained her air of being above the station in which she found herself, but her hands were gentler. Miss Dove noticed the difference. She guessed its cause. The woman suspected now that her patient was more than ordinarily ailing. Miss Dove was no longer a negligible old schoolteacher with a backache. She was an "interesting case" and, as such, cast dignity upon ministrations performed in her behalf.

A small quick flame of fear leapt in her mind. For an instant it burned steady, throwing its beams into the amorphous shadows of the future. But Miss Dove refused to look where the beams pointed.

Thomas Baker had directed her to put the whole business out of her mind. Once she had exacted obedience of him. Now that roles were reversed, she must allow him to exact it of her.

In the geography room each class, each day, was allotted a short reading period. For a prescribed number of minutes the children—keeping their posture correct and being careful not to move their lips or contort their features —had perused a prescribed number of pages. When the time was up they closed their books and listened while Miss Dove explained to them what they had just read. To read ahead—to go on, undirected, into the next chapter— was a graver misdemeanor than to fall behind. The latter was merely slothful; the former was impudent and dangerous. In such unguided sorties children were likely to collect odd impressions and form unsound opinions. The greenhorn mind, Miss Dove felt, should do its first traveling abroad in company and on a *guided* tour.

Thomas had told her, in effect, that she must not "read ahead." She forbade her fancy to turn the page.

She slept through the night and, if she dreamed at all, her dreams were of that childlike, inconsequential kind—scarcely more than echoes of a lullaby —that dissolve with returning consciousness. She awoke to hear Billie Jean telling the night nurse good-by and to see that the rain had stopped. Beyond her window the sky was opalescent gray—the color of April itself.

The morning passed quietly. Miss Dove had her bath and breakfast. Billie Jean turned the toe of the big sock. The interne made rounds.

Jincey Baker stopped in, wearing a ruffled negligee and looking remarkably like a little girl who was playing at pregnancy with a pillow stuffed under her waistband.

She had been admitted to the hospital, Jincey said, more for Tommy's peace of mind than anything. She was several days past term. If nothing definite had happened by Saturday night, Sam Tillet had promised to give Nature a nudge.

"Whatever Dr. Tillet suggests will be wise," Billie Jean said primly.

"Of course," said Jincey, making it plain that she did not question the wisdom of her obstetrician. "Right now he suggests that I keep walking. I peeped in to ask Miss Dove to wish me luck."

"I do, Virginia," said Miss Dove.

When Jincey had left to continue her promenade Billie Jean said: "I used to think she was the snootiest, dumbest brat in Liberty Hill. But she's really a good kid. She hasn't hardly seen her husband for days, and not a cheep out of her!"

"A physician cannot call his time his own," said Miss Dove.

"Nor an officer of the law, either," Billie Jean added smugly. "It's like the old folks say. 'Men must work and women must weep.'"

"I consider that an effete philosophy," said Miss Dove.

"Oh, so do I!" agreed Billie Jean, who had no inkling of the meaning of effete.

More blossoms arrived. There were two mixed bouquets from the florist (Miss Dove dispensed with them) and the dish garden that the pupils of the third grade had made under Miss Ellwood's supervision. The dish was a biscuit pan filled with moss and bordered with ferns and hepatica. In the moss was stuck a seedling cedar and nearby, in the exact center of the pan, sat a rectangular building made of red cardboard upon which the pattern of bricks had been marked in white ink.

"It's Cedar Grove!" said Billie Jean. "Oh, isn't it sweet!"

"Yes," said Miss Dove. As she examined the arrangement of the garden she saw something sweeter still. She saw a group of children absorbed in a task and aiming at perfection. She was aware of a constriction in her throat. "The ink-work is laudably neat," she said. "You may place it on the windowsill."

Just before noon there was a message from the hospital receptionist. Two out-of-town visitors wished to see Miss Dove. One had telephoned to ask permission. The other was waiting in the lobby.

"Who are they?" Miss Dove asked Billie Jean.

"Well, they're not birds of a feather, as the old folks say," said Billie Jean. "One is Mr. Lyons, the writer from New York. The other is Fred Makepeace." She looked haughty. "I suppose you know where he resides!"

"I do know," said Miss Dove. Fred was an inmate of a prison camp. "I shall be glad to see them both. They are my former pupils."

"*Mr.* Makepeace," said Billie Jean, with a flounce of her head, "was sure of his welcome. *He's* already come. If you don't mind, I'll wait outside." She walked stiffly away. Obviously, as the fiancée of a policeman, she intended to preserve herself from association with felons.

Fred Makepeace entered the room. He was a lean, sandy-haired man in the middle thirties. He was dressed in blue serge. A snow-white handkerchief protruded from his breast pocket. His shoes were polished to a lustre. He walked on the balls of his feet and his manner, as he approached the bedside, was deferential. The hand he extended in greeting was scrupulously clean.

Miss Dove gave him three fingers, like a duchess. "How d'y'do, Fred," she said. (She would have preferred to call him "Frederick" but he had not been christened so.) "You may be seated."

Fred sat on the edge of a chair. He placed his hat—a dark gray Homburg —upon his knees and folded his hands upon its crown.

Having nothing to say, Miss Dove waited for him to speak. She studied his face. She found it remarkably unchanged. It was a smooth face, neither good nor bad. There was no malice in it and very little character. The eyes, blue and cloudless as a child's, were set too wide apart.

Fred was, she knew, serving a sentence for forgery and the theft of an automobile, and so must be counted among her failures. But she did not blame herself. Rational humility had always told her that the ultimate success of a teacher depended, in some measure, upon the material with which she worked. In the last analysis one could not go behind the hand of Providence.

And yet, in Fred's case, it was possible that neither she nor Providence had failed. Fred was a follower. When rules were made clear to him he obeyed them. It was only when he made independent choices—which an unrealistic society now forced him to make—that he invariably chose wrong. Miss Dove remembered how neat his margins had been and how he had always coughed in his handkerchief. She remembered also the offerings of fruit that he'd brought her each Friday—polished apples and tangerines and heavy bunches of Malaga grapes—until she'd discovered that he had stolen them from a grocer.

"I'm not over the hill," said Fred.

"I am gratified to hear that," said Miss Dove.

"When I seen in the paper you was sick I went to my gang-boss. 'Boss,' I says, 'the only teacher that ever learned me anything is in the hospital. I want a day off to go tell her I'm preparing to reform my ways.'"

"And he gave you leave?"

"Yes, ma'am. He says, 'Why sure, Fred. I know I can trust *you!*' "

"A compliment to cherish," said Miss Dove.

There was a tentative-sounding knock at the door and Geoffrey Lyon came in. In contrast to Fred's sober formality, his attire was loud and untidy. He wore brown flannels, a tweed jacket, a yellow shirt and a tattersall waistcoat. His shoes were rusty. One of them was untied. (He had often come to school improperly buttoned; Miss Dove remembered that.)

"Miss Dove," he said, "I'm Geoffrey Lyon."

"I know you, Geoffrey," said Miss Dove.

Fred jumped up. He grinned. "Recall the face, Geoff?" he asked.

Geoffrey whistled. "Old Babe Makepeace! The best slugger Cedar Grove ever had!"

"I hear tell you're doin' pretty good in show business," said Fred.

"Fair," said Geoffrey. "I'm on my way to Hollywood now. It's a rat-race. What are you doing these days, Babe?"

Fred widened his blue eyes as if in mild surprise that anyone should be ignorant of his situation. "Me?" he said. "I'm on the roads."

His tone was so unabashed that Geoffrey missed the import of his words.

"On the road?" Geoffrey queried. "Acting or selling?"

Fred laughed. "Mostly diggin' with a pick-ax."

Miss Dove deplored levity. "Fred Makepeace is paying his debt to society," she said.

"Oh," said Geoffrey. He smiled at Fred and at Miss Dove. "That's a debt few of us ever pay."

"Exactly," said Miss Dove. She was thinking, Geoffrey guessed, of his last play which had dealt in a frivolous way with a certain form of misbehavior.

"I got in a jam Christmas a year ago," Fred explained, "and had to pass a coupla checks with another guy's name on 'em. Then I borrowed this Chrysler from a parking lot and happened to wreck it."

"Tough," said Geoffrey.

"The judge woulda let me off with a fine and a suspended sentence," Fred said. "But I didn't know where to look for the money and I never did like probation. Makes me nervous."

"I can imagine," said Geoffrey.

"So I decided to pull my time and get it over with. I'm doin' twenty-four months on the roads."

"Fred was paroled for the day on his own recognizance," said Miss Dove.

"Splendid," said Geoffrey.

Billie Jean appeared. She was careful to look only at Geoffrey. "Your time is up, gentlemen," she said.

"Say! Aren't you little Billie McVay?" said Fred.

"I am Mrs. Green," Billie Jean said, without a glance in his direction.

"Well, pardon *me!*" said Fred.

Outside the hospital in the soft Spring air the two men chatted together.

"I guess you'll see a lot of cheese-cake in Hollywood," Fred said wistfully.

"It won't affect me," Geoffrey said. "I've got a B. W. and six kids in Upper Montclair."

"You don't say!" said Fred. "I had a wife but—" he laughed without the ring of pleasure "—like the feller says, she got away!" He sighed. "Well, I'd better start rollin'. I'm goin' back to the camp but today'll cost me time. I didn't have no parole. If I'd told the boss-man I wanted to see a sick teacher he'd of given me the horse laugh. I just laid down my pick and started walkin'."

"Where'd you get the Sunday clothes?"

"I borrowed 'em from a funeral home," Fred said. "Well." A look of pain and wonder passed, like the drifting shadow of a cloud, across his face. "Did you notice how little she was?" he said. "Miss Dove, I mean."

Geoffrey nodded. "I noticed."

"Layin' in the bed not hardly bigger than a baby doll or a bird—one of them robins on the grass. If she had a husband he'd have to shake the sheets to find her. And I used to think she was Goliath."

"I know," said Geoffrey. He took out a pack of cigarettes. "Smoke?"

"Mind if I take two?" Fred asked. "One for the road."

"Take the pack," said Geoffrey.

"Thanks," Fred said. "Remember how we used to smoke in the boys' basement at Cedar Grove? Those were the days, Geoff. We'll never have it so good again!"

"Look, Babe," said Geoffrey. "When you—when they spring you, get in touch with me. I might be able to put you on to something."

"I'll do that thing," Fred said. "So long, boy. Give my regards to Marilyn Monroe."

Geoffrey watched his old schoolmate walk away. He noted how Fred hunched one shoulder as if to ward off a chilly wind. He felt creeping over him that mysterious mood of receptivity which is the courted darling of every artist. He knew, in his bones, how Fred felt and what had moved him to risk extra months of penal servitude for a brief visit to his lost childhood. He even understood himself—or almost. Why had he wanted Miss Dove with him when his first play appeared on Broadway? Sentimentality? Publicity? Ah, it had been more than that!

He looked, hardly seeing it—but *feeling* it, *feeling* it!—at the misty, low, tree-blurred skyline of Liberty Hill. In his mind a play had begun to take shape. It was the play he had always meant to write—a play woven of homespun human emotions like love and nostalgia and despair and fortitude. It was unlike the complicated, glittering things that had brought him fame. It was as simple as a Chekov!

Geoffrey tossed his cigarette into the gutter. He returned to his brother's house, went up to his room, locked the door, and put a sheet of paper on the roller of his portable typewriter. He started writing.

Once he cursed himself for being a literary leech who had no blood in his own veins and must batten upon the joys and sorrows of others. But the curse was lightly meant, and, in essence, happy. Geoffrey knew what kind of person

he was; he wouldn't have changed if he could have. Soon his present surroundings—the chintzy guest-room with the hooked rugs and the botanical
prints and the eiderdown quilts—had receded into oblivion. He was in
another world. In it there was no sound but the dialogue of people in his
mind and the steady tap-tapping of the keys.

At four-thirty or thereabout, Billie Jean began tidying the room. She
whisked about rearranging objects and flicking at imaginary dust in the im-
memorial fashion of a woman expecting important guests.

"Dr. Baker'll be here in a few minutes," she said. "I want things prettied
up."

Upon the bedside table she arranged a pitcher of fresh ice-water, two
clean glasses, and a stiff-backed loose-leaf notebook. "That's your chart," she
said. "Everything's ready if he comes while I'm out. I'll just slip down to
the nurses' lounge a minute now."

So the waiting was nearly over, thought Miss Dove. And suddenly the
protective apathy she had assumed fell away. Without the least compunction
—and realizing perfectly the breach of hospital etiquette—she reached for the
notebook. She began to read her chart.

She was not a self-conscious woman. She rarely looked into a mirror and for
many years she had been too busy weighing her impressions of others to
speculate upon their impression of her. Now, before her fascinated gaze—
neatly typed in the laconic, "un-prettied-up" language of a medical man—was
her own image as reflected in the mind of Adams Temple.

"The patient," Dr. Temple had written, "is a slender, fully developed
female aged fifty-five, showing few of the usual senile changes, lying quietly
in bed in no apparent distress, alert and collected."

She read the sentence again. It was too long for style, she thought, but
style had not been its author's object. It was grammatical. It was correctly
punctuated. It was economically expressed. And as for the truth it conveyed—
art could have done no better!

Billie Jean returned. She came and took the chart from Miss Dove's hands
—*gently but firmly*, like a teacher confiscating a small boy's comic book. In
her reproachful eyes was more sorrow than anger. "I'm surprised," she said.
"I *trusted* you!"

"I'm sorry," said Miss Dove. But she was not sorry. The thing she had
read had restored to her a sense of personal identity. Whatever tidings
Thomas might bring she could receive as became a lady. Quietly, collectedly,
and "in no apparent distress."

Thomas arrived accompanied by Mr. Porter.

The old gentleman refused a chair. "I can talk better on my feet," he said,
"and I shan't stay long."

He stood leaning on his gold-headed cane, beetling his bushy brows, thrusting his pendulous underlip, and glaring at Miss Dove. The glare, Miss Dove
knew, was a sign of that anger that is often, in the old and strong, a twin of
pity. She despised pity. She rejected Mr. Porter's with a glance.

Thomas did not beat about the bush. "Surgery is indicated, Miss Dove," he said. "The sooner the better. And now—" he bowed to Mr. Porter.

"I am not here in a private capacity," said Mr. Porter, sounding unctuous in spite of his creaking voice. "I represent Rotary!"

"Indeed," said Miss Dove.

"Indeed, yes," said Mr. Porter. "Our chapter has voted unanimously to assume entire financial responsibility for the expenses of your illness."

Miss Dove opened her lips to speak. Mr. Porter silenced her.

"Wherever you choose to go for this operation," he said. "Rochester, Boston, Philadelphia, Baltimore—Rotary is behind you!"

"And if I decline the kind offer?" said Miss Dove.

A flush swept over Mr. Porter's gaunt face. He pounded his stick. "Who are you to decline it?" he demanded. "Who gave you the right to insult your friends? To walk the world with a haughty spirit—frightening little children, turning men to stone?"

"My dear sir," said Miss Dove, "if you wish my attention you must employ a civil tone. I am not to be bullied."

"Bullied!" Mr. Porter croaked. "You talk of bullying!" He turned to Thomas. "She's always been a stiff-necked termagant. Do you think my pride hasn't suffered, seeing the daughter of my friend penniless, working for her bread, wearing outlandish clothes—"

"You have forgotten yourself, Mr. Porter," said Miss Dove.

"I have forgotten nothing," Mr. Porter rejoined. "I haven't forgotten that I made you a very civil offer once!"

Mr. Porter had once offered Miss Dove his name. That had been fifteen years before when he had been a vigorous sixty-seven and a widower of a year's standing. He was rich. He was lonely. Miss Dove was undoubtedly lonely, too, and far from rich. What could have been more suitable?

Walking up Oakwood Street with a rose in his buttonhole and a spring in his gait he had felt utterly sanguine as to the success of his errand. He had been warmed by a glow of benevolence and armed with pretty phrases with which to soothe his lady-love when she would (as it didn't occur to him she wouldn't) droop against his broad chest with bird-like chirps of gratitude. And then she had refused him. She had simply said no, thank you, and changed the subject.

Now, in this hospital room, the chagrin of that old moment was plain as a wen on his face.

"The offer was generous," said Miss Dove, "but none-the-less ridiculous."

Mr. Porter trembled. His hawk's eyes blazed. But he knew he could not sustain his rage against Miss Dove. She had once done something for him, consciously or unconsciously, that would always command his devotion.

That had been in February '33, a black month that still recurred to him in dyspeptic nightmares. There had been a run on his bank. All morning the lobby had been packed and a line of frightened customers had moved toward the teller's window withdrawing the life-blood of trade. And then, bobbing among the milling, muttering throng, Mr. Porter saw the flat black hat and

the pale pointed face of Miss Dove. Her features were composed. Only the
tip of her nose was pinker than usual and that was owing, no doubt, to the
frost in the air outside. She spoke. Her voice was not strident or even raised.
It was the crisp, precise, level voice of the geography room at Cedar Grove
School.

"Will you allow me passage, please," she said. "I wish to make a deposit."

She stared at the man at the head of the line—a man prepared to demand
the last scrapings in the till—until, like one mesmerised, he stepped aside
and allowed her to take his place. She deposited her salary check for the
month. It was a check for ninety-eight dollars. She took her time. She did
not slight those amenities that give grace to commerce in a small town. She
inquired as to the state of Mr. Porter's health and, with particularity, into
that of his wife, his cousins, his aunts and his nieces; she commented—and
whether with irony or innocence he never knew—upon the flourishing business that the bank appeared to be doing. She had just completed her transaction when the courthouse clock struck three. Banking hours were over. Mr.
Porter could close the teller's window, lower the green baize shade behind
the glass, and put his head in his hands.

By next day the bank had been able to convert a few of its intangibles into
ready cash but there had been, it transpired, no necessity for doing so. The
temper of panic had passed.

Since then, whenever he had heard anyone speak of entertaining angels
unaware, Mr. Porter had thought of Miss Dove.

"I am sure your Rotarians intended no offense," said Miss Dove, "but I
am not an object of public charity."

"Insufferable woman!" Mr. Porter sputtered. "I knew what you were the
day you were born. Those eyes! You got 'em from a taxidermist!"

The day she was born! Thomas looked at Miss Dove in wonder. Had she
really come into the world naked and helpless as other infants came? (As
Jincey's would come—but he had put anxiety resolutely aside.) The idea was
fantastic. Crazy. Thomas had an impulse to hoot in the manner of conventional persons who are confronted suddenly with modern art.

But of course the ineluctable truth remained that even the terrible Miss
Dove had begun life in the raw. She had been born in the orthodox fashion
to the off-stage accompaniment of a more than orthodox fuss on the part of
her male parent. Mr. Porter recalled the occasion with clarity.

He had set out for his office one fine morning in the autumn of 1896 when
Jefferson, the Dove's colored butler, had stopped him. The doctor was with
Mrs. Dove, Jefferson had said. The child was expected momentarily.

"Are things going badly?" Mr. Porter inquired in alarm.

"Not with Miss Betsy," Jefferson assured him. "But Mr. Phonnie! Oh,
suh—he needs you!"

Mr. Porter had hurried to the house. There in the parlor he found his
friend and saw at once that his condition was pitiable. Alphonzo Dove, ordinarily impeccably groomed, was clad in a pair of trousers over a flannel
nightshirt, a red velvet smoking jacket, and carpet slippers embroidered by

his wife in a design of pansies. His hair was a coxcomb. His elegant silken mustaches were pulled out of shape. His cheeks were unshaven. His eyes were wild.

"What can I do?" he gasped when he saw his visitor.

"Well, Phonnie," speculated Mr. Porter as his glance fell upon the brandy decanter that Jefferson had tactfully placed in full view upon the mantel, "I am told it helps to get drunk."

Alphonzo regarded him with horror. "Do you think me dead to decency?" he demanded. He groaned, covered his bloodshot eyes with his hands, and bowed as if in prayer. "Drunk!" he whispered. "While above"—he lifted a forefinger toward the ceiling—"that bright saint of heaven descends the valley of the shadow?"

(And the extravagance of Mr. Dove's language should provoke in us no snide mistrust of his sincerity. Distraught as he was, the poor man spoke truly from a noble heart. It is a sad mistake, common to our cautious times, to assume that the expression of all valid feeling falls naturally into the monosyllabic or the vernacular.)

Alphonzo paced the Aubusson carpet. He stared out the window. He flung himself down upon sofas and chairs, rose, paced, flung himself down again. He stood in the middle of the room beneath the crystal chandelier and discoursed upon the grossness of all men and the purity of all women. He cursed himself for the sins of his bachelor days which—as Mr. Porter knew— had, in reality, been few and more akin to folly than to vice.

Mr. Porter, though his sympathies were aroused and the brandy that he sipped alone was excellent, found his friend's behavior trying.

"Hush, Phonnie," he said at last. "Listen!"

The walls were thick in that house and the doors were closed, but they could not entirely muffle the shrill, imperious clamor of life itself.

"Soprano or tenor?" said Mr. Porter.

Alphonzo made a dive for the door. Mr. Porter blocked his way. "No you don't," he said. "You'll have to wait until you're sent for." He took Alphonzo by the hand, as he might have taken a child, and led him to a chair. "If all were not well they'd have told you."

After a short, but turbulent, interval of waiting, they were rewarded by the entrance of the doctor. Dr. Hurley—the original Dr. Hurley—was a dapper man with Gallic eyebrows and a step as brisk and light as that of a dancing master. He looked spruce, like an usher at a high-noon wedding. His face was as pink as the blanket bundle he carried in his arms.

"Betsy was a courageous girl and admirably equipped for her natural duty," he said. "You can see her presently, Phonnie. Meanwhile she sends you a pledge of her affection. A nice little daughter."

Alphonzo stared blankly.

"Will you accept it?" asked the doctor.

Alphonzo arose. Like a man coming in late to church he tiptoed to the doctor's side. He extended his arms, rigid as boards. The doctor laid his burden upon them.

A shiver went through Mr. Dove. His tension relaxed. His arms curved to a cradle, like a woman's arms.

Mr. Porter looked over his friend's shoulder. The baby was asleep. She was, of course, very small. Her face, folded shut, was an unlovely shade of red. Nobody could have guessed that here, wrapped in a blanket, was the public conscience of Liberty Hill!

Then she opened her eyes. They were not yet the cool, luminous gray eyes that were to freeze the marrow of sinners in Cedar Grove School. They were the eyes of the new-born—dark-blue, milky, and opaque. It was probably by accident that they seemed to focus, unflickering upon the eyes above them. But the expression in them was to endure. It was a steady look. A look of command. A look that made any man wish himself taller and straighter than he was. (Her father said afterwards that he was devoutly thankful he hadn't come to that first meeting with liquor on his breath!) Alphonzo bowed from the waist.

"Good morning, Miss Dove," he said.

Recalling that moment—so sentimental, so pretty, so buoyant with hope that had run out long ago—recalling his youth and his friend and his own child, the reckless, scapegrace son who had lived long enough to be killed at Bellau Wood—Mr. Porter felt all his fierceness desert him. He was only an old man leaning on a cane.

"It isn't charity that Liberty Hill offers you," he said gently. "It is—" He searched for a word that would satisfy her. Love? Gratitude? "It is Respect," he said.

"That," said Miss Dove with an air of *noblesse oblige*, "I shall accept with unqualified pleasure."

"Now," said Thomas, bringing the conversation back to medicine, "I've discussed your case with Dr. Hurley."

"What was young Dr. Hurley's opinion?"

"His opinion concurs with mine," Thomas said. "You have a small growth on your spine that must, if possible, be removed."

"If possible?"

"If possible," Thomas said. "Until we go in we can never be sure about the nature of any tumor."

"Oh," said Miss Dove. She understood. She was not so naive as to fail to guess the word the doctor had chosen not to use.

"All you have to decide," said Mr. Porter, "is *who* shall remove it and where!"

"Aren't you competent?" Miss Dove asked Thomas.

"Yes," Thomas said without hesitation. "I am." (Miss Dove liked men who did not pretend to diffidence.) "But there are surgeons with more experience and reputation. And I am not a Boards man."

He explained that he had not yet taken certain examinations which would qualify him as a Fellow of the American Board of Surgeons. He had completed the residency in a celebrated teaching hospital and had expected to be examined, but financial considerations had altered his plans. When he had been offered a staff-position in the new hospital in Liberty Hill he had felt obligated to accept it at once. His parents had other sons to educate.

"I plan to take Boards this summer," he said. "But in the meantime—"

"I am not a Boards *woman*," said Miss Dove.

This was true. Miss Dove had not satisfied the state Board of Education's requirements for a grade-A certificate. She had never had a course in educational psychology or classroom management. She was rated—and paid—as a sub-standard teacher.

"If you decide to go elsewhere that won't be interpreted by anyone as a reflection upon my ability," Thomas said. "The operation is extremely delicate."

"The club can charter a plane," said Mr. Porter. "There's a famous man at the Mayo Clinic—"

"Allow me to deliberate," said Miss Dove.

Mr. Porter leaned on his cane. Billie Jean stood, still as a statue, against the wall. Thomas waited at the foot of the bed. His hands rested lightly upon the rail.

Miss Dove deliberated. Her thoughts took her far into the past.

She was in the geography room. The third grade was painting maps. There was quiet in the room except for the occasional faint musical clink of a paintbrush striking the edge of a glass. Miss Dove reached for a book. As she did so she upset a box of chalk. She was mortified by the accident; she had never done such an awkward thing before.

It was a new box, scarcely broached. Its contents spilled on the floor behind the teacher's desk making a rattling sound, like a shower of pebbles. The pupils looked up. Their hands shot into the air. They were all bright-faced, glad of diversion, eager to be of help.

"You may continue painting," Miss Dove told them distantly. "I can attend to this."

To retrieve the chalk she squatted down, balancing her modest derrière upon her heels. She was thankful that her solid-front desk hid her from view for she thought a stooping position incongruous with dignity. She was arranging the sticks of chalk neatly in the box, lining them up as they'd been packed originally, when she sensed an electric quality in the silence of the room. Then something soft brushed her cheek, her neck. It fell about her shoulders. It was her hair!

Pivoting on the balls of her feet she came face to face with Thomas Baker. He held one wire hairpin between his thumb and forefinger. Half a dozen others protruded from his mouth.

For an awful moment she glimpsed ignominious defeat. The citadel of her privacy, of her immutability, had been invaded by an eight-year-old boy! She would soon be an object of derision. She wanted to shake Thomas until his bones rattled, until he choked on the hairpins.

Happily, however, an expedient occurred to her. If he was dexterous enough to remove the pins without her knowledge, he was dexterous enough to repair his mischief!

She spoke in an almost inaudible whisper close to Thomas' blushing ear. "Put each one back in its proper place," she said, and turned away to continue gathering up the chalk.

Her appearance, when she resumed her throne, was quite usual. Her face was impassive. Her hair was screwed into its customary knot at the nape of her neck.

"Remember to print your names legibly in the lower right hand corners of your margins," she had said to the class.

She had not glanced at Thomas.

Now, twenty years later, she did glance at him.

"I remember," she said, "that you had very skillful fingers."

"You had very pretty hair, Miss Dove," said Thomas.

Miss Dove did not smile. She never smiled except in a perfunctory way—a mere turning up of the corners of her thin lips—at PTA parties in the school cafeteria. But for an instant her face softened.

"I shall feel perfectly safe," she said, "in the hands of my children."

It was too much for old Mr. Porter. Wheezing back his tears, he stumped out of the room. Billie Jean followed him with a glass of water.

"Now that the air is clear of emotion," said Miss Dove to Thomas, "we can resume our discussion."

"I think we ought to do it Saturday," Thomas said. "Tomorrow. As you used to tell us, there is no merit in delay."

"None," said Miss Dove. "Tomorrow, then."

"Shall I notify your sisters?"

"Afterwards," she said.

"As you wish," said Thomas. At ten that evening, he told her, she would swallow a capsule containing a powerful soporific. She would sleep soundly. So soundly that next morning when she was given a hypodermic she might scarcely know—certainly, she wouldn't care. She would be taken to the operating room and put under general anesthesia. Because of the position of her tumor the operation for its removal would be slow. It might be lengthy. In that event, the anesthetic would be prolonged and so would its after-effects. It might well be Sunday before she really awoke.

"Where?" asked Miss Dove.

"What?"

"Where will I awake?"

Thomas shook his head. The Bakers, Miss Dove recalled, had never been good at dissembling.

"I don't know, Miss Dove," he said.

Miss Dove, as her history would bear out, was little given to swagger. But even she was not proof against that human vanity which impels one to say something memorable and gallant upon the eve of crisis.

"Here or there is immaterial," she said, with a shrug in her voice. "I have long been curious about the topography of Heaven."

Later, she reflected that the boast had been unworthy of her. It was unworthy because it was untrue. She took a rather cool view of Heaven.

She did not question the existence of that far bourne. It lay, she presumed, beyond all the horizons and solar systems and galaxies that the finite mind of man could imagine. It was an estimable country. But from hearsay, the contours of its land, the character of its fauna, and the aspect of its populace did not appeal to her. There were too many sheep there. (Silly creatures!) Golden streets were ostentatious. Rivers that flowed with milk and honey would attract flies. Faces "shining as the sun" sounded hard on the eyes. And the place held no room for improvement! Its institutions and inhabitants were perfect. How dull it would be for a teacher!

Naturally, Miss Dove had never voiced that objection. (Criticism of orthodox beliefs she considered vulgar and jejune and harmful to the masses.) She hardly knew she entertained it. Heaven was her eventual home. She would be loyal to it. Someday she would go there and accept, with what grace she could muster, beatific and perpetual idleness.

Only—she whispered to herself—not tomorrow!

Pretending to read a magazine, she thought of the places—the lowly, earthbound places—that she did long to see. They ran through her mind like snatches of poetry. The white cliffs of Dover, the Lake Country, and all the green English countryside. Paris. Rome on its Seven Hills. Rivers and deltas and black forests where bull elephants charged through the undergrowth and supple feline animals stalked their prey. The Orient. The Arctic Circle. The Northwest Passage? In Miss Dove's childhood that short route from east to west, though a lost cause to explorers, had still stirred the young with adventurous hope. She had planned to discover it herself when she grew up and the plan had never ceased haunting her.

How small and circumscribed her life had been! She had a great yearning to burst its bounds—to see, to admire, to be free!

"The day's beginning to fade," said Billie Jean. She turned on the lamp.

Supper was over. Nurses were changed. Jincey looked in again—paler this time, but still undiscouraged. Will I ever see the child? Miss Dove asked herself. Will I know whether it's a boy or girl?

There was much she wanted to know. After her retirement she had meant to study Greek and geology. She had meant to learn more about the migratory habits of birds. She regretted neglecting to verify the statement about the flavor of ants that Angela had queried long ago.

Dr. Temple came to listen to her chest. Mere hospital busy-work, Miss Dove thought impatiently; but recalling his description of herself, she was gracious to him.

"When you write to your mother, which I trust you do at regular intervals—" she began.

"Once a week," he said.

"You may tell her I do not find you unastute."

"She'll be proud to hear that," he said. "*She's* so keen that she sometimes fancies her family more obtuse than it is!"

"Do you know how ants taste?" Miss Dove asked without preamble, simply because she suddenly burned to know.

The nurse looked alarmed (was the patient wandering?) and Miss Dove herself was aware that the question had a mildly lunatic ring.

But Adams Temple—Angela's own true son!—was a young man to whom curiosity, per se, seemed a normal, wholesome appetite.

"Why, yes. My mother told me," he said. "She ate one once, when she was a little girl. They taste like sour pickles."

Fearing to unhinge her patient's mind even further, the nightnurse was more silent than usual. She sat buffing her fingernails (a boudoir rite, Miss Dove reflected, that no person of refined instinct would perform in company) and casting occasional wary glances in the direction of the bed. When the Reverend Mr. Burnham appeared she was visibly relieved. "I'll leave you with your pastor," she said and discreetly withdrew.

Alexander laid a prayerbook on the table and sat down in a chair close to the bed.

This visit, Miss Dove thought, was the final test of her power of humility. It had been hard to accept Thomas as a medical authority and harder to preserve equanimity beneath the stethoscope of young Temple and the bossy ministrations of Billie Jean. To regard Alexander Burnham as her spiritual shepherd was hardest of all.

In church she found it easy. There the familiar rhythm of the service, the candles and the organ and the vestments combined to give him a kind of exalted anonymity. He seemed less a man than a symbol of office and quite dissociate from the high-strung boy who had been a touchy problem in Cedar Grove School.

He had been an uncertain child. Too tense. Too much enamoured of magnificence to endure willingly the long stretches of mediocrity that lie between the peaks of experience. And he had been afraid. Miss Dove had done what she could. She had tried to show him that he was not unique, that—in her room at least—he was subject only to the strict but unfrightening laws of cause and effect. Once she had protected him. But from another. Not from himself.

One day a pane of glass in the window of the principal's office had been broken. After recess a baseball was found among the shattered glass on the floor. Around it in an equatorial band the name "Alexander the Great" was printed in old English script.

The principal, who liked to impose discipline in a delayed and pompous way, had waited until school was out to question the suspect. He had chosen the geography room—possibly because its climate was unfriendly to falsehood —as the scene of his inquisition. Miss Dove had sat at her desk, divorcing herself from the proceedings while her so-called superior—a man of coarser grain than Mr. Spivey—had confronted Alexander with his evidence.

"Is this your ball, Sandy?" he asked, striding down the aisle to the spot where the accused child stood.

Alexander glanced at the ball. He blenched. "Yes, sir," he said.

"You positively identify it?"

"Yes, sir." A greenish tinge crept into the boy's pallor.

The principal gave him a menacing look. "You're guilty of destroying school property, aren't you?"

Alexander swallowed. Miss Dove could see the muscle bulging in his throat as he struggled with himself. "No, sir," he said.

"You deny that you broke the window?"

"No," said Alexander. "I mean yes. I didn't break it."

The principal gave vent to a cynical laugh. "Now look, Sandy. Don't give me that guff! We all know you never let anyone else touch that ball. We—"

Miss Dove spoke. Her voice was controlled and quiet and incisive as a new-honed blade.

"The child has answered you," she said. "You asked your question. He gave you his word."

"But—" the principal began.

"There are no 'buts,'" she said. She fixed her terrible calm eyes upon the flustered man. "The incident is closed."

The principal thumped the baseball down upon the teacher's desk. "Very well," he said as he left the room, "*you* manage it!"

"I will," said Miss Dove.

For a moment Alexander stood where he was, trembling, turning greener. Then he lunged forward. He reached the sink in the corner by the sand table. He gripped its sides and bent over it retching again and again.

Miss Dove did not go to him to hold his head or wipe his mouth with a cool damp rag. She sat on at her desk, as if he did not exist, and heard him try in vain to vomit up his lie.

When, at last, he was quiet, she said: "Remember to take your baseball as you go."

Now he was a man. A man to whom other men came for advice in perplexity. A man useful in church and state. He was one of her successes, she supposed; but it was difficult to forget the boy at the sink, the boy whose name in the Book had been followed by a rare symbol—a question mark! And yet, in simple parochial duty, she must forget him now.

"Thomas has told you?" said Miss Dove.

"That he'll operate tomorrow? Yes," said Alexander. "I'm glad you're staying here. Tommy's as good as they come."

"The outcome is doubtful," she said.

"All outcomes are. Always," said Alexander.

"I do not wish to die," said Miss Dove. Now she had said it. She had used the word. She felt curiously purged.

"No. Of course not," he agreed. "It may seem strange, in view of my calling, but I do scorn the person who is resigned to death. He is ungrateful to life."

"Life—" said Miss Dove. She dwelt on the word as on a lover's name. "It is—" But she had not the eloquence to say what it was. "I have been happy," she said.

She had never said so before. She had, in fact, considered it ignoble to measure euphoria. She saw now that she had been one of the blessed simply because she had not guessed she was.

"I know," said Alexander.

"Thomas is not hopeful, is he?" she asked.

"Not very," said Alexander. "But there is a hope that transcends the medical!" He reached for the prayerbook. "Perhaps if we read from this—"

Miss Dove was grateful for his candor. She repaid it now in kind.

"Do you intend to read the general confession?" she asked.

He nodded. "In such circumstances that is customary."

"Then I must warn you," she said, "that when I repeat that prayer I do so with reservations."

"Reservations?"

"Yes," she said. "I have made mistakes. I have my human limitations. But I do not, in all honesty, find the burden of my sins intolerable. And I haven't erred and strayed like a sheep!"

"The language is archaic, I'll grant you," Alexander said. "But it contains the core of truth. All of us—"

But Miss Dove was adamant. "No," she said. "I have never spoken hypocrisy to my Maker and now is scarcely a propitious moment to begin." Her neck, propped on the pillow, looked very stiff indeed. "I am not 'a miserable offender.'"

The rector smiled. His smile was warm and engaging and bright with the good gaiety that radiates from men whose hearts are leavened by work they love. Why, Miss Dove thought, he is at ease with himself. He is the man I wished him to become.

"And I'll tell you a secret, Miss Dove," he said. "Neither am I!"

He sat with her for a while, there in the hospital room that was as small and nearly as ascetic as a monk's cell. He talked of the world outside—of his garden where the crocuses were up, of the old gnarled crabapple that was in full bud in the courthouse square and of the foreign places he had seen as a chaplain in the navy. Just before he left he said casually, almost in the manner of after-thought: "We could have our prayer now if you like. Silently, but together."

"I *should* like," said Miss Dove.

She could not know—nor did she try to guess—the nature of Alexander's petition, but her own was simple. "Whatever comes to me," she pleaded, "let me take it like a Teacher!"

The nurse came in. She carried a saucer upon which a yellow capsule reposed in one of those little fluted paper cups that usually contain chocolate creams.

Miss Dove swallowed the capsule.

After the lamp was out she lay waiting for sleep to trip her in the thoughts, gazing at the square of sky framed in the window. The sky was a deep, stained-glass blue and perfectly clear except for one long, thin line of transparent cloud. Over it innumerable stars seemed to swim and swirl like a swarm of crystal bees. Then, as if Miss Dove had stepped aside at a remove from actuality, she saw her own star—the planet Earth, her darling, which she knew in all its beauty and imperfection—hung aloft outside her window. It was no bee. No trivial celestial insect. It was a round ball as large as the globe on her schoolroom desk. It glowed with a brilliance that came not from without but from within, and it revolved slowly so that she could see the familiar patterns of its continental bodies shadowed on its surface. She had done what she could for it. Now, like a child just graduated from Cedar Grove, it was on its own—beyond her care or correction. She bade it Godspeed as it spun in the April night.

On Saturday morning at eight o'clock Dr. Baker stood in the corridor outside the operating rooms and talked with his interne, Dr. Temple. He appeared relaxed, unhurried, and steady of nerve which, as a matter of fact, he was. Just before an operation—no matter how difficult or fraught with danger—this miraculous thing always happened to him. Tranquility descended upon his spirit. Cares fell away from his mind and left it clean and sharp like a scalpel.

"The parson and the cop are in the lobby," Adams Temple said. "Potential blood donors. They both match."

"Good," said Thomas. He lit a cigarette. His hand did not shake.

"An odd pair," Adams said.

"Oh, I don't know. They both grew up here in Liberty Hill. They went to the same school."

"I talked a bit with the cop," Adams said. "He told me about his life—sketchily of course. How he pulled himself up by his bootstraps with Miss Dove's moral aid. A remarkable story."

"Bill's quite a guy," Thomas said absently.

"If he does give her a transfusion," Adams went on, "or even if he doesn't —just because he's here ready to—and this thing turns out well it will mean a lot to him. To all of you."

"You're damn right it will," said Thomas.

"Psychologically, I mean," Adams explained. "A sort of rounding out of the cycle of maturity."

Thomas smoked in silence. At the moment he wanted nothing less than to be forced into introspection. This bright, pontifical lad got on his nerves.

But Adams continued to worry his thesis. "It's like the pious Aeneas turning back into burning Troy," he said. "Remember? He took the old Anchises—his own father—on his shoulders and bore him, like a child, away from the flames."

"I follow your drift," said Thomas drily. "But I lack your classical background."

"Well," Adams told him. "*My* Miss Dove taught Latin."

Thomas tossed his cigarette into a jardiniere filled with sand. "It's time to scrub," he said. "You ought to be a psychiatrist."

"I think I shall be," Adams said. "What's surgery but sublimated butchery?"

If Adams had been a permanent interne instead of a temporary whose place would be hard to fill, Thomas might have fired him on the spot. Instead, he only laughed. "At least we don't plug our patients into the wall," he said lightly.

The operation lasted for hours. During the morning a number of callers came to the hospital. There was nothing they could do, they knew. They were drawn there, as by a magnet, to inquire, to leave their cards, and go away.

John Wesley Evans buttonholed the Reverend Mr. Burnham. He spoke feelingly of his personal reformation.

"It was like Damascus," he declared. "I'll never touch another drop!"

Alexander, who was ordinarily impatient of John Wesley's ups and downs, spoke kindly.

"Take it easy, Wes," he advised. "A day at a time."

For the most part, Billie Jean remained in her patient's empty room. Now and then, however, just for the pure pleasure of gazing on William Holloway who sat, majestic and muscular, in a brown leather lounge chair—she found an excuse for consulting the receptionist in the lobby. She was there when the delegation from Cedar Grove School arrived.

The delegation was composed of four girls and eight boys. Their faces, preternaturally clean, were solemn, brave, and scared. The girls were in Brownie dresses and the boys in Cub Scout uniforms. Their right sleeves were rolled to their shoulders.

Billie Jean met them at the door.

"Children aren't allowed without their parents," she said. "What do you want?"

"We're on important business," young David Burnham said haughtily. "A matter of life or death."

"Let me talk," said Vicky Evans. "I'm spokesman."

"Okay, big shot," said David.

"We came to give blood to Miss Dove," said Vicky. She crooked out her bare arm as if expecting to be seized and bled on the instant. She bit her lips and squinched her eyes shut.

David shoved her. "Dope! They don't do it out here. They lay you down and afterwards they give you tomato juice."

"We don't do it anywhere to folks your age," said Billie Jean.

"We're all big," piped a diminutive, pigtailed girl. "We're all over nine!"

"We have health badges," said Vicky. "Our blood's *strong!*"

Billie Jean's maternal tenderness was touched. "Listen, honeys," she said gently, "we don't need you. We've got David's daddy and Officer Holloway right here. But I know something you *can* do for Miss Dove."

"What?" asked David suspiciously, as if he knew the project would be dull.

"The proficiency test's Monday," said Billie Jean. "If she comes back to school and finds you flunked it she'll be good and mad! She'll be *terrible!* You go home and study for that!"

"Heck," someone muttered. "We know that junk!"

"Are you sure?" asked Billie Jean. In rapid succession she pointed her finger at child after child, firing questions like bullets. "What's the difference between longitude and latitude? Name the Great Lakes. The chief product of Brazil. Where is the Tropic of Capricorn?"

At each shot the children backed nearer to the door. At last they were gone.

"You managed that like a seasoned diplomat, Billie Jean," said Alexander.

Billie Jean smiled. "I wish I knew the answers!" She dabbed at her eyes. "Those cute little tykes," she murmured brokenly and hurried away.

Holloway cleared his throat. The courage of the children had moved him and Billie Jean's tears he considered womanly and genteel.

The children trailed along the sidewalk looking up at the hospital windows.

"That's where she is," said David. "That top room at the corner."

"No. That's where ladies have babies," one of his companions objected.

"Davie's right," said Vicky. "I was in there when I had my tonsils out. It's all tiled, like a bathroom. They put you on a table under a huge light and make you blow up a balloon."

"That's the ether," said David.

They stared. They tried to imagine the terrible Miss Dove lying on a table in a bathroom, puffing at a balloon. The effort was beyond them. On a common impulse they scampered off to a vacant lot where they played kick-the-can until their spirits rose so high that David called Vicky an ugly name which she, quite properly, resented. Later in the day, however, she wrote him a poem in which she told him he was her knight in armor and she was sorry she had kicked him in the stomach.

Meanwhile Miss Dove had set out on a very grand tour.

Precisely when the journey began (was it when Miss Dove had her vision of the home planet?) and how long it lasted and what ground it covered are questions impossible to answer. Even Miss Dove was baffled by them. Now and then she would find herself in a new place without knowing how she had got there and she would move on before she had a chance to clarify her recollections. She decided that as soon as she arrived at her destination—whatever that might be—she would sit down quietly in a room alone and fill in the gaps in her memory. She was not fond of gaps.

The truth is that she knew all there was to know. She had entered a realm where ordinary laws—the laws of gravity and space and time—are not constant.

At first she was being carried—in a palanquin she presumed—across a beautiful plain that spread out on either side and was dotted with clusters of buildings. Pagodas. Palaces. Temples. Bells were ringing in the distance—they made a mellow, wistful sound—and the colors of the landscape were clear and delicate. The trees had twisted trunks and their spreading, wind-flattened crowns were a soft sea-green outlined in gold. They were like the trees in a Chinese tapestry. Beneath one tree a man stood reading a book. He wore a crimson gown and a long, thin chin-beard that fell to his knees.

"Are you Marco Polo?" he called when he saw Miss Dove.

"No," she replied, finding nothing strange in his question. "I am Miss Dove of Liberty Hill!"

"Miss Dove!" he cried and made a deep obeisance.

Why, this is old Cathay! she thought. Of course. She saw now that the whole plain was encircled by a wall. She wished to explore it thoroughly—to go into its temples and its fabulous gardens and to talk to its wise men so she could tell her father all about it.

She didn't know the language of the palanquin bearers but she remembered that French was the international tongue. What was the French for "Stop"? All she could think of was "Parlez-vous Français" which did not sound right. "Attention, please!" she said in a distinct tone. But even as she spoke she saw that the scene had changed. She must have crossed the wall without noticing.

She was in the middle of a desert.

Suddenly she realized that she was not riding in a palanquin. She was sitting on a seat made of four joined hands which belonged to Thomas Baker and Alexander Burnham. The boys were grinning up at her in an impish way. They were about eleven years old. They wore red sweaters and corduroy knickers. Alexander was smoking a cigarette.

"How unseemly!" she said. "Put me down at once."

Thomas wiggled his ears. "This is *my* theatre of command," he said.

"You have never been in more grievous error," said Miss Dove. "Put me down."

"Keep your spine rigid," said Thomas. "Ready, Sandy? One—two—three—go!"

Instead of putting her down they swung her aloft. She left their hands and bounced into the air—very lightly, she remarked, like a soap-bubble—and found herself perched comfortably upon the hump of a camel.

The camel half-turned its head and looked at her with one mournful eye. "I'm not a pretty beast," it said.

Miss Dove was chagrined. Although she had dictated those words many times to the advanced first grade, she would never have been so unfeeling as to say them to a camel's face.

"Pretty is as pretty does," she said.

"I can go many days without water," the camel said. It moved off toward the flat, treeless horizon.

Miss Dove was agreeably surprised at the smoothness of its gait. She had understood that the motion of a camel was apt to be jerky and rough, but this one seemed to glide. He was, indeed, a veritable "ship of the desert." She felt borne along on a gently undulating stream.

Elaine the fair, Elaine the lovable.

Miss Dove the grim, Miss Dove the terrible—the lines flowed drowsily through her mind. She shook them off.

The desert looked exactly like the sand table desert that the third grade always made when it was introduced to Arabia. Only, of course, no table could begin to suggest this sense of illimitable space, of vastness and emptiness stretching beyond the scope of the eye or the imagination. Then, against the horizon, she saw a caravan. Its "desert ships" and their robed riders were purple. They might have been cut from the purple cardboard that the children used to suggest distance.

Miss Dove and her steed were approaching an oasis. It was a green, inviting spot—a clump of date palms around a bubbling spring.

"Could you take a sip of water?" asked the camel. His voice was like a woman's voice, soft and wheedling. "Just a little sip of water?"

Miss Dove was tempted. She would have enjoyed a sip. But pride would not permit her to be less abstemious than a beast.

"We will wait until big recess," she said.

Before long she regretted her refusal. Her mouth was dry. When, shimmering near at hand, she saw another clump of palms, she said she would now like to pause for refreshment.

"That one is a mirage," the camel said contemptuously. "You can go thirsty."

"You must employ a civil tone," said Miss Dove.

The camel snorted. It turned its head to her. Its heavy-lidded eye, its curling lips and its long yellow teeth made her think of Mr. Porter. "I made you a civil offer once," it said.

When the desert was crossed, how she dismounted from her perch, Miss Dove could not say. She only knew that before long she was in an airplane speeding over land and sea and receiving a kaleidoscope of impressions that were both strange and familiar.

The plane was not like the big liner in which, at Geoffrey Lyon's invitation, she had flown to New York. It was such a machine as she had watched rise above the county fairgrounds in the summer of 1910. She flew it herself. She sat in an open cockpit and held the stick with one hand while with the other she pressed down hard on the crown of her hat to prevent its blowing off.

It was night. The moon and stars were shining. They were very close to her or else her vision was even more acute than usual. She saw the craters on the moon and the rings around Saturn and the seventh star in the Pleiades. For an instant she let her hat take its chances while she reached out and nearly touched the Southern Cross. Below her, white in the moonlight, gleamed the remnants of antiquity—the leaning tower, the pyramids, the broken columns of the Parthenon. Black ink-blots of jungle were spilled, sprawling, over the earth; in their depths she saw the burning jewel eyes of tigers on the prowl and the great rivers winding silver to the sea. The Ganges. The Euphrates. The Nile. She knew each one by its peculiar bends and turns that she had so often traced on the schoolroom map. The sea itself. The vast, mysterious matrix of all life. Wider than the desert. Wide as the sky.

Near her some invisible person was singing an old, silly song that made her think of honeysuckle at a dormitory window.

"Come and take a ride in my ai-rr-plane
And we'll vis-it the man in the moon!"

Miss Dove sniffed. "The moon is a dead planet," she said. "A satellite of the Earth. Because of its intense cold and the lack of oxygen in its atmosphere it cannot support any form of life, animal or vegetable."

"Yes, Miss Dove," a voice replied.

The plane nosed downward. It went into a spin. Round and round and round and round into a funnel of darkness went Miss Dove. She lay fathoms deep in water. Slowly, she floated upward. She had an impression of light seeping down upon her. She had nearly reached the surface. She had reached it. There was an odor of flowers and of something else—half sweet, half sickening—pulling her down. Faces bent above her. If they would go away, move back, give her air—

She was in Paris. The chestnuts were in flower. Ladies, exquisitely gowned, strolled beside handsome gentlemen with mustaches like her father's. Wellmannered children sailed boats on a pond. Everything was suave and *comme il faut* and yet she was uneasy. Paris was a beautiful city full of beautiful names—Champs d'Élysées, Bois de Boulogne, Place de la Concorde—but she did not trust it. She would have liked to buy a book at one of the stalls along the Seine but she didn't dare lest it be an improper one. She was still thirsty but she was afraid to sit at a table at a sidewalk cafe and order a drink lest the waiter—the *garçon*—should bring her something alcoholic.

" 'Oh to be in England, now that April's here'!" she sighed.

"It's just past the channel," said a man at her elbow. Or did he say "crisis?" He had an American accent—a Liberty Hill accent. "It ought to be smooth sailing."

"Thank you," said Miss Dove. She descended a flight of rickety steps to a pier at the end of which a small steamship was bobbing on choppy water. The man called down to someone on the ship.

"She's all right," he called. "Let her sleep!"

Let her sleep, let her sleep, let her sleep—

In London she felt more at home. A bobby saluted her. "They're expecting you, mum," he said. He put her into a cab—a hansom cab—and she rode through the gray calm heart of London past the British Museum and Trafalgar Square and The Old Curiosity Shop. Big Ben struck the hour. The bells of St. Paul's and St. Ive's chimed together. The cab stopped at the gates of

Buckingham Palace. Miss Dove alighted. A soldier in a busby flung open the gate. "They're expecting you," he said.

Miss Dove went past him. A garden party was in progress. Among the guests Miss Dove spotted her mother who was dressed in black but carrying a pink silk parasol that cast rosy light upon her face and made it look young and debonair. She smiled at her daughter and continued talking gaily to a little page.

Miss Dove sat down at a round table. Presently Queen Mary joined her. The queen's manner was stately and affable. She wore a high turban covered with feathers and violets. She exuded an agreeable odor of lavendar.

"Miss Dove," she said, "I admire your hat."

"Thank you, ma'am," said Miss Dove, congratulating herself upon remembering to say 'ma'am' to the Queen. "It is not to be compared with yours. Yours is a *chapeau*."

Her Majesty stroked the feathers on her hat. "I always wash before applying scent," she said. "Would you care to see my herbaceous border?"

"Indeed, yes," said Miss Dove who was an amateur of botany.

At a respectful distance she followed her hostess. But she never saw the border. Instead, when she came to the end of the path she found herself standing on the jutting point of a cliff at the edge of a high plateau. Far below—so far that looking down made her dizzy—a narrow inlet joined two great seas that lay to left and right. Between the promontory upon which she stood and another promontory exactly like hers, a footbridge spanned the chasm. It was a flimsy-looking bridge made of wire and barrel staves and less than a yard in width. Miss Dove drew back.

"Is it London Bridge?" she asked.

"It's condition is satisfactory," said the Queen. "It's only the Northwest Passage."

"Of course," said Miss Dove. The aurora borealis spread its giant fan of colors on the sky. Far down in the water an iceberg reflected the colors and sailed serenely out to sea like a great cumulous cloud full of the setting sun.

At the further end of the bridge stood the young archeologist. He wore white flannel trousers, a dark blue blazer, a high collar and a stiff straw hat which he removed with a flourish.

"Do you know *me*, Miss Dove?" he asked and his voice, though familiar, sounded different from the voice of the young man she had talked to on the campus lawn. "I'm rather bizarre, but quite benign!"

Miss Dove crossed the bridge. She walked gingerly at first but by the time she reached the middle she had no fear of falling. On the other side of the chasm the world was bathed in pellucid gold. All the vegetation was overlaid with a patina of light. Each lacquered blade of grass stood separate from its neighbor. On every leaf on every tree the delicate vein-structure was visible.

The air had a new quality. As Miss Dove drew it into her lungs she was filled with a desire to dance, to sing, to laugh. To loosen her hair and let it blow in the wind. She had discovered, she felt, some marvelous secret that prompted the pulse of the universe.

"Under these happy auspices—" the young archeologist began and would have seized her hand.

She darted away from him.

"I must tell them!" she cried. "I must tell them!"

Once she looked back to see if he were following, but he was only standing there, decorous and unimportunate.

She ran through the town of Liberty Hill. William Holloway stared, shocked and disillusioned, as she passed him at Maple and Grant. He raised a big gloved paw to halt her. She did not halt.

She ran down the central corridor of Cedar Grove School. Mr. Spivey was standing just outside his office. His bald head was a wan day-moon in the dim academic light.

She took a long, flying leap and slid along the floor, as she had seen boys do when they thought she wasn't looking. She slid straight to the geography room and in at the door.

The room was noisy and bright with children. They were playing leap-frog over the desks. They sang and shouted and called one another rude names. The shirttails of the boys flapped behind them. The skirts of the girls belled out, blue and pink and yellow and lilac, like flowers of the field.

When they saw Miss Dove they reined in their joy. They went to their seats. They opened their notebooks and sat erect—feet on the floor, hands folded on the desks, solemn eyes to the front.

Miss Dove mounted the platform. "Attention, please," she said. She meant her voice to ring, but it came out level and precise. She wanted to say to the children: "Unclasp your little hands! Forget the rules. A fig for margins!" She wanted to tell them: "Look for the golden light and the new-veined leaf! Drink the air of Spring! Life is the only thing that matters at all. Life!"

But the spell that had fallen upon the class fell upon her. She could not speak. The only sound in the room was that of a fly buzzing against a screen. She picked up yesterday's folded newspaper, which she had saved against such an emergency. At a measured pace she walked to the window and swatted the fly.

"The Alps, I presume," said Miss Dove to the young archeologist. She was in a meadow where young goats with bells on their collars tumbled among flowers and filled the air with tinkling clatter. She pointed to a range of mountains.

"Yes. In a manner of speaking," he said. "And beyond lies—"

She did not wait to hear what lay beyond. She began to climb. Like a mountain goat she leapt from crag to crag. She was amazed at her own agility.

But when, with her companion puffing behind her, she reached what she thought must surely be the summit of the mountain, she found she was mistaken. It was only an upland pasture, a resting place, above which the true peak ascended, glassy with ice and too steep for any foot, goat or human.

From the apex of the peak stretched a steel cable down which slid a little car—a kind of basket, really, like those beneath balloons at expositions.

Alphonzo Dove stepped out of the basket. "I came down to meet you, dear child," he said. "How did you stand the trip?"

"Very well, thank you, sir," said Miss Dove. She was glad to see her father, but not at all surprised. He wore a green alpine-climbing costume. A sprig of eidelweiss was stuck into the band of his hat. An old brown vellum-bound book peeped from the pocket of his jacket. His jaunty mustaches glittered in the sun.

"You go the rest of the way by funicular," he said with a gesture toward the basket. "Don't be afraid. It's rather bizarre, but quite benign."

Bizarre. Benign. Miss Dove started. Someone else had said that. Someone else dressed in green. She turned her head.

"What are you looking for?" Alphonzo asked.

"For Thomas Baker," said Miss Dove.

"The child with the ears," said Alphonzo.

"Oh," said the archeologist, "he's not a Boards man. Are you a Boards woman?"

"No," said Miss Dove, "but I have passed my proficiency test."

"She's in no apparent distress," said her father, "though her hair is rather bizarre."

Bizarre, benign. Benign, bizarre. Bizarre, bizarre, bz-z-z-z.

She was in the funnel again. She was under water. She was floating. She was coming up—up—up—

She opened her eyes.

She was lying, of course, in her hospital bed. Beside her stood a tall iron contraption, like a floor lamp, that held a jar of clear liquid. From the bottom of the jar depended a small rubber tube that was attached by a needle to the vein in the inside bend of her elbow. Glucose, she thought correctly and knew where she was and what had happened.

From outside, beyond glass, she heard the courthouse clock striking the half, and then the sweet, dissonant ringing of churchbells. It was Sunday. Those were the bells for early service. Alexander Burnham was standing in the chancel ready to make the ways of righteousness appear amiable to his flock and to speak, out of his knowledge, of the peace that passed understanding.

She felt alert and collected.

But in an odd and bitter way she felt disappointed too. Why had she returned to this small, restricted, accustomed place? She had been free. She had breathed upland air. Why had she not gone on and scaled the glassy mountains and seen what lay beyond?

Sunlight flooded the window. The red paper schoolhouse in the dish-garden was incandescent. Why, there it is, she thought. There is Life.

She thought of all the children she had pruned and polished and kept in line, and to whom she had explained, by precept and example, the hard, the true, the simple and beautiful meaning of the human adventure. She thought of their faces lighting up with fresh wonder when they conceived, for the first time, the roundness of the earth. Of those who had gone and of those—if she dared hope—who were yet to come. For a scandalized instant, before she forgot it entirely and forever, she recalled the amorality she had been on the verge of uttering to those desk-jumping children in her dream.

She knew, with a passion of yearning, exactly where she wished to go. Not to old Cathay. Not to London or Paris or to the anomalous country beyond the hills. She wanted to walk down Oakwood, across LaFayette, up Maple, over to Grant (nodding to William Holloway) and into the portals of Cedar Grove School. She wanted to go into the geography room. To put her hat and gloves and bag in the cupboard. To unroll the big map of the world. To mount her platform and to stand there waiting for the first graders to file in—abandoning folly as they crossed her sill, greeting her soberly, one by one, in the prescribed words which told her that the day had begun to blossom.

Billie Jean was tidying the bureau. On her left hand a single diamond sparkled. She pushed the potted azalea back so far that it tilted the mirror and Miss Dove could see the nurse's reflection and that of Thomas Baker as he came into the room.

Thomas' face looked tired, like the face of a man who has forgotten about sleep. But it looked jaunty, as well—the way it had looked, she remembered, when a hard test or a baseball game had come out better than he'd had a right to expect. In the crook of either arm he carried a bundle wrapped in a blue blanket.

(Twins, thought Miss Dove. Boy twins. I shall have to keep them apart —one on the first row and one far over by the windows—even though that upsets my alphabetical seating arrangement. But would they—? Would she ever—? Hadn't something been said—something in Thomas' voice—about strangeness and benignity?)

Beneath the sheet she moved her hand slowly, fearfully, toward her right thigh. She held her thumb and forefinger curved, like a crab's pincers, in pinching position. One tweak and she would know! But suddenly she let her fingers go limp and her hand lie still. Investigation was not a patient's province.

Thomas had paused just inside the door. When he saw in the glass Billie Jean's delighted smile, he wagged his ears. He cocked one eyebrow. "What a man among men am I!" his clowning plainly bragged.

He tiptoed to the bedside. The babies began to cry. "An-ha-n-n! Ahan-a-n-nn-n!" their shrill, indignant voices went.

"Quiet, please," said Miss Dove.

Nobody—not she nor Thomas nor Billie Jean—was surprised when the babies hushed.

She gazed up at the doctor. Her eyes were gray and luminous and steady. She waited to hear the truth.

Thomas returned her gaze. His face, like the paper schoolhouse, seemed to glow from within.

He thought of what Adams Temple had said about Aeneas and Anchises and the rounded circle. He thought of Miss Dove tying Jincey's hair with the string. He saw her, standing straight as her long map-pointer, beside the desk and the globe. Then he told her what she wanted to know. He told her without wasting a word.

He stood erect. He drew a curtain of gravity over his face, making it blank of everything except decorum and sober dedication. In the reserved, deferential, uninflected accents of Cedar Grove Elementary School, he spoke at last.

"Good morning, Miss Dove," he said.

TURN ABOUT

WILLIAM FAULKNER

MARCH 5, 1932

THE AMERICAN—the older one—wore no pink Bedfords. His breeches were of plain whipcord, like the tunic. And the tunic had no long London-cut skirts, so that below the Sam Browne the tail of it stuck straight out like a tunic of a military policeman beneath his holster belt. And he wore simple putties and the easy shoes of a man of middle age, instead of Savile Row boots, and the shoes and the putties did not match in shade, and the ordnance belt did not match either of them, and the pilot's wings on his breast were just wings. But the ribbon beneath them was a good ribbon, and the insigne on his shoulders were the twin bars of a captain. He was not tall. His face was thin, a little aquiline; the eyes intelligent and a little tired. He was past twenty-five; looking at him, one thought, not Phi Beta Kappa exactly, but Skull and Bones perhaps, or possibly a Rhodes scholarship.

One of the men who faced him probably could not see him at all. He was being held on his feet by an American military policeman. He was quite drunk, and in contrast with the heavy-jawed policeman who held him erect on his long, slim, boneless legs, he looked like a masquerading girl. He was possibly eighteen, tall, with a pink-and-white face and blue eyes, and a little dull gold mustache above a mouth like a girl's mouth. He wore a pea-coat, buttoned awry and stained with recent mud, and upon his blond head, at that unmistakable and rakish swagger which no other people can ever approach or imitate, the cap of a Royal Naval officer.

"What's this, corporal?" the American captain said. "What's the trouble? He's an Englishman. You'd better let their M.P.'s take care of him."

"I know he is," the policeman said. He spoke heavily, breathing heavily, in the voice of a man under physical strain; for all his girlish delicacy of limb, the English boy was heavier—or more helpless—than he looked. "Stand up!" the policeman said. "They're officers!"

The English boy made an effort then. He pulled himself together, focusing his eyes. He swayed, throwing his arm about the policeman's neck, and with the other hand he saluted, his hand flicking, fingers curled a little, to his right ear, already swaying again and catching himself again. "Cheerio, sir," he said. "Name's not Beatty, I hope."

"No," the captain said.

"Ah," the English boy said. "Hoped not. My mistake. No offense, what?"

"No offense," the captain said quietly. But he was looking at the policeman. The second American spoke. He was a lieutenant, also a pilot. But he was not twenty-five and he wore the pink breeches, the London boots, and his tunic might have been a British tunic save for the collar.

"It's one of those navy eggs," he said. "They pick them out of the gutters here all night long. You don't come to town often enough."

"Oh," the captain said. "I've heard about them. I remember now." He also remarked now that, though the street was a busy one—it was just outside a popular café—and there were many passers, soldier, civilian, women, yet none of them so much as paused, as though it were a familiar sight. He was looking at the policeman. "Can't you take him to his ship?"

"I thought of that before the captain did," the policeman said. "He says he can't go aboard his ship after dark because he puts the ship away at sundown."

"Puts it away?"

"Stand up, sailor!" the policeman said savagely, jerking at his lax burden. "Maybe the captain can make sense out of it. Damned if I can. He says they keep the boat under the wharf. Run it under the wharf at night, and that they can't get it out again until the tide goes out tomorrow."

"Under the wharf? A boat? What is this?" He was now speaking to the lieutenant. "Do they operate some kind of aquatic motorcycles?"

"Something like that," the lieutenant said. "You've seen them—the boats. Launches, camouflaged and all. Dashing up and down the harbor. You've seen them. They do that all day and sleep in the gutters here all night."

"Oh," the captain said. "I thought those boats were ship commanders' launches. You mean to tell me they use officers just to——"

"I don't know," the lieutenant said. "Maybe they use them to fetch hot water from one ship to another. Or buns. Or maybe to go back and forth fast when they forget napkins or something."

"Nonsense," the captain said. He looked at the English boy again.

"That's what they do," the lieutenant said. "Town's lousy with them all night long. Gutters full, and their M.P.'s carting them away in batches, like nursemaids in a park. Maybe the French give them the launches to get them out of the gutters during the day."

"Oh," the captain said, "I see." But it was clear that he didn't see, wasn't listening, didn't believe what he did hear. He looked at the English boy. "Well, you can't leave him here in that shape," he said.

Again the English boy tried to pull himself together. "Quite all right, 'sure you," he said glassily, his voice pleasant, cheerful almost, quite courteous. "Used to it. Confounded rough *pavé*, though. Should force French do something about it. Visiting lads jolly well deserve decent field to play on, what?"

"And he was jolly well using all of it too," the policeman said savagely. "He must think he's a one-man team, maybe."

At that moment a fifth man came up. He was a British military police-man. "Nah then," he said. "What's this? What's this?" Then he saw the Americans' shoulder bars. He saluted. At the sound of his voice the English boy turned, swaying, peering.

"Oh, hullo, Albert," he said.

"Nah then, Mr. Hope," the British policeman said. He said to the Ameri-can policeman, over his shoulder: "What is it this time?"

"Likely nothing," the American said. "The way you guys run a war. But I'm a stranger here. Here, Take him."

"What is this, corporal?" the captain said. "What was he doing?"

"He won't call it nothing," the American policeman said, jerking his head at the British policeman. "He'll just call it a thrush or a robin or something. I turn into this street about three blocks back a while ago, and I find it blocked with a line of trucks going up from the docks, and the drivers all hollering ahead what the hell the trouble is. So I come on, and I find it is about three blocks of them, blocking the cross streets too; and I come on to the head of it where the trouble is, and I find about a dozen of the drivers out in front, holding a caucus or something in the middle of the street, and I come up and I say, 'What's going on here?' and they leave me through and I find this egg here laying—"

"Yer talking about one of His Majesty's officers, my man," the British policeman said.

"Watch yourself, corporal," the captain said. "And you found this officer—"

"He had done gone to bed in the middle of the street, with an empty basket for a pillow. Laying there with his hands under his head and his knees crossed, arguing with them about whether he ought to get up and move or not. He said that the trucks could turn back and go around by another street, but that he couldn't use any other street, because this street was his."

"His street?"

The English boy had listened, interested, pleasant. "Billet, you see," he said. "Must have order, even in war emergency. Billet by lot. This street mine; no poaching, eh? Next street Jamie Wutherspoon's. But trucks can go by that street because Jamie not using it yet. Not in bed yet. Insomnia. Knew so. Told them. Trucks go that way. See now?"

"Was that it, corporal?" the captain said.

"He told you. He wouldn't get up. He just laid there, arguing with them. He was telling one of them to go somewhere and bring back a copy of their articles of war—"

"King's Regulations; yes," the captain said.

"—and see if the book said whether he had the right of way, or the trucks. And then I got him up, and then the captain come along. And that's all. And with the captain's permission I'll now hand him over to His Maj-esty's wet nur—"

"That'll do, corporal," the captain said. "You can go. I'll see to this." The policeman saluted and went on. The British policeman was now supporting the English boy. "Can't you take him home?" the captain said. "Where are their quarters?"

"I don't rightly know, sir, if they have quarters or not. We—I usually see them about the pubs until daylight. They don't seem to use quarters."

"You mean, they really aren't off of ships?"

"Well, sir, they might be ships, in a manner of speaking. But a man would have to be a bit sleepier than him to sleep in one of them."

"I see," the captain said. He looked at the policeman. "What kind of boats are they?"

This time the policeman's voice was immediate, final and completely inflectionless. It was like a closed door. "I don't rightly know, sir."

"Oh," the captain said. "Quite. Well, he's in no shape to stay about pubs until daylight this time."

"Perhaps I can find him a bit of a pub with a back table, where he can sleep," the policeman said. But the captain was not listening. He was looking across the street, where the lights of another café fell across the pavement. The English boy yawned terrifically, like a child does, his mouth pink and frankly gaped as a child's.

The captain turned to the policeman:

"Would you mind stepping across there and asking for Captain Bogard's driver? I'll take care of Mr. Hope."

The policeman departed. The captain now supported the English boy, his hand beneath the other's arm. Again the boy yawned like a weary child. "Steady," the captain said. "The car will be here in a minute."

"Right," the English boy said through the yawn.

II

Once in the car, he went to sleep immediately with the peaceful suddenness of babies, sitting between the two Americans. But though the aerodrome was only thirty minutes away, he was awake when they arrived, apparently quite fresh, and asking for whisky. When they entered the mess he appeared quite sober, only blinking a little in the lighted room, in his raked cap and his awry-buttoned pea-jacket and a soiled silk muffler, embroidered with a club insignia which Bogard recognized to have come from a famous preparatory school, twisted about his throat.

"Ah," he said, his voice fresh, clear now, not blurred, quite cheerful, quite loud, so that the others in the room turned and looked at him. "Jolly. Whisky, what?" He went straight as a bird dog to the bar in the corner, the lieutenant following. Bogard had turned and gone on to the other end of the room, where five men sat about a card table.

"What's he admiral of?" one said.

"Of the whole Scotch navy, when I found him," Bogard said.

Another looked up. "Oh. I thought I'd seen him in town." He looked at the guest. "Maybe it's because he was on his feet that I didn't recognize him when he came in. You usually see them lying down in the gutter."

"Oh," the first said. He, too, looked around. "Is he one of those guys?"

"Sure. You've seen them. Sitting on the curb, you know, with a couple of limey M. P.'s hauling at their arms."

"Yes. I've seen them," the other said. They all looked at the English boy. He stood at the bar, talking, his voice loud, cheerful. "They all look like him too," the speaker said. "About seventeen or eighteen. They run those little boats that are always dashing in and out."

"Is that what they do?" a third said. "You mean, there's a male marine auxiliary to the Waacs? Good Lord, I sure made a mistake when I enlisted. But this war never was advertised right."

"I don't know," Bogard said. "I guess they do more than just ride around."

But they were not listening to him. They were looking at the guest. "They run by clock," the first said. "You can see the condition of one of them after sunset and almost tell what time it is. But what I don't see is, how a man that's in that shape at one o'clock every morning can even see a battleship the next day."

"Maybe when they have a message to send out to a ship," another said, "they just make duplicates and line the launches up and point them toward the ship and give each one a duplicate of the message and let them go. And the ones that miss the ship just cruise around the harbor until they hit a dock somewhere."

"It must be more than that," Bogard said.

He was about to say something else, but at that moment the guest turned from the bar and approached, carrying a glass. He walked steadily enough, but his color was high and his eyes were bright, and he was talking, loud, cheerful, as he came up.

"I say. Won't you chaps join——" He ceased. He seemed to remark something; he was looking at their breasts. "Oh, I say. You fly. All of you. Oh, good gad! Find it jolly, eh?"

"Yes," somebody said. "Jolly."

"But dangerous, what?"

"A little faster than tennis," another said. The guest looked at him, bright, affable, intent.

Another said quickly, "Bogard says you command a vessel."

"Hardly a vessel. Thanks, though. And not command. Ronnie does that. Ranks me a bit. Age."

"Ronnie?"

"Yes. Nice. Good egg. Old, though. Stickler."

"Stickler?"

"Frightful. You'd not believe it. Whenever we sight smoke and I have the glass, he sheers away. Keeps the ship hull down all the while. No beaver then. Had me two down a fortnight yesterday."

The Americans glanced at one another. "No beaver?"

"We play it. With basket masts, you see. See a basket mast. Beaver! One up. The Ergenstrasse doesn't count any more, though."

The men about the table looked at one another. Bogard spoke. "I see. When you or Ronnie see a ship with basket masts, you get a beaver on the other. I see. What is the Ergenstrasse?"

"She's German. Interned. Tramp steamer. Foremast rigged so it looks something like a basket mast. Booms, cables, I dare say. I didn't think it looked very much like a basket mast, myself. But Ronnie said yes. Called it one day. Then one day they shifted her across the basin and I called her on Ronnie. So we decided to not count her any more. See now, eh?"

"Oh," the one who had made the tennis remark said, "I see. You and Ronnie run about in the launch, playing beaver. H'm'm. That's nice. Did you ever pl——"

"Jerry," Bogard said. The guest had not moved. He looked down at the speaker, still smiling, his eyes quite wide.

The speaker still looked at the guest. "Has yours and Ronnie's boat got a yellow stern?"

"A yellow stern?" the English boy said. He had quit smiling, but his face was still pleasant.

"I thought that maybe when the boats had two captains, they might paint the sterns yellow or something."

"Oh," the guest said. "Burt and Reeves aren't officers."

"Burt and Reeves," the other said, in a musing tone. "So they go too. Do they play beaver too?"

"Jerry," Bogard said. The other looked at him. Bogard jerked his head a little. "Come over here." The other rose. They went aside. "Lay off of him," Bogard said. "I mean it, now. He's just a kid. When you were that age, how much sense did you have? Just about enough to get to chapel on time."

"My country hadn't been at war going on four years, though," Jerry said. "Here we are, spending our money and getting shot at by the clock, and it's not even our fight, and these limeys that would have been goose-stepping twelve months now if it hadn't been——"

"Shut it," Bogard said. "You sound like a Liberty Loan."

"—taking it like it was a fair or something. 'Jolly.'" His voice was now falsetto, lilting. "'But dangerous, what?'"

"Sh-h-h-h," Bogard said.

"I'd like to catch him and his Ronnie out in the harbor, just once. Any harbor. London's. I wouldn't want anything but a Jenny, either. Jenny? Hell, I'd take a bicycle and a pair of water wings! I'll show him some war."

"Well, you lay off him now. He'll be gone soon."

"What are you going to do with him?"

"I'm going to take him along this morning. Let him have Harper's place out front. He says he can handle a Lewis. Says they have one on the boat. Something he was telling me—about how he once shot out a channel-marker light at seven hundred yards."

"Well, that's your business. Maybe he can beat you."

"Beat me?"

"Playing beaver. And then you can take on Ronnie."

"I'll show him some war, anyway," Bogard said. He looked at the guest. "His people have been in it three years now, and he seems to take it like a sophomore in town for the big game." He looked at Jerry again. "But you lay off him now."

As they approached the table, the guest's voice was loud and cheerful: ". . . if he got the glasses first, he would go in close and look, but when I got them first, he'd sheer off where I couldn't see anything but the smoke. Frightful stickler. Frightful. But Ergenstrasse not counting any more. And if you make a mistake and call her, you lose two beaver from your score. If Ronnie were only to forget and call her we'd be even."

III

At two o'clock the English boy was still talking, his voice bright, innocent and cheerful. He was telling them how Switzerland had been spoiled by 1914, and instead of the vacation which his father had promised him for his sixteenth birthday, when that birthday came he and his tutor had had to do with Wales. But that he and the tutor had got pretty high and that he dared to say—with all due respect to any present who might have had the advantage of Switzerland, of course—that one could see probably as far from Wales as from Switzerland. "Perspire as much and breathe as hard, anyway," he added. And about him the Americans sat, a little hard-bitten, a little sober, somewhat older, listening to him with a kind of cold astonishment. They had been getting up for some time now and going out and returning in flying clothes, carrying helmets and goggles. An orderly entered with a tray of coffee cups, and the guest realized that for some time now he had been hearing engines in the darkness outside.

At last Bogard rose. "Come along," he said. "We'll get your togs." When they emerged from the mess, the sound of the engines was quite loud—an idling thunder. In alignment along the invisible tarmac was a vague rank of short banks of flickering blue-green fire suspended apparently in mid-air. They crossed the aerodrome to Bogard's quarters, where the lieutenant, McGinnis, sat on a cot fastening his flying boots. Bogard reached down a Sidcott suit and threw it across the cot. "Put this on," he said.

"Will I need all this?" the guest said. "Shall we be gone that long?"

"Probably," Bogard said. "Better use it. Cold upstairs."

The guest picked up the suit. "I say," he said. "I say. Ronnie and I have a do ourselves, tomor—today. Do you think Ronnie won't mind if I am a bit late? Might not wait for me."

"We'll be back before teatime," McGinnis said. He seemed quite busy with his boot. "Promise you." The English boy looked at him.

"What time should you be back?" Bogard said.

"Oh, well," the English boy said, "I dare say it will be all right. They let

Ronnie say when to go, anyway. He'll wait for me if I should be a bit late."

"He'll wait," Bogard said. "Get your suit on."

"Right," the other said. They helped him into the suit. "Never been up before," he said, chattily, pleasantly. "Dare say you can see farther than from mountains, eh?"

"See more, anyway," McGinnis said. "You'll like it."

"Oh, rather. If Ronnie only waits for me. Lark. But dangerous, isn't it?"

"Go on," McGinnis said. "You're kidding me."

"Shut your trap, Mac," Bogard said. "Come along. Want some more coffee?" He looked at the guest, but McGinnis answered:

"No. Got something better than coffee. Coffee makes such a confounded stain on the wings."

"On the wings?" the English boy said. "Why coffee on the wings?"

"Stow it, I said, Mac," Bogard said. "Come along."

They recrossed the aerodrome, approaching the muttering banks of flame. When they drew near, the guest began to discern the shape, the outlines, of the Handley-Page. It looked like a Pullman coach run upslanted aground into the skeleton of the first floor of an incomplete skyscraper. The guest looked at it quietly.

"It's larger than a cruiser," he said in his bright, interested voice. "I say, you know. This doesn't fly in one lump. You can't pull my leg. Seen them before. It comes in two parts: Captain Bogard and me in one; Mac and 'nother chap in other. What?"

"No," McGinnis said. Bogard had vanished. "It all goes up in one lump. Big lark, eh? Buzzard, what?"

"Buzzard?" the guest murmured. "Oh, I say. A cruiser. Flying. I say, now."

"And listen," McGinnis said. His hand came forth; something cold fumbled against the hand of the English boy—a bottle. "When you feel yourself getting sick, see? Take a pull at it."

"Oh, shall I get sick?"

"Sure. We all do. Part of flying. This will stop it. But if it doesn't. See?"

"What? Quite. What?"

"Not overside. Don't spew it overside."

"Not overside?"

"It'll blow back in Bogy's and my face. Can't see. Bingo. Finished. See?"

"Oh, quite. What shall I do with it?" Their voices were quiet, brief, grave as conspirators.

"Just duck your head and let her go."

"Oh, quite."

Bogard returned. "Show him how to get into the front pit, will you?" he said. McGinnis led the way through the trap. Forward, rising to the slant of the fuselage, the passage narrowed; a man would need to crawl.

"Crawl in there and keep going," McGinnis said.

"It looks like a dog kennel," the guest said.

"Doesn't it, though?" McGinnis agreed cheerfully. "Cut along with you."

Stooping, he could hear the other scuttling forward. "You'll find a Lewis gun up there, like as not," he said into the tunnel.

The voice of the guest came back: "Found it."

"The gunnery sergeant will be along in a minute and show you if it is loaded."

"It's loaded," the guest said; almost on the heels of his words the gun fired, a brief staccato burst. There were shouts, the loudest from the ground beneath the nose of the aeroplane. "It's quite all right," the English boy's voice said. "I pointed it west before I let it off. Nothing back there but Marine office and your brigade headquarters. Ronnie and I always do this before we go anywhere. Sorry if I was too soon. Oh, by the way," he added, "my name's Claude. Don't think I mentioned it."

On the ground, Bogard and two other officers stood. They had come up running. "Fired it west," one said. "How in hell does he know which way is west?"

"He's a sailor," the other said. "You forgot that."

"He seems to be a machine gunner too," Bogard said.

"Let's hope he doesn't forget that," the first said.

IV

Nevertheless, Bogard kept an eye on the silhouetted head rising from the round gunpit in the nose ten feet ahead of him. "He did work that gun, though," he said to McGinnis beside him. "He even put the drum on himself, didn't he?"

"Yes," McGinnis said. "If he just doesn't forget and think that that gun is him and his tutor looking around from a Welsh alp."

"Maybe I should not have brought him," Bogard said. McGinnis didn't answer. Bogard jockeyed the wheel a little. Ahead, in the gunner's pit, the guest's head moved this way and that continuously, looking. "We'll get there and unload and haul air for home," Bogard said. "Maybe in the dark—— Confound it, it would be a shame for his country to be in this mess for four years and him not even to see a gun pointed in his direction."

"He'll see one tonight if he don't keep his head in," McGinnis said.

But the boy did not do that. Not even when they had reached the objective and McGinnis had crawled down to the bomb toggles. And even when the searchlights found them and Bogard signaled to the other machines and dived, the two engines snarling full speed into and through the bursting shells, he could see the boy's face in the searchlight's glare, leaned far overside, coming sharply out as a spotlighted face on a stage, with an expression upon it of childlike interest and delight. "But he's firing that Lewis," Bogard thought. "Straight too"; nosing the machine farther down, watching the pin-point swing into the sights, his right hand lifted, waiting to drop into Mc-Ginnis' sight. He dropped his hand; above the noise of the engines he seemed to hear the click and whistle of the released bombs as the machine, freed of the weight, shot zooming in a long upward bounce that carried it for an instant out of the light. Then he was pretty busy for a time, coming into and through the shells again, shooting athwart another beam that caught and held long enough for him to see the English boy leaning far over the side, looking back and down past the right wing, the undercarriage. "Maybe he's read about it somewhere," Bogard thought, turning, looking back to pick up the rest of the flight.

Then it was all over, the darkness cool and empty and peaceful and almost quiet, with only the steady sound of the engines. McGinnis climbed back into the office, and standing up in his seat, he fired the colored pistol this time and stood for a moment longer, looking backward toward where the searchlights still probed and sabered. He sat down again.

"O.K.," he said. "I counted all four of them. Let's haul air." Then he looked forward. "What's become of the King's Own? You didn't hang him onto a bomb release, did you?" Bogard looked. The forward pit was empty. It was in dim silhouette again now, against the stars, but there was nothing there now save the gun. "No," McGinnis said; "there he is. See? Leaning overside. Dammit, I told him not to spew it! There he comes back." The guest's head came into view again. But again it sank out of sight.

"He's coming back," Bogard said. "Stop him. Tell him we're going to have every squadron in the Hun Channel group on top of us in thirty minutes."

McGinnis swung himself down and stooped at the entrance to the passage. "Get back!" he shouted. The other was almost out; they squatted so, face to face like two dogs, shouting at one another above the noise of the still-unthrottled engines on either side of the fabric walls. The English boy's voice was thin and high.

"Bomb!" he shrieked.

"Yes," McGinnis shouted, "they were bombs! We gave them hell! Get back, I tell you! Have every Hun in France on us in ten minutes! Get back to your gun!"

Again the boy's voice came, high, faint above the noise: "Bomb! All right?"

"Yes! Yes! All right. Back to your gun, damn you!"

McGinnis climbed back into the office. "He went back. Want me to take her awhile?"

"All right," Bogard said. He passed McGinnis the wheel. "Ease her back some. I'd just as soon it was daylight when they come down on us."

"Right," McGinnis said. He moved the wheel suddenly. "What's the matter with that right wing?" he said. "Watch it. . . . See? I'm flying on the right aileron and a little rudder. Feel it."

Bogard took the wheel a moment. "I didn't notice that. Wire somewhere, I guess. I didn't think any of those shells were that close. Watch her, though."

"Right," McGinnis said. "And so you are going with him on his boat to-morrow—today."

"Yes. I promised him. Confound it, you can't hurt a kid, you know."

"Why don't you take Collier along, with his mandolin? Then you could sail around and sing."

"I promised him," Bogard said. "Get that wing up a little."

"Right," McGinnis said.

Thirty minutes later it was beginning to be dawn; the sky was gray. Presently McGinnis said: "Well, here they come. Look at them! They look like mosquitoes in September. I hope he don't get worked up now and think he's playing beaver. If he does he'll just be one down to Ronnie, provided the devil has a beard. . . . Want the wheel?"

V

At eight o'clock the beach, the Channel, was beneath them. Throttled back, the machine drifted down as Bogard ruddered it gently into the Channel wind. His face was strained, a little tired.

McGinnis looked tired, too, and he needed a shave.

"What do you guess he is looking at now?" he said. For again the English boy was leaning over the right side of the cockpit, looking backward and downward past the right wing.

"I don't know," Bogard said. "Maybe bullet holes." He blasted the port engine. Must have the riggers——"

"He could see some closer than that," McGinnis said. "I'll swear I saw tracer going into his back at one time. Or maybe it's the ocean he's looking at. But he must have seen that when he came over from England." Then Bogard leveled off; the nose rose sharply, the sand, the curling tide edge fled alongside. Yet still the English boy hung far overside, looking backward and downward at something beneath the right wing, his face rapt, with utter and childlike interest. Until the machine was completely stopped he continued to do so. Then he ducked down, and in the abrupt silence of the engines they could hear him crawling in the passage. He emerged just as the two pilots climbed stiffly down from the office, his face bright, eager; his voice high, excited.

"Oh, I say! Oh, good gad! What a chap! What a judge of distance! If Ronnie could only have seen! Oh, good gad! Or maybe they aren't like ours —don't load themselves as soon as the air strikes them."

The Americans looked at him. "What don't what?" McGinnis said.

"The bomb. It was magnificent; I say, I shan't forget it. Oh, I say, you know! It was splendid!"

After a while McGinnis said, "The bomb?" in a fainting voice. Then the two pilots glared at each other; they said in unison: "That right wing!" Then as one they clawed down through the trap and, with the guest at their heels, they ran around the machine and looked beneath the right wing. The bomb, suspended by its tail, hung straight down like a plumb bob beside the right wheel, its tip just touching the sand. And parallel with the wheel track was the long, delicate line in the sand where its ultimate tip had dragged. Behind them the English boy's voice was high, clear, childlike:

"Frightened, myself. Tried to tell you. But realized you knew your business better than I. Skill. Marvelous. Oh, I say, I shan't forget it."

VI

A marine with a bayoneted rifle passed Bogard onto the wharf and directed him to the boat. The wharf was empty, and he didn't even see the boat until he approached the edge of the wharf and looked directly down into it and upon the backs of two stooping men in greasy dungarees, who rose and glanced briefly at him and stooped again.

It was about thirty feet long and about three feet wide. It was painted with gray-green camouflage. It was quarter-decked forward, with two blunt, raked exhaust stacks. "Good Lord," Bogard thought, "if all that deck is engine——" Just aft the deck was the control seat; he saw a big wheel, an instrument panel. Rising to a height of about a foot above the freeboard, and running from the stern forward to where the deck began, and continuing on across the after edge of the deck and thence back down the other gunwale to the stern, was a solid screen, also camouflaged, which inclosed the boat save for the width of the stern, which was open. Facing the steersman's seat like an eye was a hole in the screen about eight inches in diameter. And looking down into the long, narrow, still, vicious shape, he saw a machine gun swiveled at the stern, and he looked at the low screen—including which the whole vessel did not sit much more than a yard above water level—with its single empty forward-staring eye, and he thought quietly: "It's steel. It's made of steel." And his face was quite sober, quite thoughtful, and he drew his trench coat about him and buttoned it, as though he were getting cold.

He heard steps behind him and turned. But it was only an orderly from the aerodrome, accompanied by the marine with the rifle. The orderly was carrying a largish bundle wrapped in paper.

"From Lieutenant McGinnis, to the captain," the orderly said.

Bogard took the bundle. The orderly and the marine retreated. He opened the bundle. It contained some objects and a scrawled note. The objects were a new yellow silk sofa cushion and a Japanese parasol, obviously borrowed, and a comb and a few sheets of flimsy paper. The note said:

Couldn't find a camera anywhere and Collier wouldn't let me have his mandolin. But maybe Ronnie can play on the comb.

MAC.

Bogard looked at the objects. But his face was still quite thoughtful, quite grave. He rewrapped the things and carried the bundle on up the wharf a way and dropped it quietly into the water.

As he returned toward the invisible boat he saw two men approaching. He recognized the boy at once—tall, slender, already talking, voluble, his head bent a little toward his shorter companion, who plodded along beside him, hands in pockets, smoking a pipe. The boy still wore the pea-coat beneath a flapping oilskin, but in place of the rakish and casual cap he now wore an infantryman's soiled Balaclava helmet, with, floating behind him as though upon the sound of his voice, a curtainlike piece of cloth almost as long as a burnous.

"Hullo, there!" he cried, still a hundred yards away.

But it was the second man that Bogard was watching, thinking to himself that he had never in his life seen a more curious figure. There was something stolid about the very shape of his hunched shoulders, his slightly downlooking face. He was a head shorter than the other. His face was ruddy, too, but its mold was of a profound gravity that was almost dour. It was the face of a man of twenty who has been for a year trying, even while asleep, to look twenty-one. He wore a high-necked sweater and dungaree slacks; above this a leather jacket; and above this a soiled naval officer's warmer that reached almost to his heels and which had one shoulder strap missing and not one remaining button at all. On his head was a plaid fore-and-aft deer stalker's cap, tied on by a narrow scarf brought across and down, hiding his ears, and then wrapped once about his throat and knotted with a hangman's noose beneath his left ear. It was unbelievably soiled, and with his hands elbowdeep in his pockets and his hunched shoulders and his bent head, he looked like someone's grandmother hung, say, for a witch. Clamped upside down between his teeth was a short brier pipe.

"Here he is!" the boy cried. "This is Ronnie. Captain Bogard."

"How are you?" Bogard said. He extended his hand. The other said no word, but his hand came forth, limp. It was quite cold, but it was hard, calloused. But he said no word; he just glanced briefly at Bogard and then away. But in that instant Bogard caught something in the look, something strange—a flicker; a kind of covert and curious respect, something like a boy of fifteen looking at a circus trapezist.

But he said no word. He ducked on; Bogard watched him drop from sight over the wharf edge as though he had jumped feet first into the sea. He remarked now that the engines in the invisible boat were running.

"We might get aboard too," the boy said. He started toward the boat, then he stopped. He touched Bogard's arm. "Yonder!" he hissed. "See?" His voice was thin with excitement.

"What?" Bogard also whispered; automatically he looked backward and upward, after old habit. The other was gripping his arm and pointing across the harbor.

"There! Over there. The Ergenstrasse. They have shifted her again." Across the harbor lay an ancient, rusting, sway-backed hulk. It was small and nondescript, and, remembering, Bogard saw that the foremast was a strange mess of cables and booms, resembling—allowing for a great deal of license or looseness of imagery—a basket mast. Beside him the boy was almost chortling. "Do you think that Ronnie noticed?" he hissed. "Do you?"

"I don't know," Bogard said.

"Oh, good gad! If he should glance up and call her before he notices,

we'll be even. Oh, good gad! But come along." He went on; he was still
chortling. "Careful," he said. "Frightful ladder."

He descended first, the two men in the boat rising and saluting. Ronnie
had disappeared, save for his backside, which now filled a small hatch leading
forward beneath the deck. Bogard descended gingerly.

"Good Lord," he said. "Do you have to climb up and down this every day?"

"Frightful, isn't it?" the other said, in his happy voice. "But you know
yourself. Try to run a war with makeshifts, then wonder why it takes so
long." The narrow hull slid and surged, even with Bogard's added weight.
"Sits right on top, you see," the boy said. "Would float on a lawn, in a heavy
dew. Goes right over them like a bit of paper."

"It does?" Bogard said.

"Oh, absolutely. That's why, you see." Bogard didn't see, but he was too busy letting himself gingerly down to a sitting posture. There were no thwarts; no seats save a long, thick, cylindrical ridge which ran along the bottom of the boat from the driver's seat to the stern. Ronnie had backed into sight. He now sat behind the wheel, bent over the instrument panel. But when he glanced back over his shoulder he did not speak. His face was merely interrogatory. Across his face there was now a long smudge of grease. The boy's face was empty, too, now.

"Right," he said. He looked forward, where one of the seamen had gone. "Ready forward?" he said.

"Aye, sir," the seaman said.

The other seaman was at the stern line. "Ready aft?"

"Aye, sir."

"Cast off." The boat sheered away, purring, a boiling of water under the stern. The boy looked down at Bogard. "Silly business. Do it shipshape, though. Can't tell when silly four-striper——" His face changed again, immediate, solicitous. "I say. Will you be warm? I never thought to fetch——"

"I'll be all right," Bogard said. But the other was already taking off his oilskin. "No, no," Bogard said. "I won't take it."

"You'll tell me if you get cold?"

"Yes. Sure." He was looking down at the cylinder on which he sat. It was a half cylinder—that is, like the hotwater tank to some Gargantuan stove, sliced down the middle and bolted, open side down, to the floor plates. It was twenty feet long and more than two feet thick. Its top rose as high as the gunwales and between it and the hull on either side was just room enough for a man to place his feet to walk.

"That's Muriel," the boy said.

"Muriel?"

"Yes. The one before that was Agatha. After my aunt. The first one Ronnie and I had was Alice in Wonderland. Ronnie and I were the White Rabbit. Jolly, eh?"

"Oh, you and Ronnie have had three, have you?"

"Oh, yes," the boy said. He leaned down. "He didn't notice," he whispered. His face was again bright, gleeful. "When we come back," he said, "you watch."

"Oh," Bogard said. "The Ergenstrasse." He looked astern, and then he thought: "Good Lord! We must be going—traveling." He looked out now, broadside, and saw the harbor line fleeing past, and he thought to himself that the boat was well-nigh moving at the speed at which the Handley-Page flew, left the ground. They were beginning to bound now, even in the sheltered water, from one wave crest to the next with a distinct shock. His hand still rested on the cylinder on which he sat. He looked down at it again, following it from where it seemed to emerge beneath Ronnie's seat, to where it beveled into the stern. "It's the air in here, I suppose," he said.

"The what?" the boy said.

"The air. Stored up in here. That makes the boat ride high."

"Oh, yes. I dare say. Very likely. I hadn't thought about it." He came forward, his burnous whipping in the wind, and sat down beside Bogard. Their heads were below the top of the screen.

Astern the harbor fled, diminishing, sinking into the sea. The boat had begun to lift now, swooping forward and down, shocking almost stationary for a moment, then lifting and swooping again; a gout of spray came aboard over the bows like a flung shovelful of shot. "I wish you'd take this coat," the boy said.

Bogard didn't answer. He looked around at the bright face. "We're outside, aren't we?" he said quietly.

"Yes. . . . Do take it, won't you?"

"Thanks, no. I'll be all right. We won't be long, anyway, I guess."

"No. We'll turn soon. It won't be so bad then."

"Yes. I'll be all right when we turn." Then they did turn. The motion became easier. That is, the boat didn't bang head-on, shuddering, into the swells. They came up beneath now, and the boat fled with increased speed, with a long, sickening, yawing motion, first to one side and then the other. But it fled on, and Bogard looked astern with that same soberness with which he had first looked down into the boat. "We're going east now," he said.

"With just a spot of north," the boy said. "Makes her ride a bit better, what?"

"Yes," Bogard said. Astern there was nothing now save empty sea and the delicate needlelike cant of the machine gun against the boiling and slewing wake, and the two seamen crouching quietly in the stern. "Yes. It's easier." Then he said: "How far do we go?"

The boy leaned closer. He moved closer. His voice was happy, confidential, proud, though lowered a little: "It's Ronnie's show. He thought of it. Not that I wouldn't have, in time. Gratitude and all that. But he's the older, you see. Thinks fast. Courtesy, *noblesse oblige*—all that. Thought of it soon as I told him this morning. I said, 'Oh, I say. I've been there. I've seen it'; and he said, 'Not flying'; and I said, 'Strewth'; and he said, 'How far? No lying now'; and I said, 'Oh, far. Tremendous. Gone all night'; and he said, 'Flying all night. That must have been to Berlin'; and I said, 'I don't know. I dare say'; and he thought. I could see him thinking. Because he is the older, you see. More experience in courtesy, right thing. And he said, 'Berlin. No fun to that chap, dashing out and back with us.' And he thought and I waited, and I said, 'But we can't take him to Berlin. Too far. Don't know the way, either'; and he said—fast, like a shot—said, 'But there's Kiel'; and I knew——"

"What?" Bogard said. Without moving, his whole body sprang. "Kiel? In this?"

"Absolutely. Ronnie thought of it. Smart, even if he is a stickler. Said at once, 'Zeebrugge no show at all for that chap. Must do best we can for him. Berlin,' Ronnie said. 'My gad! Berlin.'"

"Listen," Bogard said. He had turned now, facing the other, his face quite grave. "What is this boat for?"

"For?"

"What does it do?" Then, knowing beforehand the answer to his own question, he said, putting his hand on the cylinder: "What is this in here? A torpedo, isn't it?"

"I thought you knew," the boy said.

"No," Bogard said. "I didn't know." His voice seemed to reach him from a distance, dry, cricket-like: "How do you fire it?"

"Fire it?"

"How do you get it out of the boat? When that hatch was open a while ago I could see the engines. They were right in front of the end of this tube."

"Oh," the boy said. "You pull a gadget there and the torpedo drops out astern. As soon as the screw touches the water it begins to turn, and then the torpedo is ready, loaded. Then all you have to do is turn the boat quickly and the torpedo goes on."

"You mean——" Bogard said. After a moment his voice obeyed him again. "You mean you aim the torpedo with the boat and release it and it starts moving, and you turn the boat out of the way and the torpedo passes through the same water that the boat just vacated?"

"Knew you'd catch on," the boy said. "Told Ronnie so. Airman. Tamer than yours, though. But can't be helped. Best we can do, just on water. But knew you'd catch on."

"Listen," Bogard said. His voice sounded to him quite calm. The boat fled on, yawing over the swells. He sat quite motionless. It seemed to him that he could hear himself talking to himself: "Go on. Ask him. Ask him what? Ask him how close to the ship do you have to be before you fire. . . . Listen," he said, in that calm voice. "Now, you tell Ronnie, you see. You just tell him—just say——" He could feel his voice ratting off on him again, so he stopped it. He sat quite motionless, waiting for it to come back; the boy leaning now, looking at his face. Again the boy's voice was solicitous:

"I say. You're not feeling well. These confounded shallow boats."

"It's not that," Bogard said. "I just—— Do your orders say Kiel?"

"Oh, no. They let Ronnie say. Just so we bring the boat back. This is for you. Gratitude. Ronnie's idea. Tame, after flying. But if you'd rather, eh?"

"Yes, some place closer. You see, I——"

"Quite. I see. No vacations in wartime. I'll tell Ronnie." He went forward. Bogard did not move. The boat fled in long, slewing swoops. Bogard looked quietly astern, at the scudding sea, the sky.

"My God!" he thought. "Can you beat it? Can you beat it?"

The boy came back; Bogard turned to him a face the color of dirty paper. "All right now," the boy said. "Not Kiel. Nearer place, hunting probably just as good. Ronnie says he knows you will understand." He was tugging at his pocket. He brought out a bottle. "Here. Haven't forgot last night. Do the same for you. Good for the stomach, eh?"

Bogard drank, gulping—a big one. He extended the bottle, but the boy refused. "Never touch it on duty," he said. "Not like you chaps. Tame here."

The boat fled on. The sun was already down the west. But Bogard had lost all count of time, of distance. Ahead he could see white seas through the round eye opposite Ronnie's face, and Ronnie's hand on the wheel and the granite-like jut of his profiled jaw and the dead upside-down pipe. The boat fled on.

Then the boy leaned and touched his shoulder. He half rose. The boy was pointing. The sun was reddish; against it, outside them and about two miles away, a vessel—a trawler, it looked like—at anchor swung a tall mast.

"Lightship!" the boy shouted. "Theirs." Ahead Bogard could see a low, flat mole—the entrance to a harbor. "Channel!" the boy shouted. He swept his arm in both directions. "Mines!" His voice swept back on the wind. "Place filthy with them. All sides. Beneath us too. Lark, eh?"

VII

Against the mole a fair surf was beating. Running before the seas now, the boat seemed to leap from one roller to the next; in the intervals while the screw was in the air the engine seemed to be trying to tear itself out by the roots. But it did not slow; when it passed the end of the mole the boat seemed to be standing almost erect on its rudder, like a sailfish. The mole was a mile away. From the end of it little faint lights began to flicker like fireflies. The boy leaned. "Down," he said. "Machine guns. Might stop a stray."

"What do I do?" Bogard shouted. "What can I do?"

"Stout fellow! Give them hell, what? Knew you'd like it!"

Crouching, Bogard looked up at the boy, his face wild. "I can handle the machine gun!"

"No need," the boy shouted back. "Give them first innings. Sporting. Visitors, eh?" He was looking forward. "There she is. See?" They were in the harbor now, the basin opening before them. Anchored in the channel was a big freighter. Painted midships of the hull was a huge Argentine flag. "Must get back to stations!" the boy shouted down to him. Then at that moment Ronnie spoke for the first time. The boat was hurtling along now in smoother water. Its speed did not slacken and Ronnie did not turn his head when he spoke. He just swung his jutting jaw and the clamped cold pipe a little, and said from the side of his mouth a single word:

"Beaver."

The boy, stooped over what he had called his gadget, jerked up, his expression astonished and outraged. Bogard also looked forward and saw Ronnie's arm pointing to starboard. It was a light cruiser at anchor a mile away. She had basket masts, and as he looked a gun flashed from her after turret. "Oh, damn!" the boy cried. "Oh, you putt! Oh, confound you, Ronnie! Now I'm three down!" But he had already stooped again over his gadget, his face bright and empty and alert again; not sober; just calm, waiting. Again Bogard looked forward and felt the boat pivot on its rudder and head directly for the freighter at terrific speed, Ronnie now with one hand on the wheel and the other lifted and extended at the height of his head.

But it seemed to Bogard that the hand would never drop. He crouched, not sitting, watching with a kind of quiet horror the painted flag increase like a moving picture of a locomotive taken from between the rails. Again the gun crashed from the cruiser behind them, and the freighter fired point-blank at them from its poop. Bogard heard neither shot.

"Man, man!" he shouted. "For God's sake!"

Ronnie's hand dropped. Again the boat spun on its rudder. Bogard saw the bow rise, pivoting; he expected the hull to slam broadside on into the ship. But it didn't. It shot off on a long tangent. He was waiting for it to make a wide sweep, heading seaward, putting the freighter astern, and he thought of the cruiser again. "Get a broadside, this time, once we clear the freighter," he thought. Then he remembered the freighter, the torpedo, and he looked back toward the freighter to watch the torpedo strike, and saw to his horror that the boat was now bearing down on the freighter again, in a skidding turn. Like a man in a dream, he watched himself rush down upon the ship and shoot past under her counter, still skidding, close enough to see the faces on her decks. "They missed and they are going to run down the torpedo and catch it and shoot it again," he thought idiotically.

So the boy had to touch his shoulder before he knew he was behind him. The boy's voice was quite calm: "Under Ronnie's seat there. A bit of a crank handle. If you'll just hand it to me——"

He found the crank. He passed it back; he was thinking dreamily: "Mac would say they had a telephone on board." But he didn't look at once to see what the boy was doing with it, for in that still and peaceful horror he was watching Ronnie, the cold pipe rigid in his jaw, hurling the boat at top speed round and round the freighter, so near that he could see the rivets in the plates. Then he looked aft, his face wild, importunate, and he saw what the boy was doing with the crank. He had fitted it into what was obviously a a small windlass low on one flank of the tube near the head. He glanced up and saw Bogard's face. "Didn't go that time!" he shouted cheerfully.

"Go?" Bogard shouted. "It didn't—— The torpedo——"

The boy and one of the seamen were quite busy, stooping over the windlass and the tube. "No. Clumsy. Always happening. Should think clever chaps like engineers—— Happens, though. Draw her in and try her again."

"But the nose, the cap!" Bogard shouted. "It's still in the tube, isn't it? It's all right, isn't it?"

"Absolutely. But it's working now. Loaded. Screw's started turning. Get it back and drop it clear. If we should stop or slow up it would overtake us. Drive back into the tube. Bingo! What?"

Bogard was on his feet now, turned, braced to the terrific merry-go-round of the boat. High above them the freighter seemed to be spinning on her heel like a trick picture in the movies. "Let me have that winch!" he cried.

"Steady!" the boy said. "Mustn't draw her back too fast. Jam her into the head of the tube ourselves. Same bingo! Best let us. Every cobbler to his last, what?"

"Oh, quite," Bogard said. "Oh, absolutely." It was like someone else was using his mouth. He leaned, braced, his hands on the cold tube, beside the others. He was hot inside, but his outside was cold. He could feel all his flesh jerking with cold as he watched the blunt, grained hand of the seaman turning the windlass in short, easy, inch-long arcs, while at the head of the tube the boy bent, tapping the cylinder with a spanner, lightly, his head turned with listening, delicate and deliberate as a watchmaker. The boat rushed on in those furious, slewing turns. Bogard saw a long, drooping thread loop down from somebody's mouth, between his hands, and he found that the thread came from his own mouth.

He didn't hear the boy speak, nor notice when he stood up. He just felt the boat straighten out, flinging him to his knees beside the tube. The seaman had gone back to the stern and the boy stooped again over his gadget. Bogard knelt now, quite sick. He did not feel the boat when it swung again, nor hear the gun from the cruiser which had not dared to fire and the freighter which had not been able to fire, firing again. He did not feel anything at all when he saw the huge, painted flag directly ahead and increasing with locomotive speed, and Ronnie's lifted hand drop. But this time he knew that the torpedo was gone; in pivoting and spinning this time the whole boat seemed to leave the water; he saw the bow of the boat shoot skyward like the nose of a pursuit ship going into a wingover. Then his outraged stomach denied him. He saw neither the geyser nor heard the detonation as he sprawled over the tube. He felt only a hand grasp him by the slack of his coat, and the voice of one of the seamen: "Steady all, sir. I've got you."

VIII

A voice roused him, a hand. He was half sitting in the narrow starboard runway, half lying across the tube. He had been there for quite a while; quite a while ago he had felt someone spread a garment over him. But he had not raised his head. "I'm all right," he had said. "You keep it."

"Don't need it," the boy said. "Going home now."

"I'm sorry I——" Bogard said.

"Quite. Confounded shallow boats. Turn any stomach until you get used to them. Ronnie and I both, at first. Each time. You wouldn't believe it. Believe human stomach hold so much. Here." It was the bottle. "Good drink. Take enormous one. Good for stomach."

Bogard drank. Soon he did feel better, warmer. When the hand touched him later, he found that he had been asleep.

It was the boy again. The pea-coat was too small for him; shrunken, perhaps. Below the cuffs his long, slender, girl's wrists were blue with cold. Then Bogard realized what the garment was that had been laid over him.

But before Bogard could speak, the boy leaned down, whispering; his face was gleeful: "He didn't notice!"

"What?"

"Ergenstrasse! He didn't notice that they had shifted her. Gad, I'd be just one down, then." He watched Bogard's face with bright, eager eyes. "Beaver, you know. I say. Feeling better, eh?"

"Yes," Bogard said, "I am."

"He didn't notice at all. Oh, gad! Oh, Jove!"

Bogard rose and sat on the tube. The entrance to the harbor was just ahead; the boat had slowed a little. It was just dusk. He said quietly: "Does this often happen?" The boy looked at him. Bogard touched the tube. "This. Failing to go out."

"Oh, yes. Why they put the windlass on them. That was later. Made first boat; whole thing blew up one day. So put on windlass."

"But it happens sometimes, even now? I mean, sometimes they blow up, even with the windlass?"

"Well, can't say, of course. Boats go out. Not come back. Possible. Not ever know, of course. Not heard of one captured yet, though. Possible. Not to us, though. Not yet."

"Yes," Bogard said. "Yes." They entered the harbor, the boat moving still fast, but throttled now and smooth, across the dusk-filled basin. Again the boy leaned down, his voice gleeful.

"Not a word, now!" he hissed. "Steady all!" He stood up; he raised his voice: "I say, Ronnie." Ronnie did not turn his head, but Bogard could tell that he was listening. "That Argentine ship was amusing, eh? In there. How do you suppose it got past us here? Might have stopped here as well. French would buy the wheat." He paused, diabolical—Machiavelli with the face of a strayed angel. "I say. How long has it been since we had a strange ship in here? Been months, eh?" Again he leaned, hissing. "Watch, now!" But Bogard could not see Ronnie's head move at all. "He's looking, though!" the boy whispered, breathed. And Ronnie was looking, though his head had not moved at all. Then there came into view, in silhouette against the dusk-filled sky, the vague, basketlike shape of the interned vessel's foremast. At once Ronnie's arm rose, pointing; again he spoke without turning his head, out of the side of his mouth, past the cold, clamped pipe, a single word:

"Beaver."

The boy moved like a released spring, like a heeled dog freed. "Oh, damn you!" he cried. "Oh, you putt! It's the Ergenstrasse! Oh, confound you! I'm just one down now!" He had stepped in one stride completely over Bogard, and he now leaned down over Ronnie. "What?" The boat was slowing in toward the wharf, the engine idle. "Aren't I, Ronnie? Just one down now?"

The boat drifted in; the seaman had again crawled forward onto the deck. Ronnie spoke for the third and last time. "Right," he said.

IX

"I want," Bogard said, "a case of Scotch. The best we've got. And fix it up good. It's to go to town. And I want a responsible man to deliver it." The responsible man came. "This is for a child," Bogard said, indicating the package. "You'll find him in the Street of the Twelve Hours, somewhere near the Café Twelve Hours. He'll be in the gutter. You'll know him. A child about six feet long. Any English M. P. will show him to you. If he is asleep, don't wake him. Just sit there and wait until he wakes up. Then give him this. Tell him it is from Captain Bogard."

X

About a month later a copy of the *English Gazette* which had strayed on to an American aerodrome carried the following item in the casualty lists:

MISSING: Torpedo Boat XOOI. Ensigns R. Boyce Smith and L. C. W. Hope, R. N. R., Machinist's Mate Burt and Torpedo-man Reeves, Channel Fleet, Light Torpedo Division. Failed to return from coast patrol duty.

Shortly after that the American Air Service headquarters also issued a bulletin:

For extraordinary valor over and beyond the routine of duty, Captain H. S. Bogard, with his crew, composed of Second Lieutenant Darrel McGinnis and Aviation Gunners Watts and Harper, on a daylight raid and without scout protection, destroyed with bombs an ammunition depot several miles behind the enemy's lines. From here, beset by enemy aircraft in superior numbers, these men proceeded with what bombs remained to the enemy's corps headquarters at —— and partially demolished this château, and then returned safely without loss of a man.

And regarding which exploit, it might have added, had it failed and had Captain Bogard come out of it alive, he would have been immediately and thoroughly court-martialed.

Carrying his remaining two bombs, he had dived the Handley-Page at the château where the generals sat at lunch, until McGinnis, at the toggles below him, began to shout at him, before he ever signaled. He didn't signal until he could discern separately the slate tiles of the roof. Then his hand dropped and he zoomed, and he held the aeroplane so, in its wild snarl, his lips parted, his breath hissing, thinking: "God! God! If they were all there—all the generals, the admirals, the presidents and the kings—theirs, ours —all of them."

MARY SMITH

BOOTH TARKINGTON

HENRY MILLICK CHESTER, rising early from intermittent slumbers, found himself the first of the crowded Pullman to make a toilet in the men's smoke-and-wash-room, and so had the place to himself—an advantage of high dramatic value to a person of his age and temperament, on account of the mirrors which, set at various angles, afford a fine view of the profile. Henry Millick Chester, scouring cinders and stickiness from his eyes and rouging his ears with honest friction, enriched himself of this too unfamiliar opportunity. He smiled and was warmly interested in the results of his smile in reflection, particularly in some pleasant alterations it effected upon an outline of the cheek usually invisible to the bearer. He smiled graciously, then he smiled sardonically. Other smiles he offered—the tender smile, the forbidding smile, the austere and the seductive, the haughty and the pleading, the mordant and the compassionate, the tolerant but incredulous smile of a man of the world, and the cold, ascetic smile that shows a woman that her shallow soul has been read all too easily—pastimes abandoned only with the purely decorative application of shaving lather to his girlish chin. However, as his unbeetling brow was left unobscured, he was able to pursue his physiognomical researches and to produce for his continued enlightenment a versatile repertory of frowns—the stern, the quizzical, the bitter, the treacherous, the bold, the agonized, the inquisitive, the ducal, and the frown of the husband who says: "I forgive you. Go!" A few minutes later Mr. Chester, abruptly pausing in the operation of fastening his collar, bent a sudden, passionate interest upon his right forearm, without apparent cause and with the air of never having seen it until that moment. He clenched his fingers tightly, producing a slight stringiness above the wrist, then crooked his elbow with intensity, noting this enormous effect in all the mirrors. Regretfully, he let his shirtsleeves fall and veil the rare but private beauties just discovered, rested his left hand negligently upon his hip, extended his right in a gesture of flawlessly aristocratic grace, and, with a slight inclination of his head, uttered aloud these simple but befitting words: "I thank ye, my good people." T' yoong Maister was greeting the loyal tenantry who acclaimed his return to Fielding Manor, a flowered progress thoroughly incomprehensible to the Pullman porter whose transfixed eye— glazed upon an old-gold face intruded through the narrow doorway—Mr. Chester encountered in the glass above the nickeled washbasins. The Libyan withdrew in a cloud of silence, and t' yoong Maister, flushing somewhat, resumed his toilet with annoyed precision and no more embroidery. He had yesterday completed his sophomore year; the brushes he applied to his now adult locks were those of a junior. And with a man's age had come a man's cares and responsibilities. Several long years had rolled away since for the last time he had made himself sick on a train in a club-car orgy of cubebs and sarsaparilla pop.

Zigzagging through shoe-bordered aisles of sleepers in morning dishevel- ment, he sought the dining car, where the steward escorted him to an end table for two. He would have assumed his seat with that air of negligent hauteur which was his chosen manner for public appearances, had not the train, taking a curve at high speed, heaved him into the undesirable embrace of an elderly man breakfasting across the aisle. "Keep your feet, sonny; keep your feet," said this barbarian, little witting that he addressed a member of the nineteen-something prom committee. People at the next table laughed genially, and Mr. Chester, muttering a word of hostile apology, catapulted into his assigned place, his cheeks hot with the triple outrage.

He relieved himself a little by the icy repulsion with which he countered the cordial advances of the waiter, who took his order and wished him a good morning, hoped he had slept well, declared the weather delightful and, un- answered, yet preserved his beautiful courtesy unimpaired. When this hum- ble ambassador had departed on his mission to the kitchen Henry Millick Chester, unwarrantably persuaded that all eyes were searching his every inch and angle—an impression not uncharacteristic of his years—gazed out of the window with an indifference which would have been obtrusive if any of the other breakfasters had happened to notice it. The chill exclusiveness of his expression was a rebuke to such prying members of the proletariat as might be striving to read his thoughts, and barred his fellow passengers from every privilege to his consideration. The intensely reserved gentleman was occupied with interests which were the perquisites of only his few existing peers in birth, position, and intelligence, none of whom, patently, was in that car.

He looked freezingly upon the abashed landscape, which fled in shame; nor was that wintry stare relaxed when the steward placed someone opposite him at the little table. Nay, our frosty scholar now intensified the bleakness of his isolation, retiring quite to the pole in reproval of this too close in- trusion. He resolutely denied the existence of his vis-à-vis, refused conscious- ness of its humanity, even of its sex, and then inconsistently began to perspire with the horrible impression that it was glaring at him fixedly. It was a dread- ful feeling. He felt himself growing red, and coughed vehemently to afford the public an explanation of his change of colour. At last, his suffering grown unendurable, he desperately turned his eyes full upon the newcomer. She was not looking at him at all, but down at the edge of the white cloth on her own side of the table; and she was the very prettiest girl he had ever seen in his life.

She was about his own age. Her prettiness was definitely extreme, and its fair delicacy was complete and without any imperfection whatever. She was dressed in pleasant shades of tan and brown. A brown veil misted the rim of her hat, tan gloves were folded back from her wrists; and they, and all she wore, were fresh and trim and ungrimed by the dusty journey. She was charming. Henry Millick Chester's first gasping appraisal of her was perfectly accurate, for she *was* a peach—or a rose, or anything that is dewy and fresh and delectable. She was indeed some smooth. She was the smoothest thing in the world, and the world knows it!

She looked up.

Henry Millick Chester was lost.

At the same instant that the gone feeling came over him she dropped her eyes again to the edge of the table. Who can tell if she knew what she had done?

The conversation began with appalling formalities, which preluded the most convenient placing of a sugar bowl and the replenishing of an exhausted saltcellar. Then the weather, spurned as the placative offering of the gentle waiter, fell from the lips of the princess in words of diamonds and rubies and pearls. Our Henry took up the weather where she left it; he put it to its utmost; he went forward with it, prophesying weather; he went backward with it, recalling weather; he spun it out and out, while she agreed to all he said, until this overworked weather got so stringy that each obscurely felt it to be hideous. The thread broke; fragments wandered in the air for a few moments, but disappeared; a desperate propriety descended, and they fell into silence over their eggs.

Frantically Mr. Chester searched his mind for some means to pursue the celestial encounter. According to the rules, something ought to happen that would reveal her as Patricia Beekman, the sister of his roommate, Schuyler Beekman, and to-night he should be handing the imperturbable Dawkins a wire to send: "My dear Schuyler, I married your sister this afternoon." But it seemed unlikely, because his roommate's name was Jake Schmulze, and Jake lived in Cedar Rapids; and, besides, this train wasn't coming from or going to Palm Beach—it was going to St. Louis eventually, and now hustled earnestly across the placid and largely unbutlered plains of Ohio.

Often—as everyone knows—people have been lost to each other forever through the lack of a word, and few have realized this more poignantly than our Henry, as he helplessly suffered the precious minutes to accumulate vacancy. True, he had thought of something to say, yet he abandoned it. Probably he was wiser to wait, as what he thought of saying was: "Will you be my wife?" It might seem premature, he feared.

The strain was relieved by a heavenly accident which saved the life of a romance near perishing at birth. That charming girl, relaxing slightly in her chair, made some small, indefinite, and entirely ladylike movement of restfulness that reached its gentle culmination upon the two feet of Mr. Chester which, obviously mistaken for structural adjuncts of the table, were thereby glorified and became beautiful on the mountains. He was not the man to criticise the remarkable ignorance of dining-car table architecture thus displayed, nor did he in any wise resent being mistaken up to the ankles for metal or wood. No. The light pressure of her small heels hardly indented the stout toes of his brown shoes; the soles of her slippers reposed upon his two insteps, and rapture shook his soul to its foundations, while the ineffable girl gazed lustrously out of the window, the clear serenity of her brilliant eyes making plain her complete unconsciousness of the nature of what added to her new comfort.

A terrific blush sizzled all over him, and to conceal its visible area he bent low to his coffee. She was unaware. He was transported, she—to his eyes— transfigured. Glamour diffused itself about her, sprayed about them both like showers of impalpable gold-dust, and filled the humble dining car—it filled the whole world. Transformed, seraphic waiters passed up and down the aisle in a sort of obscure radiance. A nimbus hovered faintly above the brown veil; a sacred luminosity was exhaled by the very tablecloth, where an angel's pointed fingers drummed absently.

It would be uncharitable to believe that a spirit of retaliation inspired the elderly and now replete man across the aisle, and yet, when he rose, he fell upon the neck of Henry as Henry had fallen upon his, and the shock of it jarred four shoes from the acute neighbourliness of their juxtaposition. The accursed graybeard, giggling in his senility, passed on; but that angel leaped backward in her chair while her beautiful eyes, wide open, stunned, her beautiful mouth, wide open, incredulous, gave proof that horror can look bewitching.

"Murder!" she gasped. "Were those your *feet?*"

And as he could compass no articulate reply, she grew as pink as he, murmured inaudibly, and stared at him in wider and wilder amazement.

"It—it didn't hurt," he finally managed to stammer.

At this she covered her blushes with her two hands and began to gurgle and shake with laughter. She laughed and laughed and laughed. It became a paroxysm. He laughed, too, because she laughed. Other passengers looked at them and laughed. The waiters laughed; they approved—coloured waiters always approve of laughter—and a merry spirit went abroad in the car.

At last she controlled herself long enough to ask:

"But what did you think of me?"

"It—it didn't hurt," he repeated idiotically, to his own mortification, for he passionately aspired to say something airy and winsome; but, as he couldn't think of anything like that, he had to let it go. "Oh, not at all," he added feebly.

However, "though not so deep as a well," it served, 'twas enough, for she began to laugh again, and there loomed no further barrier in the way of acquaintance. Therefore it was pleasantly without constraint, and indeed as a matter of course, that he dropped into a chair beside her half an hour later, in the observation car; and something in the way she let the *Illustrated London News* slide into the vacant chair on the other side of her might have suggested that she expected him.

"I was still wondering what you must have thought of me."

This gave him an opportunity, because he had thought out a belated reply for the first time she had said it. Hence, quick as a flash, he made the dashing rejoinder:

"It wasn't so much what I thought of you, but what I thought of myself—I thought I was in heaven!"

She must have known what pretty sounds her laughter made. She laughed a great deal. She even had a way of laughing in the middle of some of her words, and it gave them a kind of ripple. There are girls who naturally laugh like that; others learn to; a few won't, and some can't. It isn't fair to the ones that can't.

"But you oughtn't to tell me that," she said.

It was in the middle of "oughtn't" that she rippled. A pen cannot express it, neither can a typewriter, and no one has yet invented a way of writing with a flute; but the effect on Henry shows what a wonderful ripple it was. Henry trembled. From this moment she had only to ripple to make Henry tremble. Henry was more in love than he had been at breakfast. Henry was a Goner.

"Why oughtn't I to?" he demanded with white intensity. "If anything's true it's right to tell it, isn't it? I believe that everybody has a right to tell the truth, don't you?"

"Ye-es——"

"You take the case of a man that's in love," said this rather precipitate gentleman; "isn't it right for him to——"

"But suppose," she interrupted, becoming instantly serious with the introduction of the great topic—"Suppose he isn't *really* in love. Don't you think there are very few cases of people truly and deeply caring for each other?"

"There are men," he said firmly, "who know how to love truly and deeply, and could never in their lives care for anybody but the one woman they have picked out. I don't say all men feel that way; I don't think they do. But there are a few that are capable of it." The seats in an observation car are usually near neighbours, and it happened that the brown cuff of a tan sleeve, extended reposefully on the arm of her chair, just touched the back of his hand, which rested on the arm of his. This ethereally light contact continued. She had no apparent cognizance of it, but a vibrant thrill passed through him, and possibly quite a hearty little fire might have been built under him without his perceiving good cause for moving. He shook, gulped, and added: "I am!"

"But how could you be sure of that," she said thoughtfully, "until you tried?" And as he seemed about to answer, perhaps too impulsively, she checked him with a smiling, "At your age!"

"You don't know how old I am. I'm older than you!"

"How old are you?"

"Twenty-one next March."

"What day?"

"The seventh."

"That is singular!"

"Why?"

"Because," she began in a low tone and with full recognition of the solemn import of the revelation—"Because my birthday is only one day after yours. I was twenty years old the eighth of last March."

"By George!" The exclamation came from him, husky with awe.

There was a fateful silence.

"Yes, I was born on the eighth," she said slowly.

"And me on the seventh!" At such a time no man is a purist.

"It is strange," she said.

"Strange! I came into the world just one day before you did!"

They looked at each other curiously, deeply stirred. Coincidence could not account for these birthdays of theirs, nor chance for their meeting on a train "like this." Henry Millick Chester was breathless. The mysteries were glimpsed. No doubt was possible—he and the wondrous creature at his side were meant for each other, intended from the beginning of eternity.

She dropped her eyes slowly from his, but he was satisfied that she had felt the marvel precisely as he had felt it.

"Don't you think," she said gently, "that a girl has seen more of the world at twenty than a man?"

Mr. Chester well wished to linger upon the subject of birthdays; however, the line of original research suggested by her question was alluring also. "Yes —and no," he answered with admirable impartiality. "In some ways, yes. In some ways, no. For instance, you take the case of a man that's in love——"

"Well," interrupted the lady, "I think, for instance, that a girl understands men better at twenty than men do women."

"It may be," he admitted, nodding. "I like to think about the deeper things like this sometimes."

"So do I. I think they're interesting," she said with that perfect sympathy of understanding which he believed she was destined to extend to him always and in all things. "Life itself is interesting. Don't you think so?"

"I think it's the most interesting subject there can be. Real life, that is, though—not just on the surface. Now, for instance, you take the case of a man that's in——"

"Do you go in much for reading?" she asked.

"Sure. But as I was saying, you take——"

"I think reading gives us so many ideas, don't you?"

"Yes. I get a lot out of it. I——"

"I do, too. I try to read only the best things," she said. "I don't believe in reading everything, and there's so much to read nowadays that isn't really good."

"Who do you think," he inquired with deference, "is the best author now?"

It was not a question to be settled quite offhand; she delayed her answer slightly, then, with a gravity appropriate to the literary occasion, temporized: "Well, since Victor Hugo is dead, it's hard to say just who is the best."

"Yes, it is," he agreed. "We get that in the English course in college. There aren't any great authors any more. I expect probably Swinburne's the best."

She hesitated. "Perhaps; but more as a poet."

He assented. "Yes, that's so. I expect he would be classed more as a poet. Come to think of it, I believe he's dead, too. I'm not sure, though; maybe it was Beerbohm Tree—somebody like that. I've forgotten; but, anyway, it doesn't matter. I didn't mean poetry; I meant who do you think writes the best books? Mrs. Humphry Ward?"

"Yes, she's good, and so's Henry James."

"I've never read anything by Henry James. I guess I'll read some of his this summer. What's the best one to begin on?"

The exquisite pink of her cheeks extended its area almost imperceptibly. "Oh, any one. They're all pretty good. Do you care for Nature?"

"Sure thing," he returned quickly. "Do you?"

"I love it!"

"So do I. I can't do much for mathematics, though."

"Br-r!" She shivered prettily. "I hate it!"

"So do I. I can't give astronomy a whole lot, either."

She turned a softly reproachful inquiry upon him. "Oh, don't you love to look at the stars?"

In horror lest the entrancing being think him a brute, he responded with breathless haste: "Oh, rath-er-r! To look at 'em, sure thing! I meant astronomy in college; that's mostly math, you know—just figures. But stars to look at—of course that's different. Why, I look up at 'em for hours sometimes!" He believed what he was saying. "I look up at 'em, and think and think and think——"

"So do I." Her voice was low and hushed; there was something almost holy in the sound of it, and a delicate glow suffused her lovely, upraised face—like that picture of Saint Cecilia, he thought. "Oh, I love the stars! And music—and flowers——"

"And birds," he added automatically in a tone that, could it by some miracle have been heard at home, would have laid his nine-year-old brother flat on the floor in a might-be mortal swoon.

A sweet warmth centred in the upper part of his diaphragm and softly filtered throughout him. The delicious future held no doubts or shadows for him. It was assured. He and this perfect woman had absolutely identical tastes; their abhorrences and their enthusiasms marched together; they would never know a difference in all their lives to come. Destiny unrolled before him a shining pathway which they two would walk hand-in-hand through the summer days to a calm and serene autumn, respected and admired by the world, but finding ever their greatest and most sacred joy in the light of each other's eyes—that light none other than the other could evoke.

Could it be possible, he wondered, that he was the same callow boy who but yesterday pranced and exulted in the "pee-rade" of the new juniors! How absurd and purposeless that old life seemed; how far away, how futile, and how childish! Well, it was over, finished. By this time to-morrow he would have begun his business career.

Back in the old life, he had expected to go through a law school after graduating from college, subsequently to enter his father's office. That meant five years before even beginning to practice, an idea merely laughable now. There was a men's furnishing store on a popular corner at home; it was an establishment which had always attracted him, and what pleasanter way to plow the road to success than through acres of variously woven fabrics, richly coloured silks, delicate linens, silver mountings and odorous leathers, in congenial association with neckties, walking-sticks, hosiery, and stickpins? He would be at home a few hours hence, and he would not delay. After lunch he would go boldly to his father and say: "Father, I have reached man's estate and I have put away childish things. I have made up my mind upon a certain matter and you will only waste time by any effort to alter this, my firm determination. Father, I here and now relinquish all legal ambitions, for the reason that a mercantile career is more suited to my inclinations and my abilities. Father, I have met the one and only woman I can ever care for, and I intend to make her my wife. Father, you have always dealt squarely with me; I will deal squarely with you. I ask you the simple question: Will you or will you not advance me the funds to purchase an interest in Paul H. Hoy & Company's Men's Outfitting Establishment? If you will not, then I shall seek help elsewhere."

Waking dreams are as swift, sometimes, as the other kind—which, we hear, thread mazes so labyrinthine "between the opening and the closing of a door"; and a twenty-year-old fancy, fermenting in the inclosure of a six-and-seven-eighths plaid cap, effervesces with a power of sizzling and sparkling and popping.

"I believe I love music best of all," said the girl dreamily.

"Do you play?" he asked, and his tone and look were those of one who watches at the sick-bed of a valued child.

"Yes, a little."

"I love the piano." He was untroubled by any remorse for what he and some of his gang had done only two days since to a previously fine instrument in his dormitory entry. He had forgotten the dead past in his present vision, which was of a luxurious room in a spacious mansion, and a tired man of affairs coming quietly into that room—from a conference at which he had consolidated the haberdashery trade of the world—and sinking noiselessly upon a rich divan, while a beautiful woman in a dress of brown and tan, her hair slightly silvered, played to him through the twilight upon a grand piano, the only other sound in the great house being the softly murmurous voices of perfectly trained children being put to bed in a distant nursery upstairs.

"I like the stage, too," she said. "Don't you?"

"You know! Did you see The Tinkle-Dingle Girl?"

"Yes. I liked it."

"It's a peach show." He spoke with warranted authority. During the university term just finished he had gone eight times to New York, and had enriched his critical perceptions of music and the drama by ten visits to The Tinkle-Dingle Girl, two of his excursions having fallen on matinee days. "Those big birds that played the comedy parts were funny birds, weren't they?"

"The tramp and the brewer? Yes. Awfully funny."

"We'll go lots to the theatre!" He spoke eagerly and with superb simplicity, quite without consciousness that he was skipping much that would usually be thought necessarily intermediate. An enchanting vision engrossed his mind's eye. He saw himself night after night at The Tinkle-Dingle Girl, his lovely wife beside him—growing matronly, perhaps, but slenderly matronly—with a grace of years that only added to her beauty, and always wearing tan gloves and a brown veil.

The bewilderment of her expression was perhaps justified.

"What!"

At this he realized the import of what he had said and what, in a measure, it did assume. He became pinkish, then pink, then more pink; and so did she. Paralyzed, the blushing pair looked at each other throughout this duet in colour, something like a glint of alarm beginning to show through the wide astonishment in her eyes; and with the perception of this he was assailed by an acute perturbation. He had spoken thoughtlessly, even hastily, he feared; he should have given her more time. Would she rise now with chilling dignity and leave him, it might be forever? Was he to lose her just when he had found her? He shuddered at the ghastly abyss of loneliness disclosed by the possibility. But this was only the darkest moment before a radiance that shot heavenward like the flaming javelins of an equatorial sunrise.

Her eyes lowered slowly till the long, brown lashes shadowed the rose-coloured cheek and the fall of her glance came to rest upon the arms of their two chairs, where the edge of her coat sleeve just touched the knuckle of his little finger. Two people were passing in front of them; there was no one who could see; and with a lightning-swift impulse she turned her wrist and for a half second, while his heart stopped beating, touched all his fingers with her own, then as quickly withdrew her hand and turned as far away from him as the position of her chair permitted.

It was a caress of incredible brevity, and so fleeting, so airy, that it was little more than a touch of light itself, like the faint quick light from a flying star one might just glimpse on one's hand as it passed. But in our pleasant world important things have resulted from touches as evanescent as that. Nature has its uses for the ineffable.

Blazing with glory, dumb with rapture, Henry Millick Chester felt his heart rebound to its work, while his withheld breath upheaved in a gulp that half suffocated him. Thus, blinded by the revelation of the stupefying beauty of life, he sat through a heaven-stricken interval, and time was of no moment. Gradually he began to perceive, in the midst of the effulgence which surrounded the next chair like a bright mist, the adorable contour of a shoulder in a tan coat and the ravishing outline of a rosy cheek that belonged to this divine girl who was his.

By and by he became dreamily aware of other objects beyond that cheek and that shoulder, of a fat man and his fat wife on the opposite side of the car near the end. Unmistakably they were man and wife, but it seemed to Henry that they had no reason to be—such people had no right to be married. They had no obvious right to exist at all; certainly they had no right whatever to exist in that car. Their relation to each other had become a sickening commonplace, the bleakness of it as hideously evident as their overfed convexity. It was visible that they looked upon each other as inevitable nuisances which had to be tolerated. They were horrible. Had Love ever known these people? It was unthinkable! For lips such as theirs to have pronounced the name of the god would have been blasphemy; for those fat hands ever to have touched, desecration! Henry hated the despicable pair.

All at once his emotion changed: he did not hate them, he pitied them. From an immense height he looked down with compassion upon their wretched condition. He pitied everybody except himself and the roseate being beside him; they floated together upon a tiny golden cloud, alone in the vast sky at an immeasurable altitude above the squalid universe. A wave of pity for the rest of mankind flooded over him, but most of all he pitied that miserable, sodden, befleshed old married couple.

He was dimly aware of a change that came over these fat people, a strangeness; but he never did realize that at this crisis his eyes, fixed intently upon them and aided by his plastic countenance, had expressed his feelings and sentiments regarding them in the most lively and vivid way. For at the moment when the stout gentleman laid his paper down, preparatory to infuriated inquiry, both he and his wife were expunged from Henry's consciousness forever and were seen of him thenceforth no more than if they had been ether and not solid flesh. The exquisite girl had been pretending to pick a thread out of her left sleeve with her right hand—but now at last she leaned back in her chair and again turned her face partly toward Henry. Her under lip was caught in slightly beneath her upper teeth, as if she had been doing something that possibly she oughtn't to be doing, and though the pause in the conversation had been protracted—it is impossible to calculate how long—her charming features were still becomingly overspread with rose. She looked toward her rapt companion, not at him, and her eyes were preoccupied, tender, and faintly embarrassed.

The pause continued.

He leaned a little closer to her. And he looked at her and looked at her and looked at her. At intervals his lips moved as if he were speaking, and yet he was thinking wordlessly. Leaning thus toward her, his gaze and attitude had all the intensity of one who watches a ninth-inning tie in the deciding game of a championship series. And as he looked and looked and looked, the fat man and his wife, quite unaware of their impalpability, also looked and looked and looked in grateful fascination.

"Did you——" Henry Millick Chester finally spoke these words in a voice he had borrowed, evidently from a stranger, for it did not fit his throat and was so deep that it disappeared—it seemed to fall down a coal-hole and ended in a dusty choke. "Did you——" he began again, two octaves higher, and immediately squeaked out. He said "Did you" five times before he subjugated the other two words.

"Did you—mean that?"

"What?" Her own voice was so low that he divined rather than heard what she said. He leaned even a little closer—and the fat man nudged his wife, who elbowed his thumb out of her side morbidly: she wasn't missing anything.

"Did you—did you mean that?"

"Mean what?"

"That!"

"I don't know what you mean."

"When you—when you—oh, you know!"

"No, I don't."

"When you—when you took my hand."

"I!"

With sudden, complete self-possession she turned quickly to face him, giving him a look of half-shocked, half-amused astonishment.

"When I took your hand?" she repeated incredulously. "What are you saying?"

"You—you know," he stammered. "A while ago when—when—you—you——"

"I didn't do anything of the kind!" Impending indignation began to cloud the delicate face ominously. "Why in the world should I?"

"But you——"

"I didn't!" She cut him off sharply. "I couldn't. Why, it wouldn't have been nice! What made you dream I would do a thing like that? How dare you imagine such things!"

At first dumfounded, then appalled, he took the long, swift, sickening descent from his golden cloud with his mouth open, but it snapped tight at the bump with which he struck the earth. He lay prone, dismayed, abject. The lovely witch could have made him believe anything; at least it is the fact that for a moment she made him believe he had imagined that angelic little caress; and perhaps it was the sight of his utter subjection that melted her. For she flashed upon him suddenly with a dazing smile, and then, blushing again but more deeply than before, her whole attitude admitting and yielding, she offered full and amazing confession, her delicious laugh rippling tremulously throughout every word of it.

"It must have been an accident—partly!"

"I love you!" he shouted.

The translucent fat man and his wife groped for each other feverishly, and a coloured porter touched Henry Millick Chester on the shoulder.

"Be in Richmon' less'n fi' minutes now," said the porter. He tapped the youth's shoulder twice more; it is his office to awaken the rapt dreamer. "Richmon', In'iana, less'n fi' minutes now," he repeated more slowly.

Henry gave him a stunned and dishevelled "What?"

"You get off Richmon', don't you?"

"What of it? We haven't passed Dayton yet."

"Yessuh, long 'go. Pass' Dayton eight-fifty. Be in Richmon' mighty quick now."

The porter appeared to be a malicious liar. Henry appealed pitifully to the girl.

"But we haven't passed Dayton?"

"Yes, just after you sat down by me. We stopped several minutes."

"Yessuh. Train don't stop no minutes in Richmon' though," said the porter with a hard laugh, waving his little broom at some outlying freight cars they were passing. "Gittin' in now. I got you' bag on platfawm."

"I don't want to be brushed," Henry said, almost sobbing. "For heaven's sake, get out!"

Porters expect anything. This one went away solemnly without even lifting his eyebrows.

The brakes were going on.

One class of railway tragedies is never recorded, though it is the most numerous of all and fills the longest list of heartbreaks; the statics ignore it, yet no train ever leaves its shed, or moves, that is not party to it. It is time and overtime that the safety-device inventors should turn their best attention to it, so that the happy day may come at last when we shall see our common carriers equipped with something to prevent these lovers' partings.

The train began to slow down.

Henry Millick Chester got waveringly to his feet; she rose at the same time and stood beside him.

"I am no boy," he began, hardly knowing what he said, but automatically quoting a fragment from his forthcoming address to his father. "I have reached man's estate and I have met the only——" He stopped short with an exclamation of horror. "You—you haven't even told me your name!"

"My name?" the girl said, a little startled.

"Yes! And your address!"

"I'm not on my way home now," she said. "I've been visiting in New York and I'm going to St. Louis to make another visit."

"But your name!"

She gave him an odd glance of mockery, a little troubled.

"You mightn't like my name!"

"Oh, please, please!"

"Besides, do you think it's quite proper for me to——"

"Oh, please! To talk of that now! Please!" The train had stopped.

The glint of a sudden decision shone in the lovely eyes. "I'll write it for you so you won't forget."

She went quickly to the writing desk at the end of the compartment, he with her, the eyes of the fat man and his wife following them like two pairs of searchlights swung by the same mechanism.

"And where you live," urged Henry. "I shall write to you every day." He drew a long, deep breath and threw back his head. "Till the day—the day when I come for you."

"Don't look over my shoulder." She laughed shyly, wrote hurriedly upon a loose sheet, placed it in an envelope, sealed the envelope, and then, as he reached to take it, withheld it tantalizingly. "No. It's my name and where I live, but you can't have it. Not till you've promised not to open it until the train is clear out of the station."

Outside the window sounded the twice-repeated "Awl aboh-oh," and far ahead a fatal bell was clanging.

"I promise," he gulped.

"Then take it!"

With a strange, new-born masterfulness he made a sudden impetuous gesture and lifted both the precious envelope and the fingers that inclosed it to his lips. Then he turned and dashed to the forward end of the car where a porter remained untipped as Henry leaped from the already rapidly moving steps of the car to the ground. Instantly the wonderful girl was drawn past him, leaning and waving from the railed rear platform whither she had run for this farewell. And in the swift last look that they exchanged there was in her still-flushing, lovely face a light of tenderness and of laughter, of kindness and of something like a fleeting regret.

The train gained momentum, skimming onward and away, the end of the observation car dwindling and condensing into itself like a magician's disappearing card, while a white handkerchief, waving from the platform, quickly became an infinitesimal shred of white—and then there was nothing. The girl was gone.

Probably Henry Millick Chester owes his life to the fact that there are no gates between the station building and the tracks at Richmond. For gates and a ticket-clipping official might have delayed Henry's father in the barely successful dash he made to drag from the path of a backing local a boy wholly lost to the outward world in a state of helpless puzzlement, which already threatened to become permanent as he stared and stared at a sheet of railway notepaper whereon was written in a charming hand:

      Mary Smith
           Chicago
                Ill.

CLERICAL ERROR

JAMES GOULD COZZENS

THERE were three steps down from the street door. Then the store extended, narrow and low between the book-packed walls, sixty or seventy feet to a little cubbyhole of an office where a large sallow man worked under a shaded desk-lamp. He had heard the street door open, and he looked that way a moment, peering intently through his spectacles. Seeing only a thin, stiffly erect gentleman with a small cropped white mustache, standing hesitant before the table with the sign *Any Book 50 Cents*, he returned to the folded copy of a religious weekly on the desk in front of him. He looked at the obituary column again, pulled a pad toward him and made a note. When he had finished, he saw, upon looking up again, that the gentleman with the white mustache had come all the way down the store.

"Yes, sir?" he said, pushing the papers aside. "What can I do for you?"

The gentleman with the white mustache stared at him keenly. "I am addressing the proprietor, Mr. Joreth?" he said.

"Yes, sir. You are."

"Quite so. My name is Ingalls—Colonel Ingalls."

"I'm glad to know you, Colonel. What can I—"

"I see that the name does not mean anything to you."

Mr. Joreth took off his spectacles, looked searchingly. "Why, no, sir. I am afraid not. Ingalls. No. I don't know anyone by that name."

Colonel Ingalls thrust his stick under his arm and drew an envelope from his inner pocket. He took a sheet of paper from it, unfolded the sheet, scowled at it a moment, and tossed it onto the desk. "Perhaps," he said, "this will refresh your memory."

Mr. Joreth pulled his nose a moment, looked harder at Colonel Ingalls, replaced his spectacles. "Oh," he said, "a bill. Yes. You must excuse me. I do much of my business by mail with people I've never met personally. 'The Reverend Doctor Godfrey Ingalls, Saint John's Rectory.' Ah, yes, yes—"

"The late Doctor Ingalls was my brother. This bill is obviously an error. He would never have ordered, received, or wished to read any of these works. Naturally, no such volumes were found among his effects."

First published in *Redbook*. Copyright © 1935 by James Gould Cozzens. Reprinted by permission of Brandt & Brandt.

"Hm," said Mr. Joreth. "Yes, I see." He read down the itemized list, coughed, as though in embarrassment. "I see. Now, let me check my records a moment." He dragged down a vast battered folio from the shelf before him. "*G, H, I—*" he muttered. "*Ingalls.* Ah, now—"

"There is no necessity for that," said Colonel Ingalls. "It is, of course, a mistake. A strange one, it seems to me. I advise you strongly to be more careful. If you choose to debase yourself by surreptitiously selling works of the sort, that is your business. But—"

Mr. Joreth nodded several times, leaned back. "Well, Colonel," he said, "you're entitled to your opinion. I don't sit in judgment on the tastes of my customers. Now, in this case, there seems unquestionably to have been an order for the books noted from the source indicated. On the fifteenth of last May I filled the order. Presumably they arrived. What became of them, then, is no affair of mine; but in view of your imputation, I might point out that such literature is likely to be kept in a private place and read privately. For eight successive months I sent a statement. I have never received payment. Of course, I was unaware that the customer was, didn't you say, deceased. Hence my reference to legal action on this last. I'm very sorry to have—"

"You unmitigated scoundrel!" roared Colonel Ingalls. "Do you really mean definitely to maintain that Doctor Ingalls purchased such books? Let me tell you—"

Mr. Joreth said: "My dear sir, one moment, if you please! Are you in a position to be so positive? I imply nothing about the purchaser. I mean to maintain nothing, except that I furnished goods, for which I am entitled to payment. I am a poor man. When people do not pay me, what can I do but—"

"Why, you infamous—"

Mr. Joreth held up his hand. "Please, please!" he protested. "I think you are taking a most unjust and unjustified attitude, Colonel. This account has run a long while. I've taken no action. I am well aware of the unpleasantness which would be caused for many customers if a bill for books of this sort was made public. The circumstances aren't by any means unique, my dear sir; a list of my confidential customers would no doubt surprise you."

Colonel Ingalls said carefully: "Be good enough to show me my brother's original order."

"Ah," said Mr. Joreth. He pursed his lips. "That's unfair of you, Colonel. You are quite able to see that I wouldn't have it. It would be the utmost imprudence for me to keep on file anything which could cause so much trouble. I have the carbon of an invoice, which is legally sufficient, under the circumstances, I think. You see my position."

"Clearly," said Colonel Ingalls. "It is the position of a dirty knave and a blackguard, and I shall give myself the satisfaction of thrashing you." He whipped the stick from under his arm. Mr. Joreth slid agilely from his seat, caught the telephone off the desk, kicking a chair into the Colonel's path.

"Operator," he said, "I want a policeman." Then he jerked open a drawer, plucked a revolver from it. "Now, my good sir," he said, his back against the wall, "we shall soon see. I have put up with a great deal of abuse from you, but there are limits. To a degree I understand your provocation, though it doesn't excuse your conduct. If you choose to take yourself out of here at once and send me a check for the amount due me, we will say no more."

Colonel Ingalls held the stick tight in his hand. "I think I will wait for the officer," he said with surprising composure. "I was too hasty. In view of your list of so-called customers, which you think would surprise me, there are doubtless other people to be considered—"

The stick in his hand leaped, sudden and slashing, catching Mr. Joreth over the wrist. The revolver flew free, clattered along the floor, and Colonel Ingalls kicked it behind him. "It isn't the sort of thing the relatives of a clergyman would like to have made public, is it? When you read of the death of one, what is to keep you from sending a bill? Very often they must pay and shut up. A most ingenious scheme, sir."

Mr. Joreth clasped his wrist, wincing. "I am at loss to understand this non-sense," he said. "How dare you—"

"Indeed?" said Colonel Ingalls. "Ordinarily, I might be at loss myself, sir; but in this case I think you put your foot in it, sir! I happen to be certain that my late brother ordered no books from you, that he did not keep them in private or read them in private. It was doubtless not mentioned in the obituary, but for fifteen years previous to his death Doctor Ingalls had the misfortune to be totally blind. . . . There, sir, is the policeman you sent for."

THE SUICIDE CLUB

ROBERT LOUIS STEVENSON

STORY OF THE YOUNG MAN WITH THE CREAM TARTS

DURING his residence in London, the accomplished Prince Florizel of Bohemia gained the affection of all classes by the seduction of his manner and by a well-considered generosity. He was a remarkable man even by what was known of him; and that was but a small part of what he actually did. Although of a placid temper in ordinary circumstances, and accustomed to take the world with as much philosophy as any ploughman, the Prince of Bohemia was not without a taste for ways of life more adventurous and eccentric than that to which he was destined by his birth. Now and then, when he fell into a low humor, when there was no laughable play to witness in any of the London theatres, and when the season of the year was unsuitable to those field sports in which he excelled all competitors, he would summon his confidant and Master of the Horse, Colonel Geraldine, and bid him prepare himself against an evening ramble. The Master of the Horse was a young officer of a brave and even temerarious disposition. He greeted the news with delight, and hastened to make ready. Long practice and a varied acquaintance of life had given him a singular facility in disguise; he could adapt not only his face and bearing, but his voice and almost his thoughts, to those of any rank, character, or nation; and in this way he diverted attention from the Prince, and sometimes gained admission for the pair into strange societies. The civil authorities were never taken into the secret of these adventures; the imperturbable courage of the one and the ready invention and chivalrous devotion of the other had brought them through a score of dangerous passes; and they grew in confidence as time went on.

One evening in March they were driven by a sharp fall of sleet into an Oyster Bar in the immediate neighborhood of Leicester Square. Colonel Geraldine was dressed and painted to represent a person connected with the Press in reduced circumstances; while the Prince had, as usual, travestied his appearance by the addition of false whiskers and a pair of large adhesive eyebrows. These lent him a shaggy and weather-beaten air, which, for one of his urbanity, formed the most impenetrable disguise. Thus equipped, the commander and his satellite sipped their brandy and soda in security.

The bar was full of guests, both male and female; but though more than one of these offered to fall into talk with our adventurers, none of them promised to grow interesting upon a nearer acquaintance. There was nothing present but the lees of London and the commonplace of disrespectability; and the Prince had already fallen to yawning, and was beginning to grow weary of the whole excursion, when the swing doors were pushed violently open, and a young man, followed by a couple of commissionaires, entered the bar. Each of the commissionaires carried a large dish of cream tarts under a cover, which they at once removed; and the young man made the round of the company, and pressed these confections upon everyone's acceptance with an exaggerated courtesy. Sometimes his offer was laughingly accepted; sometimes it was firmly, or even harshly, rejected. In these latter cases the newcomer always ate the tart himself, with some more or less humorous commentary.

At last he accosted Prince Florizel.

"Sir," said he, with a profound obeisance, proffering the tart at the same time between his thumb and forefinger, "will you so far honor an entire stranger? I can answer for the quality of the pastry, having eaten two dozen and three of them myself since five o'clock."

"I am in the habit," replied the Prince, "of looking not so much to the nature of a gift as to the spirit in which it is offered."

"The spirit, sir," returned the young man, with another bow, "is one of mockery."

"Mockery?" repeated Florizel. "And whom do you propose to mock?"

"I am not here to expound my philosophy," replied the other, "but to distribute these cream tarts. If I mention that I heartily include myself in the ridicule of the transaction, I hope you will consider honor satisfied and condescend. If not, you will constrain me to eat my twenty-eighth, and I own to being weary of the exercise."

"You touch me," said the Prince, "and I have all the will in the world to rescue you from this dilemma, but upon one condition. If my friend and I eat your cakes—for which we have neither of us any natural inclination— we shall expect you to join us at supper by way of recompense."

The young man seemed to reflect.

"I have still several dozen upon hand," he said at last; "and that will make it necessary for me to visit several more bars before my great affair is concluded. This will take some time; and if you are hungry——"

The Prince interrupted him with a polite gesture.

"My friend and I will accompany you," he said; "for we have already a deep interest in your very agreeable mode of passing an evening. And now that the preliminaries of peace are settled, allow me to sign the treaty for both."

And the Prince swallowed the tart with the best grace imaginable.

"It is delicious," said he.

"I perceive you are a connoisseur," replied the young man.

Colonel Geraldine likewise did honor to the pastry; and every one in that bar having now either accepted or refused his delicacies, the young man with the cream tarts led the way to another and similar establishment. The two commissionaires, who seemed to have grown accustomed to their absurd employment, followed immediately after; and the Prince and the Colonel brought up the rear, arm in arm, and smiling to each other as they went. In this order the company visited two other taverns, where scenes were enacted of a like nature to that already described—some refusing, some accepting, the favors of this vagabond hospitality, and the young man himself eating each rejected tart.

On leaving the third saloon the young man counted his store. There were but nine remaining, three in one tray and six in the other.

"Gentlemen," said he, addressing himself to his two new followers, "I am unwilling to delay your supper. I am positively sure you must be hungry. I feel that I owe you a special consideration. And on this great day for me, when I am closing a career of folly by my most conspicuously silly action, I wish to behave handsomely to all who give me countenance. Gentlemen, you shall wait no longer. Although my constitution is shattered by previous excesses, at the risk of my life I liquidate the suspensory condition."

With these words he crushed the nine remaining tarts into his mouth, and swallowed them at a single movement each. Then, turning to the commissionaires, he gave them a couple of sovereigns.

"I have to thank you," said he, "for your extraordinary patience."

And he dismissed them with a bow apiece. For some seconds he stood looking at the purse from which he had just paid his assistants, then, with a laugh, he tossed it into the middle of the street, and signified his readiness for supper.

In a small French restaurant in Soho, which had enjoyed an exaggerated reputation for some little while, but had already begun to be forgotten, and in a private room up two pair of stairs, the three companions made a very elegant supper, and drank three or four bottles of champagne, talking the while upon indifferent subjects. The young man was fluent and gay, but he laughed louder than was natural in a person of polite breeding; his hands trembled violently, and his voice took sudden and surprising inflections, which seemed to be independent of his will. The dessert had been cleared away, and all three had lighted their cigars, when the Prince addressed him in these words:

"You will, I am sure, pardon my curiosity. What I have seen of you has greatly pleased but even more puzzled me. And though I should be loth to seem indiscreet, I must tell you that my friend and I are persons very well worthy to be entrusted with a secret. We have many of our own, which we are continually revealing to improper ears. And if, as I suppose, your story is a silly one, you need have no delicacy with us, who are two of the silliest men in England. My name is Godall, Theophilus Godall; my friend is Major Alfred Hammersmith—or at least, such is the name by which he chooses to be known. We pass our lives entirely in the search for extravagant adventures; and there is no extravagance with which we are not capable of sympathy."

"I like you, Mr. Godall," returned the young man; "you inspire me with a natural confidence; and I have not the slightest objection to your friend, the Major; whom I take to be a nobleman in masquerade. At least, I am sure he is no soldier."

The Colonel smiled at this compliment to the perfection of his art; and the young man went on in a more animated manner.

"There is every reason why I should not tell you my story. Perhaps that is just the reason why I am going to do so. At least, you seem so well prepared to hear a tale of silliness that I cannot find it in my heart to disappoint you. My name, in spite of your example, I shall keep to myself. My age is not essential to the narrative. I am descended from my ancestors by ordinary generation, and from them I inherited the very eligible human tenement which I still occupy and a fortune of three hundred pounds a year. I suppose they also handed on to me a hare-brain humor, which it has been my chief delight to indulge. I received a good education. I can play the violin nearly well enough to earn money in the orchestra of a penny gaff, but not quite. The same remark applies to the flute and the French horn. I learned enough of whist to lose about a hundred a year at that scientific game. My acquaintance with French was sufficient to enable me to squander money in Paris with almost the same facility as in London. In short, I am a person full of manly accomplishments. I have had every sort of adventure, including a duel about nothing. Only two months ago I met a young lady exactly suited to my taste in mind and body; I found my heart melt; I saw that I had come upon my fate at last, and was in the way to fall in love. But when I came to reckon up what remained to me of my capital, I found it amounted to something less than four hundred pounds! I ask you fairly—can a man who respects himself fall in love on four hundred pounds? I concluded, certainly not; left the presence of my charmer, and slightly accelerating my usual rate of expenditure, came this morning to my last eighty pounds. This I divided into two equal parts; forty I reserved for a particular purpose; the remaining forty I was to dissipate before the night. I have passed a very entertaining day, and played many farces besides that of the cream tarts which procured me the advantage of your acquaintance; for I was determined, as I told you, to bring a foolish career to a still more foolish conclusion; and when you saw me throw my purse into the street, the forty pounds were at an end. Now you know me as well as I know myself: a fool but consistent in his folly; and, as I will ask you to believe, neither a whimperer nor a coward."

From the whole tone of the young man's statement it was plain that he harbored very bitter and contemptuous thoughts about himself. His auditors were led to imagine that his love affair was nearer his heart than he admitted, and that he had a design on his own life. The farce of the cream tarts began to have very much the air of a tragedy in disguise.

"Why, is this not odd," broke out Geraldine, giving a look to Prince Florizel, "that we three fellows should have met by the merest accident in so large a wilderness as London, and should be so nearly in the same condition?"

"How?" cried the young man. "Are you, too, ruined? Is this supper a folly like my cream tarts? Has the devil brought three of his own together for a last carouse?"

"The devil, depend upon it, can sometimes do a very gentlemanly thing," returned Prince Florizel; "and I am so much touched by this coincidence, that, although we are not entirely in the same case, I am going to put an end to the disparity. Let your heroic treatment of the last cream tarts be my example."

So saying, the Prince drew out his purse and took from it a small bundle of bank-notes.

"You see, I was a week or so behind you, but I mean to catch you up and come neck and neck into the winning-post," he continued. "This," laying one of the notes upon the table, will suffice for the bill. As for the rest—"

He tossed them into the fire, and they went up the chimney in a single blaze.

The young man tried to catch his arm, but as the table was between them his interference came too late.

"Unhappy man," he cried, "you should not have burned them all! You should have kept forty pounds."

"Forty pounds!" repeated the Prince. "Why, in heaven's name, forty pounds?"

"Why not eighty?" cried the Colonel; "for to my certain knowledge there must have been a hundred in the bundle."

"It was only forty pounds he needed," said the young man gloomily. "But without them there is no admission. The rule is strict. Forty pounds for each. Accursed life, where a man cannot even die without money!"

The Prince and the Colonel exchanged glances.

"Explain yourself," said the latter. "I have still a pocket-book tolerably well lined, and I need not say how readily I would share my wealth with Godall. But I must know to what end; you must certainly tell us what you mean."

The young man seemed to awaken; he looked uneasily from one to the other, and his face flushed deeply.

"You are not fooling me?" he asked. "You are indeed ruined men like me?"

"Indeed, I am for my part," replied the Colonel.

"And for mine," said the Prince, "I have given you proof. Who but a ruined man would throw his notes into the fire? The action speaks for itself."

"A ruined man—yes," returned the other suspiciously, "or else a millionaire."

"Enough, sir," said the Prince; "I have said so, and I am not accustomed to have my word remain in doubt."

"Ruined?" said the young man. "Are you ruined, like me? Are you, after a life of indulgence, come to such a pass that you can only indulge yourself in one thing more? Are you"—he kept lowering his voice as he went on—"are you going to give yourselves that last indulgence! Are you going to avoid the consequences of your folly by the one infallible and easy path? Are you going to give the slip to the sheriff's officers of conscience by the one open door?"

Suddenly he broke off and attempted to laugh.

"Here is your health!" he cried, emptying his glass, "and good night to you, my merry ruined men."

Colonel Geraldine caught him by the arm as he was about to rise.

"You lack confidence in us," he said, "and you are wrong. To all your questions I make answer in the affirmative. But I am not so timid, and can speak the Queen's English plainly. We, too, like yourself, have had enough of life, and are determined to die. Sooner or later, alone or together, we meant to seek out death and beard him where he lies ready. Since we have met you, and your case is more pressing, let it be to-night—and at once—and, if you will, all three together. Such a penniless trio," he cried, "should go arm in arm into the halls of Pluto, and give each other some countenance among the shades!"

Geraldine had hit exactly on the manners and intonations that became the part he was playing. The Prince himself was disturbed, and looked over at his confidant with a shade of doubt. As for the young man, the flush came back darkly into his cheek, and his eyes threw out a spark of light.

"You are the men for me!" he cried, with an almost terrible gaiety. "Shake hands upon the bargain!" (his hand was cold and wet). "You little know in what a company you will begin the march! You little know in what a happy moment for yourselves you partook of my cream tarts! I am only a unit, but I am a unit in an army. I know Death's private door. I am one of his familiars, and can show you into eternity without ceremony and yet without scandal."

They called upon him eagerly to explain his meaning.

"Can you muster eighty pounds between you?" he demanded.

Geraldine ostentatiously consulted his pocket-book, and replied in the affirmative.

"Fortunate beings!" cried the young man. "Forty pounds is the entry money of the Suicide Club."

"The Suicide Club," said the Prince, "why, what the devil is that?"

"Listen," said the young man; "this is the age of conveniences, and I have to tell you of the last perfection of the sort. We have affairs in different places; and hence railways were invented. Railways separated us infallibly from our friends; and so telegraphs were made that we might communicate speedily at great distances. Even in hotels we have lifts to spare us a climb of some hundred steps. Now, we know that life is only a stage to play the fool upon as long as the part amuses us. There was one more convenience lacking to modern comfort; a decent, easy way to quit that stage; the back stairs to liberty; or, as I said this moment, Death's private door. This, my two fellow-rebels, is supplied by the Suicide Club. Do not suppose that you and I are alone, or even exceptional, in the highly reasonable desire that we profess. A large number of our fellow-men, who have grown heartily sick of the performance in which they are expected to join daily and all their lives long, are only kept from flight by one or two considerations. Some have families who would be shocked, or even blamed, if the matter became public; others have a weakness at heart and recoil from the circumstances of death. That is, to some extent, my own experience. I cannot put a pistol to my head and draw the trigger; for something stronger than myself withholds the act; and although I loathe life, I have not strength enough in my body to take hold of death and be done with it. For such as I, and for all who desire to be out of the coil without posthumous scandal, the Suicide Club has been inaugurated. How this has been managed, what is its history, or what may be its ramifications in other lands, I am myself uninformed; and what I know of its constitution, I am not at liberty to communicate to you. To this extent, however, I am at your service. If you are truly tired of life, I will introduce you to-night to a meeting; and if not to-night, at least some time within the week, you will be easily relieved of your existences. It is now (consulting his watch) eleven; by half-past, at latest, we must leave this place; so that you have half an hour before you to consider my proposal. It is more serious than a cream tart," he added, with a smile; "and I suspect more palatable."

"More serious, certainly," returned Colonel Geraldine; "and as it is so much more so, will you allow me five minutes' speech in private with my friend, Mr. Godall?"

"It is only fair," answered the young man. "If you will permit, I will retire."

"You will be very obliging," said the Colonel.

As soon as the two were alone—"What," said Prince Florizel, "is the use of this confabulation, Geraldine? I see you are flurried, whereas my mind is very tranquilly made up. I will see the end of this."

"Your Highness," said the Colonel, turning pale; "let me ask you to consider the importance of your life, not only to your friends, but to the public interest. 'If not to-night,' said this madman; but supposing that to-night some irreparable disaster were to overtake your Highness's person, what, let me ask you, what would be my despair, and what the concern and disaster of a great nation?"

"I will see the end of this," repeated the Prince in his most deliberate tones; "and have the kindness, Colonel Geraldine, to remember and respect your word of honor as a gentleman. Under no circumstances, recollect, nor without my special authority, are you to betray the incognito under which I choose to go abroad. These were my commands, which I now reiterate. And now," he added, "let me ask you to call for the bill."

Colonel Geraldine bowed in submission; but he had a very white face as he summoned the young man of the cream tarts, and issued his directions to the waiter. The Prince preserved his undisturbed demeanor, and described a Palais Royal farce to the young suicide with great humor and gusto. He avoided the Colonel's appealing looks without ostentation, and selected another cheroot with more than usual care. Indeed, he was now the only man of the party who kept any command over his nerves.

The bill was discharged, the Prince giving the whole change of the note to the astonished waiter; and the three drove off in a four wheeler. They were not long upon the way before the cab stopped at the entrance to a rather dark court. Here all descended.

After Geraldine had paid the fare, the young man turned, and addressed Prince Florizel as follows:

"It is still time, Mr. Godall, to make good your escape into thralldom. And for you too, Major Hammersmith. Reflect well before you take another step; and if your hearts say no—here are the cross-roads."

"Lead on, sir," said the Prince. "I am not the man to go back from a thing once said."

"Your coolness does me good," replied their guide. "I have never seen anyone so unmoved at this conjuncture; and yet you are not the first whom I have escorted to this door. More than one of my friends has preceded me, where I knew I must shortly follow. But this is of no interest to you. Wait me here for only a few moments; I shall return as soon as I have arranged the preliminaries of your introduction."

And with that the young man, waving his hand to his companions, turned into the court, entered a doorway and disappeared.

"Of all our follies," said Colonel Geraldine in a low voice, "this is the wildest and most dangerous."

"I perfectly believe so," returned the Prince.

"We have still," pursued the Colonel, "a moment to ourselves. Let me beseech your Highness to profit by the opportunity and retire. The consequences of this step are so dark, and may be so grave, that I feel myself justified in pushing a little farther than usual the liberty which your Highness is so condescending as to allow me in private."

"Am I to understand that Colonel Geraldine is afraid?" asked his Highness, taking his cheroot from his lips, and looking keenly into the other's face.

"My fear is certainly not personal," replied the other proudly; "of that your Highness may rest well assured."

"I had supposed as much," returned the Prince, with undisturbed good humor; "but I was unwilling to remind you of the difference in our stations. No more—no more," he added, seeing Geraldine about to apologize, "you stand excused."

And he smoked placidly, leaning against a railing, until the young man returned.

"Well," he asked, "has our reception been arranged?"

"Follow me," was the reply. "The President will see you in the cabinet. And let me warn you to be frank in your answers. I have stood your guarantee; but the club requires a searching inquiry before admission; for the indiscretion of a single member would lead to the dispersion of the whole society forever."

The Prince and Geraldine put their heads together for a moment. "Bear me out in this," said the one; and "bear me out in that," said the other; and by boldly taking up the characters of men with whom both were acquainted, they had come to an agreement in a twinkling, and were ready to follow their guide into the President's cabinet.

There were no formidable obstacles to pass. The outer door stood open; the door of the cabinet was ajar; and there, in a small but very high apartment, the young man left them once more.

"He will be here immediately," he said with a nod, as he disappeared.

Voices were audible in the cabinet through the folding-doors which formed one end; and now and then the noise of a champagne cork, followed by a burst of laughter, intervened among the sounds of conversation. A single tall window looked out upon the river and the embankment; and by the disposition of the lights they judged themselves not far from Charing Cross station. The furniture was scanty, and the coverings worn to the thread; and there was nothing movable except a hand-bell in the centre of a round table, and the hats and coats of a considerable party hung round the wall on pegs.

"What sort of a den is this?" said Geraldine.

"That is what I have come to see," replied the Prince. "If they keep live devils on the premises, the thing may grow amusing."

Just then the folding-door was opened no more than was necessary for the passage of a human body; and there entered at the same moment a louder buzz of talk, and the redoubtable President of the Suicide Club. The President was a man of fifty or upwards; large and rambling in his gait, with shaggy side-whiskers, a bald top to his head, and a veiled gray eye, which now and then emitted a twinkle. His mouth, which embraced a large cigar, he kept continually screwing round and round and from side to side, as he looked sagaciously and coldly at the strangers. He was dressed in light tweeds, with his neck very open, in a striped shirt collar; and carried a minute book under one arm.

"Good evening," said he, after he had closed the door behind him. "I am told you wish to speak with me."

"We have a desire, sir, to join the Suicide Club," replied the Colonel.

The President rolled his cigar about in his mouth.

"What is that?" he said abruptly.

"Pardon me," returned the Colonel, "but I believe you are the person best qualified to give us information on that point."

"I?" cried the President. "A Suicide Club? Come, come! this is a frolic for All Fools' Day. I can make allowances for gentlemen who get merry in their liquor; but let there be an end to this."

"Call your Club what you will," said the Colonel, "you have some company behind these doors, and we insist on joining it."

"Sir," returned the President, curtly, "you have made a mistake. This is a private house, and you must leave it instantly."

The Prince had remained quietly in his seat throughout this little colloquy; but now, when the Colonel looked over to him, as much as to say, "Take your answer and come away, for God's sake!" he drew his cheroot from his mouth, and spoke:

"I have come here," said he, "upon the invitation of a friend of yours. He has doubtless informed you of my intention in thus intruding on your party. Let me remind you that a person in my circumstances has exceedingly little to bind him, and is not at all likely to tolerate much rudeness. I am a very quiet man, as a usual thing; but, my dear sir, you are either going to oblige me in the little matter of which you are aware, or you shall very bitterly repent that you ever admitted me to your antechamber."

The President laughed aloud.

"That is the way to speak," said he. "You are a man who is a man. You know the way to my heart, and can do what you like with me. Will you," he continued, addressing Geraldine, "will you step aside for a few minutes? I shall finish first with your companion, and some of the club's formalities require to be fulfilled in private."

With these words he opened the door of a small closet, into which he shut the Colonel.

"I believe in you," he said to Florizel, as soon as they were alone; "but are you sure of your friend?"

"Not so sure as I am of myself, though he has more cogent reasons," answered Florizel, "but sure enough to bring him here without alarm. He has had enough to cure the most tenacious man of life. He was cashiered the other day for cheating at cards."

"A good reason, I daresay," replied the President; "at least, we have another in the same case, and I feel sure of him. Have you also been in the Service, may I ask?"

"I have," was the reply; "but I was too lazy, I left it early."

"What is your reason for being tired of life?" pursued the President.

"The same, as near as I can make out," answered the Prince; "unadulterated laziness."

The President started. D——n it," said he, "you must have something better than that."

"I have no more money," added Florizel. "That is also a vexation, without doubt. It brings my sense of idleness to an acute point."

The President rolled his cigar round in his mouth for some seconds, directing his gaze straight into the eyes of this unusual neophyte; but the Prince supported his scrutiny with unabashed good temper.

"If I had not a deal of experience," said the President at last, "I should turn you off. But I know the world; and this much any way, that the most frivolous excuses for a suicide are often the toughest to stand by. And when I downright like a man, as I do you, sir, I would rather strain the regulation than deny him."

The Prince and the Colonel, one after the other, were subjected to a long and particular interrogatory—the Prince alone; but Geraldine in the presence of the Prince, so that the President might observe the countenance of the one while the other was being warmly cross-examined. The result was satisfactory; and the President, after having booked a few details of each case, produced a form of oath to be accepted. Nothing could be conceived more passive than the obedience promised, or more stringent than the terms by which the juror bound himself. The man who forfeited a pledge so awful could scarcely have a rag of honor or any of the consolations of religion left to him. Florizel signed the document, but not without a shudder; the Colonel followed his example with an air of great depression. Then the President received the entry money; and without more ado, introduced the two friends into the smoking-room of the Suicide Club.

The smoking-room of the Suicide Club was the same height as the cabinet into which it opened, but much larger, and papered from top to bottom with an imitation of oak wainscot. A large and cheerful fire and a number of gas jets illuminated the company. The Prince and his follower made the number up to eighteen. Most of the party were smoking, and drinking champagne; a feverish hilarity reigned, with sudden and rather ghastly pauses.

"Is this a full meeting?" asked the Prince.

"Middling," said the President. "By the way," he added, "if you have any money, it is usual to offer some champagne. It keeps up a good spirit, and is one of my own little perquisites."

"Hammersmith," said Florizel, "I may leave the champagne to you."

And with that he turned away and began to go round among the guests. Accustomed to play the host in the highest circles, he charmed and dominated all whom he approached; there was something at once winning and authoritative in his address; and his extraordinary coolness gave him yet another distinction in this half maniacal society. As he went from one to another he kept both his eyes and ears open, and soon began to gain a general idea of the people among whom he found himself. As in all other places of resort, one type predominated: people in the prime of youth, with every show of intelligence and sensibility in their appearance, but with little promise of strength or the quality that makes success. Few were much above thirty, and not a few were still in their teens. They stood, leaning on tables and shifting on their feet; sometimes they smoked extraordinarily fast, and sometimes they let their cigars go out; some talked well, but the conversation of others was plainly the result of nervous tension, and was equally without wit or purport. As each new bottle of champagne was opened, there was a manifest improvement in gaiety. Only two were seated—one in a chair in the recess of the window, with his head hanging and his hands plunged deep into his trouser pockets, pale, visibly moist with perspiration, saying never a word, a very wreck of soul and body; the other sat on the divan close by the chimney, and attracted notice by a trenchant dissimilarity from all the rest. He was probably upwards of forty, but he looked fully ten years older; and Florizel thought he had never seen a man more naturally hideous, nor one more ravaged by disease and ruinous excitements. He was no more than skin and bone, was partly paralyzed, and wore spectacles of such unusual power, that his eyes appeared through the glasses greatly magnified and distorted in shape. Except the Prince and the President, he was the only person in the room who preserved the composure of ordinary life.

There was little decency among the members of the club. Some boasted of the disgraceful actions, the consequences of which had reduced them to seek refuge in death; and the others listened without disapproval. There was a tacit understanding against moral judgments; and whoever passed the club doors enjoyed already some of the immunities of the tomb. They drank to each other's memories, and to those of notable suicides in the past. They compared and developed their different views of death—some declaring that it was no more than blackness and cessation; others full of a hope that that very night they should be scaling the stars and commercing with the mighty dead.

"To the eternal memory of Baron Trenck, the type of suicides!" cried one. "He went out of a small cell into a smaller, that he might come forth again to freedom."

"For my part," said a second, "I wish no more than a bandage for my eyes and cotton for my ears. Only they have no cotton thick enough in this world."

A third was for reading the mysteries of life in a future state; and a fourth professed that he would never have joined the club, if he had not been induced to believe in Mr. Darwin.

"I could not bear," said this remarkable suicide, "to be descended from an ape."

Altogether, the Prince was disappointed by the bearing and conversation of the members.

"It does not seem to me," he thought, "a matter for so much disturbance. If a man has made up his mind to kill himself, let him do it, in God's name, like a gentleman. This flutter and big talk is out of place."

In the meanwhile Colonel Geraldine was a prey to the blackest apprehensions; the club and its rules were still a mystery, and he looked round the room for some one who should be able to set his mind at rest. In this survey his eye lighted on the paralytic person with the strong spectacles; and seeing him so exceedingly tranquil, he besought the President, who was going in and out of the room under a pressure of business, to present him to the gentleman on the divan.

The functionary explained the needlessness of all such formalities within the club, but nevertheless presented Mr. Hammersmith to Mr. Malthus.

Mr. Malthus looked at the Colonel curiously, and then requested him to take a seat upon his right.

"You are a newcomer," he said, "and wish information? You have come to the proper source. It is two years since I first visited this charming club."

The Colonel breathed again. If Mr. Malthus had frequented the place for two years there could be little danger for the Prince in a single evening. But Geraldine was none the less astonished, and began to suspect a mystification.

"What!" cried he, "two years! I thought—but indeed I see I have been made the subject of a pleasantry."

"By no means," replied Mr. Malthus mildly. "My case is peculiar. I am not, properly speaking, a suicide at all; but, as it were, an honorary member. I rarely visit the club twice in two months. My infirmity and the kindness of the President have procured me these little immunities, for which besides I pay at an advanced rate. Even as it is my luck has been extraordinary."

"I am afraid," said the Colonel, "that I must ask you to be more explicit. You must remember that I am still most imperfectly acquainted with the rules of the club."

"An ordinary member who comes here in search of death like yourself," replied the paralytic, "returns every evening until fortune favors him. He can, even if he is penniless, get board and lodging from the President—very fair, I believe, and clean, although, of course, not luxurious; that could hardly be, considering the exiguity (if I may so express myself) of the subscription. And then the President's company is a delicacy in itself."

"Indeed!" cried Geraldine, "he had not greatly prepossessed me."

"Ah!" said Mr. Malthus, "you do not know the man: the drollest fellow! What stories! What cynicism! He knows life to admiration and, between ourselves, is probably the most corrupt rogue in Christendom."

"And he also," asked the Colonel, "is a permanency—like yourself, if I may say so without offence?"

"Indeed, he is a permanency in a very different sense from me," replied Mr. Malthus. "I have been graciously spared, but I must go at last. Now he never plays. He shuffles and deals for the club, and makes the necessary arrangements. That man, my dear Mr. Hammersmith, is the very soul of ingenuity. For three years he has pursued in London his useful and, I think I may add, his artistic calling; and not so much as a whisper of suspicion has been once aroused. I believe him myself to be inspired. You doubtless remember the celebrated case, six months ago, of the gentleman who was accidentally poisoned in a chemist's shop? That was one of the least rich, one of the least racy, of his notions; but then, how simple! and how safe!"

"You astound me," said the Colonel. "Was that unfortunate gentleman one of the——" He was about to say "victims"; but bethinking himself in time, he substituted—"members of the club?"

In the same flash of thought, it occurred to him that Mr. Malthus himself had not at all spoken in the tone of one who is in love with death; and he added hurriedly:

"But I perceive I am still in the dark. You speak of shuffling and dealing; pray for what end? And since you seem rather unwilling to die than otherwise, I must own that I cannot conceive what brings you here at all."

"You say truly that you are in the dark," replied Mr. Malthus with more animation. "Why, my dear sir, this club is the temple of intoxication. If my enfeebled health could support the excitement more often, you may depend upon it I should be more often here. It requires all the sense of duty engendered by a long habit of ill-health and careful regimen, to keep me from excess in this, which is, I may say, my last dissipation. I have tried them all, sir," he went on, laying his hand on Geraldine's arm, "all without exception, and I declare to you, upon my honor, there is not one of them that has not been grossly and untruthfully overrated. People trifle with love. Now, I deny that love is a strong passion. Fear is the strong passion; it is with fear that you must trifle, if you wish to taste the intense joys of living. Envy me—envy me, sir," he added with a chuckle, "I am a coward!"

Geraldine could scarcely repress a movement of repulsion for this deplorable wretch; but he commanded himself with an effort, and continued his inquiries.

"How, sir," he asked, "is the excitement so artfully prolonged? and where is there any element of uncertainty?"

"I must tell you how the victim for every evening is selected," returned Mr. Malthus; "and not only the victim, but another member, who is to be the instrument in the club's hands, and death's high priest for that occasion."

"Good God!" said the Colonel, "do they then kill each other?"

"The trouble of suicide is removed in that way," returned Malthus with a nod.

"Merciful Heavens!" ejaculated the Colonel, "and may you—may I—may the—my friend, I mean—may any of us be pitched upon this evening as the slayer of another man's body and immortal spirit? Can such things be possible among men born of women? Oh! infamy of infamies!"

He was about to rise in his horror, when he caught the Prince's eye. It was fixed upon him from across the room with a frowning and angry stare. And in a moment Geraldine recovered his composure.

"After all," he added, "why not? And since you say the game is interesting, *vogue la galère*—I follow the club!"

Mr. Malthus had keenly enjoyed the Colonel's amazement and disgust. He had the vanity of wickedness; and it pleased him to see another man give way to a generous movement, while he felt himself, in his entire corruption, superior to such emotions.

"You now, after your first moment of surprise," said he, "are in a position to appreciate the delights of our society. You can see how it combines the excitement of a gaming-table, a duel, and a Roman amphitheatre. The Pagans did well enough; I cordially admire the refinement of their minds; but it has been reserved for a Christian country to attain this extreme, this quintessence, this absolute of poignancy. You will understand how vapid are all amusements to a man who has acquired a taste for this one. The game we play," he continued, "is one of extreme simplicity. A full pack—but I perceive you are about to see the thing in progress. Will you lend me the help of your arm? I am unfortunately paralyzed."

Indeed, just as Mr. Malthus was beginning his description, another pair of folding-doors was thrown open, and the whole club began to pass, not without some hurry, into the adjoining room. It was similar in every respect to the one from which it was entered, but somewhat differently furnished. The centre was occupied by a long green table, at which the President sat shuffling a pack of cards with great particularity. Even with the stick and the Colonel's arm, Mr. Malthus walked with so much difficulty that everyone was seated before this pair and the Prince, who had waited for them, entered the apartment; and, in consequence, the three took seats close together at the lower end of the board.

"It is a pack of fifty-two," whispered Mr. Malthus. "Watch for the ace of spades, which is the sign of death, and the ace of clubs, which designates the official of the night. Happy, happy young men!" he added. "You have good eyes, and can follow the game. Alas! I cannot tell an ace from a deuce across the table."

And he proceeded to equip himself with a second pair of spectacles.

"I must at least watch the faces," he explained.

The Colonel rapidly informed his friend of all that he had learned from the honorary member, and of the horrible alternative that lay before them. The Prince was conscious of a deadly chill and a contraction about his heart; he swallowed with difficulty, and looked from side to side like a man in a maze.

"One bold stroke," whispered the Colonel, "and we may still escape."

But the suggestion recalled the Prince's spirits.

"Silence!" said he. "Let me see that you can play like a gentleman for any stake, however serious."

And he looked about him, once more to all appearance at his ease, although his heart beat thickly, and he was conscious of an unpleasant heat in his bosom. The members were all very quiet and intent; everyone was pale, but none so pale as Mr. Malthus. His eyes protruded; his head kept nodding involuntarily upon his spine; his hands found their way, one after the other, to his mouth, where they made clutches at his tremulous and ashen lips. It was plain that the honorary member enjoyed his membership on very startling terms.

"Attention, gentlemen!" said the President.

And he began slowly dealing the cards about the table in the reverse direction, pausing until each man had shown his card. Nearly everyone hesitated; and sometimes you would see a player's fingers stumble more than once before he could turn over the momentous slip of pasteboard. As the Prince's turn drew nearer, he was conscious of a growing and almost suffocating excitement; but he had somewhat of the gambler's nature, and recognized almost with astonishment that there was a degree of pleasure in his sensations. The nine of clubs fell to his lot; the three of spades was dealt to Geraldine; and the queen of hearts to Mr. Malthus, who was unable to suppress a sob of relief. The young man of the cream tarts almost immediately afterwards turned over the ace of clubs, and remained frozen with horror, the card still resting on his finger; he had not come there to kill, but to be killed; and the Prince, in his generous sympathy with his position, almost forgot the peril that still hung over himself and his friend.

The deal was coming round again, and still Death's card had not come out. The players held their respiration, and only breathed by gasps. The Prince received another club; Geraldine had a diamond; but when Mr. Malthus turned up his card a horrible noise, like that of something breaking, issued from his mouth; and he rose from his seat and sat down again, with no sign of his paralysis. It was the ace of spades. The honorary member had trifled once too often with his terrors.

Conversation broke out again almost at once. The players relaxed their rigid attitudes, and began to rise from the table and stroll back by twos and threes into the smoking-room. The President stretched his arms and yawned, like a man who had finished his day's work. But Mr. Malthus sat in his place, with his head in his hands, and his hands upon the table, drunk and motionless—a thing stricken down.

The Prince and Geraldine made their escape at once. In the cold night air their horror of what they had witnessed was redoubled.

"Alas!" cried the Prince, "to be bound by an oath in such a matter! to allow this wholesale trade in murder to be continued with profit and impunity! If I but dared to forfeit my pledge!"

"That is impossible for your Highness," replied the Colonel, whose honor is the honor of Bohemia. "But I dare, and may with propriety, forfeit mine."

"Geraldine," said the Prince, "if your honor suffers in any of the adventures into which you follow me, not only will I never pardon you, but—what I believe will much more sensibly affect you—I should never forgive myself."

"I receive your Highness's commands," replied the Colonel. "Shall we go from this accursed spot?"

"Yes," said the Prince. "Call a cab in Heaven's name, and let me try to forget in slumber the memory of this night's disgrace."

But it was notable that he carefully read the name of the court before he left it.

The next morning, as soon as the Prince was stirring, Colonel Geraldine brought him a daily newspaper, with the following paragraph marked:

"Melancholy Accident.—This morning, about two o'clock, Mr. Bartholomew Malthus, of 16 Chepstow Place, Westbourne Grove, on his way home from a party at a friend's house, fell over the upper parapet in Trafalgar Square, fracturing his skull and breaking a leg and an arm. Death was instantaneous. Mr. Malthus, accompanied by a friend, was engaged in looking for a cab at the time of the unfortunate occurrence. As Mr. Malthus was paralytic, it is thought that his fall may have been occasioned by another seizure. The unhappy gentleman was well known in the most respectable circles, and his loss will be widely and deeply deplored."

"If ever a soul went straight to Hell," said Geraldine solemnly, "it was that paralytic man's."

The Prince buried his face in his hands, and remained silent.

"I am almost rejoiced," continued the Colonel, "to know that he is dead. But for our young man of the cream tarts I confess my heart bleeds."

"Geraldine," said the Prince, raising his face, "that unhappy lad was last night as innocent as you and I; and this morning the guilt of blood is on his soul. When I think of the President, my heart grows sick within me. I do not know how it shall be done, but I shall have that scoundrel at my mercy as there is a God in heaven. What an experience, what a lesson, was that game of cards!"

"One," said the Colonel, "never to be repeated."

The Prince remained so long without replying, that Geraldine grew alarmed.

"You cannot mean to return," he said. "You have suffered too much and seen too much horror already. The duties of your high position forbid the repetition of the hazard."

"There is much in what you say," replied Prince Florizel, "and I am not altogether pleased with my own determination. Alas! in the clothes of the greatest potentate, what is there but a man? I never felt my weakness more acutely than now, Geraldine, but it is stronger than I. Can I cease to interest myself in the fortunes of the unhappy young man who supped with us some hours ago? Can I leave the President to follow his nefarious career unwatched? Can I begin an adventure so entrancing, and not follow it to an end? No, Geraldine; you ask of the Prince more than the man is able to perform. To-night, once more, we take our places at the table of the Suicide Club."

Colonel Geraldine fell upon his knees.

"Will your Highness take my life?" he cried. "It is his—his freely; but do not, O do not! let him ask me to countenance so terrible a risk."

"Colonel Geraldine," replied the Prince, with some haughtiness of manner, "your life is absolutely your own. I only looked for obedience; and when that is unwillingly rendered, I shall look for that no longer. I add one word: your importunity in this affair has been sufficient."

The Master of the Horse regained his feet at once. "Your Highness," he said, "may I be excused in my attendance this afternoon? I dare not, as an honorable man, venture a second time into that fatal house until I have perfectly ordered my affairs. Your Highness shall meet, I promise him, with no more opposition from the most devoted and grateful of his servants."

"My dear Geraldine," returned Prince Florizel, "I always regret when you oblige me to remember my rank. Dispose of your day as you think fit, but be here before eleven in the same disguise."

The club, on this second evening, was not so fully attended; and when Geraldine and the Prince arrived, there were not above half-a-dozen persons in the smoking-room. His Highness took the President aside and congratulated him warmly on the demise of Mr. Malthus.

"I like," he said, "to meet with capacity, and certainly find much of it in you. Your profession is of a very delicate nature, but I see you are well qualified to conduct it with success and secrecy."

The President was somewhat affected by these compliments from one of his Highness's superior bearing. He acknowledged them almost with humility.

"Poor Malthy!" he added, "I shall hardly know the club without him. The most of my patrons are boys, sir, and poetical boys, who are not much company for me. Not but what Malthy had some poetry, too; but it was of a kind that I could understand."

"I can readily imagine you should find yourself in sympathy with Mr. Malthus," returned the Prince. "He struck me as a man of a very original disposition."

The young man of the cream tarts was in the room, but painfully depressed and silent. His late companions sought in vain to lead him into conversation.

"How bitterly I wish," he cried, "that I had never brought you to this infamous abode! Begone, while you are clean-handed. If you could have heard the old man scream as he fell, and the noise of his bones upon the pavement! Wish me, if you have any kindness to so fallen a being—wish the ace of spades for me to-night!"

A few more members dropped in as the evening went on, but the club did not muster more than the devil's dozen when they took their places at the table. The Prince was again conscious of a certain joy in his alarms; but he was astonished to see Geraldine so much more self-possessed than on the night before.

"It is extraordinary," thought the Prince, "that a will, made or unmade, should so greatly influence a young man's spirit."

"Attention, gentlemen!" said the President, and he began to deal.

Three times the cards went all round the table, and neither of the marked cards had yet fallen from his hand. The excitement as he began the fourth distribution was overwhelming. There were just cards enough to go once more entirely round. The Prince, who sat second from the dealer's left, would receive, in the reverse mode of dealing practiced at the club, the second last card. The third player turned up a black ace—it was the ace of clubs. The next received a diamond, the next a heart, and so on; but the ace of spades was still undelivered. At last Geraldine, who sat upon the Prince's left, turned his card; it was an ace, but the ace of hearts.

When Prince Florizel saw his fate upon the table in front of him, his heart stood still. He was a brave man, but the sweat poured off his face. There were exactly fifty chances out of a hundred that he was doomed. He reversed the card; it was the ace of spades. A loud roaring filled his brain, and the table swam before his eyes. He heard the player on his right break into a fit of laughter that sounded between mirth and disappointment; he saw the company rapidly dispersing, but his mind was full of other thoughts. He recognized how foolish, how criminal, had been his conduct. In perfect health, in the prime of his years, the heir to a throne, he had gambled away his future and that of a brave and loyal country. "God," he cried, "God forgive me!" And with that, the confusion of his senses passed away, and he regained his self-possession in a moment.

To his surprise Geraldine had disappeared. There was no one in the card-room but his destined butcher consulting with the President, and the young man of the cream tarts, who slipped up to the Prince and whispered in his ear:

"I would give a million, if I had it, for your luck."

His Highness could not help reflecting, as the young man departed, that he would have sold his opportunity for a much more moderate sum.

The whispered conference now came to an end. The holder of the ace of clubs left the room with a look of intelligence, and the President, approaching the unfortunate Prince, proffered him his hand.

"I am pleased to have met you, sir," said he, "and pleased to have been in a position to do you this trifling service. At least, you cannot complain of delay. On the second evening—what a stroke of luck!"

The Prince endeavored in vain to articulate something in response, but his mouth was dry and his tongue seemed paralyzed.

"You feel a little sickish?" asked the President, with some show of solicitude. "Most gentlemen do. Will you take a little brandy?"

The Prince signified in the affirmative, and the other immediately filled some of the spirit into a tumbler.

"Poor old Malthy!" ejaculated the President, as the Prince drained the glass. "He drank near upon a pint, and little enough good it seemed to do him!"

"I am more amenable to treatment," said the Prince, a good deal revived. "I am my own man again at once, as you perceive. And so, let me ask you, what are my directions?"

"You will proceed along the Strand in the direction of the City, and on the left-hand pavement, until you meet the gentleman who has just left the room. He will continue your instructions, and him you will have the kindness to obey; the authority of the club is vested in his person for the night. And now," added the President, "I wish you a pleasant walk."

Florizel acknowledged the salutation rather awkwardly, and took his leave. He passed through the smoking-room, where the bulk of the players were still consuming champagne, some of which he had himself ordered and paid for; and he was surprised to find himself cursing them in his heart. He put on his hat and great coat in the cabinet, and selected his umbrella from a corner. The familiarity of these acts, and the thought that he was about them for the last time, betrayed him into a fit of laughter which sounded unpleasantly in his own ears. He conceived a reluctance to leave the cabinet, and turned instead to the window. The sight of the lamps and the darkness recalled him to himself.

"Come, come, I must be a man," he thought, "and tear myself away."

At the corner of Box Court three men fell upon Prince Florizel and he was unceremoniously thrust into a carriage, which at once drove rapidly away. There was already an occupant.

"Will your Highness pardon my zeal?" said a well-known voice.

The Prince threw himself upon the Colonel's neck in a passion of relief. "How can I ever thank you?" he cried. "And how was this effected?"

Although he had been willing to march upon his doom, he was overjoyed to yield to friendly violence, and return once more to life and hope.

"You can thank me effectually enough," replied the Colonel, "by avoiding all such dangers in the future. And as for your second question, all has been managed by the simplest means. I arranged this afternoon with a celebrated detective. Secrecy has been promised and paid for. Your own servants have been principally engaged in the affair. The house in Box Court has been surrounded since nightfall, and this, which is one of your own carriages, has been awaiting you for nearly an hour."

"And the miserable creature who was to have slain me—what of him?" inquired the Prince.

"He was pinioned as he left the club," replied the Colonel, "and now awaits your sentence at the Palace, where he will soon be joined by his accomplices."

"Geraldine," said the Prince, "you have saved me against my explicit orders, and you have done well. I owe you not only my life, but a lesson; and

I should be unworthy of my rank if I did not show myself grateful to my teacher. Let it be yours to choose the manner."

There was a pause, during which the carriage continued to speed through the streets, and the two men were each buried in his own reflections. The silence was broken by Colonel Geraldine.

"Your Highness," said he, "has by this time a considerable body of prisoners. There is at least one criminal among the number to whom justice should be dealt. Our oath forbids us all recourse to law; and discretion would forbid it equally if the oath were loosened. May I inquire your Highness's intention?"

"It is decided," answered Florizel; "the President must fall in duel. It only remains to choose his adversary."

"Your Highness has permitted me to name my own recompense," said the Colonel. "Will he permit me to ask the appointment of my brother? It is an honorable post, but I dare assure your Highness that the lad will acquit himself with credit."

"You ask me an ungracious favor," said the Prince, "but I must refuse you nothing."

The Colonel kissed his hand with the greatest affection; and at that moment the carriage rolled under the archway of the Prince's splendid residence.

An hour after, Florizel in his official robes, and covered with all the orders of Bohemia, received the members of the Suicide Club.

"Foolish and wicked men," said he, "as many of you as have been driven into this strait by the lack of fortune shall receive employment and remuneration from my officers. Those who suffer under a sense of guilt must have recourse to a higher and more generous Potentate than I. I feel pity for all of you, deeper than you can imagine; to-morrow you shall tell me your stories; and as you answer more frankly, I shall be the more able to remedy your misfortunes. As for you," he added, turning to the President, "I should only offend a person of your parts by any offer of assistance; but I have instead a piece of diversion to propose to you. Here," laying his hand on the shoulder of Colonel Geraldine's young brother, "is an officer of mine who desires to make a little tour upon the Continent; and I ask you, as a favor, to accompany him on this excursion. Do you," he went on, changing his tone, "do you shoot well with the pistol? Because you may have need of that accomplishment. When two men go traveling together, it is best to be prepared for all. Let me add that, if by any chance you should lose young Mr. Geraldine upon the way, I shall always have another member of my household to place at your disposal; and I am known, Mr. President, to have long eyesight, and as long an arm."

With these words, said with much sternness, the Prince concluded his address. Next morning the members of the club were suitably provided for by his munificence, and the President set forth upon his travels, under the supervision of Mr. Geraldine, and a pair of faithful and adroit lackeys, well trained in the Prince's household. Not content with this, discreet agents were put in possession of the house of Box Court, and all letters of visitors for the Suicide Club or its officials were to be examined by Prince Florizel in person.

Here (says my Arabian author) *ends* THE STORY OF THE YOUNG MAN WITH THE CREAM TARTS, *who is now a comfortable householder in Wigmore Street, Cavendish Square. The number, for obvious reasons, I suppress.*

EIGHTEEN OAK TIES

TIM PRIDGEN

LITTLE Burney Lanksher was five years old and he had on pants. Not his pants. Pants. He was not interested in them. They had more to do with Grantville than with him. His ma put him in them, every-day shirt and all, like something in a bucket, whenever his pa took him to Grantville. Whoever went to the railroad with his pa, Jack or Pep or Burney, wore the pants. They stayed on because they had a gallus. They were big, stiff corduroys, cut down, but did not fit. But you wore them when you went to Grantville.

Burney reached up to his almost white tow hair and scratched a mosquito bite. His hair was stiff and bristly with little ridges in it where yesterday his ma, in preparation for the trip, cut it dam'-nigh all off. Quietly, while Nigger mule pounded his hoofs in the grit-pomp, pomp, Burney watched the left wheel, at the front of the one-horse wagon, turn over. He paid no atten-tion to the wide spread scene of white sandhills, covered thinly with scrub oaks and wire grass, with a few tall, long-leaf pines reaching up. His eyes sought the thing that moved most. Grit worked in between the tire and the felloe and popped. The axle was worn and the wheel leaned first in and now out, as it turned. Pa had stuffed soft soap into the hub yesterday and the axle didn't squeak as almost always it did. When the sand rut ran with water, down near the branches, the wheels made purling sounds, like music. But it was a long way between branches and Nigger mule went so slow. Burney twisted in his brown pants, sighed, looked up at his pa on the same seat and smiled.

"Reckon we'll see a train?" he asked.

His pa was a gaunt, quiet man with a drooping black mustache. He wore a dark felt hat with dust caked into the brim of it. Over his faded hickory shirt, bed-ticking galluses crossed where his long back bent, to lean on his knees, while he sat and drove.

His pa did not answer at once, did not move, only said: "Chr-r-r-k, chr-r-r-k!" to Nigger mule. Then he slowly switched his tobacco from one cheek to the other, and spat over the right wheel.

First published in *Cavalcade Magazine*. Reprinted by permission of Fremont C. Peck.

"Reckon not," he drawled. "We got to go and come. Extry special business."

"Why-y-y, pa?" Burney wanted to see a train.

"Impawtant business, I told you. Life and death, like. Got to hurry. Now shet up. I got things on my mind."

"Wished I could see a train," Burney said futilely, easily, like a breeze blowing.

Almost they were at Grantville. It was a big place. It had a railroad and a depot and two stores, a big one and a little one. And the section master's house. Already they could see the station. It was a flat little building with a dull red tin roof and lead colored paint on the sides, with brown stripes at the corners. The paint was peeling off in dry splinters.

Burney's pa drove on by the big time store and lumbered over the railroad track toward Jerry Merdy's little store. He drove up to a tree and stopped, stepping to the ground and hitching Nigger mule to a limb. Burney clambered out. They spoke to Jerry, on the store porch, and walked toward the railroad tool house, where the section force was working.

Cap'n Darney, the section master, was a tall, red-faced, thin man, well-dressed in clean overalls, with a big gold watch chain hung across his chest. He made a lot of money, some said $110 a month.

"I come to see you about getting out some tiars, cap'n," Burney's pa told him.

"Oak ties?" Cap'n Darney said, looking sideways, like he was listening for something bad.

"No. Pine tiars."

The section master shook his head.

"They ain't buyin' none. They want oak ties."

Burney's pa's lips closed tight and his Adam's apple went up and down, as if he swallowed. He didn't say anything.

"I was scared of that," he said quietly. "I don't practically never have no luck."

"How's that?" asked the Cap'n.

"Well—it's this way. Me and Henry and Bill—we can get out pine tiars all right. But if I put enough pressure on my little old b'iler to saw oak tiars—she'll bust, shore."

"I wouldn't want to be around no b'iler when it busts," Cap'n Darney said. "Somebody's liable to git killed."

"That's the trouble."

"Well—maybe—after Christmas—"

Burney's pa shook his head so quick that Cap'n Darney stopped talking.

"I can't wait until after Christmas. My cotton wasn't wuth shucks this year and I'm out of money. I got to scrape up some, short off. My wife's in a delicate way, and some other time won't do."

"Oh, in a case like that, Doc Reynolds'll trust you."

"No, cap'n."

Again Burney's pa shook his head.

"No. I ain't never asked him to trust me. I allus had the notion that if he knew the cash money was waitin', he'd come quicker and do better. That's human nature. I got a mighty fine wife, cap'n, and I ain't takin' no chances. A womern has hard enough time with everything in her favor."

"That's right," Cap'n Darney agreed.

"Wish to goodness the railroad was buyin' pine tiars."

"Wish so. You reckon your b'iler would really bust?"

"Reckon so."

"Well—maybe—after Christmas—"

"Can't wait. Now—lemme see—fifteen dollars for Doc Reynolds and seven dollars for Granny Boyce—that's twenty-two dollars. How much you payin' for oak tiars?"

"Dollar twenty-five. Eighteen would come to twenty-two-fifty. But you ain't figuring on sawing oak ties with a weak b'iler, are you?"

Burney looked up without much interest at his tall, sad pa. He never saw a boiler burst. No boilers he ever saw burst.

"Maybe not. Maybe so. Hadn't thought much about it," his pa said, turning back toward Nigger mule. Burney wondered why the section master looked after them so strangely.

As they walked along the track, Burney's pa kept looking down at the ties on which they walked.

"Don't see why a train can't run on pine tiars the same as oak tiars," he complained.

Burney didn't care. He was getting tired and sleepy. He yawned. His pa took off his corduroy pants at the wagon, made a pillow in the wagon bed, and it was dark when he woke up at home.

The next morning when he got up and had breakfast he found his pa and Henry and Bill had hitched Nigger mule to the wagon and were loading axes and saws for a trip to the woods.

Burney's ma was sitting in the doorway, her hands under her apron watching them. She was thin and blue-eyed and tired-looking and Burney thought her very beautiful.

"Anybody seen that piece of hay war I had in the barn?" his pa asked, coming up to her.

"What you want with hay war?" she asked suspiciously. "You going to tie down the valve and cut oak tiars?"

Burney's pa laughed loudly. He laughed until he bent over.

"What a fool question," he declared. "Don't you know we can't saw oak tiars with that b'iler?"

"Are you?" she asked. "Won't the railroad buy pine tiars?"

"Who said the railroad wouldn't buy pine tiars?" he demanded.

"The man," Burney spoke up, "said he didn't want no pine tiars."

"Ah-h-h!" Burney's pa said, "you didn't hear him right."

"Don't do it! Don't you dare do it!" Burney's ma said.

She stood up and grasped him by the shirt. Her eyes were hard and bright. She kind of shook his pa and her voice sounded as if she hurt. Burney thought she was going to cry and felt angry at his pa.

"Now Bessie," his pa said, speaking tenderly, taking her hands and making her sit down. "Don't concern yourself with men's business. You've got plenty to worry about without that."

He turned and went to the wagon. Henry and Bill were waiting for him. Henry was sixteen and had big, wide shoulders and wore brogan shoes. Bill was only fourteen and was barefoot. They drove off, the wagon and the tools clattering as the wheels ran over roots in the lane. Burney's ma sat in the doorway and looked after them. Her chin was trembling, and Burney wondered why.

That was a very poor day for Burney. The other children, Jack and Jill and Pep and Millie, went out and played, but his mother's drawn, white face continued before him and he remained at her side. She said nothing and let him stay.

An hour later they began to hear, far away, the sharp bite of axes in trees. She gazed that way with strained eyes and he looked at her and was troubled.

He went into the front room to look at the pictures on the newspapers which were pasted on the walls, but when he called to her to come and tell him what words spelled, she would not. That was puzzling. She always had. She liked to spell the words for him, and, when she knew, tell him what they meant.

More strangely still, she would not come when he called to her to tell him about the picture which hung over the fireplace. It was in an old-fashioned frame, a queer man with a big plume on his hat and a sword under his cape. That, Burney's ma always told him proudly, was his grampa's grampa, and a great fine gentleman. Burney did not understand that. His pa had no sword.

But today his ma would not come to him and talk about the man with the plume, but sat in her splint-bottom chair at the door and listened to the axes chopping.

It became noon and she grew angry. She left her place at the door and went to the kitchen. She built a fire in the cookstove and heated a pot of beans. When these were warm, she poured them in a dish and set it on the table so solidly it almost broke.

"Come and get it!" she called out the door to the children, and her voice was harsh and ill-tempered. She, herself, ate nothing, but sat at the door and listened to the axes. Burney ate and went back to her side.

For a time there was quiet in the woods, but still his mother sat and listened and looked, as if she could see and hear every move they made. Now and then she sighed, but she never smiled. Burney tried to make her smile by rubbing her hand over his short hair, but she pushed him away, and continued to look always in the direction of his tall, sad pa, who was out there in the woods getting out tiars.

Millie was a big girl of twelve. She asked if she might take the twins down in the woods where her pa was.

"No!" his ma snapped. "No!"

All the children looked on, strangely quiet, passed around her and went out to play, but Burney gathered to himself the grimness which wore at her heart and sat with her, suffering and not knowing why. He yawned and slept awhile.

There finally came a rumbling sound from the woods, which Burney knew was the noise from the boiler and engine, followed by the scream of the little circular saw as it bit into the first log. Burney's ma seemed to feel that scream as something that was like a chill. She leaned forward in her chair, grasping it and holding on until her fingers were white.

The wind changed and the rumble of the mill could not be heard. She sat for a long time listening and could hear nothing. Then, as the sun moved westward, she carried her little chair to the porch and sat in the shade of a clematis vine. There, whitely, she listened and now and then could hear the whine of the saw in the hard logs.

For the remainder of the day she sat until the sun was sinking into a black cloud. A thunderstorm began to rumble and Burney could not say which noise was which, whether it was the storm or the sawmill which made those sharp, exploding sounds. Nor could his mother. She was afraid of storms, but when the thunder ripped through the sky she did not move, but sat still, staring toward the woods, saying prayers in shrill, whispered words to God.

Then, before long, there was a clatter down the lane and Nigger mule came galloping in, bumping the wagon over the roots, heading for the stable before the storm broke. Henry and Bill went on to the barn, but Burney's pa jumped to the ground and came to the house.

He took Burney's ma's hands and lifted her upright from the chair and she took both his hands in hers and rubbed them softly. Their eyes had a sort of glow as they looked at each other, but Burney's ma and pa never were great hands to say much.

"Well—we got 'em all out—eighteen good oak tiars," his pa said, leading the way to the wash basin on the back porch shelf.

"I've been pretty lazy, myself," his ma said. "Jest set around all day."

ULTIMA THULE

JOHN GALSWORTHY

ULTIMA THULE! The words come into my head this winter night. That is why I write down the story, as I know it, of a little old friend.

I used to see him first in Kensington Gardens, where he came in the afternoons, accompanied by a very small girl. One would see them silent before a shrub or flower, or with their heads inclined to heaven before a tree, or leaning above water and the ducks, or stretched on their stomachs watching a beetle, or on their backs watching the sky. Often they would stand holding crumbs out to the birds, who would perch about them, and even drop on their arms little white marks of affection and esteem. They were admittedly a noticeable couple. The child, who was fair-haired and elfinlike, with dark eyes and a pointed chin, wore clothes that seemed somewhat hard put to it. And, if the two were not standing still, she went along pulling at his hand, eager to get there; and, since he was a very little, light old man, he seemed always in advance of his own feet. He was garbed, if I remember, in a daverdy brown overcoat and broad-brimmed soft grey hat, and his trousers, what was visible of them, were tucked into half-length black gaiters which tried to join with very old brown shoes. Indeed, his costume did not indicate any great share of prosperity. But it was his face that riveted attention. Thin, cherry-red, and wind-dried as old wood, it had a special sort of brightness, with its spikes and waves of silvery hair, and blue eyes which seemed to shine. Rather mad, I used to think. Standing by the rails of an enclosure, with his withered lips pursed and his cheeks drawn in till you would think the wind might blow through them, he would emit the most enticing trills and pipings, exactly imitating various birds.

Those who rouse our interest are generally the last people we speak to, for interest seems to set up a kind of special shyness; so it was long before I made his acquaintance. But one day by the Serpentine, I saw him coming along alone, looking sad, but still with that queer brightness about him. He sat down on my bench with his little dried hands on his thin little knees, and began talking to himself in a sort of whisper. Presently I caught the

From *Caravan* by John Galsworthy (Charles Scribner's Sons, 1925).

words: "God cannot be like us." And for fear that he might go on uttering such precious remarks that were obviously not intended to be heard, I had either to go away or else address him. So, on an impulse, I said:

"Why?"

He turned without surprise.

"I've lost my landlady's little girl," he said. "Dead! And only seven years old."

"That little thing I used to watch you with?"

"Did you? Did you? I'm glad you saw her."

"I used to see you looking at flowers, and trees, and those ducks."

His face brightened wistfully. "Yes; she was a great companion to an old man like me." And he relapsed into his contemplation of the water. He had a curious, precise way of speaking, that matched his pipchinesque little old face. At last he again turned to me those blue youthful eyes which seemed to shine out of a perfect little nest of crow's-feet.

"We were great friends! But I couldn't expect it. Things don't last, do they?" I was glad to notice that his voice was getting cheerful. "When I was in the orchestra at the Harmony Theatre, it never used to occur to me that some day I shouldn't play there any more. One felt like a bird. That's the beauty of music, sir. You lose yourself; like that blackbird there." He imitated the note of a blackbird so perfectly that I could have sworn the bird started.

"Birds and flowers! Wonderful things; wonderful! Why, even a buttercup——!" He pointed at one of those little golden flowers with his toe. "Did you ever see such a marvellous thing?" And he turned his face up at me. "And yet, somebody told me once that they don't agree with cows. Now can that be? I'm not a countryman—though I was born at Kingston."

"The cows do well enough on them," I said, "in my part of the world. In fact, the farmers say they like to see buttercups."

"I'm glad to hear you say that. I was always sorry to think they disagreed." When I got up to go, he rose, too.

"I take it as very kind of you," he said, "to have spoken to me."

"The pleasure was mine. I am generally to be found hereabouts in the afternoons any time you like a talk."

"Delighted," he said; "delighted. I make friends of the creatures and flowers as much as possible, but they can't always make us understand." And after we had taken off our respective hats, he reseated himself, with his hands on his knees.

Next time I came across him standing by the rails of an enclosure, and, in his arms, an old and really wretched-looking cat.

"I don't like boys," he said, without preliminary of any sort. "What do you think they were doing to this poor old cat? Dragging it along by a string to drown it; see where it's cut into the fur! I think boys despise the old and weak!" He held it out to me. At the ends of those little sticks of arms the beast looked more dead than alive; I had never seen a more miserable creature.

"I think a cat," he said, "is one of the most marvellous things in the world. Such a depth of life in it."

And, as he spoke, the cat opened its mouth as if protesting at that assertion. It *was* the sorriest-looking beast.

"What are you going to do with it?"

"Take it home; it looks to me as if it might die."

"You don't think that might be more merciful?"

"It depends; it depends. I shall see. I fancy a little kindness might do a great deal for it. It's got plenty of spirit. I can see from its eye."

"May I come along with you a bit?"

"Oh!" he said; "delighted."

We walked on side by side, exciting the derision of nearly everyone we passed—his face looked so like a mother's when she is feeding her baby!

"You'll find this'll be quite a different cat to-morrow," he said. "I shall have to get in, though, without my landlady seeing; a funny woman! I have two or three strays already."

"Can I help in any way?"

"Thank you," he said. "I shall ring the area bell, and as she comes out below I shall go in above. She'll think it's boys. They *are* like that."

"But doesn't she do your rooms, or anything?"

A smile puckered his face. "I've only one; I do it myself. Oh, it'd never do to have her about, even if I could afford it. But," he added, "if you're so kind as to come with me to the door, you might engage her by asking where Mr. Thompson lives. That's me. In the musical world my name was Moronelli; not that I have Italian blood in me, of course."

"And shall I come up?"

"Honoured; but I live very quietly."

We passed out of the gardens at Lancaster Gate, where all the house-fronts seem so successful, and out of it into a little street that was extremely like a grubby child trying to hide under its mother's skirts. Here he took a newspaper from his pocket and wrapped it round the cat.

"She's a funny woman," he repeated; "Scotch descent, you know." Suddenly he pulled an area bell and scuttled up the steps.

When he had opened the door, however, I saw before him in the hall a short, thin woman dressed in black, with a sharp and bumpy face. Her voice sounded brisk and resolute.

"What have you got there, Mr. Thompson?"

"Newspaper, Mrs. March."

"Oh, indeed! Now, you're not going to take that cat upstairs!"

The little old fellow's voice acquired a sudden shrill determination. "Stand aside, please. If you stop me, I'll give you notice. The cat is going up. It's ill, and it is going up."

It was then I said:

"Does Mr. Thompson live here?"

In that second he shot past her, and ascended.

"That's him," she said; "and I wish it wasn't, with his dirty cats. Do you want him?"

"I do."

"He lives at the top." Then, with a grudging apology: "I can't help it; he tries me—he's very trying."

"I am sure he is."

She looked at me. The longing to talk that comes over those who answer bells all day, and the peculiar Scottish desire to justify oneself, rose together in that face which seemed all promontories dried by an east wind.

"Ah!" she said; "he is. I don't deny his heart; but he's got no sense of anything. Goodness knows what he hasn't got up there. I wonder I keep him. An old man like that ought to know better; half-starving himself to feed them." She paused, and her eyes, which had a cold and honest glitter, searched me closely.

"If you're going up," she said, "I hope you'll give him good advice. He never lets me in. I wonder I keep him."

There were three flights of stairs, narrow, clean, and smelling of oilcloth. Selecting one of two doors at random, I knocked. His silvery head and bright, pinched face were cautiously poked out.

"Ah!" he said; "I thought it might be her!"

The room, which was fairly large, had a bare floor with little on it save a camp-bed and chest of drawers with jug and basin. A large bird-cage on the wall hung wide open. The place smelt of soap and a little of beasts and birds. Into the walls, whitewashed over a green wall-paper which stared through in places, were driven nails with their heads knocked off, on to which bits of wood had been spiked, so that they stood out as bird-perches high above the ground. Over the open window a piece of wire-netting had been fixed. A little spirit-stove and an old dressing-gown hanging on a peg completed the accoutrements of a room which one entered with a certain diffidence. He had not exaggerated. Besides the new cat, there were three other cats and four birds, all—save one, a bullfinch—invalids. The cats kept close to the walls, avoiding me, but wherever my little old friend went they followed him with their eyes. The birds were in the cage, except the bullfinch, which had perched on his shoulder.

"How on earth," I said, "do you manage to keep cats and birds in one room?"

"There is danger," he answered, "but I have not had a disaster yet. Till their legs or wings are mended, they hardly come out of the cage; and after that they keep up on my perches. But they don't stay long, you know, when they're once well. That wire is only put over the window while they're mending; it'll be off to-morrow for this lot."

"And then they'll go?"

"Yes. The sparrow first, and then the two thrushes."

"And this fellow?"

"Ask him," he said. "Would *you* go, bully?" But the bullfinch did not deign to answer.

"And were all those cats, too, in trouble?"

"Yes," he said. "They wouldn't want me if they weren't."

Thereupon he began to warm some blue-looking milk, contemplating the new cat, which he had placed in a round basket close to the little stove, while the bullfinch sat on his head. It seemed time to go.

"Delighted to see you, sir," he said, "any day." And, pointing up at the bullfinch on his head, he added: "Did you ever see anything so wonderful as that bird? The size of its heart! Really marvellous."

To the rapt sound of that word marvellous, and full of the memory of his mysterious brightness while he stood pointing upward to the bird perched on his thick, silvery hair, I went.

The landlady was still at the bottom of the stairs, and began at once. "So you found him! I don't know why I keep him. Of course, he was kind to my little girl." I saw tears gather in her eyes.

"With his cats and his birds, I wonder I keep him! But where would he go? He's no relations, and no friends—not a friend in the world, I think! He's a character. Lives on air—feeding them cats! I've no patience with them, eating him up. He never lets me in. Cats and birds! I wonder I keep him. Losing himself for those rubbishy things! It's my belief he was always like that; and that's why he never got on. He's no sense of anything."

And she gave me a shrewd look, wondering, no doubt, what the deuce I had come about.

I did not come across him again in the gardens for some time, and went at last to pay him a call. At the entrance to a mews just round the corner of his grubby little street, I found a knot of people collected round one of those bears that are sometimes led through the less conspicuous streets of our huge towns. The yellowish beast was sitting up in deference to its master's rod, uttering little grunts, and moving its uplifted snout from side to side, in the way bears have. But it seemed to be extracting more amusement than money from its audience.

"Let your bear down off its hind legs and I'll give you a penny." And suddenly I saw my little old friend under his flopping grey hat, amongst the spectators, all taller than himself. But the bear's master only grinned and prodded the animal in the chest. He evidently knew a good thing when he saw it.

"I'll give you twopence to let him down."

Again the bear-man grinned. "More!" he said, and again prodded the bear's chest. The spectators were laughing now.

"Threepence! And if you don't let him down for that, I'll hit you in the eye."

The bear-man held out his hand. "All a-right," he said, "threepence: I let him down."

I saw the coins pass and the beast dropping on his forefeet; but just then a policeman coming in sight, the man led his bear off, and I was left alone with my little old friend.

"I wish I had that poor bear," he said: "I could teach him to be happy. But, even if I could buy him, what could I do with him up there? She's such a funny woman."

He looked quite dim, but brightened as we went along.

"A bear," he said, "is really an extraordinary animal. What wise little eyes he has! I do think he's a marvellous creation! My cats will have to go without their dinner, though. I was going to buy it with that threepence."

I begged to be allowed the privilege.

"Willingly!" he said. "Shall we go in here? They like cod's head best."

While we stood waiting to be served I saw the usual derisive smile pass over the fishmonger's face. But my little old friend by no means noticed it; he was too busy looking at the fish. "A fish is a marvellous thing, when you come to think of it," he murmured. "Look at its scales. Did you ever see such mechanism?"

We bought five cod's heads, and I left him carrying them in a bag, evidently lost in the anticipation of five cats eating them.

After that I saw him often, going with him sometimes to buy food for his cats, which seemed ever to increase in numbers. His talk was always of his strays, and the marvels of creation, and that time of his life when he played the flute at the Harmony Theatre. He had been out of a job, it seemed, for more than ten years; and, when questioned, only sighed and answered: "Don't talk about it, please!"

His bumpy landlady never failed to favour me with a little conversation. She was one of those women who have terrific consciences, and terrible grudges against them.

"I never get out," she would say.

"Why not?"

"Couldn't leave the house."

"It won't run away!"

But she would look at me as if she thought it might, and repeat:

"Oh! I never get out."

An extremely Scottish temperament.

Considering her descent, however, she was curiously devoid of success, struggling on apparently from week to week, cleaning, and answering the bell, and never getting out, and wondering why she kept my little old friend; just as he struggled on from week to week, getting out and collecting strays, and discovering the marvels of creation, and finding her a funny woman. Their hands were joined, one must suppose, by that dead child.

One July afternoon, however, I found her very much upset. He had been taken dangerously ill three days before.

"There he is," she said; "can't touch a thing. It's my belief he's done for himself, giving his food away all these years to those cats of his. I shooed 'em out to-day, the nasty creatures; they won't get in again."

"Oh!" I said, "you shouldn't have done that. It'll only make him miserable."

She flounced her head up. "Hoh!" she said: "I wonder I've kept him all this time, with his birds and his cats dirtying my house. And there he lies, talking gibberish about them. He made me write to a Mr. Jackson, of some theatre or other—I've no patience with him. And that little bullfinch all the time perching on his pillow, the dirty little thing! I'd have turned it out, too, only it wouldn't let me catch it."

"What does the doctor say?"

"Double pneumonia—caught it getting his feet wet, after some stray, I'll be bound. I'm nursing him. There has to be someone with him all the time."

He was lying very still when I went up, with the sunlight falling across the foot of his bed, and, sure enough, the bullfinch perching on his pillow. In that high fever he looked brighter than ever. He was not exactly delirious, yet not exactly master of his thoughts.

"Mr. Jackson! He'll be here soon. Mr. Jackson! He'll do it for me. I can ask him, if I die. A funny woman. I don't want to eat; I'm not a great eater —I want my breath, that's all."

At sound of his voice the bullfinch fluttered off the pillow and flew round and round the room, as if alarmed at something new in the tones that were coming from its master.

Then he seemed to recognise me. "I think I'm going to die," he said; "I'm very weak. It's lucky there's nobody to mind. If only he'd come soon. I wish" —and he raised himself with feeble excitement—"I wish you'd take that wire off the window; I want my cats. She turned them out. I want him to promise me to take them, and bully-boy, and feed them with my money, when I'm dead."

Seeing that excitement was certainly worse for him than cats, I took the wire off. He fell back, quiet at once; and presently, first one and then another cat came stealing in, till there were four or five seated against the walls. The moment he ceased to speak the bullfinch, too, came back to his pillow. His eyes looked most supernaturally bright, staring out of his little, withered-up old face at the sunlight playing on his bed; he said just audibly: "Did you ever see anything more wonderful than that sunlight? It's really marvellous!" After that he fell into a sort of doze or stupor. And I continued to sit there in the window, relieved, but rather humiliated, that he had not asked me to take care of his cats and bullfinch.

Presently there came the sound of a motor-car in the little street below. And almost at once the landlady appeared. For such an abrupt woman, she entered very softly.

"Here he is," she whispered.

I went out and found a gentleman, perhaps sixty years of age, in a black coat, buff waistcoat, gold watch-chain, light trousers, patent-leather boots, and a wonderfully shining hat. His face was plump and red, with a glossy grey moustache; indeed, he seemed to shine everywhere, save in the eyes, which were of a dull and somewhat liverish hue.

"Mr. Jackson?"

"The same. How is the little old chap?"

Opening the door of the next room, which I knew was always empty, I beckoned Mr. Jackson in.

"He's really very ill; I'd better tell you what he wants to see you about."

He looked at me with that air of "You can't get at me—whoever you may be," which belongs to the very successful.

"Right-o!" he said. "Well?"

I described the situation. "He seems to think," I ended, "that you'll be kind enough to charge yourself with his strays, in case he should die."

Mr. Jackson prodded the unpainted washstand with his gold-headed cane. "Is he really going to kick it?"

"I'm afraid so; he's nothing but skin, bone, and spirit, as it is."

"H'm! Stray cats, you say, and a bird! Well, there's no accounting. He was always a cracky little chap. So that's it! When I got the letter I wondered what the deuce! We pay him his five quid a quarter regular to this day. To tell truth, he deserved it. Thirty years he was at our shop; never missed a night. First-rate flute he was. He ought never to have given it up, though I always thought it showed a bit of heart in him. If a man don't look after number one, he's as good as gone; that's what I've always found. Why, I was no more than he was when I started. Shouldn't have been worth a plum if I'd gone on his plan, that's certain." And he gave that profound chuckle which comes from the very stomach of success. "We were having a rocky time at the Harmony; had to cut down everything we could—music, well, that came about first. Little old Moronelli, as we used to call him— old Italian days before English names came in, you know—he was far the best of the flutes; so I went to him and said: 'Look here, Moronelli, which of these other boys had better go?' 'Oh!' he said—I remember his funny little old mug now—'has one of them to go, Mr. Jackson? Timminsa'—that was the elder—'he's a wife and family; and Smetoni'—Smith, you know—'he's only a boy. Times are bad for flutes.' 'I know it's a bit hard,' I said, 'but this theatre's goin' to be run much cheaper; one of 'em's got to get.' 'Oh!' he said, 'dear me!' he said. What a funny little old chap it was! Well—what do you think? Next day I had his resignation. Give you my word I did my best to turn him. Why, he was sixty then if he was a day—at sixty a man don't get jobs in a hurry. But not a bit of it! All he'd say was: 'I shall get a place all right!' But that's it, you know—he never did. Too long in one shop. I heard by accident he was on the rocks; that's how I make him that allowance. But that's the sort of hopeless little old chap he is—no idea of himself. Cats! Why not? I'll take his old cats on; don't you let him worry about that. I'll see to his bird, too. If I can't give 'em a better time than ever they have here, it'll be funny!" And, looking round the little empty room, he again uttered that profound chuckle: "Why, he was with us at the Harmony thirty years—that's time, you know; I made my fortune in it."

"I'm sure," I said, "it'll be a great relief to him."

"Oh! Ah! That's all right. You come down to my place"—he handed me a card: 'Mr. Cyril Porteous Jackson, Ultima Thule, Wimbledon'—"and see how I fix 'em up. But if he's really going to kick it, I'd like to have a look at the little old chap, just for old times' sake."

We went, as quietly as Mr. Jackson's bright boots would permit, into his room, where the landlady was sitting gazing angrily at the cats. She went out without noise, flouncing her head as much as to say: "Well, now you can see what I have to go through, sitting up here. I never get out."

Our little old friend was still in that curious stupor. He seemed unconscious, but his blue eyes were not closed, staring brightly out before them at things we did not see. With his silvery hair and his flushed frailty, he had an unearthly look. After standing perhaps three minutes at the foot of the bed, Mr. Jackson whispered:

"Well, he does look queer. Poor little old chap! You tell him from me I'll look after his cats and bird; he needn't worry. And now, I think I won't keep the car. Makes me feel a bit throaty, you know. Don't move; he might come to."

And, leaning all the weight of his substantial form on those bright and creaking toes, he made his way to the door, flashed at me a diamond ring, whispered hoarsely: "So long! That'll be all right!" and vanished. And soon I heard the whirring of his car and just saw the top of his shiny hat travelling down the little street.

Some time I sat on there, wanting to deliver that message. An uncanny vigil in the failing light, with those five cats—yes, five at least—lying or sitting against the walls, staring like sphinxes at their motionless protector. I could not make out whether it was he in his stupor with his bright eyes that fascinated them, or the bullfinch perched on his pillow, who they knew perhaps might soon be in their power. I was glad when the landlady came up and I could leave the message with her.

When she opened the door to me next day at six o'clock I knew that he was gone. There was about her that sorrowful, unmistakable importance, that peculiar mournful excitement, which hovers over houses where death has entered.

"Yes," she said, "he went this morning. Never came round after you left. Would you like to see him?"

We went up.

He lay, covered with a sheet, in the darkened room. The landlady pulled the window-curtains apart. His face, as white now almost as his silvery head, had in the sunlight a radiance like that of a small, bright angel gone to sleep. No growth of hair, such as comes on most dead faces, showed on those frail cheeks that were now smooth and lineless as porcelain. And on the sheet above his chest the bullfinch sat, looking into his face.

The landlady let the curtains fall, and we went out.

"I've got the cats in here"—she pointed to the room where Mr. Jackson and I had talked—"all ready for that gentleman when he sends. But that little bird, I don't know what to do; he won't let me catch him, and there he sits. It makes me feel all funny."

It had made me feel all funny, too.

"He hasn't left the money for his funeral. Dreadful, the way he never thought about himself. I'm glad I kept him, though." And, not to my astonishment, she suddenly began to cry.

A wire was sent to Mr. Jackson, and on the day of the funeral I went down to "Ultima Thule," Wimbledon, to see if he had carried out his promise.

He had. In the grounds, past the vinery, an outhouse had been cleaned and sanded, with cushions placed at intervals against the wall, and a little trough of milk. Nothing could have been more suitable or luxurious.

"How's that?" he said. "I've done it thoroughly." But I noticed that he looked a little glum.

"The only thing," he said, "is the cats. First night they seemed all right; and the second, there were three of 'em left. But to-day the gardener tells me there's not the ghost of one anywhere. It's not for want of feeding. They've had tripe, and liver, and milk—as much as ever they liked. And cod's heads, you know—they're very fond of them. I must say it's a bit of a disappointment to me."

As he spoke, a sandy cat which I perfectly remembered, for it had only half of its left ear, appeared in the doorway, and stood, crouching, with its green eyes turned on us; then, hearing Mr. Jackson murmur, "Puss, puss!" it ran for its life, slinking almost into the ground, and vanished among some shrubs.

Mr. Jackson sighed. "Perversity of the brutes!" he said. He led me back to the house through a conservatory full of choice orchids. A gilt bird-cage was hanging there, one of the largest I had ever seen, replete with every luxury the heart of bird could want.

"Is that for the bullfinch?" I asked him.

"Oh!" he said; "didn't you know? The little beggar wouldn't let himself be caught, and the second morning, when they went up, there he lay on the old chap's body, dead. I thought it was very touchin'. But I kept the cage hung up for you to see that I should have given him a good time here. Oh, yes, 'Ultima Thule' would have done him well!"

And from a bright leather case Mr. Jackson offered me a cigar.

The question I had long been wishing to ask him slipped out of me then: "Do you mind telling me why you called your house 'Ultima Thule?'"

"Why?" he said. "Found it on the gate. Think it's rather distingué, don't you?" and he uttered his profound chuckle.

"First-rate. The whole place is the last word in comfort."

"Very good of you to say so," he said. "I've laid out a goodish bit on it. A man must have a warm corner to end his days in. 'Ultima Thule,' as you say—it isn't bad. There's success about it, somehow."

And with that word in my ears, and in my eyes a vision of the little old fellow in his "Ultima Thule," with the bullfinch lying dead on a heart that had never known success, I travelled back to town.

1914.

ANTY BLIGH

JOHN MASEFIELD

ONE night in the tropics I was "farmer" in the middle watch—that is, I had neither "wheel" nor "look-out" to stand during the four hours I stayed on deck. We were running down the North-east Trades, and the ship was sailing herself, and the wind was gentle, and it was very still on board, the blocks whining as she rolled, and the waves talking, and the wheel-chains clanking, and a light noise aloft of pattering and tapping. The sea was all pale with moonlight, and from the lamp-room door, where the watch was mustered, I could see a red stain on the water from the port sidelight. The mate was walking the weather side of the poop, while the boatswain sat on the booby-hatch humming an old tune and making a sheath for his knife. The watch were lying on the deck, out of the moonlight, in the shadow of the break of the poop. Most of them were sleeping, propped against the bulkhead. One of them was singing a new chanty he had made, beating out the tune with his pipe-stem, in a little quiet voice that fitted the silence of the night.

> *Ha! Ha! Why don't you blow?*
> *O ho!*
> *Come, roll him over,*

repeated over and over again, as though he could never tire of the beauty of the words and the tune.

Presently he got up from where he was and came over to me. He was one of the best men we had aboard—a young Dane who talked English like a native. We had had business dealings during the dog watch, some hours before, and he had bought a towel from me, and I had let him have it cheap, as I had one or two to spare. He sat down beside me, and began a conversation, discussing a number of sailor matters, such as the danger of sleeping in the moonlight, the poison supposed to lurk in cold boiled potatoes, and the folly of having a good time in port. From these we passed to the consideration of piracy, colouring our talk with anecdotes of pirates. "Ah, there was no pirate," said my friend, "like old Anty Bligh of Bristol. Dey hung old Anty Bligh off of

Reprinted by kind permission of the Society of Authors and Dr. John Masefield, O.M.

the Brazils. He was the core and the strands of an old rogue, old Anty Bligh was. Dey hung old Anty Bligh on Fernando Noronha, where the prison is. And he walked after, Anty Bligh did. That shows how bad he was." "How did he walk?" I asked. "Let's hear about him." "Oh, they jest hung him," replied my friend, "like they'd hang any one else, and they left him on the gallows after. Dey thought old Anty was too bad to bury, I guess. And there was a young Spanish captain on the island in dem times. Frisco Baldo his name was. He was a terror. So the night dey hung old Anty, Frisco was getting gorgeous wid some other captains in a kind of a drinking shanty. And de other captains say to Frisco, 'I bet you a month's pay you won't go and put a rope round Anty's legs.' And 'I bet you a new suit of clothes you won't put a bowline around Anty's ankles.' And 'I bet you a cask of wine you won't put Anty's feet in a noose.' 'I bet you I will,' says Frisco Baldo. 'What's a dead man anyways,' he says, 'and why should I be feared of Anty Bligh? Give us a rope,' he says, 'and I'll lash him up with seven turns, like a sailor would a hammock.' So he drinks up his glass, and gets a stretch of rope, and out he goes into the dark to where the gallows stood. It was a new moon dat time, and it was as dark as the end of a sea-boot and as blind as the toe. And the gallows was right down by the sea dat time because old Anty Bligh was a pirate. So he comes up under the gallows, and there was old Anty Bligh hanging. And 'Way-ho, Anty,' he says. 'Lash and carry, Anty,' he says. 'I'm going to lash you up like a hammock.' So he slips a bowline around Anty's feet." . . . Here my informant broke off his yarn to light his pipe. After a few puffs he went on.

"Now when a man's hanged in hemp," he said gravely, "you mustn't never touch him with what killed him, for fear he should come to life on you. You mark that. Don't you forget it. So soon as ever Frisco Baldo sets that bowline around Anty's feet, old Anty looks down from his noose, and though it was dark, Frisco Baldo could see him plain enough. 'Thank you, young man,' said Anty; 'just cast that turn off again. Burn my limbs,' he says, 'if you ain't got a neck! And now climb up here,' he says, 'and take my neck out of the noose. I'm as dry as a cask of split peas.' Now you may guess that Frisco Baldo feller he come out all over in a cold sweat. 'Git a gait on you,' says Anty. 'I ain't going to wait up here to please you.' So Frisco Baldo climbs up, and a sore job he had of it getting the noose off Anty. 'Git a gait on you,' says Anty, 'and go easy with them clumsy hands of yours. You'll give me a sore throat,' he says, 'the way you're carrying on. Now don't let me fall plop,' says Anty. 'Lower away handsomely,' he says. 'I'll make you a weary one if you let me fall plop,' he says. So Frisco lowers away handsomely, and Anty comes to the ground, with the rope off him, only he still had his head to one side like he'd been hanged. 'Come here to me,' he says. So Frisco Baldo goes over to him. And Anty he jest put one arm round his neck, and gripped him tight and cold. 'Now march,' he says; 'march me down to the grog shop and get me a dram. None of your six-water dollops, neither,' he says; 'I'm as dry as a foul block,' he says. So Frisco and Anty they go to the grog shop, and all the while Anty's cold fingers was playing down Frisco's neck. And when they

got to der grog shop der captains was all fell asleep. So Frisco takes the bottle
of rum and Anty laps it down like he'd been used to it. 'Ah!' he says, 'thank
ye,' he says, 'and now down to the Mole with ye,' he says, 'and we'll take a
boat,' he says; 'I'm going to England,' he says, 'to say good-bye to me mother.'
So Frisco he come out all over in a cold sweat, for he was feared of the sea;
but Anty's cold fingers was fiddling on his neck, so he t'ink he better go. And
when dey come to der Mole there was a boat there—one of these perry-acks,
as they call them—and Anty he says, 'You take the oars,' he says. 'I'll steer,' he
says, 'and every time you catch a crab,' he says, 'you'll get such a welt as you'll
remember.' So Frisco shoves her off and rows out of the harbour, with old
Anty Bligh at the tiller, telling him to put his beef on and to watch out he
didn't catch no crabs. And he rowed, and he rowed, and he rowed, and every
time he caught a crab—whack! he had it over the sconce with the tiller. And
der perry-ack it went a great holy big skyoot, ninety knots in der quarter of
an hour, so they soon sees the Bull Point Light and der Shutter Light, and
then the lights of Bristol. 'Oars,' said Anty. 'Lie on your oars,' he says; 'we
got way enough.' Then dey make her fast to a dock-side and dey goes ashore,
and Anty has his arm round Frisco's neck, and 'March,' he says; 'step lively,'
he says; 'for Johnny comes marching home,' he says. By and by they come to a
little house with a light in the window. 'Knock at the door,' says Anty. So
Frisco knocks, and in they go. There was a fire burning in the room and some
candles on the table, and there, by the fire, was a very old, ugly woman in a
red flannel dress, and she'd a ring in her nose and a black cutty pipe between
her lips. 'Good evening, mother,' says Anty. 'I come home,' he says. But the
old woman she just looks at him but never says nothing. 'It's your son Anty
that's come home to you,' he says again. So she looks at him again and,
'Aren't you ashamed of yourself, Anty,' she says, 'coming home the way you
are? Don't you repent your goings-on?' she says. 'Dying disgraced,' she says,
'in a foreign land, with none to lay you out.' 'Mother,' he says, 'I repent in
blood,' he says. 'You'll not deny me my rights?' he says. 'Not since you repent,' she says. 'Them as repents I got no quarrel with. You was always a bad
one, Anty,' she says, 'but I hoped you'd come home in the end. Well, and
now you're come,' she says. 'And I must bathe that throat of yours,' she
says. 'It looks as though you been hit by something.' 'Be quick, mother,' he
says; 'it's after midnight now,' he says.

"So she washed him in wine, the way you wash a corpse, and put him in
a white linen shroud, with a wooden cross on his chest, and two silver pieces
on his eyes, and a golden marigold between his lips. And together they carried him to the perry-ack and laid him in the stern sheets. 'Give way, young
man,' she says; 'give way like glory. Pull, my heart of blood,' she says, 'or
we'll have the dawn on us.' So he pulls, that Frisco Baldo does, and the
perry-ack makes big southing—a degree a minute—and they comes ashore at
the Mole just as the hens was settling to their second sleep. 'To the church-
yard,' says the old woman; 'you take his legs.' So they carries him to the
churchyard at the double. Git a gait on you,' says Anty. 'I feel the dawn in
my bones,' he says. 'My wraith'll chase you if you ain't in time,' he says.

And there was an empty grave, and they put him in, and shovelled in the clay, and the old woman poured out a bottle on the top of it. 'It's holy water,' she says. 'It's make his wraith rest easy.' Then she runs down to the sea's edge and gets into the perry-ack. And immediately she was hull down beyond the horizon, and the sun came up out of the sea, and the cocks cried cock-a-doodle in the henroost, and Frisco Baldo falls down into a swound. He was a changed man from that out."

"Lee for brace," said the mate above us. "Quit your chinning there, and go forward to the rope."

SAM WELLER MAKES HIS BOW

CHARLES DICKENS

THERE are in London several old inns, once the headquarters of celebrated coaches in the days when coaches performed their journeys in a graver and more solemn manner than they do in these times; but which have now degenerated into little more than the abiding and booking places of country waggons. The reader would look in vain for any of these ancient hostelries, among the Golden Crosses and Bull and Mouths, which rear their stately fronts in the improved streets of London. If he would light upon any of these old places, he must direct his steps to the obscurer quarters of the town; and there in some secluded nooks he will find several, still standing with a kind of gloomy sturdiness, amidst the modern innovations which surround them.

In the Borough especially, there still remain some half dozen old inns, which have preserved their external features unchanged, and which have escaped alike the rage for public improvement, and the encroachments of private speculation. Great, rambling, queer, old places they are, with galleries, and passages, and staircases, wide enough and antiquated enough to furnish materials for a hundred ghost stories, supposing we should ever be reduced to the lamentable necessity of inventing any, and that the world should exist long enough to exhaust the innumerable veracious legends connected with old London Bridge, and its adjacent neighbourhood on the Surrey side.

It was in the yard of one of these inns—of no less celebrated a one than the White Hart—that a man was busily employed in brushing the dirt off a pair of boots, early on the morning succeeding the events narrated in the last chapter. He was habited in a coarse-striped waistcoat, with black calico sleeves, and blue glass buttons; drab breeches and leggings. A bright red handkerchief was wound in a very loose and unstudied style round his neck, and an old white hat was carelessly thrown on one side of his head. There were two rows of boots before him, one cleaned and the other dirty, and at every addition he made to the clean row, he paused from his work, and contemplated its results with evident satisfaction.

The yard presented none of that bustle and activity which are the usual

characteristics of a large coach inn. Three or four lumbering waggons, each with a pile of goods beneath its ample canopy, about the height of the second-floor window of an ordinary house, were stowed away beneath a lofty roof which extended over one end of the yard; and another, which was probably to commence its journey that morning, was drawn out into the open space. A double tier of bedroom galleries, with old clumsy balustrades, ran round two sides of the straggling area, and a double row of bells to correspond, sheltered from the weather by a little sloping roof, hung over the door lead-ing to the bar and coffee-room. Two or three gigs and chaise-carts were wheeled up under different little sheds and pent-houses; and the occasional heavy tread of a cart-horse, or rattling of a chain at the further end of the yard, announced to anybody who cared about the matter, that the stable lay in that direction. When we add that a few boys in smock frocks were lying asleep on heavy packages, wool-packs, and other articles that were scattered about on heaps of straw, we have described as fully as need be the general appearance of the yard of the White Hart Inn, High Street, Borough, on the particular morning in question.

A loud ringing of one of the bells, was followed by the appearance of a smart chambermaid in the upper sleeping gallery, who, after tapping at one of the doors, and receiving a request from within, called over the balus-trades—

"Sam!"

"Hallo," replied the man with the white hat.

"Number twenty-two wants his boots."

"Ask number twenty-two, wether he'll have 'em now, or wait till he gets 'em," was the reply.

"Come, don't be a fool, Sam," said the girl, coaxingly, "the gentleman wants his boots directly."

"Well, you *are* a nice young 'ooman for a musical party, you are," said the boot-cleaner. "Look at these here boots—eleven pair o' boots; and one shoe as b'longs to number six, with the wooden leg. The eleven boots is to be called at half-past eight and the shoe at nine. Who's number twenty-two, that's to put all the others out? No, no; reg'lar rotation, as Jack Ketch said, wen he tied the men up. Sorry to keep you a waitin', sir, but I'll attend to you directly."

Saying which, the man in the white hat set to work upon a top-boot with increased assiduity.

There was another loud ring; and the bustling old landlady of the White Hart made her appearance in the opposite gallery.

"Sam," cried the landlady, "where's that lazy, idle—why, Sam—oh, there you are; why don't you answer?"

"Wouldn't be gen-teel to answer, 'till you'd done talking," replied Sam, gruffly.

"Here, clean them shoes for number seventeen directly, and take 'em to private sitting-room, number five, first floor."

The landlady flung a pair of lady's shoes into the yard, and bustled away.

"Number five," said Sam, as he picked up the shoes, and taking a piece of chalk from his pocket, made a memorandum of their destination on the soles—"Lady's shoes and private sittin' room! I suppose *she* didn't come in the waggin."

"She came in early this morning," cried the girl, who was still leaning over the railing of the gallery, "with a gentleman in a hackney-coach, and it's him as wants his boots, and you'd better do 'em, that's all about it."

"Vy didn't you say so before," said Sam, with great indignation, singling out the boots in question from the heap before him. "For all I know'd he vas one o' the regular threepennies. Private room! and a lady too! If he's anything of a gen'lm'n, he's vorth a shillin' a day, let alone the arrands."

Stimulated by this inspiring reflection, Mr. Samuel brushed away with such hearty good will, that in a few minutes the boots and shoes, with a polish which would have struck envy to the soul of the amiable Mr. Warren (for they used Day and Martin at the White Hart), had arrived at the door of number five.

"Come in," said a man's voice, in reply to Sam's rap at the door.

Sam made his best bow, and stepped into the presence of a lady and gentleman seated at breakfast. Having officiously deposited the gentleman's boots right and left at his feet, and the lady's shoes right and left at hers, he backed towards the door.

"Boots," said the gentleman.

"Sir," said Sam, closing the door, and keeping his hand on the knob of the lock.

"Do you know—what's a-name—Doctors' Commons?"

"Yes, sir."

"Where is it?"

"Paul's Church-yard, sir; low archway on the carriage-side, bookseller's at one corner, hot-el on the other, and two porters in the middle as touts for licences."

"Touts for licences!" said the gentleman.

"Touts for licences," replied Sam. "Two coves in vhite aprons—touches their hats wen you walk in—'Licence, sir, licence?' Queer sort, them, and their mas'rs too, sir—Old Baily Proctors—and no mistake."

"What do they do?" inquired the gentleman.

"Do! You, sir! That an't the wost on it, neither. They puts things into old gen'lm'n's heads as they never dreamed of. My father, sir, wos a coachman. A widower he wos, and fat enough for anything—uncommon fat, to be sure. His missus dies, and leaves him four hundred pound. Down he goes to the Commons, to see the lawyer and draw the blunt—wery smart—top boots on—nosegay in his buttonhole—broad-brimmed tile—green shawl— quite the gen'lm'n. Goes through the archvay, thinking how he should inwest the money—up comes the touter, touches his hat—'Licence, sir, licence?'— 'What's that?' says my father.—'Licence, sir,' says he.—'What licence?' says my father.—'Marriage licence,' says the touter.—'Dash my veskit,' says my father, 'I never thought o' that.'—'I think you wants one, sir,' says the touter.

My father pulls up, and thinks a bit—'No,' says he, 'damme, I'm too old, b'sides I'm a many sizes too large,' says he.—'Not a bit on it, sir,' says the touter.—'Think not?' says my father.—'I'm sure not,' says he; 'we married a gen'lm'n twice your size, last Monday.'—'Did you, though,' said my father.— 'To be sure, we did,' says the touter, 'you're a babby to him—this way, sir— this way!'—and sure enough my father walks arter him, like a tame monkey behind a horgan, into a little back office, vere a feller sat among dirty papers and tin boxes, making believe he was busy. 'Pray take a seat, vile I makes out the affidavit, sir,' says the lawyer.—'Thankee, sir,' says my father, and down he sat, and stared with all his eyes, and his mouth vide open, at the names on the boxes. 'What's your name, sir,' says the lawyer.—'Tony Weller,' says my father.—'Parish?' says the lawyer.—'Belle Savage,' says my father; for he stopped there wen he drove up, and he know'd nothing about parishes, *he* didn't.—'And what's the lady's name?' says the lawyer. My father was struck all of a heap. 'Blessed if I know,' says he.—'Not know!' says the lawyer.—'No more nor you do,' says my father, 'can't I put that in arterwards?'—'Impossible!' says the lawyer.—'Wery well,' says my father, after he'd thought a moment, 'put down Mrs. Clarke.'—'What Clarke?' says the lawyer, dipping his pen in the ink.—'Susan Clarke, Markis o' Granby, Dorking,' says my father; 'she'll have me, if I ask, I des-say—I never said nothing to her, but she'll have me, I know.' The licence was made out, and she *did* have him, and what's more she's got him now; and *I* never had any of the four hundred pound, worse luck. Beg your pardon, sir," said Sam, when he had concluded, "but wen I gets on this here grievance, I runs on like a new barrow vith the wheel greased." Having said which, and having paused for an instant to see whether he was wanted for anything more, Sam left the room.

"Half-past nine—just the time—off at once," said the gentleman, whom we need hardly introduce as Mr. Jingle.

"Time—for what?" said the spinster aunt, coquettishly.

"Licence, dearest of angels—give notice at the church—call you mine, to-morrow"—said Mr. Jingle, and he squeezed the spinster aunt's hand.

"The licence!" said Rachael, blushing.

"The licence," repeated Mr. Jingle—

> "*In hurry, post-haste for a licence,*
> *In hurry, ding dong I come back.*"

"How you run on," said Rachael.

"Run on—nothing to the hours, days, weeks, months, years, when we're united—*run* on—they'll fly on—bolt—mizzle—steam-engine—thousand-horse power—nothing to it."

"Can't—can't we be married before to-morrow morning?" inquired Rachael.

"Impossible—can't be—notice at the church—leave the licence to-day— ceremony come off to-morrow."

"I am so terrified, lest my brother should discover us!" said Rachael.

"Discover—nonsense—too much shaken by the break down—besides—extreme caution—gave up the post-chaise—walked on—took a hackney-coach—came to the Borough—last place in the world that he'd look in—ha! ha!—capital notion that—very."

"Don't be long," said the spinster, affectionately, as Mr. Jingle stuck the pinched-up hat on his head.

"Long away from *you?*—Cruel charmer," and Mr. Jingle skipped playfully up to the spinster aunt, imprinted a chaste kiss upon her lips, and danced out of the room.

"Dear man!" said the spinster as the door closed after him.

"Rum old girl," said Mr. Jingle, as he walked down the passage.

It is painful to reflect upon the perfidy of our species; and we will not, therefore, pursue the thread of Mr. Jingle's meditations, as he wended his way to Doctors' Commons. It will be sufficient for our purpose to relate, that escaping the snares of the dragons in white aprons, who guard the entrance to that enchanted region, he reached the Vicar General's office in safety, and having procured a highly flattering address on parchment, from the Archbishop of Canterbury, to his "trusty and well-beloved Alfred Jingle and Rachael Wardle, greeting," he carefully deposited the mystic document in his pocket, and retraced his steps in triumph to the Borough.

He was yet on his way to the White Hart, when two plump gentlemen and one thin one entered the yard, and looked round in search of some authorised person of whom they could make a few inquiries. Mr. Samuel Weller happened to be at that moment engaged in burnishing a pair of painted tops, the personal property of a farmer who was refreshing himself with a slight lunch of two or three pounds of cold beef and a pot or two of porter, after the fatigues of the Borough market; and to him the thin gentleman straightway advanced.

"My friend," said the thin gentleman.

"You're one o' the adwice gratis order," thought Sam, "or you wouldn't be so werry fond o' me all at once." But he only said—"Well, sir."

"My friend," said the thin gentleman, with a conciliatory hem—"Have you got many people stopping here, now? Pretty busy. Eh?"

Sam stole a look at the inquirer. He was a little high-dried man, with a dark squeezed-up face, and small restless black eyes, that kept winking and twinkling on each side of his little inquisitive nose, as if they were playing a perpetual game of peep-bo with that feature. He was dressed all in black, with boots as shiny as his eyes, a low white neckcloth, and a clean shirt with a frill to it. A gold watch-chain, and seals, depended from his fob. He carried his black kid gloves *in* his hands, not *on* them; and as he spoke, thrust his wrists beneath his coat-tails, with the air of a man who was in the habit of propounding some regular posers.

"Pretty busy, eh?" said the little man.

"Oh, werry well, sir," replied Sam, "we shan't be bankrupts, and we shan't make our fort'ns. We eats our biled mutton without capers, and don't care for horse-radish wen we can get beef."

"Ah," said the little man, "you're a wag, an't you?"

"My eldest brother was troubled with that complaint," said Sam; "it may be catching—I used to sleep with him."

"This is a curious old house of yours," said the little man, looking round him.

"If you'd sent word you was a coming, we'd ha' had it repaired," replied the imperturbable Sam.

The little man seemed rather baffled by these several repulses, and a short consultation took place between him and the two plump gentlemen. At its conclusion, the little man took a pinch of snuff from an oblong silver box, and was apparently on the point of renewing the conversation, when one of the plump gentlemen, who in addition to a benevolent countenance, possessed a pair of spectacles, and a pair of black gaiters, interfered—

"The fact of the matter is," said the benevolent gentleman, "that my friend here (pointing to the other plump gentleman) will give you half a guinea, if you'll answer one or two—"

"Now, my dear sir—my dear sir," said the little man, "pray, allow me—my dear sir, the very first principle to be observed in these cases, is this: if you place a matter in the hands of a professional man, you must in no way interfere in the progress of the business; you must repose implicit confidence in him. Really, Mr. (he turned to the other plump gentleman, and said)—I forget your friend's name."

"Pickwick," said Mr. Wardle, for it was no other than that jolly personage.

"Ah, Pickwick—really Mr. Pickwick, my dear sir, excuse me—I shall be happy to receive any private suggestions of yours, as *amicus curiæ*, but you must see the impropriety of your interfering with my conduct in this case, with such an *ad captandum* argument as the offer of half a guinea. Really, my dear sir, really;" and the little man took an argumentative pinch of snuff, and looked very profound.

"My only wish, sir," said Mr. Pickwick, "was to bring this very unpleasant matter to as speedy a close as possible."

"Quite right—quite right," said the little man.

"With which view," continued Mr. Pickwick, "I made use of the argument which my experience of men has taught me is the most likely to succeed in any case."

"Ay, ay," said the little man, "very good, very good, indeed; but you should have suggested it to *me*. My dear sir, I'm quite certain you cannot be ignorant of the extent of confidence which must be placed in professional men. If any authority can be necessary on such a point, my dear sir, let me refer you to the well-known case in Barnwell and——"

"Never mind George Barnwell," interrupted Sam, who had remained a wondering listener during this short colloquy; "every body knows vhat sort of a case his was, tho' it's always been my opinion, mind you, that the young 'ooman deserved scragging a precious sight more than he did. Hows'ever, that's neither here nor there. You want me to accept of half a guinea. Werry well, I'm agreeable: I can't say no fairer than that, can I, sir? (Mr. Pickwick smiled.) Then the next question is, what the devil do you want with me, as the man said wen he see the ghost?"

"We want to know—" said Mr. Wardle.

"Now my dear sir—my dear sir," interposed the busy little man.

Mr. Wardle shrugged his shoulders, and was silent.

"We want to know," said the little man, solemnly; "and we ask the question of you, in order that we may not awaken apprehensions inside—we want to know who you've got in this house, at present?"

"Who there is in the house!" said Sam, in whose mind the inmates were always represented by that particular article of their costume, which came under his immediate superintendence. "There's a wooden leg in number six; there's a pair of Hessians in thirteen; there's two pair of halves in the commercial; there's these here painted tops in the snuggery inside the bar; and five more tops in the coffee-room."

"Nothing more?" said the little man.

"Stop a bit," replied Sam, suddenly recollecting himself. "Yes; there's a pair of Wellingtons a good deal worn, and a pair o' lady's shoes, in number five."

"What sort of shoes?" hastily inquired Wardle, who, together with Mr. Pickwick, had been lost in bewilderment at the singular catalogue of visitors.

"Country make," replied Sam.

"Any maker's name?"

"Brown."

"Where of?"

"Muggleton."

"It *is* them," exclaimed Wardle. "By Heavens, we've found them."

"Hush!" said Sam. "The Wellingtons has gone to Doctors' Commons."

"No," said the little man.

"Yes, for a licence."

"We're in time," exclaimed Wardle. "Show us the room; not a moment is to be lost."

"Pray, my dear sir—pray," said the little man; "caution, caution." He drew from his pocket a red silk purse, and looked very hard at Sam as he drew out a sovereign.

Sam grinned expressively.

"Show us into the room at once, without announcing us," said the little man, "and it's yours."

Sam threw the painted tops into a corner, and led the way through a dark passage, and up a wide staircase. He paused at the end of a second passage, and held out his hand.

"Here it is," whispered the attorney, as he deposited the money in the hand of their guide.

The man stepped forward for a few paces, followed by the two friends and their legal adviser. He stopped at a door.

"Is this the room?" murmured the little gentleman.

Sam nodded assent.

Old Wardle opened the door; and the whole three walked into the room just as Mr. Jingle, who had that moment returned, had produced the licence to the spinster aunt.

The spinster uttered a loud shriek, and, throwing herself in a chair, covered her face with her hands. Mr. Jingle crumpled up the licence, and thrust it into his coat-pocket. The unwelcome visitors advanced into the middle of the room.

"You—you are a nice rascal, arn't you?" exclaimed Wardle, breathless with passion.

"My dear sir, my dear sir," said the little man, laying his hat on the table. "Pray, consider—pray. Defamation of character: action for damages. Calm yourself, my dear sir, pray—"

"How dare you drag my sister from my house?" said the old man.

"Ay—ay—very good," said the little gentleman, "you may ask that. How dare you, sir?—eh, sir?"

"Who the devil are you?" inquired Mr. Jingle, in so fierce a tone, that the little gentleman involuntarily fell back a step or two.

"Who is he, you scoundrel," interposed Wardle. "He's my lawyer, Mr. Perker, of Gray's Inn. Perker, I'll have this fellow prosecuted—indicted—I'll —I'll—I'll ruin him. And you," continued Mr. Wardle, turning abruptly round to his sister, "you, Rachael, at a time of life when you ought to know better, what do you mean by running away with a vagabond, disgracing your family, and making yourself miserable. Get on your bonnet, and come back. Call a hackney-coach there, directly, and bring this lady's bill, d'ye hear— d'ye hear?"

"Cert'nly, sir," replied Sam, who had answered Wardle's violent ringing of the bell with a degree of celerity which must have appeared marvellous to anybody who didn't know that his eye had been applied to the outside of the keyhole during the whole interview.

"Get on your bonnet," repeated Wardle.

"Do nothing of the kind," said Jingle. "Leave the room, sir—no business here—lady's free to act as she pleases—more than one-and-twenty."

"More than one-and-twenty!" ejaculated Wardle, contemptuously. "More than one-and-forty!"

"I an't," said the spinster aunt, her indignation getting the better of her determination to faint.

"You are," replied Wardle, "you're fifty if you're an hour."

Here the spinster aunt uttered a loud shriek, and became senseless.

"A glass of water," said the humane Mr. Pickwick, summoning the landlady.

"A *glass* of water!" said the passionate Wardle. "Bring a bucket, and throw it all over her; it'll do her good, and she richly deserves it."

"Ugh, you brute!" ejaculated the kind-hearted landlady. "Poor dear." And with sundry ejaculations of "Come now, there's a dear—drink a little of this —it'll do you good—don't give way so—there's a love," &c., &c., the landlady, assisted by a chamber-maid, proceeded to vinegar the forehead, beat the hands, titillate the nose, and unlace the stays of the spinster aunt, and to administer such other restoratives as are usually applied by compassionate females to ladies who are endeavouring to ferment themselves into hysterics.

"Coach is ready, sir," said Sam, appearing at the door.

"Come along," cried Wardle. "I'll carry her down stairs."

At this proposition, the hysterics came on with redoubled violence.

The landlady was about to enter a very violent protest against this proceeding, and had already given vent to an indignant inquiry whether Mr. Wardle considered himself a lord of creation, when Mr. Jingle interposed—

"Boots," said he, "get me an officer."

"Stay, stay," said little Mr. Perker. "Consider, sir, consider."

"I'll *not* consider," replied Jingle. "She's her own mistress—see who dares to take her away—unless she wishes it."

"I *won't* be taken away," murmured the spinster aunt. "I *don't* wish it." (Here there was a frightful relapse.)

"My dear sir," said the little man, in a low tone, taking Mr. Wardle and Mr. Pickwick apart: "My dear sir, we're in a very awkward situation. It's a distressing case—very; I never knew one more so; but really, my dear sir, really we have no power to control this lady's actions. I warned you before we came, my dear sir, that there was nothing to look to but a compromise."

There was a short pause.

"What kind of compromise would you recommend?" inquired Mr. Pickwick.

"Why, my dear sir, our friend's in an unpleasant position—very much so. We must be content to suffer some pecuniary loss."

"I'll suffer any, rather than submit to this disgrace, and let her, fool as she is, be made miserable for life," said Wardle.

"I rather think it can be done," said the bustling little man. "Mr. Jingle, will you step with us into the next room for a moment?"

Mr. Jingle assented, and the quartette walked into an empty apartment.

"Now, sir," said the little man, as he carefully closed the door, "is there no way of accommodating this matter—step this way, sir, for a moment—into this window, sir, where we can be alone—there, sir, there, pray sit down, sir. Now, my dear sir, between you and I, we know very well, my dear sir, that you have run off with this lady for the sake of her money. Don't frown, sir, don't frown; I say, between you and I, *we* know it. We are both men of the world, and *we* know very well that our friends here, are not—eh?"

Mr. Jingle's face gradually relaxed; and something distantly resembling a wink quivered for an instant in his left eye.

"Very good, very good," said the little man, observing the impression he had made. "Now the fact is, that beyond a few hundreds, the lady has little or nothing till the death of her mother—fine old lady, my dear sir."

"*Old*," said Mr. Jingle, briefly but emphatically.

"Why, yes," said the attorney with a slight cough. "You are right, my dear sir, she is *rather* old. She comes of an old family though, my dear sir; old in every sense of the word. The founder of that family came into Kent, when

Julius Cæsar invaded Britain;—only one member of it, since, who hasn't lived to eighty-five, and *he* was beheaded by one of the Henrys. The old lady is not seventy-three now, my dear sir." The little man paused, and took a pinch of snuff.

"Well," cried Mr. Jingle.

"Well, my dear sir—you don't take snuff!—ah! so much the better—expensive habit—well, my dear sir, you're a fine young man, man of the world—able to push your fortune, if you had capital, eh?"

"Well," said Mr. Jingle again.

"Do you comprehend me?"

"Not quite."

"Don't you think—now, my dear sir, I put it to you, *don't* you think—that fifty pounds and liberty, would be better than Miss Wardle and expectation?"

"Won't do—not half enough!" said Mr. Jingle rising.

"Nay, nay, my dear sir," remonstrated the little attorney, seizing him by the button. "Good round sum—a man like you could treble it in no time—great deal to be done with fifty pounds, my dear sir."

"More to be done with a hundred and fifty," replied Mr. Jingle, coolly.

"Well, my dear sir, we won't waste time in splitting straws," resumed the little man, "say—say—seventy."

"Won't do," said Mr. Jingle.

"Don't go away, my dear sir—pray don't hurry," said the little man. "Eighty; come: I'll write you a cheque at once."

"Won't do," said Mr. Jingle.

"Well, my dear sir, well," said the little man, still detaining him; "just tell me what *will* do."

"Expensive affair," said Mr. Jingle. "Money out of pocket—posting, nine pounds; licence, three—that's twelve—compensation, a hundred—hundred and twelve—Breach of honour—and loss of the lady—"

"Yes, my dear sir, yes," said the little man, with a knowing look, "never mind the last two items. That's a hundred and twelve—say a hundred—come."

"And twenty," said Mr. Jingle.

"Come, come, I'll write you a cheque," said the little man; and down he sat at the table for that purpose.

"I'll make it payable the day after to-morrow," said the little man, with a look towards Mr. Wardle; "and we can get the lady away, meanwhile." Mr. Wardle sullenly nodded assent.

"A hundred," said the little man.

"And twenty," said Mr. Jingle.

"My dear sir," remonstrated the little man.

"Give it him," interposed Mr. Wardle, "and let him go."

The cheque was written by the little gentleman, and pocketed by Mr. Jingle.

"Now, leave this house instantly!" said Wardle, starting up.

"My dear sir," urged the little man.

"And mind," said Mr. Wardle, "that nothing should have induced me to make this compromise—not even a regard for my family—if I had not known that the moment you got any money in that pocket of yours, you'd go to the devil faster, if possible, than you would without it—"

THE CROXLEY MASTER

A. CONAN DOYLE

I

MR. ROBERT MONTGOMERY was seated at his desk, his head upon his hands, in a state of the blackest despondency. Before him was the open ledger with the long columns of Dr. Oldacre's prescriptions. At his elbow lay the wooden tray with the labels in various partitions, the cork box, the lumps of twisted sealing-wax, while in front a rank of empty bottles waited to be filled. But his spirits were too low for work. He sat in silence, with his fine shoulders bowed and his head upon his hands.

Outside, through the grimy surgery window over a foreground of blackened brick and slate, a line of enormous chimneys like Cyclopean pillars upheld the lowering, dun-coloured cloud-bank. For six days in the week they spouted smoke, but to-day the furnace fires were banked, for it was Sunday. Sordid and polluting gloom hung over a district blighted and blasted by the greed of man. There was nothing in the surroundings to cheer a desponding soul, but it was more than his dismal environment which weighed upon the medical assistant.

His trouble was deeper and more personal. The winter session was approaching. He should be back again at the University completing the last year which would give him his medical degree; but, alas! he had not the money with which to pay his class fees, nor could he imagine how he could procure it. Sixty pounds were wanted to make his career, and it might have been as many thousands for any chance there seemed to be of his obtaining it.

He was roused from his black meditation by the entrance of Dr. Oldacre himself, a large, clean-shaven, respectable man, with a prim manner and an austere face. He had prospered exceedingly by the support of the local Church interest, and the rule of his life was never by word or action to run a risk of offending the sentiment which had made him. His standard of respectability and of dignity was exceedingly high, and he expected the same from his assistants. His appearance and words were always vaguely benevolent. A sudden impulse came over the despondent student. He would test the reality of this philanthropy.

"I beg your pardon, Dr. Oldacre," said he, rising from his chair; "I have a great favour to ask of you."

The doctor's appearance was not encouraging. His mouth suddenly tightened, and his eyes fell.

"Yes, Mr. Montgomery?"

"You are aware, sir, that I need only one more session to complete my course."

"So you have told me."

"It is very important to me, sir."

"Naturally."

"The fees, Dr. Oldacre, would amount to about sixty pounds."

"I am afraid that my duties call me elsewhere, Mr. Montgomery."

"One moment, sir! I had hoped, sir, that perhaps, if I signed a paper promising you interest upon your money, you would advance this sum to me. I will pay you back, sir, I really will. Or, if you like, I will work it off after I am qualified."

The doctor's lips had thinned into a narrow line. His eyes were raised again, and sparkled indignantly.

"Your request is unreasonable, Mr. Montgomery. I am surprised that you should have made it. Consider, sir, how many thousands of medical students there are in this country. No doubt there are many of them who have a difficulty in finding their fees. Am I to provide for them all? Or why should I make an exception in your favour? I am grieved and disappointed, Mr. Montgomery, that you should have put me into the painful position of having to refuse you." He turned upon his heel, and walked with offended dignity out of the surgery.

The student smiled bitterly, and turned to his work of making up the morning prescriptions. It was poor and unworthy work—work which any weakling might have done as well, and this was a man of exceptional nerve and sinew. But, such as it was, it brought him his board and £1 a week, enough to help him during the summer months and let him save a few pounds towards his winter keep. But those class fees! Where were they to come from? He could not save them out of his scanty wage. Dr. Oldacre would not advance them. He saw no way of earning them. His brains were fairly good, but brains of that quality were a drug in the market. He only excelled in his strength; and where was he to find a customer for that? But the ways of Fate are strange, and his customer was at hand.

"Look y'ere!" said a voice at the door.

Montgomery looked up, for the voice was a loud and rasping one. A young man stood at the entrance—a stocky, bull-necked young miner, in tweed Sunday clothes and an aggressive necktie. He was a sinister-looking figure, with dark, insolent eyes, and the jaw and throat of a bulldog.

"Look y'ere!" said he again. "Why hast thou not sent t' medicine oop as thy master ordered?"

Montgomery had become accustomed to the brutal frankness of the Northern worker. At first it had enraged him, but after a time he had grown callous to it, and accepted it as it was meant. But this was something different. It was insolence—brutal, overbearing insolence, with physical menace behind it.

"What name?" he asked coldly.

"Barton. Happen I may give thee cause to mind that name, yoong man. Mak' oop t' wife's medicine this very moment, look ye, or it will be the worse for thee."

Montgomery smiled. A pleasant sense of relief thrilled softly through him. What blessed safety-valve was this through which his jangled nerves might find some outlet. The provocation was so gross, the insult so unprovoked, that he could have none of those qualms which take the edge off a man's mettle. He finished sealing the bottle upon which he was occupied, and he addressed it and placed it carefully in the rack.

"Look here!" said he, turning round to the miner, "your medicine will be made up in its turn and sent down to you. I don't allow folk in the surgery. Wait outside in the waiting-room, if you wish to wait at all."

"Yoong man," said the miner, "thou's got to mak' t' wife's medicine here, and now, and quick, while I wait and watch thee, or else happen thou might need some medicine thysel' before all is over."

"I shouldn't advise you to fasten a quarrel upon me." Montgomery was speaking in the hard, staccato voice of a man who is holding himself in with difficulty. "You'll save trouble if you'll go quietly. If you don't you'll be hurt. Ah, you would? Take it, then!"

The blows were almost simultaneous—a savage swing which whistled past Montgomery's ear and a straight drive which took the workman on the chin. Luck was with the assistant. That single whizzing uppercut, and the way in which it was delivered, warned him that he had a formidable man to deal with. But if he had underrated his antagonist, his antagonist had also underrated him, and had laid himself open to a fatal blow.

The miner's head had come with a crash against the corner of the surgery shelves, and he had dropped heavily on to the ground. There he lay with his bandy legs drawn up and his hands thrown abroad, the blood trickling over the surgery tiles.

"Had enough?" asked the assistant, breathing fiercely through his nose.

But no answer came. The man was insensible. And then the danger of his position came upon Montgomery, and he turned as white as his antagonist. A Sunday, the immaculate Dr. Oldacre with his pious connection, a savage brawl with a patient; he would irretrievably lose his situation if the facts came out. It was not much of a situation, but he could not get another without a reference, and Oldacre might refuse him one. Without money for his classes, and without a situation—what was to become of him? It was absolute ruin.

But perhaps he could escape exposure after all. He seized his insensible adversary, dragged him out into the centre of the room, loosened his collar, and squeezed the surgery sponge over his face. He sat up at last with a gasp and a scowl.

"Domn thee, thou's spoilt my necktie," said he, mopping up the water from his breast.

"I'm sorry I hit you so hard," said Montgomery, apologetically.

"Thou hit me hard! I could stan' such fly-flappin' all day. 'Twas this here press that cracked my pate for me, and thou art a looky man to be able to boast as thou hast outed me. And now I'd be obliged to thee if thou wilt give me t' wife's medicine."

Montgomery gladly made it up and handed it to the miner.

"You are weak still," said he. "Won't you stay awhile and rest?"

"T' wife wants her medicine," said the man, and lurched out at the door.

The assistant, looking after him, saw him rolling with an uncertain step down the street, until a friend met him, and they walked on arm-in-arm. The man seemed in his rough Northern fashion to bear no grudge, and so Montgomery's fears left him. There was no reason why the doctor should know anything about it. He wiped the blood from the floor, put the surgery in order, and went on with his interrupted task, hoping that he had come scathless out of a very dangerous business.

Yet all day he was aware of a sense of vague uneasiness which sharpened into dismay when, late in the afternoon, he was informed that three gentlemen had called and were waiting for him in the surgery. A coroner's inquest, a descent of detectives, an invasion of angry relatives—all sorts of possibilities rose to scare him. With tense nerves and a rigid face he went to meet his visitors.

They were a very singular trio. Each was known to him by sight; but what on earth the three could be doing together, and, above all, what they could expect from *him*, was a most inexplicable problem.

The first was Sorley Wilson, the son of the owner of the Nonpareil Coalpit. He was a young blood of twenty, heir to a fortune, a keen sportsman, and down for the Easter Vacation from Magdalene College. He sat now upon the edge of the surgery table, looking in thoughtful silence at Montgomery, and twisting the ends of his small, black, waxed moustache.

The second was Purvis, the publican, owner of the chief beershop, and well known as the local bookmaker. He was a coarse, clean-shaven man, whose fiery face made a singular contrast with his ivory-white bald head. He had shrewd, light-blue eyes with foxy lashes, and he also leaned forward in silence from his chair, a fat, red hand upon either knee, and stared critically at the young assistant.

So did the third visitor, Fawcett, the horsebreaker, who leaned back, his long, thin legs, with their box-cloth riding-gaiters, thrust out in front of him, tapping his protruding teeth with his riding-whip, with anxious thought in every line of his rugged, bony face. Publican, exquisite, and horsebreaker were all three equally silent, equally earnest, and equally critical. Montgomery, seated in the midst of them, looked from one to the other.

"Well, gentlemen?" he observed, but no answer came.

The position was embarrassing.

"No," said the horsebreaker, at last. "No. It's off. It's nowt."

"Stand oop, lad; let's see thee standin'." It was the publican who spoke.

Montgomery obeyed. He would learn all about it, no doubt, if he were patient. He stood up and turned slowly round, as if in front of his tailor.

"It's off! It's off!" cried the horsebreaker. "Why, mon, the Master would break him over his knee."

"Oh, that be hanged for a yarn!" said the young Cantab. "You can drop out if you like, Fawcett, but I'll see this thing through, if I have to do it alone. I don't hedge a penny. I like the cut of him a great deal better than I liked Ted Barton."

"Look at Barton's shoulders, Mr. Wilson."

"Lumpiness isn't always strength. Give me nerve and fire and breed. That's what wins."

"Ay, sir, you have it theer—you have it theer!" said the fat, red-faced publican, in a thick, suety voice. "It's the same wi' poops. Get 'em clean-bred an' fine, an' they'll yark the thick 'uns—yark 'em out o' their skins."

"He's ten good pund on the light side," growled the horsebreaker.

"He's a welter weight, anyhow."

"A hundred and thirty."

"A hundred and fifty, if he's an ounce."

"Well, the Master doesn't scale much more than that."

"A hundred and seventy-five."

"That was when he was hog-fat and living high. Work the grease out of him, and I lay there's no great difference between them. Have you been weighed lately, Mr. Montgomery?"

It was the first direct question which had been asked him. He had stood in the midst of them, like a horse at a fair, and he was just beginning to wonder whether he was more angry or amused.

"I am just eleven stone," said he.

"I said that he was a welter weight."

"But suppose you was trained?" said the publican. "Wot then?"

"I am always in training."

"In a manner of speakin', no doubt, he *is* always in trainin'," remarked the horsebreaker. "But trainin' for everyday work ain't the same as trainin' with a trainer; and I dare bet, with all respec' to your opinion, Mr. Wilson, that there's half a stone of tallow on him at this minute."

The young Cantab put his fingers on the assistant's upper arm. Then with his other hand on his wrist he bent the forearm sharply, and felt the biceps, as round and hard as a cricket-ball, spring up under his fingers.

"Feel that!" said he.

The publican and horsebreaker felt it with an air of reverence.

"Good lad! He'll do yet!" cried Purvis.

"Gentlemen," said Montgomery, "I think that you will acknowledge that I have been very patient with you. I have listened to all that you have to say about my personal appearance, and now I must really beg that you will have the goodness to tell me what is the matter."

They all sat down in their serious, business-like way.

"That's easy done, Mr. Montgomery," said the fat-voiced publican. "But before sayin' anything we had to wait and see whether, in a way of speakin', there was any need for us to say anything at all. Mr. Wilson thinks there is. Mr. Fawcett, who has the same right to his opinion, bein' also a backer and one o' the committee, thinks the other way."

"I thought him too light built, and I think so now," said the horsebreaker, still tapping his prominent teeth with the metal head of his riding-whip. "But happen he may pull through; and he's a fine-made, buirdly young chap, so if you mean to back him, Mr. Wilson——"

"Which I do."

"And you, Purvis?"

"I ain't one to go back, Fawcett."

"Well, I'll stan' to my share of the purse."

"And well I knew you would," said Purvis, "for it would be somethin' new to find Isaac Fawcett as a spoilsport. Well, then, we make up the hundred for the stake among us, and the fight stands—always supposin' the young man is willin'."

"Excuse all this rot, Mr. Montgomery," said the University man, in a genial voice. "We've begun at the wrong end, I know, but we'll soon straighten it out, and I hope that you will see your way to falling in with our views. In the first place, you remember the man whom you knocked out this morning? He is Barton—the famous Ted Barton."

"I'm sure, sir, you may well be proud to have outed him in one round," said the publican. "Why, it took Morris, the ten-stone-six champion, a deal more trouble than that before he put Barton to sleep. You've done a fine performance, sir, and happen you'll do a finer, if you give yourself the chance."

"I never heard of Ted Barton, beyond seeing the name on a medicine label," said the assistant.

"Well, you may take it from me that he's a slaughterer," said the horse-breaker. "You've taught him a lesson that he needed, for it was always a word and a blow with him, and the word alone was worth five shillin' in a public court. He won't be so ready now to shake his nief in the face of every one he meets. However, that's neither here nor there."

Montgomery looked at them in bewilderment.

"For goodness' sake, gentlemen, tell me what it is you want me to do!" he cried.

"We want you to fight Silas Craggs, better known as the Master of Croxley."

"But why?"

"Because Ted Barton was to have fought him next Saturday. He was the champion of the Wilson coal-pits, and the other was the Master of the iron-folk down at the Croxley smelters. We'd matched our man for a purse of a hundred against the Master. But you've queered our man, and he can't face such a battle with a two-inch cut at the back of his head. There's only one thing to be done, sir, and that is for you to take his place. If you can lick Ted Barton you may lick the Master of Croxley; but if you don't we're done, for there's no one else who is in the same street with him in this district. It's twenty rounds, two-ounce gloves, Queensberry rules, and a decision on points if you fight to the finish."

For a moment the absurdity of the thing drove every other thought out of Montgomery's head. But then there came a sudden revulsion. A hundred pounds!—all he wanted to complete his education was lying there ready to his hand if only that hand were strong enough to pick it up. He had thought bitterly that morning that there was no market for his strength, but here was one where his muscle might earn more in an hour than his brains in a year. But a chill of doubt came over him.

"How can I fight for the coal-pits?" said he. "I am not connected with them."

"Eh, lad, but thou art!" cried old Purvis. "We've got it down in writin', and it's clear enough. 'Anyone connected with the coal-pits.' Doctor Oldacre is the coal-pit club doctor; thou art his assistant. What more can they want?"

"Yes, that's right enough," said the Cantab. "It would be a very sporting thing of you, Mr. Montgomery, if you would come to our help when we are in such a hole. Of course, you might not like to take the hundred pounds; but I have no doubt that, in the case of your winning, we could arrange that it should take the form of a watch or piece of plate, or any other shape which might suggest itself to you. You see, you are responsible for our having lost our champion, so we really feel that we have a claim upon you."

"Give me a moment, gentlemen. It is very unexpected. I am afraid the doctor would never consent to my going—in fact, I am sure that he would not."

"But he need never know—not before the fight, at any rate. We are not bound to give the name of our man. So long as he is within the weight limits on the day of the fight, that is all that concerns any one."

The adventure and the profit would either of them have attracted Montgomery. The two combined were irresistible.

"Gentlemen," said he, "I'll do it!"

The three sprang from their seats. The publican had seized his right hand, the horse-dealer his left, and the Cantab slapped him on the back.

"Good lad! good lad!" croaked the publican. "Eh, mon, but if thou yark him, thou'll rise in one day from being just a common doctor to the best-known mon 'twixt here and Bradford. Thou are a witherin' tyke, thou art, and no mistake; and if thou beat the Master of Croxley, thou'll find all the beer thou want for the rest of thy life waiting for thee at the Four Sacks."

"It is the most sporting thing I ever heard of in my life," said young Wilson. "By George, sir, if you pull it off, you've got the constituency in your pocket, if you care to stand. You know the outhouse in my garden?"

"Next the road?"

"Exactly. I turned it into a gymnasium for Ted Barton. You'll find all you want there: clubs, punching-ball, bars, dumb-bells, everything. Then you'll want a sparring partner. Ogilvy has been acting for Barton, but we don't think that he is class enough. Barton bears you no grudge. He's a good-hearted fellow, though cross-grained with strangers. He looked upon you as a stranger this morning, but he says he knows you now. He is quite ready to spar with you for practice, and he will come at any hour you will name."

"Thank you; I will let you know the hour," said Montgomery; and so the committee departed jubilant upon their way.

The medical assistant sat for a little time in the surgery turning it over in his mind. He had been trained originally at the University by the man who had been middle-weight champion in his day. It was true that his teacher was long past his prime, slow upon his feet and stiff in his joints, but even so he was still a tough antagonist; but Montgomery had found at last that he could more than hold his own with him. He had won the University medal, and his teacher, who had trained so many students, was emphatic in his opinion that he had never had one who was in the same class with him. He had been exhorted to go in for the Amateur Championships, but he had no particular ambition in that direction. Once he had put on the gloves with Hammer Tunstall in a booth at a fair, and had fought three rattling rounds, in which he had the worst of it, but had made the prize-fighter stretch himself to the uttermost. There was his whole record, and was it enough to encourage him to stand up to the Master of Croxley? He had never heard of the Master before, but then he had lost touch of the ring during the last few years of hard work. After all, what did it matter? If he won, there was the money, which meant so much to him. If he lost, it would only mean a thrashing. He could take punishment without flinching, of that he was certain. If there were only one chance in a hundred of pulling it off, then it was worth his while to attempt it.

Dr. Oldacre, new come from church, with an ostentatious prayer-book in his kid-gloved hand, broke in upon his meditation.

"You don't go to service, I observe, Mr. Montgomery," said he, coldly.

"No, sir; I have had some business to detain me."

"It is very near to my heart that my household should set a good example. There are so few educated people in this district that a great responsibility devolves upon us. If we do not live up to the highest, how can we expect these poor workers to do so? It is a dreadful thing to reflect that the parish takes a great deal more interest in an approaching glove-fight than in their religious duties."

"A glove-fight, sir?" said Montgomery, guiltily.

"I believe that to be the correct term. One of my patients tell me that it is the talk of the district. A local ruffian, a patient of ours, by the way, is matched against a pugilist over at Croxley. I cannot understand why the law does not step in and stop so degrading an exhibition. It is really a prize-fight."

"A glove-fight, you said."

"I am informed that a two-ounce glove is an evasion by which they dodge the law, and make it difficult for the police to interfere. They contend for a sum of money. It seems dreadful and almost incredible—does it not?—to think that such scenes can be enacted within a few miles of our peaceful home. But you will realize, Mr. Montgomery, that while there are such influences for us to counteract, it is very necessary that we should live up to our highest."

The doctor's sermon would have had more effect if the assistant had not once or twice had occasion to test his highest and come upon it at unexpectedly humble elevations. It is always so particularly easy to "compound for sins we're most inclined to by damning those we have no mind to." In any case, Montgomery felt that of all the men concerned in such a fight—promoters, backers, spectators—it is the actual fighter who holds the strongest and most honourable position. His conscience gave him no concern upon the subject. Endurance and courage are virtues, not vices, and brutality is, at least, better than effeminacy.

There was a little tobacco-shop at the corner of the street, where Montgomery got his bird's-eye and also his local information, for the shopman was a garrulous soul, who knew everything about the affairs of the district. The assistant strolled down there after tea and asked, in a casual way, whether the tobacconist had ever heard of the Master of Croxley.

"Heard of him! Heard of him!" the little man could hardly articulate in his astonishment. "Why, sir, he's the first mon o' the district, an' his name's as

well known in the West Riding as the winner o' t' Derby. But Lor', sir"—
here he stopped and rummaged among a heap of papers. "They are makin' a
fuss about him on account o' his fight wi' Ted Barton, and so the *Croxley
Herald* has his life an' record, an' here it is, an' thou canst read it for thysel'."

The sheet of the paper which he held up was a lake of print around an
islet of illustration. The latter was a coarse wood-cut of a pugilist's head and
neck set in a cross-barred jersey. It was a sinister but powerful face, the face
of a debauched hero, clean-shaven, strongly eyebrowed, keen-eyed, with a
huge, aggressive jaw, and an animal dewlap beneath it. The long, obstinate
cheeks ran flush up to the narrow, sinister eyes. The mighty neck came down
square from the ears and curved outwards into shoulders, which had lost
nothing at the hands of the local artist. Above was written "Silas Craggs,"
and beneath, "The Master of Croxley."

"Thou'll find all about him there, sir," said the tobacconist. "He's a
witherin' tyke, he is, and w're proud to have him in the county. If he hadn't
broke his leg he'd have been champion of England."

"Broke his leg, has he?"

"Yes, and it set badly. They ca' him owd K behind his bock, for thot is
how his two legs look. But his arms—well, if they was both stropped to a
bench, as the sayin' is, I wonder where the champion of England would be
then."

"I'll take this with me," said Montgomery; and putting the paper into his
pocket he returned home.

It was not a cheering record which he read there. The whole history of
the Croxley Master was given in full, his many victories, his few defeats.

"Born in 1857," said the provincial biographer, "Silas Craggs, better known
in sporting circles as The Master of Croxley, is now in his fortieth year."

"Hang it, I'm only twenty-three," said Montgomery to himself, and read
on more cheerfully.

"Having in his youth shown a surprising aptitude for the game, he fought
his way up among his comrades, until he became the recognized champion
of the district and won the proud title which he still holds. Ambitious of a
more than local fame, he secured a patron, and fought his first fight against
Jack Barton, of Birmingham, in May, 1880, at the old Loiterers' Club.
Craggs, who fought at ten-stone-two at the time, had the better of fifteen rattling rounds, and gained an award on points against the Midlander. Having
disposed of James Dunn, of Rotherhithe, Cameron, of Glasgow, and a youth
named Fernie, he was thought so highly of by the fancy that he was matched
against Ernest Willox, at that time middle-weight champion of the North of
England, and defeated him in a hard-fought battle, knocking him out in the
tenth round after a punishing contest. At this period it looked as if the very
highest honours of the ring were within the reach of the young Yorkshireman,
but he was laid upon the shelf by a most unfortunate accident. The kick of
a horse broke his thigh, and for a year he was compelled to rest himself.
When he returned to his work the fracture had set badly, and his activity
was much impaired. It was owing to this that he was defeated in seven rounds

by Willox, the man whom he had previously beaten, and afterwards by James Shaw, of London, though the latter acknowledged that he had found the toughest customer of his career. Undismayed by his reverses, the Master adapted the style of his fighting to his physical disabilities, and resumed his career of victory—defeating Norton (the black), Bobby Wilson, and Levi Cohen, the latter a heavy-weight. Conceding two stone, he fought a draw with the famous Billy McQuire, and afterwards, for a purse of fifty pounds, he defeated Sam Hare at the Pelican Club, London. In 1891 a decision was given against him upon a foul when fighting a winning fight against Jim Taylor, the Australian middle-weight, and so mortified was he by the decision, that he withdrew from the ring. Since then he has hardly fought at all save to accommodate any local aspirant who may wish to learn the difference between a bar-room scramble and a scientific contest. The latest of these ambitious souls comes from the Wilson coal-pits, which have undertaken to put up a stake of £100 and back their local champion. There are various rumours afloat as to who their representative is to be, the name of Ted Barton being freely mentioned; but the betting, which is seven to one on the Master against any untried man, is a fair reflection of the feeling of the community."

Montgomery read it over twice, and it left him with a very serious face. No light matter this, which he had undertaken; no battle with a rough-and-tumble fighter who presumed upon a local reputation. The man's record showed that he was first class—or nearly so. There were a few points in his favour, and he must make the most of them. There was age—twenty-three against forty. There was an old ring proverb that "Youth will be served," but the annals of the ring offer a great number of exceptions. A hard veteran, full of cool valour and ring-craft, could give ten or fifteen years and a beating to most striplings. He could not rely too much upon his advantage in age. But then there was the lameness; that must surely count for a great deal. And, lastly, there was the chance that the Master might underrate his opponent, that he might be remiss in his training, and refuse to abandon his usual way of life, if he thought that he had an easy task before him. In a man of his age and habits this seemed very possible. Montgomery prayed that it might be so. Meanwhile, if his opponent were the best man whoever jumped the ropes into a ring, his own duty was clear. He must prepare himself carefully, throw away no chance, and do the very best that he could. But he knew enough to appreciate the difference which exists in boxing, as in every sport, between the amateur and the professional. The coolness, the power of hitting, above all the capability of taking punishment, count for so much. Those specially developed, gutta-percha-like abdominal muscles of the hardened pugilist will take without flinching a blow which would leave another man writhing on the ground. Such things are not to be acquired in a week, but all that could be done in a week should be done.

The medical assistant had a good basis to start from. He was 5 feet 11 inches—tall enough for anything on two legs, as the old ring men used to say —lithe and spare, with the activity of a panther, and a strength which had hardly yet ever found its limitations. His muscular development was finely hard, but his power came rather from that higher nerve-energy which counts for nothing upon a measuring tape. He had the well-curved nose and the widely opened eye which never yet were seen upon the face of a craven, and behind everything he had the driving force, which came from the knowledge that his whole career was at stake upon the contest. The three backers rubbed their hands when they saw him at work punching the ball in the gymnasium next morning; and Fawcett, the horsebreaker, who had written to Leeds to hedge his bets, sent a wire to cancel the letter, and to lay another fifty at the market price of seven to one.

Montgomery's chief difficulty was to find time for his training without any interference from the doctor. His work took him a large part of the day, but as the visiting was done on foot, and considerable distances had to be traversed, it was a training in itself. For the rest, he punched the swinging ball and worked with the dumb-bells for an hour every morning and evening, and boxed twice a day with Ted Barton in the gymnasium, gaining as much profit as could be got from a rushing, two-handed slogger. Barton was full of admiration for his cleverness and quickness, but doubtful about his strength. Hard hitting was the feature of his own style, and he exacted it from others. "Lord, sir, that's a turble poor poonch for an eleven-stone man!" he would cry. "Thou wilt have to hit harder than that afore t' Master will know that thou art theer. Ah, thot's better, mon, thot's fine!" he would add, as his opponent lifted him across the room on the end of a right counter. "Thot's how I likes to feel 'em. Happen thou'lt pull through yet." He chuckled with joy when Montgomery knocked him into a corner. "Eh, mon, thou art comin' along grand. Thou hast fair yarked me off my legs. Do it again, lad, do it again!"

The only part of Montgomery's training which came within the doctor's observation was his diet, and that puzzled him considerably.

"You will excuse my remarking, Mr. Montgomery, that you are becoming rather particular in your tastes. Such fads are not to be encouraged in one's youth. Why do you eat toast with every meal?"

"I find that it suits me better than bread, sir."

"It entails unnecessary work upon the cook. I observe, also, that you have turned against potatoes."

"Yes, sir; I think that I am better without them."

"And you no longer drink your beer?"

"No, sir."

"These causeless whims and fancies are very much to be deprecated, Mr. Montgomery. Consider how many there are to whom these very potatoes and this very beer would be most acceptable."

"No doubt, sir. But at present I prefer to do without them."

They were sitting alone at lunch, and the assistant thought that it would be a good opportunity of asking leave for the day of the fight.

"I should be glad if you could let me have leave for Saturday, Doctor Oldacre."

"It is very inconvenient upon so busy a day."

"I should do a double day's work on Friday so as to leave everything in order. I should hope to be back in the evening."

"I am afraid I cannot spare you, Mr. Montgomery."

This was a facer. If he could not get leave he would go without it.

"You will remember, Doctor Oldacre, that when I came to you it was understood that I should have a clear day every month. I have never claimed one. But now there are reasons why I wish to have a holiday upon Saturday."

Doctor Oldacre gave in with a very bad grace.

"Of course, if you insist upon your formal rights, there is no more to be said, Mr. Montgomery, though I feel that it shows a certain indifference to my comfort and the welfare of the practice. Do you still insist?"

"Yes, sir."

"Very good. Have your way."

The doctor was boiling over with anger, but Montgomery was a valuable assistant—steady, capable, and hard working—and he could not afford to lose him. Even if he had been prompted to advance those class fees, for which his assistant had appealed, it would have been against his interests to do so, for he did not wish him to qualify, and he desired him to remain in his subordinate position, in which he worked so hard for so small a wage. There was something in the cool insistence of the young man, a quiet resolution in his voice as he claimed his Saturday, which aroused his curiosity.

"I have no desire to interfere unduly with your affairs, Mr. Montgomery, but were you thinking of having a day in Leeds upon Saturday?"

"No, sir."

"In the country?"

"Yes, sir."

"You are very wise. You will find a quiet day among the wild flowers a very valuable restorative. Had you thought of any particular direction?"

"I am going over Croxley way."

"Well, there is no prettier country when once you are past the iron-works. What could be more delightful than to lie upon the Fells, basking in the sunshine, with perhaps some instructive and elevating book as your companion? I should recommend a visit to the ruins of St. Bridget's Church, a very interesting relic of the early Norman era. By the way, there is one objection which I see to your going to Croxley on Saturday. It is upon that date, as I am informed, that that ruffianly glove-fight takes place. You may find yourself molested by the blackguards whom it will attract."

"I will take my chance of that, sir," said the assistant.

On the Friday night, which was the last before the fight, Montgomery's three backers assembled in the gymnasium and inspected their man as he went through some light exercises to keep his muscles supple. He was certainly in splendid condition, his skin shining with health, and his eyes with energy and confidence. The three walked round him and exulted.

"He's simply rippling!" said the undergraduate. "By Gad, you've come out of it splendidly. You're as hard as a pebble, and fit to fight for your life."

"Happen he's a trifle on the fine side," said the publican. "Runs a bit light at the loins, to my way of thinkin'."

"What weight to-day?"

"Ten-stone-eleven," the assistant answered.

"That's only three pund off in a week's trainin'," said the horsebreaker. "He said right when he said that he was in condition. Well, it's fine stuff all there is of it, but I'm none so sure as there is enough." He kept poking his finger into Montgomery, as if he were one of his horses. "I hear that the Master will scale a hundred and sixty odd at the ring-side."

"But there's some of that which he'd like well to pull off and leave behind wi' his shirt," said Purvis. "I hear they've had a rare job to get him to drop his beer, and if it had not been for that great red-headed wench of his they'd never ha' done it. She fair scratted the face off a potman that had brought him a gallon from t' Chequers. They say the hussy is his sparrin' partner, as well as his sweetheart, and that his poor wife is just breakin' her heart over it. Hullo, young 'un, what do you want?"

The door of the gymnasium had opened, and a lad about sixteen, grimy and black with soot and iron, stepped into the yellow glare of the oil-lamp. Ted Barton seized him by the collar.

"See here, thou yoong whelp, this is private, and we want noan o' thy spyin'!"

"But I maun speak to Mr. Wilson."

The young Cantab stepped forward.

"Well, my lad, what is it?"

"It's aboot t' fight, Mr. Wilson, sir. I wanted to tell your mon somethin' aboot t' Maister."

"We've no time to listen to gossip, my boy. We know all about the Master."

"But thou doant, sir. Nobody knows but me and mother, and we thought as we'd like thy mon to know, sir, for we want him to fair bray him."

"Oh, you want the Master fair brayed, do you? So do we. Well, what have you to say?"

"Is this your mon, sir?"

"Well, suppose it is?"

"Then it's him I want to tell aboot it. T' Maister is blind o' the left eye."

"Nonsense!"

"It's true, sir. Not stone blind, but rarely fogged. He keeps it secret, but mother knows, and so do I. If thou slip him on the left side he can't cop thee. Thou'll find it right as I tell thee. And mark him when he sinks his right. 'Tis his best blow, his right upper-cut. T' Maister's finisher, they ca' it at t' works. It's a turble blow, when it do come home."

"Thank you, my boy. This is information worth having about his sight," said Wilson. "How came you to know so much? Who are you?"

"I'm his son, sir."

Wilson whistled.

"And who sent you to us?"

"My mother. I maun get back to her again."

"Take this half-crown."

"No, sir, I don't seek money in comin' here. I do it——"

"For love?" suggested the publican.

"For hate!" said the boy, and darted off into the darkness.

"Seems to me t' red-headed wench may do him more harm than good, after all," remarked the publican. "And now, Mr. Montgomery, sir, you've done enough for this evenin', and a nine-hours' sleep is the best trainin' before a battle. Happen this time to-morrow night you'll be safe back again with your one hundred pounds in your pocket."

II

Work was struck at one o'clock at the coal-pits and the iron-works, and the fight was arranged for three. From the Croxley Furnaces, from Wilson's Coal-pits, from the Heartsease Mine, from the Dodd Mills, from the Leverworth Smelters the workmen came trooping, each with his fox-terrier or his lurcher at his heels. Warped with labour and twisted by toil, bent double by week-long work in the cramped coal galleries, or half-blinded with years spent in front of white-hot fluid metal, these men still gilded their harsh and hopeless lives by their devotion to sport. It was their one relief, the only thing which could distract their minds from sordid surroundings, and give them an interest beyond the blackened circle which inclosed them. Literature, art, science, all these things were beyond their horizon; but the race, the football match, the cricket, the fight, these were things which they could understand, which they could speculate upon in advance and comment upon afterwards. Sometimes brutal, sometimes grotesque, the love of sport is still one of the great agencies which make for the happiness of our people. It lies very deeply in the springs of our nature, and when it has been educated out, a higher, more refined nature may be left, but it will not be of that robust British type which has left its mark so deeply on the world. Every one of these ruddled workers, slouching with his dog at his heels to see something of the fight, was a true unit of his race.

It was a squally May day, with bright sunbursts and driving showers. Montgomery worked all morning in the surgery getting his medicine made up.

"The weather seems so very unsettled, Mr. Montgomery," remarked the doctor, "that I am inclined to think that you had better postpone your little country excursion until a later date."

"I am afraid that I must go to-day, sir."

"I have just had an intimation that Mrs. Potter, at the other side of Angleton, wishes to see me. It is probable that I shall be there all day. It will be extremely inconvenient to leave the house empty so long."

"I am very sorry, sir, but I must go," said the assistant, doggedly.

The doctor saw that it would be useless to argue, and departed in the worst of bad tempers upon his mission. Montgomery felt easier now that he was gone. He went up to his room, and packed his running-shoes, his fighting-drawers, and his cricket-sash into a handbag. When he came down Mr. Wilson was waiting for him in the surgery.

"I hear the doctor has gone."

"Yes; he is likely to be away all day."

"I don't see that it matters much. It's bound to come to his ears by to-night."

"Yes; it's serious with me, Mr. Wilson. If I win, it's all right. I don't mind telling you that the hundred pounds will make all the difference to me. But if I lose, I shall lose my situation, for, as you say, I can't keep it secret."

"Never mind. We'll see you through among us. I only wonder the doctor has not heard, for it's all over the country that you are to fight the Croxley Champion. We've had Armitage up about it already. He's the Master's backer, you know. He wasn't sure that you were eligible. The Master said he wanted you whether you were eligible or not. Armitage has money on, and would have made trouble if he could. But I showed him that you came within the conditions of the challenge, and he agreed that it was all right. They think they have a soft thing on."

"Well, I can only do my best," said Montgomery.

They lunched together; a silent and rather nervous repast, for Montgomery's mind was full of what was before him, and Wilson had himself more money at stake than he cared to lose.

Wilson's carriage and pair were at the door, the horses with blue-and-white rosettes at their ears, which were the colours of the Wilson Coal-pits, well known on many a football field. At the avenue gate a crowd of some hundred pitmen and their wives gave a cheer as the carriage passed. To the assistant it all seemed dream-like and extraordinary—the strangest experience of his life, but with a thrill of human action and interest in it which made it passionately absorbing. He lay back in the open carriage and saw the fluttering handkerchiefs from the doors and windows of the miners' cottages. Wilson had pinned a blue-and-white rosette upon his coat, and every one knew him as their champion. "Good luck, sir! good luck to thee!" they shouted from the roadside. He felt that it was like some unromantic knight riding down to sordid lists, but there was something of chivalry in it all the same. He fought for others as well as for himself. He might fail from want of skill or strength, but deep in his sombre soul he vowed that it should never be for want of heart.

Mr. Fawcett was just mounting into his high-wheeled, spidery dogcart, with his little bit of blood between the shafts. He waved his whip and fell in behind the carriage. They overtook Purvis, the tomato-faced publican, upon the road, with his wife in her Sunday bonnet. They also dropped into the procession, and then, as they traversed the seven miles of the high road to Croxley, their two-horsed, rosetted carriage became gradually the nucleus of a comet with a loosely radiating tail. From every side-road came the miners' carts, the humble, ramshackle traps, black and bulging, with their loads of noisy, foul-tongued, open-hearted partisans. They trailed for a long quarter of a mile behind them—cracking, whipping, shouting, galloping, swearing. Horsemen and runners were mixed with the vehicles. And then suddenly a squad of the Sheffield Yeomanry, who were having their annual training in those parts, clattered and jingled out of a field, and rode as an escort to the carriage. Through the dust-clouds round him Montgomery saw the gleaming brass helmets, the bright coats, and the tossing heads of the chargers, the delighted brown faces of the troopers. It was more dream-like than ever.

And then, as they approached the monstrous uncouth line of bottle-shaped buildings which marked the smeltingworks of Croxley, their long, writhing snake of dust was headed off by another but longer one which wound across their path. The main road into which their own opened was filled by the rushing current of traps. The Wilson contingent halted until the others should get past. The iron-men cheered and groaned, according to their humour, as they whirled past their antagonist. Rough chaff flew back and forwards like iron nuts and splinters of coal. "Brought him up, then!" "Got t' hearse for to fetch him back?" "Where's t' owd K-legs?" "Mon, mon, have thy photograph took—'twill mind thee of what thou used to look!" "He fight?—he's now't but a half-baked doctor!" "Happen he'll doctor thy Croxley Champion afore he's through wi't."

So they flashed at each other as the one side waited and the other passed. Then there came a rolling murmur swelling into a shout, and a great break with four horses came clattering along, all streaming with salmon-pink ribbons. The driver wore a white hat with pink rosette, and beside him, on the high seat, were a man and a woman—she with her arm round his waist. Montgomery had one glimpse of them as they flashed past: he with a furry cap drawn low over his brow, a great frieze coat, and a pink comforter round his throat; she brazen, red-headed, bright-coloured, laughing excitedly. The Master, for it was he, turned as he passed, gazed hard at Montgomery, and gave him a menacing, gap-toothed grin. It was a hard, wicked face, blue-jowled and craggy, with long, obstinate cheeks and inexorable eyes. The break behind was full of patrons of the sport—flushed iron-foremen, heads of departments, managers. One was drinking from a metal flask, and raised it to Montgomery as he passed; and then the crowd thinned, and the Wilson cortège with their dragoons swept in at the rear of the others.

The road led away from Croxley, between curving green hills, gashed and polluted by the searchers for coal and iron. The whole country had been gutted, and vast piles of refuse and mountains of slag suggested the mighty chambers which the labour of man had burrowed beneath. On the left the road curved up to where a huge building, roofless and dismantled, stood crumbling and forlorn, with the light shining through the windowless squares.

"That's the old Arrowsmith's factory. That's where the fight is to be," said Wilson. "How are you feeling now?"

"Thank you. I was never better in my life," Montgomery answered.

"By Gad, I like your nerve!" said Wilson, who was himself flushed and uneasy. "You'll give us a fight for our money, come what may. That place on the right is the office, and that has been set aside as the dressing- and weighing-room."

The carriage drove up to it amidst the shouts of the folk upon the hillside. Lines of empty carriages and traps curved down upon the winding road, and a black crowd surged round the door of the ruined factory. The seats, as a huge placard announced, were five shillings, three shillings, and a shilling, with half-price for dogs. The takings, deducting expenses, were to go to the winner, and it was already evident that a larger stake than a hundred pounds was in question. A babel of voices rose from the door. The workers wished to bring their dogs in free. The men scuffled. The dogs barked. The crowd was a whirling, eddying pool surging with a roar up to the narrow cleft which was its only outlet.

The break, with its salmon-coloured streamers and four reeking horses, stood empty before the door of the office; Wilson, Purvis, Fawcett, and Montgomery passed in.

There was a large, bare room inside with square, clean patches upon the grimy walls, where pictures and almanacs had once hung. Worn linoleum covered the floor, but there was no furniture save some benches and a deal table with a ewer and a basin upon it. Two of the corners were curtained off. In the middle of the room was a weighing-chair. A hugely fat man, with a salmon tie and a blue waistcoat with birds'-eye spots, came bustling up to them. It was Armitage, the butcher and grazier, well known for miles round as a warm man, and the most liberal patron of sport in the Riding.

"Well, well," he grunted, in a thick, fussy, wheezy voice, "you have come, then. Got your man? Got your man?"

"Here he is, fit and well. Mr. Montgomery, let me present you to Mr. Armitage."

"Glad to meet you, sir. Happy to make your acquaintance. I make bold to say, sir, that we of Croxley admire your courage, Mr. Montgomery, and that our only hope is a fair fight and no favour and the best man win. That's our sentiment at Croxley."

"And it is my sentiment also," said the assistant.

"Well, you can't say fairer than that, Mr. Montgomery. You've taken a large contrac' in hand, but a large contrac' may be carried through, sir, as anyone that knows my dealings could testify. The Master is ready to weigh in!"

"So am I."

"You must weigh in the buff."

Montgomery looked askance at the tall, red-headed woman who was standing gazing out of the window.

"That's all right," said Wilson. "Get behind the curtain and put on your fighting-kit."

He did so, and came out the picture of an athlete, in white, loose drawers, canvas shoes, and the sash of a well-known cricket club round his waist. He was trained to a hair, his skin gleaming like silk, and every muscle rippling down his broad shoulders and along his beautiful arms as he moved them. They bunched into ivory knobs, or slid into long, sinuous curves, as he raised or lowered his hands.

"What thinkest thou o' that?" asked Ted Barton, his second, of the woman in the window.

She glanced contemptuously at the young athlete.

"It's but a poor kindness thou dost him to put a thread-paper yoong gentleman like yon against a mon as is a mon. Why, my Jock would throttle him wi' one hond lashed behind him."

"Happen he may—happen not," said Barton. "I have but twa pund in the world, but it's on him, every penny, and no hedgin'. But here's t' Maister, and rarely fine he do look."

The prize-fighter had come out from his curtain, a squat, formidable figure, monstrous in chest and arms, limping slightly on his distorted leg. His skin had none of the freshness and clearness of Montgomery's, but was dusky and mottled, with one huge mole amid the mat of tangled black hair which thatched his mighty breast. His weight bore no relation to his strength, for those huge shoulders and great arms, with brown, sledge-hammer fists, would have fitted the heaviest man that ever threw his cap into a ring. But his loins and legs were slight in proportion. Montgomery, on the other hand, was as symmetrical as a Greek statue. It would be an encounter between a man who was specially fitted for one sport, and one who was equally capable of any. The two looked curiously at each other: a bulldog, and a high-bred, clean-limbed terrier, each full of spirit.

"How do you do?"

"How do?" The Master grinned again, and his three jagged front teeth gleamed for an instant. The rest had been beaten out of him in twenty years of battle. He spat upon the floor. "We have a rare fine day for't."

"Capital," said Montgomery.

"That's the good feelin' I like," wheezed the fat butcher. "Good lads, both of them!—prime lads!—hard meat an' good bone. There's no ill-feelin'."

"If he downs me, Gawd bless him!" said the Master.

"An' if we down him, Gawd help him!" interrupted the woman.

"Haud thy tongue, wench!" said the Master, impatiently. "Who art thou to put in thy word? Happen I might draw my hand across thy face."

The woman did not take the threat amiss.

"Wilt have enough for thy hand to do, Jock," said she. "Get quit o' this gradely man afore thou turn on me."

The lovers' quarrel was interrupted by the entrance of a new-comer, a gentleman with a fur-collared overcoat and a very shiny top-hat—a top-hat of a degree of glossiness which is seldom seen five miles from Hyde Park. This hat he wore at the extreme back of his head, so that the lower surface of the brim made a kind of frame for his high, bald forehead, his keen eyes, his rugged and yet kindly face. He bustled in with the quiet air of possession with which the ring-master enters the circus.

"It's Mr. Stapleton, the referee from London," said Wilson. "How do you do, Mr. Stapleton? I was introduced to you at the big fight at the Corinthian Club, in Piccadilly."

"Ah, I dare say," said the other, shaking hands. "Fact is, I'm introduced to so many that I can't undertake to carry their names. Wilson, is it? Well, Mr. Wilson, glad to see you. Couldn't get a fly at the station, and that's why I'm late."

"I'm sure, sir," said Armitage, "we should be proud that anyone so well known in the boxing world should come down to our little exhibition."

"Not at all. Not at all. Anything in the interest of boxin'. All ready? Men weighed?"

"Weighing now, sir."

"Ah, just as well I should see it done. Seen you before, Craggs. Saw you fight your second battle against Willox. You had beaten him once, but he came back on you. What does the indicator say?—one hundred and sixty-three pounds—two off for the kit—one hundred and sixty-one. Now, my lad, you jump. My goodness, what colours are you wearing?"

"The Anonymi Cricket Club."

"What right have you to wear them? I belong to the club myself."

"So do I."

"You an amateur?"

"Yes, sir."

"And you are fighting for a money prize?"

"Yes."

"I suppose you know what you are doing. You realize that you're a professional pug from this onwards, and that if ever you fight again——"

"I'll never fight again."

"Happen you won't," said the woman, and the Master turned a terrible eye upon her.

"Well, I suppose you know your own business best. Up you jump. One hundred and fifty-one, minus two, one hundred and forty-nine—twelve pounds' difference, but youth and condition on the other scale. Well, the sooner we get to work the better, for I wish to catch the seven-o'clock express at Hellifield. Twenty three-minute rounds, with one minute intervals, and Queensberry rules. Those are the conditions, are they not?"

"Yes, sir."

"Very good, then, we may go across."

The two combatants had overcoats thrown over their shoulders, and the whole party, backers, fighters, seconds, and the referee, filed out of the room. A police inspector was waiting for them in the road. He had a notebook in his hand—that terrible weapon which awes even the London cabman.

"I must take your names, gentlemen, in case it should be necessary to proceed for breach of peace."

"You don't mean to stop the fight?" cried Armitage, in a passion of indignation. "I'm Mr. Armitage, of Croxley, and this is Mr. Wilson, and we'll be responsible that all is fair and as it should be."

"I'll take the names in case it should be necessary to proceed," said the inspector, impassively.

"But you know me well."

"If you was a dook or even a judge it would be all the same," said the inspector. "It's the law, and there's an end. I'll not take upon myself to stop the fight, seeing that gloves are to be used, but I'll take the names of all concerned. Silas Craggs, Robert Montgomery, Edward Barton, James Stapleton of London. Who seconds Silas Craggs?"

"I do," said the woman. "Yes, you can stare, but it's my job, and no one else's. Anastasia's the name—four a's."

"Craggs?"

"Johnson. Anastasia Johnson. If you jug him, you can jug me."

"Who talked of juggin', ye fool?" growled the Master. "Coom on, Mr. Armitage, for I'm fair sick o' this loiterin'."

The inspector fell in with the procession, and proceeded, as they walked up the hill, to bargain in his official capacity for a front seat, where he could safeguard the interests of the law, and in his private capacity to lay out thirty shillings at seven to one with Mr. Armitage.

Through the door they passed, down a narrow lane walled with a dense bank of humanity, up a wooden ladder to a platform, over a rope which was slung waist-high from four corner stakes, and then Montgomery realized that he was in that ring in which his immediate destiny was to be worked out. On the stake at one corner there hung a blue-and-white streamer. Barton led him across, the overcoat dangling loosely from his shoulders, and he sat down on a wooden stool. Barton and another man, both wearing white sweaters, stood beside him. The so-called ring was a square, twenty feet each way. At the opposite angle was the sinister figure of the Master, with his red-headed woman and a rough-faced friend to look after him. At each corner were metal basins, pitchers of water, and sponges.

During the hubbub and uproar of the entrance Montgomery was too bewildered to take things in. But now there was a few minutes' delay, for the referee had lingered behind, and so he looked quietly about him. It was a sight to haunt him for a lifetime. Wooden seats had been built in, sloping upwards to the tops of the walls. Above, instead of a ceiling, a great flight of crows passed slowly across a square of grey cloud. Right up to the topmost benches the folk were banked—broadcloth in front, corduroys and fustian behind; faces turned everywhere upon him. The grey reek of the pipes filled the building, and the air was pungent with the acrid smell of cheap, strong tobacco. Everywhere among the human faces were to be seen the heads of the dogs. They growled and yapped from the back benches. In that dense mass of humanity one could hardly pick out individuals, but Montgomery's eyes caught the brazen gleam of the helmets held upon the knees of the ten yeomen of his escort. At the very edge of the platform sat the reporters, five of them: three locals, and two all the way from London. But where was the all-important referee? There was no sign of him, unless he were in the centre of that angry swirl of men near the door.

Mr. Stapleton had stopped to examine the gloves which were to be used, and entered the building after the combatants. He had started to come down that narrow lane with the human walls which led to the ring. But already it had gone abroad that the Wilson champion was a gentleman, and that another gentleman had been appointed as referee. A wave of suspicion passed through the Croxley folk. They would have one of their own people for a referee. They would not have a stranger. His path was stopped as he made for the ring. Excited men flung themselves in front of him; they waved their fists in his face and cursed him. A woman howled vile names in his ear. Somebody struck at him with an umbrella. "Go thou back to Lunnon. We want noan o' thee. Go thou back!" they yelled.

Stapleton with his shiny hat cocked backwards, and his large, bulging forehead swelling from under it, looked round him from beneath his bushy brows. He was in the centre of a savage and dangerous mob. Then he drew his watch from his pocket and held it dial upwards in his palm.

"In three minutes," said he, "I will declare the fight off."

They raged round him. His cool face and that aggressive top-hat irritated them. Grimy hands were raised. But it was difficult, somehow, to strike a man who was so absolutely indifferent.

"In two minutes I declare the fight off."

They exploded into blasphemy. The breath of angry men smoked into his placid face. A gnarled, grimy fist vibrated at the end of his nose. "We tell thee we want noan o' thee. Get thou back where thou com'st from."

"In one minute I declare the fight off."

Then the calm persistence of the man conquered the swaying, mutable, passionate crowd.

"Let him through, mon. Happen there'll be no fight after a'."

"Let him through."

"Bill, thou loomp, let him pass. Dost want the fight declared off?"

"Make room for the referee!—room for the Lunnon referee!"

And half pushed, half carried, he was swept up to the ring. There were two chairs by the side of it, one for him and one for the timekeeper. He sat down, his hands on his knees, his hat at a more wonderful angle than ever, impassive but solemn, with the aspect of one who appreciates his responsibilities.

Mr. Armitage, the portly butcher, made his way into the ring and held up two fat hands, sparkling with rings, as a signal for silence.

"Gentlemen!" he yelled. And then in a crescendo shriek, "Gentlemen!"

"And ladies!" cried somebody, for indeed there was a fair sprinkling of women among the crowd. "Speak up, owd man!" shouted another. "What price pork chops?" cried somebody at the back. Everybody laughed, and the dogs began to bark. Armitage waved his hands amidst the uproar as if he were conducting an orchestra. At last the babel thinned into silence.

"Gentlemen," he yelled, "the match is between Silas Craggs, whom we call the Master of Croxley, and Robert Montgomery, of the Wilson Coalpits. The match was to be under eleven eight. When they were weighed just now Craggs weighed eleven seven, and Montgomery ten nine. The conditions of the contest are—the best of twenty three-minute rounds with two-ounce gloves. Should the fight run to its full length it will, of course, be decided upon points. Mr. Stapleton, the well-known London referee, has kindly consented to see fair play. I wish to say that Mr. Wilson and I, the chief backers of the two men, have every confidence in Mr. Stapleton, and that we beg that you accept his rulings without dispute."

He then turned from one combatant to the other, with a wave of his hand.

III

"Montgomery—Craggs!" said he.

A great hush fell over the huge assembly. Even the dogs stopped yapping; one might have thought that the monstrous room was empty. The two men had stood up, the small white gloves over their hands. They advanced from their corners and shook hands: Montgomery gravely, Craggs with a smile. Then they fell into position. The crowd gave a long sigh—the intake of a thousand excited breaths. The referee tilted his chair on to its back legs, and looked moodily critical from the one to the other.

It was strength against activity—that was evident from the first. The Master stood stolidly upon his K-leg. It gave him a tremendous pedestal; one could hardly imagine his being knocked down. And he could pivot round upon it with extraordinary quickness; but his advance or retreat was ungainly. His frame, however, was so much larger and broader than that of the student, and his brown, massive face looked so resolute and menacing, that the hearts of the Wilson party sank within them. There was one heart, however, which had not done so. It was that of Robert Montgomery.

Any nervousness which he may have had completely passed away now that he had his work before him. Here was something definite—this hard-faced, deformed Hercules to beat, with a career as the price of beating him. He glowed with the joy of action; it thrilled through his nerves. He faced his man with little in-and-out steps, breaking to the left, breaking to the right, feeling his way, while Craggs, with a dull, malignant eye, pivoted slowly upon his weak leg, his left arm half extended, his right sunk low across the mark. Montgomery led with his left, and then led again, getting lightly home each time. He tried again, but the Master had his counter ready, and Montgomery reeled back from a harder blow than he had given. Anastasia, the woman, gave a shrill cry of encouragement, and her man let fly his right. Montgomery ducked under it, and in an instant the two were in each other's arms.

"Break away! Break away!" said the referee.

The Master struck upwards on the break, and shook Montgomery with the blow. Then it was "time." It had been a spirited opening round. The people buzzed into comment and applause. Montgomery was quite fresh, but the hairy chest of the Master was rising and falling. The man passed a sponge over his head, while Anastasia flapped the towel before him. "Good lass! Good lass!" cried the crowd, and cheered her.

The men were up again, the Master grimly watchful, Montgomery as alert as a kitten. The Master tried a sudden rush, squattering along with his awkward gait, but coming faster than one would think. The student slipped aside and avoided him. The Master stopped, grinned, and shook his head. Then he motioned with his hand as an invitation to Montgomery to come to him. The student did so and led with his left, but got a swinging right counter in the ribs in exchange. The heavy blow staggered him, and the Master came scrambling in to complete his advantage; but Montgomery, with his greater activity, kept out of danger until the call of "time." A tame round, and the advantage with the Master.

"T' Maister's too strong for him," said a smelter to his neighbour.

"Ay; but t'other's a likely lad. Happen we'll see some sport yet. He can joomp rarely."

"But t' Maister can stop and hit rarely. Happen he'll mak' him joomp when he gets his neif upon him."

They were up again, the water glistening upon their faces. Montgomery led instantly and got his right home with a sounding smack upon the Master's forehead. There was a shout from the colliers, and "Silence! Order!" from the referee. Montgomery avoided the counter and scored with his left. Fresh applause, and the referee upon his feet in indignation. "No comments, gentlemen, if *you* please, during the rounds."

"Just bide a bit!" growled the Master.

"Don't talk—fight!" said the referee, angrily.

Montgomery rubbed in the point by a flush hit upon the mouth, and the Master shambled back to his corner like an angry bear, having had all the worst of the round.

"Where's that seven to one?" shouted Purvis, the publican. "I'll take six to one!"

There were no answers.

"Five to one!" There were givers at that. Purvis booked them in a tattered notebook.

Montgomery began to feel happy. He lay back with his legs outstretched, his back against the corner-post and one gloved hand upon each rope. What a delicious minute it was between each round. If he could only keep out of harm's way, he must surely wear this man out before the end of twenty rounds. He was so slow that all his strength went for nothing. "You're fightin' a winnin' fight—a winnin' fight," Ted Barton whispered in his ear. "Go canny; tak' no chances; you have him proper."

But the Master was crafty. He had fought so many battles with his maimed limb that he knew how to make the best of it. Warily and slowly he manœuvred round Montgomery, stepping forward and yet again forward until he had imperceptibly backed him into his corner. The student suddenly saw a flash of triumph upon the grim face, and a gleam in the dull, malignant eyes. The Master was upon him. He sprang aside and was on the ropes. The Master smashed in one of his terrible upper-cuts, and Montgomery half broke it with his guard. The student sprang the other way and was against the other converging rope. He was trapped in the angle. The Master sent in another, with a hoggish grunt which spoke of the energy behind it. Montgomery ducked, but got a jab from the left upon the mark. He closed with his man. "Break away! Break away!" cried the referee. Montgomery disengaged and got a swinging blow on the ear as he did so. It had been a damaging round for him, and the Croxley people were shouting their delight.

"Gentlemen, I will *not* have this noise!" Stapleton roared. "I have been accustomed to preside at a well-conducted club, and not at a bear-garden." This little man, with the tilted hat and the bulging forehead, dominated the whole assembly. He was like a headmaster among his boys. He glared round him, and nobody cared to meet his eye.

Anastasia had kissed the Master when he resumed his seat. "Good lass. Do't again!" cried the laughing crowd, and the angry Master shook his glove at her, as she flapped her towel in front of him. Montgomery was weary and a little sore, but not depressed. He had learned something. He would not again be tempted into danger.

For three rounds the honours were fairly equal. The student's hitting was the quicker, the Master's the harder. Profiting by his lesson, Montgomery kept himself in the open, and refused to be herded into a corner. Sometimes the Master succeeded in rushing him to the side-ropes, but the younger man slipped away, or closed, and then disengaged. The monotonous "Break away! Break away!" of the referee broke in upon the quick, low patter of rubber-soled shoes, the dull thud of the blows, and the sharp, hissing breath of two tired men.

The ninth round found both of them in fairly good condition. Montgomery's head was still singing from the blow that he had in the corner, and one of his thumbs pained him acutely and seemed to be dislocated. The Master showed no sign of a touch, but his breathing was the more laboured, and a long line of ticks upon the referee's paper showed that the student had a good show of points. But one of this iron-man's blows was worth three of his, and he knew that without the gloves he could not have stood for three rounds against him. All the amateur work that he had done was the merest tapping and flapping when compared to those frightful blows, from arms toughened by the shovel and the crowbar.

It was the tenth round, and the fight was half over. The betting was now only three to one, for the Wilson champion had held his own much better than had been expected. But those who knew the ring-craft as well as the staying-power of the old prize-fighter knew that the odds were still a long way in his favour.

"Have a care of him!" whispered Barton, as he sent his man up to the scratch. "Have a care! He'll play thee a trick, if he can."

But Montgomery saw, or imagined he saw, that his antagonist was tiring. He looked jaded and listless, and his hands drooped a little from their position. His own youth and condition were beginning to tell. He sprang in and brought off a fine left-handed lead. The Master's return lacked his usual fire. Again Montgomery led, and again he got home. Then he tried his right upon the mark, and the Master guarded it downwards.

"Too low! Too low! A foul! A foul!" yelled a thousand voices.

The referee rolled his sardonic eyes slowly round. "Seems to me this buildin' is chock-full of referees," said he.

The people laughed and applauded, but their favour was as immaterial to him as their anger.

"No applause, please! This is not a theatre!" he yelled.

Montgomery was very pleased with himself. His adversary was evidently in a bad way. He was piling on his points and establishing a lead. He might as well make hay while the sun shone. The Master was looking all abroad. Montgomery popped one upon his blue jowl and got away without a return. And then the Master suddenly dropped both his hands and began rubbing his thigh. Ah! that was it, was it! He had muscular cramp.

"Go in! Go in!" cried Teddy Barton.

Montgomery sprang wildly forward, and the next instant was lying half senseless, with his neck nearly broken, in the middle of the ring.

The whole round had been a long conspiracy to tempt him within reach of one of those terrible right-hand upper-cuts for which the Master was famous. For this the listless, weary bearing, for this the cramp in the thigh. When Montgomery had sprang in so hotly he had exposed himself to such a blow as neither flesh nor blood could stand. Whizzing up from below with a rigid arm, which put the Master's eleven stone into its force, it struck him under the jaw: he whirled half round, and fell a helpless and half-paralysed mass. A vague groan and murmur, inarticulate, too excited for words, rose from the great audience. With open mouths and staring eyes they gazed at the twitching and quivering figure.

"Stand back! Stand right back!" shrieked the referee, for the Master was standing over his man ready to give him the *coup-de-grâce* as he rose.

"Stand back, Craggs, this instant!" Stapleton repeated.

The Master sank his hands sulkily and walked backwards to the rope with his ferocious eyes fixed upon his fallen antagonist. The timekeeper called the seconds. If ten of them passed before Montgomery rose to his feet, the fight was ended. Ted Barton wrung his hands and danced about in an agony in his corner.

As if in a dream—a terrible nightmare—the student could hear the voice of the timekeeper—three—four—five—he got up on his hand—six—seven—he was on his knee, sick, swimming, faint, but resolute to rise. Eight—he was up, and the Master was on him like a tiger, lashing savagely at him with both hands. Folk held their breath as they watched those terrible blows, and anticipated the pitiful end—so much more pitiful where a game but helpless man refuses to accept defeat.

Strangely automatic is the human brain. Without volition, without effort, there shot into the memory of this bewildered, staggering, half-stupefied man the one thing which could have saved him—that blind eye of which the Master's son had spoken. It was the same as the other to look at, but Montgomery remembered that he had said that it was the left. He reeled to the left side, half felled by a drive which lit upon his shoulder. The Master pivoted round upon his leg and was at him in an instant.

"Yark him, lad! yark him!" screamed the woman.

"Hold your tongue!" said the referee.

Montgomery slipped on the left again and yet again; but the Master was too quick and clever for him. He struck round and got him full on the face as he tried once more to break away. Montgomery's knees weakened under him, and he fell with a groan on the floor. This time he knew that he was done. With bitter agony he realized, as he groped blindly with his hands, that he could not possibly raise himself. Far away and muffled he heard, amid the murmurs of the multitude, the fateful voice of the timekeeper counting off the seconds.

"One—two—three—four—five—six——"

"Time!" said the referee.

Then the pent-up passion of the great assembly broke loose. Croxley gave a deep groan of disappointment. The Wilsons were on their feet, yelling with delight. There was still a chance for them. In four more seconds their man would have been solemnly counted out. But now he had a minute in which to recover. The referee looked round with relaxed features and laughing eyes. He loved this rough game, this school for humble heroes, and it was pleasant to him to intervene as a *deus ex machina* at so dramatic a moment. His chair and his hat were both tilted at an extreme angle; he and the timekeeper smiled at each other. Ted Barton and the other second had rushed out and thrust an arm each under Montgomery's knee, the other behind his loins, and so carried him back to his stool. His head lolled upon his shoulder, but a douche of cold water sent a shiver through him, and he started and looked round him.

"He's a' right!" cried the people round. "He's a rare brave lad. Good lad! Good lad!" Barton poured some brandy into his mouth. The mists cleared a little, and he realized where he was and what he had to do. But he was still very weak, and he hardly dared to hope that he could survive another round.

"Seconds out of the ring!" cried the referee. "Time!"

The Croxley Master sprang eagerly off his stool.

"Keep clear of him! Go easy for a bit," said Barton; and Montgomery walked out to meet his man once more.

He had had two lessons—the one when the Master got him into his corner, the other when he had been lured into mixing it up with so powerful an antagonist. Now he would be wary. Another blow would finish him; he could afford to run no risks. The Master was determined to follow up his advantage, and rushed at him, slogging furiously right and left. But Montgomery was too young and active to be caught. He was strong upon his legs once more, and his wits had all come back to him. It was a gallant sight—

the line-of-battleship trying to pour its overwhelming broadside into the frigate, and the frigate manœuvring always so as to avoid it. The Master tried all his ring-craft. He coaxed the student up by pretended inactivity; he rushed at him with furious rushes towards the ropes. For three rounds he exhausted every wile in trying to get at him. Montgomery during all this time was conscious that his strength was minute by minute coming back to him. The spinal jar from an upper-cut is overwhelming, but evanescent. He was losing all sense of it beyond a great stiffness of the neck. For the first round after his downfall he had been content to be entirely on the defensive, only too happy if he could stall off the furious attacks of the Master. In the second he occasionally ventured upon a light counter. In the third he was smacking back merrily where he saw an opening. His people yelled their approval of him at the end of every round. Even the iron-workers cheered him with that fine unselfishness which true sport engenders. To most of them, unspiritual and unimaginative, the sight of this clean-limbed young Apollo, rising above disaster and holding on while consciousness was in him to his appointed task, was the greatest thing their experience had ever known.

But the Master's naturally morose temper became more and more murderous at this postponement of his hopes. Three rounds ago the battle had been in his hands; now it was all to do over again. Round by round his man was recovering his strength. By the fifteenth he was strong again in wind and limb. But the vigilant Anastasia saw something which encouraged her.

"That bash in t' ribs is telling on him, Jock," she whispered. "Why else should he be gulping t' brandy? Go in, lad, and thou hast him yet."

Montgomery had suddenly taken the flask from Barton's hand, and had a deep pull at the contents. Then, with his face a little flushed, and with a curious look of purpose, which made the referee stare hard at him, in his eyes, he rose for the sixteenth round.

"Game as a pairtridge!" cried the publican, as he looked at the hard-set face.

"Mix it oop, lad; mix it oop!" cried the iron-men to their Master.

And then a hum of exultation ran through their ranks as they realized that their tougher, harder, stronger man held the vantage, after all.

Neither of the men showed much sign of punishment. Small gloves crush and numb, but they do not cut. One of the Master's eyes was even more flush with his cheek than Nature had made it. Montgomery had two or three livid marks upon his body, and his face was haggard, save for that pink spot which the brandy had brought into either cheek. He rocked a little as he stood opposite his man, and his hands drooped as if he felt the gloves to be an unutterable weight. It was evident that he was spent and desperately weary. If he received one other blow it must surely be fatal to him. If he brought one home, what power could there be behind it, and what chance was there of its harming the colossus in front of him? It was the crisis of the fight. This round must decide it. "Mix it oop, lad; mix it oop!" the iron-men whooped. Even the savage eyes of the referee were unable to restrain the excited crowd.

Now, at last, the chance had come for Montgomery. He had learned a lesson from his more experienced rival. Why should he not play his own game upon him? He was spent, but not nearly so spent as he pretended. That brandy was to call up his reserves, to let him have strength to take full advantage of the opening when it came. It was thrilling and tingling through his veins, at the very moment when he was lurching and rocking like a beaten man. He acted his part admirably. The Master felt that there was an easy task before him, and rushed in with ungainly activity to finish it once for all. He slap-banged away left and right, boring Montgomery up against the ropes, swinging in his ferocious blows with those animal grunts which told of the vicious energy behind them.

But Montgomery was too cool to fall a victim to any of those murderous upper-cuts. He kept out of harm's way with a rigid guard, an active foot, and a head which was swift to duck. And yet he contrived to present the same appearance of a man who is hopelessly done. The Master, weary from his own shower of blows, and fearing nothing from so weak a man, dropped his hand for an instant, and at that instant Montgomery's right came home.

It was a magnificent blow, straight, clean, crisp, with the force of the loins and the back behind it. And it landed where he had meant it to—upon the exact point of that blue-grained chin. Flesh and blood could not stand such a blow in such a place. Neither valour nor hardihood can save the man to whom it comes. The Master fell backwards, flat, prostrate, striking the ground with so simultaneous a clap that it was like a shutter falling from a wall. A yell which no referee could control broke from the crowded benches as the giant went down. He lay upon his back, his knees a little drawn up, his huge chest panting. He twitched and shook, but could not move. His feet pawed convulsively once or twice. It was no use. He was done. "Eight—nine—ten!" said the timekeeper, and the roar of a thousand voices, with a deafening clap like the broadside of a ship, told that the Master of Croxley was the Master no more.

Montgomery stood half dazed, looking down at the huge, prostrate figure. He could hardly realize that it was indeed all over. He saw the referee motion towards him with his hand. He heard his name bellowed in triumph from every side. And then he was aware of some one rushing towards him; he caught a glimpse of a flushed face and an aureole of flying red hair, a gloveless fist struck him between the eyes, and he was on his back in the ring beside his antagonist, while a dozen of his supporters were endeavouring to secure the frantic Anastasia. He heard the angry shouting of the referee, the screaming of the furious woman, and the cries of the mob. Then something seemed to break like an over-stretched banjo-string, and he sank into the deep, deep, mist-girt abyss of unconsciousness.

The dressing was like a thing in a dream, and so was a vision of the Master with the grin of a bulldog upon his face, and his three teeth amiably protruded. He shook Montgomery heartily by the hand.

"I would have been rare pleased to shake thee by the throttle, lad, a short

while syne," said he. "But I bear no ill-feelin' again' thee. It was a rare poonch that brought me down—I have not had a better since my second fight wi' Billy Edwards in '89. Happen thou might think o' goin' further wi' this business. If thou dost, and want a trainer, there's not much inside t' ropes as I don't know. Or happen thou might like to try it wi' me old style and bare knuckles. Thou hast but to write to t' iron-works to find me."

But Montgomery disclaimed any such ambition. A canvas bag with his share—one hundred and ninety sovereigns—was handed to him, of which he gave ten to the Master, who also received some share of the gate-money. Then, with young Wilson escorting him on one side, Purvis on the other, and

Fawcett carrying his bag behind, he went in triumph to his carriage, and drove amid a long roar, which lined the highway like a hedge for the seven miles, back to his starting-point.

"It's the greatest thing I ever saw in my life. By George, it's ripping!" cried Wilson, who had been left in a kind of ecstasy by the events of the day. "There's a chap over Barnsley way who fancies himself a bit. Let us spring you on him, and let him see what he can make of you. We'll put up a purse—won't we, Purvis? You shall never want a backer."

"At his weight," said the publican, "I'm behind him, I am, for twenty rounds, and no age, country, or colour barred."

"So am I!" cried Fawcett; "middle-weight champion of the world, that's what he is—here, in the same carriage with us."

But Montgomery was not to be beguiled.

"No; I have my own work to do now."

"And what may that be?"

"I'll use this money to get my medical degree."

"Well, we've plenty of doctors, but you're the only man in the Riding that could smack the Croxley Master off his legs. However, I suppose you know your own business best. When you're a doctor, you'd best come down into these parts, and you'll always find a job waiting for you at the Wilson Coal-pits."

Montgomery had returned by devious ways to the surgery. The horses were smoking at the door and the doctor was just back from his long journey. Several patients had called in his absence, and he was in the worst of tempers.

"I suppose I should be glad that you have come back at all, Mr. Montgomery!" he snarled. "When next you elect to take a holiday, I trust it will not be at so busy a time."

"I am sorry, sir, that you should have been inconvenienced."

"Yes, sir, I have been exceedingly inconvenienced." Here, for the first time, he looked hard at the assistant. "Good heavens, Mr. Montgomery, what have you been doing with your left eye?"

It was where Anastasia had lodged her protest.

Montgomery laughed. "It is nothing, sir," said he.

"And you have a livid mark under your jaw. It is, indeed, terrible that my representative should be going about in so disreputable a condition. How did you receive these injuries?"

"Well, sir, as you know, there was a little glove-fight to-day over at Croxley."

"And you got mixed up with that brutal crowd?"

"I *was* rather mixed up with them."

"And who assaulted you?"

"One of the fighters."

"Which of them?"

"The Master of Croxley."

"Good heavens! Perhaps you interfered with him?"

"Well, to tell the truth, I did a little."

"Mr. Montgomery, in such a practice as mine, intimately associated as it is with the highest and most progressive elements of our small community, it is impossible——"

But just then the tentative bray of a cornet-player searching for his keynote jarred upon their ears, and an instant later the Wilson Colliery brass band was in full cry with "See the Conquering Hero Comes," outside the surgery window. There was a banner waving, and a shouting crowd of miners.

"What is it? What does it mean?" cried the angry doctor.

"It means, sir, that I have, in the only way which was open to me, earned the money which is necessary for my education. It is my duty, Doctor Old-acre, to warn you that I am about to return to the University, and that you should lose no time in appointing my successor."

FRANÇOIS VILLON MEETS A WOMAN

JOHN ERSKINE

FRANÇOIS VILLON, poet in flight, turned on his side, woke in a state of panic, and tried to recall where he was.

The light was gray, an hour before dawn.

The stamp of a horse! Had they found him? He sat up on the hay-mow.

No, it was the farmer below, working at the cow. He could hear the swish of milk in the pail. Master Villon collapsed upon his stolen bed.

God, but he was hungry! Just listen to that milk! And in the farm kitchen, for honest care-free men, there would be eggs and bread, perhaps a slice of pig or chicken.

His thoughts went back to the wrongs he had suffered. Old stories, all of them. Except Marguerite, of course. Before Marguerite—Catherine. If ever he got his hands on Catherine again, he'd cut her throat. Or break her neck. Or strangle her slowly, till her beautiful eyes popped out. There's woman-kind for you—take your love while the pocket is full, leave you in your bad hour.

And Noah Jolis, who to please Catherine had beaten him—and Margot, his fat sister—and Robin Turgis, of the Pine Cone Tavern, who had Margot for wife and deserved no better!

These memories pained him most when the stomach was empty, hunger and indignation being twins. With that one windfall of food, five miles out of Paris, he had recovered a modicum of Christian charity. Except for Catherine. Heaven be his aid, he would hate her to the end.

There was of course that affair at the College of Navarre, the prick to his conscience which made flight easier, the strongest excuse he had given the provost to stretch his neck. Fortunately, the provost didn't yet connect him with the crime. Meanwhile Master Villon reflected that justice is a slippery thing, hard to define and rarely enforced. All theft is disorderly and should if possible be avoided. To rob a church is sin. And unprofitable. From the college chapel his share had been one false piece of silver and four genuine sous. The provost would do his duty as to the four sous, but the worshiper who had offered the bad piece would be free to go to church again.

Because he loved Catherine, he had told her the truth. You can't cheat a girl you really love, and she had been the first to make him wish he were a decent man. But when she learned his danger she drove him into the night, and when he came back desperate she had those ruffians at the door, to beat him up. And Noah Jolis, standing by, laughed. Noah might be sleeping with her now.

The farmer below, having exhausted the cow, was climbing the ladder for hay. Master Villon held his breath, in prudence rather than in fear. The lout would do no worse than swear at him.

The pitchfork touched his left leg and drew an involuntary grunt. His hand went to his knife, by instinct, but the peasant didn't wait. Master Villon heard a thump as the fellow slid down the ladder and hit the ground, then made for the farmhouse, where a dog barked, asking to be unchained.

Master Villon, having finished his sleep for the day, got over the farm wall and plied his legs, the scratched one and the sound, along the river road, toward the southeast.

His head was dizzy by the time he came to the château, two hours before noon. Villages on the way had been few and sleepy-looking, yet he had skirted them all. The château seemed austere, not the sort of place the provost's men would stop at. Master Villon found the gate and pulled the bell-chain.

He could hear the tinkle inside, but no one answered. He pulled once more. The house was, as you might say, dead.

It wouldn't do to climb the front wall, not in the broad sun, but around at the back, where you might expect a garden, an old apple tree furnished a screen for his gymnastics, and once down among the rosebushes he aimed straight for the kitchen door.

Locked tight. All the doors. To his regret Master Villon was forced to enter by an unshuttered window.

At the foot of the stairs, in the main hall, he halloed, to establish an honorable relation with the inmates, but only the echo was roused. Having eased his conscience, he sought the kitchen from the inside; that door also was bolted. Had Master Villon been a man to despair, his weakened knees would have sunk under him altogether.

But while there was still a pencil of strength in his legs he mounted the stairs and inspected the richly garnished bedrooms where those could sleep whose fathers, he reflected, had done their stealing for them.

And in one room he paused, with extra bitterness: a woman's boudoir, laced and silken. A wardrobe for her gowns—a massive dresser full no doubt of whatever went next to her delicate skin—a canopied bed with a blue pillow. He could see the white thing resting there, head cushioned, eyelids closed. Catherine! Damn her!

From the window he learned why the house was silent. In yonder vineyard the servants, male and female, gathered grapes. Among them must be the cook.

So the woman who used this room was on a journey with her husband,

and the servants expected no early return. Doubtless a handsome creature with a selfish heart, like Catherine's, and an itch to see the world, and her husband would rather be home but she needed watching. The devil help the man! Master Villon would walk on.

Before he walked, however, he pulled out the trays of the dresser, he being thorough in all his visits, and the contents were what he had supposed, dainty, intimate and troubling—fresh-laundered, scented, neatly folded.

On a pair of black stockings, in the middle of the top drawer, lay a shining gold piece.

What heaven sends, heaven sends! The muscles were working again in Master Villon's legs as he dusted down the road in search of meat and drink.

Midway through the afternoon he found what belonged to him, where the Seine forks with another river, and a tree-shaded town nested between shores. The inn was called "La Belle Image." There was a woman's face on the sign. Master Villon removed his hat, ran his hand over his bald head, stroked his long nose, and recognized the will of God.

When he opened the door the inn-keeper, missing baggage and means of transportation, remained at ease in his chair, with his apron on.

"Food!" said Master Villon. "Beef, red wine, bread!" With that he stepped over the bench by the inn table and thrust his tired legs underneath.

"Money?" said the man in the chair.

Master Villon rang his gold piece on the board, at which music the host rose, as to Gabriel's horn.

"Put your bonnet on the nail yonder," said he, "while I fry an egg. There's a roast on the spit but it won't be cooked through till sundown."

"An egg," said Master Villon, ringing the nail with his hat, "will render appetite endurable without killing it. Let cheese and ale be included in this temporary sustenance."

In a moment his cheeks were full of bread and cheese, and without ale he would have choked, so ravenously he went at it, but before the egg was fried a coach thundered up to the inn door, and Master Villon had been too close to his plate to note the direction it came from. Moreover, there was a convoy of three horsemen, well armed.

While the inn-keeper was out in front, bowing to this unusual company, Master Villon got his hat from the peg, found a window in the taproom, and sought the picturesque bushes along the river bank.

Once there, he repented of his haste. Though screened from possible pursuers, he couldn't inquire whether he really was pursued. His shelter had no look-out. Why hadn't he examined the coachload first? There, someone was hunting him now!

It was a girl of nineteen or twenty, swinging her sunhat by the ribbon, a reasonably tall young woman with engaging endowments of person and, it seemed, qualities of mind. To Master Villon, who had expected the provost, she was beauty itself. His own quick black eyes observed that hers were brown, wide-set with long lashes. When she saw him she betrayed neither astonishment nor fear nor boldness. She accepted him with the rest of the sunset-colored landscape. Her linen gown, plain but well-fitted, hid little of a bosom which Catherine would have envied—a gray dress, a broad white collar, a blue ribbon at her throat. Of what such a body might say to a man, her sincere eyes were not aware. By her hands, had he seen nothing else, he would have known a lady.

"I couldn't wait," she said.

Master Villon bowed cautiously.

"Father says the river is loveliest at this bend. After dinner it would be too dark."

Master Villon, who had given the river no study, turned to look at it.

"The dark green of the trees over there, the purple shadows, the dreamy slide of the water—it *is* the best hour, wouldn't you say?"

Master Villon returned her smile. "I have enjoyed none better."

"Do you come often?"

He shook his head. "Seldom."

"Then you don't live in Corbeil?"

Attending to the name of the town, he let slip the truth. "My home is in Paris."

"From choice?" she asked sympathetically, then corrected herself. "Of course I don't really know Paris."

"I can see that," said he.

She laughed. "Father will have a fit. You stay at the inn?"

They walked back side by side.

"How," she asked, "do you pass the time, when you are in Paris?"

He couldn't tell her he was a thief. Nor a Master of Arts—not in that dusty jacket, with the knife slung from his belt. "I lack a reputable profession," said he. "I am a bad poet."

She laughed again, to deride his modesty, but her father at the inn door was displeased. "You detain us all from dinner, Louise!"

A tall gentleman with white beard trimmed to a point, neat mustaches, keen eyes.

"I found a poet in the river," said she, unrebuked.

"My lady honored me," said Master Villon, bowing to the tall man. "François des Loges, at your service."

The keen eyes fastened on him. "Which Des Loges?"

"There is but one of me," said Master Villon, "born, such as I am, in Paris or near-by."

"Are you sure?"

"I am not," said Master Villon. "I take my mother's word for it."

The tall man held out his hand, not yet letting go with his eyes. "The Seigneur de Grigny, at *your* service."

Master Villon knew the Seigneur de Grigny did not like him, but he had faced adverse opinion before, and just then the inn-keeper summoned them to dinner.

"The egg was wasted," he complained. "I thought you had left without paying."

"Your river view," said Master Villon, "is worth a dozen eggs."

"Not to mention," said the girl, "the pleasure of conversation with me. Will you sit at our end of the table, master poet?"

From then on the inn-keeper thought well of him, whatever may have been in the seigneur's mind, and the girl with her cheerful questions gave him scarcely an interval for soup-swallowing.

"Do you write poems every day, or only while you are at home?"

Master Villon broke off a piece of bread. "As heaven decides, my lady."

"What are your poems about? Love?"

The seigneur looked up, to watch his reply.

"I deal with that theme, from time to time. Also with hate."

"Hate? That wouldn't be poetry!"

Her father interrupted. "Monsieur des Loges, have you ever eaten at the king's table?"

Master Villon shook his head, his mouth being full.

"You know my friend, D'Estouteville?"

Master Villon swallowed hard. "Who?"

"The Provost of Paris."

Knowing the provost entirely too well, Master Villon shied away. "The Duke of Orleans is a friend of mine, in a sense my protector."

"Ah!" said the girl. "There's a poet for you!"

The seigneur smiled, ever so slightly. "I *thought* we had met before."

Master Villon let the subject die, more willingly as the girl looked up, ready with another idea.

"The fine folk kill each other, don't they?"

"Where?"

"Paris. Father says so. And the poor starve. Don't they, Father?"

The seigneur was examining his knife, which edge to cut with.

"In all cities," said Master Villon, "there is mischief. The evil with the good. We have the river, this same river, and the islands, and the markets, and the churches, of course, and the inns, and the streets."

"Leave nothing out," said the seigneur. "Mention the jail."

"Father!" said the girl, brushing aside the discordant suggestion. "The streets," she went on, "are crooked and crowded."

"Men and women," said Master Villon. "Give me those, and I can live."

The seigneur's eyes almost lifted, then chose not to.

"The women," said the girl, pleased with her inexperience for knowing so much. "You don't need the men. Why did you come away?"

There was no impertinence in her questions, only a cordial turning-over as of a book's pages, to get at the plot quickly.

"In summer," said he, "when the town is hot, I take to the road."

She laughed. "For peace?"

"Among other things."

"And even here a woman interrupts!"

"Louise," said the seigneur, "talk less and eat. We must be on our journey."

"Father, if Monsieur des Loges is homeward bound—you are, aren't you?"

He was, so long as the seigneur listened. To be headed openly for Paris might establish credit.

"Then he can ride with us, can't he? There's room in the coach."

"Unless I walk," said Master Villon hastily, "I miss the flavor of travel."

"You're not walking to Paris?" said the girl. "Not with your trunk on your back?"

"On these short rambles, my lady, I exchange the convenience of luggage for an easier touch of earth and weather."

"So far as our paths are the same," said the seigneur, with unforeseen complacence, "we shall be glad of your company, Monsieur des Loges."

Master Villon had met danger too often not to recognize the signs. The tall man must have something up his sleeve.

"At any other time, my lord——"

"Now!" said the girl. "We won't take no."

So the inn-keeper, who had his ear out, came to the side of the seigneur's chair, and at his invitation recited from memory the cost of feeding one gentleman and one daughter, together with one coachman, one footman, and three outriders, who ate in the kitchen, together with five horses, who ate in the stall.

"Monsieur des Loges," said the seigneur, more affable than the inn-keeper himself, "since you are for the moment my guest, will you give me the pleasure——"

"A thousand thanks," said Master Villon, starting to fish in his pocket, "but I happen to have——"

"There was also," said the inn-keeper, "an egg, cooked though not consumed. Half a pound of cheese. A quart of ale."

"Naturally," said the seigneur, untying his purse. "Will you now fetch the coach?"

So the horses clattered up, the footman held the door, the girl stepped in, Master Villon with his gold piece unbroken took the seat on her left side, the seigneur the place of honor on the right. The inn-keeper waved them off into the darkness, but no one noticed him.

They rode in silence, because the highway was rough, and for better reasons. Twice the girl spoke, but since it would have been equally appropriate for her father or the poet to reply, each left the privilege to the other.

"Suppose I hadn't cared to look at the river!"

Master Villon was estimating his chances of slipping away. Sooner or later the coach would stop. Should he thank them bravely, affect the light-hearted minstrel, and walk on humming a tune? Or should he dodge behind the coach and run?

"I feel as though we'd been absent a lifetime!"

He wouldn't run. He had no wish to slip away. Her knee was touching his, and if he could reform his impulses so as not to emphasize the pressure, she might continue to believe he was the upholstery.

To steady himself against the jolting of the coach, he put his hand down, where he expected to find the leather cushion between them, but her hand was resting there.

"Pardon!" He drew back from the warm softness, wondering at his flush of shame.

A moment later the seigneur roused himself, leaned forward to look out the window, recognized a gleam in the night.

"We are home," said he. "Monsieur des Loges, might we interrupt your walk a second time by providing you with a bed?"

Master Villon saw a trap. "My lord, your kindness is already beyond measure. With your permission——"

The girl put her hand on his, and held it there.

"My lord, with your permission I will accept an honor which I do not deserve."

Hardly were the words out of him when the coach wheeled through the gate of the château from which he had stolen the piece of gold.

There was such a twist of conscience around his heart that he turned faint, standing in the great hall at the foot of the stairs, with the servants of the house greeting the man and his daughter, and the outriders helping in with the bags.

"Home again, and how I've missed my room!" said the girl, running up to be sure it was still there. Master Villon felt the sweat spring on his brow.

"Monsieur des Loges," said her father, leading the way to a small office behind the stairs, "if you'll draw the other bench to my desk, we'll share a bottle before we sleep. I like to wash out the dust."

Master Villon wiped his forehead with his hat, and sat down.

"My dear wife," continued the seigneur as the butler poured, "was a Des Loges. Louise des Loges. God rest her soul! I have been curious, ever since we met, as to the nearness of blood."

The butler having withdrawn, the white-bearded man raised a red glass, and Master Villon, for want of other ingenuity, returned the salute but did not drink.

"So far as the records are known," the seigneur went on, smacking his lips and stroking his mustache, "no Des Loges was ever a poet. A weakness for the arts was first detected in my side of the family."

Master Villon heard the girl coming from her room upstairs.

"Until this afternoon I had understood that no Des Loges was ever born in Paris, none at least of the authorized strain. . . . This wine is excellent— or would you prefer——"

Master Villon had counted her slow steps down the stairs, till she stood before them, calm but pale.

"Father, our house has been entered!"

The seigneur looked at her. "Nonsense! The servants were here. Nonsense!"

"My things have been moved around. The dresser has been searched. A gold piece is gone."

"Monsieur des Loges will form a sad opinion of us," said the tall man, rising with no great hurry. "Shall we examine the evidence, Monsieur des Loges?"

Though he pronounced the name somewhat too often, as it seemed to Master Villon, there was nothing for it but to follow them up the staircase and look again at what, to his regret, he had already seen.

"In the morning," said her father, finishing what you might call a surface survey, "I'll have it out with our people. You'd better not sleep here tonight, Louise."

"But of course I will! This is my room!"

"Then I'll show Monsieur des Loges to his bed across the hall," said her father, as docile as you could wish.

"Good night, poet," said she, quite herself again, holding out both hands for him to kiss. "I was silly to speak of this accident. Rest well!"

"There's a gown on the bed, Monsieur des Loges, and my other pair of slippers," said her father, closing the shutters against the night air. "Shall I send up some fruit, to nibble on?"

Master Villon cleared his throat. "I need nothing."

"Good dreams, then. I rise early but my daughter is usually late. Take your time."

Master Villon put off his shoes and stretched on the bed. The seigneur had removed the candle and the shutters were locked, unless a practised ear could mistake. In the hall below waited, no doubt, the men who had ridden beside the coach.

Yet it wasn't danger that kept him awake, but the gold piece and the girl to whom it belonged. Her hand on his! If she alone still thought generously of him, what might she learn at dawn?

Strange that he should melt before a creature so childlike, he who had shunned innocence and paid tribute rather to what was scarred and scorched. At the goodness which knows little, he had laughed. But lying there on the bed he wished the gold piece were where it should have stayed. He wished he could return with her to the river bank and admire the sunset. He wished he were—whatever she imagined him to be.

If her father intended to hold him till the Des Loges records could be examined, the provost might happen along with his rope, and if the girl were looking on while they searched his pockets, she would recognize the money and know he deserved to swing.

If on the other hand he could put the money back, then even if he hanged——

Calculating the hours by the growing wear on his patience, Master Villon gave the household ample time to fall asleep. With his shoes in his hand he then drew open his door, inch by inch. Diagonally to the left, if he could remember the precise angle——

When his groping fingers told him her door was not entirely closed, he stepped back, as from peril. It couldn't be true! Of another woman, yes, but not of her! How many times had he thanked fortune for a ripe adventure dropped in his hands! But now he wasn't thankful. His heart ached with fear that she might be like all the rest.

Well, he would restore the gold piece and take his chance with the watchmen downstairs. In every house, no matter how timid, one window is overlooked. . . . The dresser would be to the right—the top drawer.

In the darkness he fancied he could trace the figure on the bed. He tried not to breathe. The top drawer came out, noiseless . . . he smoothed down the folded black stockings . . . he laid the coin gently, felt it sink upon the fabric.

To his horror the lovely form sat up in bed, struck a vigorous flint, lighted a candle.

"François Villon," said the seigneur, bringing his boots down on the floor and rising fully clad, "the compliment which you meditated, the tribute to my daughter and therefore indirectly to me, is not acceptable. On your rambles, as I observed, you wear no sword, but happily I possess two. Take your choice!"

Master Villon, very weary of life at that moment, raised a limp hand and grasped one of the hilts her father was holding toward him in the candle gloom.

"There is more space in the hall," said the man, kicking a chair out of the way, "but it will be a pleasure to kill you here."

"Father! No!"

They both turned and saw her at the door, candle in hand, clad somewhat hastily in a trailing night-robe.

"Go back to my room, daughter!"

"You mustn't kill him! He meant no harm!"

"The worst rascal in France," said her father. "At the inn table I knew him. He accepted my hospitality, then stole here to dishonor you. I was sure he would."

Master Villon dropped his sword on the girl's bed, with the hilt toward the seigneur. "I'm not in the mood," said he. "Run the blade through me, and be done with it!"

The seigneur reached for the bell-cord. "You're no gentleman, François Villon. The two swords were for my daughter's sake, and because you happened to borrow my wife's name. Bring a rope," he went on as the outriders stuck their heads in. "We'll hang him from the window."

"Not from *my* window!" pleaded the girl. "Not from this house! I couldn't live here! I'd see his body swinging outside! I'd——"

"You have your mother's practical sense," said the seigneur. "Why soil a good home? François Villon, have the courtesy to be hanged elsewhere. I'll give you six hours' start. It is now past midnight. At seven or eight in the morning my dogs and my men will join you, under some convenient tree."

The outriders took him by the elbows and rushed him down the stairs.

"My hat," said Master Villon, "I left it in the office."

"His hat!" exclaimed the seigneur. "Give it to him. His hat!"

When they kicked him through the gate, she was standing by her father, motionless, with the night-robe around her.

Nine o'clock or thereabouts, next morning, she was walking in the rose garden when a bough cracked in the apple tree over the wall. The fruit that bounced at her feet was Master Villon.

She began to smile, then turned white. "Father is looking for you."

"I saw him ride off, my lady."

"I'm sorry you returned."

"My lady, do you regret our meeting in the first place?"

For a moment she stared at the ground.

"As Father said, you took his hospitality and then you——"

"He was playing a trick," said Master Villon with some heat. "He was catching a fly in honey. Hospitality should be too sacred for treacherous use!"

"You and Father may debate that, if you wish. I wasn't treacherous. I liked you. You knew I did. Yet you came looking for me where—where you thought I was."

Master Villon did not laugh at the sequence of her ideas; his mind was on what he must now tell her, and how she would take it.

"You believe, with your father, that I entered your room to possess you? I had no such purpose! The next time I come there, yes, but not last night."

She put those honest brown eyes on him. "Why did you come?"

"To return your gold piece."

For once she flinched, under the full blow of that news.

"That's how it came back! Then you are a thief!"

"I was. Until I met you."

They stood silent, the longest of moments.

"Why did you return this morning? Just to make certain that I knew the worst?"

"No!" said he, with sudden vigor. "To learn whether you too enjoy stamping on those who are found out!"

She may not have understood him. Or perhaps she did.

"The gold piece is not important. Not in the slightest!"

"To me," he said, "it is. Very!"

He bowed, hat on heart, as though closing the episode for the time being, and she watched while he climbed the wall, took hold of the apple bough for a safe purchase, and leapt to the turf outside.

FATHER AND THE COOK

CLARENCE DAY, JR.

I

ONE late afternoon when Father came up from downtown, he found his home much upset. Our cook had walked out and left us. I was a child of four, George was two, and there was a new baby besides. Mother was ill. She hadn't been able to leave us to go to an agency. And as she was no hand at cooking herself, the outlook for dinner was poor.

This state of affairs was unprecedented in all Father's experience. In his father's home, they never changed their servants suddenly; they seldom changed them at all; and as his mother was a past mistress of cooking, he had always been doubly protected. Since his marriage, he had had to live a much bumpier life. But this was the worst yet.

He asked Mother, who was lying in bed, what she was going to do about it. There were no telephones then, and she couldn't do anything at all, at the moment; but she said she would try to go to an agency in the morning and see what she could find. "In the morning? Good God!" Father said. "Where is the place, anyhow?" And he clapped on his hat and strode out again, over toward Sixth Avenue.

As I heard the story years afterward, it was late when he got there, and he bounded up the front stoop two or three steps at a time, and went quickly into the little office, where the gaslights were burning. He had never been in such a place before, and to his surprise it was empty, except for a severe-looking woman who sat at a desk at one side. "Where do you keep 'em?" he urgently demanded, his mind on the question of dinner.

She looked at him, got out her pen, and opened a large book deliberately. "I will take your name and address," she informed him, "and then, if you please, you may give me the details as to what kind of person you require and when you would wish her to call."

But Father had no time, he told her, for any damned fol-de-rol. "Where do you keep 'em?" he said again. She was standing in the way of his dinner. I can imagine how his face must have reddened and how his eyes must have blazed at her. "I am asking you where you keep them!" he roared.

"Why, the girls are in there," the lady explained, to calm him, "but clients are not allowed in that room. If you will tell me the kind of position you wish me to fill for you, I will have one come out."

Before she'd half finished, Father had thrown open the door and gone in. There sat a crowd of the girls, young and old, sickly and brawny, of all shapes and sizes; some ugly, some pretty and trim and stylish, some awkward; nurses, ladies' maids, waitresses, washerwomen, and cooks.

The manager was by now at Father's elbow, trying to make him get out, and insisting that he tell her the position he wished her to fill. But Father was swiftly glancing around at the crowd, and he paid no attention. He noticed a little woman in the corner, with honest gray eyes, who sat there, shrewd-looking and quiet. He pointed his cane over at her and said, "I'll take that one."

The manager was flustered, but still she kept trying to enforce her authority. She protested she didn't yet know the position. . . .

"Cook," Father said, "cook."

"But Margaret doesn't wish to be a cook, she wants—"

"You can cook, can't you?" Father demanded.

Margaret's plain little face was still pink with excitement and pleasure at being chosen above all that roomful by such a masterful gentleman. Father had probably smiled at her, too, for they liked each other at once. Well, she said, she had cooked for one family.

"Of course she can cook," Father said.

He said afterward, when describing the incident, "I knew at once she could cook."

The manager didn't like this at all. The discipline of the office was spoiled. "If you are going to take her anyhow," she said acidly, "what day would you wish her to come, and will you please give me your name?"

"Yes, yes," Father said, without giving it. "Come on, Margaret." And he planked down the fee and walked out.

Margaret followed him through the door and trotted over to our home at his heels. He sent her down to the kitchen immediately, while he went upstairs to dress.

"I don't know why you make such a fuss about engaging new servants. It's simple enough," he said comfortably to Mother that evening, after Margaret's first dinner.

It was the first of a long series, for she stayed with us twenty-six years.

II

In the summers, when we went to the country, our usual plan was to hire a temporary cook to go with us, so that Margaret could stay in town. We hated to leave her, but the idea was that somebody must stay to take care of the house. There were no electric burglar alarms in those days, and few special watchmen. Little Margaret made a pretty small watchman, for she was no size at all, but she had an indomitable spirit. So we'd leave her on guard while we went up to our summer home in Harrison with a substitute cook.

But this didn't work well. No matter how few the substitute's faults were, Father had no patience with them. One summer, I remember, there was a nice woman, Delia, who got on well with Mother because she was so obliging and pleasant, but who didn't suit Father at all. "I don't give a damn how obliging she is," he kept saying. "If she won't oblige me by cooking something fit to eat, she can go."

This didn't sound unreasonable, but Delia cooked well enough for the rest of us, and Mother hated to risk getting someone else who'd be temperamental. Our dining-room consequently became a battleground morning and night. At breakfast, Father would put down his coffee cup in disgust and roar: "Slops! Damn it, slops! Does she call this confounded mess coffee? Isn't there a damned soul in Westchester County who knows how to make coffee but me? I swear to God I can't even imagine how she concocts such atrocities. I come down to this room hungry every morning, and she tries to fill me with slops! Take it away, I tell you!" he would bellow to the waitress. "Take this accursed mess away!" And while she and Delia were frantically hurrying to make a fresh pot, he would savagely devour his omelet and bacon, and declare that his breakfast was ruined.

The longer Delia stayed with us, the more alarmed Father became. He ate heartily, as Mother kept pointing out to him, but he said he didn't feel nourished. He said it was no use to argue about it; he felt all gone inside. One night after he had had a four-course dinner, he fretfully got up from the table, went into the library with his cigar, and moaned that he was starved. His moans were, as always, full-throated, and they came from the heart. Every now and then, when his miserable condition seemed to strike him afresh, he laid down his book and shouted "Starved! Starved!" in a grief-stricken roar.

When Mother went in the library to quiet him, he told her he'd be damned if he'd stand it. "I refuse to be sent to my grave, do you hear me, by that infernal bog-trotting imbecile you keep in my kitchen."

"Now Clare, a Japanese is coming tomorrow, I told you. This is Delia's last night. I do hope you'll like Tobo. He won't know our ways right at the start, of course, but he is a very good cook."

Father was appeased for the moment by the dismissal of Delia. But the next night, when he found that the first dish was too Oriental, he said in an annoyed tone to Mother, "Will you kindly explain to your man Tobo that I am not a coolie?" And after eating the rest of his dinner, he pushed his plate away and went up to his bedroom, declaring vehemently that he was poisoned. He undressed, lay down on his sofa, and filled the air with deep groans.

From time to time he stopped and dozed a little, or listened to what he could hear of our talk. His feeling was that we shouldn't be talking at all. We ought to be sitting with bowed heads in silence until he recovered. "Poisoned!" he suddenly boomed, to remind us. "Oh, God! I am poisoned!"

At this point, Mother, who was down in the library, laughed. Father heard her. He jumped up from his sofa and marched from his bedroom indignantly into the hall. "I'm a sick man!" he thundered robustly. "And nobody in this house gives a damn!"

Mother hurried upstairs to see what he wanted. He insisted on her rubbing his back. Sick or well, that always soothed him, and he would have liked her to do it for hours. He loved to close his eyes, with someone's hand moving quietly on him, while a feeling of comfort flowed into his thoughts and his nerves.

Mother didn't think much of rubbing, however. She didn't like it herself. When anyone rubbed her, she stiffened and resisted at once. Consequently she had no idea of the right way to do it. When she had to rub Father, she always got tired of it in a very few minutes.

She gave him some hasty little rubs and digs as well as she could, but just as he was beginning to relax, she said, "There now, Clare, that's enough." Father was so disappointed by this that it reminded him that he was poisoned, and the only cure he could think of was the dismissal of Tobo.

The next day old Margaret was sent for to come at once to the country, and the house in town was locked up and left to take care of itself.

She came in a hack from the Harrison station. She was an odd sight. Her face looked familiar in her little black bonnet, tied under her chin, but she seemed strangely swollen and bulky; she stuck out in queer places; and as she crowded through the back door, she bruised me with her hard, bony hip. Only it wasn't her hip, it turned out; it was her favorite saucepan, which was tied to her waist under her skirt. Several large spoons, a dipper, a skillet, and two pair of shoes were made fast under it elsewhere. In her arms she had some bundles wrapped in newspapers, which Mother thought at first held her clothes, but when Margaret opened them we found they contained cheeses, melons, fresh coffee, a leg of lamb, some sweet potatoes, and other provisions. Margaret had no faith at all in being able to buy any supplies in the country. She had brought as complete a larder to Harrison as though we were at the North Pole.

"But didn't you bring any clothes with you, Margaret? Not even an apron?" asked Mother.

Little Margaret pursed her lips closely together and didn't answer at first. Then, as Mother stood waiting, she said unwillingly, "I have me other clothes on me."

She had wanted to have her hands free, it seemed, to bring us something good to eat. So under her street dress she was wearing two other dresses on that hot summer day, a collection of stiffly starched petticoats, three aprons, two night-gowns, and pretty much all the rest of her wardrobe.

As she was climbing upstairs to unpeel and unpack herself, Father saw her. "Is that you, Margaret?" he called, suddenly feeling much better. "Thank God!"

III

Old Margaret was just the kind of cook that we wanted. Lots of cooks can do rich dishes well. Margaret couldn't. But she cooked simple, everyday dishes in a way that made our mouths water. Her apple pies were the most satisfying pies I've ever tasted. Her warmed-up potatoes were so delicious I could have made my whole dinner of them.

Yet even Margaret sometimes miscalculated. A large, royal-looking steak would be set before Father, which, upon being cut into, would turn out to be too underdone. Father's face would darken with disappointment. If the earth had begun to wobble and reel in its orbit he could scarcely have been more disapproving. He would raise his foot, under the table, and stamp slowly and heavily three times on the rug. Thud; thud; thud.

At this solemn signal, we would hear Margaret leave the kitchen below us and come clumping step by step up the stairs to the dining-room door.

"Margaret, look at that steak."

Margaret would step nearer and peer with a shocked look at the platter. "The Lord bless us and save us," she would say to herself in a low voice. She would then seize the platter and make off with it, to better it the best way she could, and Father would gloomily wait and eat a few vegetables and pour out a fresh glass of claret.

Father and Margaret were united by the intense interest they both took in cooking. Each understood the other instinctively. They had a complete fellow-feeling. Mother's great interest was in babies—she had never been taught how to cook. All she wanted was to keep Father pleased somehow; and if it was too difficult she didn't always care about even that.

At table it was Father who carved the fowl, or sliced the roast lamb or beef. I liked to watch him whet the knife and go at it. He had such a fine, easy hand. To a hungry boy, he seemed overdeliberate and exact in his strokes, yet in a moment or two he had done. And usually the cooking had been as superb as the carving. Sometimes it was so perfect that Father's face would crinkle with pleasure, and with a wink at us he'd summon Margaret with his usual three measured thumps. She would appear, clutching her skirts with both hands, and looking worried. "What's wanting?" she'd ask.

"Margaret," Father would tell her affectionately, "that fricasseed chicken is *good.*"

Margaret would turn her wrinkled face aside, and look down, and push the flat of her hand out toward Father. It was the same gesture she used when she said "Get along with you" to flatterers. She couldn't say that to Father, but she would beam at him, and turn and go out, and stump back down the dark little stairs without ever a word.

Every once in a while, when the household bills were getting too high, a platter with three tiny French chops on it would be placed before Father, and a larger dish full of cold corned beef or Irish stew before Mother. At this sight we boys would stop talking and become round-eyed and still.

Father would look over at Mother's dish to see if it seemed appetizing, for he often said there was nothing better than one of Margaret's stews. The stew usually seemed possible enough to him, yet not quite what he wanted. He would then ask Mother if she'd have a chop.

Mother always said, "No."

"They look nice and juicy," Father would urge her, but she would say again she didn't want any, and turn her eyes away from the platter.

Father would then look around at the rest of us, doubtfully. He had four sons, all with appetites. He would clear his throat as though getting ready to offer a chop to each boy in turn; but he usually compromised by saying, "Will anyone else have a chop?"

"No, Clare," Mother would quickly and impatiently reply, "they're for you. The rest of us are going to have stew tonight." And she'd smile brightly but a little watchfully around at us boys, to be sure that we were making no fuss about it, while she hurried to get the thing settled.

We boys would then earnestly watch Father while he ate the three chops. Not that we didn't like Margaret's stew, which was the best in the world, but we regarded dinner as a special occasion, and we often had stew for lunch.

If some of us had taken up Father's offer, and left him with only one chop or none, I suppose that he would have asked Mother, "Where are the rest of the chops?" and been very cross about it when she told him there weren't any more. But his offer of them to us was sincere, though it cost him a struggle. He wanted plenty of food bought for everyone. His instincts were generous. Only, it made him cross if he suffered for those generous instincts.

Long after Margaret died, Father was speaking one night of how good her things always had tasted.

"I wish she could hear you," said Mother. She smiled tenderly at the thought of that gallant and dear little figure. "If anybody ever was sure of going to Heaven," she added, "I know it was Margaret."

This struck Father as a recommendation of the place. He took a sip of cognac and said casually, "I'll look her up when I get there. I'll have her take care of me."

Mother started to say something but checked herself.

"What's the matter?" he asked.

"Well, Clare dear," said Mother, "Margaret must be in some special part of Heaven, she was so good. You'd be very fortunate, Clare, to get to the same part as Margaret."

"Hah!" Father said, suddenly scowling. "I'll make a devil of a row if I don't."

THE GRAVE GRASS QUIVERS

MACKINLAY KANTOR

W E WERE alone, out there in the soft spring sunshine. There
was no one to disturb us. We dug silently, carefully.

The clinging, black earth came up at every shovelful—moist
and alive with the richness of the prairies. We had been digging for ten
minutes, when my shovel struck against something. It struck again, and something cracked.

After that, it wasn't long before we began to uncover things. "Murdered,"
Doc said, once, and then he didn't talk any more.

It began in Doc Martindale's office, which, as soon as he retired, was to
be my office, on a cool spring afternoon in 1921.

"How's it going?" asked Doc.

"I guess it'll be pretty slow here, to live," I said, childishly.

"Not much excitement," agreed Doc. He went to the door and picked up
a copy of the *Cottonwood Herald* which a boy had just tossed over the banis-
ters. . . . "Yes, local news is slow, pretty slow. There's a sample of a Cottonwood thriller."

It told of the plans for Arbor Day. The children of the public schools
were going to set out some trees as a memorial to the local boys who had
died in the World War.

. . . and selected as their choice, American elms. The trees will be
planted on the Louis Wilson farm, above the Coon River. Mr. Wilson
has agreed to donate a small plot of ground for this purpose. It is
thought that these trees, standing on a high hill above the river and
overlooking a majestic view of our city will be a fitting memorial.

Ceremonies are to begin at 2 p.m., and it is urged that all local people attend. Rev. J. Medley Williams of the Baptist Church will deliver
a——

Doc pulled his gray beard and laughed. "A few meetings, a church social, once in a while a fire or an auto accident! Once in a blue moon we have a divorce. Life comes—and goes—without much hullabaloo."

Then I had to laugh also, and a bit sheepishly. "I guess I'm rather silly. Of course those are the important things in most people's lives. But I would like to get called in on a nice, exciting murder once in awhile!"

Doc was silent for a moment. He appeared to be thinking heavily, as if he had taken me seriously. "Murders," he said, after a moment. "Once before the war, a Mexican section worker stabbed his wife. Then back in '96, an insane farmer shot his neighbor. But, come to think about it, those are the only murders we've ever had here in all my years of practice." He seemed much impressed. "Think of that, think of that! Only two murders since 1861."

"And who," I inquired idly, "was murdered in 1861?"

He tugged at his beard again, and cleared his throat. "Well," he said, slowly, "it was my father and my brother."

"Oh." And I scarcely knew what to say. "I'm sorry, Doctor, I——"

"No matter." He shrugged. "It's a long time. I was just a boy then."

My curiosity was aroused. "What are the details, Doctor? That is, if you don't——"

"Oh, I don't mind. . . . Sit down and take it easy." He fumbled around for his matches, and his fat, brown cigar had been fogging the room for several minutes before he began to talk.

"My brother Titus—he was a lot older—had run away from home when he was small, and gone West with some folks. He didn't come back until the spring of '61. And when he came, what a time!"

He laughed his short, dry laugh.

"Titus had struck it rich. He had about seven thousand dollars in gold with him.

"Pa and Titus decided to take the gold to Hamilton. There was a sort of bank opened up there, and the folks were afraid to risk keeping so much money around home.

"They were pretty careful, too, and didn't tell around town much about what they planned. They started out at night, figuring to get clear away from Cottonwood and the settlers who knew them, before daylight. Pa and Titus were big strapping men. They looked very strong, setting up on the board laid across the plank wagon box, and Titus carried a navy revolver on his hip and a Sharps rifle across his knees."

Doc Martindale shifted his fat, bumpy body in his old swivel chair. "And that," he said, "was the last we ever saw them.

"On the evening of the second day after my folks left," Doc Martindale continued, "a farmer from the Salt Creek neighborhood rode up in front of our house, and said that he had seen our team down in a clump of willows by Little Hell Slough, hitched to a wagon, and that the men folks were not with the wagon. The team had been dragging around, and tried to go home, but they got hung up in the willows."

Old Doc was silent for several minutes.

"That was a terrible night," he said, simply. "Before we all got down to Little Hell Slough—most of the neighbors were with us—we found the team in those willows, pretty muddy and hungry, and tangled up in the harness, too.

"None of the stuff in the wagon had been taken except—sure: the gold was gone. The blankets were still there, and Titus's rifle, but his navy revolver wasn't anywhere around. And there was no other sign of Pa and Titus.

"I drove Ma and the girls home, in that wagon. Ma sat there beside me on the board, stiff and solemn. Once she said, 'Georgie, if they're gone and gone for good, you'll get the man who did it. Won't you?' I began to cry, of course. I says, 'Yes, Ma. I'll take care of you always, Ma. . . . But if they're dead, it wasn't a man who killed 'em. It was men. One man wouldn't be a match for Titus alone.'"

Doc was buried in the thickening shadows of the office. I couldn't see his face any more.

"Then I went back with the men. We searched the river, up and down the hills around Cottonwood, too, clear down to the East Fork. And never found a thing.

"In that wagon there was just one clue—just one thing which made it certain in our minds that they were dead. That was a little spot of dried blood on the floor of the wagon, right behind the seat. About half as big as your hand. Seemed like, if they'd been shot off the wagon, there'd have been more blood. Then, too, the horses were a fairly young team and they might have cut loose and run away if any shooting had started.

"It was always the general opinion that the murderers had disposed of the bodies in the river. But, personally, I always hung to the idea that Titus and Pa were killed in some mysterious way, and their bodies buried. The fact is that the entire community searched for a week, and then gave it up. No other clue was ever discovered, and no further information of any kind was ever unearthed.

"I didn't quit searching for months. Eli Goble helped me, too; he worked like grim death. But we couldn't find a thing."

I asked, "Who was Eli Goble?"

There was the dull scraping of Doc's shoes on the floor. "Seems to me that you cashed a check this noon, boy. Where did you cash it?"

Somewhat perplexed, I told him. "At the bank across the street."

"Well, that's Eli Goble. And where are you living temporarily—until you can find rooms or an apartment to your liking?"

"At the—Oh, of course, Doctor. The Goble Hotel."

He chuckled. "Everything in this town's Goble, boy. He came here in '59 with a man named Goble, but that wasn't Eli's real name. He had heard that his folks came from Ohio, but didn't know anything about it. You see, his family was killed in the Mint Valley massacre, about 1840, and he had been kidnaped by the Indians. Lived with the Sioux until he was sixteen —could talk the language like a native, too. In fact, lots of folks used to think he was part Indian. But he wasn't. And during the search, he thought all the trailing experience which he had had when among the Indians, might be of some account. But even that didn't help. We couldn't find a thing."

I said, slowly, "And he's rich, now?"

Doc sighed, and began to hunt around for the light switch. "Suspecting Eli Goble, are you?" He chuckled. "I don't believe anybody ever did, before. He never had a cent to his name for years after that. A few months later he enlisted in the army, served all through the war, and didn't come back here till 1867. In the meantime, through someone he met in the army, he had been trying to get track of his family. And eventually he succeeded. Found the original family, back in Ohio. He got what money was coming to him, brought it out here to Cottonwood, invested it carefully, and made good. He retained the name of Goble, for convenience's sake. Now he's almost ninety, but he's one of the richest men in the state, and one of the tightest. He never lets go of a nickel until the Goddess of Liberty yells for mercy."

The big yellow light hissed into being. It glared down on the white-enameled table, the glistening cabinets and instruments, the old desk and rows of books. Doc Martindale stood there in the middle of the office and nodded his head. "That's the story, boy. Real live mystery, just sixty years old this spring. . . ."

We were just putting on our hats, and Doc was struggling into his old brown slicker, when the telephone rang. Martindale took up the receiver. "Doctor Martindale speaking."

"Oh," he said, after a moment. "Well." And then he winked quickly at me above the telephone. "Did you use any of that stimulant I left last time? . . . Yes. I'm leaving the office, now, to go home, and I'll stop in. Yes."

He replaced the receiver on its hook. "Speak of the devil," he said. "Eli Goble's just had another heart attack. Nothing to get excited about. He has them frequently, but in between times he's up and down and around. We'll stop in to see him for a minute."

The Goble house was only a few minutes' drive from the main business streets. . . . Lights glowed from most of the windows, as we came up the sidewalk. "You can tell that Eli's flat on his back," said Doc. "If he was around, he wouldn't let them burn all that electricity."

The old man watched us from his pillow, with black, red-rimmed eyes, deeply sunk beneath the moldy fuzz of his eyebrows. . . . He was breathing heavily.

"Well, Eli. How do you feel? This is Dr. Patterson, Eli."

The old man seemed to glare broodingly at me.

"Don't feel—so—good," Goble managed with difficulty. "Plagued heart seems—like—played out on me."

Martindale began to open his bag. "Oh, nothing to worry about, Eli. We'll fix it all up right." He made a perfunctory examination. "You'll feel better to-morrow, Eli. Sleep tight."

The old man mumbled and coughed; and we went down the shadowy stairway, through the gloomy, over-ornate hall, and out to the front door.

It was four o'clock the next afternoon when Doc Martindale and I arrived at the office, following a round of calls on widely separated cases. Beyond a few hasty reports to the girl whom Doc Martindale kept in his office
during the mid-day hours, we had enjoyed no contact with the town of Cottonwood since 10 a.m.

When we returned in Doc's old touring car, it was to find the *Cottonwood
Herald* spread on the table with plenty of black ink decorating the front
page.

ELI GOBLE GIVES PARK TO CITY

Local Businessman and Pioneer
Settler Decides on Memorial

Plans Changed for Tomorrow's Dedication

At a special meeting of the city council this afternoon, it was unanimously agreed to accept the gift tendered by Eli Goble, revered Civil
War veteran and early settler in Cottonwood, who today offered to give
the town of Cottonwood some thirty acres of beautiful woodland, to
be known as "Goble Memorial Park."

It is understood that Mr. Goble has been ill, and that is the reason
for a delay in his plans.

"The grand old man of Crockett County" stipulated in the terms of
his gift that the proposed Memorial Grove of trees should be set out
somewhere in the new park area. This necessitated a hasty change in
plans. Instead of being planted on the north hill, on the Louis Wilson
farm above the Coon River, the trees will be set out on the brow of
the east hill, which is included in the thirty acres donated by Mr. Goble.

A big parade, forming in the city hall square, and proceeding across
the east bridge toward the new park, will officially open the Arbor Day
ceremonies at two o'clock tomorrow afternoon. Following an invocation
by Rev. J. Medley Williams, the Cottonwood city band will——

We leaned there, side by side with our hands upon the desk, and read
that newspaper story.

Doc tapped the paper with his forefinger. "I'll go on record as saying," he
declared, "that this is the first thing Eli Goble ever gave away in his life—
at least the first thing in which there wasn't some chance of his getting value
received out of it. And I don't see what he can get out of this, except glory.
. . . Eli doesn't care a rap for glory. Listen to Editor Nollins calling him,
'the grand old man of Crockett County.' That's because Eli holds a mortgage
on the *Herald* building."

Two patients drifted in for examination. . . . When I left, an hour later,
I looked back to see Doctor Martindale sitting there in his swivel chair, a
tired hulk, still reading the *Cottonwood Herald*.

At five-thirty in the morning, Old Doc was beating on my door. I arose, startled, and feeling that nothing short of peritonitis or a breech delivery could have made him summon me so insistently.

He came into the hotel room and waited while I threw on my clothes. "What is it?" I asked, between splashes of cold water.

"We're going out and do a little digging," he said.

I nodded. "Appendectomy? Or what?"

"Nothing so unimportant," Doc replied. And his eyes looked as if he had been awake all night—red-rimmed and circled. . . . "Real digging. No one will know where we are. If Mrs. Gustafson takes a notion to sink and die while we're away, she'll just have to sink and die." He said it with seeming brutality. I was still too sleepy to press him for more details, or to wonder what it was all about.

But when we got out to the curbing in front of the hotel, and I glanced into the rear seat of Doc's car, there lay two spades, a scoop-shovel and a pick ax.

I turned with an exclamation of astonishment.

"Get in," said Doc. And I did, without any more words. He drove down Main Street, north on Kowa Avenue, and under the Burlington viaduct. We seemed to be heading north of town. Two minutes later our car was making the Coon River bridge rattle and bang in every loose joint.

"This is the Louis Wilson farm," said Doc. "Hm. I reckon we can turn here past the Cedar school, and drive down the lane past the timber."

At the furthest corner of the cornfield we climbed out, taking the shovels and ax with us. Doc was breathing hoarsely, but the strange pallor had left his face. . . . His eyes were bright and intent; there was something almost furious in their gleam.

He led me through a fringe of oak timberland, skirting two brushy ravines, and coming out on a sloping knoll where one solitary oak tree stood, stunted and twisted by many winds. The grass beneath our feet was coarse, tangled, flat-bladed. Native prairie sod, without a doubt. . . . Far away, a band of crows was circling over the river, cawing with faint and raucous cries.

"This is the north hill," said Doc. "There's the town."

It was a very high hill, this bald mound on which we stood. Beneath us the Coon River swung in a flat band of glistening brown.

The thin, brittle grass of the barren hill was tufted with hundreds of pale, lilac-pastel flowers. The blossoms grew on short, fuzzy stems; the petals shaded from white to purple, with a heart of yellow in each flower.

"They're beautiful," I said, "I never saw anything like them before. What are they?"

"Wind-flowers. Easter flowers. Or I guess the more modern name is pasque-flower. Pretty things, aren't they? One of the earliest we have around here. . . . Well, I'm going to get busy."

Doc dropped the shovel he was carrying, and I was just as willing to relinquish the heavy load in my own arms. I went over and sat down against the gnarled oak tree, which was the only tree on all that bald, brownish hill.

A million facts and statements and conjectures seemed boiling in my brain; I could make nothing out of them.

Before my eyes, Doc Martindale was behaving in a very strange manner. He was walking slowly in vague, indefinite circles, his eyes staring at the ground in front of him. Occasionally he would move up beyond the brow of the hill and sweep the surrounding area with his eyes. I had the strange notion that Doctor George Martindale, after unloading the sad story of his youth, had taken two days in going deliberately and completely insane.

He thrust a small piece of stick into the ground, moved away, surveyed the spot carefully, and then came back to set up another stick, several feet from the first. He repeated this process two more times. He now had an uneven rectangle, eight or ten feet long, marked at its corners by the bits of stick. "We'll try it here," he said.

Without another word, he removed his coat, lifted the pickax, and sent its point into the ground.

I cried, "Wait a minute! Won't people down in the town see us up here?"

"They'll think we're cows or pigs," said Doc.

And, as I have said before, we were alone—out there in the thin sunshine of early morning. We dug silently. Neither of us spoke a word. After Doc had penetrated some two feet in depth, at one side of the rectangle, he moved out toward the middle of the space he had marked. I followed, with my shovel.

We had been digging for about ten minutes, when we began to find things.

"Murdered," said Doc.

We were finding them, picking out the disordered relics from the rich earth where they had lain so long. Tibiæ, ribs . . . phalanges . . . the rusty remains of an ancient revolver.

Doc straightened up, and spoke to me gently. His face was set and strained; it might have been cast in iron. "There's a sheet and a grain sack or two in the car," he said. "Will you go over and bring them?"

I was glad of the opportunity to get away for a few minutes. When I came back, Doc had most of the bones covered with his coat. The knees of his trousers were dark and earthy; he had been kneeling in the loose mold of the grave, picking out the smaller fragments.

"I want a witness," he said, shortly. "Take a look at this." From beneath the coat he withdrew a human skull and turned it slowly for me to see. There was a complete and noticeable fracture, such as might have been caused by the blow of a sharp ax. "The other is the same way," he added, and replaced the skull tenderly.

Then I spoke for the first time. "Can you identify them?"

"Easily," he said. "There's a Masonic pocket-piece, the revolver, and knives and things. . . . The pocket-piece is the best bet. It's engraved with Pa's name. Not corroded at all. I rubbed it up and could read the engraving."

Wisely, he made no attempt to identify or isolate the separate skeletons. The bones made awkward bundles, in the grain sacks. We worked slowly, carrying them and the shovels back to the car. I was too stunned by the

grim reality to ask any questions. We went away and left that uneven black hole in the middle of the blooming wind-flowers.

Back in town, we went to Doc Martindale's garage, behind his little house on Omaha Street, and left the bundles there. Then we hurried to the office; fortunately there had been no phone calls at either house or office. It was after seven o'clock, and yet I had no desire for breakfast.

Doc sat at his desk and thumbed through a stack of old letters and note-books. "Clell Howard's living in Long Beach," he muttered. "Got his address somewhere. . . . And Eph Spokesman is with his niece out in Port-land. I've got to send telegrams right away." Then, strangely enough, he seemed to discover me standing there. "You go around and look at Mrs. Gustafson and that greenstick fracture and the little Walker boy; tell them I'm busy on an emergency case. Don't say a word to anybody."

"I won't," I promised.

He said, "And be sure you don't forget the parade. It forms at 2 p.m., at the city hall square. You'll want to see that." And then he turned back to his rummaging.

I had all of the bedfast patients bandaged and dosed and sprayed and examined before 1.30 p.m. At two o'clock I was standing, with a group of pleasant and gossipy citizens, on the steps of the Cottonwood city hall. The triangular "square" was blooming with the gay sweaters and dresses of hundreds of school children who darted wildly underfoot, seething and yelling in a mad half-holiday.

At twenty minutes after two, the crowd was somewhat impatient. There had been a large turn-out; the Boy Scouts were there, and the members of the American Legion, chafing and shifting in line. There was even a huge truck, splashed with vivid bunting, on which were the grove of memorial elms all ready to be set out, their dirt-encrusted roots sticking from beneath the scarlet shimmer of flags, like so many witches' claws.

This crowd was waiting for Eli Goble, albeit waiting impatiently. If a man was so kind as to give away thirty acres of land, one could at least expect him to show up for the dedication.

It was almost two-thirty before a big Cadillac touring car slid around the corner by the Phillips's oil station, and the crowds in that vicinity began a desultory hand-clapping. Yes, it was Eli Goble. I could see that bearded, skeleton shape sitting hunched in the rear seat, a Navajo blanket across his knees. His narrow-eyed son, vice-president of the bank, was driving.

Some fortunate fate had directed me to take up my station on those steps, above the mass of children. For I had a clear and unobstructed view of Doc Martindale, accompanied by a fat, pink-faced man who seemed very nervous, emerging from a dark stairway across the street.

I vaulted over the concrete railing beside me, and shouldered through the knotted humanity. Once or twice I had a quick glance at Doc and the pink-faced man, over the heads of the crowd. They were walking rapidly toward the corner where the Goble car was parked; the pink-faced man was drawing a folded paper from his pocket, and he seemed more nervous than ever.

We reached the corner simultaneously. A benign citizen, who wore a white silk badge, "Chairman," fluttering from his coat, was leaning at the side of the car, conversing with Eli Goble and his son.

"Daniel," said Doc Martindale.

The chairman turned.

"Get up on the city hall steps," Doc directed him, "and announce to the crowd that Mr. Goble's physician refuses to allow him to participate in the exercises. Then get them started with their parade."

Daniel began to stammer and sputter.

"Go 'long with you," ordered Doc, firmly. He opened the door of the back seat, and he and the pink-faced man slid in beside Eli Goble. And then Doc saw me standing there. "Get in the front seat, Dr. Patterson," he called, and before I knew it, I was sitting beside Vincent Goble, who was too excited to even bow.

"I don't understand this," he said importantly. "You're carrying things off with a very high hand, Doctor Martindale. It is my father's wish that——"

Doc's lips were thin and firm beneath his scraggly beard. "You keep your mouth shut, Vincent," he said. Vincent Goble gasped. "Drive around the corner on Queen Street, out of this crowd, and pull up at the curb."

The younger man's face was flaming with rage, but he obeyed the command. The Cadillac purred ahead, past the corner, past the alley, past the crowd. A block away it drew up beside the curb.

Vincent Goble and I swung around to face the trio in back. Eli Goble sat in the middle, clutching and contracting his hands against the red triangles of the Navajo blanket.

"Go ahead, Ed," said Doctor Martindale.

The little pink-faced man gasped apologetically, and fluttered the folds of the paper in his hand. He began a whispered jumble of phrases: "As sheriff of Crockett County, it is my duty to place you, Eli Goble, under arrest. You are charged with the murder of Titus Martindale, and William Martindale, on or about the twenty-fourth of April, in the year 1861——"

Vincent Goble snarled. The old man still sat there, motionless except for the parchment hands which twisted in his lap. "Ain't true," he managed to whisper. "It—ain't true."

"You cowards!" cried his son. The banker's face was livid. "You'd devil the very life out of an old man with some crazy superstition like that! You'd——"

Doc Martindale said, "Drive up to the sheriff's office, Vincent. We want to talk things over."

"Like hell I will! Like——"

Ed Maxon, the sheriff, gulped fearfully. "Yes, Mr. Goble. That's right. Have to ask you to bring your father up to my office."

And so, we went. Vincent, cursing beneath his breath, Doc Martindale silent as the tomb, Ed Maxon twisting and rubbing a damp hand around his collar. And Eli Goble sitting there under the blanket, his eyes like black caverns, and saying: "I—never done it. You'll see. I never done—that."

"You saw the gold at the house. And made up your mind——"

"No."

"You followed them out there on the east prairie. Or maybe you were lying there, waiting for them."

"I never—done it."

"Say, Doctor Martindale! If my father should have another heart attack and die while you're questioning him——"

"Now, Mr. Goble, you——"

"I'm a physician, Vincent. And Eli's my patient. I'll look out for him if he starts to faint. . . . Eli, you killed them from ambush."

"I never. Never did."

"Then you left the bodies in the wagon, took the team, and drove out to the north hill. It was a long drive—must have taken hours to get out there. But you figured that nobody ever went up there, and it was away from the beaten track, and would be a good place to hide the bodies."

"I–I–George, I'm an old man. I——"

"Damn you, Martindale! You——"

"Sit down, Vincent, and shut up. I'm not going to fool with anybody to-day. . . . Let's take your pulse, Eli. . . . Hm. Guess you can stand it. All right. You buried them out on the north hill. Maybe you drove the wagon back and forth over the grave—an Indian trick. Trick you learned from the Sioux. And probably you scattered lots of grass and brush around."

"No. No."

"Titus had his gun strapped on; you left them in the ground, just as they were. You didn't take anything out of the wagon except those buckskin bags. Then you drove clear around town again, forded the river opposite Salt Creek, and drove over by Little Hell Slough. You left the team there, and skinned out. Took the gold somewhere and hid it, probably."

"Ain't so. Lie. . . ."

"Then you laid low, and waited to join in the search. You were clever, Eli. Clever as an Indian. . . . You helped me search, too. Oh, how we searched! We even went right across that north hill. But we never saw anything that looked like a grave. . . . You kept it covered up, Eli. You were smart."

"Don't. . . . Don't talk so—I can't——"

"By God, you let my father alone!——"

"Now, Mr. Goble. Please. Control yourself. Please——"

"You concluded that seven thousand dollars was a big fortune. Well, it was. Worth waiting for. So you enlisted in the army, took your chances—I'll give you credit for nerve there, Eli—and turned up after the war with that story about finding your relatives and your family property back in Ohio. Yes, you were smart."

"I never—never done it."

"Why did you give this park to the city?"

"Mmmmm. I——"

"The *Herald* carried that Arbor Day announcement, night before last. And right away you had a heart attack. And the next morning you came out with that gift to the city. *Provided*——"

"Vincent. Vincent. Make 'em let me——"

"I'll——"

"Here, hold him!"

"I've got him. Now, Mr. Goble, you'll have to sit down."

"Don't be a fool, Vincent. This is true—all true. It's taken me sixty years to find out, but I've found out. . . . You gave that park to the city of Cottonwood, Eli Goble, *provided* that they set out the memorial grove over there, on the east hill, instead of on the north hill. You didn't want anybody digging on the north hill, did you? It had never occurred to you to buy Louis Wilson's farm, so there wouldn't be a chance of people digging that ground up."

"No. . . . Don't talk so, George! . . . Old. I'm an old an'——"

"Well, it was the first thing you ever gave away, in your life. And it set me to thinking. I thought, 'Why didn't Eli want that memorial grove planted up there?' And then, I began to understand things. I went up there this morning. Doctor Patterson was with me—I have a witness to what I am now about to relate. He saw me dig; he saw me find things. I found *them*, Eli."

Vincent Goble was slumped forward, his head buried in his hands. Eli sat there in the sheriff's big chair, staring across the table. He seemed to be looking squarely through the opposite wall.

"They were murdered, Eli. Their skulls had been broken. A heavy, sharp blow at the back of each skull. I found them."

The old man's lips were gray and rubbery. He whispered. "No, I never done it. Can't prove it was me."

"A hatchet, Eli. Someone had thrown a hatchet—or maybe two hatchets, in quick succession. They were sitting on that wagon board, in the bright moonlight. It would have been easy for anyone who could throw a tomahawk."

Doc fumbled in the breast pocket of his coat, and brought out three folded squares of yellow paper. "I'll read to you all," he said calmly. "Three telegrams. The first one I sent myself, early this morning, to Clell Howard, in Long Beach, California, and to Ephriam Spokesman in Portland, Oregon. . . . Remember those names, Eli? . . . Clell was mayor here, once. And Eph Spokesman—everybody knew him. Here's my telegram: 'Please reply by wire completely and at my expense. During the old days at Cottonwood, what man was skillful at throwing a knife or hatchet. Search your recollection and reply at once.'

"Here's the first reply I got. It came from Ephriam Spokesman's niece. Came about eleven o'clock. You can read it yourself, gentlemen. It says, 'Uncle Eph very sick but says man named Goble thought to be a half-breed was only one who could throw hatchet. Wants to hear full details why you ask.'

"Along about eleven-forty-five, I got a telegram from Clell Howard. Here it is: 'Hello old neighbor regards to you. Am almost ninety but recall perfectly how I lost five dollars betting Eli Goble couldn't stick hatchet ten times in succession in big tree by Halsey blacksmith shop.'"

The room was perfectly still, except for the hoarse sputtering in Eli Goble's throat. "No," he whispered tremulously. "No."

Doc Martindale pointed to the further corner of the dusty old room. There was a table, which none of us had noticed before, and on that table was a white sheet, rumpled and bulky. . . . "Eli," said Doc, quietly. "They're over there. In the corner."

The aged man stiffened in his chair. His back arched up, the shoulders quaking; his claw hands seemed wrenching a chunk of wood from the table in front of him.

"Father!" his son cried.

Eli Goble shook his head, and dropped back in his chair, his deep-set eyes dull with a flat, blue light. "The dead," he whispered. "They found me. . . . They're here in this room. I done it. I killed them. Titus and Bill. Yes. Yes."

Vincent Goble dropped down, his head buried in his arms, and began to sob—big, gulping sobs. The sheriff twisted nervously in his seat.

"George. You—you gonna send me to—prison? You gonna have them—hang me? I'm old . . . I done it. Yes."

Doc Martindale cleared his throat. "Yes, you are old, Eli. Lot older than I am. It's too late, now, to do anything about it. I told my mother I'd get the man, and—But I can't see what good it would do, now, to send you to jail or even try you for murder."

Sheriff Maxon wiped his forehead. "The law," he said shrilly, "the law must take its course! Eli Goble, you must——"

"No," said Old Doc, decisively. "I'm running this show, Ed. Without me, without my testimony and the case I've built up, there isn't any show against Eli. I won't prosecute him, or furnish evidence."

"But he confessed to this murder!" shrilled Maxon. "He——"

Doc nodded. "Orally. Yes, but what if Vincent and Dr. Patterson and myself all swear that he never confessed? What if I destroy—the evidence!"

Maxon shook his head and bit his lips.

"How much is your father worth?" asked Doc of Vincent Goble.

The banker lifted his face, on which the weary, baffled tears were still wet. "Couple of million, I guess."

"All yours," whispered Eli. "All yours . . ."

"Maybe," Doc nodded. "Seven thousand dollars. Quite a nest egg, in those days. Like fifty thousand, now. Or even more. . . . No, gentlemen. Money won't do me any good. It can't bring back Titus and my father. But it can still do good. Yes."

Eli Goble's eyes had closed, like dark windows on which ragged curtains had been drawn. "I've seen 'em—I've seen 'em. Always. Since I got old—they come back. . . . I had to give in. Yes."

"You'll go home," said Doc. "I'll give you something to put you to sleep. Then, after you have a little rest and get your strength back, you'll have a lawyer up at your house. . . . You will give, to this county in which you live, one million dollars for the purpose of founding and endowing a modern hospital, where every inhabitant can secure the best medical and surgical attention, free of charge. How does that sound?"

Head still buried in his arms, Vincent Goble nodded drunkenly. His father had opened his eyes and was shivering, still staring through the blank wall ahead of him. "Yes. Anything. . . . I give—anything. But take me away.

I want to go—home. . . . I'm old. I don't want to stay in—this room. I don't want to stay with—*them*."

After Eli Goble was in bed, and asleep, Doc and I came out into the damp warmth of the spring afternoon. Martindale looked ten years older than he did the day before. "After this," he said, "after everything is taken care of, I'll let things go. . . . You look after the practice beginning next Monday."

Our feet sounded flat and talkative, echoing on the long sidewalk. "One thing," I said. "I can't understand how you found the place. I can see how you reasoned out the rest—about that grove and about Eli Goble's not wanting the trees planted up there. But how did you know where to dig? We could have been up there for days, turning the soil."

Doc felt in his pocket for a cigar which wasn't there. "Wind-flowers," he said quietly. "They were scattered all over that hill. Beautiful, like you said. . . . But I knew enough to dig where there were no wind-flowers. The grass on that hill looked pretty much alike, all over, but there weren't any flowers growing in that place I marked off. Those little purple flowers are funny. They only grow on native soil. You can't get them to grow where the sod has ever been turned."

THE KING WAITS

CLEMENCE DANE

THE morning was a Friday, the month was May; it was the twenty-eighth year of the Eighth Henry's reign over England, and it needed five minutes to be noon. On Richmond Hill, under the great spring-leaved oak, stood Henry the King. His outstretched hand commanded silence, and his huntsmen stilled the restless coupled hounds in dumb show, with furtive, sidelong glances, fearing that outstretched jewel-laden hand, that arrogant glance. Who will disobey Harry the King, calling in that furious voice for silence? Even the midday sun, as a little cloud slipped from its face, poured down such an answering concentration of heat upon the green hill-side that the noon hush seemed an act of grace from one royalty to another. There was instantly no sound at all save the panting of the half-throttled hounds and the dry whisper of innumerable caterpillars hissing in innumerable leaves; for there was a blight that spring in the oak-woods.

For one minute—two—three—the silence endured; then a burst of wind broke it: and all the trees in Richmond Park began once more to strain, creak, rustle, and the scent of the May drifted by again in gusts, and high overhead the clouds too renewed their voyage eastward through the heavenly blue. Over the Tower of London, as the wind lulled once more, they banked together again, a white tower of the sky.

Far below the scent of the white may drifted over the town and in through the windows, doorways, and courtyards of the Tower, and over the Tower green. Through slits in the wall the river sparkled in the noon sunshine; but still it lacked four minutes to be noon.

Across the green to the new scaffold came Anne the Queen, dressed in black damask with a white cape, and her hat was in the fashion. The Lieutenant of the Tower helped her to mount the steps. She had her glance and her nod for the waiting swordsman; then she looked down upon her friends and upon her enemies gathered close about her harsh death-bed; said to them that which was in her mind to say; adjusted her dress and freed the small neck; then knelt. But she would not let friend or enemy cover her eyes, and though she knelt she did not bow her head, but looked again

Reprinted by permission of the author and Pearn, Pollinger and Higham, Ltd.

keenly upon the silenced crowd: and for the last time called upon the ready
blood to flush her cheeks.

She had always been able to redden thus into beauty when she chose;
and now the hot blood did not fail her. It was at its old trick, brightening
her black eyes: and this was ever the sign of crisis with her. With that
sudden flush she had won her game—how often?—with this king and husband
who had now beaten her. She felt a strange pang of longing to remember,
to finger once again her glorious victories over time, absence, malice, envy,
a queen, a cardinal, a king—and her own resentful heart.

She was not used to deny herself any wish; so, lifting her head, she let the
spell work for the last time: and her executioner, meeting that full glance,
hesitated and turned aside, as if his part were not yet ready to be played.
Again he advanced: again she looked at him, and had the last triumph of
her beauty as she won her respite. He would wait her pleasure for a minute,
no more than a minute; but she knew now that the tales they had told of
drowning men were true. The dying see their lives in a minute: she, dying,
would see again her life.

She turned her eyes away from the frightened faces of her women, from
faithful Mary Wyatt's weeping agony: she looked in turn upon her gaoler
Kingston, on courteous Gwynn clutching in his hand her last gift, on thank-
less Cromwell, on Suffolk's exultant face. But here her glance checked, her
very heart checked on its beat, for beside Suffolk, her enemy, stood a nearer
enemy; it seemed to her that her husband's eyes glittered at her, set in a
younger, comelier countenance. So Henry had sent his bastard to watch her
die! She smiled to herself as she thought that it was like him, like her fool
and tyrant, her Henry, husband, king! She thought that he himself would
have been glad to watch her die: he could not for his dignity, so he sent his
left-hand son, young Richmond. Yes, to act thus was like Henry, and young
Richmond, watching her, was very like Henry: she had seen on many a May
morning that eager parting of the full, pinched mouth, that glistening of
small, hard eyes.

Suddenly her thirty-odd years of life began to speed across her eyeballs,
quickly and softly, like the scudding clouds above her speeding over the
Tower in the spring wind. Childhood and youth at Hever Castle—in a flash
she saw those spring years pass, and herself journeying to France in the train
of Henry's sister. Little thought fifteen-year-old Anne Boleyn that she would
ever call the Queen of France sister! But she saw herself, nevertheless, all
unconscious, dancing, dressing, laughing, learning, learning always to be a
queen. And so home again to England, to the Court at Windsor Castle, like
that last lone small cloud above her scudding across the sky to join the massed
castles of the air. And there she saw herself for a little while serving the
good dull Katharine; but she had no memory of Katharine's lord, Henry
King of England. Another face and form flitted across her eyeballs, of
another Henry—Henry Percy, heir to the dukedom of Northumberland.

A high wind drove in upon the clouds as she watched, and scattered them
all ways, while the executioner whispered with his underling. Thus bois-

terously, she thought, had Henry the King driven in upon love and lovers. Henry Percy is rated by the butcher's son, Wolsey, the hated cardinal; and his father summoned; and shamed Anne is dismissed the Court.

Home again goes Anne to Hever, her marriage and her heart broken, and never knows, so innocent is this earlier Anne, why misfortune cut off her happiness at a blow, like a skilled swordsman striking off a queen's head. But when a guest arrived at Hever Castle—then Anne knows!

Henry the King comes to Hever very sure of his welcome. And indeed her father and her stepmother may scour the county for fish, flesh, fowl and fruits in their season; and summon country gentlemen and ladies, and handsome boys and pleasant girls, to make feasts and plan pleasures for the King. But Maistresse Anne keeps her chamber. Henry is master of Hever, not of Anne. Anne knows now who has parted her, with Wolsey's help, from Henry Percy, true love, first love, and she will teach that greedy mouth, those glistening eyes, a lesson. Henry the King is the singular good lord and favourable prince of Sir Thomas and Lady Boleyn; but Maistresse Anne Boleyn keeps her chamber. Let the King learn what it means to part lovers! Let him wait and chafe and learn!

She watched him in memory once more as he rode away from Hever, an angry, hungry king, spurring his horse. She watched him and his train dwindling in the distance to such ant-like folk and swallowed up by young green and pure white may hedges, under just such a blue sky in just such windy weather. What a wind! There's no sound at all in the world but the hurry of the royal wind. When will it strike twelve? Is it a minute or a lifetime since she knelt?

More clouds scud across the sky, more years scud across her dying eyes. She saw again her father, and smiled as she remembered that he, too, had been among those who condemned her. Strange father! Coward father! But he had liked his new title, all those years ago—Viscount Rochford sounded well; and her sister's husband was glad enough to be Gentleman of the Privy Chamber; and for herself there was a place at Court again, and jewels! (But Henry Percy is exiled to Northumberland!) Once more she saw that greedy mouth; once more she fell very humbly on her knees, summoned the lovely blood to her cheek, and said her say to Henry the King:

"Your wife I cannot be, both in respect of mine own unworthiness, and also because you have a queen already. Your mistress I will not be."

And so home again to Hever in just such soft blue weather, to read humble letters from a once blustering king, who knows now what it means to be a lover parted from his love. How did his letter go?

"I beseech you earnestly to let me know your real mind as to the love between us. . . . If it does not please you to answer me in writing, let me know some place where I may have it by word of mouth; and I will go thither with all my heart. No more for fear of tiring you."

But he tires her none the less, and she will not go to meet him. Let him wait! Let him wait his four years!

They scud by like clouds, as her cheek burns with a new memory of hate and reckoning. What of Wolsey? How shall Wolsey be paid if Anne pines at Hever while the King waits unsatisfied?

So Anne Boleyn comes to town again and serves the Queen again, and takes her place at last as King's bliss: queens it at Hampton, at Windsor, and at Greenwich, and holds her state in the Cardinal's own York House. How else should Wolsey be taught what it is to part lovers? (But Henry Percy has married a wife and will not come again!) Let Wolsey learn what he has to pay for crossing "the foolish girl yonder in the Court."

She saw herself again, while Katharine, her mistress, sat weeping and praying and sewing with her dull maids, reigning at the feasts the shaken Cardinal prepared for her; saw herself May Queen on May mornings and Lady of the Revels on Christmas Eves; till, at the Greenwich midnight masque, the French ambassador watching, she danced (mark it, butcher's son!) in public with the King, the flush upon her cheek, and listened afterwards to Henry's own song:—

> The eagle force subdues each bird that flies:
> What metal can resist the flaming fire?
> Doth not the sun dazzle the clearest eyes,
> And melt the ice and make the frost retire?

The ice, indeed, is melting, Lord Cardinal! You were not wise to go to France; less wise when you returned to dissuade a king from changing old queens for new. Anne Boleyn has other weapons than her brilliant eyes, her burning cheek, her dancing feet, and quick tongue. Henry has been jealous once; he shall be jealous again! King Henry is not the only lover who sings to Anne his own verses. Besides, Tom Wyatt has a look of Henry Percy (married, out of sight, never out of mind!), and is a bolder man than Percy.

She lived again through the day when Henry stole a ring from her finger and swaggered out to play at bowls with Wyatt. Again she watched all from her window, and heard all—King Henry crying out that he wins: and Wyatt telling him that, by his leave, it is not so!—and Henry's chuckle as he points with his new-ringed finger, crying:

"Wyatt, I tell thee, it is mine!"

But Wyatt, too, wears a keepsake under his Court suit over his heart. What can a poet and a lover do but draw from that hiding-place the jewel swinging on its chain.

"Give me leave to measure the cast with this, and I have good hopes yet it will be mine!"

Once again she saw him stoop, measure, and prove winner; and rise to face the Tudor thunderstorm.

"It may be so, but then I am deceived." And away storms Henry to her chamber crying—"What is Wyatt to you?"

She remembered how easily then she dealt with him and his jealousies: how she struck her bargain: and how, five years later, while she, the new-made Marchioness of Pembroke, sat on the King's knee, and he kissed her, not caring who saw, she heard Wyatt's voice singing to her new ladies-in-waiting his farewell song—

> *Forget not yet thine own approved,*
> *The which so constant hath thee loved,*
> *Whose steadfast faith has never moved;*
> *Forget not yet!*

Poor Tom Wyatt! The scent of the may drifts across the scaffold like the scent of the rose-water that it was his office to pour upon her hands on her coronation day. And there was another May morning to remember—the best to remember!

The flush on her cheek deepened, and her head sank as she saw herself three years ago, only three years ago, journeying to the Tower, this same Tower that now witnessed her last journey's end. She saw the press of cheering folk at Greenwich, the branches of the oaks cracking under the weight of citizens, the may-bushes clambered over, with gaping faces thrust out, scratched and red and laughable between the pure clots of bloom. She saw again the Lord Mayor and his scarlet haberdashers, and felt the jewels on his glove dent her fingers as she put her hand in his that he might lead her to the State barge.

It waited for her on the breast of the sparkling river, the same sparkling river sparkling now through slits in her prison walls. But then the river was alive with pageantry, and instead of black damask she wore cloth of gold; and the world was full of noise where now was deadly silence and the executioner's foot behind her, breaking the silence.

But her mind rejected utterly that stealthy sound: it was filled with memories of the glorious noises—the cries of all the people and the tinkling of the fluttering, bell-sewn flags as the barge poled out into mid-stream with fifty lesser barges following. All London moved that May morning with her towards the Tower, so that her progress turned the very Thames back upon its course. (Why not when she, Anne Boleyn, had already turned back history, shaken Spain, defeated Rome, killed a cardinal, and wrecked a queen?) The great fiery dragon spat fire from the foist, and from the bachelor barge came trumpet-calls once more, and, from the maiden's barge, unceasing high-pitched singing, sweet as the singing of the waking birds had been when she met Henry Percy, not Henry of England, by stealth under the Greenwich hawthorn trees. Well, she had avenged that lost sweetness! Wolsey had parted her from Henry Percy, and where was Wolsey now? fallen, as she was falling: dead, as she in another instant must lie dead! But Henry Percy had been gaoler to the great cardinal before the end, had led the cardinal, his legs bound beneath his horse's belly like any other felon, to his prison and his grave. She had taught the greatest man in England what it cost to part lovers.

A smile lit up her face as she remembered that lesson, and the watchers saw it and wondered, and weeping Mary Wyatt called her in her heart "saint" and "innocent"; and young Richmond thought of his father, waiting on

Richmond Hill for the boom of the cannon, and wondered if he should report that inexplicable, triumphant smile. How slowly the man from Calais goes about his business! Look, he swings his sword! Does the kneeling creature know that the French executioner is swinging his sword?

But Anne did not see the present. She was smiling at her achieved past. She saw that she had done what she set out to do, unafraid. She could say, when her sins rose up and looked at her, that she had never, in life or death, been made afraid. She had been fit mother for kings and queens: and—who knows? Wheels turn!—her Elizabeth might yet rule England, like her mother, unafraid! She saw again so clearly, lying open before her, the book of prophecies found once in her room, hidden there to frighten her by friends of Katharine. There had been a picture of Henry and weeping Katharine, and herself between them, kneeling at the block even as she knelt now. But when her frightened maid called out, "If this were prophesied of me, I would not have him, were he emperor!" she had answered—

"I am resolved to have him, that my issue may be royal, whatever may become of me."

She murmured the words again half aloud, and heard Mary's gasp from the scaffold foot—"She prays!" and saw the sudden upward flash of faces, watching a movement that she heard behind her but could not see. What? had so many years, had her whole life flashed before her eyes in so brief a minute? Yet the minute was too long, it seemed, for these watchers! They grew impatient and would hurry her into death. Let them know that the Queen dies at her own minute, not at theirs! Not thus had they hurried her two years ago from Greenwich landing to the Tower. They had led her slowly to the Tower then, that all the town might see her beauty. And Henry, her king and husband, had met her in the gateway and welcomed her most joyfully. She felt again upon her lips his loving kiss, and his great arm flung about her neck.

It fell upon her neck again like an all-ending blow; and there was a booming in her ears. . . .

The echoes of the gun went rolling round and out over the Tower walls, went rolling over the City and its suburbs, went rolling with the river up to Richmond Hill. Henry the King, motionless beneath the oak, like a painted monarch, like a card-king of hearts, heard the heavy voice and understood the awaited, welcome message.

He started joyfully from his trance and, stripping a little ring from his finger, flung it into a bloom-laden may-thorn bush ten yards away.

"The deed is done!" cried Henry. "Uncouple the hounds and away!"

He clambered to his saddle while the statues of his huntsmen, his horses, and his hounds came to life about him, and, spurring his eager beast, led the hunt westward, ever westward, towards Wiltshire and Jane Seymour, and his wedding morrow.

BABYLON REVISITED

F. SCOTT FITZGERALD

FEBRUARY 21, 1931

"AND where's Mr. Campbell?" Charlie asked.

"Gone to Switzerland. Mr. Campbell's a pretty sick man, Mr. Wales."

"I'm sorry to hear that. And George Hardt?" Charlie inquired.

"Back in America, gone to work."

"And where is the snow bird?"

"He was in here last week. Anyway, his friend, Mr. Schaeffer, is in Paris."

Two familiar names from the long list of a year and a half ago. Charlie scribbled an address in his notebook and tore out the page.

"If you see Mr. Schaeffer, give him this," he said. "It's my brother-in-law's address. I haven't settled on a hotel yet."

He was not really disappointed to find Paris was so empty. But the stillness in the bar was strange, almost portentous.

It was not an American bar any more—he felt polite in it, and not as if he owned it. It had gone back into France. He had felt the stillness from the moment he got out of the taxi and saw the doorman, usually in a frenzy of activity at this hour, gossiping with a *chasseur* by the servants' entrance.

Passing through the corridor, he heard only a single, bored voice in the once-clamorous women's room. When he turned into the bar he traveled the twenty feet of green carpet with his eyes fixed straight ahead by old habit; and then, with his foot firmly on the rail, he turned and surveyed the room, encountering only a single pair of eyes that fluttered up from a newspaper in the corner. Charlie asked for the head barman, Paul, who in the latter days of the bull market had come to work in his own custom-built car—disembarking, however, with due nicety at the nearest corner. But Paul was at his country house today and Alix was giving him his information.

"No, no more. I'm going slow these days."

Alix congratulated him: "Hope you stick to it, Mr. Wales. You were going pretty strong a couple of years ago."

"I'll stick to it all right," Charlie assured him. "I've stuck to it for over a year and a half now."

"How do you find conditions in America?"

"I haven't been to America for months. I'm in business in Prague, representing a couple of concerns there. They don't know about me down there." He smiled faintly. "Remember the night of George Hardt's bachelor dinner here? . . . By the way, what's become of Claude Fessenden?"

Alix lowered his voice confidentially: "He's in Paris, but he doesn't come here any more. Paul doesn't allow it. He ran up a bill of thirty thousand francs, charging all his drinks and his lunches, and usually his dinner, for more than a year. And when Paul finally told him he had to pay, he gave him a bad check."

Alix pressed his lips together and shook his head.

"I don't understand it, such a dandy fellow. Now he's all bloated up——" He made a plump apple of his hands.

A thin world, resting on a common weakness, shredded away now like tissue paper. Turning, Charlie saw a group of effeminate young men installing themselves in a corner.

"Nothing affects them," he thought. "Stocks rise and fall, people loaf or work, but they go on forever." The place oppressed him. He called for the dice and shook with Alix for the drink.

"Here for long, Mr. Wales?"

"I'm here for four or five days to see my little girl."

"Oh-h! You have a little girl?"

Outside, the fire-red, gas-blue, ghost-green signs shone smokily through the tranquil rain. It was late afternoon and the streets were in movement; the *bistros* gleamed. At the corner of the Boulevard des Capucines he took a taxi. The Place de la Concorde moved by in pink majesty; they crossed the logical Seine, and Charlie felt the sudden provincial quality of the left bank.

"I spoiled this city for myself," he thought. "I didn't realize it, but the days came along one after another, and then two years were gone, and everything was gone, and I was gone."

He was thirty-five, a handsome man, with the Irish mobility of his face sobered by a deep wrinkle between his eyes. As he rang his brother-in-law's bell in the Rue Palatine, the wrinkle deepened till it pulled down his brows; he felt a cramping sensation in his belly. From behind the maid who opened the door darted a lovely little girl of nine who shrieked "Daddy!" and flew up, struggling like a fish, into his arms. She pulled his head around by one ear and set her cheek against his.

"My old pie," he said.

"Oh, daddy, daddy, daddy, daddy, dads, dads, dads!"

She drew him into the salon, where the family waited, a boy and girl his daughter's age, his sister-in-law and her husband. He greeted Marion with his voice pitched carefully to avoid either feigned enthusiasm or dislike, but her response was more frankly tepid, and she minimized her expression of unshakable distrust by directing her regard toward his child. The two men clasped hands in a friendly way and Lincoln Peters rested his for a moment on Charlie's shoulder.

The room was warm and comfortably American. The three children moved intimately about, playing through the yellow oblongs that led to other rooms; the cheer of six o'clock spoke in the eager smacks of the fire and the sounds of French activity in the kitchen. But Charlie did not relax; his heart sat up rigidly in his body and he drew confidence from his daughter, who from time to time came close to him, holding in her arms the doll he had brought.

"Really extremely well," he declared in answer to Lincoln's question. "There's a lot of business there that isn't moving at all, but we're doing even better than ever. In fact, damn well. I'm bringing my sister over from America next month to keep house for me. In fact, my income is bigger than it was when I had money. You see, the Czechs——"

His boasting was for a specific purpose; but after a moment, seeing a faint restiveness in Lincoln's eye, he changed the subject:

"Those are fine children of yours, well brought up, good manners."

"We think Honoria's a great little girl too."

Marion Peters came back into the little salon. She was a tall woman with worried eyes, who had once possessed a fresh American loveliness. Charlie had never been sensitive to it and was always surprised when people spoke of how pretty she had been. From the first there had been an instinctive antipathy between them.

"Well, how do you find Honoria?" she asked.

"Wonderful. I was astonished how much she's grown in ten months. All the children are looking well."

"We haven't had a doctor for a year. How do you like being back in Paris?"

"It seems very funny to see so few Americans around."

"I'm delighted," Marion said vehemently. "Now at least you can go into a store without their assuming you're a millionaire. We've suffered like everybody, but on the whole it's a good deal pleasanter."

"But it was nice while it lasted," Charlie said. "We were a sort of royalty, almost infallible, with a sort of magic around us. In the bar this afternoon"— he stumbled, seeing his mistake—"there wasn't a man I knew."

She looked at him keenly. "I should think you'd have had enough of bars."

"I only stayed a minute. I take one drink every afternoon, and no more."

"Don't you want a cocktail before dinner?" Lincoln asked.

"I take only one drink every afternoon, and I've had that."

"I hope you keep to it," said Marion.

Her dislike was evident in the coldness with which she spoke, but Charlie only smiled; he had larger plans. Her very aggressiveness gave him an advantage, and he knew enough to wait. He wanted them to initiate the discussion of what they knew had brought him to Paris.

Honoria was to spend the following afternoon with him. At dinner he couldn't decide whether she was most like him or her mother. Fortunate if she didn't combine the traits of both that had brought them to disaster. A great wave of protectiveness went over him. He thought he knew what to do for her. He believed in character; he wanted to jump back a whole generation and trust in character again as the eternally valuable element.

Everything wore out now. Parents expected genius, or at least brilliance, and both the forcing of children and the fear of forcing them, the fear of warping natural abilities, were poor substitutes for that long, careful watchfulness, that checking and balancing and reckoning of accounts, the end of which was that there should be no slipping below a certain level of duty and integrity.

That was what the elders had been unable to teach plausibly since the break between the generations ten or twelve years ago.

He left soon after dinner, but not to go home. He was curious to see Paris by night with clearer and more judicious eyes. He bought a *strapontin* for the Casino and watched Josephine Baker go through her chocolate arabesques.

After an hour he left and strolled toward Montmartre, up the Rue Pigalle into the Place Blanche. The rain had stopped and there were a few people in evening clothes disembarking from taxis in front of cabarets, and *cocottes* prowling singly or in pairs, and many Negroes. He passed a lighted door from which issued music, and stopped with the sense of familiarity; it was Brick-top's, where he had parted with so many hours and so much money. A few doors farther on he found another ancient rendezvous and incautiously put his head inside. Immediately an eager orchestra burst into sound, a pair of professional dancers leaped to their feet and a maître d'hôtel swooped toward him, crying, "Crowd just arriving, sir!" But he withdrew quickly.

"You have to be damn drunk," he thought.

Zelli's was closed, the bleak and sinister cheap hotels surrounding it were dark; up in the Rue Blanche there was more light and a local, colloquial French crowd. The Poet's Cave had disappeared, but the two great mouths of the Café of Heaven and the Café of Hell still yawned—even devoured, as he watched, the meager contents of a tourist bus—a German, a Japanese, and an American couple who glanced at him with frightened eyes.

So much for the effort and ingenuity of Montmartre. All the catering to vice and waste was on an utterly childish scale, and he suddenly realized the meaning of the word "dissipate"—to dissipate into thin air; to make nothing out of something. In the little hours of the night every move from place to place was an enormous human jump, an increase of paying for the privilege of slower and slower motion.

He remembered thousand-franc notes given to an orchestra for playing a single number, hundred-franc notes tossed to a doorman for calling a cab.

But it hadn't been given for nothing.

It had been given, even the most wildly squandered sum, as an offering to destiny that he might not remember the things most worth remembering, the things that now he would always remember—his child taken from his control, his wife escaped to a grave in Vermont.

In the glare of a *brasserie* a woman spoke to him. He bought her some eggs and coffee, and then, eluding her encouraging stare, gave her a twenty-franc note and took a taxi to his hotel.

II

He woke upon a fine fall day—football weather. The depression of yesterday was gone and he liked the people on the streets. At noon he sat opposite Honoria at the Grand Vatel, the only restaurant he could think of not reminiscent of champagne dinners and long luncheons that began at two and ended in a blurred and vague twilight.

"Now, how about vegetables? Oughtn't you to have some vegetables?"

"Well, yes."

"Here's *épinards* and *choux-fleur* and carrots and haricots."

"I'd like *choux-fleur.*"

"Wouldn't you like to have two vegetables?"

"I usually only have one at lunch."

The waiter was pretending to be inordinately fond of children. *"Qu'elle est mignonne la petite? Elle parle exactement comme une française."*

"How about dessert? Shall we wait and see?"

The waiter disappeared. Honoria looked at him expectantly.

"What are we going to do?"

"First we're going to that toy store in the Rue St. Honoré and buy you anything you like. And then we're going to the vaudeville at the Empire."

She hesitated. "I like it about the vaudeville, but not the toy store."

"Why not?"

"Well, you brought me this doll." She had it with her. "And I've got lots of things. And we're not rich any more, are we?"

"We never were. But today you are to have anything you want."

"All right," she agreed resignedly.

He had always been fond of her, but when there had been her mother and a French nurse he had been inclined to be strict; now he extended himself, reached out for a new tolerance; he must be both parents to her and not shut any of her out of communication.

"I want to get to know you," he said gravely. "First let me introduce myself. My name is Charles J. Wales, of Prague."

"Oh, daddy!" her voice cracked with laughter.

"And who are you, please?" he persisted, and she accepted a rôle immediately: "Honoria Wales, Rue Palatine, Paris."

"Married or single?"

"No, not married. Single."

He indicated the doll. "But I see you have a child, madame."

Unwilling to disinherit it, she took it to her heart and thought quickly: "Yes, I've been married, but I'm not married now. My husband is dead."

He went on quickly, "And the child's name?"

"Simone. That's after my best friend at school."

"I'm very pleased that you're doing so well at school."

"I'm third this month," she boasted. "Elsie"—that was her cousin—"is only about eighteenth, and Richard is about at the bottom."

"You like Richard and Elsie, don't you?"

"Oh, yes. I like Richard quite well and I like her all right."

Cautiously and casually he asked: "And Aunt Marion and Uncle Lincoln—which do you like best?"

"Oh, Uncle Lincoln, I guess."

He was increasingly aware of her presence. As they came in, a murmur of "What an adorable child" followed them, and now the people at the next table bent all their silences upon her, staring as if she were something no more conscious than a flower.

"Why don't I live with you?" she asked suddenly. "Because mamma's dead?"

"You must stay here and learn more French. It would have been hard for daddy to take care of you so well."

"I don't really need much taking care of any more. I do everything for myself."

Going out of the restaurant, a man and a woman unexpectedly hailed him!

"Well, the old Wales!"

"Hello there, Lorraine. . . . Dunc."

Sudden ghosts out of the past: Duncan Schaeffer, a friend from college. Lorraine Quarrles, a lovely, pale blonde of thirty; one of a crowd who had helped them make months into days in the lavish times of two years ago.

"My husband couldn't come this year," she said, in answer to his question. "We're poor as hell. So he gave me two hundred a month and told me I could do my worst on that. . . . This your little girl?"

"What about sitting down?" Duncan asked.

"Can't do it." He was glad for an excuse.

As always, he felt Lorraine's passionate, provocative attraction, but his own rhythm was different now.

"Well, how about dinner?" she asked.

"I'm not free. Give me your address and let me call you."

"Charlie, I believe you're sober," she said judicially. "I honestly believe he's sober, Dunc. Pinch him and see if he's sober."

Charlie indicated Honoria with his head. They both laughed.

"What's your address?" said Duncan skeptically.

He hesitated, unwilling to give the name of his hotel.

"I'm not settled yet. I'd better call you. We're going to see the vaudeville at the Empire."

"There! That's what I want to do," Lorraine said. "I want to see some clowns and acrobats and jugglers. That's just what we'll do, Dunc."

"We've got to do an errand first," said Charlie. "Perhaps we'll see you there."

"All right, you snob. . . . Good-by, beautiful little girl."

"Good-by." Honoria bobbed politely.

Somehow, an unpleasant encounter, Charlie thought. They liked him because he was functioning, because he was serious; they wanted to see him, because he was stronger than they were now, because they wanted to draw a certain sustenance from his strength.

At the Empire, Honoria proudly refused to sit upon her father's folded coat. She was already an individual with a code of her own, and Charlie was more and more absorbed by the desire of putting a little of himself into her before she crystallized utterly. It was hopeless to try to know her in so short a time.

Between the acts they came upon Duncan and Lorraine in the lobby where the band was playing.

"Have a drink?"

"All right, but not up at the bar. We'll take a table."

"The perfect father."

Listening abstractedly to Lorraine, Charlie watched Honoria's eyes leave them all, and he followed them wistfully about the room, wondering what they saw. He met them and she smiled.

"I liked that lemonade," she said.

What had she said? What had he expected? Going home in a taxi afterward, he pulled her over until her head rested against his chest.

"Darling, do you ever think about your mother?"

"Yes, sometimes," she answered vaguely.

"I don't want you to forget her. Have you got a picture of her?"

"Yes, I think so. Anyhow, Aunt Marion has. Why don't you want me to forget her?"

"She loved you very much."

"I loved her too."

They were silent for a moment.

"Daddy, I want to come and live with you," she said suddenly.

His heart leaped; he had wanted it to come like this.

"Aren't you perfectly happy?"

"Yes, but I love you better than anybody. And you love me better than anybody, don't you, now that mummy's dead?"

"Of course I do. But you won't always like me best, honey. You'll grow up and meet somebody your own age and go marry him and forget you ever had a daddy."

"Yes, that's true," she agreed tranquilly.

He didn't go in. He was coming back at nine o'clock and he wanted to keep himself fresh and new for the thing he must say then.

"When you're safe inside, just show yourself in that window."

"All right. Good-by, dads, dads, dads, dads."

He waited in the dark street until she appeared, all warm and glowing, in the window above and kissed her fingers out into the night.

III

They were waiting. Marion sat behind empty coffee cups in a dignified black dinner dress that just faintly suggested mourning. Lincoln was walking up and down with the animation of one who had already been talking. They were as anxious as he was to get into the question. He opened it almost immediately:

"I suppose you know what I want to see you about—why I really came to Paris."

Marion fiddled with the glass grapes on her necklace and frowned.

"I'm awfully anxious to have a home," he continued. "And I'm awfully anxious to have Honoria in it. I appreciate your taking in Honoria for her mother's sake, but things have changed now"—he hesitated and then continued strongly—"changed radically with me, and I want to ask you to reconsider the matter. It would be silly for me to deny that about two years ago I was acting badly——"

Marion looked up at him with hard eyes.

"—but all that's over. As I told you, I haven't had more than a drink a day for over a year, and I take that drink deliberately, so that the idea of alcohol won't get too big in my imagination. You see the idea?"

"No," said Marion succinctly.

"It's a sort of stunt I set myself. It keeps the matter in proportion."

"I get you," said Lincoln. "You don't want to admit it's got any attraction for you."

"Something like that. Sometimes I forget and don't take it. But I try to take it. Anyhow, I couldn't afford to drink in my position. The people I represent are more than satisfied with what I've done, and I'm bringing my sister over from Burlington to keep house for me, and I want awfully to have Honoria too. You know that even when her mother and I weren't getting along well I never let anything that happened touch Honoria. I know she's fond of me and I know I'm able to take care of her and—well, there you are. How do you feel about it?"

He knew that now he would have to take a beating. It would last an hour or two hours, and it would be difficult, but if he modulated his inevitable resentment to the chastened attitude of the reformed sinner, he might win his point in the end. "Keep your temper," he told himself. "You don't want to be justified. You want Honoria."

Lincoln spoke first: "We've been talking it over ever since we got your letter last month. We're happy to have Honoria here. She's a dear little thing, and we're glad to be able to help her, but of course that isn't the question——"

Marion interrupted suddenly. "How long are you going to stay sober, Charlie?" she asked.

"Permanently, I hope."

"How can anybody count on that?"

"You know I never did drink heavily until I gave up business and came over here with nothing to do. Then Helen and I began to run around with——"

"Please leave Helen out of it. I can't bear to hear you talk about her like that."

He stared at her grimly; he had never been certain how fond of each other the sisters were in life.

"My drinking only lasted about a year and a half—from the time we came over until I—collapsed."

"It was time enough."

"It was time enough," he agreed.

"My duty is entirely to Helen," she said. "I try to think what she would have wanted me to do. Frankly, from the night you did that terrible thing you haven't really existed for me. I can't help that. She was my sister."

"Yes."

"When she was dying she asked me to look out for Honoria. If you hadn't been in a sanitarium then, it might have helped matters."

He had no answer.

"I'll never in my life be able to forget the morning when Helen knocked at my door, soaked to the skin and shivering, and said you'd locked her out."

Charlie gripped the sides of the chair. This was more difficult than he expected; he wanted to launch out into a long expostulation and explanation, but he only said: "The night I locked her out——" and she interrupted, "I don't feel up to going over that again."

After a moment's silence Lincoln said: "We're getting off the subject. You want Marion to set aside her legal guardianship and give you Honoria. I think the main point for her is whether she has confidence in you or not."

"I don't bame Marion," Charlie said slowly, "but I think she can have entire confidence in me. I had a good record up to three years ago. Of course, it's within human possibilities I might go wrong any time. But if we wait much longer I'll lose Honoria's childhood and my chance for a home. I'll simply lose her, don't you see?"

"Yes, I see," said Lincoln.

"Why didn't you think of all this before?" Marion asked.

"I suppose I did, from time to time, but Helen and I were getting along badly. When I consented to the guardianship, I was flat on my back in a sanitarium and the market had cleaned me out of every sou. I knew I'd acted badly, and I thought if it would bring any peace to Helen, I'd agree to anything. But now it's different. I'm well, I'm functioning, I'm behaving damn well, so far as——"

"Please don't swear at me," Marion said.

He looked at her, startled. With each remark the force of her dislike became more and more apparent. She had built up all her fear of life into one wall and faced it toward him. This trivial reproof was possibly the result of some trouble with the cook several hours before. Charlie became increasingly alarmed at leaving Honoria in this atmosphere of hostility against himself; sooner or later it would come out, in a word here, a shake of the head there, and some of that distrust would be irrevocably implanted in Honoria. But he pulled his temper down out of his face and shut it up inside him; he had won a point, for Lincoln realized the absurdity of Marion's remark and asked her lightly since when she had objected to the word "damn."

"Another thing," Charlie said: "I'm able to give her certain advantages now. I'm going to take a French governess to Prague with me. I've got a lease on a new apartment——"

He stopped, realizing that he was blundering. They couldn't be expected to accept with equanimity the fact that his income was again twice as large as their own.

"I suppose you can give her more luxuries than we can," said Marion. "When you were throwing away money we were living along watching every ten francs. . . . I suppose you'll start doing it again."

"Oh, no," he said. "I've learned. I worked hard for ten years, you know—until I got lucky in the market, like so many people. Terribly lucky. It didn't seem any use working any more, so I quit. It won't happen again."

There was a long silence. All of them felt their nerves straining, and for the first time in a year Charlie wanted a drink. He was sure now that Lincoln Peters wanted him to have his child.

Marion shuddered suddenly; part of her saw that Charlie's feet were planted on the earth now, and her own maternal feeling recognized the naturalness of his desire; but she had lived for a long time with a prejudice—a prejudice founded on a curious disbelief in her sister's happiness, and which, in the shock of one terrible night, had turned to hatred for him. It had all happened at a point in her life where the discouragement of ill-health and adverse circumstances made it necessary for her to believe in tangible villainy and a tangible villain.

"I can't help what I think!" she cried out suddenly. "How much you were responsible for Helen's death, I don't know. It's something you'll have to square with your own conscience."

An electric current of agony surged through him; for a moment he was almost on his feet, an unuttered sound echoing in his throat. He hung on to himself for a moment, another moment.

"Hold on there," said Lincoln uncomfortably. "I never thought you were responsible for that."

"Helen died of heart trouble," Charlie said dully.

"Yes, heart trouble." Marion spoke as if the phrase had another meaning for her.

Then, in the flatness that followed her outburst, she saw him plainly and she knew he had somehow arrived at control over the situation. Glancing at her husband, she found no help from him, and as abruptly as if it were a matter of no importance, she threw up the sponge.

"Do what you like!" she cried, springing up from her chair. "She's your child. I'm not the person to stand in your way. I think if it were my child I'd rather see her——" She managed to check herself. "You two decide it. I can't stand this. I'm sick. I'm going to bed."

She hurried from the room; after a moment Lincoln said:

"This has been a hard day for her. You know how strongly she feels——" His voice was almost apologetic: "When a woman gets an idea in her head."

"Of course."

"It's going to be all right. I think she sees now that you—can provide for the child, and so we can't very well stand in your way or Honoria's way."

"Thank you, Lincoln."

"I'd better go along and see how she is."

"I'm going."

He was still trembling when he reached the street, but a walk down the

Rue Bonaparte to the quais set him up, and as he crossed the Seine, dotted with many cold moons, he felt exultant. But back in his room he couldn't sleep. The image of Helen haunted him. Helen whom he had loved so until they had senselessly begun to abuse each other's love and tear it into shreds. On that terrible February night that Marion remembered so vividly, a slow quarrel that had gone on for hours. There was a scene at the Florida, and then he attempted to take her home, and then Helen kissed Ted Wilder at a table, and what she had hysterically said. Charlie's departure and, on his arrival home, his turning the key in the lock in wild anger. How could he know she would arrive an hour later alone, that there would be a snow-storm in which she wandered about in slippers for an hour, too confused to find a taxi? Then the aftermath, her escaping pneumonia by a miracle, and all the attendant horror. They were "reconciled," but that was the begin-ning of the end, and Marion, who had seen with her own eyes and who imagined it to be one of many scenes from her sister's martyrdom, never forgot.

Going over it again brought Helen nearer, and in the white, soft light that steals upon half sleep near morning he found himself talking to her again. She said that he was perfectly right about Honoria and that she wanted Honoria to be with him. She said she was glad he was being good and doing better. She said a lot of other things—very friendly things—but she was in a swing in a white dress, and swinging faster and faster all the time, so that at the end he could not hear clearly all that she said.

IV

He woke up feeling happy. The door of the world was open again. He made plans, vistas, futures for Honoria and himself, but suddenly he grew sad, remembering all the plans he and Helen had made. She had not planned to die. The present was the thing—work to do and someone to love. But not to love too much, for Charlie had read in D. H. Lawrence about the injury that a father can do to a daughter, or a mother to a son by attaching them too closely. Afterward, out in the world, the child would seek in the marriage partner the same blind, unselfish tenderness and, failing in all hu-man probability to find it, develop a grudge against love and life.

It was another bright, crisp day. He called Lincoln Peters at the bank where he worked and asked if he could count on taking Honoria when he left for Prague. Lincoln agreed that there was no reason for delay. One thing —the legal guardianship. Marion wanted to retain that a while longer. She was upset by the whole matter, and it would oil things if she felt that the situation was still in her control for another year. Charlie agreed, wanting only the tangible, visible child.

Then the question of a governess. Charlie sat in a gloomy agency and talked to a buxom Breton peasant whom he knew he couldn't endure. There were others whom he could see tomorrow.

He lunched with Lincoln Peters at the Griffon, trying to keep down his exultation.

"There's nothing quite like your own child," Lincoln said. "But you understand how Marion feels too."

"She's forgotten how hard I worked for seven years there," Charlie said. "She just remembers one night."

"There's another thing." Lincoln hesitated. "While you and Helen were tearing around Europe throwing money away, we were just getting along. I didn't touch any of the prosperity because I never got ahead enough to carry anything but my insurance. I think Marion felt there was some kind of injustice in it—you not even working and getting richer and richer."

"It went just as quick as it came," said Charlie.

"A lot did. And a lot of it stayed in the hands of *chasseurs* and saxophone players and maîtres d'hôtel—well, the big party's over now. I just said that to explain Marion's feeling about those crazy years. If you drop in about six o'clock tonight before Marion's too tired, we'll settle the details on the spot."

Back at his hotel, Charlie took from his pocket a *pneumatique* that Lincoln had given him at luncheon. It had been redirected by Paul from the hotel bar.

Dear Charlie: You were so strange when we saw you the other day that I wondered if I did something to offend you. If so, I'm not conscious of it. In fact, I have thought about you too much for the past year, and it's always been in the back of my mind that I might see you if I came over here. We did have such good times that crazy spring, like the night you and I stole the butcher's tricycle, and the time we tried to call on the president and you had the old derby and the wire cane. Everybody seems so old lately, but I don't feel old a bit. Couldn't we get together sometime today for old time's sake? I've got a vile hang-over for the moment, but will be feeling better this afternoon and will look for you about five at the bar.

Always devotedly,
LORRAINE.

His first feeling was one of awe that he had actually, in his mature years, stolen a tricycle and pedaled Lorraine all over the Étoile between the small hours and dawn. In retrospect it was a nightmare. Locking out Helen didn't fit in with any other act of his life, but the tricycle incident did—it was one of many. How many weeks or months of dissipation to arrive at that condition of utter irresponsibility?

He tried to picture how Lorraine had appeared to him then—very attractive; so much so that Helen had been jealous. Yesterday, in the restaurant, she had seemed trite, blurred, worn away. He emphatically did not want to see her, and he was glad no one knew at what hotel he was staying. It was a relief to think of Honoria, to think of Sundays spent with her and of saying good morning to her and of knowing she was there in his house at night, breathing quietly in the darkness.

At five he took a taxi and bought presents for all the Peters'—a piquant cloth doll, a box of Roman soldiers, flowers for Marion, big linen handkerchiefs for Lincoln.

He saw, when he arrived in the apartment, that Marion had accepted the inevitable. She greeted him now as though he were a recalcitrant member of the family, rather than a menacing outsider. Honoria had been told she was going, and Charlie was glad to see that her tact was sufficient to conceal her excessive happiness. Only on his lap did she whisper her delight and the question "When?" before she slipped away.

He and Marion were alone for a minute in the room, and on an impulse he spoke out boldly:

"Family quarrels are bitter things. They don't go according to my rules. They're not like aches or wounds; they're more like splits in the skin that won't heal because there's not enough material. I wish you and I could be on better terms."

"Some things are hard to forget," she answered. "It's a question of confidence. If you behave yourself in the future I won't have any criticism." There was no answer to this, and presently she asked, "When do you propose to take her?"

"As soon as I can get a governess. I hoped the day after tomorrow."

"That's impossible. I've got to get her things in shape. Not before Saturday."

He yielded. Coming back into the room, Lincoln offered him a drink.

"I'll take my daily whisky," he said.

It was warm here, it was a home, people together by a fire. The children felt very safe and important; the mother and father were serious, watchful. They had things to do for the children more important than his visit here. A spoonful of medicine was, after all, more important than the strained relations between Marion and himself. They were not dull people, but they were very much in the grip of life and circumstances, and their gestures as they turned in a cramped space lacked largeness and grace. He wondered if he couldn't do something to get Lincoln out of that rut at the bank.

There was a long peal at the doorbell; the maid crossed the room and went down the corridor. The door opened upon another long ring, and then voices, and the three in the salon looked up expectantly; Richard moved to bring the corridor within his range of vision, and Marion rose. Then the maid came along the corridor, closely followed by the voices, which developed under the light into Duncan Schaeffer and Lorraine Quarrles.

They were gay, they were hilarious, they were roaring with laughter. For a moment Charlie was astounded; then he realized they had got the address he had left at the bar.

"Ah-h-h!" Duncan wagged his finger roguishly at Charlie. "Ah-h-h!"

They both slid down into another cascade of laughter. Anxious and at a loss, Charlie shook hands with them quickly and presented them to Lincoln and Marion. Marion nodded, scarcely speaking. She had drawn back a step toward the fire; her little girl stood beside her, and Marion put an arm about her shoulder.

With growing annoyance at the intrusion, Charlie waited for them to explain themselves. After some concentration Duncan said:

"We came to take you to dinner. Lorraine and I insist that all this shi-shi, cagy business has got to stop."

Charlie came closer to them, as if to force them backward down the corridor.

"Sorry, but I can't. Tell me where you'll be and we'll call you in half an hour."

This made no impression. Lorraine sat down suddenly on the side of a chair, and focusing her eyes on Richard, cried, "Oh, what a nice little boy! Come here, little boy." Richard glanced at his mother, but did not move. With a perceptible shrug of her shoulders, Lorraine turned back to Charlie:

"Come on out to dinner. Be yourself, Charlie. Come on."

"How about a little drink?" said Duncan to the room at large.

Lincoln Peters had been somewhat uneasily occupying himself by swinging Honoria from side to side with her feet off the ground.

"I'm sorry, but there isn't a thing in the house," he said. "We just this minute emptied the only bottle."

"All the more reason coming to dinner," Lorraine assured Charlie.

"I can't," said Charlie almost sharply. "You two go have dinner and I'll phone you."

"Oh, you will, will you?" Her voice became suddenly unpleasant. "All right, we'll go along. But I remember, when you used to hammer on my door, I used to be enough of a good sport to give you a drink. Come on, Dunc."

Still in slow motion, with blurred, angry faces, with uncertain feet, they retired along the corridor.

"Good night," Charlie said.

"Good night!" responded Lorraine emphatically.

When he went back into the salon Marion had not moved, only now her son was standing in the circle of her other arm. Lincoln was still swinging Honoria back and forth like a pendulum from side to side.

"What an outrage!" Charlie broke out. "What an absolute outrage!"

Neither of them answered. Charlie dropped into an armchair, picked up his drink, set it down again and said:

"People I haven't seen for two years having the colossal nerve——"

He broke off. Marion had made the sound "Oh!" in one swift, furious breath, turned her body from him with a jerk and left the room.

Lincoln set down Honoria carefully.

"You children go in and start your soup," he said, and when they obeyed, he said to Charlie:

"Marion's not well and she can't stand shocks. That kind of people make her really physically sick."

"I didn't tell them to come here. They wormed this address out of Paul at the bar. They deliberately——"

"Well, it's too bad. It doesn't help matters. Excuse me a minute."

Left alone, Charlie sat tense in his chair. In the next room he could hear the children eating, talking in monosyllables, already oblivious of the scene among their elders. He heard a murmur of conversation from a farther room and then the ticking bell of a phone picked up, and in a panic he moved to the other side of the room and out of earshot.

In a minute Lincoln came back. "Look here, Charlie. I think we'd better call off dinner for tonight. Marion's in bad shape."

"Is she angry with me?"

"Sort of," he said, almost roughly. "She's not strong and——"

"You mean she's changed her mind about Honoria."

"She's pretty bitter right now. I don't know. You phone me at the bank tomorrow."

"I wish you'd explain to her I never dreamed these people would come here. I'm just as sore as you are."

"I couldn't explain anything to her now."

Charlie got up. He took his coat and hat and started down the corridor. Then he opened the door of the dining room and said in a strange voice, "Good night, children."

Honoria rose and ran around the table to hug him.

"Good night, sweetheart," he said vaguely, and then trying to make his voice more tender, trying to conciliate something, "Good night, dear children."

V

Charlie went directly to the bar with the furious idea of finding Lorraine and Duncan, but they were not there, and he realized that in any case there was nothing he could do. He had not touched his drink at the Peters', and now he ordered a whisky-and-soda. Paul came over to say hello.

"It's a great change," he said sadly. "We do about half the business we did. So many fellows I hear about back in the States lost everything, maybe not in the first crash, but then in the second, and now when everything keeps going down. Your friend George Hardt lost every cent, I hear. Are you back in the States?"

"No, I'm in business in Prague."

"I heard that you lost a lot in the crash."

"I did," and he added grimly, "but I lost everything I wanted in the boom."

"Selling short."

"Something like that."

Again the memory of those days swept over him like a nightmare—the people they had met traveling; then people who couldn't add a row of figures or speak a coherent sentence. The little man Helen had consented to dance with at the ship's party, who had insulted her ten feet from the table; the human mosaic of pearls who sat behind them at the Russian ballet and, when the curtain rose on a scene, remarked to her companion: "Luffly; just luffly. Zomebody ought to baint a bicture of it." Men who locked their wives out in the snow, because the snow of twenty-nine wasn't real snow. If you didn't want it to be snow, you just paid some money.

He went to the phone and called the Peters' apartment; Lincoln himself answered.

"I called up because, as you can imagine, this thing is on my mind. Has Marion said anything definite?"

"Marion's sick," Lincoln answered shortly. "I know this thing isn't altogether your fault, but I can't have her go to pieces about this. I'm afraid we'll have to let it slide for six months; I can't take the chance of working her up to this state again."

"I see."

"I'm sorry, Charlie."

He went back to his table. His whisky glass was empty, but he shook his head when Alix looked at it questioningly. There wasn't much he could do now except send Honoria some things; he would send her a lot of things tomorrow. He thought rather angrily that that was just money—he had given so many people money.

"No, no more," he said to another waiter. "What do I owe you?"

He would come back some day; they couldn't make him pay forever. But he wanted his child, and nothing was much good now, beside that fact. He wasn't young any more, with a lot of nice thoughts and dreams to have by himself. He was absolutely sure Helen wouldn't have wanted him to be so alone.

THE BOWMEN

ARTHUR MACHEN

IT WAS during the retreat of the eighty thousand, and the authority of the censorship is sufficient excuse for not being more explicit. But it was on the most awful day of that awful time, on the day when ruin and disaster came so near that their shadow fell over London far away; and, without any certain news, the hearts of men failed within them and grew faint; as if the agony of the army in the battlefield had entered into their souls.

On this dreadful day, then, when three hundred thousand men in arms with all their artillery swelled like a flood against the little English company, there was one point above all other points in our battle line that was for a time in awful danger, not merely of defeat, but of utter annihilation. With the permission of the censorship and of the military expert, this corner may, perhaps, be described as a salient, and if this angle were crushed and broken, then the English force as a whole would be shattered, the Allied left would be turned, and Sedan would inevitably follow.

All the morning the German guns had thundered and shrieked against this corner, and against the thousand or so of men who held it. The men joked at the shells, and found funny names for them, and had bets about them, and greeted them with scraps of music-hall songs. But the shells came on and burst, and tore good Englishmen limb from limb, and tore brother from brother, and as the heat of the day increased so did the fury of that terrific cannonade. There was no help, it seemed. The English artillery was good, but there was not nearly enough of it; it was being steadily battered into scrap iron.

There comes a moment in a storm at sea when people say to one another: "It is at its worst; it can blow no harder," and then there is a blast ten times more fierce than any before it. So it was in these British trenches.

There were no stouter hearts in the whole world than the hearts of these men; but even they were appalled as this seven-times-heated hell of the German cannonade fell upon them and overwhelmed them and destroyed them.

And at this very moment they saw from their trenches that a tremendous host was moving against their lines. Five hundred of the thousand remained, and as far as they could see the German infantry was pressing on against them, column upon column, a grey world of men, ten thousand of them, as it appeared afterwards.

There was no hope at all. They shook hands, some of them. One man improvised a new version of the battle-song, *Good-bye, Good-bye to Tipperary*, ending with "And we shan't get there." And they all went on firing steadily. The officers pointed out that such an opportunity for high-class, fancy shooting might never occur again; the Germans dropped line after line; the Tipperary humorist asked: "What price Sidney Street?" And the few machine guns did their best. But everybody knew it was of no use. The dead grey bodies lay in companies and battalions, as others came on and on, and they swarmed and stirred and advanced from beyond and beyond.

"World without end. Amen," said one of the British soldiers with some irrelevance as he took aim and fired. And then he remembered—he says he cannot think why or wherefore—a queer vegetarian restaurant in London where he had once or twice eaten eccentric dishes of cutlets made of lentils and nuts that pretended to be steak. On all the plates in this restaurant there was printed a figure of St. George in blue, with the motto, *Adsit Sanctus Georgius*—May St. George be a present help to the English. This soldier happened to know Latin and other useless things, and now, as he fired at his man in the grey advancing mass—three hundred yards away—he uttered the pious vegetarian motto. He went on firing to the end, and at last Bill on his right had to clout him cheerfully over the head to make him stop, pointing out as he did so that the King's ammunition cost money and was not lightly to be wasted in drilling funny patterns into dead Germans.

For as the Latin scholar uttered his invocation he felt something between a shudder and an electric shock pass through his body. The roar of the battle died down in his ears to a gentle murmur; instead of it, he says, he heard a great voice and a shout louder than a thunder-peal crying: "Array, array, array!"

His heart grew hot as a burning coal, it grew cold as ice within him, as it seemed to him that a tumult of voices answered to his summons. He heard, or seemed to hear, thousands shouting: "St. George! St. George!"

"Ha! messire; ha! sweet Saint, grant us good deliverance!"

"St. George for merry England!"

"Harow! Harow! Monseigneur St. George, succour us."

"Ha! St. George! Ha! St. George! a long bow and a strong bow."

"Heaven's Knight, aid us!"

And as the soldier heard these voices he saw before him, beyond the trench, a long line of shapes, with a shining about them. They were like men who drew the bow, and with another shout their cloud of arrows flew singing and tingling through the air towards the German hosts.

The other men in the trench were firing all the while. They had no hope; but they aimed just as if they had been shooting at Bisley.

Suddenly one of them lifted up his voice in the plainest English. "Gawd help us!" he bellowed to the man next to him, "but we're blooming marvels! Look at those grey . . . gentlemen, look at them! D'ye see them? They're not going down in dozens, nor in 'undreds; it's thousands, it is. Look! look! there's a regiment gone while I'm talking to ye."

"Shut it!" the other soldier bellowed, taking aim, "what are ye gassing about?"

But he gulped with astonishment even as he spoke, for, indeed, the grey men were falling by the thousands. The English could hear the guttural scream of the German officers, the crackle of their revolvers as they shot the reluctant; and still line after line crashed to the earth.

All the while the Latin-bred soldier heard the cry:

"Harow! Harow! Monseigneur, dear Saint, quick to our aid! St. George help us!"

"High Chevalier, defend us!"

The singing arrows fled so swift and thick that they darkened the air; the heathen horde melted from before them.

"More machine guns!" Bill yelled to Tom.

"Don't hear them," Tom yelled back. "But, thank God, anyway; they've got it in the neck."

In fact, there were ten thousand dead German soldiers left before that salient of the English army, and consequently there was no Sedan. In Germany, a country ruled by scientific principles, the great general staff decided that the contemptible English must have employed shells containing an unknown gas of a poisonous nature, as no wounds were discernible on the bodies of the dead German soldiers. But the man who knew what nuts tasted like when they called themselves steak knew also that St. George had brought his Agincourt bowmen to help the English.

THE MURDER OF ROGER ACKROYD

AGATHA CHRISTIE

I. DR. SHEPPARD AT THE BREAKFAST TABLE

MRS. FERRARS died on the night of the 16th–17th September—a Thursday. I was sent for at eight o'clock on the morning of Friday the 17th. There was nothing to be done. She had been dead some hours.

It was just a few minutes after nine when I reached home once more. I opened the front door with my latchkey, and purposely delayed a few moments in the hall, hanging up my hat and the light overcoat that I had deemed a wise precaution against the chill of an early autumn morning. To tell the truth, I was considerably upset and worried. I am not going to pretend that at that moment I foresaw the events of the next few weeks. I emphatically did not do so. But my instinct told me that there were stirring times ahead.

From the dining-room on my left there came the rattle of tea-cups and the short, dry cough of my sister Caroline.

"Is that you, James?" she called.

An unnecessary question, since who else could it be? To tell the truth, it was precisely my sister Caroline who was the cause of my few minutes' delay. The motto of the mongoose family, so Mr. Kipling tells us, is: "Go and find out." If Caroline ever adopts a crest, I should certainly suggest a mongoose rampant. One might omit the first part of the motto. Caroline can do any amount of finding out by sitting placidly at home. I don't know how she manages it, but there it is. I suspect that the servants and the tradesmen constitute her Intelligence Corps. When she goes out, it is not to gather in information, but to spread it. At that, too, she is amazingly expert.

It was really this last named trait of hers which was causing me these pangs of indecision. Whatever I told Caroline now concerning the demise of Mrs. Ferrars would be common knowledge all over the village within the space of an hour and a half. As a professional man, I naturally aim at discretion. Therefore I have got into the habit of continually withholding all information possible from my sister. She usually finds out just the same, but I have the moral satisfaction of knowing that I am in no way to blame.

Mrs. Ferrars's husband died just over a year ago, and Caroline has constantly asserted, without the least foundation for the assertion, that his wife poisoned him.

She scorns my invariable rejoinder that Mr. Ferrars died of acute gastritis, helped on by habitual over-indulgence in alcoholic beverages. The symptoms of gastritis and arsenical poisoning are not, I agree, unlike, but Caroline bases her accusation on quite different lines.

"You've only got to look at her," I have heard her say.

Mrs. Ferrars, though not in her first youth, was a very attractive woman, and her clothes, though simple, always seemed to fit her very well, but all the same, lots of women buy their clothes in Paris and have not, on that account, necessarily poisoned their husbands.

As I stood hesitating in the hall, with all this passing through my mind, Caroline's voice came again, with a sharper note in it.

"What on earth are you doing out there, James? Why don't you come and get your breakfast?"

"Just coming, my dear," I said hastily. "I've been hanging up my overcoat."

"You could have hung up half a dozen overcoats in this time."

She was quite right. I could have.

I walked into the dining-room, gave Caroline the accustomed peck on the cheek, and sat down to eggs and bacon. The bacon was rather cold.

"You've had an early call," remarked Caroline.

"Yes," I said. "King's Paddock. Mrs. Ferrars."

"I know," said my sister.

"How did you know?"

"Annie told me."

Annie is the house parlormaid. A nice girl, but an inveterate talker.

There was a pause. I continued to eat eggs and bacon. My sister's nose, which is long and thin, quivered a little at the tip, as it always does when she is interested or excited over anything.

"Well?" she demanded.

"A bad business. Nothing to be done. Must have died in her sleep."

"I know," said my sister again.

This time I was annoyed.

"You can't know," I snapped. "I didn't know myself until I got there, and I haven't mentioned it to a soul yet. If that girl Annie knows, she must be a clairvoyant."

"It wasn't Annie who told me. It was the milkman. He had it from the Ferrars' cook."

As I say, there is no need for Caroline to go out to get information. She sits at home, and it comes to her.

My sister continued:

"What did she die of? Heart failure?"

"Didn't the milkman tell you that?" I inquired sarcastically.

Sarcasm is wasted on Caroline. She takes it seriously and answers accordingly.

"He didn't know," she explained.

After all, Caroline was bound to hear sooner or later. She might as well hear from me.

"She died of an overdose of veronal. She's been taking it lately for sleeplessness. Must have taken too much."

"Nonsense," said Caroline immediately. "She took it on purpose. Don't tell me!"

It is odd how, when you have a secret belief of your own which you do not wish to acknowledge, the voicing of it by some one else will rouse you to a fury of denial. I burst immediately into indignant speech.

"There you go again," I said. "Rushing along without rhyme or reason. Why on earth should Mrs. Ferrars wish to commit suicide? A widow, fairly young still, very well off, good health, and nothing to do but enjoy life. It's absurd."

"Not at all. Even you must have noticed how different she has been looking lately. It's been coming on for the last six months. She's looked positively hag-ridden. And you have just admitted that she hasn't been able to sleep."

"What is your diagnosis?" I demanded coldly. "An unfortunate love affair, I suppose?"

My sister shook her head.

"*Remorse*," she said, with great gusto.

"Remorse?"

"Yes. You never would believe me when I told you she poisoned her husband. I'm more than ever convinced of it now."

"I don't think you're very logical," I objected. "Surely if a woman committed a crime like murder, she'd be sufficiently cold-blooded to enjoy the fruits of it without any weak-minded sentimentality such as repentance."

Caroline shook her head.

"There probably are women like that—but Mrs. Ferrars wasn't one of them. She was a mass of nerves. An overmastering impulse drove her on to get rid of her husband because she was the sort of person who simply can't endure suffering of any kind, and there's no doubt that the wife of a man like Ashley Ferrars must have had to suffer a good deal——"

I nodded.

"And ever since she's been haunted by what she did. I can't help feeling sorry for her."

I don't think Caroline ever felt sorry for Mrs. Ferrars whilst she was alive. Now that she has gone where (presumably) Paris frocks can no longer be worn, Caroline is prepared to indulge in the softer emotions of pity and comprehension.

I told her firmly that her whole idea was nonsense. I was all the more firm because I secretly agreed with some part, at least, of what she had said. But it is all wrong that Caroline should arrive at the truth simply by a kind of inspired guesswork. I wasn't going to encourage that sort of thing. She will go round the village airing her views, and every one will think that she is doing so on medical data supplied by me. Life is very trying.

"Nonsense," said Caroline, in reply to my strictures. "You'll see. Ten to one she's left a letter confessing everything."

"She didn't leave a letter of any kind," I said sharply, and not seeing where the admission was going to land me.

"Oh!" said Caroline. "So you *did* inquire about that, did you? I believe, James, that in your heart of hearts, you think very much as I do. You're a precious old humbug."

"One always has to take the possibility of suicide into consideration," I said repressively.

"Will there be an inquest?"

"There may be. It all depends. If I am able to declare myself absolutely satisfied that the overdose was taken accidentally, an inquest might be dispensed with."

"And are you absolutely satisfied?" asked my sister shrewdly.

I did not answer, but got up from table.

II. WHO'S WHO IN KING'S ABBOT

Before I proceed further with what I said to Caroline and what Caroline said to me, it might be as well to give some idea of what I should describe as our local geography. Our village, King's Abbot, is, I imagine, very much like any other village. Our big town is Cranchester, nine miles away. We have a large railway station, a small post office, and two rival "General Stores." Able-bodied men are apt to leave the place early in life, but we are rich in unmarried ladies and retired military officers. Our hobbies and recreations can be summed up in the one word, "gossip."

There are only two houses of any importance in King's Abbot. One is King's Paddock, left to Mrs. Ferrars by her late husband. The other, Fernly Park, is owned by Roger Ackroyd. Ackroyd has always interested me by being a man more impossibly like a country squire than any country squire could really be. He reminds one of the red-faced sportsmen who always appeared early in the first act of an old-fashioned musical comedy, the setting being the village green. They usually sang a song about going up to London. Nowadays we have revues, and the country squire has died out of musical fashion.

Of course, Ackroyd is not really a country squire. He is an immensely successful manufacturer of (I think) wagon wheels. He is a man of nearly fifty years of age, rubicund of face and genial of manner. He is hand and glove with the vicar, subscribes liberally to parish funds (though rumor has it that he is extremely mean in personal expenditure), encourages cricket matches, Lads' Clubs, and Disabled Soldiers' Institutes. He is, in fact, the life and soul of our peaceful village of King's Abbot.

Now when Roger Ackroyd was a lad of twenty-one, he fell in love with, and married, a beautiful woman some five or six years his senior. Her name was Paton, and she was a widow with one child. The history of the marriage was short and painful. To put it bluntly, Mrs. Ackroyd was a dipsomaniac. She succeeded in drinking herself into her grave four years after her marriage.

In the years that followed, Ackroyd showed no disposition to make a second matrimonial adventure. His wife's child by her first marriage was only seven years old when his mother died. He is now twenty-five. Ackroyd has always regarded him as his own son, and has brought him up accordingly, but he has been a wild lad and a continual source of worry and trouble to his stepfather. Nevertheless we are all very fond of Ralph Paton in King's Abbot. He is such a good-looking youngster for one thing.

As I said before, we are ready enough to gossip in our village. Everybody noticed from the first that Ackroyd and Mrs. Ferrars got on very well together. After her husband's death, the intimacy became more marked. They were always seen about together, and it was freely conjectured that at the end of her period of mourning, Mrs. Ferrars would become Mrs. Roger Ackroyd. It was felt, indeed, that there was a certain fitness in the thing. Roger Ackroyd's wife had admittedly died of drink. Ashley Ferrars had been a drunkard for many years before his death. It was only fitting that these two victims of alcoholic excess should make up to each other for all that they had previously endured at the hands of their former spouses.

The Ferrars only came to live here just over a year ago, but a halo of gossip has surrounded Ackroyd for many years past. All the time that Ralph Paton was growing up to manhood, a series of lady housekeepers presided over Ackroyd's establishment, and each in turn was regarded with lively suspicion by Caroline and her cronies. It is not too much to say that for at least fifteen years the whole village has confidently expected Ackroyd to marry one of his housekeepers. The last of them, a redoubtable lady called Miss Russell, has reigned undisputed for five years, twice as long as any of her predecessors. It is felt that but for the advent of Mrs. Ferrars, Ackroyd could hardly have escaped. That—and one other factor—the unexpected arrival of a widowed sister-in-law with her daughter from Canada. Mrs. Cecil Ackroyd, widow of Ackroyd's ne'er-do-well younger brother, has taken up her residence at Fernly Park, and has succeeded, according to Caroline, in putting Miss Russell in her proper place.

I don't know exactly what a "proper place" constitutes—it sounds chilly and unpleasant—but I know that Miss Russell goes about with pinched lips, and what I can only describe as an acid smile, and that she professes the utmost sympathy for "poor Mrs. Ackroyd—dependent on the charity of her husband's brother. The bread of charity is so bitter, is it not? I should be quite miserable if I did not work for my living."

I don't know what Mrs. Cecil Ackroyd thought of the Ferrars affair when it came on the tapis. It was clearly to her advantage that Ackroyd should remain unmarried. She was always very charming—not to say gushing—to Mrs. Ferrars when they met. Caroline says that proves less than nothing.

Such have been our preoccupations in King's Abbot for the last few years. We have discussed Ackroyd and his affairs from every standpoint. Mrs. Ferrars has fitted into her place in the scheme.

Now there has been a rearrangement of the kaleidoscope. From a mild discussion of probable wedding presents, we have been jerked into the midst of tragedy.

Revolving these and sundry other matters in my mind, I went mechanically on my round. I had no cases of special interest to attend, which was, perhaps, as well, for my thoughts returned again and again to the mystery of Mrs. Ferrars's death. Had she taken her own life? Surely, if she had done so, she would have left some word behind to say what she contemplated doing. Women, in my experience, if they once reach the determination to commit suicide, usually wish to reveal the state of mind that led to the fatal action. They covet the limelight.

When had I last seen her? Not for over a week. Her manner then had been normal enough considering—well—considering everything.

Then I suddenly remembered that I had seen her, though not to speak to, only yesterday. She had been walking with Ralph Paton, and I had been surprised because I had had no idea that he was likely to be in King's Abbot.

I thought, indeed, that he had quarreled finally with his stepfather. Nothing had been seen of him down here for nearly six months. They had been walking along, side by side, their heads close together, and she had been talking very earnestly.

I think I can safely say that it was at this moment that a foreboding of the future first swept over me. Nothing tangible as yet—but a vague premonition of the way things were setting. That earnest *tête-à-tête* between Ralph Paton and Mrs. Ferrars the day before struck me disagreeably.

I was still thinking of it when I came face to face with Roger Ackroyd.

"Sheppard!" he exclaimed. "Just the man I wanted to get hold of. This is a terrible business."

"You've heard then?"

He nodded. He had felt the blow keenly, I could see. His big red cheeks seemed to have fallen in, and he looked a positive wreck of his usual jolly, healthy self.

"It's worse than you know," he said quietly. "Look here, Sheppard, I've got to talk to you. Can you come back with me now?"

"Hardly. I've got three patients to see still, and I must be back by twelve to see my surgery patients."

"Then this afternoon—no, better still, dine to-night. At seven-thirty? Will that suit you?"

"Yes—I can manage that all right. What's wrong? Is it Ralph?"

I hardly knew why I said that—except, perhaps, that it had so often been Ralph.

Ackroyd stared blankly at me as though he hardly understood. I began to realize that there must be something very wrong indeed somewhere. I had never seen Ackroyd so upset before.

"Ralph?" he said vaguely. "Oh! no, it's not Ralph. Ralph's in London—— Damn! Here's old Miss Ganett coming. I don't want to have to talk to her about this ghastly business. See you to-night, Sheppard. Seven-thirty."

I nodded, and he hurried away, leaving me wondering. Ralph in London? But he had certainly been in King's Abbot the preceding afternoon. He must have gone back to town last night or early this morning, and yet Ackroyd's manner had conveyed quite a different impression. He had spoken as though Ralph had not been near the place for months.

I had no time to puzzle the matter out further. Miss Ganett was upon me, thirsting for information. Miss Ganett has all the characteristics of my sister Caroline, but she lacks that unerring aim in jumping to conclusions which lends a touch of greatness to Caroline's maneuvers. Miss Ganett was breathless and interrogatory.

Wasn't it sad about poor dear Mrs. Ferrars? A lot of people were saying she had been a confirmed drug-taker for years. So wicked the way people went about saying things. And yet, the worst of it was, there was usually a grain of truth somewhere in these wild statements. No smoke without fire! They were saying too that Mr. Ackroyd had found out about it, and had broken off the engagement—because there *was* an engagement. She, Miss Ganett, had proof positive of that. Of course I must know all about it—doctors always did—but they never tell?

And all this with a sharp beady eye on me to see how I reacted to these suggestions. Fortunately long association with Caroline has led me to preserve an impassive countenance, and to be ready with small non-committal remarks.

On this occasion I congratulated Miss Ganett on not joining in ill-natured gossip. Rather a neat counterattack, I thought. It left her in difficulties, and before she could pull herself together, I had passed on.

I went home thoughtful, to find several patients waiting for me in the surgery.

I had dismissed the last of them, as I thought, and was just contemplating a few minutes in the garden before lunch when I perceived one more patient waiting for me. She rose and came towards me as I stood somewhat surprised.

I don't know why I should have been, except that there is a suggestion of cast iron about Miss Russell, a something that is above the ills of the flesh.

Ackroyd's housekeeper is a tall woman, handsome but forbidding in appearance. She has a stern eye, and lips that shut tightly, and I feel that if I were an under housemaid or a kitchenmaid I should run for my life whenever I heard her coming.

"Good-morning, Dr. Sheppard," said Miss Russell. "I should be much obliged if you would take a look at my knee."

I took a look, but, truth to tell, I was very little wiser when I had done so. Miss Russell's account of vague pains was so unconvincing that with a woman of less integrity of character I should have suspected a trumped-up tale. It did cross my mind for one moment that Miss Russell might have deliberately invented this affection of the knee in order to pump me on the subject of Mrs. Ferrars's death, but I soon saw that there, at least, I had misjudged her. She made a brief reference to the tragedy, nothing more. Yet she certainly seemed disposed to linger and chat.

"Well, thank you very much for this bottle of liniment, doctor," she said at last. "Not that I believe it will do the least good."

I didn't think it would either, but I protested in duty bound. After all, it couldn't do any harm, and one must stick up for the tools of one's trade.

"I don't believe in all these drugs," said Miss Russell, her eyes sweeping over my array of bottles disparagingly. "Drugs do a lot of harm. Look at the cocaine habit."

"Well, as far as that goes——"

"It's very prevalent in high society."

I'm sure Miss Russell knows far more about high society than I do. I didn't attempt to argue with her.

"Just tell me this, doctor," said Miss Russell. "Suppose you are really a slave of the drug habit. Is there any cure?"

One cannot answer a question like that offhand. I gave her a short lecture on the subject, and she listened with close attention. I still suspected her of seeking information about Mrs. Ferrars.

"Now, veronal, for instance——" I proceeded.

But, strangely enough, she didn't seem interested in veronal. Instead she changed the subject, and asked me if it was true that there were certain poisons so rare as to baffle detection.

"Ah!" I said. "You've been reading detective stories."

She admitted that she had.

"The essence of a detective story," I said, "is to have a rare poison—if possible something from South America, that nobody has ever heard of—something that one obscure tribe of savages use to poison their arrows with. Death is instantaneous, and Western science is powerless to detect it. That is the kind of thing you mean?"

"Yes. Is there really such a thing?"

I shook my head regretfully.

"I'm afraid there isn't. There's *cuare*, of course."

I told her a good deal about cuare, but she seemed to have lost interest once more. She asked me if I had any in my poison cupboard, and when I replied in the negative I fancy I fell in her estimation.

She said she must be getting back, and I saw her out at the surgery door just as the luncheon gong went.

I should never have suspected Miss Russell of a fondness for detective stories. It pleases me very much to think of her stepping out of the housekeeper's room to rebuke a delinquent housemaid, and then returning to a comfortable perusal of *The Mystery of the Seventh Death*, or something of the kind.

III. THE MAN WHO GREW VEGETABLE MARROWS

I told Caroline at lunch time that I should be dining at Fernly. She expressed no objection—on the contrary—

"Excellent," she said. "You'll hear all about it. By the way, what is the trouble with Ralph?"

"With Ralph?" I said, surprised; "there isn't any."

"Then why is he staying at the Three Boars instead of at Fernly Park?"

I did not for a minute question Caroline's statement that Ralph Paton was staying at the local inn. That Caroline said so was enough for me.

"Ackroyd told me he was in London," I said. In the surprise of the moment I departed from my valuable rule of never parting with information.

"Oh!" said Caroline. I could see her nose twitching as she worked on this.

"He arrived at the Three Boars yesterday morning," she said. "And he's still there. Last night he was out with a girl."

That did not surprise me in the least. Ralph, I should say, is out with a girl most nights of his life. But I did rather wonder that he chose to indulge in the pastime in King's Abbot instead of in the gay metropolis.

"One of the barmaids?" I asked.

"No. That's just it. He went out to meet her. I don't know who she is." (Bitter for Caroline to have to admit such a thing.)

"But I can guess," continued my indefatigable sister.

I waited patiently.

"His cousin."

"Flora Ackroyd?" I exclaimed in surprise.

Flora Ackroyd is, of course, no relation whatever really to Ralph Paton, but Ralph has been looked upon for so long as practically Ackroyd's own son, that cousinship is taken for granted.

"Flora Ackroyd," said my sister.

"But why not go to Fernly if he wanted to see her?"

"Secretly engaged," said Caroline, with immense enjoyment. "Old Ackroyd won't hear of it, and they have to meet this way."

I saw a good many flaws in Caroline's theory, but I forbore to point them out to her. An innocent remark about our new neighbor created a diversion.

The house next door, The Larches, has recently been taken by a stranger. To Caroline's extreme annoyance, she has not been able to find out anything about him, except that he is a foreigner. The Intelligence Corps has proved a broken reed. Presumably the man has milk and vegetables and joints of meat and occasional whitings just like everybody else, but none of the people who make it their business to supply these things seem to have acquired any information. His name, apparently, is Mr. Porrott—a name which conveys an odd feeling of unreality. The one thing we do know about him is that he is interested in the growing of vegetable marrows.

But that is certainly not the sort of information that Caroline is after. She wants to know where he comes from, what he does, whether he is married, what his wife was, or is, like, whether he has children, what his mother's maiden name was—and so on. Somebody very like Caroline must have invented the questions on passports, I think.

"My dear Caroline," I said. "There's no doubt at all about what the man's profession has been. He's a retired hairdresser. Look at that mustache of his."

Caroline dissented. She said that if the man was a hairdresser, he would have wavy hair—not straight. All hairdressers did.

I cited several hairdressers personally known to me who had straight hair, but Caroline refused to be convinced.

"I can't make him out at all," she said in an aggrieved voice. "I borrowed some garden tools the other day, and he was most polite, but I couldn't get anything out of him. I asked him point blank at last whether he was a Frenchman, and he said he wasn't—and somehow I didn't like to ask him any more."

I began to be more interested in our mysterious neighbor. A man who is capable of shutting up Caroline and sending her, like the Queen of Sheba, empty away must be something of a personality.

"I believe," said Caroline, "that he's got one of those new vacuum cleaners——"

I saw a meditated loan and the opportunity of further questioning gleaming from her eye. I seized the chance to escape into the garden. I am rather fond of gardening. I was busily exterminating dandelion roots when a shout of warning sounded from close by and a heavy body whizzed by my ear and fell at my feet with a repellant squelch. It was a vegetable marrow!

I looked up angrily. Over the wall, to my left, there appeared a face. An egg-shaped head, partially covered with suspiciously black hair, two immense mustaches, and a pair of watchful eyes. It was our mysterious neighbor, Mr. Porrott.

He broke at once into fluent apologies.

"I demand of you a thousand pardons, monsieur. I am without defense. For some months now I cultivate the marrows. This morning suddenly I enrage myself with these marrows. I send them to promenade themselves—alas!

not only mentally but physically. I seize the biggest. I hurl him over the wall. Monsieur, I am ashamed. I prostrate myself."

Before such profuse apologies, my anger was forced to melt. After all, the wretched vegetable hadn't hit me. But I sincerely hoped that throwing large vegetables over walls was not our new friend's hobby. Such a habit could hardly endear him to us as a neighbor.

The strange little man seemed to read my thoughts.

"Ah! no," he exclaimed. "Do not disquiet yourself. It is not with me a habit. But can you figure to yourself, monsieur, that a man may work towards a certain object, may labor and toil to attain a certain kind of leisure and occupation, and then find that, after all, he yearns for the old busy days, and the old occupations that he thought himself so glad to leave?"

"Yes," I said slowly. "I fancy that that is a common enough occurrence. I myself am perhaps an instance. A year ago I came into a legacy—enough to enable me to realize a dream. I have always wanted to travel, to see the world. Well, that was a year ago, as I said, and—I am still here."

My little neighbor nodded.

"The chains of habit. We work to attain an object, and the object gained, we find that what we miss is the daily toil. And mark you, monsieur, my work was interesting work. The most interesting work there is in the world."

"Yes?" I said encouragingly. For the moment the spirit of Caroline was strong within me.

"The study of human nature, monsieur!"

"Just so," I said kindly.

Clearly a retired hairdresser. Who knows the secrets of human nature better than a hairdresser?

"Also, I had a friend—a friend who for many years never left my side. Occasionally of an imbecility to make one afraid, nevertheless he was very dear to me. Figure to yourself that I miss even his stupidity. His *naïveté*, his honest outlook, the pleasure of delighting and surprising him by my superior gifts—all these I miss more than I can tell you."

"He died?" I asked sympathetically.

"Not so. He lives and flourishes—but on the other side of the world. He is now in the Argentine."

"In the Argentine," I said enviously.

I have always wanted to go to South America. I sighed, and then looked up to find Mr. Porrott eyeing me sympathetically. He seemed an understanding little man.

"You will go there, yes?" he asked.

I shook my head with a sigh.

"I could have gone," I said, "a year ago. But I was foolish—and worse than foolish—greedy. I risked the substance for the shadow."

"I comprehend," said Mr. Porrott. "You speculated?"

I nodded mournfully, but in spite of myself I felt secretly entertained. This ridiculous little man was so portentously solemn.

"Not the Porcupine Oilfields?" he asked suddenly.

I stared.

"I thought of them, as a matter of fact, but in the end I plumped for a gold mine in Western Australia."

My neighbor was regarding me with a strange expression which I could not fathom.

"It is Fate," he said at last.

"What is Fate?" I asked irritably.

"That I should live next to a man who seriously considers Porcupine Oilfields, and also West Australian Gold Mines. Tell me, have you also a penchant for auburn hair?"

I stared at him open-mouthed, and he burst out laughing.

"No, no, it is not the insanity that I suffer from. Make your mind easy. It was a foolish question that I put to you there, for, see you, my friend of whom I spoke was a young man, a man who thought all women good, and most of them beautiful. But you are a man of middle age, a doctor, a man who knows the folly and the vanity of most things in this life of ours. Well, well, we are neighbors. I beg of you to accept and present to your excellent sister my best marrow."

He stooped, and with a flourish produced an immense specimen of the tribe, which I duly accepted in the spirit in which it was offered.

"Indeed," said the little man cheerfully, "this has not been a wasted morning. I have made the acquaintance of a man who in some ways resembles my far-off friend. By the way, I should like to ask you a question. You doubtless know every one in this tiny village. Who is the young man with the very dark hair and eyes, and the handsome face. He walks with his head flung back, and an easy smile on his lips?"

The description left me in no doubt.

"That must be Captain Ralph Paton," I said slowly.

"I have not seen him about here before?"

"No, he has not been here for some time. But he is the son—adopted son, rather—of Mr. Ackroyd of Fernly Park."

My neighbor made a slight gesture of impatience.

"Of course, I should have guessed. Mr. Ackroyd spoke of him many times."

"You know Mr. Ackroyd?" I said, slightly surprised.

"Mr. Ackroyd knew me in London—when I was at work there. I have asked him to say nothing of my profession down here."

"I see," I said, rather amused by this patent snobbery, as I thought it.

But the little man went on with an almost grandiloquent smirk.

"One prefers to remain incognito. I am not anxious for notoriety. I have not even troubled to correct the local version of my name."

"Indeed," I said, not knowing quite what to say.

"Captain Ralph Paton," mused Mr. Porrott. "And so he is engaged to Mr. Ackroyd's niece, the charming Miss Flora."

"Who told you so?" I asked, very much surprised.

"Mr. Ackroyd. About a week ago. He is very pleased about it—has long desired that such a thing should come to pass, or so I understood from him. I even believe that he brought some pressure to bear upon the young man. That is never wise. A young man should marry to please himself—not to please a stepfather from whom he has expectations."

My ideas were completely upset. I could not see Ackroyd taking a hairdresser into his confidence, and discussing the marriage of his niece and stepson with him. Ackroyd extends a genial patronage to the lower orders, but he has a very great sense of his own dignity. I began to think that Porrott couldn't be a hairdresser after all.

To hide my confusion, I said the first thing that came into my head.

"What made you notice Ralph Paton? His good looks?"

"No, not that alone—though he is unusually good-looking for an Englishman—what your lady novelists would call a Greek god. No, there was something about that young man that I did not understand."

He said the last sentence in a musing tone of voice which made an indefinable impression upon me. It was as though he was summing up the boy by the light of some inner knowledge that I did not share. It was that impression that was left with me, for at that moment my sister's voice called me from the house.

I went in. Caroline had her hat on, and had evidently just come in from the village. She began without preamble.

"I met Mr. Ackroyd."

"Yes?" I said.

"I stopped him, of course, but he seemed in a great hurry, and anxious to get away."

I have no doubt but that that was the case. He would feel towards Caroline much as he had felt towards Miss Ganett earlier in the day—perhaps more so. Caroline is less easy to shake off.

"I asked him at once about Ralph. He was absolutely astonished. Had no idea the boy was down here. He actually said he thought I must have made a mistake. I! A mistake!"

"Ridiculous," I said. "He ought to have known you better."

"Then he went on to tell me that Ralph and Flora are engaged."

"I know that too," I interrupted, with modest pride.

"Who told you?"

"Our new neighbor."

Caroline visibly wavered for a second or two, much as a roulette ball might coyly hover between two numbers. Then she declined the tempting red herring.

"I told Mr. Ackroyd that Ralph was staying at the Three Boars."

"Caroline," I said, "do you never reflect that you might do a lot of harm with this habit of yours of repeating everything indiscriminately?"

"Nonsense," said my sister. "People ought to know things. I consider it my duty to tell them. Mr. Ackroyd was very grateful to me."

"Well?" I said, for there was clearly more to come.

"I think he went straight off to the Three Boars, but if so he didn't find Ralph there."

"No?"

"No. Because as I was coming back through the wood——"

"Coming back through the wood?" I interrupted.

Caroline had the grace to blush.

"It was such a lovely day," she exclaimed. "I thought I would make a little round. The woods with their autumnal tints are so perfect at this time of year."

Caroline does not care a hang for woods at any time of year. Normally she regards them as places where you get your feet damp, and where all kinds of unpleasant things may drop on your head. No, it was good sound mongoose instinct which took her to our local wood. It is the only place adjacent to the village of King's Abbot where you can talk with a young woman unseen by the whole of the village. It adjoins the Park of Fernly.

"Well," I said, "go on."

"As I say, I was just coming back through the wood when I heard voices."

Caroline paused.

"Yes?"

"One was Ralph Paton's—I knew it at once. The other was a girl's. Of course I didn't mean to listen——"

"Of course not," I interjected, with patent sarcasm—which was, however, wasted on Caroline.

"But I simply couldn't help overhearing. The girl said something—I didn't quite catch what it was, and Ralph answered. He sounded very angry. 'My dear girl,' he said. 'Don't you realize that it is quite on the cards the old man will cut me off with a shilling? He's been pretty fed up with me for the last few years. A little more would do it. And we need the dibs, my dear. I shall be a very rich man when the old fellow pops off. He's mean as they make 'em, but he's rolling in money really. I don't want him to go altering his will. You leave it to me, and don't worry.' Those were his exact words. I remember them perfectly. Unfortunately, just then I stepped on a dry twig or something, and they lowered their voices and moved away. I couldn't, of course, go rushing after them, so wasn't able to see who the girl was."

"That must have been most vexing," I said. "I suppose, though, you hurried on to the Three Boars, felt faint, and went into the bar for a glass of brandy, and so were able to see if both the barmaids were on duty?"

"It wasn't a barmaid," said Caroline unhesitatingly. "In fact, I'm almost sure that it was Flora Ackroyd, only——"

"Only it doesn't seem to make sense," I agreed.

"But if it wasn't Flora, who could it have been?"

Rapidly my sister ran over a list of maidens living in the neighborhood, with profuse reasons for and against.

When she paused for breath, I murmured something about a patient, and slipped out.

I proposed to make my way to the Three Boars. It seemed likely that Ralph Paton would have returned there by now.

I knew Ralph very well—better, perhaps, than any one else in King's Abbot, for I had known his mother before him, and therefore I understood much in him that puzzled others. He was, to a certain extent, the victim of heredity. He had not inherited his mother's fatal propensity for drink, but nevertheless he had in him a strain of weakness. As my new friend of this morning had declared, he was extraordinarily handsome. Just on six feet, perfectly proportioned, with the easy grace of an athlete, he was dark, like his mother, with a handsome, sunburnt face always ready to break into a smile. Ralph Paton was of those born to charm easily and without effort. He was self-indulgent and extravagant, with no veneration for anything on earth, but he was lovable nevertheless, and his friends were all devoted to him.

Could I do anything with the boy? I thought I could.

On inquiry at the Three Boars I found that Captain Paton had just come in. I went up to his room and entered unannounced.

For a moment, remembering what I had heard and seen, I was doubtful of my reception, but I need have had no misgivings.

"Why, it's Sheppard! Glad to see you."

He came forward to meet me, hand outstretched, a sunny smile lighting up his face.

"The one person I am glad to see in this infernal place."

I raised my eyebrows.

"What's the place been doing?"

He gave a vexed laugh.

"It's a long story. Things haven't been going well with me, doctor. But have a drink, won't you?"

"Thanks," I said, "I will."

He pressed the bell, then, coming back, threw himself into a chair.

"Not to mince matters," he said gloomily, "I'm in the devil of a mess. In fact, I haven't the least idea what to do next."

"What's the matter?" I asked sympathetically.

"It's my confounded stepfather."

"What has he done?"

"It isn't what he's done yet, but what he's likely to do."

The bell was answered, and Ralph ordered the drinks. When the man had gone again, he sat hunched in the arm-chair, frowning to himself.

"Is it really—serious?" I asked.

He nodded.

"I'm fairly up against it this time," he said soberly.

The unusual ring of gravity in his voice told me that he spoke the truth. It took a good deal to make Ralph grave.

"In fact," he continued, "I can't see my way ahead. . . . I'm damned if I can."

"If I could help——" I suggested diffidently.

But he shook his head very decidedly.

"Good of you, doctor. But I can't let you in on this. I've got to play a lone hand."

He was silent a minute and then repeated in a slightly different tone of voice:—

"Yes—I've got to play a lone hand. . . ."

IV. DINNER AT FERNLY

It was just a few minutes before half-past seven when I rang the front door bell of Fernly Park. The door was opened with admirable promptitude by Parker, the butler.

The night was such a fine one that I had preferred to come on foot. I stepped into the big square hall and Parker relieved me of my overcoat. Just then Ackroyd's secretary, a pleasant young fellow by the name of Raymond, passed through the hall on his way to Ackroyd's study, his hands full of papers.

"Good-evening, doctor. Coming to dine? Or is this a professional call?"

The last was in allusion to my black bag, which I had laid down on the oak chest.

I explained that I expected a summons to a confinement case at any moment, and so had come out prepared for an emergency call. Raymond nodded, and went on his way, calling over his shoulder:—

"Go into the drawing-room. You know the way. The ladies will be down in a minute. I must just take these papers to Mr. Ackroyd, and I'll tell him you're here."

On Raymond's appearance Parker had withdrawn, so I was alone in the hall. I settled my tie, glanced in a large mirror which hung there, and crossed to the door directly facing me, which was, as I knew, the door of the drawing-room.

I noticed, just as I was turning the handle, a sound from within—the shutting down of a window, I took it to be. I noted it, I may say, quite mechanically, without attaching any importance to it at the time.

I opened the door and walked in. As I did so, I almost collided with Miss Russell, who was just coming out. We both apologized.

For the first time I found myself appraising the housekeeper and thinking what a handsome woman she must once have been—indeed, as far as that goes, still was. Her dark hair was unstreaked with gray, and when she had a color, as she had at this minute, the stern quality of her looks was not so apparent.

Quite subconsciously I wondered whether she had been out, for she was breathing hard, as though she had been running.

"I'm afraid I'm a few minutes early," I said.

"Oh! I don't think so. It's gone half-past seven, Dr. Sheppard." She paused a minute before saying, "I—didn't know you were expected to dinner to-night. Mr. Ackroyd didn't mention it."

I received a vague impression that my dining there displeased her in some way, but I couldn't imagine why.

"How's the knee?" I inquired.

"Much the same, thank you, doctor. I must be going now. Mrs. Ackroyd will be down in a moment. I—I only came in here to see if the flowers were all right."

She passed quickly out of the room. I strolled to the window, wondering at her evident desire to justify her presence in the room. As I did so, I saw what, of course, I might have known all the time had I troubled to give my mind to it, namely, that the windows were long French ones opening on the terrace. The sound I had heard, therefore, could not have been that of a window being shut down.

Quite idly, and more to distract my mind from painful thoughts than for any other reason, I amused myself by trying to guess what could have caused the sound in question.

Coals on the fire? No, that was not the kind of noise at all. A drawer of the bureau pushed in? No, not that.

Then my eye was caught by what, I believe, is called a silver table, the lid of which lifts, and through the glass of which you can see the contents. I crossed over to it, studying the things. There were one or two pieces of old silver, a baby shoe belonging to King Charles the First, some Chinese jade figures, and quite a number of African implements and curios. Wanting to examine one of the jade figures more closely, I lifted the lid. It slipped through my fingers and fell.

At once I recognized the sound I had heard. It was this same table lid being shut down gently and carefully. I repeated the action once or twice for my own satisfaction. Then I lifted the lid to scrutinize the contents more closely.

I was still bending over the open silver table when Flora Ackroyd came into the room.

Quite a lot of people do not like Flora Ackroyd, but nobody can help admiring her. And to her friends she can be very charming. The first thing that strikes you about her is her extraordinary fairness. She has the real Scandinavian pale gold hair. Her eyes are blue—blue as the waters of a Norwegian fiord, and her skin is cream and roses. She has square, boyish shoulders and slight hips. And to a jaded medical man it is very refreshing to come across such perfect health.

A simple straightforward English girl—I may be old-fashioned, but I think the genuine article takes a lot of beating.

Flora joined me by the silver table, and expressed heretical doubts as to King Charles I ever having worn the baby shoe.

"And anyway," continued Miss Flora, "all this making a fuss about things because some one wore or used them seems to me all nonsense. They're not wearing or using them now. The pen that George Eliot wrote *The Mill on the Floss* with—that sort of thing—well, it's only just a pen after all. If you're really keen on George Eliot, why not get *The Mill on the Floss* in a cheap edition and read it."

"I suppose you never read such old out-of-date stuff, Miss Flora?"

"You're wrong, Dr. Sheppard. I love *The Mill on the Floss*."

I was rather pleased to hear it. The things young women read nowadays and profess to enjoy positively frighten me.

"You haven't congratulated me yet, Dr. Sheppard," said Flora. "Haven't you heard?"

She held out her left hand. On the third finger of it was an exquisitely set single pearl.

"I'm going to marry Ralph, you know," she went on. "Uncle is very pleased. It keeps me in the family, you see."

I took both her hands in mine.

"My dear," I said, "I hope you'll be very happy."

"We've been engaged for about a month," continued Flora in her cool voice, "but it was only announced yesterday. Uncle is going to do up Crossstones, and give it to us to live in, and we're going to pretend to farm. Really, we shall hunt all the winter, town for the season, and then go yachting. I love the sea. And, of course, I shall take a great interest in the parish affairs, and attend all the Mothers' Meetings."

Just then Mrs. Ackroyd rustled in, full of apologies for being late.

I am sorry to say I detest Mrs. Ackroyd. She is all chains and teeth and bones. A most unpleasant woman. She has small pale flinty blue eyes, and however gushing her words may be, those eyes of hers always remain coldly speculative.

I went across to her, leaving Flora by the window. She gave me a handful of assorted knuckles and rings to squeeze, and began talking volubly.

Had I heard about Flora's engagement? So suitable in every way. The dear young things had fallen in love at first sight. Such a perfect pair, he so dark and she so fair.

"I can't tell you, my dear Dr. Sheppard, the relief to a mother's heart."

Mrs. Ackroyd sighed—a tribute to her mother's heart, whilst her eyes remained shrewdly observant of me.

"I was wondering. You are such an old friend of dear Roger's. We know how much he trusts to your judgment. So difficult for me—in my position, as poor Cecil's widow. But there are so many tiresome things—settlements, you know—all that. I fully believe that Roger intends to make settlements upon dear Flora, but, as you know, he is just a *leetle* peculiar about money. Very usual, I've heard, amongst men who are captains of industry. I wondered, you know, if you could just *sound* him on the subject? Flora is so fond of you. We feel you are quite an old friend, although we have only really known you just over two years."

Mrs. Ackroyd's eloquence was cut short as the drawing-room door opened once more. I was pleased at the interruption. I hate interfering in other people's affairs, and I had not the least intention of tackling Ackroyd on the subject of Flora's settlements. In another moment I should have been forced to tell Mrs. Ackroyd as much.

"You know Major Blunt, don't you, doctor?"

"Yes, indeed," I said.

A lot of people know Hector Blunt—at least by repute. He has shot more wild animals in unlikely places than any man living, I suppose. When you mention him, people say: "Blunt—you don't mean the big game man, do you?"

His friendship with Ackroyd has always puzzled me a little. The two men are so totally dissimilar. Hector Blunt is perhaps five years Ackroyd's junior. They made friends early in life, and though their ways have diverged, the friendship still holds. About once in two years Blunt spends a fortnight at Fernly, and an immense animal's head, with an amazing number of horns which fixes you with a glazed stare as soon as you come inside the front door, is a permanent reminder of the friendship.

Blunt had entered the room now with his own peculiar, deliberate, yet soft-footed tread. He is a man of medium height, sturdily and rather stockily built. His face is almost mahogany-colored, and is peculiarly expressionless. He has gray eyes that give the impression of always watching something that is happening very far away. He talks little, and what he does say is said jerkily, as though the words were forced out of him unwillingly.

He said now: "How are you, Sheppard?" in his usual abrupt fashion, and then stood squarely in front of the fireplace looking over our heads as though he saw something very interesting happening in Timbuctoo.

"Major Blunt," said Flora, "I wish you'd tell me about these African things. I'm sure you know what they all are."

I have heard Hector Blunt described as a woman hater, but I noticed that he joined Flora at the silver table with what might be described as alacrity. They bent over it together.

I was afraid Mrs. Ackroyd would begin talking about settlements again, so I made a few hurried remarks about the new sweet pea. I knew there was a new sweet pea because the *Daily Mail* had told me so that morning. Mrs. Ackroyd knows nothing about horticulture, but she is the kind of woman who likes to appear well-informed about the topics of the day, and she, too, reads the *Daily Mail*. We were able to converse quite intelligently until Ackroyd and his secretary joined us, and immediately afterwards Parker announced dinner.

My place at table was between Mrs. Ackroyd and Flora. Blunt was on Mrs. Ackroyd's other side, and Geoffrey Raymond next to him.

Dinner was not a cheerful affair. Ackroyd was visibly preoccupied. He looked wretched, and ate next to nothing. Mrs. Ackroyd, Raymond, and I kept the conversation going. Flora seemed affected by her uncle's depression, and Blunt relapsed into his usual taciturnity.

Immediately after dinner Ackroyd slipped his arm through mine and led me off to his study.

"Once we've had coffee, we shan't be disturbed again," he explained. "I told Raymond to see to it that we shouldn't be interrupted."

I studied him quietly without appearing to do so. He was clearly under the influence of some strong excitement. For a minute or two he paced up and down the room, then, as Parker entered with the coffee tray, he sank into an arm-chair in front of the fire.

The study was a comfortable apartment. Book-shelves lined one wall of it. The chairs were big and covered in dark blue leather. A large desk stood by the window and was covered with papers neatly docketed and filed. On a round table were various magazines and sporting papers.

"I've had a return of that pain after food lately," remarked Ackroyd casually, as he helped himself to coffee. "You must give me some more of those tablets of yours."

It struck me that he was anxious to convey the impression that our conference was a medical one. I played up accordingly.

"I thought as much. I brought some up with me."

"Good man. Hand them over now."

"They're in my bag in the hall. I'll get them."

Ackroyd arrested me.

"Don't you trouble. Parker will get them. Bring in the doctor's bag, will you, Parker?"

"Very good, sir."

Parker withdrew. As I was about to speak, Ackroyd threw up his hand.

"Not yet. Wait. Don't you see I'm in such a state of nerves that I can hardly contain myself?"

I saw that plainly enough. And I was very uneasy. All sorts of forebodings assailed me.

Ackroyd spoke again almost immediately.

"Make certain that window's closed, will you?" he asked.

Somewhat surprised, I got up and went to it. It was not a French window, but one of the ordinary sash type. The heavy blue velvet curtains were drawn in front of it, but the window itself was open at the top.

Parker reëntered the room with my bag while I was still at the window.

"That's all right," I said, emerging again into the room.

"You've put the latch across?"

"Yes, yes. What's the matter with you, Ackroyd?"

The door had just closed behind Parker, or I would not have put the question.

Ackroyd waited just a minute before replying.

"I'm in hell," he said slowly, after a minute. "No, don't bother with those damned tablets. I only said that for Parker. Servants are so curious. Come here and sit down. The door's closed too, isn't it?"

"Yes. Nobody can overhear; don't be uneasy."

"Sheppard, nobody knows what I've gone through in the last twenty-four hours. If a man's house ever fell in ruins about him, mine has about me. This business of Ralph's is the last straw. But we won't talk about that now. It's the other—the other——! I don't know what to do about it. And I've got to make up my mind soon."

"What's the trouble?"

Ackroyd remained silent for a minute or two. He seemed curiously averse to begin. When he did speak, the question he asked came as a complete surprise. It was the last thing I expected.

"Sheppard, you attended Ashley Ferrars in his last illness, didn't you?"

"Yes, I did."

He seemed to find even greater difficulty in framing his next question.

"Did you never suspect—did it ever enter your head—that—well, that he might have been poisoned?"

I was silent for a minute or two. Then I made up my mind what to say. Roger Ackroyd was not Caroline.

"I'll tell you the truth," I said. "At the time I had no suspicion whatever, but since—well, it was mere idle talk on my sister's part that first put the idea into my head. Since then I haven't been able to get it out again. But, mind you, I've no foundation whatever for that suspicion."

"He *was* poisoned," said Ackroyd.

He spoke in a dull heavy voice.

"Who by?" I asked sharply.

"His wife."

"How do you know that?"

"She told me so herself."

"When?"

"Yesterday! My God! yesterday! It seems ten years ago."

I waited a minute, and then he went on.

"You understand, Sheppard, I'm telling you this in confidence. It's to go no further. I want your advice—I can't carry the whole weight by myself. As I said just now, I don't know what to do."

"Can you tell me the whole story?" I said. "I'm still in the dark. How did Mrs. Ferrars come to make this confession to you?"

"It's like this. Three months ago I asked Mrs. Ferrars to marry me. She refused. I asked her again and she consented, but she refused to allow me to make the engagement public until her year of mourning was up. Yesterday I called upon her, pointed out that a year and three weeks had now elapsed since her husband's death, and that there could be no further objection to making the engagement public property. I had noticed that she had been very strange in her manner for some days. Now, suddenly, without the least warning, she broke down completely. She—she told me everything. Her hatred of her brute of a husband, her growing love for me, and the—the dreadful means she had taken. Poison! My God! It was murder in cold blood."

I saw the repulsion, the horror, in Ackroyd's face. So Mrs. Ferrars must have seen it. Ackroyd is not the type of the great lover who can forgive all for love's sake. He is fundamentally a good citizen. All that was sound and wholesome and law-abiding in him must have turned from her utterly in that moment of revelation.

"Yes," he went on, in a low, monotonous voice, "she confessed everything. It seems that there is one person who has known all along—who has been blackmailing her for huge sums. It was the strain of that that drove her nearly mad."

"Who was the man?"

Suddenly before my eyes there arose the picture of Ralph Paton and Mrs. Ferrars side by side. Their heads so close together. I felt a momentary throb of anxiety. Supposing—oh! but surely that was impossible. I remembered the frankness of Ralph's greeting that very afternoon. Absurd!

"She wouldn't tell me his name," said Ackroyd slowly. "As a matter of fact, she didn't actually say that it was a man. But of course——"

"Of course," I agreed. "It must have been a man. And you've no suspicion at all?"

For answer Ackroyd groaned and dropped his head into his hands.

"It can't be," he said. "I'm mad even to think of such a thing. No, I won't even admit to you the wild suspicion that crossed my mind. I'll tell you this much, though. Something she said made me think that the person in question might be actually among my household—but that can't be so. I must have misunderstood her."

"What did you say to her?" I asked.

"What could I say? She saw, of course, the awful shock it had been to me. And then there was the question, what was my duty in the matter? She had made me, you see, an accessory after the fact. She saw all that, I think, quicker than I did. I was stunned, you know. She asked me for twenty-four hours—made me promise to do nothing till the end of that time. And she steadfastly refused to give me the name of the scoundrel who had been blackmailing her. I suppose she was afraid that I might go straight off and hammer him, and then the fat would have been in the fire as far as she was concerned. She told me that I should hear from her before twenty-four hours had passed. My God! I swear to you, Sheppard, that it never entered my head what she meant to do. Suicide! And I drove her to it."

"No, no," I said. "Don't take an exaggerated view of things. The responsibility for her death doesn't lie at your door."

"The question is, what am I to do now? The poor lady is dead. Why rake up past trouble?"

"I rather agree with you," I said.

"But there's another point. How am I to get hold of that scoundrel who drove her to death as surely as if he'd killed her. He knew of the first crime, and he fastened on to it like some obscene vulture. She's paid the penalty. Is he to go scot-free?"

"I see," I said slowly. "You want to hunt him down? It will mean a lot of publicity, you know."

"Yes, I've thought of that. I've zigzagged to and fro in my mind."

"I agree with you that the villain ought to be punished, but the cost has got to be reckoned."

Ackroyd rose and walked up and down. Presently he sank into the chair again.

"Look here, Sheppard, suppose we leave it like this. If no word comes from her, we'll let the dead things lie."

"What do you mean by word coming from her?" I asked curiously.

"I have the strongest impression that somewhere or somehow she must have left a message for me—before she went. I can't argue about it, but there it is."

I shook my head.

"She left no letter or word of any kind. I asked."

"Sheppard, I'm convinced that she did. And more, I've a feeling that by deliberately choosing death, she wanted the whole thing to come out, if only to be revenged on the man who drove her to desperation. I believe that if I could have seen her then, she would have told me his name and bid me go for him for all I was worth."

He looked at me.

"You don't believe in impressions?"

"Oh, yes, I do, in a sense. If, as you put it, word should come from her——"

I broke off. The door opened noiselessly and Parker entered with a salver on which were some letters.

"The evening post, sir," he said, handing the salver to Ackroyd.

Then he collected the coffee cups and withdrew.

My attention, diverted for a moment, came back to Ackroyd. He was staring like a man turned to stone at a long blue envelope. The other letters he had let drop to the floor.

"*Her writing,*" he said in a whisper. "She must have gone out and posted it last night, just before—before——"

He ripped open the envelope and drew out a thick enclosure. Then he looked up sharply.

"You're sure you shut the window?" he said.

"Quite sure," I said, surprised. "Why?"

"All this evening I've had a queer feeling of being watched, spied upon. What's that——?"

He turned sharply. So did I. We both had the impression of hearing the latch of the door give ever so slightly. I went across to it and opened it. There was no one there.

"Nerves," murmured Ackroyd to himself.

He unfolded the thick sheets of paper, and read aloud in a low voice.

"*My dear, my very dear Roger,—A life calls for a life. I see that—I saw it in your face this afternoon. So I am taking the only road open to me. I leave to you the punishment of the person who has made my life a hell upon earth for the last year. I would not tell you the name this afternoon, but I propose to write it to you now. I have no children or near relations to be spared, so do not fear publicity. If you can, Roger, my very dear Roger, forgive me the wrong I meant to do you, since when the time came, I could not do it after all. . . .*"

Ackroyd, his finger on the sheet to turn it over, paused.

"Sheppard, forgive me, but I must read this alone," he said unsteadily. "It was meant for my eyes, and my eyes only."

He put the letter in the envelope and laid it on the table.

"Later, when I am alone."

"No," I cried impulsively, "read it now."

Ackroyd stared at me in some surprise.

"I beg your pardon," I said, reddening. "I do not mean read it aloud to me. But read it through whilst I am still here."

Ackroyd shook his head.

"No, I'd rather wait."

But for some reason, obscure to myself, I continued to urge him.

"At least, read the name of the man," I said.

Now Ackroyd is essentially pig-headed. The more you urge him to do a thing, the more determined he is not to do it. All my arguments were in vain.

The letter had been brought in at twenty minutes to nine. It was just on ten minutes to nine when I left him, the letter still unread. I hesitated with my hand on the door handle, looking back and wondering if there was anything I had left undone. I could think of nothing. With a shake of the head I passed out and closed the door behind me.

I was startled by seeing the figure of Parker close at hand. He looked embarrassed, and it occurred to me that he might have been listening at the door.

What a fat, smug, oily face the man had, and surely there was something decidedly shifty in his eye.

"Mr. Ackroyd particularly does not want to be disturbed," I said coldly. "He told me to tell you so."

"Quite so, sir. I—I fancied I heard the bell ring."

This was such a palpable untruth that I did not trouble to reply. Preceding me to the hall, Parker helped me on with my overcoat, and I stepped out into the night. The moon was overcast and everything seemed very dark and still. The village church clock chimed nine o'clock as I passed through the lodge gates. I turned to the left towards the village, and almost cannoned into a man coming in the opposite direction.

"This the way to Fernly Park, mister?" asked the stranger in a hoarse voice.

I looked at him. He was wearing a hat pulled down over his eyes, and his coat collar turned up. I could see little or nothing of his face, but he seemed a young fellow. The voice was rough and uneducated.

"These are the lodge gates here," I said.

"Thank you, mister." He paused, and then added, quite unnecessarily, "I'm a stranger in these parts, you see."

He went on, passing through the gates as I turned to look after him.

The odd thing was that his voice reminded me of some one's voice that I knew, but whose it was I could not think.

Ten minutes later I was at home once more. Caroline was full of curiosity to know why I had returned so early. I had to make up a slightly fictitious account of the evening in order to satisfy her, and I had an uneasy feeling that she saw through the transparent device.

At ten o'clock I rose, yawned, and suggested bed. Caroline acquiesced.

It was Friday night, and on Friday night I wind the clocks. I did it as usual, whilst Caroline satisfied herself that the servants had locked up the kitchen properly.

It was a quarter past ten as we went up the stairs. I had just reached the top when the telephone rang in the hall below.

"Mrs. Bates," said Caroline immediately.

"I'm afraid so," I said ruefully.

I ran down the stairs and took up the receiver.

"What?" I said. "What? Certainly, I'll come at once."

I ran upstairs, caught up my bag, and stuffed a few extra dressings into it.

"Parker telephoning," I shouted to Caroline, "from Fernly. They've just found Roger Ackroyd murdered."

V. MURDER

I got out the car in next to no time, and drove rapidly to Fernly. Jumping out, I pulled the bell impatiently. There was some delay in answering, and I rang again.

Then I heard the rattle of the chain and Parker, his impassivity of countenance quite unmoved, stood in the open doorway.

I pushed past him into the hall.

"Where is he?" I demanded sharply.

"I beg your pardon, sir?"

"Your master. Mr. Ackroyd. Don't stand there staring at me, man. Have you notified the police?"

"The police, sir? Did you say the police?" Parker stared at me as though I were a ghost.

"What's the matter with you, Parker? If, as you say, your master has been murdered——"

A gasp broke from Parker.

"The master? Murdered? Impossible, sir!"

It was my turn to stare.

"Didn't you telephone to me, not five minutes ago, and tell me that Mr. Ackroyd had been found murdered?"

"Me, sir? Oh! no indeed, sir. I wouldn't dream of doing such a thing."

"Do you mean to say it's all a hoax? That there's nothing the matter with Mr. Ackroyd?"

"Excuse me, sir, did the person telephoning use my name?"

"I'll give you the exact words I heard. '*Is that Dr. Sheppard? Parker, the butler at Fernly, speaking. Will you please come at once, sir. Mr. Ackroyd has been murdered.*'"

Parker and I stared at each other blankly.

"A very wicked joke to play, sir," he said at last, in a shocked tone. "Fancy saying a thing like that."

"Where is Mr. Ackroyd?" I asked suddenly.

"Still in the study, I fancy, sir. The ladies have gone to bed, and Major Blunt and Mr. Raymond are in the billiard room."

"I think I'll just look in and see him for a minute," I said. "I know he didn't want to be disturbed again, but this odd practical joke has made me uneasy. I'd just like to satisfy myself that he's all right."

"Quite so, sir. It makes me feel quite uneasy myself. If you don't object to my accompanying you as far as the door, sir——?"

"Not at all," I said. "Come along."

I passed through the door on the right, Parker on my heels, traversed the little lobby where a small flight of stairs led upstairs to Ackroyd's bedroom, and tapped on the study door.

There was no answer. I turned the handle, but the door was locked.

"Allow me, sir," said Parker.

Very nimbly, for a man of his build, he dropped on one knee and applied his eye to the keyhole.

"Key is in the lock all right, sir," he said, rising. "On the inside. Mr. Ackroyd must have locked himself in and possibly just dropped off to sleep."

I bent down and verified Parker's statement.

"It seems all right," I said, "but, all the same, Parker, I'm going to wake your master up. I shouldn't be satisfied to go home without hearing from his own lips that he's quite all right."

So saying, I rattled the handle and called out, "Ackroyd, Ackroyd, just a minute."

But still there was no answer. I glanced over my shoulder.

"I don't want to alarm the household," I said hesitatingly.

Parker went across and shut the door from the big hall through which we had come.

"I think that will be all right now, sir. The billiard room is at the other side of the house, and so are the kitchen quarters and the ladies' bedrooms."

I nodded comprehendingly. Then I banged once more frantically on the door, and stooping down, fairly bawled through the keyhole:—

"Ackroyd, Ackroyd! It's Sheppard. Let me in."

And still—silence. Not a sign of life from within the locked room. Parker and I glanced at each other.

"Look here, Parker," I said, "I'm going to break this door in—or rather, we are. I'll take the responsibility."

"If you say so, sir," said Parker, rather doubtfully.

"I do say so. I'm seriously alarmed about Mr. Ackroyd."

I looked round the small lobby and picked up a heavy oak chair. Parker and I held it between us and advanced to the assault. Once, twice, and three times we hurled it against the lock. At the third blow it gave, and we staggered into the room.

Ackroyd was sitting as I had left him in the arm-chair before the fire. His head had fallen sideways, and clearly visible, just below the collar of his coat, was a shining piece of twisted metalwork.

Parker and I advanced till we stood over the recumbent figure. I heard the butler draw in his breath with a sharp hiss.

"Stabbed from be'ind," he murmured. "'Orrible!"

He wiped his moist brow with his handkerchief, then stretched out a hand gingerly towards the hilt of the dagger.

"You mustn't touch that," I said sharply. "Go at once to the telephone and ring up the police station. Inform them of what has happened. Then tell Mr. Raymond and Major Blunt."

"Very good, sir."

Parker hurried away, still wiping his perspiring brow.

I did what little had to be done. I was careful not to disturb the position of the body, and not to handle the dagger at all. No object was to be attained by moving it. Ackroyd had clearly been dead some little time.

Then I heard young Raymond's voice, horror-stricken and incredulous, outside.

"What do you say? Oh! impossible! Where's the doctor?"

He appeared impetuously in the doorway, then stopped dead, his face very white. A hand put him aside, and Hector Blunt came past him into the room.

"My God!" said Raymond from behind him; "it's true, then."

Blunt came straight on till he reached the chair. He bent over the body, and I thought that, like Parker, he was going to lay hold of the dagger hilt. I drew him back with one hand.

"Nothing must be moved," I explained. "The police must see him exactly as he is now."

Blunt nodded in instant comprehension. His face was expressionless as ever, but I thought I detected signs of emotion beneath the stolid mask. Geoffrey Raymond had joined us now, and stood peering over Blunt's shoulder at the body.

"This is terrible," he said in a low voice.

He had regained his composure, but as he took off the pince-nez he habitually wore and polished them I observed that his hand was shaking.

"Robbery, I suppose," he said. "How did the fellow get in? Through the window? Has anything been taken?"

He went towards the desk.

"You think it's burglary?" I said slowly.

"What else could it be? There's no question of suicide, I suppose?"

"No man could stab himself in such a way," I said confidently. "It's murder right enough. But with what motive?"

"Roger hadn't an enemy in the world," said Blunt quietly. "Must have been burglars. But what was the thief after? Nothing seems to be disarranged."

He looked round the room. Raymond was still sorting the papers on the desk.

"There seems nothing missing, and none of the drawers show signs of having been tampered with," the secretary observed at last. "It's very mysterious."

Blunt made a slight motion with his head.

"There are some letters on the floor here," he said.

I looked down. Three or four letters still lay where Ackroyd had dropped them earlier in the evening.

But the blue envelope containing Mrs. Ferrars's letter had disappeared. I half opened my mouth to speak, but at that moment the sound of a bell pealed through the house. There was a confused murmur of voices in the hall, and then Parker appeared with our local inspector and a police constable.

"Good-evening, gentlemen," said the inspector. "I'm terribly sorry for this! A good kind gentleman like Mr. Ackroyd. The butler says it is murder. No possibility of accident or suicide, doctor?"

"None whatever," I said.

"Ah! A bad business."

He came and stood over the body.

"Been moved at all?" he asked sharply.

"Beyond making certain that life was extinct—an easy matter—I have not disturbed the body in any way."

"Ah! And everything points to the murderer having got clear away—for the moment, that is. Now then, let me hear all about it. Who found the body?"

I explained the circumstances carefully.

"A telephone message, you say? From the butler?"

"A message that I never sent," declared Parker earnestly. "I've not been near the telephone the whole evening. The others can bear me out that I haven't."

"Very odd, that. Did it sound like Parker's voice, doctor?"

"Well—I can't say I noticed. I took it for granted, you see."

"Naturally. Well, you got up here, broke in the door, and found poor Mr. Ackroyd like this. How long should you say he had been dead, doctor?"

"Half an hour at least—perhaps longer," I said.

"The door was locked on the inside, you say? What about the window?"

"I myself closed and bolted it earlier in the evening at Mr. Ackroyd's request."

The inspector strode across to it and threw back the curtains.

"Well, it's open now anyway," he remarked.

True enough, the window was open, the lower sash being raised to its fullest extent.

The inspector produced a pocket torch and flashed it along the sill outside.

"This is the way he went all right," he remarked, "*and* got in. See here."

In the light of the powerful torch, several clearly defined footmarks could be seen. They seemed to be those of shoes with rubber studs in the soles. One particularly clear one pointed inwards, another, slightly overlapping it, pointed outwards.

"Plain as a pikestaff," said the inspector. "Any valuables missing?"

Geoffrey Raymond shook his head.

"Not so that we can discover. Mr. Ackroyd never kept anything of particular value in this room."

"H'm," said the inspector. "Man found an open window. Climbed in, saw Mr. Ackroyd sitting there—maybe he'd fallen asleep. Man stabbed him from behind, then lost his nerve and made off. But he's left his tracks pretty clearly. We ought to get hold of *him* without much difficulty. No suspicious strangers been hanging about anywhere?"

"Oh!" I said suddenly.

"What is it, doctor?"

"I met a man this evening—just as I was turning out of the gate. He asked me the way to Fernly Park."

"What time would that be?"

"Just nine o'clock. I heard it chime the hour as I was turning out of the gate."

"Can you describe him?"

I did so to the best of my ability.

The inspector turned to the butler.

"Any one answering that description come to the front door?"

"No, sir. No one has been to the house at all this evening."

"What about the back?"

"I don't think so, sir, but I'll make inquiries."

He moved towards the door, but the inspector held up a large hand.

"No, thanks. I'll do my own inquiring. But first of all I want to fix the time a little more clearly. When was Mr. Ackroyd last seen alive?"

"Probably by me," I said, "when I left at—let me see—about ten minutes to nine. He told me that he didn't wish to be disturbed, and I repeated the order to Parker."

"Just so, sir," said Parker respectfully.

"Mr. Ackroyd was certainly alive at half-past nine," put in Raymond, "for I heard his voice in here talking."

"Who was he talking to?"

"That I don't know. Of course, at the time I took it for granted that it was Dr. Sheppard who was with him. I wanted to ask him a question about some papers I was engaged upon, but when I heard the voices I remembered that he had said he wanted to talk to Dr. Sheppard without being disturbed, and I went away again. But now it seems that the doctor had already left?"

I nodded.

"I was at home by a quarter past nine," I said. "I didn't go out again until I received the telephone call."

"Who could have been with him at half-past nine?" queried the inspector. "It wasn't you, Mr.—er——"

"Major Blunt," I said.

"Major Hector Blunt?" asked the inspector, a respectful tone creeping into his voice.

Blunt merely jerked his head affirmatively.

"I think we've seen you down here before, sir," said the inspector. "I didn't recognize you for the moment, but you were staying with Mr. Ackroyd a year ago last May."

"June," corrected Blunt.

"Just so, June it was. Now, as I was saying, it wasn't you with Mr. Ackroyd at nine-thirty this evening?"

Blunt shook his head.

"Never saw him after dinner," he volunteered.

The inspector turned once more to Raymond.

"You didn't overhear any of the conversation going on, did you, sir?"

"I did catch just a fragment of it," said the secretary, "and, supposing as I did that it was Dr. Sheppard who was with Mr. Ackroyd, that fragment struck me as distinctly odd. As far as I can remember, the exact words were these. Mr. Ackroyd was speaking. 'The calls on my purse have been so frequent of late'—that is what he was saying—'of late, that I fear it is impossible for me to accede to your request. . . .' I went away again at once, of course, so did not hear any more. But I rather wondered because Dr. Sheppard——"

"——Does not ask for loans for himself or subscriptions for others," I finished.

"A demand for money," said the inspector musingly. "It may be that here we have a very important clew." He turned to the butler. "You say, Parker, that nobody was admitted by the front door this evening?"

"That's what I say, sir."

"Then it seems almost certain that Mr. Ackroyd himself must have admitted this stranger. But I don't quite see——"

The inspector went into a kind of day-dream for some minutes.

"One thing's clear," he said at length, rousing himself from his absorption. "Mr. Ackroyd was alive and well at nine-thirty. That is the last moment at which he is known to have been alive."

Parker gave vent to an apologetic cough which brought the inspector's eyes on him at once.

"Well?" he said sharply.

"If you'll excuse me, sir, Miss Flora saw him after that."

"Miss Flora?"

"Yes, sir. About a quarter to ten that would be. It was after that that she told me Mr. Ackroyd wasn't to be disturbed again to-night."

"Did he send her to you with that message?"

"Not exactly, sir. I was bringing a tray with soda and whisky when Miss Flora, who was just coming out of this room, stopped me and said her uncle didn't want to be disturbed."

The inspector looked at the butler with rather closer attention than he had bestowed on him up to now.

"You'd already been told that Mr. Ackroyd didn't want to be disturbed, hadn't you?"

Parker began to stammer. His hands shook.

"Yes, sir. Yes, sir. Quite so, sir."

"And yet you were proposing to do so?"

"I'd forgotten, sir. At least I mean, I always bring the whisky and soda about that time, sir, and ask if there's anything more, and I thought—well, I was doing as usual without thinking."

It was at this moment that it began to dawn upon me that Parker was most suspiciously flustered. The man was shaking and twitching all over.

"H'm," said the inspector. "I must see Miss Ackroyd at once. For the moment we'll leave this room exactly as it is. I can return here after I've heard what Miss Ackroyd has to tell me. I shall just take the precaution of shutting and bolting the window."

This precaution accomplished, he led the way into the hall and we followed him. He paused a moment, as he glanced up at the little staircase, then spoke over his shoulder to the constable.

"Jones, you'd better stay here. Don't let any one go into that room."

Parker interposed deferentially.

"If you'll excuse me, sir. If you were to lock the door into the main hall, nobody could gain access to this part. That staircase leads only to Mr. Ackroyd's bedroom and bathroom. There is no communication with the other part of the house. There once was a door through, but Mr. Ackroyd had it blocked up. He liked to feel that his suite was entirely private."

To make things clear and explain the position, I have appended a rough sketch of the right-hand wing of the house. The small staircase leads, as Parker explained, to a big bedroom (made by two being knocked into one) and an adjoining bathroom and lavatory.

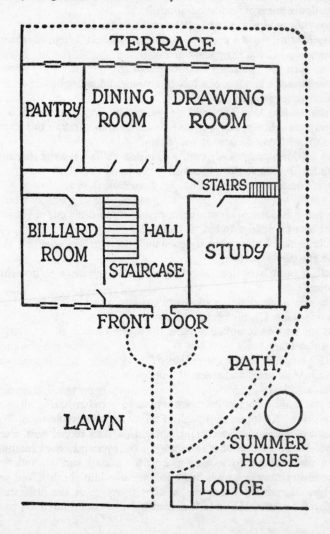

The inspector took in the position at a glance. We went through into the large hall and he locked the door behind him, slipping the key into his pocket. Then he gave the constable some low-voiced instructions, and the latter prepared to depart.

"We must get busy on those shoe tracks," explained the inspector. "But first of all, I must have a word with Miss Ackroyd. She was the last person to see her uncle alive. Does she know yet?"

Raymond shook his head.

"Well, no need to tell her for another five minutes. She can answer my questions better without being upset by knowing the truth about her uncle. Tell her there's been a burglary, and ask her if she would mind dressing and coming down to answer a few questions."

It was Raymond who went upstairs on this errand.

"Miss Ackroyd will be down in a minute," he said, when he returned. "I told her just what you suggested."

In less than five minutes Flora descended the staircase. She was wrapped in a pale pink silk kimono. She looked anxious and excited.

The inspector stepped forward.

"Good-evening, Miss Ackroyd," he said civilly. "We're afraid there's been an attempt at robbery, and we want you to help us. What's this room—the billiard room? Come in here and sit down."

Flora sat down composedly on the wide divan which ran the length of the wall, and looked up at the inspector.

"I don't quite understand. What has been stolen? What do you want me to tell you?"

"It's just this, Miss Ackroyd. Parker here says you came out of your uncle's study at about a quarter to ten. Is that right?"

"Quite right. I had been to say good-night to him."

"And the time is correct?"

"Well, it must have been about then. I can't say exactly. It might have been later."

"Was your uncle alone, or was there any one with him?"

"He was alone. Dr. Sheppard had gone."

"Did you happen to notice whether the window was open or shut?"

Flora shook her head.

"I can't say. The curtains were drawn."

"Exactly. And your uncle seemed quite as usual?"

"I think so."

"Do you mind telling us exactly what passed between you?"

Flora paused a minute, as though to collect her recollections.

"I went in and said, 'Good-night, uncle, I'm going to bed now. I'm tired to-night.' He gave a sort of grunt, and—I went over and kissed him, and he said something about my looking nice in the frock I had on, and then he told me to run away as he was busy. So I went."

"Did he ask specially not to be disturbed?"

"Oh! yes, I forgot. He said: 'Tell Parker I don't want anything more to-night, and that he's not to disturb me.' I met Parker just outside the door and gave him uncle's message."

"Just so," said the inspector.

"Won't you tell me what it is that has been stolen?"

"We're not quite—certain," said the inspector hesitatingly.

A wide look of alarm came into the girl's eyes. She started up.

"What is it? You're hiding something from me?"

Moving in his usual unobtrusive manner, Hector Blunt came between her and the inspector. She half stretched out her hand, and he took it in both of his, patting it as though she were a very small child, and she turned to him as though something in his stolid, rocklike demeanor promised comfort and safety.

"It's bad news, Flora," he said quietly. "Bad news for all of us. Your Uncle Roger——"

"Yes?"

"It will be a shock to you. Bound to be. Poor Roger's dead."

Flora drew away from him, her eyes dilating with horror.

"When?" she whispered. "When?"

"Very soon after you left him, I'm afraid," said Blunt gravely.

Flora raised her hand to her throat, gave a little cry, and I hurried to catch her as she fell. She had fainted, and Blunt and I carried her upstairs and laid her on her bed. Then I got him to wake Mrs. Ackroyd and tell her the news. Flora soon revived, and I brought her mother to her, telling her what to do for the girl. Then I hurried downstairs again.

VI. THE TUNISIAN DAGGER

I met the inspector just coming from the door which led into the kitchen quarters.

"How's the young lady, doctor?"

"Coming round nicely. Her mother's with her."

"That's good. I've been questioning the servants. They all declare that no one has been to the back door to-night. Your description of that stranger was rather vague. Can't you give us something more definite to go upon?"

"I'm afraid not," I said regretfully. "It was a dark night, you see, and the fellow had his coat collar well pulled up and his hat squashed down over his eyes."

"H'm," said the inspector. "Looked as though he wanted to conceal his face. Sure it was no one you know?"

I replied in the negative, but not as decidedly as I might have done. I remembered my impression that the stranger's voice was not unfamiliar to me. I explained this rather haltingly to the inspector.

"It was a rough, uneducated voice, you say?"

I agreed, but it occurred to me that the roughness had been of an almost exaggerated quality. If, as the inspector thought, the man had wished to hide his face, he might equally well have tried to disguise his voice.

"Do you mind coming into the study with me again, doctor? There are one or two things I want to ask you."

I acquiesced. Inspector Davis unlocked the door of the lobby, we passed through, and he locked the door again behind him.

"We don't want to be disturbed," he said grimly. "And we don't want any eavesdropping either. What's all this about blackmail?"

"Blackmail!" I exclaimed, very much startled.

"Is it an effort of Parker's imagination? Or is there something in it?"

"If Parker heard anything about blackmail," I said slowly, "he must have been listening outside this door with his ear glued against the keyhole."

Davis nodded.

"Nothing more likely. You see, I've been instituting a few inquiries as to what Parker has been doing with himself this evening. To tell the truth, I didn't like his manner. The man knows something. When I began to question him, he got the wind up, and plumped out some garbled story of blackmail."

I took an instant decision.

"I'm rather glad you've brought the matter up," I said. "I've been trying to decide whether to make a clean breast of things or not. I'd already practically decided to tell you everything, but I was going to wait for a favorable opportunity. You might as well have it now."

And then and there I narrated the whole events of the evening as I have set them down here. The inspector listened keenly, occasionally interjecting a question.

"Most extraordinary story I ever heard," he said, when I had finished. "And you say that letter has completely disappeared? It looks bad—it looks very bad indeed. It gives us what we've been looking for—a motive for the murder."

I nodded.

"I realize that."

"You say that Mr. Ackroyd hinted at a suspicion he had that some member of his household was involved? Household's rather an elastic term."

"You don't think that Parker himself might be the man we're after?" I suggested.

"It looks very like it. He was obviously listening at the door when you came out. Then Miss Ackroyd came across him later bent on entering the study. Say he tried again when she was safely out of the way. He stabbed Ackroyd, locked the door on the inside, opened the window, and got out that way, and went round to a side door which he had previously left open. How's that?"

"There's only one thing against it," I said slowly. "If Ackroyd went on reading that letter as soon as I left, as he intended to do, I don't see him continuing to sit on here and turn things over in his mind for another hour. He'd have had Parker in at once, accused him then and there, and there would have been a fine old uproar. Remember, Ackroyd was a man of choleric temper."

"Mightn't have had time to go on with the letter just then," suggested the inspector. "We know some one was with him at half-past nine. If that visitor turned up as soon as you left, and after he went, Miss Ackroyd came in to say good-night—well, he wouldn't be able to go on with the letter until close upon ten o'clock."

"And the telephone call?"

"Parker sent that all right—perhaps before he thought of the locked door and open window. Then he changed his mind—or got in a panic—and decided to deny all knowledge of it. That was it, depend upon it."

"Ye-es," I said rather doubtfully.

"Anyway, we can find out the truth about the telephone call from the exchange. If it was put through from here, I don't see how any one else but Parker could have sent it. Depend upon it, he's our man. But keep it dark—we don't want to alarm him just yet, till we've got all the evidence. I'll see to it he doesn't give us the slip. To all appearances we'll be concentrating on your mysterious stranger."

He rose from where he had been sitting astride the chair belonging to the desk, and crossed over to the still form in the arm-chair.

"The weapon ought to give us a clew," he remarked, looking up. "It's something quite unique—a curio, I should think, by the look of it."

He bent down, surveying the handle attentively, and I heard him give a grunt of satisfaction. Then, very gingerly, he pressed his hands down below the hilt and drew the blade out from the wound. Still carrying it so as not to touch the handle, he placed it in a wide china mug which adorned the mantelpiece.

"Yes," he said, nodding at it. "Quite a work of art. There can't be many of them about."

It was indeed a beautiful object. A narrow, tapering blade, and a hilt of elaborately intertwined metals of curious and careful workmanship. He touched the blade gingerly with his finger, testing its sharpness, and made an appreciative grimace.

"Lord, what an edge," he exclaimed. "A child could drive that into a man —as easy as cutting butter. A dangerous sort of toy to have about."

"May I examine the body properly now?" I asked.

He nodded.

"Go ahead."

I made a thorough examination.

"Well?" said the inspector, when I had finished.

"I'll spare you the technical language," I said. "We'll keep that for the inquest. The blow was delivered by a right-handed man standing behind him, and death must have been instantaneous. By the expression on the dead man's face, I should say that the blow was quite unexpected. He probably died without knowing who his assailant was."

"Butlers can creep about as soft-footed as cats," said Inspector Davis.

"There's not going to be much mystery about this crime. Take a look at the hilt of that dagger."

I took the look.

"I dare say they're not apparent to you, but I can see them clearly enough." He lowered his voice. *"Fingerprints!"*

He stood off a few steps to judge of his effect.

"Yes," I said mildly. "I guessed that."

I do not see why I should be supposed to be totally devoid of intelligence. After all, I read detective stories, and the newspapers, and am a man of quite average ability. If there had been toe marks on the dagger handle, now, that would have been quite a different thing. I would then have registered any amount of surprise and awe.

I think the inspector was annoyed with me for declining to get thrilled. He picked up the china mug and invited me to accompany him to the billiard room.

"I want to see if Mr. Raymond can tell us anything about this dagger," he explained.

Locking the outer door behind us again, we made our way to the billiard room, where we found Geoffrey Raymond. The inspector held up his exhibit.

"Ever seen this before, Mr. Raymond?"

"Why—I believe—I'm almost sure that is a curio given to Mr. Ackroyd by Major Blunt. It comes from Morocco—no, Tunis. So the crime was committed with that? What an extraordinary thing. It seems almost impossible, and yet there could hardly be two daggers the same. May I fetch Major Blunt?"

Without waiting for an answer, he hurried off.

"Nice young fellow that," said the inspector. "Something honest and ingenuous about him."

I agreed. In the two years that Geoffrey Raymond has been secretary to Ackroyd, I have never seen him ruffled or out of temper. And he has been, I know, a most efficient secretary.

In a minute or two Raymond returned, accompanied by Blunt.

"I was right," said Raymond excitedly. "It *is* the Tunisian dagger."

"Major Blunt hasn't looked at it yet," objected the inspector.

"Saw it the moment I came into the study," said the quiet man.

"You recognized it then?"

Blunt nodded.

"You said nothing about it," said the inspector suspiciously.

"Wrong moment," said Blunt. "Lot of harm done by blurting out things at the wrong time."

He returned the inspector's stare placidly enough.

The latter grunted at last and turned away. He brought the dagger over to Blunt.

"You're quite sure about it, sir. You identify it positively?"

"Absolutely. No doubt whatever."

"Where was this—er—curio usually kept? Can you tell me that, sir?"

It was the secretary who answered.

"In the silver table in the drawing-room."

"What?" I exclaimed.

The others looked at me.

"Yes, doctor?" said the inspector encouragingly.

"It's nothing."

"Yes, doctor?" said the inspector again, still more encouragingly.

"It's so trivial," I explained apologetically. "Only that when I arrived for dinner I heard the lid of the silver table being shut down in the drawing-room."

I saw profound skepticism and a trace of suspicion on the inspector's countenance.

"How did you know it was the silver table lid?"

I was forced to explain in detail—a long, tedious explanation which I would infinitely rather not have had to make.

The inspector heard me to the end.

"Was the dagger in its place when you were looking over the contents?" he asked.

"I don't know," I said. "I can't say I remember noticing it—but, of course, it may have been there all the time."

"We'd better get hold of the housekeeper," remarked the inspector, and pulled the bell.

A few minutes later Miss Russell, summoned by Parker, entered the room.

"I don't think I went near the silver table," she said, when the inspector had posed his question. "I was looking to see that all the flowers were fresh. Oh! yes, I remember now. The silver table was open—which it had no business to be, and I shut the lid down as I passed."

She looked at him aggressively.

"I see," said the inspector. "Can you tell me if this dagger was in its place then?"

Miss Russell looked at the weapon composedly.

"I can't say, I'm sure," she replied. "I didn't stop to look. I knew the family would be down any minute, and I wanted to get away."

"Thank you," said the inspector.

There was just a trace of hesitation in his manner, as though he would have liked to question her further, but Miss Russell clearly accepted the words as a dismissal, and glided from the room.

"Rather a Tartar, I should fancy, eh?" said the inspector, looking after her. "Let me see. This silver table is in front of one of the windows, I think you said, doctor?"

Raymond answered for me.

"Yes, the left-hand window."

"And the window was open?"

"They were both ajar."

"Well, I don't think we need go into the question much further. Some-body—I'll just say somebody—could get that dagger any time he liked, and

exactly when he got it doesn't matter in the least. I'll be coming up in the morning with the chief constable, Mr. Raymond. Until then, I'll keep the key of that door. I want Colonel Melrose to see everything exactly as it is. I happen to know that he's dining out the other side of the county, and, I believe, staying the night. . . ."

We watched the inspector take up the jar.

"I shall have to pack this carefully," he observed. "It's going to be an important piece of evidence in more ways than one."

A few minutes later as I came out of the billiard room with Raymond, the latter gave a low chuckle of amusement.

I felt the pressure of his hand on my arm, and followed the direction of his eyes. Inspector Davis seemed to be inviting Parker's opinion of a small pocket diary.

"A little obvious," murmured my companion. "So Parker is the suspect, is he? Shall we oblige Inspector Davis with a set of our fingerprints also?"

He took two cards from the card tray, wiped them with his silk handkerchief, then handed one to me and took the other himself. Then, with a grin, he handed them to the police inspector.

"Souvenirs," he said. "No. 1, Dr. Sheppard; No. 2, my humble self. One from Major Blunt will be forthcoming in the morning."

Youth is very buoyant. Even the brutal murder of his friend and employer could not dim Geoffrey Raymond's spirits for long. Perhaps that is as it should be. I do not know. I have lost the quality of resilience long since myself.

It was very late when I got back, and I hoped that Caroline would have gone to bed. I might have known better.

She had hot cocoa waiting for me, and whilst I drank it, she extracted the whole history of the evening from me. I said nothing of the blackmailing business, but contented myself with giving her the facts of the murder.

"The police suspect Parker," I said, as I rose to my feet and prepared to ascend to bed. "There seems a fairly clear case against him."

"Parker!" said my sister. "Fiddlesticks! That inspector must be a perfect fool. Parker indeed! Don't tell me."

With which obscure pronouncement we went up to bed.

VII. I LEARN MY NEIGHBOR'S PROFESSION

On the following morning I hurried unforgivably over my round. My excuse can be that I had no very serious cases to attend. On my return Caroline came into the hall to greet me.

"Flora Ackroyd is here," she announced in an excited whisper.

"What?"

I concealed my surprise as best I could.

"She's very anxious to see you. She's been here half an hour."

Caroline led the way into our small sitting-room, and I followed.

Flora was sitting on the sofa by the window. She was in black and she sat nervously twisting her hands together. I was shocked by the sight of her face. All the color had faded away from it. But when she spoke her manner was as composed and resolute as possible.

"Dr. Sheppard, I have come to ask you to help me."

"Of course he'll help you, my dear," said Caroline.

I don't think Flora really wished Caroline to be present at the interview. She would, I am sure, have infinitely preferred to speak to me privately. But she also wanted to waste no time, so she made the best of it.

"I want you to come to The Larches with me."

"The Larches?" I queried, surprised.

"To see that funny little man?" exclaimed Caroline.

"Yes. You know who he is, don't you?"

"We fancied," I said, "that he might be a retired hairdresser."

Flora's blue eyes opened very wide.

"Why, he's Hercule Poirot! You know who I mean—the private detective. They say he's done the most wonderful things—just like detectives do in books. A year ago he retired and came to live down here. Uncle knew who he was, but he promised not to tell any one, because M. Poirot wanted to live quietly without being bothered by people."

"So that's who he is," I said slowly.

"You've heard of him, of course?"

"I'm rather an old fogey, as Caroline tells me," I said, "but I *have* just heard of him."

"Extraordinary!" commented Caroline.

I don't know what she was referring to—possibly her own failure to discover the truth.

"You want to go and see him?" I asked slowly. "Now why?"

"To get him to investigate this murder, of course," said Caroline sharply. "Don't be so stupid, James."

I was not really being stupid. Caroline does not always understand what I am driving at.

"You haven't got confidence in Inspector Davis?" I went on.

"Of course she hasn't," said Caroline. "I haven't either."

Any one would have thought it was Caroline's uncle who had been murdered.

"And how do you know he would take up the case?" I asked. "Remember he has retired from active work."

"That's just it," said Flora simply. "I've got to persuade him."

"You are sure you are doing wisely?" I asked gravely.

"Of course she is," said Caroline. "I'll go with her myself if she likes."

"I'd rather the doctor came with me if you don't mind, Miss Sheppard," said Flora.

She knows the value of being direct on certain occasions. Any hints would certainly have been wasted on Caroline.

"You see," she explained, following directness with tact, "Dr. Sheppard being the doctor, and having found the body, he would be able to give all the details to M. Poirot."

"Yes," said Caroline grudgingly, "I see that."

I took a turn or two up and down the room.

"Flora," I said gravely, "be guided by me. I advise you not to drag this detective into the case."

Flora sprang to her feet. The color rushed into her cheeks.

"I know why you say that," she cried. "But it's exactly for that reason I'm so anxious to go. You're afraid! But I'm not. I know Ralph better than you do."

"Ralph," said Caroline. "What has Ralph got to do with it?"

Neither of us heeded her.

"Ralph may be weak," continued Flora. "He may have done foolish things in the past—wicked things even—but he wouldn't murder any one."

"No, no," I exclaimed. "I never thought it of him."

"Then why did you go to the Three Boars last night?" demanded Flora, "on your way home—after uncle's body was found?"

I was momentarily silenced. I had hoped that that visit of mine would remain unnoticed.

"How did you know about that?" I countered.

"I went there this morning," said Flora. "I heard from the servants that Ralph was staying there—"

I interrupted her.

"You had no idea that he was in King's Abbot?"

"No. I was astounded. I couldn't understand it. I went there and asked for him. They told me, what I suppose they told you last night, that he went out at about nine o'clock yesterday evening—and—and never came back."

Her eyes met mine defiantly, and as though answering something in my look, she burst out:—

"Well, why shouldn't he? He might have gone—anywhere. He may even have gone back to London."

"Leaving his luggage behind?" I asked gently.

Flora stamped her foot.

"I don't care. There must be a simple explanation."

"And that's why you want to go to Hercule Poirot? Isn't it better to leave things as they are? The police don't suspect Ralph in the least, remember. They're working on quite another tack."

"But that's just it," cried the girl. "They do suspect him. A man from Cranchester turned up this morning—Inspector Raglan, a horrid, weasely little man. I found he had been to the Three Boars this morning before me. They told me all about his having been there, and the questions he had asked. He must think Ralph did it."

"That's a change of mind from last night, if so," I said slowly. "He doesn't believe in Davis's theory that it was Parker then?"

"Parker indeed," said my sister, and snorted.

Flora came forward and laid her hand on my arm.

"Oh! Dr. Sheppard, let us go at once to this M. Poirot. He will find out the truth."

"My dear Flora," I said gently, laying my hand on hers. "Are you quite sure it is the truth we want?"

She looked at me, nodding her head gravely.

"You're not sure," she said. "I am. I know Ralph better than you do."

"Of course he didn't do it," said Caroline, who had been keeping silent with great difficulty. "Ralph may be extravagant, but he's a dear boy, and has the nicest manners."

I wanted to tell Caroline that large numbers of murderers have had nice manners, but the presence of Flora restrained me. Since the girl was determined, I was forced to give in to her and we started at once, getting away before my sister was able to fire off any more pronouncements beginning with her favorite words, "Of course."

An old woman with an immense Breton cap opened the door of The Larches to us. M. Poirot was at home, it seemed.

We were ushered into a little sitting-room arranged with formal precision, and there, after the lapse of a minute or so, my friend of yesterday came to us.

"Monsieur le docteur," he said, smiling. "Mademoiselle."

He bowed to Flora.

"Perhaps," I began, "you have heard of the tragedy which occurred last night."

His face grew grave.

"But certainly I have heard. It is horrible. I offer mademoiselle all my sympathy. In what way can I serve you?"

"Miss Ackroyd," I said, "wants you to—to——"

"To find the murderer," said Flora in a clear voice.

"I see," said the little man. "But the police will do that, will they not?"

"They might make a mistake," said Flora. "They are on their way to make a mistake now, I think. Please, M. Poirot, won't you help us? If—if it is a question of money——"

Poirot held up his hand.

"Not that, I beg of you, mademoiselle. Not that I do not care for money." His eyes showed a momentary twinkle. "Money, it means much to me and always has done. No, if I go into this, you must understand one thing clearly. *I shall go through with it to the end.* The good dog, he does not leave the scent, remember! You may wish that, after all, you had left it to the local police."

"I want the truth," said Flora, looking him straight in the eyes.

"All the truth?"

"All the truth."

"Then I accept," said the little man quietly. "And I hope you will not regret those words. Now, tell me all the circumstances."

"Dr. Sheppard had better tell you," said Flora. "He knows more than I do."

Thus enjoined, I plunged into a careful narrative, embodying all the facts I have previously set down. Poirot listened carefully, inserting a question here and there, but for the most part sitting in silence, his eyes on the ceiling.

I brought my story to a close with the departure of the inspector and myself from Fernly Park the previous night.

"And now," said Flora, as I finished, "tell him all about Ralph."

I hesitated, but her imperious glance drove me on.

"You went to this inn—this Three Boars—last night on your way home?" asked Poirot, as I brought my tale to a close. "Now exactly why was that?"

I paused a moment to choose my words carefully.

"I thought some one ought to inform the young man of his stepfather's death. It occurred to me after I had left Fernly that possibly no one but myself and Mr. Ackroyd were aware that he was staying in the village."

Poirot nodded.

"Quite so. That was your only motive in going there, eh?"

"That was my only motive," I said stiffly.

"It was not to—shall we say—reassure yourself about *ce jeune homme?*"

"Reassure myself?"

"I think, M. le docteur, that you know very well what I mean, though you pretend not to do so. I suggest that it would have been a relief to you if you had found that Captain Paton had been at home all the evening."

"Not at all," I said sharply.

The little detective shook his head at me gravely.

"You have not the trust in me of Miss Flora," he said. "But no matter. What we have to look at is this—Captain Paton is missing, under circumstances which call for an explanation. I will not hide from you that the matter looks grave. Still, it may admit of a perfectly simple explanation."

"That's just what I keep saying," cried Flora eagerly.

Poirot touched no more upon that theme. Instead he suggested an immediate visit to the local police. He thought it better for Flora to return home, and for me to be the one to accompany him there and introduce him to the officer in charge of the case.

We carried out this plan forthwith. We found Inspector Davis outside the police station looking very glum indeed. With him was Colonel Melrose, the chief constable, and another man whom, from Flora's description of "weaselly," I had no difficulty in recognizing as Inspector Raglan, from Cranchester.

I know Melrose fairly well, and I introduced Poirot to him and explained the situation. The chief constable was clearly vexed, and Inspector Raglan looked as black as thunder. Davis, however, seemed slightly exhilarated by the sight of his superior officer's annoyance.

"The case is going to be plain as a pikestaff," said Raglan. "Not the least need for amateurs to come butting in. You'd think any fool would have seen the way things were last night, and then we shouldn't have lost twelve hours."

He directed a vengeful glance at poor Davis, who received it with perfect stolidity.

"Mr. Ackroyd's family must, of course, do what they see fit," said Colonel Melrose. "But we cannot have the official investigation hampered in any way. I know M. Poirot's great reputation, of course," he added courteously.

"The police can't advertise themselves, worse luck," said Raglan.

It was Poirot who saved the situation.

"It is true that I have retired from the world," he said. "I never intended to take up a case again. Above all things, I have a horror of publicity. I must beg, that in the case of my being able to contribute something to the solution of the mystery, my name may not be mentioned."

Inspector Raglan's face lightened a little.

"I've heard of some very remarkable successes of yours," observed the colonel, thawing.

"I have had much experience," said Poirot quietly. "But most of my successes have been obtained by the aid of the police. I admire enormously your English police. If Inspector Raglan permits me to assist him, I shall be both honored and flattered."

The inspector's countenance became still more gracious.

Colonel Melrose drew me aside.

"From all I hear, this little fellow's done some really remarkable things," he murmured. "We're naturally anxious not to have to call in Scotland Yard.

Raglan seems very sure of himself, but I'm not quite certain that I agree with him. You see, I—er—know the parties concerned better than he does. This fellow doesn't seem out after kudos, does he? Would work in with us unobtrusively, eh?"

"To the greater glory of Inspector Raglan," I said solemnly.

"Well, well," said Colonel Melrose breezily in a louder voice, "we must put you wise to the latest developments, M. Poirot."

"I thank you," said Poirot. "My friend, Dr. Sheppard, said something of the butler being suspected."

"That's all bunkum," said Raglan instantly. "These high-class servants get in such a funk that they act suspiciously for nothing at all."

"The fingerprints?" I hinted.

"Nothing like Parker's." He gave a faint smile, and added: "And yours and Mr. Raymond's don't fit either, doctor."

"What about those of Captain Ralph Paton?" asked Poirot quietly.

I felt a secret admiration for the way he took the bull by the horns. I saw a look of respect creep into the inspector's eye.

"I see you don't let the grass grow under your feet, Mr. Poirot. It will be a pleasure to work with you, I'm sure. We're going to take that young gentleman's fingerprints as soon as we can lay hands upon him."

"I can't help thinking you're mistaken, inspector," said Colonel Melrose warmly. "I've known Ralph Paton from a boy upward. He'd never stoop to murder."

"Maybe not," said the inspector tonelessly.

"What have you got against him?" I asked.

"Went out just on nine o'clock last night. Was seen in neighborhood of Fernly Park somewhere about nine-thirty. Not been seen since. Believed to be in serious money difficulties. I've got a pair of his shoes here—shoes with rubber studs in them. He had two pairs, almost exactly alike. I'm going up now to compare them with those footmarks. The constable is up there seeing that no one tampers with them."

"We'll go at once," said Colonel Melrose. "You and M. Poirot will accompany us, will you not?"

We assented, and all drove up in the colonel's car. The inspector was anxious to get at once to the footmarks, and asked to be put down at the lodge. About half-way up the drive, on the right, a path branched off which led round to the terrace and the window of Ackroyd's study.

"Would you like to go with the inspector, M. Poirot?" asked the chief constable, "or would you prefer to examine the study?"

Poirot chose the latter alternative. Parker opened the door to us. His manner was smug and deferential, and he seemed to have recovered from his panic of the night before.

Colonel Melrose took a key from his pocket, and unlocking the door which led into the lobby, he ushered us through into the study.

"Except for the removal of the body, M. Poirot, this room is exactly as it was last night."

"And the body was found—where?"

As precisely as possible, I described Ackroyd's position. The arm-chair still stood in front of the fire.

Poirot went and sat down in it.

"The blue letter you speak of, where was it when you left the room?"

"Mr. Ackroyd had laid it down on this little table at his right hand."

Poirot nodded.

"Except for that, everything was in its place?"

"Yes, I think so."

"Colonel Melrose, would you be so extremely obliging as to sit down in this chair a minute. I thank you. Now, M. le docteur, will you kindly indicate to me the exact position of the dagger?"

I did so, whilst the little man stood in the doorway.

"The hilt of the dagger was plainly visible from the door then. Both you and Parker could see it at once?"

"Yes."

Poirot went next to the window.

"The electric light was on, of course, when you discovered the body?" he asked over his shoulder.

I assented, and joined him where he was studying the marks on the window-sill.

"The rubber studs are the same pattern as those in Captain Paton's shoes," he said quietly.

Then he came back once more to the middle of the room. His eye traveled round, searching everything in the room with a quick, trained glance.

"Are you a man of good observation, Dr. Sheppard?" he asked at last.

"I think so," I said, surprised.

"There was a fire in the grate, I see. When you broke the door down and found Mr. Ackroyd dead, how was the fire? Was it low?"

I gave a vexed laugh.

"I—I really can't say. I didn't notice. Perhaps Mr. Raymond or Major Blunt——"

The little man opposite me shook his head with a faint smile.

"One must always proceed with method. I made an error of judgment in asking you that question. To each man his own knowledge. You could tell me the details of the patient's appearance—nothing there would escape you. If I wanted information about the papers on that desk, Mr. Raymond would have noticed anything there was to see. To find out about the fire, I must ask the man whose business it is to observe such things. You permit——"

He moved swiftly to the fireplace and rang the bell.

After a lapse of a minute or two Parker appeared.

"The bell rang, sir," he said hesitatingly.

"Come in, Parker," said Colonel Melrose. "This gentleman wants to ask you something."

Parker transferred a respectful attention to Poirot.

"Parker," said the little man, "when you broke down the door with Dr.

Sheppard last night, and found your master dead, what was the state of the fire?"

Parker replied without a pause.

"It had burned very low, sir. It was almost out."

"Ah!" said Poirot. The exclamation sounded almost triumphant. He went on:—

"Look round you, my good Parker. Is this room exactly as it was then?"

The butler's eye swept round. It came to rest on the windows.

"The curtains were drawn, sir, and the electric light was on."

Poirot nodded approval.

"Anything else?"

"Yes, sir, this chair was drawn out a little more."

He indicated a big grandfather chair to the left of the door between it and the window. I append a plan of the room with the chair in question marked with an X.

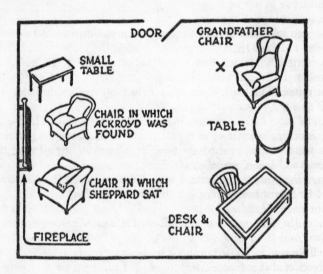

"Just show me," said Poirot.

The butler drew the chair in question out a good two feet from the wall, turning it so that the seat faced the door.

"*Voilà ce qui est curieux*," murmured Poirot. "No one would want to sit in a chair in such a position, I fancy. Now who pushed it back into place again, I wonder? Did you, my friend?"

"No, sir," said Parker. "I was too upset with seeing the master and all."

Poirot looked across at me.

"Did you, doctor?"

I shook my head.

"It was back in position when I arrived with the police, sir," put in Parker. "I'm sure of that."

"Curious," said Poirot again.

"Raymond or Blunt must have pushed it back," I suggested. "Surely it isn't important?"

"It is completely unimportant," said Poirot. "That is why it is so interesting," he added softly.

"Excuse me a minute," said Colonel Melrose. He left the room with Parker.

"Do you think Parker is speaking the truth?" I asked.

"About the chair, yes. Otherwise I do not know. You will find, M. le docteur, if you have much to do with cases of this kind, that they all resemble each other in one thing."

"What is that?" I asked curiously.

"Every one concerned in them has something to hide."

"Have I?" I asked, smiling.

Poirot looked at me attentively.

"I think you have," he said quietly.

"But——"

"Have you told me everything known to you about this young man Paton?" He smiled as I grew red. "Oh! do not fear. I will not press you. I shall learn it in good time."

"I wish you'd tell me something of your methods," I said hastily, to cover my confusion. "The point about the fire, for instance?"

"Oh! that was very simple. You leave Mr. Ackroyd at—ten minutes to nine, was it not?"

"Yes, exactly, I should say."

"The window is then closed and bolted and the door unlocked. At a quarter past ten when the body is discovered, the door is locked and the window is open. Who opened it? Clearly only Mr. Ackroyd himself could have done so, and for one of two reasons. Either because the room became unbearably hot (but since the fire was nearly out and there was a sharp drop in temperature last night, that cannot be the reason), or because he admitted some one that way. And if he admitted some one that way, it must have been some one well known to him, since he had previously shown himself uneasy on the subject of that same window."

"It sounds very simple," I said.

"Everything is simple, if you arrange the facts methodically. We are concerned now with the personality of the person who was with him at nine-thirty last night. Everything goes to show that that was the individual admitted by the window, and though Mr. Ackroyd was seen alive later by Miss Flora, we cannot approach a solution of the mystery until we know who that visitor was. The window may have been left open after his departure and so afforded entrance to the murderer, or the same person may have returned a second time. Ah! here is the colonel who returns."

Colonel Melrose entered with an animated manner.

"That telephone call has been traced at last," he said. "It did not come from here. It was put through to Dr. Sheppard at 10.15 last night from a public call office at King's Abbot station. And at 10.23 the night mail leaves for Liverpool."

VIII. INSPECTOR RAGLAN IS CONFIDENT

We looked at each other.

"You'll have inquiries made at the station, of course?" I said.

"Naturally, but I'm not over-sanguine as to the result. You know what that station is like."

I did. King's Abbot is a mere village, but its station happens to be an important junction. Most of the big expresses stop there, and trains are shunted, re-sorted, and made up. It has two or three public telephone boxes. At that time of night three local trains come in close upon each other, to catch the connection with the express for the north which comes in at 10.19 and leaves at 10.23. The whole place is in a bustle, and the chances of one particular person being noticed telephoning or getting into the express are very small indeed.

"But why telephone at all?" demanded Melrose. "That is what I find so extraordinary. There seems no rhyme or reason in the thing."

Poirot carefully straightened a china ornament on one of the bookcases.

"Be sure there was a reason," he said over his shoulder.

"But what reason could it be?"

"When we know that, we shall know everything. This case is very curious and very interesting."

There was something almost indescribable in the way he said those last words. I felt that he was looking at the case from some peculiar angle of his own, and what he saw I could not tell.

He went to the window and stood there, looking out.

"You say it was nine o'clock, Dr. Sheppard, when you met this stranger outside the gate?"

He asked the question without turning round.

"Yes," I replied. "I heard the church clock chime the hour."

"How long would it take him to reach the house—to reach this window, for instance?"

"Five minutes at the outside. Two or three minutes only if he took the path at the right of the drive and came straight here."

"But to do that he would have to know the way. How can I explain myself?—it would mean that he had been here before—that he knew his surroundings."

"That is true," replied Colonel Melrose.

"We could find out, doubtless, if Mr. Ackroyd had received any strangers during the past week?"

"Young Raymond could tell us that," I said.

"Or Parker," suggested Colonel Melrose.

"*Ou tous les deux,*" suggested Poirot, smiling.

Colonel Melrose went in search of Raymond, and I rang the bell once more for Parker.

Colonel Melrose returned almost immediately, accompanied by the young secretary, whom he introduced to Poirot. Geoffrey Raymond was fresh and debonair as ever. He seemed surprised and delighted to make Poirot's acquaintance.

"No idea you'd been living among us incognito, M. Poirot," he said. "It will be a great privilege to watch you at work—— Hallo, what's this?"

Poirot had been standing just to the left of the door. Now he moved aside suddenly, and I saw that while my back was turned he must have swiftly drawn out the arm-chair till it stood in the position Parker had indicated.

"Want me to sit in the chair whilst you take a blood test?" asked Raymond good-humoredly. "What's the idea?"

"M. Raymond, this chair was pulled out—so—last night when Mr. Ackroyd was found killed. Some one moved it back again into place. Did you do so?"

The secretary's reply came without a second's hesitation.

"No, indeed I didn't. I don't even remember that it was in that position, but it must have been if you say so. Anyway, somebody else must have moved it back to its proper place. Have they destroyed a clew in doing so? Too bad!"

"It is of no consequence," said the detective. "Of no consequence whatever. What I really want to ask you is this, M. Raymond: Did any stranger come to see Mr. Ackroyd during this past week?"

The secretary reflected for a minute or two, knitting his brows, and during the pause Parker appeared in answer to the bell.

"No," said Raymond at last. "I can't remember any one. Can you, Parker?"

"I beg your pardon, sir?"

"Any stranger coming to see Mr. Ackroyd this week?"

The butler reflected for a minute or two.

"There was the young man who came on Wednesday, sir," he said at last. "From Curtis and Troute, I understood he was."

Raymond moved this aside with an impatient hand.

"Oh! yes, I remember, but that is not the kind of stranger this gentleman means." He turned to Poirot. "Mr. Ackroyd had some idea of purchasing a dictaphone," he explained. "It would have enabled us to get through a lot more work in a limited time. The firm in question sent down their representative, but nothing came of it. Mr. Ackroyd did not make up his mind to purchase."

Poirot turned to the butler.

"Can you describe this young man to me, my good Parker?"

"He was fair-haired, sir, and short. Very neatly dressed in a blue serge suit. A very presentable young man, sir, for his station in life."

Poirot turned to me.

"The man you met outside the gate, doctor, was tall, was he not?"

"Yes," I said. "Somewhere about six feet, I should say."

"There is nothing in that, then," declared the Belgian. "I thank you, Parker."

The butler spoke to Raymond.

"Mr. Hammond has just arrived, sir," he said. "He is anxious to know if he can be of any service, and he would be glad to have a word with you."

"I'll come at once," said the young man. He hurried out. Poirot looked inquiringly at the chief constable.

"The family solicitor, M. Poirot," said the latter.

"It is a busy time for this young M. Raymond," murmured M. Poirot. "He has the air efficient, that one."

"I believe Mr. Ackroyd considered him a most able secretary."

"He has been here—how long?"

"Just on two years, I fancy."

"His duties he fulfills punctiliously. Of that I am sure. In what manner does he amuse himself? Does he go in for *le sport?*"

"Private secretaries haven't much time for that sort of thing," said Colonel Melrose, smiling. "Raymond plays golf, I believe. And tennis in the summer time."

"He does not attend the courses—I should say the running of the horses?"

"Race meetings? No, I don't think he's interested in racing."

Poirot nodded and seemed to lose interest. He glanced slowly round the study.

"I have seen, I think, all that there is to be seen here."

I, too, looked round.

"If those walls could speak," I murmured.

Poirot shook his head.

"A tongue is not enough," he said. "They would have to have also eyes and ears. But do not be too sure that these dead things"—he touched the top of the bookcase as he spoke—"are always dumb. To me they speak some-times—chairs, tables—they have their message!"

He turned away towards the door.

"What message?" I cried. "What have they said to you to-day?"

He looked over his shoulder and raised one eyebrow quizzically.

"An opened window," he said. "A locked door. A chair that apparently moved itself. To all three I say, 'Why?' and I find no answer."

He shook his head, puffed out his chest, and stood blinking at us. He looked ridiculously full of his own importance. It crossed my mind to wonder whether he was really any good as a detective. Had his big reputation been built up on a series of lucky chances?

I think the same thought must have occurred to Colonel Melrose, for he frowned.

"Anything more you want to see, M. Poirot?" he inquired brusquely.

"You would perhaps be so kind as to show me the silver table from which the weapon was taken? After that, I will trespass on your kindness no longer."

We went to the drawing-room, but on the way the constable waylaid the colonel, and after a muttered conversation the latter excused himself and left us together. I showed Poirot the silver table, and after raising the lid once or twice and letting it fall, he pushed open the window and stepped out on the terrace. I followed him.

Inspector Raglan had just turned the corner of the house, and was coming towards us. His face looked grim and satisfied.

"So there you are, M. Poirot," he said. "Well, this isn't going to be much of a case. I'm sorry, too. A nice enough young fellow gone wrong."

Poirot's face fell, and he spoke very mildly.

"I'm afraid I shall not be able to be of much aid to you, then?"

"Next time, perhaps," said the inspector soothingly. "Though we don't have murders every day in this quiet little corner of the world."

Poirot's gaze took on an admiring quality.

"You have been of a marvelous promptness," he observed. "How exactly did you go to work, if I may ask?"

"Certainly," said the inspector. "To begin with—method. That's what I always say—method!"

"Ah!" cried the other. "That, too, is my watchword. Method, order, and the little gray cells."

"The cells?" said the inspector, staring.

"The little gray cells of the brain," explained the Belgian.

"Oh, of course; well, we all use them, I suppose."

"In a greater or lesser degree," murmured Poirot. "And there are, too, differences in quality. Then there is the psychology of a crime. One must study that."

"Ah!" said the inspector, "you've been bitten with all this psychoanalysis stuff? Now, I'm a plain man——"

"Mrs. Raglan would not agree, I am sure, to that," said Poirot, making him a little bow.

Inspector Raglan, a little taken aback, bowed.

"You don't understand," he said, grinning broadly. "Lord, what a lot of difference language makes. I'm telling you how I set to work. First of all, method. Mr. Ackroyd was last seen alive at a quarter to ten by his niece, Miss Flora Ackroyd. That's fact number one, isn't it?"

"If you say so."

"Well, it is. At half-past ten, the doctor here says that Mr. Ackroyd has been dead at least half an hour. You stick to that, doctor?"

"Certainly," I said. "Half an hour or longer."

"Very good. That gives us exactly a quarter of an hour in which the crime must have been committed. I make a list of every one in the house, and work through it, setting down opposite their names where they were and what they were doing between the hour of 9.45 and 10 p.m."

He handed a sheet of paper to Poirot. I read it over his shoulder. It ran as follows, written in a neat script:—

Major Blunt.—In billiard room with Mr. Raymond.
    (*Latter confirms.*)
Mr. Raymond.—Billiard room. (See above.)

Mrs. Ackroyd.—9.45 *watching billiard match. Went up to bed* 9.55. (*Raymond and Blunt watched her up staircase.*)

Miss Ackroyd.—*Went straight from her uncle's room upstairs.* (*Confirmed by Parker, also housemaid, Elsie Dale.*)

Servants:—

Parker.—*Went straight to butler's pantry.* (*Confirmed by housekeeper, Miss Russell, who came down to speak to him about something at* 9.47, *and remained at least ten minutes.*)

Miss Russell.—*As above. Spoke to housemaid, Elsie Dale, upstairs at* 9.45.

Ursula Bourne (*parlormaid*).—*In her own room until* 9.55. *Then in Servants' Hall.*

Mrs. Cooper (*cook*).—*In Servants' Hall.*

Gladys Jones (*second housemaid*).—*In Servants' Hall.*

Elsie Dale.—*Upstairs in bedroom. Seen there by Miss Russell and Miss Flora Ackroyd.*

Mary Thripp (*kitchenmaid*).—*Servants' Hall.*

"The cook has been here seven years, the parlormaid eighteen months, and Parker just over a year. The others are new. Except for something fishy about Parker, they all seem quite all right."

"A very complete list," said Poirot, handing it back to him. "I am quite sure that Parker did not do the murder," he added gravely.

"So is my sister," I struck in. "And she's usually right." Nobody paid any attention to my interpolation.

"That disposes pretty effectually of the household," continued the inspector. "Now we come to a very grave point. The woman at the lodge—Mary Black—was pulling the curtains last night when she saw Ralph Paton turn in at the gate and go up towards the house."

"She is sure of that?" I asked sharply.

"Quite sure. She knows him well by sight. He went past very quickly and turned off by the path to the right, which is a short cut to the terrace."

"And what time was that?" asked Poirot, who had sat with an immovable face.

"Exactly twenty-five minutes past nine," said the inspector gravely.

There was a silence. Then the inspector spoke again.

"It's all clear enough. It fits in without a flaw. At twenty-five minutes past nine, Captain Paton is seen passing the lodge; at nine-thirty or thereabouts, Mr. Geoffrey Raymond hears some one in here asking for money and Mr. Ackroyd refusing. What happens next? Captain Paton leaves the same way—through the window. He walks along the terrace, angry and baffled. He comes to the open drawing-room window. Say it's now a quarter to ten. Miss Flora Ackroyd is saying good-night to her uncle. Major Blunt, Mr. Raymond, and Mrs. Ackroyd are in the billiard room. The drawing-room is empty. He steals in, takes the dagger from the silver table, and returns to the study window. He slips off his shoes, climbs in, and—well, I don't need to go into details. Then he slips out again and goes off. Hadn't the nerve to go back to the inn. He makes for the station, rings up from there——"

"Why?" said Poirot softly.

I jumped at the interruption. The little man was leaning forward. His eyes shone with a queer green light.

For a moment Inspector Raglan was taken aback by the question.

"It's difficult to say exactly why he did that," he said at last. "But murderers do funny things. You'd know that if you were in the police force. The cleverest of them make stupid mistakes sometimes. But come along and I'll show you those footprints."

We followed him round the corner of the terrace to the study window. At a word from Raglan a police constable produced the shoes which had been obtained from the local inn.

The inspector laid them over the marks.

"They're the same," he said confidently. "That is to say, they're not the same pair that actually made these prints. He went away in those. This is a pair just like them, but older—see how the studs are worn down."

"Surely a great many people wear shoes with rubber studs in them?" asked Poirot.

"That's so, of course," said the inspector. "I shouldn't put so much stress on the footmarks if it wasn't for everything else."

"A very foolish young man, Captain Ralph Paton," said Poirot thoughtfully. "To leave so much evidence of his presence."

"Ah! well," said the inspector, "it was a dry, fine night, you know. He left no prints on the terrace or on the graveled path. But, unluckily for him, a spring must have welled up just lately at the end of the path from the drive. See here."

A small graveled path joined the terrace a few feet away. In one spot, a few yards from its termination, the ground was wet and boggy. Crossing this wet place there were again the marks of footsteps, and amongst them the shoes with rubber studs.

Poirot followed the path on a little way, the inspector by his side.

"You noticed the women's footprints?" he said suddenly.

The inspector laughed.

"Naturally. But several different women have walked this way—and men as well. It's a regular short cut to the house, you see. It would be impossible to sort out all the footsteps. After all, it's the ones on the window-sill that are really important."

Poirot nodded.

"It's no good going farther," said the inspector, as we came in view of the drive. "It's all graveled again here, and hard as it can be."

Again Poirot nodded, but his eyes were fixed on a small garden house—a kind of superior summer-house. It was a little to the left of the path ahead of us, and a graveled walk ran up to it.

Poirot lingered about until the inspector had gone back towards the house. Then he looked at me.

"You must have indeed been sent from the good God to replace my friend Hastings," he said, with a twinkle. "I observe that you do not quit my side. How say you, Dr. Sheppard, shall we investigate that summer-house? It interests me."

He went up to the door and opened it. Inside, the place was almost dark. There were one or two rustic seats, a croquet set, and some folded deck-chairs.

I was startled to observe my new friend. He had dropped to his hands and knees and was crawling about the floor. Every now and then he shook his head as though not satisfied. Finally, he sat back on his heels.

"Nothing," he murmured. "Well, perhaps it was not to be expected. But it would have meant so much——"

He broke off, stiffening all over. Then he stretched out his hand to one of the rustic chairs. He detached something from one side of it.

"What is it?" I cried. "What have you found?"

He smiled, unclosing his hand so that I should see what lay in the palm of it. A scrap of stiff white cambric.

I took it from him, looked at it curiously, and then handed it back.

"What do you make of it, eh, my friend?" he asked, eyeing me keenly.

"A scrap torn from a handkerchief," I suggested, shrugging my shoulders.

He made another dart and picked up a small quill—a goose quill by the look of it.

"And that?" he cried triumphantly. "What do you make of that?"

I only stared.

He slipped the quill into his pocket, and looked again at the scrap of white stuff.

"A fragment of a handkerchief?" he mused. "Perhaps you are right. But remember this—*a good laundry does not starch a handkerchief.*"

He nodded at me triumphantly, then he put away the scrap carefully in his pocket-book.

IX. THE GOLDFISH POND

We walked back to the house together. There was no sign of the inspector. Poirot paused on the terrace and stood with his back to the house, slowly turning his head from side to side.

"*Une belle propriété,*" he said at last appreciatively. "Who inherits it?"

His words gave me almost a shock. It is an odd thing, but until that moment the question of inheritance had never come into my head. Poirot watched me keenly.

"It is a new idea to you, that," he said at last. "You had not thought of it before—eh?"

"No," I said truthfully. "I wish I had."

He looked at me again curiously.

"I wonder just what you mean by that," he said thoughtfully. "Ah! no," as I was about to speak. "*Inutile!* You would not tell me your real thought."

"Every one has something to hide," I quoted, smiling.

"Exactly."

"You still believe that?"

"More than ever, my friend. But it is not easy to hide things from Hercule Poirot. He has a knack of finding out."

He descended the steps of the Dutch garden as he spoke.

"Let us walk a little," he said over his shoulder. "The air is pleasant to-day."

I followed him. He led me down a path to the left enclosed in yew hedges. A walk led down the middle, bordered on each side with formal flower beds, and at the end was a round paved recess with a seat and a pond of goldfish. Instead of pursuing the path to the end, Poirot took another which wound up the side of a wooded slope. In one spot the trees had been cleared away, and a seat had been put. Sitting there one had a splendid view over the countryside, and one looked right down on the paved recess and the goldfish pond.

"England is very beautiful," said Poirot, his eyes straying over the prospect. Then he smiled. "And so are English girls," he said in a lower tone. "Hush, my friend, and look at the pretty picture below us."

It was then that I saw Flora. She was moving along the path we had just left and she was humming a little snatch of song. Her step was more dancing than walking, and in spite of her black dress, there was nothing but joy in her whole attitude. She gave a sudden pirouette on her toes, and her black draperies swung out. At the same time she flung her head back and laughed outright.

As she did so a man stepped out from the trees. It was Hector Blunt.

The girl started. Her expression changed a little.

"How you startled me—I didn't see you."

Blunt said nothing, but stood looking at her for a minute or two in silence.

"What I like about you," said Flora, with a touch of malice, "is your cheery conversation."

I fancy that at that Blunt reddened under his tan. His voice, when he spoke, sounded different—it had a curious sort of humility in it.

"Never was much of a fellow for talking. Not even when I was young."

"That was a very long time ago, I suppose," said Flora gravely.

I caught the undercurrent of laughter in her voice, but I don't think Blunt did.

"Yes," he said simply, "it was."

"How does it feel to be Methuselah?" asked Flora.

This time the laughter was more apparent, but Blunt was following out an idea of his own.

"Remember the Johnny who sold his soul to the devil? In return for being made young again? There's an opera about it."

"Faust, you mean?"

"That's the beggar. Rum story. Some of us would do it if we could."

"Any one would think you were creaking at the joints to hear you talk," cried Flora, half vexed, half amused.

Blunt said nothing for a minute or two. Then he looked away from Flora into the middle distance and observed to an adjacent tree trunk that it was about time he got back to Africa.

"Are you going on another expedition—shooting things?"

"Expect so. Usually do, you know—shoot things, I mean."

"You shot that head in the hall, didn't you?"

Blunt nodded. Then he jerked out, going rather red, as he did so:—

"Care for some decent skins any time? If so, I could get 'em for you."

"Oh! please do," cried Flora. "Will you really? You won't forget?"

"I shan't forget," said Hector Blunt.

He added, in a sudden burst of communicativeness:—

"Time I went. I'm no good in this sort of life. Haven't got the manners for it. I'm a rough fellow, no use in society. Never remember the things one's expected to say. Yes, time I went."

"But you're not going at once," cried Flora. "Not—not while we're in all this trouble. Oh! please. If you go——"

She turned away a little.

"You want me to stay?" asked Blunt.

He spoke deliberately but quite simply.

"We all——"

"I meant you personally," said Blunt, with directness.

Flora turned slowly back again and met his eyes.

"I want you to stay," she said, "if—if that makes any difference."

"It makes all the difference," said Blunt.

There was a moment's silence. They sat down on the stone seat by the goldfish pond. It seemed as though neither of them knew quite what to say next.

"It—it's such a lovely morning," said Flora at last. "You know, I can't help feeling happy, in spite—in spite of everything. That's awful, I suppose?"

"Quite natural," said Blunt. "Never saw your uncle until two years ago, did you? Can't be expected to grieve very much. Much better to have no humbug about it."

"There's something awfully consoling about you," said Flora. "You make things so simple."

"Things are simple as a rule," said the big game hunter.

"Not always," said Flora.

Her voice had lowered itself, and I saw Blunt turn and look at her, bringing his eyes back from (apparently) the coast of Africa to do so. He evidently put his own construction on her change of tone, for he said, after a minute or two, in rather an abrupt manner:—

"I say, you know, you mustn't worry. About that young chap, I mean. Inspector's an ass. Everybody knows—utterly absurd to think he could have done it. Man from outside. Burglar chap. That's the only possible solution."

Flora turned to look at him.

"You really think so?"

"Don't you?" said Blunt quickly.

"I—oh, yes, of course."

Another silence, and then Flora burst out:—

"I'm—I'll tell you why I felt so happy this morning. However heartless you think me, I'd rather tell you. It's because the lawyer has been—Mr. Hammond. He told us about the will. Uncle Roger has left me twenty thousand pounds. Think of it—twenty thousand beautiful pounds."

Blunt looked surprised.

"Does it mean so much to you?"

"Mean much to me? Why, it's everything. Freedom—life—no more scheming and scraping and lying——"

"Lying?" said Blunt, sharply interrupting.

Flora seemed taken aback for a minute.

"You know what I mean," she said uncertainly. "Pretending to be thankful for all the nasty castoff things rich relations give you. Last year's coats and skirts and hats."

"Don't know much about ladies' clothes; should have said you were always very well turned out."

"It's cost me something, though," said Flora in a low voice. "Don't let's talk of horrid things. I'm so happy I'm free. Free to do what I like. Free not to——"

She stopped suddenly.

"Not to what?" asked Blunt quickly.

"I forget now. Nothing important."

Blunt had a stick in his hand, and he thrust it into the pond, poking at something.

"What are you doing, Major Blunt?"

"There's something bright down there. Wondered what it was—looks like a gold brooch. Now I've stirred up the mud and it's gone."

"Perhaps it's a crown," suggested Flora. "Like the one Mélisande saw in the water."

"Mélisande," said Blunt reflectively—"she's in an opera, isn't she?"

"Yes, you seem to know a lot about operas."

"People take me sometimes," said Blunt sadly. "Funny idea of pleasure —worse racket than the natives make with their tom-toms."

Flora laughed.

"I remember Mélisande," continued Blunt, "married an old chap old enough to be her father."

He threw a small piece of flint into the goldfish pond. Then, with a change of manner, he turned to Flora.

"Miss Ackroyd, can I do anything? About Paton, I mean. I know how dreadfully anxious you must be."

"Thank you," said Flora in a cold voice. "There is really nothing to be done. Ralph will be all right. I've got hold of the most wonderful detective in the world, and he's going to find out all about it."

For some time I had felt uneasy as to our position. We were not exactly eavesdropping, since the two in the garden below had only to lift their heads to see us. Nevertheless, I should have drawn attention to our presence before now, had not my companion put a warning pressure on my arm. Clearly he wished me to remain silent.

But now he rose briskly to his feet, clearing his throat.

"I demand pardon," he cried. "I cannot allow mademoiselle thus extravagantly to compliment me, and not draw attention to my presence. They say the listener hears no good of himself, but that is not the case this time. To spare my blushes, I must join you and apologize."

He hurried down the path with me close behind him, and joined the others by the pond.

"This is M. Hercule Poirot," said Flora. "I expect you've heard of him."

Poirot bowed.

"I know Major Blunt by reputation," he said politely. "I am glad to have encountered you, monsieur. I am in need of some information that you can give me."

Blunt looked at him inquiringly.

"When did you last see M. Ackroyd alive?"

"At dinner."

"And you neither saw nor heard anything of him after that?"

"Didn't see him. Heard his voice."

"How was that?"

"I strolled out on the terrace——"

"Pardon me, what time was this?"

"About half-past nine. I was walking up and down smoking in front of the drawing-room window. I heard Ackroyd talking in his study——"

Poirot stooped and removed a microscopic weed.

"Surely you couldn't hear voices in the study from that part of the terrace," he murmured.

He was not looking at Blunt, but I was, and to my intense surprise, I saw the latter flush.

"Went as far as the corner," he explained unwillingly.

"Ah! indeed?" said Poirot.

In the mildest manner he conveyed an impression that more was wanted.

"Thought I saw—a woman disappearing into the bushes. Just a gleam of white, you know. Must have been mistaken. It was while I was standing at the corner of the terrace that I heard Ackroyd's voice speaking to that secretary of his."

"Speaking to Mr. Geoffrey Raymond?"

"Yes—that's what I supposed at the time. Seems I was wrong."

"Mr. Ackroyd didn't address him by name?"

"Oh, no."

"Then, if I may ask, why did you think——?"

Blunt explained laboriously.

"Took it for granted that it *would* be Raymond, because he had said just before I came out that he was taking some papers to Ackroyd. Never thought of it being anybody else."

"Can you remember what the words you heard were?"

"Afraid I can't. Something quite ordinary and unimportant. Only caught a scrap of it. I was thinking of something else at the time."

"It is of no importance," murmured Poirot. "Did you move a chair back against the wall when you went into the study after the body was discovered?"

"Chair? No—why should I?"

Poirot shrugged his shoulders but did not answer. He turned to Flora.

"There is one thing I should like to know from you, mademoiselle. When you were examining the things in the silver table with Dr. Sheppard, was the dagger in its place, or was it not?"

Flora's chin shot up.

"Inspector Raglan has been asking me that," she said resentfully. "I've told him, and I'll tell you. I'm perfectly certain the dagger was *not* there. He thinks it was and that Ralph sneaked it later in the evening. And—and he doesn't believe me. He thinks I'm saying it to—to shield Ralph."

"And aren't you?" I asked gravely.

Flora stamped her foot.

"You, too, Dr. Sheppard! Oh! it's too bad."

Poirot tactfully made a diversion.

"It is true what I heard you say, Major Blunt. There is something that glitters in this pond. Let us see if I can reach it."

He knelt down by the pond, baring his arm to the elbow, and lowered it in very slowly, so as not to disturb the bottom of the pond. But in spite of all his precautions the mud eddied and swirled, and he was forced to draw his arm out again empty-handed.

He gazed ruefully at the mud upon his arm. I offered him my handkerchief, which he accepted with fervent protestations of thanks. Blunt looked at his watch.

"Nearly lunch time," he said. "We'd better be getting back to the house."

"You will lunch with us, M. Poirot?" asked Flora. "I should like you to meet my mother. She is—very fond of Ralph."

The little man bowed.

"I shall be delighted, mademoiselle."

"And you will stay, too, won't you, Dr. Sheppard?"

I hesitated.

"Oh, do!"

I wanted to, so I accepted the invitation without further ceremony.

We set out towards the house, Flora and Blunt walking ahead.

"What hair," said Poirot to me in a low tone, nodding towards Flora. "The real gold! They will make a pretty couple. She and the dark, handsome Captain Paton. Will they not?"

I looked at him inquiringly, but he began to fuss about a few microscopic drops of water on his coat sleeve. The man reminded me in some ways of a cat. His green eyes and his finicking habits.

"And all for nothing, too," I said sympathetically. "I wonder what it was in the pond?"

"Would you like to see?" asked Poirot.

I stared at him. He nodded.

"My good friend," he said gently and reproachfully, "Hercule Poirot does not run the risk of disarranging his costume without being sure of attaining his object. To do so would be ridiculous and absurd. I am never ridiculous."

"But you brought your hand out empty," I objected.

"There are times when it is necessary to have discretion. Do you tell your patients everything—everything, doctor? I think not. Nor do you tell your excellent sister everything either, is it not so? Before showing my empty hand, I dropped what it contained into my other hand. You shall see what that was."

He held out his left hand, palm open. On it lay a little circlet of gold. A woman's wedding ring.

I took it from him.

"Look inside," commanded Poirot.

I did so. Inside was an inscription in fine writing:—

From R., March 13th.

I looked at Poirot, but he was busy inspecting his appearance in a tiny pocket glass. He paid particular attention to his mustaches, and none at all to me. I saw that he did not intend to be communicative.

X. THE PARLORMAID

We found Mrs. Ackroyd in the hall. With her was a small dried-up little man, with an aggressive chin and sharp gray eyes, and "lawyer" written all over him.

"Mr. Hammond is staying to lunch with us," said Mrs. Ackroyd. "You know Major Blunt, Mr. Hammond? And dear Dr. Sheppard—also a close friend of poor Roger's. And, let me see——"

She paused, surveying Hercule Poirot in some perplexity.

"This is M. Poirot, mother," said Flora. "I told you about him this morning."

"Oh! yes," said Mrs. Ackroyd vaguely. "Of course, my dear, of course. He is to find Ralph, is he not?"

"He is to find out who killed uncle," said Flora.

"Oh! my dear," cried her mother. "Please! My poor nerves. I am a wreck this morning, a positive wreck. Such a dreadful thing to happen. I can't help feeling that it must have been an accident of some kind. Roger was so fond of handling queer curios. His hand must have slipped, or something."

This theory was received in polite silence. I saw Poirot edge up to the lawyer, and speak to him in a confidential undertone. They moved aside into the embrasure of the window. I joined them—then hesitated.

"Perhaps I'm intruding," I said.

"Not at all," cried Poirot heartily. "You and I, M. le docteur, we investigate this affair side by side. Without you I should be lost. I desire a little information from the good Mr. Hammond."

"You are acting on behalf of Captain Ralph Paton, I understand," said the lawyer cautiously.

Poirot shook his head.

"Not so. I am acting in the interests of justice. Miss Ackroyd has asked me to investigate the death of her uncle."

Mr. Hammond seemed slightly taken aback.

"I cannot seriously believe that Captain Paton can be concerned in this crime," he said, "however strong the circumstantial evidence against him may be. The mere fact that he was hard pressed for money——"

"Was he hard pressed for money?" interpolated Poirot quickly.

The lawyer shrugged his shoulders.

"It was a chronic condition with Ralph Paton," he said dryly. "Money went through his hands like water. He was always applying to his stepfather."

"Had he done so of late? During the last year, for instance?"

"I cannot say. Mr. Ackroyd did not mention the fact to me."

"I comprehend. Mr. Hammond, I take it that you are acquainted with the provisions of Mr. Ackroyd's will?"

"Certainly. That is my principal business here to-day."

"Then, seeing that I am acting for Miss Ackroyd, you will not object to telling me the terms of that will?"

"They are quite simple. Shorn of legal phraseology, and after paying certain legacies and bequests——"

"Such as——?" interrupted Poirot.

Mr. Hammond seemed a little surprised.

"A thousand pounds to his housekeeper, Miss Russell; fifty pounds to the cook, Emma Cooper; five hundred pounds to his secretary, Mr. Geoffrey Raymond. Then to various hospitals——"

Poirot held up his hand.

"Ah! the charitable bequests, they interest me not."

"Quite so. The income on ten thousand pounds' worth of shares to be paid to Mrs. Cecil Ackroyd during her lifetime. Miss Flora Ackroyd inherits twenty thousand pounds outright. The residue—including this property, and the shares in Ackroyd and Son—to his adopted son, Ralph Paton."

"Mr. Ackroyd possessed a large fortune?"

"A very large fortune. Captain Paton will be an exceedingly wealthy young man."

There was a silence. Poirot and the lawyer looked at each other.

"Mr. Hammond," came Mrs. Ackroyd's voice plaintively from the fireplace.

The lawyer answered the summons. Poirot took my arm and drew me right into the window.

"Regard the irises," he remarked in rather a loud voice. "Magnificent, are they not? A straight and pleasing effect."

At the same time I felt the pressure of his hand on my arm, and he added in a low tone:—

"Do you really wish to aid me? To take part in this investigation?"

"Yes, indeed," I said eagerly. "There's nothing I should like better. You don't know what a dull old fogey's life I lead. Never anything out of the ordinary."

"Good, we will be colleagues then. In a minute or two I fancy Major Blunt will join us. He is not happy with the good mamma. Now there are some things I want to know—but I do not wish to seem to want to know them. You comprehend? So it will be your part to ask the questions."

"What questions do you want me to ask?" I asked apprehensively.

"I want you to introduce the name of Mrs. Ferrars."

"Yes?"

"Speak of her in a natural fashion. Ask him if he was down here when her husband died. You understand the kind of thing I mean. And while he replies, watch his face without seeming to watch it. C'est compris?"

There was no time for more, for at that minute, as Poirot had prophesied, Blunt left the others in his abrupt fashion and came over to us.

I suggested strolling on the terrace, and he acquiesced. Poirot stayed behind.

I stopped to examine a late rose.

"How things change in the course of a day or so," I observed. "I was up here last Wednesday, I remember, walking up and down this same terrace. Ackroyd was with me—full of spirits. And now—three days later—Ackroyd's dead, poor fellow, Mrs. Ferrars's dead—you knew her, didn't you? But of course you did."

Blunt nodded his head.

"Had you seen her since you'd been down this time?"

"Went with Ackroyd to call. Last Tuesday, think it was. Fascinating woman—but something queer about her. Deep—one would never know what she was up to."

I looked into his steady gray eyes. Nothing there surely. I went on:—

"I suppose you'd met her before."

"Last time I was here—she and her husband had just come here to live." He paused a minute and then added: "Rum thing, she had changed a lot between then and now."

"How—changed?" I asked.

"Looked ten years older."

"Were you down here when her husband died?" I asked, trying to make the question sound as casual as possible.

"No. From all I heard it would be a good riddance. Uncharitable, perhaps, but the truth."

I agreed.

"Ashley Ferrars was by no means a pattern husband," I said cautiously.

"Blackguard, I thought," said Blunt.

"No," I said, "only a man with more money than was good for him."

"Oh! money! All the troubles in the world can be put down to money— or the lack of it."

"Which has been your particular trouble?" I asked.

"I've enough for what I want. I'm one of the lucky ones."

"Indeed."

"I'm not too flush just now, as a matter of fact. Came into a legacy a year ago, and like a fool let myself be persuaded into putting it into some wild-cat scheme."

I sympathized, and narrated my own similar trouble.

Then the gong pealed out, and we all went in to lunch. Poirot drew me back a little.

"Eh! bien?"

"He's all right," I said. "I'm sure of it."

"Nothing—disturbing?"

"He had a legacy just a year ago," I said. "But why not? Why shouldn't he? I'll swear the man is perfectly square and aboveboard."

"Without doubt, without doubt," said Poirot soothingly. "Do not upset yourself."

He spoke as though to a fractious child.

We all trooped into the dining-room. It seemed incredible that less than twenty-four hours had passed since I last sat at that table.

Afterwards, Mrs. Ackroyd took me aside and sat down with me on a sofa.

"I can't help feeling a little hurt," she murmured, producing a handkerchief of the kind obviously not meant to be cried into. "Hurt, I mean, by Roger's lack of confidence in me. That twenty thousand pounds ought to have been left to *me*—not to Flora. A mother could be trusted to safeguard the interests of her child. A lack of trust, I call it."

"You forget, Mrs. Ackroyd," I said, "Flora was Ackroyd's own niece, a blood relation. It would have been different had you been his sister instead of his sister-in-law."

"As poor Cecil's widow, I think my feelings ought to have been considered," said the lady, touching her eyelashes gingerly with the handkerchief. "But Roger was always most peculiar—not to say *mean*—about money matters. It has been a most difficult position for both Flora and myself. He did not even give the poor child an allowance. He would pay her bills, you know, and even that with a good deal of reluctance and asking what she wanted all those fal-lals for—so like a man—but—now I've forgotten what it was I was going to say! Oh, yes, not a penny we could call our own, you know. Flora resented it—yes, I must say she resented it—very strongly. Though devoted to her uncle, of course. But any girl would have resented it. Yes, I must say Roger had very strange ideas about money. He wouldn't even buy new face towels, though I told him the old ones were in holes. And then," proceeded Mrs. Ackroyd, with a sudden leap highly characteristic of her conversation, "to leave all that money—a thousand pounds—fancy, a thousand pounds!—to that woman."

"What woman?"

"That Russell woman. Something very queer about her, and so I've always said. But Roger wouldn't hear a word against her. Said she was a woman of great force of character, and that he admired and respected her. He was always going on about her rectitude and independence and moral worth. *I* think there's something fishy about her. She was certainly doing her best to marry Roger. But I soon put a stop to that. She's always hated me. Naturally. I saw through her."

I began to wonder if there was any chance of stemming Mrs. Ackroyd's eloquence, and getting away.

Mr. Hammond provided the necessary diversion by coming up to say good-by. I seized my chance and rose also.

"About the inquest," I said. "Where would you prefer it to be held. Here, or at the Three Boars?"

Mrs. Ackroyd stared at me with a dropped jaw.

"The inquest?" she asked, the picture of consternation. "But surely there won't have to be an inquest?"

Mr. Hammond gave a dry little cough and murmured, "Inevitable. Under the circumstances," in two short little barks.

"But surely Dr. Sheppard can arrange——"

"There are limits to my powers of arrangement," I said dryly.

"If his death was an accident——"

"He was murdered, Mrs. Ackroyd," I said brutally.

She gave a little cry.

"No theory of accident will hold water for a minute."

Mrs. Ackroyd looked at me in distress. I had no patience with what I thought was her silly fear of unpleasantness.

"If there's an inquest, I—I shan't have to answer questions and all that, shall I?" she asked.

"I don't know what will be necessary," I answered. "I imagine Mr. Raymond will take the brunt of it off you. He knows all the circumstances, and can give formal evidence of identification."

The lawyer assented with a little bow.

"I really don't think there is anything to dread, Mrs. Ackroyd," he said. "You will be spared all unpleasantness. Now, as to the question of money, have you all you need for the present? I mean," he added, as she looked at him inquiringly, "ready money. Cash, you know. If not, I can arrange to let you have whatever you require."

"That ought to be all right," said Raymond, who was standing by. "Mr. Ackroyd cashed a cheque for a hundred pounds yesterday."

"A hundred pounds?"

"Yes. For wages and other expenses due to-day. At the moment it is still intact."

"Where is this money? In his desk?"

"No, he always kept his cash in his bedroom. In an old collar-box, to be accurate. Funny idea, wasn't it?"

"I think," said the lawyer, "we ought to make sure the money is there before I leave."

"Certainly," agreed the secretary. "I'll take you up now. . . . Oh! I forgot. The door's locked."

Inquiry from Parker elicited the information that Inspector Raglan was in the housekeeper's room asking a few supplementary questions. A few minutes later the inspector joined the party in the hall, bringing the key with him. He unlocked the door and we passed into the lobby and up the small staircase. At the top of the stairs the door into Ackroyd's bedroom stood open. Inside the room it was dark, the curtains were drawn, and the bed was turned down just as it had been last night. The inspector drew the curtains, letting in the sunlight, and Geoffrey Raymond went to the top drawer of a rosewood bureau.

"He kept his money like that, in an unlocked drawer. Just fancy," commented the inspector.

The secretary flushed a little.

"Mr. Ackroyd had perfect faith in the honesty of all the servants," he said hotly.

"Oh! quite so," said the inspector hastily.

Raymond opened the drawer, took out a round leather collar-box from the back of it, and opening it, drew out a thick wallet.

"Here is the money," he said, taking out a fat roll of notes. "You will find the hundred intact, I know, for Mr. Ackroyd put it in the collar-box in my presence last night when he was dressing for dinner, and of course it has not been touched since."

Mr. Hammond took the roll from him and counted it. He looked up sharply.

"A hundred pounds, you said. But there is only sixty here."

Raymond stared at him.

"Impossible," he cried, springing forward. Taking the notes from the other's hand, he counted them aloud.

Mr. Hammond had been right. The total amounted to sixty pounds.

"But—I can't understand it," cried the secretary, bewildered.

Poirot asked a question.

"You saw Mr. Ackroyd put this money away last night when he was dressing for dinner? You are sure he had not paid away any of it already?"

"I'm sure he hadn't. He even said, 'I don't want to take a hundred pounds down to dinner with me. Too bulgy.'"

"Then the affair is very simple," remarked Poirot. "Either he paid out that forty pounds sometime last evening, or else it has been stolen."

"That's the matter in a nutshell," agreed the inspector. He turned to Mrs. Ackroyd. "Which of the servants would come in here yesterday evening?"

"I suppose the housemaid would turn down the bed."

"Who is she? What do you know about her?"

"She's not been here very long," said Mrs. Ackroyd. "But she's a nice ordinary country girl."

"I think we ought to clear this matter up," said the inspector. "If Mr. Ackroyd paid that money away himself, it may have a bearing on the mystery of the crime. The other servants all right, as far as you know?"

"Oh, I think so."

"Not missed anything before?"

"No."

"None of them leaving, or anything like that?"

"The parlormaid is leaving."

"When?"

"She gave notice yesterday, I believe."

"To you?"

"Oh, no. I have nothing to do with the servants. Miss Russell attends to the household matters."

The inspector remained lost in thought for a minute or two. Then he nodded his head and remarked, "I think I'd better have a word with Miss Russell, and I'll see the girl Dale as well."

Poirot and I accompanied him to the housekeeper's room. Miss Russell received us with her usual sang-froid.

Elsie Dale had been at Fernly five months. A nice girl, quick at her duties, and most respectable. Good references. The last girl in the world to take anything not belonging to her.

"What about the parlormaid?"

"She, too, was a most superior girl. Very quiet and ladylike. An excellent worker."

"Then why is she leaving?" asked the inspector.

Miss Russell pursed up her lips.

"It was none of my doing. I understand Mr. Ackroyd found fault with her yesterday afternoon. It was her duty to do the study, and she disarranged some of the papers on his desk, I believe. He was very annoyed about it, and she gave notice. At least, that is what I understood from her, but perhaps you'd like to see her yourselves?"

The inspector assented. I had already noticed the girl when she was waiting on us at lunch. A tall girl, with a lot of brown hair rolled tightly away at the back of her neck, and very steady gray eyes. She came in answer to the housekeeper's summons, and stood very straight with those same gray eyes fixed on us.

"You are Ursula Bourne?" asked the inspector.

"Yes, sir."

"I understand you are leaving?"

"Yes, sir."

"Why is that?"

"I disarranged some papers on Mr. Ackroyd's desk. He was very angry about it, and I said I had better leave. He told me to go as soon as possible."

"Were you in Mr. Ackroyd's bedroom at all last night? Tidying up or anything?"

"No, sir. That is Elsie's work. I never went near that part of the house."

"I must tell you, my girl, that a large sum of money is missing from Mr. Ackroyd's room."

At last I saw her roused. A wave of color swept over her face.

"I know nothing about any money. If you think I took it, and that that is why Mr. Ackroyd dismissed me, you are wrong."

"I'm not accusing you of taking it, my girl," said the inspector. "Don't flare up so."

The girl looked at him coldly.

"You can search my things if you like," she said disdainfully. "But you won't find anything."

Poirot suddenly interposed.

"It was yesterday afternoon that Mr. Ackroyd dismissed you—or you dismissed yourself, was it not?" he asked.

The girl nodded.

"How long did the interview last?"

"The interview?"

"Yes, the interview between you and Mr. Ackroyd in the study?"

"I—I don't know."

"Twenty minutes? Half an hour?"

"Something like that."

"Not longer?"

"Not longer than half an hour, certainly."

"Thank you, mademoiselle."

I looked curiously at him. He was rearranging a few objects on the table, setting them straight with precise fingers. His eyes were shining.

"That'll do," said the inspector.

Ursula Bourne disappeared. The inspector turned to Miss Russell.

"How long has she been here? Have you got a copy of the reference you had with her?"

Without answering the first question, Miss Russell moved to an adjacent bureau, opened one of the drawers, and took out a handful of letters clipped together with a patent fastener. She selected one and handed it to the inspector.

"H'm," said he. "Reads all right. Mrs. Richard Folliott, Marby Grange, Marby. Who's this woman?"

"Quite good county people," said Miss Russell.

"Well," said the inspector, handing it back, "let's have a look at the other one, Elsie Dale."

Elsie Dale was a big fair girl, with a pleasant but slightly stupid face. She answered our questions readily enough, and showed much distress and concern at the loss of the money.

"I don't think there's anything wrong with her," observed the inspector, after he had dismissed her.

"What about Parker?"

Miss Russell pursed her lips together and made no reply.

"I've a feeling there's something wrong about that man," the inspector continued thoughtfully. "The trouble is that I don't quite see when he got his opportunity. He'd be busy with his duties immediately after dinner, and he's got a pretty good alibi all through the evening. I know, for I've been devoting particular attention to it. Well, thank you very much, Miss Russell. We'll leave things as they are for the present. It's highly probable Mr. Ackroyd paid that money away himself."

The housekeeper bade us a dry good-afternoon, and we took our leave.

I left the house with Poirot.

"I wonder," I said, breaking the silence, "what the papers the girl disarranged could have been for Ackroyd to have got into such a state about them? I wonder if there is any clew there to the mystery?"

"The secretary said there were no papers of particular importance on the desk," said Poirot quietly.

"Yes, but——" I paused.

"It strikes you as odd that Ackroyd should have flown into a rage about so trivial a matter?"

"Yes, it does rather."

"But was it a trivial matter?"

"Of course," I admitted, "we don't know what those papers may have been. But Raymond certainly said——"

"Leave M. Raymond out of it for a minute. What did you think of that girl?"

"Which girl? The parlormaid?"

"Yes, the parlormaid. Ursula Bourne."

"She seemed a nice girl," I said hesitatingly.

Poirot repeated my words, but whereas I had laid a slight stress on the fourth word, he put it on the second.

"She *seemed* a nice girl—yes."

Then, after a minute's silence, he took something from his pocket and handed it to me.

"See, my friend, I will show you something. Look there."

The paper he had handed me was that compiled by the inspector and given by him to Poirot that morning. Following the pointing finger, I saw a small cross marked in pencil opposite the name Ursula Bourne.

"You may not have noticed it at the time, my good friend, but there was one person on this list whose alibi had no kind of confirmation. Ursula Bourne."

"You don't think——"

"Dr. Sheppard, I dare to think anything. Ursula Bourne may have killed Mr. Ackroyd, but I confess I can see no motive for her doing so. Can you?"

He looked at me very hard—so hard that I felt uncomfortable.

"Can you?" he repeated.

"No motive whatsoever," I said firmly.

His gaze relaxed. He frowned and murmured to himself:—

"Since the blackmailer was a man, it follows that she cannot be the blackmailer, then——"

I coughed.

"As far as that goes——" I began doubtfully.

He spun round on me.

"What? What are you going to say?"

"Nothing. Nothing. Only that, strictly speaking, Mrs. Ferrars in her letter mentioned a *person*—she didn't actually specify a man. But we took it for granted, Ackroyd and I, that it *was* a man."

Poirot did not seem to be listening to me. He was muttering to himself again.

"But then it is possible after all—yes, certainly it is possible—but then— ah! I must rearrange my ideas. Method, order; never have I needed them more. Everything must fit in—in its appointed place—otherwise I am on the wrong tack."

He broke off, and whirled round upon me again.

"Where is Marby?"

"It's on the other side of Cranchester."

"How far away?"

"Oh!—fourteen miles, perhaps."

"Would it be possible for you to go there? To-morrow, say?"

"To-morrow? Let me see, that's Sunday. Yes, I could arrange it. What do you want me to do there?"

"See this Mrs. Folliott. Find out all you can about Ursula Bourne."

"Very well. But—I don't much care for the job."

"It is not the time to make difficulties. A man's life may hang on this."

"Poor Ralph," I said with a sigh. "You believe him to be innocent, though?"

Poirot looked at me very gravely.

"Do you want to know the truth?"

"Of course."

"Then you shall have it. My friend, everything points to the assumption that he is guilty."

"What!" I exclaimed.

Poirot nodded.

"Yes, that stupid inspector—for he is stupid—has everything pointing his way. I seek for the truth—and the truth leads me every time to Ralph Paton. Motive, opportunity, means. But I will leave no stone unturned. I promised Mademoiselle Flora. And she was very sure, that little one. But very sure indeed."

XI. POIROT PAYS A CALL

I was slightly nervous when I rang the bell at Marby Grange the following afternoon. I wondered very much what Poirot expected to find out. He had entrusted the job to me. Why? Was it because, as in the case of questioning Major Blunt, he wished to remain in the background? The wish, intelligible in the first case, seemed to me quite meaningless here.

My meditations were interrupted by the advent of a smart parlormaid.

Yes, Mrs. Folliott was at home. I was ushered into a big drawing-room, and looked round me curiously as I waited for the mistress of the house. A large bare room, some good bits of old china, and some beautiful etchings, shabby covers and curtains. A lady's room in every sense of the term.

I turned from the inspection of a Bartolozzi on the wall as Mrs. Folliott came into the room. She was a tall woman, with untidy brown hair, and a very winning smile.

"Dr. Sheppard," she said hesitatingly.

"That is my name," I replied. "I must apologize for calling upon you like this, but I wanted some information about a parlormaid previously employed by you, Ursula Bourne."

With the utterance of the name the smile vanished from her face, and all the cordiality froze out of her manner. She looked uncomfortable and ill at ease.

"Ursula Bourne?" she said hesitatingly.

"Yes," I said. "Perhaps you don't remember the name?"

"Oh, yes, of course. I—I remember perfectly."

"She left you just over a year ago, I understand?"

"Yes. Yes, she did. That is quite right."

"And you were satisfied with her whilst she was with you? How long was she with you, by the way?"

"Oh! a year or two—I can't remember exactly how long. She—she is very capable. I'm sure you will find her quite satisfactory. I didn't know she was leaving Fernly. I hadn't the least idea of it."

"Can you tell me anything about her?" I asked.

"Anything about her?"

"Yes, where she comes from, who her people are—that sort of thing?"

Mrs. Folliott's face wore more than ever its frozen look.

"I don't know at all."

"Who was she with before she came to you?"

"I'm afraid I don't remember."

There was a spark of anger now underlying her nervousness. She flung up her head in a gesture that was vaguely familiar.

"Is it really necessary to ask all these questions?"

"Not at all," I said, with an air of surprise and a tinge of apology in my manner. "I had no idea you would mind answering them. I am very sorry."

Her anger left her and she became confused again.

"Oh! I don't mind answering them. I assure you I don't. Why should I? It—it just seemed a little odd, you know. That's all. A little odd."

One advantage of being a medical practitioner is that you can usually tell when people are lying to you. I should have known from Mrs. Folliott's manner, if from nothing else, that she did mind answering my questions— minded intensely. She was thoroughly uncomfortable and upset, and there was plainly some mystery in the background. I judged her to be a woman quite unused to deception of any kind, and consequently rendered acutely uneasy when forced to practice it. A child could have seen through her.

But it was also clear that she had no intention of telling me anything further. Whatever the mystery centering around Ursula Bourne might be, I was not going to learn it through Mrs. Folliott.

Defeated, I apologized once more for disturbing her, took my hat and departed.

I went to see a couple of patients and arrived home about six o'clock. Caroline was sitting beside the wreck of tea things. She had that look of suppressed exultation on her face which I know only too well. It is a sure sign with her, of either the getting or the giving of information. I wondered which it had been.

"I've had a very interesting afternoon," began Caroline as I dropped into my own particular easy chair, and stretched out my feet to the inviting blaze in the fireplace.

"Have you?" I asked. "Miss Ganett drop in to tea?"

Miss Ganett is one of the chief of our newsmongers.

"Guess again," said Caroline with intense complacency.

I guessed several times, working slowly through all the members of Caroline's Intelligence Corps. My sister received each guess with a triumphant shake of the head. In the end she volunteered the information herself.

"M. Poirot!" she said. "Now what do you think of that?"

I thought a good many things of it, but I was careful not to say them to Caroline.

"Why did he come?" I asked.

"To see me, of course. He said that knowing my brother so well, he hoped he might be permitted to make the acquaintance of his charming sister—your charming sister, I've got mixed up, but you know what I mean."

"What did he talk about?" I asked.

"He told me a lot about himself and his cases. You know that Prince Paul of Mauretania—the one who's just married a dancer?"

"Yes?"

"I saw a most intriguing paragraph about her in Society Snippets the other day, hinting that she was really a Russian Grand Duchess—one of the Czar's daughters who managed to escape from the Bolsheviks. Well, it seems that M. Poirot solved a baffling murder mystery that threatened to involve them both. Prince Paul was beside himself with gratitude."

"Did he give him an emerald tie pin the size of a plover's egg?" I inquired sarcastically.

"He didn't mention it. Why?"

"Nothing," I said. "I thought it was always done. It is in detective fiction anyway. The super detective always has his rooms littered with rubies and pearls and emeralds from grateful Royal clients."

"It's very interesting to hear about these things from the inside," said my sister complacently.

It would be—to Caroline. I could not but admire the ingenuity of M. Hercule Poirot, who had selected unerringly the case of all others that would most appeal to an elderly maiden lady living in a small village.

"Did he tell you if the dancer was really a Grand Duchess?" I inquired.

"He was not at liberty to speak," said Caroline importantly.

I wondered how far Poirot had strained the truth in talking to Caroline—probably not at all. He had conveyed his innuendoes by means of his eyebrows and his shoulders.

"And after all this," I remarked, "I suppose you were ready to eat out of his hand."

"Don't be coarse, James. I don't know where you get these vulgar expressions from."

"Probably from my only link with the outside world—my patients. Unfortunately my practice does not lie amongst Royal princes and interesting Russian émigrés."

Caroline pushed her spectacles up and looked at me.

"You seem very grumpy, James. It must be your liver. A blue pill, I think, to-night."

To see me in my own home, you would never imagine that I was a doctor of medicine. Caroline does the home prescribing both for herself and me.

"Damn my liver," I said irritably. "Did you talk about the murder at all?"

"Well, naturally, James. What else is there to talk about locally? I was able to set M. Poirot right upon several points. He was very grateful to me. He said I had the makings of a born detective in me—and a wonderful psychological insight into human nature."

Caroline was exactly like a cat that is full to overflowing with rich cream. She was positively purring.

"He talked a lot about the little gray cells of the brain, and of their functions. His own, he says, are of the first quality."

"He would say so," I remarked bitterly. "Modesty is certainly not his middle name."

"I wish you would not be so horribly American, James. He thought it very important that Ralph should be found as soon as possible, and induced to come forward and give an account of himself. He says that his disappearance will produce a very unfortunate impression at the inquest."

"And what did you say to that?"

"I agreed with him," said Caroline importantly. "And I was able to tell him the way people were already talking about it."

"Caroline," I said sharply, "did you tell M. Poirot what you overheard in the wood that day?"

"I did," said Caroline complacently.

I got up and began to walk about.

"You realize what you're doing, I hope," I jerked out. "You're putting a halter round Ralph Paton's neck as surely as you're sitting in that chair."

"Not at all," said Caroline, quite unruffled. "I was surprised *you* hadn't told him."

"I took very good care not to," I said. "I'm fond of that boy."

"So am I. That's why I say you're talking nonsense. I don't believe Ralph did it, and so the truth can't hurt him, and we ought to give M. Poirot all the help we can. Why, think, very likely Ralph was out with that identical girl on the night of the murder, and if so, he's got a perfect alibi."

"If he's got a perfect alibi," I retorted, "why doesn't he come forward and say so?"

"Might get the girl into trouble," said Caroline sapiently. "But if M. Poirot gets hold of her, and puts it to her as her duty, she'll come forward of her own accord and clear Ralph."

"You seem to have invented a romantic fairy story of your own," I said. "You read too many trashy novels, Caroline. I've always told you so."

I dropped into my chair again.

"Did Poirot ask you any more questions?" I inquired.

"Only about the patients you had that morning."

"The patients?" I demanded, unbelievingly.

"Yes, your surgery patients. How many and who they were."

"Do you mean to say you were able to tell him that?" I demanded.

Caroline is really amazing.

"Why not?" asked my sister triumphantly. "I can see the path up to the surgery door perfectly from this window. And I've got an excellent memory, James. Much better than yours, let me tell you."

"I'm sure you have," I murmured mechanically.

My sister went on, checking the names on her fingers.

"There was old Mrs. Bennett, and that boy from the farm with the bad finger, Dolly Grice to have a needle out of her finger; that American steward off the liner. Let me see—that's four. Yes, and old George Evans with his ulcer. And lastly——"

She paused significantly.

"Well?"

Caroline brought out her climax triumphantly. She hissed in the most approved style—aided by the fortunate number of s's at her disposal.

"*Miss Russell!*"

She sat back in her chair and looked at me meaningly, and when Caroline looks at you meaningly, it is impossible to miss it.

"I don't know what you mean," I said, quite untruthfully. "Why shouldn't Miss Russell consult me about her bad knee?"

"Bad knee," said Caroline. "Fiddlesticks! No more bad knee than you and I. She was after something else."

"What?" I asked.

Caroline had to admit that she didn't know.

"But depend upon it, that was what he was trying to get at, M. Poirot, I mean. There's something fishy about that woman, and he knows it."

"Precisely the remark Mrs. Ackroyd made to me yesterday," I said. "That there was something fishy about Miss Russell."

"Ah!" said Caroline darkly, "Mrs. Ackroyd! There's another!"

"Another what?"

Caroline refused to explain her remarks. She merely nodded her head several times, rolled up her knitting, and went upstairs to don the high mauve silk blouse and the gold locket which she calls dressing for dinner.

I stayed there staring into the fire and thinking over Caroline's words. Had Poirot really come to gain information about Miss Russell, or was it only Caroline's tortuous mind that interpreted everything according to her own ideas?

There had certainly been nothing in Miss Russell's manner that morning to arouse suspicion. At least——

I remembered her persistent conversation on the subject of drug-taking and from that she had led the conversation to poisons and poisoning. But there was nothing in that. Ackroyd had not been poisoned. Still, it was odd. . . .

I heard Caroline's voice, rather acid in note, calling from the top of the stairs.

"James, you will be late for dinner."

I put some coal on the fire and went upstairs obediently.

It is well at any price to have peace in the home.

XII. ROUND THE TABLE

A joint inquest was held on Monday.

I do not propose to give the proceedings in detail. To do so would only be to go over the same ground again and again. By arrangement with the police, very little was allowed to come out. I gave evidence as to the cause of Ackroyd's death and the probable time. The absence of Ralph Paton was commented on by the coroner, but not unduly stressed.

Afterwards, Poirot and I had a few words with Inspector Raglan. The inspector was very grave.

"It looks bad, Mr. Poirot," he said. "I'm trying to judge the thing fair and square. I'm a local man, and I've seen Captain Paton many times in Cranchester. I'm not wanting him to be the guilty one—but it's bad whichever way you look at it. If he's innocent, why doesn't he come forward? We've got evidence against him, but it's just possible that that evidence could be explained away. Then why doesn't he give an explanation?"

A lot more lay behind the inspector's words than I knew at the time. Ralph's description had been wired to every port and railway station in England. The police everywhere were on the alert. His rooms in town were watched, and any houses he had been known to be in the habit of frequenting. With such a *cordon* it seemed impossible that Ralph should be able to evade detection. He had no lugguage, and, as far as any one knew, no money.

"I can't find any one who saw him at the station that night," continued the inspector. "And yet he's well known down here, and you'd think somebody would have noticed him. There's no news from Liverpool either."

"You think he went to Liverpool?" queried Poirot.

"Well, it's on the cards. That telephone message from the station, just three minutes before the Liverpool express left—there ought to be something in that."

"Unless it was deliberately intended to throw you off the scent. That might just possibly be the point of the telephone message."

"That's an idea," said the inspector eagerly. "Do you really think that's the explanation of the telephone call?"

"My friend," said Poirot gravely, "I do not know. But I will tell you this: I believe that when we find the explanation of that telephone call we shall find the explanation of the murder."

"You said something like that before, I remember," I observed, looking at him curiously.

Poirot nodded.

"I always come back to it," he said seriously.

"It seems to me utterly irrelevant," I declared.

"I wouldn't say that," demurred the inspector. "But I must confess I think Mr. Poirot here harps on it a little too much. We've better clews than that. The fingerprints on the dagger, for instance."

Poirot became suddenly very foreign in manner, as he often did when excited over anything.

"M. l'Inspecteur," he said, "beware of the blind—the blind—*comment dire?* —the little street that has no end to it."

Inspector Raglan stared, but I was quicker.

"You mean a blind alley?" I said.

"That is it—the blind street that leads nowhere. So it may be with those fingerprints—they may lead you nowhere."

"I don't see how that can well be," said the police officer. "I suppose you're hinting that they're faked? I've read of such things being done, though I can't say I've ever come across it in my experience. But fake or true—they're bound to lead *somewhere*."

Poirot merely shrugged his shoulders, flinging out his arms wide.

The inspector then showed us various enlarged photographs of the fingerprints, and proceeded to become technical on the subject of loops and whorls.

"Come now," he said at last, annoyed by Poirot's detached manner, "you've got to admit that those prints were made by some one who was in the house that night?"

"*Bien entendu,*" said Poirot, nodding his head.

"Well, I've taken the prints of every member of the household, every one, mind you, from the old lady down to the kitchenmaid."

I don't think Mrs. Ackroyd would enjoy being referred to as the old lady. She must spend a considerable amount on cosmetics.

"Every one's," repeated the inspector fussily.

"Including mine," I said dryly.

"Very well. None of them correspond. That leaves us two alternatives. Ralph Paton, or the mysterious stranger the doctor here tells us about. When we get hold of those two——"

"Much valuable time may have been lost," broke in Poirot.

"I don't quite get you, Mr. Poirot."

"You have taken the prints of every one in the house, you say," murmured Poirot. "Is that the exact truth you are telling me there, M. l'Inspecteur?"

"Certainly."

"Without overlooking any one?"

"Without overlooking any one."

"The quick or the dead?"

For a moment the inspector looked bewildered at what he took to be a religious observation. Then he reacted slowly.

"You mean——"

"The dead, M. l'Inspecteur."

The inspector still took a minute or two to understand.

"I am suggesting," said Poirot placidly, "that the fingerprints on the dagger handle are those of Mr. Ackroyd himself. It is an easy matter to verify. His body is still available."

"But why? What would be the point of it? You're surely not suggesting suicide, Mr. Poirot?"

"Ah! no. My theory is that the murderer wore gloves or wrapped something round his hand. After the blow was struck, he picked up the victim's hand and closed it round the dagger handle."

"But why?"

Poirot shrugged his shoulders again.

"To make a confusing case even more confusing."

"Well," said the inspector, "I'll look into it. What gave you the idea in the first place?"

"When you were so kind as to show me the dagger and draw attention to the fingerprints. I know very little of loops and whorls—see, I confess my ignorance frankly. But it did occur to me that the position of the prints was somewhat awkward. Not so would I have held a dagger in order to strike. Naturally, with the right hand brought up over the shoulder backwards, it would have been difficult to put it in exactly the right position."

Inspector Raglan stared at the little man. Poirot, with an air of great unconcern, flecked a speck of dust from his coat sleeve.

"Well," said the inspector, "it's an idea. I'll look into it all right, but don't you be disappointed if nothing comes of it."

He endeavored to make his tone kindly and patronizing. Poirot watched him go off. Then he turned to me with twinkling eyes.

"Another time," he observed, "I must be more careful of his *amour propre*. And now that we are left to our own devices, what do you think, my good friend, of a little reunion of the family?"

The "little reunion," as Poirot called it, took place about half an hour later. We sat round the table in the dining-room at Fernly—Poirot at the head of the table, like the chairman of some ghastly board meeting. The servants were not present, so we were six in all. Mrs. Ackroyd, Flora, Major Blunt, young Raymond, Poirot, and myself.

When every one was assembled, Poirot rose and bowed.

"Messieurs, mesdames, I have called you together for a certain purpose." He paused. "To begin with, I want to make a very special plea to mademoiselle."

"To me?" said Flora.

"Mademoiselle, you are engaged to Captain Ralph Paton. If any one is in his confidence, you are. I beg you, most earnestly, if you know of his whereabouts, to persuade him to come forward. One little minute"—as Flora raised her head to speak—"say nothing till you have well reflected. Mademoiselle, his position grows daily more dangerous. If he had come forward at once, no matter how damning the facts, he might have had a chance of explaining them away. But this silence—this flight—what can it mean? Surely only one thing, knowledge of guilt. Mademoiselle, if you really believe in his innocence, persuade him to come forward before it is too late."

Flora's face had gone very white.

"Too late!" she repeated, very low.

Poirot leant forward, looking at her.

"See now, mademoiselle," he said very gently, "it is Papa Poirot who asks you this. The old Papa Poirot who has much knowledge and much experience. I would not seek to entrap you, mademoiselle. Will you not trust me—and tell me where Ralph Paton is hiding?"

The girl rose, and stood facing him.

"M. Poirot," she said in a clear voice, "I swear to you—swear solemnly—that I have no idea where Ralph is, and that I have neither seen him nor heard from him either on the day of—of the murder, or since."

She sat down again. Poirot gazed at her in silence for a minute or two, then he brought his hand down on the table with a sharp rap.

"*Bien!* That is that," he said. His face hardened. "Now I appeal to these others who sit round this table, Mrs. Ackroyd, Major Blunt, Dr. Sheppard, Mr. Raymond. You are all friends and intimates of the missing man. If you know where Ralph Paton is hiding, speak out."

There was a long silence. Poirot looked to each in turn.

"I beg of you," he said in a low voice, "speak out."

But still there was silence, broken at last by Mrs. Ackroyd.

"I must say," she observed in a plaintive voice, "that Ralph's absence is most peculiar—most peculiar indeed. Not to come forward at such a time. It looks, you know, as though there were something *behind* it. I can't help thinking, Flora dear, that it was a very fortunate thing your engagement was never formally announced."

"Mother!" cried Flora angrily.

"Providence," declared Mrs. Ackroyd. "I have a devout belief in Providence —a divinity that shapes our ends, as Shakespeare's beautiful line runs."

"Surely you don't make the Almighty directly responsible for thick ankles, Mrs. Ackroyd, do you?" asked Geoffrey Raymond, his irresponsible laugh ringing out.

His idea was, I think, to loosen the tension, but Mrs. Ackroyd threw him a glance of reproach and took out her handkerchief.

"Flora has been saved a terrible amount of notoriety and unpleasantness. Not for a moment that I think dear Ralph had anything to do with poor Roger's death. I *don't* think so. But then I have a trusting heart—I always have had, ever since a child. I am loath to believe the worst of any one. But, of course, one must remember that Ralph was in several air raids as a young boy. The results are apparent long after, sometimes, they say. People are not responsible for their actions in the least. They lose control, you know, without being able to help it."

"Mother," cried Flora, "you don't think Ralph did it?"

"Come, Mrs. Ackroyd," said Blunt.

"I don't know what to think," said Mrs. Ackroyd tearfully. "It's all very upsetting. What would happen to the estate, I wonder, if Ralph were found guilty?"

Raymond pushed his chair away from the table violently. Major Blunt remained very quiet, looking thoughtfully at her. "Like shell-shock, you know," said Mrs. Ackroyd obstinately, "and I dare say Roger kept him very short of money—with the best intentions, of course. I can see you are all against me, but I do think it is very odd that Ralph has not come forward, and I must say I am thankful Flora's engagement was never announced formally."

"It will be to-morrow," said Flora in a clear voice.

"Flora!" cried her mother, aghast.

Flora had turned to the secretary.

"Will you send the announcement to the *Morning Post* and the *Times*, please, Mr. Raymond."

"If you are sure that it is wise, Miss Ackroyd," he replied gravely.

She turned impulsively to Blunt.

"You understand," she said. "What else can I do? As things are, I must stand by Ralph. Don't you see that I must?"

She looked very searchingly at him, and after a long pause he nodded abruptly.

Mrs. Ackroyd burst out into shrill protests. Flora remained unmoved. Then Raymond spoke.

"I appreciate your motives, Miss Ackroyd. But don't you think you're being rather precipitate? Wait a day or two."

"To-morrow," said Flora, in a clear voice. "It's no good, mother, going on like this. Whatever else I am, I'm not disloyal to my friends."

"M. Poirot," Mrs. Ackroyd appealed tearfully, "can't you say anything at all?"

"Nothing to be said," interpolated Blunt. "She's doing the right thing. I'll stand by her through thick and thin."

Flora held out her hand to him.

"Thank you, Major Blunt," she said.

"Mademoiselle," said Poirot, "will you let an old man congratulate you on your courage and your loyalty? And will you not misunderstand me if I ask you—ask you most solemnly—to postpone the announcement you speak of for at least two days more?"

Flora hesitated.

"I asked it in Ralph Paton's interests as much as in yours, mademoiselle. You frown. You do not see how that can be. But I assure you that it is so. *Pas de blagues*. You put the case into my hands—you must not hamper me now."

Flora paused a few minutes before replying.

"I do not like it," she said at last, "but I will do what you say."

She sat down again at the table.

"And now, messieurs et mesdames," said Poirot rapidly, "I will continue with what I was about to say. Understand this, I mean to arrive at the truth. The truth, however ugly in itself, is always curious and beautiful to the seeker after it. I am much aged, my powers may not be what they were." Here he clearly expected a contradiction. "In all probability this is the last case I shall ever investigate. But Hercule Poirot does not end with a failure. Messieurs et mesdames, I tell you, I mean to *know*. And I shall know—in spite of you all."

He brought out the last words provocatively, hurling them in our face as it were. I think we all flinched back a little, excepting Geoffrey Raymond, who remained good humored and imperturbable as usual.

"How do you mean—in spite of us all?" he asked, with slightly raised eyebrows.

"But—just that, monsieur. Every one of you in this room is concealing something from me." He raised his hand as a faint murmur of protest arose. "Yes, yes, I know what I am saying. It may be something unimportant—trivial—which is supposed to have no bearing on the case, but there it is. *Each one of you has something to hide.* Come, now, am I right?"

His glance, challenging and accusing, swept round the table. And every pair of eyes dropped before his. Yes, mine as well.

"I am answered," said Poirot, with a curious laugh. He got up from his seat. "I appeal to you all. Tell me the truth—the whole truth." There was a silence. "Will no one speak?"

He gave the same short laugh again.

"*C'est dommage,*" he said, and went out.

XIII. THE GOOSE QUILL

That evening, at Poirot's request, I went over to his house after dinner. Caroline saw me depart with visible reluctance. I think she would have liked to have accompanied me.

Poirot greeted me hospitably. He had placed a bottle of Irish whisky (which I detest) on a small table, with a soda water siphon and a glass. He himself was engaged in brewing hot chocolate. It was a favorite beverage of his, I discovered later.

He inquired politely after my sister, whom he declared to be a most interesting woman.

"I'm afraid you've been giving her a swelled head," I said dryly. "What about Sunday afternoon?"

He laughed and twinkled.

"I always like to employ the expert," he remarked obscurely, but he refused to explain the remark.

"You got all the local gossip anyway," I remarked. "True, and untrue."

"And a great deal of valuable information," he added quietly.

"Such as——?"

He shook his head.

"Why not have told me the truth?" he countered. "In a place like this, all Ralph Paton's doings were bound to be known. If your sister had not happened to pass through the wood that day somebody else would have done so."

"I suppose they would," I said grumpily. "What about this interest of yours in my patients?"

Again he twinkled.

"Only one of them, doctor. Only one of them."

"The last?" I hazarded.

"I find Miss Russell a study of the most interesting," he said evasively.

"Do you agree with my sister and Mrs. Ackroyd that there is something fishy about her?" I asked.

"Eh? What do you say—fishy?"

I explained to the best of my ability.

"And they say that, do they?"

"Didn't my sister convey as much to you yesterday afternoon?"

"*C'est possible.*"

"For no reason whatever," I declared.

"*Les femmes,*" generalized Poirot. "They are marvelous! They invent haphazard—and by miracle they are right. Not that it is that, really. Women observe subconsciously a thousand little details, without knowing that they are doing so. Their subconscious mind adds these little things together—and they call the result intuition. Me, I am very skilled in psychology. I know these things."

He swelled his chest out importantly, looking so ridiculous, that I found it difficult not to burst out laughing. Then he took a small sip of his chocolate, and carefully wiped his mustache.

"I wish you'd tell me," I burst out, "what you really think of it all?"

He put down his cup.

"You wish that?"

"I do."

"You have seen what I have seen. Should not our ideas be the same?"

"I'm afraid you're laughing at me," I said stiffly. "Of course, I've no experience of matters of this kind."

Poirot smiled at me indulgently.

"You are like the little child who wants to know the way the engine works. You wish to see the affair, not as the family doctor sees it, but with the eye of a detective who knows and cares for no one—to whom they are all strangers and all equally liable to suspicion."

"You put it very well," I said.

"So I give you then, a little lecture. The first thing is to get a clear history of what happened that evening—always bearing in mind that the person who speaks may be lying."

I raised my eyebrows.

"Rather a suspicious attitude."

"But necessary—I assure you, necessary. Now first—Dr. Sheppard leaves the house at ten minutes to nine. How do I know that?"

"Because I told you so."

"But you might not be speaking the truth—or the watch you went by might be wrong. But Parker also says that you left the house at ten minutes to nine. So we accept that statement and pass on. At nine o'clock you run into a man—and here we come to what we will call the Romance of the Mysterious Stranger—just outside the Park gates. How do I know that that is so?"

"I told you so," I began again, but Poirot interrupted me with a gesture of impatience.

"Ah! but it is that you are a little stupid to-night, my friend. *You* know that it is so—but how am *I* to know? *Eh bien*, I am able to tell you that the Mysterious Stranger was not a hallucination on your part, because the maid of a Miss Ganett met him a few minutes before you did, and of her too he inquired the way to Fernly Park. We accept his presence, therefore, and we can be fairly sure of two things about him—that he was a stranger to the neighborhood, and that whatever his object in going to Fernly, there was no great secrecy about it, since he twice asked the way there."

"Yes," I said, "I see that."

"Now I have made it my business to find out more about this man. He had a drink at the Three Boars, I learn, and the barmaid there says that he spoke with an American accent and mentioned having just come over from the States. Did it strike you that he had an American accent?"

"Yes, I think he had," I said, after a minute or two, during which I cast my mind back; "but a very slight one."

"*Précisément*. There is also this which, you will remember, I picked up in the summer-house?"

He held out to me the little quill. I looked at it curiously. Then a memory of something I had read stirred in me.

Poirot, who had been watching my face, nodded.

"Yes, heroin 'snow.' Drug-takers carry it like this, and sniff it up the nose."

"Diamorphine hydrochloride," I murmured mechanically.

"This method of taking the drug is very common on the other side. Another proof, if we wanted one, that the man came from Canada or the States."

"What first attracted your attention to that summer-house?" I asked curiously.

"My friend the inspector took it for granted that any one using that path did so as a short cut to the house, but as soon as I saw the summer-house, I realized that the same path would be taken by any one using the summer-house as a rendezvous. Now it seems fairly certain that the stranger came neither to the front nor to the back door. Then did some one from the house go out and meet him? If so, what could be a more convenient place than that little summer-house? I searched it with the hope that I might find some clew inside. I found two, the scrap of cambric and the quill."

"And the scrap of cambric?" I asked curiously. "What about that?"

Poirot raised his eyebrows.

"You do not use your little gray cells," he remarked dryly. "The scrap of starched cambric should be obvious."

"Not very obvious to me." I changed the subject. "Anyway," I said, "this man went to the summer-house to meet somebody. Who was that somebody?"

"Exactly the question," said Poirot. "You will remember that Mrs. Ackroyd and her daughter came over from Canada to live here?"

"Is that what you meant to-day when you accused them of hiding the truth?"

"Perhaps. Now another point. What did you think of the parlormaid's story?"

"What story?"

"The story of her dismissal. Does it take half an hour to dismiss a servant? Was the story of those important papers a likely one? And remember, though she says she was in her bedroom from nine-thirty until ten o'clock, there is no one to confirm her statement."

"You bewilder me," I said.

"To me it grows clearer. But tell me now your own ideas and theories."

I drew a piece of paper from my pocket.

"I just scribbled down a few suggestions," I said apologetically.

"But excellent—you have method. Let us hear them."

I read out in a somewhat embarrassed voice.

"To begin with, one must look at the thing logically——"

"Just what my poor Hastings used to say," interrupted Poirot, "but alas! he never did so."

"*Point No.* 1.—Mr. Ackroyd was heard talking to some one at half-past nine.

"*Point No.* 2.—At some time during the evening Ralph Paton must have come in through the window, as evidenced by the prints of his shoes.

"*Point No.* 3.—Mr. Ackroyd was nervous that evening, and would only have admitted some one he knew.

"*Point No.* 4.—The person with Mr. Ackroyd at nine-thirty was asking for money. We know Ralph Paton was in a scrape.

"*These four points go to show that the person with Mr. Ackroyd at nine-thirty was Ralph Paton. But we know that Mr. Ackroyd was alive at a quarter to ten, therefore it was not Ralph who killed him. Ralph left the window open. Afterwards the murderer came in that way.*"

"And who was the murderer?" inquired Poirot.

"The American stranger. He may have been in league with Parker, and possibly in Parker we have the man who blackmailed Mrs. Ferrars. If so, Parker may have heard enough to realize the game was up, have told his accomplice so, and the latter did the crime with the dagger which Parker gave him."

"It is a theory that," admitted Poirot. "Decidedly you have cells of a kind. But it leaves a good deal unaccounted for."

"Such as——?"

"The telephone call, the pushed-out chair——"

"Do you really think the latter important?" I interrupted.

"Perhaps not," admitted my friend. "It may have been pulled out by accident, and Raymond or Blunt may have shoved it into place unconsciously under the stress of emotion. Then there is the missing forty pounds."

"Given by Ackroyd to Ralph," I suggested. "He may have reconsidered his first refusal."

"That still leaves one thing unexplained."

"What?"

"Why was Blunt so certain in his own mind that it was Raymond with Mr. Ackroyd at nine-thirty?"

"He explained that," I said.

"You think so? I will not press the point. Tell me instead, what were Ralph Paton's reasons for disappearing?"

"That's rather more difficult," I said slowly. "I shall have to speak as a medical man. Ralph's nerves must have gone phut! If he suddenly found out that his uncle had been murdered within a few minutes of his leaving him—after, perhaps, a rather stormy interview—well, he might get the wind up and clear right out. Men have been known to do that—act guiltily when they're perfectly innocent."

"Yes, that is true," said Poirot. "But we must not lose sight of one thing."

"I know what you're going to say," I remarked: "motive. Ralph Paton inherits a great fortune by his uncle's death."

"That is one motive," agreed Poirot.

"One?"

"*Mais oui.* Do you realize that there are three separate motives staring us in the face? Somebody certainly stole the blue envelope and its contents. That is one motive. Blackmail! Ralph Paton may have been the man who blackmailed Mrs. Ferrars. Remember, as far as Hammond knew, Ralph Paton had not applied to his stepfather for help of late. That looks as though he were being supplied with money elsewhere. Then there is the fact that he was in some—how do you say—scrape?—which he feared might get to his stepfather's ears. And finally there is the one you have just mentioned."

"Dear me," I said, rather taken aback. "The case does seem black against him."

"Does it?" said Poirot. "That is where we disagree, you and I. Three motives—it is almost too much. I am inclined to believe that, after all, Ralph Paton is innocent."

XIV. MRS. ACKROYD

After the evening talk I have just chronicled, the affair seemed to me to enter on a different phase. The whole thing can be divided into two parts, each clear and distinct from the other. Part I. ranges from Ackroyd's death on the Friday evening to the following Monday night. It is the straightforward narrative of what occurred, as presented to Hercule Poirot. I was at Poirot's elbow the whole time. I saw what he saw. I tried my best to read his mind. As I know now, I failed in this latter task. Though Poirot showed me all his discoveries—as, for instance, the gold wedding ring—he held back the vital and yet logical impressions that he formed. As I came to know later, this secrecy was characteristic of him. He would throw out hints and suggestions, but beyond that he would not go.

As I say, up till the Monday evening, my narrative might have been that of Poirot himself. I played Watson to his Sherlock. But after Monday our ways diverged. Poirot was busy on his own account. I got to hear of what he was doing, because, in King's Abbot, you get to hear of everything, but he did not take me into his confidence beforehand. And I, too, had my own preoccupations.

On looking back, the thing that strikes me most is the piecemeal character of this period. Every one had a hand in the elucidation of the mystery. It was rather like a jig-saw puzzle to which every one contributed their own little piece of knowledge or discovery. But their task ended there. To Poirot alone belongs the renown of fitting those pieces into their correct place.

Some of the incidents seemed at the time irrelevant and unmeaning. There was, for instance, the question of the black boots. But that comes later. . . . To take things strictly in chronological order, I must begin with the summons from Mrs. Ackroyd.

She sent for me early on Tuesday morning, and since the summons sounded an urgent one, I hastened there, expecting to find her *in extremis*.

The lady was in bed. So much did she concede to the etiquette of the situation. She gave me her bony hand, and indicated a chair drawn up to the bedside.

"Well, Mrs. Ackroyd," I said, "and what's the matter with you?"

I spoke with that kind of spurious geniality which seems to be expected of general practitioners.

"I'm prostrated," said Mrs. Ackroyd in a faint voice. "Absolutely prostrated. It's the shock of poor Roger's death. They say these things often aren't felt at the *time*, you know. It's the reaction afterwards."

It is a pity that a doctor is precluded by his profession from being able sometimes to say what he really thinks.

I would have given anything to be able to answer "Bunkum!"

Instead, I suggested a tonic. Mrs. Ackroyd accepted the tonic. One move in the game seemed now to be concluded. Not for a moment did I imagine that I had been sent for because of the shock occasioned by Ackroyd's death. But Mrs. Ackroyd is totally incapable of pursuing a straight-forward course on any subject. She always approaches her object by tortuous means. I wondered very much why it was she had sent for me.

"And then that scene—yesterday," continued my patient.

She paused as though expecting me to take up a cue.

"What scene?"

"Doctor, how can you? Have you forgotten? That dreadful little Frenchman—or Belgian—or whatever he is. Bullying us all like he did. It has quite upset me. Coming on top of Roger's death."

"I'm very sorry, Mrs. Ackroyd," I said.

"I don't know what he meant—shouting at us like he did. I should hope I know my duty too well to *dream* of concealing anything. I have given the police *every* assistance in my power."

Mrs. Ackroyd paused, and I said, "Quite so." I was beginning to have a glimmering of what all the trouble was about.

"No one can say that I have failed in my duty," continued Mrs. Ackroyd. "I am sure Inspector Raglan is perfectly satisfied. Why should this little up-start of a foreigner make a fuss? A most ridiculous-looking creature he is too—just like a comic Frenchman in a revue. I can't think why Flora in-sisted on bringing him into the case. She never said a word to me about it. Just went off and did it on her own. Flora is too independent. I am a woman of the world and her mother. She should have come to me for advice first."

I listened to all this in silence.

"What does he think? That's what I want to know. Does he actually imagine I'm hiding something? He—he—positively *accused* me yesterday."

I shrugged my shoulders.

"It is surely of no consequence, Mrs. Ackroyd," I said. "Since you are not concealing anything, any remarks he may have made do not apply to you."

Mrs. Ackroyd went off at a tangent, after her usual fashion.

"Servants are so tiresome," she said. "They gossip, and talk amongst them-selves. And then it gets round—and all the time there's probably nothing in it at all."

"Have the servants been talking?" I asked. "What about?"

Mrs. Ackroyd cast a very shrewd glance at me. It quite threw me off my balance.

"I was sure *you'd* know, doctor, if any one did. You were with M. Poirot all the time, weren't you?"

"I was."

"Then of course you know. It was that girl, Ursula Bourne, wasn't it? Naturally—she's leaving. She *would* want to make all the trouble she could. Spiteful, that's what they are. They're all alike. Now, you being there, doctor, you must know exactly what she did say? I'm most anxious that no wrong impression should get about. After all, you don't repeat every little detail to the police, do you? There are family matters sometimes—nothing to do with the question of the murder. But if the girl was spiteful, she may have made out all sorts of things."

I was shrewd enough to see that a very real anxiety lay behind these out-pourings. Poirot had been justified in his premises. Of the six people round the table yesterday, Mrs. Ackroyd at least had had something to hide. It was for me to discover what that something might be.

"If I were you, Mrs. Ackroyd," I said brusquely, "I should make a clean breast of things."

She gave a little scream.

"Oh! doctor, how can you be so abrupt. It sounds as though—as though—— And I can explain everything so simply."

"Then why not do so," I suggested.

Mrs. Ackroyd took out a frilled handkerchief, and became tearful.

"I thought, doctor, that you might put it to M. Poirot—explain it, you know—because it's so difficult for a foreigner to see our point of view. And you don't know—nobody could know—what I've had to contend with. A martyrdom—a long martyrdom. That's what my life has been. I don't like to speak ill of the dead—but there it is. Not the smallest bill, but it had all to be gone over—just as though Roger had had a few miserly hundreds a year instead of being (as Mr. Hammond told me yesterday) one of the wealthiest men in these parts."

Mrs. Ackroyd paused to dab her eyes with the frilled handkerchief.

"Yes," I said encouragingly. "You were talking about bills?"

"Those dreadful bills. And some I didn't like to show Roger at all. They were things a man wouldn't understand. He would have said the things weren't necessary. And of course they mounted up, you know, and they kept coming in——"

She looked at me appealingly, as though asking me to condole with her on this striking peculiarity.

"It's a habit they have," I agreed.

And the tone altered—became quite abusive. "I assure you, doctor, I was becoming a nervous wreck. I couldn't sleep at nights. And a dreadful fluttering round the heart. And then I got a letter from a Scotch gentleman—as a matter of fact there were two letters—both Scotch gentlemen. Mr. Bruce MacPherson was one, and the other was Colin MacDonald. Quite a coincidence."

"Hardly that," I said dryly. "They are usually Scotch gentlemen, but I suspect a foreign strain in their ancestry."

"Ten pounds to ten thousand on note of hand alone," murmured Mrs. Ackroyd reminiscently. "I wrote to one of them, but it seemed there were difficulties."

She paused.

I gathered that we were just coming to delicate ground. I have never known any one more difficult to bring to the point.

"You see," murmured Mrs. Ackroyd, "it's all a question of expectations, isn't it? Testamentary expectations. And though, of course, I expected that Roger would provide for me, I didn't *know*. I thought that if only I could glance over a copy of his will—not in any sense of vulgar prying—but just so that I could make my own arrangements."

She glanced sideways at me. The position was now very delicate indeed. Fortunately words, ingeniously used, will serve to mask the ugliness of naked facts.

"I could only tell this to you, dear Dr. Sheppard," said Mrs. Ackroyd rapidly. "I can trust you not to misjudge me, and to represent the matter in the right light to M. Poirot. It was on Friday afternoon——"

She came to a stop and swallowed uncertainly.

"Yes," I repeated encouragingly. "On Friday afternoon. Well?"

"Every one was out, or so I thought. And I went into Roger's study—I had some real reason for going there—I mean, there was nothing underhand about it. And as I saw all the papers heaped on the desk, it just came to me, like a flash: 'I wonder if Roger keeps his will in one of the drawers of the desk.' I'm so impulsive, always was, from a child. I do things on the spur of the moment. He'd left his keys—very careless of him—in the lock of the top drawer."

"I see," I said helpfully. "So you searched the desk. Did you find the will?"

Mrs. Ackroyd gave a little scream, and I realized that I had not been sufficiently diplomatic.

"How dreadful it sounds. But it wasn't at all like that really."

"Of course it wasn't," I said hastily. "You must forgive my unfortunate way of putting things."

"You see, men are so peculiar. In dear Roger's place, I should not have objected to revealing the provisions of my will. But men are so secretive. One is forced to adopt little subterfuges in self-defence."

"And the result of the little subterfuge?" I asked.

"That's just what I'm telling you. As I got to the bottom drawer, Bourne came in. Most awkward. Of course I shut the drawer and stood up, and I called her attention to a few specks of dust on the surface. But I didn't like the way she looked—quite respectful in manner, but a very nasty light in her eyes. Almost contemptuous, if you know what I mean. I never have liked that girl very much. She's a good servant, and she says M'am, and doesn't object to wearing caps and aprons (which I declare to you a lot of them do nowadays), and she can say 'Not at home' without scruples if she has to answer the door instead of Parker, and she doesn't have those peculiar gurgling noises inside which so many parlormaids seem to have when they wait at table— Let me see, where was I?"

"You were saying, that in spite of several valuable qualities, you never liked Bourne."

"No more I do. She's—odd. There's something different about her from the others. Too well educated, that's my opinion. You can't tell who are ladies and who aren't nowadays."

"And what happened next?" I asked.

"Nothing. At least, Roger came in. And I thought he was out for a walk. And he said: 'What's all this?' and I said, 'Nothing. I just came in to fetch *Punch*.' And I took *Punch* and went out with it. Bourne stayed behind. I heard her asking Roger if she could speak to him for a minute. I went straight up to my room, to lie down. I was very upset."

There was a pause.

"You will explain to M. Poirot, won't you? You can see for yourself what a trivial matter the whole thing was. But, of course, when he was so stern about concealing things, I thought of this at once. Bourne may have made some extraordinary story out of it, but you can explain, can't you?"

"That is all?" I said. "You have told me everything?"

"Ye-es," said Mrs. Ackroyd. "Oh! yes," she added firmly.

But I had noted the momentary hesitation, and I knew that there was still something she was keeping back. It was nothing less than a flash of sheer genius that prompted me to ask the question I did.

"Mrs. Ackroyd," I said, "was it you who left the silver table open?"

I had my answer in the blush of guilt that even rouge and powder could not conceal.

"How did you know?" she whispered.

"It was you, then?"

"Yes—I—you see—there were one or two pieces of old silver—very interesting. I had been reading up the subject and there was an illustration of quite a small piece which had fetched an immense sum at Christy's. It looked to me just the same as the one in the silver table. I thought I would take it up to London with me when I went—and—and have it valued. Then if it really was a valuable piece, just think what a charming surprise it would have been for Roger."

I refrained from comments, accepting Mrs. Ackroyd's story on its merits. I even forbore to ask her why it was necessary to abstract what she wanted in such a surreptitious manner.

"Why did you leave the lid open?" I asked. "Did you forget?"

"I was startled," said Mrs. Ackroyd. "I heard footsteps coming along the terrace outside. I hastened out of the room and just got up the stairs before Parker opened the front door to you."

"That must have been Miss Russell," I said thoughtfully. Mrs. Ackroyd had revealed to me one fact that was extremely interesting. Whether her designs upon Ackroyd's silver had been strictly honorable I neither knew nor cared. What did interest me was the fact that Miss Russell must have entered the drawing-room by the window, and that I had not been wrong when I judged her to be out of breath with running. Where had she been? I thought of the summer-house and the scrap of cambric.

"I wonder if Miss Russell has her handkerchiefs starched!" I exclaimed on the spur of the moment.

Mrs. Ackroyd's start recalled me to myself, and I rose.

"You think you can explain to M. Poirot?" she asked anxiously.

"Oh, certainly. Absolutely."

I got away at last, after being forced to listen to more justifications of her conduct.

The parlormaid was in the hall, and it was she who helped me on with my overcoat. I observed her more closely than I had done heretofore. It was clear that she had been crying.

"How is it," I asked, "that you told us that Mr. Ackroyd sent for you on Friday to his study? I hear now that it was *you* who asked to speak to *him?*"

For a minute the girl's eyes dropped before mine.

Then she spoke.

"I meant to leave in any case," she said uncertainly.

I said no more. She opened the front door for me. Just as I was passing out, she said suddenly in a low voice:—

"Excuse me, sir, is there any news of Captain Paton?"

I shook my head, looking at her inquiringly.

"He ought to come back," she said. "Indeed—indeed he ought to come back."

She was looking at me with appealing eyes.

"Does no one know where he is?" she asked.

"Do you?" I said sharply.

She shook her head.

"No, indeed. I know nothing. But any one who was a friend to him would tell him this: he ought to come back."

I lingered, thinking that perhaps the girl would say more. Her next question surprised me.

"When do they think the murder was done? Just before ten o'clock?"

"That is the idea," I said. "Between a quarter to ten and the hour."

"Not earlier? Not before a quarter to ten?"

I looked at her attentively. She was so clearly eager for a reply in the affirmative.

"That's out of the question," I said. "Miss Ackroyd saw her uncle alive at a quarter to ten."

She turned away, and her whole figure seemed to droop.

"A handsome girl," I said to myself as I drove off. "An exceedingly handsome girl."

Caroline was at home. She had had a visit from Poirot and was very pleased and important about it.

"I am helping him with the case," she explained.

I felt rather uneasy. Caroline is bad enough as it is. What will she be like with her detective instincts encouraged?

"Are you going round the neighborhood looking for Ralph Paton's mysterious girl?" I inquired.

"I might do that on my own account," said Caroline. "No, this is a special thing M. Poirot wants me to find out for him."

"What is it?" I asked.

"He wants to know whether Ralph Paton's boots were black or brown," said Caroline with tremendous solemnity.

I stared at her. I see now that I was unbelievably stupid about these boots. I failed altogether to grasp the point.

"They were brown shoes," I said. "I saw them."

"Not shoes, James, boots. M. Poirot wants to know whether a pair of boots Ralph had with him at the hotel were brown or black. A lot hangs on it."

Call me dense if you like. I didn't see.

"And how are you going to find out?" I asked.

Caroline said there would be no difficulty about that. Our Annie's dearest friend was Miss Ganett's maid, Clara. And Clara was walking out with the Boots at the Three Boars. The whole thing was simplicity itself, and by the aid of Miss Ganett, who coöperated loyally, at once giving Clara leave of absence, the matter was rushed through at express speed.

It was when we were sitting down to lunch that Caroline remarked, with would-be unconcern:—

"About those boots of Ralph Paton's."

"Well," I said, "what about them?"

"M. Poirot thought they were probably brown. He was wrong. They're black."

And Caroline nodded her head several times. She evidently felt that she had scored a point over Poirot.

I did not answer. I was puzzling over what the color of a pair of Ralph Paton's boots had to do with the case.

XV. GEOFFREY RAYMOND

I was to have a further proof that day of the success of Poirot's tactics. That challenge of his had been a subtle touch born of his knowledge of human nature. A mixture of fear and guilt had wrung the truth from Mrs. Ackroyd. She was the first to react.

That afternoon when I returned from seeing my patients, Caroline told me that Geoffrey Raymond had just left.

"Did he want to see me?" I asked, as I hung up my coat in the hall.

Caroline was hovering by my elbow.

"It was M. Poirot he wanted to see," she said. "He'd just come from The Larches. M. Poirot was out. Mr. Raymond thought that he might be here, or that you might know where he was."

"I haven't the least idea."

"I tried to make him wait," said Caroline, "but he said he would call back at The Larches in half an hour, and went away down the village. A great pity, because M. Poirot came in practically the minute after he left."

"Came in here?"

"No, to his own house."

"How do you know?"

"The side window," said Caroline briefly.

It seemed to me that we had now exhausted the topic. Caroline thought otherwise.

"Aren't you going across?"

"Across where?"

"To The Larches, of course."

"My dear Caroline," I said, "what for?"

"Mr. Raymond wanted to see him very particularly," said Caroline. "You might hear what it's all about."

I raised my eyebrows.

"Curiosity is not my besetting sin," I remarked coldly. "I can exist comfortably without knowing exactly what my neighbors are doing and thinking."

"Stuff and nonsense, James," said my sister. "You want to know just as much as I do. You're not so honest, that's all. You always have to pretend."

"Really, Caroline," I said, and retired into my surgery.

Ten minutes later Caroline tapped at the door and entered. In her hand she held what seemed to be a pot of jam.

"I wonder, James," she said, "if you would mind taking this pot of medlar jelly across to M. Poirot? I promised it to him. He has never tasted any home-made medlar jelly."

"Why can't Annie go?" I asked coldly.

"She's doing some mending. I can't spare her."

Caroline and I looked at each other.

"Very well," I said, rising. "But if I take the beastly thing, I shall just leave it at the door. You understand that?"

My sister raised her eyebrows.

"Naturally," she said. "Who suggested you should do anything else?"

The honors were with Caroline.

"If you *do* happen to see M. Poirot," she said, as I opened the front door, "you might tell him about the boots."

It was a most subtle parting shot. I wanted dreadfully to understand the enigma of the boots. When the old lady with the Breton cap opened the door to me, I found myself asking if M. Poirot was in, quite automatically.

Poirot sprang up to meet me, with every appearance of pleasure.

"Sit down, my good friend," he said. "The big chair? This small one? The room is not too hot, no?"

I thought it was stifling, but refrained from saying so. The windows were closed, and a large fire burned in the grate.

"The English people, they have a mania for the fresh air," declared Poirot. "The big air, it is all very well outside, where it belongs. Why admit it to the house? But let us not discuss such banalities. You have something for me, yes?"

"Two things," I said. "First—this—from my sister."

I handed over the pot of medlar jelly.

"How kind of Mademoiselle Caroline. She has remembered her promise. And the second thing?"

"Information—of a kind."

And I told him of my interview with Mrs. Ackroyd. He listened with interest, but not much excitement.

"It clears the ground," he said thoughtfully. "And it has a certain value as confirming the evidence of the housekeeper. She said, you remember, that she found the silver table lid open and closed it down in passing."

"What about her statement that she went into the drawing-room to see if the flowers were fresh?"

"Ah! we never took that very seriously, did we, my friend? It was patently an excuse, trumped up in a hurry, by a woman who felt it urgent to explain her presence—which, by the way, you would probably never have thought of questioning. I considered it possible that her agitation might arise from the fact that she had been tampering with the silver table, but I think now that we must look for another cause."

"Yes," I said. "Whom did she go out to meet? And why?"

"You think she went to meet some one?"

"I do."

Poirot nodded.

"So do I," he said thoughtfully.

There was a pause.

"By the way," I said, "I've got a message for you from my sister. Ralph Paton's boots were black, not brown."

I was watching him closely as I gave the message, and I fancied that I saw a momentary flicker of discomposure. If so, it passed almost immediately.

"She is absolutely positive they are not brown?"

"Absolutely."

"Ah!" said Poirot regretfully. "That is a pity."

And he seemed quite crestfallen.

He entered into no explanations, but at once started a new subject of conversation.

"The housekeeper, Miss Russell, who came to consult you on that Friday morning—is it indiscreet to ask what passed at the interview—apart from the medical details, I mean?"

"Not at all," I said. "When the professional part of the conversation was over, we talked for a few minutes about poisons, and the ease or difficulty of detecting them, and about drug-taking and drug-takers."

"With special reference to cocaine?" asked Poirot.

"How did you know?" I asked, somewhat surprised.

For answer, the little man rose and crossed the room to where newspapers were filed. He brought me a copy of the *Daily Budget*, dated Friday, 16th September, and showed me an article dealing with the smuggling of cocaine. It was a somewhat lurid article, written with an eye to picturesque effect.

"That is what put cocaine into her head, my friend," he said.

I would have catechized him further, for I did not quite understand his meaning, but at that moment the door opened and Geoffrey Raymond was announced.

He came in fresh and debonair as ever, and greeted us both.

"How are you, doctor? M. Poirot, this is the second time I've been here this morning. I was anxious to catch you."

"Perhaps I'd better be off," I suggested rather awkwardly.

"Not on my account, doctor. No, it's just this," he went on, seating himself at a wave of invitation from Poirot, "I've got a confession to make."

"*En verité?*" said Poirot, with an air of polite interest.

"Oh, it's of no consequence, really. But, as a matter of fact, my conscience has been pricking me ever since yesterday afternoon. You accused us all of keeping back something, M. Poirot. I plead guilty. I've had something up my sleeve."

"And what is that, M. Raymond?"

"As I say, it's nothing of consequence—just this. I was in debt—badly, and that legacy came in the nick of time. Five hundred pounds puts me on my feet again with a little to spare."

He smiled at us both with that engaging frankness that made him such a likable youngster.

"You know how it is. Suspicious looking policemen—don't like to admit you were hard up for money—think it will look bad to them. But I was a fool, really, because Blunt and I were in the billiard room from a quarter to ten onwards, so I've got a watertight alibi and nothing to fear. Still, when you thundered out that stuff about concealing things, I felt a nasty prick of conscience, and I thought I'd like to get it off my mind."

He got up again and stood smiling at us.

"You are a very wise young man," said Poirot, nodding at him with approval. "See you, when I know that any one is hiding things from me, I suspect that the thing hidden may be something very bad indeed. You have done well."

"I'm glad I'm cleared from suspicion," laughed Raymond. "I'll be off now."

"So that is that," I remarked, as the door closed behind the young secretary.

"Yes," agreed Poirot. "A mere bagatelle—but if he had not been in the billiard room—who knows? After all, many crimes have been committed for the sake of less than five hundred pounds. It all depends on what sum is sufficient to break a man. A question of the relativity, is it not so? Have you reflected, my friend, that many people in that house stood to benefit by Mr. Ackroyd's death? Mrs. Ackroyd, Miss Flora, young Mr. Raymond, the housekeeper, Miss Russell. Only one, in fact, does not, Major Blunt."

His tone in uttering that name was so peculiar that I looked up, puzzled.

"I don't quite understand you," I said.

"Two of the people I accused have given me the truth."

"You think Major Blunt has something to conceal also?"

"As for that," remarked Poirot nonchalantly, "there is a saying, is there not, that Englishmen conceal only one thing—their love? And Major Blunt, I should say, is not good at concealments."

"Sometimes," I said, "I wonder if we haven't rather jumped to conclusions on one point."

"What is that?"

"We've assumed that the blackmailer of Mrs. Ferrars is necessarily the murderer of Mr. Ackroyd. Mightn't we be mistaken?"

Poirot nodded energetically.

"Very good. Very good indeed. I wondered if that idea would come to you. Of course it is possible. But we must remember one point. The letter disappeared. Still, that, as you say, may not necessarily mean that the murderer took it. When you first found the body, Parker may have abstracted the letter unnoticed by you."

"Parker?"

"Yes, Parker. I always come back to Parker—not as the murderer—no, he did not commit the murder; but who is more suitable than he as the mysterious scoundrel who terrorized Mrs. Ferrars? He may have got his information about Mr. Ferrars's death from one of the King's Paddock servants. At any rate, he is more likely to have come upon it than a casual guest such as Blunt, for instance."

"Parker might have taken the letter," I admitted. "It wasn't till later that I noticed it was gone."

"How much later? After Blunt and Raymond were in the room, or before?"

"I can't remember," I said slowly. "I think it was before—no, afterwards. Yes, I'm almost sure it was afterwards."

"That widens the field to three," said Poirot thoughtfully. "But Parker is the most likely. It is in my mind to try a little experiment with Parker. How say you, my friend, will you accompany me to Fernly?"

I acquiesced, and we set out at once. Poirot asked to see Miss Ackroyd, and presently Flora came to us.

"Mademoiselle Flora," said Poirot, "I have to confide in you a little secret. I am not yet satisfied of the innocence of Parker. I propose to make a little experiment with your assistance. I want to reconstruct some of his actions on that night. But we must think of something to tell him—ah! I have it. I wish to satisfy myself as to whether voices in the little lobby could have been heard outside on the terrace. Now, ring for Parker, if you will be so good."

I did so, and presently the butler appeared, suave as ever.

"You rang, sir?"

"Yes, my good Parker. I have in mind a little experiment. I have placed Major Blunt on the terrace outside the study window. I want to see if any one there could have heard the voices of Miss Ackroyd and yourself in the lobby that night. I want to enact that little scene over again. Perhaps you would fetch the tray or whatever it was you were carrying?"

Parker vanished, and we repaired to the lobby outside the study door. Presently we heard a chink in the outer hall, and Parker appeared in the doorway carrying a tray with a siphon, a decanter of whisky, and two glasses on it.

"One moment," cried Poirot, raising his hand and seemingly very excited. "We must have everything in order. Just as it occurred. It is a little method of mine."

"A foreign custom, sir," said Parker. "Reconstruction of the crime they call it, do they not?"

He was quite imperturbable as he stood there politely waiting on Poirot's orders.

"Ah! he knows something, the good Parker," cried Poirot. "He has read of those things. Now, I beg you, let us have everything of the most exact. You came from the outer hall—so. Mademoiselle was—where?"

"Here," said Flora, taking up her stand just outside the study door.

"Quite right, sir," said Parker.

"I had just closed the door," continued Flora.

"Yes, miss," agreed Parker. "Your hand was still on the handle as it is now."

"Then *allez*," said Poirot. "Play me the little comedy."

Flora stood with her hand on the door handle, and Parker came stepping through the door from the hall, bearing the tray.

He stopped just inside the door. Flora spoke.

"Oh! Parker. Mr. Ackroyd doesn't want to be disturbed again to-night."

"Is that right?" she added in an undertone.

"To the best of my recollection, Miss Flora," said Parker, "but I fancy you

used the word evening instead of night." Then, raising his voice in a somewhat theatrical fashion: "Very good, miss. Shall I lock up as usual?"

"Yes, please."

Parker retired through the door, Flora followed him, and started to ascend the main staircase.

"Is that enough?" she asked over her shoulder.

"Admirable," declared the little man, rubbing his hands. "By the way, Parker, are you sure there were two glasses on the tray that evening? Who was the second one for?"

"I always bring two glasses, sir," said Parker. "Is there anything further?"

"Nothing. I thank you."

Parker withdrew, dignified to the last.

Poirot stood in the middle of the hall frowning. Flora came down and joined us.

"Has your experiment been successful?" she asked. "I don't quite understand, you know——"

Poirot smiled admiringly at her.

"It is not necessary that you should," he said. "But tell me, were there indeed two glasses on Parker's tray that night?"

Flora wrinkled her brows a minute.

"I really can't remember," she said. "I think there were. Is—is that the object of your experiment?"

Poirot took her hand and patted it.

"Put it this way," he said. "I am always interested to see if people will speak the truth."

"And did Parker speak the truth?"

"I rather think he did," said Poirot thoughtfully.

A few minutes later saw us retracing our steps to the village.

"What was the point of that question about the glasses?" I asked curiously.

Poirot shrugged his shoulders.

"One must say something," he remarked. "That particular question did as well as any other."

I stared at him.

"At any rate, my friend," he said more seriously, "I know now something I wanted to know. Let us leave it at that."

XVI. AN EVENING AT MAH JONG

That night we had a little Mah Jong party. This kind of simple entertainment is very popular in King's Abbot. The guests arrive in goloshes and waterproofs after dinner. They partake of coffee and later of cake, sandwiches, and tea.

On this particular night our guests were Miss Ganett and Colonel Carter, who lives near the church. A good deal of gossip is handed round at these evenings, sometimes seriously interfering with the game in progress. We used to play bridge—chatty bridge of the worst description. We find Mah Jong much more peaceful. The irritated demand as to why on earth your partner did not lead a certain card is entirely done away with, and though we still express criticisms frankly, there is not the same acrimonious spirit.

"Very cold evening, eh, Sheppard?" said Colonel Carter, standing with his back to the fire. Caroline had taken Miss Ganett to her own room, and was there assisting her to disentangle herself from her many wraps. "Reminds me of the Afghan passes."

"Indeed?" I said politely.

"Very mysterious business this about poor Ackroyd," continued the colonel, accepting a cup of coffee. "A deuce of a lot behind it—that's what I say. Between you and me, Sheppard, I've heard the word blackmail mentioned!"

The colonel gave me the look which might be tabulated "one man of the world to another."

"A woman in it, no doubt," he said. "Depend upon it, a woman in it."

Caroline and Miss Ganett joined us at this minute. Miss Ganett drank coffee whilst Caroline got out the Mah Jong box and poured out the tiles upon the table.

"Washing the tiles," said the colonel facetiously. "That's right—washing the tiles, as we used to say in the Shanghai Club."

It is the private opinion of both Caroline and myself that Colonel Carter has never been in the Shanghai Club in his life. More, that he has never been farther east than India, where he juggled with tins of bully beef and plum and apple jam during the Great War. But the colonel is determinedly military, and in King's Abbot we permit people to indulge their little idiosyncrasies freely.

"Shall we begin?" said Caroline.

We sat round the table. For some five minutes there was complete silence, owing to the fact that there is tremendous secret competition amongst us as to who can build their wall quickest.

"Go on, James," said Caroline at last. "You're East Wind."

I discarded a tile. A round or two proceeded, broken by the monotonous remarks of "Three Bamboos," "Two Circles," "Pung," and frequently from Miss Ganett "Unpung," owing to that lady's habit of too hastily claiming tiles to which she had no right.

"I saw Flora Ackroyd this morning," said Miss Ganett. "Pung—no—Unpung. I made a mistake."

"Four Circles," said Caroline. "Where did you see her?"

"She didn't see *me*," said Miss Ganett, with that tremendous significance only to be met with in small villages.

"Ah!" said Caroline interestedly. "Chow."

"I believe," said Miss Ganett, temporarily diverted, "that it's the right thing nowadays to say 'Chee' not 'Chow.'"

"Nonsense," said Caroline. "I have always said '*Chow.*'"

"In the Shanghai Club," said Colonel Carter, "they say '*Chow.*'"

Miss Ganett retired, crushed.

"What were you saying about Flora Ackroyd?" asked Caroline, after a moment or two devoted to the game. "Was she with any one?"

"Very much so," said Miss Ganett.

The eyes of the two ladies met, and seemed to exchange information.

"Really," said Caroline interestedly. "Is that it? Well, it doesn't surprise me in the least."

"We're waiting for you to discard, Miss Caroline," said the colonel. He sometimes affects the pose of the bluff male, intent on the game and indifferent to gossip. But nobody is deceived.

"If you ask me," said Miss Ganett. ("Was that a Bamboo you discarded, dear? Oh! no, I see now—it was a Circle.) As I was saying, if you ask me, Flora's been exceedingly lucky. Exceedingly lucky she's been."

"How's that, Miss Ganett?" asked the colonel. "I'll Pung that Green Dragon. How do you make out that Miss Flora's been lucky? Very charming girl and all that, I know."

"I mayn't know very much about crime," said Miss Ganett, with the air of one who knows everything there is to know, "but I can tell you one thing. The first question that's always asked is 'Who last saw the deceased alive?' And the person who did is regarded with suspicion. Now, Flora Ackroyd last saw her uncle alive. It might have looked very nasty for her—very nasty indeed. It's my opinion—and I give it for what it's worth, that Ralph Paton is staying away on her account, to draw suspicion away from her."

"Come, now," I protested mildly, "you surely can't suggest that a young girl like Flora Ackroyd is capable of stabbing her uncle in cold blood?"

"Well, I don't know," said Miss Ganett. "I've just been reading a book from the library about the underworld of Paris, and it says that some of the worst women criminals are young girls with the faces of angels."

"That's in France," said Caroline instantly.

"Just so," said the colonel. "Now, I'll tell you a very curious thing—a story that was going round the Bazaars in India. . . ."

The colonel's story was one of interminable length, and of curiously little interest. A thing that happened in India many years ago cannot compare for a moment with an event that took place in King's Abbot the day before yesterday.

It was Caroline who brought the colonel's story to a close by fortunately going Mah Jong. After the slight unpleasantness always occasioned by my corrections of Caroline's somewhat faulty arithmetic, we started a new hand.

"East Wind passes," said Caroline. "I've got an idea of my own about Ralph Paton. Three Characters. But I'm keeping it to myself for the present."

"Are you, dear?" said Miss Ganett. "Chow—I mean Pung."

"Yes," said Caroline firmly.

"Was it all right about the boots?" asked Miss Ganett. "Their being black, I mean?"

"Quite all right," said Caroline.

"What was the point, do you think?" asked Miss Ganett.

Caroline pursed up her lips, and shook her head with an air of knowing all about it.

"Pung," said Miss Ganett. "No—Unpung. I suppose that now the doctor's in with M. Poirot he knows all the secrets?"

"Far from it," I said.

"James is so modest," said Caroline. "Ah! a concealed Kong."

The colonel gave vent to a whistle. For the moment gossip was forgotten.

"Your own wind, too," he said. "*And* you've got two Pungs of Dragons. We must be careful. Miss Caroline's out for a big hand."

We played for some minutes with no irrelevant conversation.

"This M. Poirot now," said Colonel Carter, "is he really such a great detective?"

"The greatest the world has ever known," said Caroline solemnly. "He had to come here incognito to avoid publicity."

"Chow," said Miss Ganett. "Quite wonderful for our little village, I'm sure. By the way, Clara—my maid, you know—is great friends with Elsie, the housemaid at Fernly, and what do you think Elsie told her? That there's been a lot of money stolen, and it's her opinion—Elsie's—I mean, that the parlormaid had something to do with it. She's leaving at the month, and she's crying a good deal at night. If you ask me, the girl is very likely in league with a *gang*. She's always been a queer girl—she's not friends with any of the girls round here. She goes off by herself on her days out—very unnatural, I call it, and most suspicious. I asked her once to come to our Girls' Friendly Evenings, but she refused, and then I asked her a few questions about her home and her family—all that sort of thing, and I'm bound to say I considered her manner most impertinent. Outwardly very respectful—but she shut me up in the most barefaced way."

Miss Ganett stopped for breath, and the colonel, who was totally uninterested in the servant question, remarked that in the Shanghai Club brisk play was the invariable rule.

We had a round of brisk play.

"That Miss Russell," said Caroline. "She came here pretending to consult James on Friday morning. It's my opinion she wanted to see where the poisons were kept. Five Characters."

"Chow," said Miss Ganett. "What an extraordinary idea. I wonder if you can be right."

"Talking of poisons," said the colonel. "Eh—what? Haven't I discarded? Oh! Eight Bamboos."

"Mah Jong!" said Miss Ganett.

Caroline was very much annoyed.

"One Red Dragon," she said regretfully, "and I should have had a hand of three doubles."

"I've had two Red Dragons all the time," I mentioned.

"So exactly like you, James," said Caroline reproachfully. "You've no conception of the spirit of the game."

I myself thought I had played rather cleverly. I should have had to pay Caroline an enormous amount if she had gone Mah Jong. Miss Ganett's Mah Jong was of the poorest variety possible, as Caroline did not fail to point out to her.

East Wind passed, and we started a new hand in silence.

"What I was going to tell you just now was this," said Caroline.

"Yes?" said Miss Ganett encouragingly.

"My idea about Ralph Paton, I mean."

"Yes, dear," said Miss Ganett, still more encouragingly. "Chow!"

"It's a sign of weakness to Chow so early," said Caroline severely. "You should go for a big hand."

"I know," said Miss Ganett. "You were saying—about Ralph Paton, you know?"

"Yes. Well, I've a pretty shrewd idea where he is."

We all stopped to stare at her.

"This is very interesting, Miss Caroline," said Colonel Carter. "All your own idea, eh?"

"Well, not exactly. I'll tell you about it. You know that big map of the county we have in the hall?"

We all said Yes.

"As M. Poirot was going out the other day, he stopped and looked at it, and he made some remark—I can't remember exactly what it was. Something about Cranchester being the only big town anywhere near us—which is true, of course. But after he had gone—it came to me suddenly."

"What came to you?"

"His meaning. Of course Ralph is in Cranchester."

It was at that moment that I knocked down the rack that held my pieces. My sister immediately reproved me for clumsiness, but half-heartedly. She was intent on her theory.

"Cranchester, Miss Caroline?" said Colonel Carter. "Surely not Cranchester! It's so near."

"That's exactly it," cried Caroline triumphantly. "It seems quite clear by now that he didn't get away from here by train. He must simply have walked into Cranchester. And I believe he's there still. No one would dream of his being so near at hand."

I pointed out several objections to the theory, but when once Caroline has got something firmly into her head, nothing dislodges it.

"And you think M. Poirot has the same idea," said Miss Ganett thoughtfully. "It's a curious coincidence, but I was out for a walk this afternoon on the Cranchester road, and he passed me in a car coming from that direction."

We all looked at each other.

"Why, dear me," said Miss Ganett suddenly, "I'm Mah Jong all the time, and I never noticed it."

Caroline's attention was distracted from her own inventive exercises. She pointed out to Miss Ganett that a hand consisting of mixed suits and too many Chows was hardly worth going Mah Jong on. Miss Ganett listened imperturbably and collected her counters.

"Yes, dear, I know what you mean," she said. "But it rather depends on what kind of a hand you have to start with, doesn't it?"

"You'll never get the big hands if you don't go for them," urged Caroline.

"Well, we must all play our own way, mustn't we?" said Miss Ganett. She looked down at her counters. "After all, I'm up, so far."

Caroline, who was considerably down, said nothing.

East Wind passed, and we set to once more. Annie brought in the tea things. Caroline and Miss Ganett were both slightly ruffled as is often the case during one of these festive evenings.

"If you would only play a leetle quicker, dear," said Caroline, as Miss Ganett hesitated over her discard. "The Chinese put down the tiles so quickly it sounds like little birds pattering."

For some few minutes we played like the Chinese.

"You haven't contributed much to the sum of information, Sheppard," said Colonel Carter genially. "You're a sly dog. Hand in glove with the great detective, and not a hint as to the way things are going."

"James is an extraordinary creature," said Caroline. "He can *not* bring himself to part with information."

She looked at me with some disfavor.

"I assure you," I said, "that I don't know anything. Poirot keeps his own counsel."

"Wise man," said the colonel with a chuckle. "He doesn't give himself away. But they're wonderful fellows, these foreign detectives. Up to all sorts of dodges, I believe."

"Pung," said Miss Ganett, in a tone of quiet triumph. "And Mah Jong."

The situation became more strained. It was annoyance at Miss Ganett's going Mah Jong for the third time running which prompted Caroline to say to me as we built a fresh wall:—

"You are too tiresome, James. You sit there like a dead head, and say nothing at all!"

"But, my dear," I protested, "I have really nothing to say—that is, of the kind you mean."

"Nonsense," said Caroline, as she sorted her hand. "You *must* know something interesting."

I did not answer for a moment. I was overwhelmed and intoxicated. I had read of there being such a thing as the Perfect Winning—going Mah Jong on one's original hand. I had never hoped to hold the hand myself.

With suppressed triumph I laid my hand face upwards on the table.

"As they say in the Shanghai Club," I remarked, "Tin-ho—the Perfect Winning!"

The colonel's eyes nearly bulged out of his head.

"Upon my soul," he said. "What an extraordinary thing. I never saw that happen before!"

It was then that I went on, goaded by Caroline's gibes, and rendered reckless by my triumph.

"And as to anything interesting," I said. "What about a gold wedding ring with a date and 'From R.' inside?"

I pass over the scene that followed. I was made to say exactly where this treasure was found. I was made to reveal the date.

"March 13th," said Caroline. "Just six months ago. Ah!"

Out of the babel of excited suggestions and suppositions three theories were evolved:—

1. That of Colonel Carter: that Ralph was secretly married to Flora. The first or most simple solution.

2. That of Miss Ganett: that Roger Ackroyd had been secretly married to Mrs. Ferrars.

3. That of my sister: that Roger Ackroyd had married his housekeeper, Miss Russell.

A fourth or super-theory was propounded by Caroline later as we went up to bed.

"Mark my words," she said suddenly, "I shouldn't be at all surprised if Geoffrey Raymond and Flora weren't married."

"Surely it would be 'From G.,' not 'From R.' then," I suggested.

"You never know. Some girls call men by their surnames. And you heard what Miss Ganett said this evening—about Flora's carryings on."

Strictly speaking, I had not heard Miss Ganett say anything of the kind, but I respected Caroline's knowledge of innuendoes.

"How about Hector Blunt," I hinted. "If it's anybody——"

"Nonsense," said Caroline. "I dare say he admires her—may even be in love with her. But depend upon it a girl isn't going to fall in love with a man old enough to be her father when there's a good-looking young secretary about. She may encourage Major Blunt just as a blind. Girls are very artful. But there's one thing I *do* tell you, James Sheppard. Flora Ackroyd does not care a penny piece for Ralph Paton, and never has. You can take it from me."

I took it from her meekly.

XVII. PARKER

It occurred to me the next morning that under the exhilaration produced by Tin-ho, or the Perfect Winning, I might have been slightly indiscreet. True, Poirot had not asked me to keep the discovery of the ring to myself. On the other hand, he had said nothing about it whilst at Fernly, and as far as I knew, I was the only person aware that it had been found. I felt distinctly guilty. The fact was by now spreading through King's Abbot like wildfire. I was expecting wholesale reproaches from Poirot any minute.

The joint funeral of Mrs. Ferrars and Roger Ackroyd was fixed for eleven o'clock. It was a melancholy and impressive ceremony. All the party from Fernly were there.

After it was over, Poirot, who had also been present, took me by the arm, and invited me to accompany him back to The Larches. He was looking very grave, and I feared that my indiscretion of the night before had got round to his ears. But it soon transpired that his thoughts were occupied by something of a totally different nature.

"See you," he said. "We must act. With your help I propose to examine a witness. We will question him, we will put such fear into him that the truth is bound to come out."

"What witness are you talking of?" I asked, very much surprised.

"Parker!" said Poirot. "I asked him to be at my house this morning at twelve o'clock. He should await us there at this very minute."

"What do you think," I ventured, glancing sideways at his face.

"I know this—that I am not satisfied."

"You think that it was he who blackmailed Mrs. Ferrars?"

"Either that, or——"

"Well?" I said, after waiting a minute or two.

"My friend, I will say this to you—I hope it was he."

The gravity of his manner, and something indefinable that tinged it, reduced me to silence.

On arrival at The Larches, we were informed that Parker was already there awaiting our return. As we entered the room, the butler rose respectfully.

"Good-morning, Parker," said Poirot pleasantly. "One instant, I pray of you."

He removed his overcoat and gloves.

"Allow me, sir," said Parker, and sprang forward to assist him. He deposited the articles neatly on a chair by the door. Poirot watched him with approval.

"Thank you, my good Parker," he said. "Take a seat, will you not? What I have to say may take some time."

Parker seated himself with an apologetic bend of the head.

"Now what do you think I asked you to come here for this morning—eh?"

Parker coughed.

"I understood, sir, that you wished to ask me a few questions about my late master—private like."

"Précisément," said Poirot, beaming. "Have you made many experiments in blackmail?"

"Sir!"

The butler sprang to his feet.

"Do not excite yourself," said Poirot placidly. "Do not play the farce of the honest, injured man. You know all there is to know about the blackmail, is it not so?"

"Sir, I—I've never—never been——"

"Insulted," suggested Poirot, "in such a way before. Then why, my excellent Parker, were you so anxious to overhear the conversation in Mr. Ackroyd's study the other evening, after you had caught the word blackmail?"

"I wasn't—I——"

"Who was your last master?" rapped out Poirot suddenly.

"My last master?"

"Yes, the master you were with before you came to Mr. Ackroyd."

"A Major Ellerby, sir——"

Poirot took the words out of his mouth.

"Just so, Major Ellerby. Major Ellerby was addicted to drugs, was he not? You traveled about with him. When he was in Bermuda there was some trouble—a man was killed. Major Ellerby was partly responsible. It was hushed up. But you knew about it. How much did Major Ellerby pay you to keep your mouth shut?"

Parker was staring at him open-mouthed. The man had gone to pieces, his cheeks shook flabbily.

"You see, me, I have made inquiries," said Poirot pleasantly. "It is as I say. You got a good sum then as blackmail, and Major Ellerby went on paying you until he died. Now I want to hear about your latest experiment."

Parker still stared.

"It is useless to deny. Hercule Poirot *knows*. It is so, what I have said about Major Ellerby, is it not?"

As though against his will, Parker nodded reluctantly once. His face was ashen pale.

"But I never hurt a hair of Mr. Ackroyd's head," he moaned. "Honest to God, sir, I didn't. I've been afraid of this coming all the time. And I tell you I didn't—I didn't kill him."

His voice rose almost to a scream.

"I am inclined to believe you, my friend," said Poirot. "You have not the nerve—the courage. But I must have the truth."

"I'll tell you anything, sir, anything you want to know. It's true that I tried to listen that night. A word or two I heard made me curious. And Mr. Ackroyd's wanting not to be disturbed, and shutting himself up with the doctor the way he did. It's God's own truth what I told the police. I heard the word blackmail, sir, and well——"

He paused.

"You thought there might be something in it for you?" suggested Poirot smoothly.

"Well—well, yes, I did, sir. I thought that if Mr. Ackroyd was being black-mailed, why shouldn't I have a share of the pickings?"

A very curious expression passed over Poirot's face. He leaned forward.

"Had you any reason to suppose before that night that Mr. Ackroyd was being blackmailed?"

"No, indeed, sir. It was a great surprise to me. Such a regular gentleman in all his habits."

"How much did you overhear?"

"Not very much, sir. There seemed what I might call a spite against me. Of course I had to attend to my duties in the pantry. And when I did creep along once or twice to the study it was no use. The first time Dr. Sheppard came out and almost caught me in the act, and another time Mr. Raymond passed me in the big hall and went that way, so I knew it was no use; and when I went with the tray, Miss Flora headed me off."

Poirot stared for a long time at the man, as if to test his sincerity. Parker returned his gaze earnestly.

"I hope you believe me, sir. I've been afraid all along the police would rake up that old business with Major Ellerby and be suspicious of me in consequence."

"*Eh bien*," said Poirot at last. "I am disposed to believe you. But there is one thing I must request of you—to show me your bank-book. You have a bank-book, I presume?"

"Yes, sir, as a matter of fact, I have it with me now."

With no sign of confusion, he produced it from his pocket. Poirot took the slim, green-covered book and perused the entries.

"Ah! I perceive you have purchased £500 of National Savings Certificates this year?"

"Yes, sir. I have already over a thousand pounds saved—the result of my connection with—er—my late master, Major Ellerby. And I have had quite a little flutter on some horses this year—very successful. If you remember, sir, a rank outsider won the Jubilee. I was fortunate enough to back it—£20."

Poirot handed him back the book.

"I will wish you good-morning. I believe that you have told me the truth. If you have not—so much the worse for you, my friend."

When Parker had departed, Poirot picked up his overcoat once more.

"Going out again?" I asked.

"Yes, we will pay a little visit to the good M. Hammond."

"You believe Parker's story?"

"It is credible enough on the face of it. It seems clear that—unless he is a very good actor indeed—he genuinely believes it was Ackroyd himself who was the victim of blackmail. If so, he knows nothing at all about the Mrs. Ferrars business."

"Then in that case—who——"

"*Précisément!* Who? But our visit to M. Hammond will accomplish one purpose. It will either clear Parker completely or else——"

"Well?"

"I fall into the bad habit of leaving my sentences unfinished this morning," said Poirot apologetically. "You must bear with me."

"By the way," I said, rather sheepishly, "I've got a confession to make. I'm afraid I have inadvertently let out something about that ring."

"What ring?"

"The ring you found in the goldfish pond."

"Ah! yes," said Poirot, smiling broadly.

"I hope you're not annoyed? It was very careless of me."

"But not at all, my good friend, not at all. I laid no commands upon you. You were at liberty to speak of it if you so wished. She was interested, your sister?"

"She was indeed. It created a sensation. All sorts of theories are flying about."

"Ah! And yet it is so simple. The true explanation leapt to the eye, did it not?"

"Did it?" I said dryly.

Poirot laughed.

"The wise man does not commit himself," he observed. "Is not that so? But here we are at M. Hammond's."

The lawyer was in his office, and we were ushered in without any delay. He rose and greeted us in his dry, precise manner.

Poirot came at once to the point.

"Monsieur, I desire from you certain information, that is, if you will be so good as to give it to me. You acted, I understand, for the late Mrs. Ferrars of King's Paddock?"

I noticed the swift gleam of surprise which showed in the lawyer's eyes, before his professional reserve came down once more like a mask over his face.

"Certainly. All her affairs passed through our hands."

"Very good. Now, before I ask you to tell me anything, I should like you to listen to the story Dr. Sheppard will relate to you. You have no objection, have you, my friend, to repeating the conversation you had with Mr. Ackroyd last Friday night?"

"Not in the least," I said, and straightway began the recital of that strange evening.

Hammond listened with close attention.

"That is all," I said, when I had finished.

"Blackmail," said the lawyer thoughtfully.

"You are surprised?" asked Poirot.

The lawyer took off his pince-nez and polished them with his handkerchief.

"No," he replied, "I can hardly say that I am surprised. I have suspected something of the kind for some time."

"That brings us," said Poirot, "to the information for which I am asking. If any one can give us an idea of the actual sums paid, you are the man, monsieur."

"I see no object in withholding the information," said Hammond, after a moment or two. "During the past year, Mrs. Ferrars has sold out certain securities, and the money for them was paid into her account and not re-invested. As her income was a large one, and she lived very quietly after her husband's death, it seems certain that these sums of money were paid away for some special purpose. I once sounded her on the subject, and she said that she was obliged to support several of her husband's poor relations. I let the matter drop, of course. Until now, I have always imagined that the money was paid to some woman who had had a claim on Ashley Ferrars. I never dreamed that Mrs. Ferrars herself was involved."

"And the amount?" asked Poirot.

"In all, I should say the various sums totaled at least twenty thousand pounds."

"Twenty thousand pounds!" I exclaimed. "In one year!"

"Mrs. Ferrars was a very wealthy woman," said Poirot dryly. "And the penalty for murder is not a pleasant one."

"Is there anything else that I can tell you?" inquired Mr. Hammond.

"I thank you, no," said Poirot, rising. "All my excuses for having deranged you."

"Not at all, not at all."

"The word derange," I remarked, when we were outside again, "is applicable to mental disorder only."

"Ah!" cried Poirot, "never will my English be quite perfect. A curious language. I should then have said disarranged, *n'est ce pas?*"

"Disturbed is the word you had in mind."

"I thank you, my friend. The word exact, you are zealous for it. *Eh bien*, what about our friend Parker now? With twenty thousand pounds in hand, would he have continued being a butler? *Je ne pense pas*. It is, of course, possible that he banked the money under another name, but I am disposed to believe he spoke the truth to us. If he is a scoundrel, he is a scoundrel on a mean scale. He has not the big ideas. That leaves us as a possibility, Raymond, or—well—Major Blunt."

"Surely not Raymond," I objected. "Since we know that he was desperately hard up for a matter of five hundred pounds."

"That is what he says, yes."

"And as to Hector Blunt——"

"I will tell you something as to the good Major Blunt," interrupted Poirot. "It is my business to make inquiries. I make them. *Eh bien*—that legacy of which he speaks, I have discovered that the amount of it was close upon twenty thousand pounds. What do you think of that?"

I was so taken aback that I could hardly speak.

"It's impossible," I said at last. "A well-known man like Hector Blunt."

Poirot shrugged his shoulders.

"Who knows? At least he is a man with big ideas. I confess that I hardly see him as a blackmailer, but there is another possibility that you have not even considered."

"What is that?"

"The fire, my friend. Ackroyd himself may have destroyed that letter, blue envelope and all, after you left him."

"I hardly think that likely," I said slowly. "And yet—of course, it may be so. He might have changed his mind."

We had just arrived at my house, and on the spur of the moment I invited Poirot to come in and take pot luck.

I thought Caroline would be pleased with me, but it is hard to satisfy one's women folk. It appears that we were eating chops for lunch—the kitchen staff being regaled on tripe and onions. And two chops set before three people are productive of embarrassment.

But Caroline is seldom daunted for long. With magnificent mendacity, she explained to Poirot that although James laughed at her for doing so, she adhered strictly to a vegetarian diet. She descanted ecstatically on the delights of nut cutlets (which I am quite sure she has never tasted) and ate a Welsh rarebit with gusto and frequent cutting remarks as to the dangers of "flesh" foods.

Afterwards, when we were sitting in front of the fire and smoking, Caroline attacked Poirot directly.

"Not found Ralph Paton yet?" she asked.

"Where should I find him, mademoiselle?"

"I thought, perhaps, you'd found him in Cranchester," said Caroline, with intense meaning in her tone.

Poirot looked merely bewildered.

"In Cranchester? But why in Cranchester?"

I enlightened him with a touch of malice.

"One of our ample staff of private detectives happened to see you in a car on the Cranchester road yesterday," I explained.

Poirot's bewilderment vanished. He laughed heartily.

"Ah, that! A simple visit to the dentist, *c'est tout*. My tooth, it aches. I go there. My tooth, it is at once better. I think to return quickly. The dentist, he says No. Better to have it out. I argue. He insists. He has his way! That particular tooth, it will never ache again."

Caroline collapsed rather like a pricked balloon.

We fell to discussing Ralph Paton.

"A weak nature," I insisted. "But not a vicious one."

"Ah!" said Poirot. "But weakness, where does it end?"

"Exactly," said Caroline. "Take James here—weak as water, if I weren't about to look after him."

"My dear Caroline," I said irritably, "can't you talk without dragging in personalities?"

"You *are* weak, James," said Caroline, quite unmoved. "I'm eight years older than you are—oh! I don't mind M. Poirot knowing that——"

"I should never have guessed it, mademoiselle," said Poirot, with a gallant little bow.

"Eight years older. But I've always considered it my duty to look after you. With a bad bringing up, Heaven knows what mischief you might have got into by now."

"I might have married a beautiful adventuress," I murmured, gazing at the ceiling, and blowing smoke rings.

"Adventuress!" said Caroline, with a snort. "If we're talking of adventuresses——"

She left the sentence unfinished.

"Well?" I said, with some curiosity.

"Nothing. But I can think of some one not a hundred miles away."

Then she turned to Poirot suddenly.

"James sticks to it that you believe some one in the house committed the murder. All I can say is, you're wrong."

"I should not like to be wrong," said Poirot. "It is not—how do you say—my *metier*?"

"I've got the facts pretty clearly," continued Caroline, taking no notice of Poirot's remark, "from James and others. As far as I can see, of the people in the house, only two *could* have had the chance of doing it. Ralph Paton and Flora Ackroyd."

"My dear Caroline——"

"Now, James, don't interrupt me. I know what I'm talking about. Parker met her *outside* the door, didn't he? He didn't hear her uncle saying good-night to her. She could have killed him then and there."

"Caroline."

"I'm not saying she *did*, James. I'm saying she *could* have done. As a matter of fact, though Flora is like all these young girls nowadays, with no veneration for their betters and thinking they know best on every subject under the sun, I don't for a minute believe she'd kill even a chicken. But there it is. Mr. Raymond and Major Blunt have alibis. Mrs. Ackroyd's got an alibi. Even that Russell woman seems to have one—and a good job for her it is she has. Who is left? Only Ralph and Flora! And say what you will, I don't believe Ralph Paton is a murderer. A boy we've known all our lives."

Poirot was silent for a minute, watching the curling smoke rise from his cigarette. When at last he spoke, it was in a gentle far-away voice that produced a curious impression. It was totally unlike his usual manner.

"Let us take a man—a very ordinary man. A man with no idea of murder in his heart. There is in him somewhere a strain of weakness—deep down. It has so far never been called into play. Perhaps it never will be—and if so he will go to his grave honored and respected by every one. But let us suppose that something occurs. He is in difficulties—or perhaps not that even. He may stumble by accident on a secret—a secret involving life or death to some one. And his first impulse will be to speak out—to do his duty as an honest citizen. And then the strain of weakness tells. Here is a chance of money—a great amount of money. He wants money—he desires it—and it is so easy. He has to do nothing for it—just keep silence. That is the beginning. The desire for money grows. He must have more—and more! He is intoxicated by the gold mine which has opened at his feet. He becomes greedy. And in his greed he overreaches himself. One can press a man as far as one likes—but with a woman one must not press too far. For a woman has at heart a great desire to speak the truth. How many husbands who have deceived their wives go comfortably to their graves, carrying their secret with them! How many wives who have deceived their husbands wreck their lives by throwing the fact in those same husbands' teeth! They have been pressed too far. In a reckless moment (which they will afterwards regret, *bien entendu*) they fling safety to the winds and turn at bay, proclaiming the truth with great momentary satisfaction to themselves. So it was, I think, in this case. The strain was too great. And so there came your proverb, the death of the goose that laid the golden eggs. But that is not the end. Exposure faced the man of whom we are speaking. And he is not the same man he was—say, a year ago. His moral fiber is blunted. He is desperate. He is fighting a losing battle, and he is prepared to take any means that come to his hand, for exposure means ruin to him. And so—the dagger strikes!"

He was silent for a moment. It was as though he had laid a spell upon the room. I cannot try to describe the impression his words produced. There was something in the merciless analysis, and the ruthless power of vision which struck fear into both of us.

"Afterwards," he went on softly, "the danger removed, he will be himself again, normal, kindly. But if the need again arises, then once more he will strike."

Caroline roused herself at last.

"You are speaking of Ralph Paton," she said. "You may be right, you may not, but you have no business to condemn a man unheard."

The telephone bell rang sharply. I went out into the hall, and took off the receiver.

"What?" I said. "Yes. Dr. Sheppard speaking."

I listened for a minute or two, then replied briefly. Replacing the receiver, I went back into the drawing-room.

"Poirot," I said, "they have detained a man at Liverpool. His name is Charles Kent, and he is believed to be the stranger who visited Fernly that night. They want me to go to Liverpool at once and identify him."

XVIII. CHARLES KENT

Half an hour later saw Poirot, myself, and Inspector Raglan in the train on the way to Liverpool. The inspector was clearly very excited.

"We may get a line on the blackmailing part of the business, if on nothing else," he declared jubilantly. "He's a rough customer, this fellow, by what I heard over the phone. Takes dope, too. We ought to find it easy to get what we want out of him. If there was the shadow of a motive, nothing's more likely than that he killed Mr. Ackroyd. But in that case, why is young Paton keeping out of the way? The whole thing's a muddle—that's what it is. By the way, M. Poirot, you were quite right about those fingerprints. They were Mr. Ackroyd's own. I had rather the same idea myself, but I dismissed it as hardly feasible."

I smiled to myself. Inspector Raglan was so very plainly saving his face.

"As regards this man," said Poirot, "he is not yet arrested, eh?"

"No, detained under suspicion."

"And what account does he give of himself?"

"Precious little," said the inspector, with a grin. "He's a wary bird, I gather. A lot of abuse, but very little more."

On arrival at Liverpool I was surprised to find that Poirot was welcomed with acclamation. Superintendent Hayes, who met us, had worked with Poirot over some case long ago, and had evidently an exaggerated opinion of his powers.

"Now we've got M. Poirot here we shan't be long," he said cheerfully. "I thought you'd retired, moosior?"

"So I had, my good Hayes, so I had. But how tedious is retirement! You cannot imagine to yourself the monotony with which day comes after day."

"Very likely. So you've come to have a look at our own particular find? Is this Dr. Sheppard? Think you'll be able to identify him, sir?"

"I'm not very sure," I said doubtfully.

"How did you get hold of him?" inquired Poirot.

"Description was circulated, as you know. In the press and privately. Not much to go on, I admit. This fellow has an American accent all right, and he doesn't deny that he was near King's Abbot that night. Just asks what the hell it is to do with us, and that he'll see us in — before he answers any questions."

"Is it permitted that I, too, see him?" asked Poirot.

The superintendent closed one eye knowingly.

"Very glad to have you, sir. You've got permission to do anything you please. Inspector Japp of Scotland Yard was asking after you the other day. Said he'd heard you were connected unofficially with this case. Where's Captain Paton hiding, sir, can you tell me that?"

"I doubt if it would be wise at the present juncture," said Poirot primly, and I bit my lips to prevent a smile.

The little man really did it very well.

After some further parley, we were taken to interview the prisoner.

He was a young fellow, I should say not more than twenty-two or three. Tall, thin, with slightly shaking hands, and the evidences of considerable physical strength somewhat run to seed. His hair was dark, but his eyes were blue and shifty, seldom meeting a glance squarely. I had all along cherished the illusion that there was something familiar about the figure I had met that night, but if this were indeed he, I was completely mistaken. He did not remind me in the least of any one I knew.

"Now then, Kent," said the superintendent, "stand up. Here are some visitors come to see you. Recognize any of them?"

Kent glared at us sullenly, but did not reply. I saw his glance waver over the three of us, and come back to rest on me.

"Well, sir," said the superintendent to me, "what do you say?"

"The height's the same," I said, "and as far as general appearance goes it might well be the man in question. Beyond that, I couldn't go."

"What the hell's the meaning of all this?" asked Kent. "What have you got against me? Come on, out with it! What am I supposed to have done?"

I nodded my head.

"It's the man," I said. "I recognize the voice."

"Recognize my voice, do you? Where do you think you heard it before?"

"On Friday evening last, outside the gates of Fernly Park. You asked me the way there."

"I did, did I?"

"Do you admit it?" asked the inspector.

"I don't admit anything. Not till I know what you've got on me."

"Have you not read the papers in the last few days?" asked Poirot, speaking for the first time.

The man's eyes narrowed.

"So that's it, is it? I saw an old gent had been croaked at Fernly. Trying to make out I did the job, are you?"

"You were there that night," said Poirot quietly.

"How do you know, mister?"

"By this." Poirot took something from his pocket and held it out.

It was the goose quill we had found in the summer-house.

At the sight of it the man's face changed. He half held out his hand.

"Snow," said Poirot thoughtfully. "No, my friend, it is empty. It lay where you dropped it in the summer-house that night."

Charles Kent looked at him uncertainly.

"You seem to know a hell of a lot about everything, you little foreign cock duck. Perhaps you remember this: the papers say that the old gent was croaked between a quarter to ten and ten o'clock?"

"That is so," agreed Poirot.

"Yes, but is it really so? That's what I'm getting at."

"This gentleman will tell you," said Poirot.

He indicated Inspector Raglan. The latter hesitated, glanced at Superintendent Hayes, then at Poirot, and finally, as though receiving sanction, he said:—

"That's right. Between a quarter to ten and ten o'clock."

"Then you've nothing to keep me here for," said Kent. "I was away from Fernly Park by twenty-five minutes past nine. You can ask at the Dog and Whistle. That's a saloon about a mile out of Fernly on the road to Cranchester. I kicked up a bit of a row there, I remember. As near as nothing to quarter to ten, it was. How about that?"

Inspector Raglan wrote down something in his note-book.

"Well?" demanded Kent.

"Inquiries will be made," said the inspector. "If you've spoken the truth, you won't have anything to complain about. What were you doing at Fernly Park anyway?"

"Went there to meet some one."

"Who?"

"That's none of your business."

"You'd better keep a civil tongue in your head, my man," the superintendent warned him.

"To hell with a civil tongue. I went there on my own business, and that's all there is to it. If I was clear away before the murder was done, that's all that concerns the cops."

"Your name, it is Charles Kent," said Poirot. "Where were you born?"

The man stared at him, then he grinned.

"I'm a full-blown Britisher all right," he said.

"Yes," said Poirot meditatively, "I think you are. I fancy you were born in Kent."

The man stared.

"Why's that? Because of my name? What's that to do with it? Is a man whose name is Kent bound to be born in that particular county?"

"Under certain circumstances, I can imagine he might be," said Poirot very deliberately. "Under certain circumstances, you comprehend."

There was so much meaning in his voice as to surprise the two police officers. As for Charles Kent, he flushed a brick red, and for a moment I thought he was going to spring at Poirot. He thought better of it, however, and turned away with a kind of laugh.

Poirot nodded as though satisfied, and made his way out through the door. He was joined presently by the two officers.

"We'll verify that statement," remarked Raglan. "I don't think he's lying, though. But he's got to come clear with a statement as to what he was doing at Fernly. It looks to me as though we'd got our blackmailer all right. On the other hand, granted his story's correct, he couldn't have had anything to do with the actual murder. He'd got ten pounds on him when he was arrested—rather a large sum. I fancy that forty pounds went to him— the numbers of the notes didn't correspond, but of course he'd have changed them first thing. Mr. Ackroyd must have given him the money, and he made off with it as fast as possible. What was that about Kent being his birthplace? What's that got to do with it?"

"Nothing whatever," said Poirot mildly. "A little idea of mine, that was all. Me, I am famous for my little ideas."

"Are you really?" said Raglan, studying him with a puzzled expression.

The superintendent went into a roar of laughter.

"Many's the time I've heard Inspector Japp say that. M. Poirot and his little ideas! Too fanciful for me, he'd say, but always something in them."

"You mock yourself at me," said Poirot, smiling; "but never mind. The old ones they laugh last sometimes, when the young, clever ones do not laugh at all."

And nodding his head at them in a sage manner, he walked out into the street.

He and I lunched together at an hotel. I know now that the whole thing lay clearly unravelled before him. He had got the last thread he needed to lead him to the truth.

But at the time I had no suspicion of the fact. I overestimated his general self-confidence, and I took it for granted that the things which puzzled me must be equally puzzling to him.

My chief puzzle was what the man Charles Kent could have been doing at Fernly. Again and again I put the question to myself and could get no satisfactory reply. At last I ventured a tentative query to Poirot. His reply was immediate.

"*Mon ami*, I do not think; I know."

"Really?" I said incredulously.

"Yes, indeed. I suppose now that to you it would not make sense if I said that he went to Fernly that night because he was born in Kent?"

I stared at him.

"It certainly doesn't seem to make sense to me," I said dryly.

"Ah!" said Poirot pityingly. "Well, no matter. I have still my little idea."

XIX. FLORA ACKROYD

As I was returning from my round the following morning, I was hailed by Inspector Raglan. I pulled up, and the inspector mounted on the step.

"Good-morning, Dr. Sheppard," he said. "Well, that alibi is all right enough."

"Charles Kent's?"

"Charles Kent's. The barmaid at the Dog and Whistle, Sally Jones, she remembers him perfectly. Picked out his photograph from among five others. It was just a quarter to ten when he came into the bar, and the Dog and Whistle is well over a mile from Fernly Park. The girl mentions that he had a lot of money on him—she saw him take a handful of notes out of his pocket. Rather surprised her, it did, seeing the class of fellow he was, with a pair of boots clean dropping off him. That's where that forty pounds went right enough."

"The man still refuses to give an account of his visit to Fernly?"

"Obstinate as a mule he is. I had a chat with Hayes at Liverpool over the wire this morning."

"Hercule Poirot says he knows the reason the man went there that night," I observed.

"Does he?" cried the inspector eagerly.

"Yes," I said maliciously. "He says he went there because he was born in Kent."

I felt a distinct pleasure in passing on my own discomfiture.

Raglan stared at me for a moment or two uncomprehendingly. Then a grin overspread his weaselly countenance and he tapped his forehead significantly.

"Bit gone here," he said. "I've thought so for some time. Poor old chap, so that's why he had to give up and come down here. In the family, very likely. He's got a nephew who's quite off his crumpet."

"Poirot has?" I said, very surprised.

"Yes. Hasn't he ever mentioned him to you? Quite docile, I believe, and all that, but mad as a hatter, poor lad."

"Who told you that?"

Again a grin showed itself on Inspector Raglan's face.

"Your sister, Miss Sheppard, she told me all about it."

Really, Caroline is amazing. She never rests until she knows the last details of everybody's family secrets. Unfortunately, I have never been able to instill into her the decency of keeping them to herself.

"Jump in, inspector," I said, opening the door of the car. "We'll go up to The Larches together, and acquaint our Belgian friend with the latest news."

"Might as well, I suppose. After all, even if he is a bit balmy, it was a useful tip he gave me about those fingerprints. He's got a bee in his bonnet about the man Kent, but who knows—there may be something useful behind it."

Poirot received us with his usual smiling courtesy.

He listened to the information we had brought him, nodding his head now and then.

"Seems quite O.K., doesn't it?" said the inspector rather gloomily. "A chap can't be murdering some one in one place when he's drinking in the bar in another place a mile away."

"Are you going to release him?"

"Don't see what else we can do. We can't very well hold him for obtaining money on false pretences. Can't prove a ruddy thing."

The inspector tossed a match into the grate in a disgruntled fashion. Poirot retrieved it and put it neatly in a little receptacle designed for the purpose. His action was purely mechanical. I could see that his thoughts were on something very different.

"If I were you," he said at last, "I should not release the man Charles Kent yet."

"What do you mean?"

Raglan stared at him.

"What I say. I should not release him yet."

"You don't think he can have had anything to do with the murder, do you?"

"I think probably not—but one cannot be certain yet."

"But haven't I just told you——"

Poirot raised a hand protestingly.

"*Mais oui, mais oui.* I heard. I am not deaf—nor stupid, thank the good God! But see you, you approach the matter from the wrong—the wrong—premises, is not that the word?"

The inspector stared at him heavily.

"I don't see how you make that out. Look here, we know Mr. Ackroyd was alive at a quarter to ten. You admit that, don't you?"

Poirot looked at him for a moment, then shook his head with a quick smile.

"I admit nothing that is not—*proved!*"

"Well, we've got proof enough of that. We've got Miss Flora Ackroyd's evidence."

"That she said good-night to her uncle? But me—I do not always believe what a young lady tells me—no, not even when she is charming and beautiful."

"But hang it all, man, Parker saw her coming out of the door."

"No." Poirot's voice rang out with sudden sharpness. "That is just what he did not see. I satisfied myself of that by a little experiment the other day—you remember, doctor? Parker saw her *outside* the door, with her hand on the handle. He did not see her come out of the room."

"But—where else could she have been?"

"Perhaps on the stairs."

"The stairs?"

"That is my little idea—yes."

"But those stairs only lead to Mr. Ackroyd's bedroom."

"Precisely."

And still the inspector stared.

"You think she'd been up to her uncle's bedroom? Well, why not? Why should she lie about it?"

"Ah! that is just the question. It depends on what she was doing there, does it not?"

"You mean—the money? Hang it all, you don't suggest that it was Miss Ackroyd who took that forty pounds?"

"I suggest nothing," said Poirot. "But I will remind you of this. Life was not very easy for that mother and daughter. There were bills—there was constant trouble over small sums of money. Roger Ackroyd was a peculiar man over money matters. The girl might be at her wit's end for a comparatively small sum. Figure to yourself then what happens. She has taken the money, she descends the little staircase. When she is half-way down she hears the chink of glass from the hall. She has not a doubt of what it is—Parker coming to the study. At all costs she must not be found on the stairs—Parker will not forget it, he will think it odd. If the money is missed, Parker is sure to remember having seen her come down those stairs. She has just time to rush down to the study door—with her hand on the handle to show that she has just come out, when Parker appears in the doorway. She says the first thing that comes into her head, a repetition of Roger Ackroyd's orders earlier in the evening, and then goes upstairs to her own room."

"Yes, but later," persisted the inspector, "she must have realized the vital importance of speaking the truth? Why, the whole case hinges on it!"

"Afterwards," said Poirot dryly, "it was a little difficult for Mademoiselle Flora. She is told simply that the police are here and that there has been a robbery. Naturally she jumps to the conclusion that the theft of the money has been discovered. Her one idea is to stick to her story. When she learns that her uncle is dead she is panic-stricken. Young women do not faint nowadays, monsieur, without considerable provocation. *Eh bien!* there it is. She is bound to stick to her story, or else confess everything. And a young and pretty girl does not like to admit that she is a thief—especially before those whose esteem she is anxious to retain."

Raglan brought his fist down with a thump on the table.

"I'll not believe it," he said. "It's—it's not credible. And you—you've known this all along?"

"The possibility has been in my mind from the first," admitted Poirot. "I was always convinced that Mademoiselle Flora was hiding something from us. To satisfy myself, I made the little experiment I told you of. Dr. Sheppard accompanied me."

"A test for Parker, you said it was," I remarked bitterly.

"*Mon ami,*" said Poirot apologetically, "as I told you at the time, one must say something."

The inspector rose.

"There's only one thing for it," he declared. "We must tackle the young lady right away. You'll come up to Fernly with me, M. Poirot?"

"Certainly. Dr. Sheppard will drive us up in his car."

I acquiesced willingly.

On inquiry for Miss Ackroyd, we were shown into the billiard room. Flora and Major Hector Blunt were sitting on the long window seat.

"Good-morning, Miss Ackroyd," said the inspector. "Can we have a word or two alone with you?"

Blunt got up at once and moved to the door.

"What is it?" asked Flora nervously. "Don't go, Major Blunt. He can stay, can't he?" she asked, turning to the inspector.

"That's as you like," said the inspector dryly. "There's a question or two it's my duty to put to you, miss, but I'd prefer to do so privately, and I dare say you'd prefer it also."

Flora looked keenly at him. I saw her face grow whiter. Then she turned and spoke to Blunt.

"I want you to stay—please—yes, I mean it. Whatever the inspector has to say to me, I'd rather you heard it."

Raglan shrugged his shoulders.

"Well, if you will have it so, that's all there is to it. Now, Miss Ackroyd, M. Poirot here has made a certain suggestion to me. He suggests that you weren't in the study at all last Friday night, that you never saw Mr. Ackroyd to say good-night to him, that instead of being in the study you were on the stairs leading down from your uncle's bedroom when you heard Parker coming across the hall."

Flora's gaze shifted to Poirot. He nodded back at her.

"Mademoiselle, the other day, when we sat round the table, I implored you to be frank with me. What one does not tell to Papa Poirot he finds out. It was that, was it not? See, I will make it easy for you. You took the money, did you not?"

"The money," said Blunt sharply.

There was a silence which lasted for at least a minute.

Then Flora drew herself up and spoke.

"M. Poirot is right. I took that money. I stole. I am a thief—yes, a common, vulgar little thief. Now you know! I am glad it has come out. It's been a nightmare, these last few days!" She sat down suddenly and buried her face in her hands. She spoke huskily through her fingers. "You don't know what my life has been since I came here. Wanting things, scheming for them, lying, cheating, running up bills, promising to pay—oh! I hate myself when I think of it all! That's what brought us together, Ralph and I. We were both weak! I understood him, and I was sorry—because I'm the same underneath. We're not strong enough to stand alone, either of us. We're weak, miserable, despicable things."

She looked at Blunt and suddenly stamped her foot.

"Why do you look at me like that—as though you couldn't believe? I may be a thief—but at any rate I'm real now. I'm not lying any more. I'm not pretending to be the kind of girl you like, young and innocent and simple. I don't care if you never want to see me again. I hate myself, despise myself —but you've got to believe one thing, if speaking the truth would have made things better for Ralph, I would have spoken out. But I've seen all along that it wouldn't be better for Ralph—it makes the case against him blacker than ever. I was not doing him any harm by sticking to my lie."

"Ralph," said Blunt. "I see—always Ralph."

"You don't understand," said Flora hopelessly. "You never will."

She turned to the inspector.

"I admit everything; I was at my wit's end for money. I never saw my uncle that evening after he left the dinner-table. As to the money, you can take what steps you please. Nothing could be worse than it is now!"

Suddenly she broke down again, hid her face in her hands, and rushed from the room.

"Well," said the inspector in a flat tone, "so that's that."

He seemed rather at a loss what to do next.

Blunt came forward.

"Inspector Raglan," he said quietly, "that money was given to me by Mr. Ackroyd for a special purpose. Miss Ackroyd never touched it. When she says she did, she is lying with the idea of shielding Captain Paton. The truth is as I said, and I am prepared to go into the witness box and swear to it."

He made a kind of jerky bow, then turning abruptly, he left the room. Poirot was after him in a flash. He caught the other up in the hall.

"Monsieur—a moment, I beg of you, if you will be so good."

"Well, sir?"

Blunt was obviously impatient. He stood frowning down on Poirot.

"It is this," said Poirot rapidly: "I am not deceived by your little fantasy. No, indeed. It was truly Miss Flora who took the money. All the same it is well imagined what you say—it pleases me. It is very good what you have done there. You are a man quick to think and to act."

"I'm not in the least anxious for your opinion, thank you," said Blunt coldly.

He made once more as though to pass on, but Poirot, not at all offended, laid a detaining hand on his arm.

"Ah! but you are to listen to me. I have more to say. The other day I spoke of concealments. Very well, all along have I seen what you are concealing. Mademoiselle Flora, you love her with all your heart. From the first moment you saw her, is it not so? Oh! let us not mind saying these things—why must one in England think it necessary to mention love as though it were some disgraceful secret? You love Mademoiselle Flora. You seek to conceal that fact from the world. That is very good—that is as it should be. But take the advice of Hercule Poirot—do not conceal it from mademoiselle herself."

Blunt had shown several signs of restlessness whilst Poirot was speaking, but the closing words seemed to rivet his attention.

"What d'you mean by that?" he said sharply.

"You think that she loves the Capitaine Ralph Paton—but I, Hercule Poirot, tell you that that is not so. Mademoiselle Flora accepted Captain Paton to please her uncle, and because she saw in the marriage a way of escape from her life here which was becoming frankly insupportable to her. She liked him, and there was much sympathy and understanding between them. But love—no! It is not Captain Paton Mademoiselle Flora loves."

"What the devil do you mean?" asked Blunt.

I saw the dark flush under his tan.

"You have been blind, monsieur. Blind! She is loyal, the little one. Ralph Paton is under a cloud, she is bound in honor to stick by him."

I felt it was time I put in a word to help on the good work.

"My sister told me the other night," I said encouragingly, "that Flora had never cared a penny piece for Ralph Paton, and never would. My sister is always right about these things."

Blunt ignored my well-meant efforts. He spoke to Poirot.

"D'you really think——" he began, and stopped.

He is one of those inarticulate men who find it hard to put things into words.

Poirot knows no such disability.

"If you doubt me, ask her yourself, monsieur. But perhaps you no longer care to—the affair of the money——"

Blunt gave a sound like an angry laugh.

"Think I'd hold that against her? Roger was always a queer chap about money. She got in a mess and didn't dare tell him. Poor kid. Poor lonely kid."

Poirot looked thoughtfully at the side door.

"Mademoiselle Flora went into the garden, I think," he murmured.

"I've been every kind of a fool," said Blunt abruptly. "Rum conversation we've been having. Like one of those Danish plays. But you're a sound fellow, M. Poirot. Thank you."

He took Poirot's hand and gave it a grip which caused the other to wince in anguish. Then he strode to the side door and passed out into the garden.

"Not every kind of a fool," murmured Poirot, tenderly nursing the injured member. "Only one kind—the fool in love."

XX. MISS RUSSELL

Inspector Raglan had received a bad jolt. He was not deceived by Blunt's valiant lie any more than we had been. Our way back to the village was punctuated by his complaints.

"This alters everything, this does. I don't know whether you've realized it, Monsieur Poirot?"

"I think so, yes, I think so," said Poirot. "You see, me, I have been familiar with the idea for some time."

Inspector Raglan, who had only had the idea presented to him a short half-hour ago, looked at Poirot unhappily, and went on with his discoveries.

"Those alibis now. Worthless! Absolutely worthless. Got to start again. Find out what every one was doing from nine-thirty onwards. Nine-thirty—that's the time we've got to hang on to. You were quite right about the man Kent—we don't release him yet awhile. Let me see now—nine-forty-five at the Dog and Whistle. He might have got there in a quarter of an hour if he ran. It's just possible that it was his voice Mr. Raymond heard talking to Mr. Ackroyd—asking for money which Mr. Ackroyd refused. But one thing's clear —it wasn't he who sent the telephone message. The station is half a mile in the other direction—over a mile and a half from the Dog and Whistle, and he was at the Dog and Whistle until about ten minutes past ten. Dang that telephone call! We always come up against it."

"We do indeed," agreed Poirot. "It is curious."

"It's just possible that if Captain Paton climbed into his uncle's room and found him there murdered, *he* may have sent it. Got the wind up, thought he'd be accused, and cleared out. That's possible, isn't it?"

"Why should he have telephoned?"

"May have had doubts if the old man was really dead. Thought he'd get the doctor up there as soon as possible, but didn't want to give himself away. Yes, I say now, how's that for a theory? Something in that, I should say."

The inspector swelled his chest out importantly. He was so plainly delighted with himself that any words of ours would have been quite superfluous.

We arrived back at my house at this minute, and I hurried in to my surgery patients, who had all been waiting a considerable time, leaving Poirot to walk to the police station with the inspector.

Having dismissed the last patient, I strolled into the little room at the back of the house which I call my workshop—I am rather proud of the home-made wireless set I turned out. Caroline hates my workroom. I keep my tools there, and Annie is not allowed to wreak havoc with a dustpan and brush. I was just adjusting the interior of an alarm clock which had been denounced as wholly unreliable by the household, when the door opened and Caroline put her head in.

"Oh! there you are, James," she said, with deep disapproval. "M. Poirot wants to see you."

"Well," I said, rather irritably, for her sudden entrance had startled me and I had let go of a piece of delicate mechanism, "if he wants to see me, he can come in here."

"In here?" said Caroline.

"That's what I said—in here."

Caroline gave a sniff of disapproval and retired. She returned in a moment or two, ushering in Poirot, and then retired again, shutting the door with a bang.

"Aha! my friend," said Poirot, coming forward and rubbing his hands. "You have not got rid of me so easily, you see!"

"Finished with the inspector?" I asked.

"For the moment, yes. And you, you have seen all the patients?"

"Yes."

Poirot sat down and looked at me, tilting his egg-shaped head on one side, with the air of one who savors a very delicious joke.

"You are in error," he said at last. "You have still one patient to see."

"Not you?" I exclaimed in surprise.

"Ah, not me, *bien entendu*. Me, I have the health magnificent. No, to tell you the truth, it is a little *complot* of mine. There is some one I wish to see, you understand—and at the same time it is not necessary that the whole village should intrigue itself about the matter—which is what would happen if the lady were seen to come to my house—for it is a lady. But to you she has already come as a patient before."

"Miss Russell!" I exclaimed.

"*Précisément.* I wish much to speak with her, so I send her the little note and make the appointment in your surgery. You are not annoyed with me?"

"On the contrary," I said. "That is, presuming I am allowed to be present at the interview?"

"But naturally! In your own surgery!"

"You know," I said, throwing down the pincers I was holding, "it's extraordinarily intriguing, the whole thing. Every new development that arises is like the shake you give to a kaleidoscope—the thing changes entirely in aspect. Now, why are you so anxious to see Miss Russell?"

Poirot raised his eyebrows.

"Surely it is obvious?" he murmured.

"There you go again," I grumbled. "According to you everything is obvious. But you leave me walking about in a fog."

Poirot shook his head genially at me.

"You mock yourself at me. Take the matter of Mademoiselle Flora. The inspector was surprised—but you—you were not."

"I never dreamed of her being the thief," I expostulated.

"That—perhaps no. But I was watching your face and you were not—like Inspector Raglan—startled and incredulous."

I thought for a minute or two.

"Perhaps you are right," I said at last. "All along I've felt that Flora was keeping back something—so the truth, when it came, was subconsciously expected. It upset Inspector Raglan very much indeed, poor man."

"Ah! *pour ça, oui!* The poor man must rearrange all his ideas. I profited by his state of mental chaos to induce him to grant me a little favor."

"What was that?"

Poirot took a sheet of notepaper from his pocket. Some words were written on it, and he read them aloud.

"The police have, for some days been seeking for Captain Ralph Paton, the stepson of Mr. Ackroyd of Fernly Park, whose death occurred under such tragic circumstances last Friday. Captain Paton has been found at Liverpool, where he was on the point of embarking for America."

He folded up the piece of paper again.

"That, my friend, will be in the newspapers to-morrow morning."

I stared at him, dumbfounded.

"But—but it isn't true! He's not at Liverpool!"

Poirot beamed on me.

"You have the intelligence so quick! No, he has not been found at Liverpool. Inspector Raglan was very loath to let me send this paragraph to the press, especially as I could not take him into my confidence. But I assured him most solemnly that very interesting results would follow its appearance in print, so he gave in, after stipulating that he was, on no account, to bear the responsibility."

I stared at Poirot. He smiled back at me.

"It beats me," I said at last, "what you expect to get out of that."

"You should employ your little gray cells," said Poirot gravely.

He rose and came across to the bench.

"It is that you have really the love of the machinery," he said, after inspecting the débris of my labors.

Every man has his hobby. I immediately drew Poirot's attention to my home-made wireless. Finding him sympathetic, I showed him one or two little inventions of my own—trifling things, but useful in the house.

"Decidedly," said Poirot, "you should be an inventor by trade, not a doctor. But I hear the bell—that is your patient. Let us go into the surgery."

Once before I had been struck by the remnants of beauty in the housekeeper's face. This morning I was struck anew. Very simply dressed in black, tall, upright and independent as ever, with her big dark eyes and an unwonted flush of color in her usually pale cheeks, I realized that as a girl she must have been startlingly handsome.

"Good-morning, mademoiselle," said Poirot. "Will you be seated? Dr. Sheppard is so kind as to permit me the use of his surgery for a little conversation I am anxious to have with you."

Miss Russell sat down with her usual composure. If she felt any inward agitation, it did not display itself in any outward manifestation.

"It seems a queer way of doing things, if you'll allow me to say so," she remarked.

"Miss Russell—I have news to give you."

"Indeed!"

"Charles Kent has been arrested at Liverpool."

Not a muscle of her face moved. She merely opened her eyes a trifle wider, and asked, with a tinge of defiance:

"Well, what of it?"

But at that moment it came to me—the resemblance that had haunted me all along, something familiar in the defiance of Charles Kent's manner. The two voices, one rough and coarse, the other painfully ladylike—were strangely the same in timbre. It was of Miss Russell that I had been reminded that night outside the gates of Fernly Park.

I looked at Poirot, full of my discovery, and he gave me an imperceptible nod.

In answer to Miss Russell's question, he threw out his hands in a thoroughly French gesture.

"I thought you might be interested, that is all," he said mildly.

"Well, I'm not particularly," said Miss Russell. "Who is this Charles Kent anyway?"

"He is a man, mademoiselle, who was at Fernly on the night of the murder."

"Really?"

"Fortunately for him, he has an alibi. At a quarter to ten he was at a public-house a mile from here."

"Lucky for him," commented Miss Russell.

"But we still do not know what he was doing at Fernly—who it was he went to meet, for instance."

"I'm afraid I can't help you at all," said the housekeeper politely. "Nothing came to *my* ears. If that is all——"

She made a tentative movement as though to rise. Poirot stopped her.

"It is not quite all," he said smoothly. "This morning fresh developments have arisen. It seems now that Mr. Ackroyd was murdered, not at a quarter to ten, but *before*. Between ten minutes to nine, when Dr. Sheppard left, and a quarter to ten."

I saw the color drain from the housekeeper's face, leaving it dead white. She leaned forward, her figure swaying.

"But Miss Ackroyd said—Miss Ackroyd said——"

"Miss Ackroyd has admitted that she was lying. She was never in the study at all that evening."

"Then——?"

"Then it would seem that in this Charles Kent we have the man we are looking for. He came to Fernly, can give no account of what he was doing there——"

"I can tell you what he was doing there. He never touched a hair of old Ackroyd's head—he never went near the study. He didn't do it, I tell you."

She was leaning forward. That iron self-control was broken through at last. Terror and desperation were in her face.

"M. Poirot! M. Poirot! Oh, do believe me."

Poirot got up and came to her. He patted her reassuringly on the shoulder.

"But yes—but yes, I will believe. I had to make you speak, you know."

For an instant suspicion flared up in her.

"Is what you said true?"

"That Charles Kent is suspected of the crime? Yes, that is true. You alone can save him, by telling the reason for his being at Fernly."

"He came to see me." She spoke in a low, hurried voice. "I went out to meet him——"

"In the summer-house, yes, I know."

"How do you know?"

"Madmoiselle, it is the business of Hercule Poirot to know things. I know that you went out earlier in the evening, that you left a message in the summer-house to say what time you would be there."

"Yes, I did. I had heard from him—saying he was coming. I dared not let him come to the house. I wrote to the address he gave me and said I would meet him in the summer-house, and described it to him so that he would be able to find it. Then I was afraid he might not wait there patiently, and I ran out and left a piece of paper to say I would be there about ten minutes past nine. I didn't want the servants to see me, so I slipped out through the drawing-room window. As I came back, I met Dr. Sheppard, and I fancied that he would think it queer. I was out of breath, for I had been running. I had no idea that he was expected to dinner that night."

She paused.

"Go on," said Poirot. "You went out to meet him at ten minutes past nine. What did you say to each other?"

"It's difficult. You see——"

"Mademoiselle," said Poirot, interrupting her, "in this matter I must have the whole truth. What you tell us need never go beyond these four walls. Dr. Sheppard will be discreet, and so shall I. See, I will help you. This Charles Kent, he is your son, is he not?"

She nodded. The color had flamed into her cheeks.

"No one has ever known. It was long ago—long ago—down in Kent. I was not married. . . ."

"So you took the name of the county as a surname for him. I understand."

"I got work. I managed to pay for his board and lodging. I never told him that I was his mother. But he turned out badly, he drank, then took to drugs. I managed to pay his passage out to Canada. I didn't hear of him for a year or two. Then, somehow or other, he found out that I was his mother. He wrote asking me for money. Finally, I heard from him back in this country again. He was coming to see me at Fernly, he said. I dared not let him come to the house. I have always been considered so—so very respectable. If any one got an inkling—it would have been all up with my post as housekeeper. So I wrote to him in the way I have just told you."

"And in the morning you came to see Dr. Sheppard?"

"Yes. I wondered if something could be done. He was not a bad boy—before he took to drugs."

"I see," said Poirot. "Now let us go on with the story. He came that night to the summer-house?"

"Yes, he was waiting for me when I got there. He was very rough and abusive. I had brought with me all the money I had, and I gave it to him. We talked a little, and then he went away."

"What time was that?"

"It must have been between twenty and twenty-five minutes past nine. It was not yet half-past when I got back to the house."

"Which way did he go?"

"Straight out the same way he came, by the path that joined the drive just inside the lodge gates."

Poirot nodded.

"And you, what did you do?"

"I went back to the house. Major Blunt was walking up and down the terrace smoking, so I made a detour to get round to the side door. It was then just on half-past nine, as I tell you."

Poirot nodded again. He made a note or two in a microscopic note-book.

"I think that is all," he said thoughtfully.

"Ought I——" She hesitated. "Ought I to tell all this to Inspector Raglan?"

"It may come to that. But let us not be in a hurry. Let us proceed slowly, with due order and method. Charles Kent is not yet formally charged with murder. Circumstances may arise which will render your story unnecessary."

Miss Russell rose.

"Thank you very much, M. Poirot," she said. "You have been very kind—very kind indeed. You—you do believe me, don't you? That Charles had nothing to do with this wicked murder!"

"There seems no doubt that the man who was talking to Mr. Ackroyd in the library at nine-thirty could not possibly have been your son. Be of good courage, mademoiselle. All will yet be well."

Miss Russell departed. Poirot and I were left together.

"So that's that," I said. "Every time we come back to Ralph Paton. How did you manage to spot Miss Russell as the person Charles Kent came to meet? Did you notice the resemblance?"

"I had connected her with the unknown man long before we actually came face to face with him. As soon as we found that quill. The quill suggested dope, and I remembered your account of Miss Russell's visit to you. Then I found the article on cocaine in that morning's paper. It all seemed very clear. She had heard from some one that morning—some one addicted to drugs, she read the article in the paper, and she came to you to ask a few tentative questions. She mentioned cocaine, since the article in question was on cocaine. Then, when you seemed too interested, she switched hurriedly to the subject of detective stories and untraceable poisons. I suspected a son or a brother, or some other undesirable male relation. Ah! but I must go. It is the time of the lunch."

"Stay and lunch with us," I suggested.

Poirot shook his head. A faint twinkle came into his eye.

"Not again to-day. I should not like to force Mademoiselle Caroline to adopt a vegetarian diet two days in succession."

It occurred to me that there was not much which escaped Hercule Poirot.

XXI. THE PARAGRAPH IN THE PAPER

Caroline, of course, had not failed to see Miss Russell come to the surgery door. I had anticipated this, and had ready an elaborate account of the lady's bad knee. But Caroline was not in a cross-questioning mood. Her point of view was that she knew what Miss Russell had really come for and that I didn't.

"Pumping you, James," said Caroline. "Pumping you in the most shameless manner, I've not a doubt. It's no good interrupting. I dare say you hadn't the least idea she was doing it even. Men *are* so simple. She knows that you are in M. Poirot's confidence, and she wants to find out things. Do you know what I think, James?"

"I couldn't begin to imagine. You think so many extraordinary things."

"It's no good being sarcastic. I think Miss Russell knows more about Mr. Ackroyd's death than she is prepared to admit."

Caroline leaned back triumphantly in her chair.

"Do you really think so?" I said absently.

"You are very dull to-day, James. No animation about you. It's that liver of yours."

Our conversation then dealt with purely personal matters.

The paragraph inspired by Poirot duly appeared in our daily paper the next morning. I was in the dark as to its purpose, but its effect on Caroline was immense.

She began by stating, most untruly, that she had said as much all along. I raised my eyebrows, but did not argue. Caroline, however, must have felt a prick of conscience, for she went on:—

"I mayn't have actually mentioned Liverpool, but I knew he'd try to get away to America. That's what Crippen did."

"Without much success," I reminded her.

"Poor boy, and so they've caught him. I consider, James, that it's your duty to see that he isn't hung."

"What do you expect me to do?"

"Why, you're a medical man, aren't you? You've known him from a boy upwards. Not mentally responsible. That's the line to take, clearly. I read only the other day that they're very happy in Broadmoor—it's quite like a high-class club."

But Caroline's words had reminded me of something.

"I never knew that Poirot had an imbecile nephew," I said curiously.

"Didn't you? Oh, he told me all about it. Poor lad. It's a great grief to all the family. They've kept him at home so far, but it's getting to such a pitch that they're afraid he'll have to go into some kind of institution."

"I suppose you know pretty well everything there is to know about Poirot's family by this time," I said, exasperated.

"Pretty well," said Caroline complacently. "It's a great relief to people to be able to tell all their troubles to some one."

"It might be," I said, "if they were ever allowed to do so spontaneously. Whether they enjoy having confidences screwed out of them by force is another matter."

Caroline merely looked at me with the air of a Christian martyr enjoying martyrdom.

"You are so self-contained, James," she said. "You hate speaking out, or parting with any information yourself, and you think everybody else must be just like you. I should hope that I never screw confidences out of anybody. For instance, if M. Poirot comes in this afternoon, as he said he might do, I shall not dream of asking him who it was arrived at his house early this morning."

"Early this morning?" I queried.

"Very early," said Caroline. "Before the milk came. I just happened to be looking out of the window—the blind was flapping. It was a man. He came in a closed car, and he was all muffled up. I couldn't get a glimpse of his face. But I will tell you *my* idea, and you'll see that I'm right."

"What's your idea?"

Caroline dropped her voice mysteriously.

"A Home Office expert," she breathed.

"A Home Office expert," I said, amazed. "My dear Caroline!"

"Mark my words, James, you'll see that I'm right. That Russell woman was here that morning after your poisons. Roger Ackroyd might easily have been poisoned in his food that night."

I laughed out loud.

"Nonsense," I cried. "He was stabbed in the neck. You know that as well as I do."

"After death, James," said Caroline; "to make a false clew."

"My good woman," I said, "I examined the body, and I know what I'm talking about. That wound wasn't inflicted after death—it was the cause of death, and you need make no mistake about it."

Caroline merely continued to look omniscient, which so annoyed me that I went on:—

"Perhaps you will tell me, Caroline, if I have a medical degree or if I have not?"

"You have the medical degree, I dare say, James—at least, I mean I know you have. But you've no imagination whatever."

"Having endowed you with a treble portion, there was none left over for me," I said dryly.

I was amused to notice Caroline's maneuvers that afternoon when Poirot duly arrived. My sister, without asking a direct question, skirted the subject of the mysterious guest in every way imaginable. By the twinkle in Poirot's eyes, I saw that he realized her object. He remained blandly impervious, and blocked her bowling so successfully that she herself was at a loss how to proceed.

Having, I suspect, quietly enjoyed the little game, he rose to his feet and suggested a walk.

"It is that I need to reduce the figure a little," he explained. "You will come with me, doctor? And perhaps later Miss Caroline will give us some tea."

"Delighted," said Caroline. "Won't your—er—guest come in also?"

"You are too kind," said Poirot. "But no, my friend reposes himself. Soon you must make his acquaintance."

"Quite an old friend of yours, so somebody told me," said Caroline, making one last valiant effort.

"Did they?" murmured Poirot. "Well, we must start."

Our tramp took us in the direction of Fernly. I had guessed beforehand that it might do so. I was beginning to understand Poirot's methods. Every little irrelevancy had a bearing upon the whole.

"I have a commission for you, my friend," he said at last. "To-night, at my house, I desire to have a little conference. You will attend, will you not?"

"Certainly," I said.

"Good. I need also all those in the house—that is to say: Mrs. Ackroyd, Mademoiselle Flora, Major Blunt, M. Raymond. I want you to be my ambassador. This little reunion is fixed for nine o'clock. You will ask them—yes?"

"With pleasure; but why not ask them yourself?"

"Because they will then put the questions: Why? What for? They will demand what my idea is. And, as you know, my friend, I much dislike to have to explain my little ideas until the time comes."

I smiled a little.

"My friend Hastings, he of whom I told you, used to say of me that I was the human oyster. But he was unjust. Of facts, I keep nothing to myself. But to every one his own interpretation of them."

"When do you want me to do this?"

"Now, if you will. We are close to the house."

"Aren't you coming in?"

"No, me, I will promenade myself in the grounds. I will rejoin you by the lodge gates in a quarter of an hour's time."

I nodded, and set off on my task. The only member of the family at home proved to be Mrs. Ackroyd, who was sipping an early cup of tea. She received me very graciously.

"So grateful to you, doctor," she murmured, "for clearing up that little matter with M. Poirot. But life is one trouble after another. You have heard about Flora, of course?"

"What exactly?" I asked cautiously.

"This new engagement. Flora and Hector Blunt. Of course not such a good match as Ralph would have been. But after all, happiness comes first. What dear Flora needs is an older man—some one steady and reliable, and then Hector is really a very distinguished man in his way. You saw the news of Ralph's arrest in the paper this morning?"

"Yes," I said, "I did."

"Horrible." Mrs. Ackroyd closed her eyes and shuddered. "Geoffrey Raymond was in a terrible way. Rang up Liverpool. But they wouldn't tell him anything at the police station there. In fact, they said they hadn't arrested Ralph at all. Mr. Raymond insists that it's all a mistake—a—what do they call it?—*canard* of the newspaper's. I've forbidden it to be mentioned before the servants. Such a terrible disgrace. Fancy if Flora had actually been married to him."

Mrs. Ackroyd shut her eyes in anguish. I began to wonder how soon I should be able to deliver Poirot's invitation.

Before I had time to speak, Mrs. Ackroyd was off again.

"You were here yesterday, weren't you, with that dreadful Inspector Raglan? Brute of a man—he terrified Flora into saying she took that money from poor Roger's room. And the matter was so simple, really. The dear child wanted to borrow a few pounds, didn't like to disturb her uncle since he'd given strict orders against it, but knowing where he kept his notes she went there and took what she needed."

"Is that Flora's account of the matter?" I asked.

"My dear doctor, you know what girls are nowadays. So easily acted on by suggestion. You, of course, know all about hypnosis and that sort of thing.

The inspector shouts at her, says the word 'steal' over and over again, until the poor child gets an inhibition—or is it a complex?—I always mix up those two words—and actually thinks herself that she has stolen the money. I saw at once how it was. But I can't be too thankful for the whole misunderstanding in one way—it seems to have brought those two together—Hector and Flora, I mean. And I assure you that I have been very much worried about Flora in the past: why, at one time I actually thought there was going to be some kind of understanding between her and young Raymond. Just think of it!" Mrs. Ackroyd's voice rose in shrill horror. "A private secretary —with practically no means of his own."

"It would have been a severe blow to you," I said. "Now, Mrs. Ackroyd, I've got a message for you from M. Hercule Poirot."

"For me?"

Mrs. Ackroyd looked quite alarmed.

I hastened to reassure her, and I explained what Poirot wanted.

"Certainly," said Mrs. Ackroyd rather doubtfully, "I suppose we must come if M. Poirot says so. But what is it all about? I like to know beforehand."

I assured the lady truthfully that I myself did not know any more than she did.

"Very well," said Mrs. Ackroyd at last, rather grudgingly, "I will tell the others, and we will be there at nine o'clock."

Thereupon I took my leave, and joined Poirot at the agreed meeting-place.

"I've been longer than a quarter of an hour, I'm afraid," I remarked. "But once that good lady starts talking it's a matter of the utmost difficulty to get a word in edgeways."

"It is of no matter," said Poirot. "Me, I have been well amused. This park is magnificent."

We set off homewards. When we arrived, to our great surprise Caroline, who had evidently been watching for us, herself opened the door.

She put her fingers to her lips. Her face was full of importance and excitement.

"Ursula Bourne," she said, "the parlormaid from Fernly. She's here! I've put her in the dining-room. She's in a terrible way, poor thing. Says she must see M. Poirot at once. I've done all I could. Taken her a cup of hot tea. It really goes to one's heart to see any one in such a state."

"In the dining-room?" asked Poirot.

"This way," I said, and flung open the door.

Ursula Bourne was sitting by the table. Her arms were spread out in front of her, and she had evidently just lifted her head from where it had been buried. Her eyes were red with weeping.

"Ursula Bourne," I murmured.

But Poirot went past me with outstretched hands.

"No," he said, "that is not quite right, I think. It is not Ursula Bourne, is it, my child—but Ursula Paton? Mrs. Ralph Paton."

XXII. URSULA'S STORY

For a moment or two the girl looked mutely at Poirot. Then, her reserve breaking down completely, she nodded her head once, and burst into an outburst of sobs.

Caroline pushed past me, and putting her arm round the girl, patted her on the shoulder.

"There, there, my dear," she said soothingly, "it will be all right. You'll see—everything will be all right."

Buried under curiosity and scandal-mongering there is a lot of kindness in Caroline. For the moment, even the interest of Poirot's revelation was lost in the sight of the girl's distress.

Presently Ursula sat up and wiped her eyes.

"This is very weak and silly of me," she said.

"No, no, my child," said Poirot kindly. "We can all realize the strain of this last week."

"It must have been a terrible ordeal," I said.

"And then to find that you knew," continued Ursula. "How did you know? Was it Ralph who told you?"

Poirot shook his head.

"You know what brought me to you to-night," went on the girl. "*This*—"

She held out a crumpled piece of newspaper, and I recognized the paragraph that Poirot had had inserted.

"It says that Ralph has been arrested. So everything is useless. I need not pretend any longer."

"Newspaper paragraphs are not always true, mademoiselle," murmured Poirot, having the grace to look ashamed of himself. "All the same, I think you will do well to make a clean breast of things. The truth is what we need now."

The girl hesitated, looking at him doubtfully.

"You do not trust me," said Poirot gently. "Yet all the same you came here to find me, did you not? Why was that?"

"Because I don't believe that Ralph did it," said the girl in a very low voice. "And I think that you are clever, and will find out the truth. And also——"

"Yes?"

"I think you are kind."

Poirot nodded his head several times.

"It is very good that—yes, it is very good. Listen, I do in verity believe that this husband of yours is innocent—but the affair marches badly. If I am to save him, I must know all there is to know—even if it should seem to make the case against him blacker than before."

"How well you understand," said Ursula.

"So you will tell me the whole story, will you not? From the beginning."

"You're not going to send *me* away, I hope," said Caroline, settling herself comfortably in an arm-chair. "What I want to know," she continued, "is why this child was masquerading as a parlormaid?"

"Masquerading?" I queried.

"That's what I said. Why did you do it, child? For a wager?"

"For a living," said Ursula dryly.

And encouraged, she began the story which I reproduce here in my own words.

Ursula Bourne, it seemed, was one of a family of seven—impoverished Irish gentlefolk. On the death of her father, most of the girls were cast out into the world to earn their own living. Ursula's eldest sister was married to Captain Folliott. It was she whom I had seen that Sunday, and the cause of her embarrassment was clear enough now. Determined to earn her living and not attracted to the idea of being a nursery governess—the one profession open to an untrained girl, Ursula preferred the job of parlormaid. She scorned to label herself a "lady parlormaid." She would be the real thing, her reference being supplied by her sister. At Fernly, despite an aloofness which, as has been seen, caused some comment, she was a success at her job—quick, competent, and thorough.

"I enjoyed the work," she explained. "And I had plenty of time to myself."

And then came her meeting with Ralph Paton, and the love affair which culminated in a secret marriage. Ralph had persuaded her into that, somewhat against her will. He had declared that his stepfather would not hear of his marrying a penniless girl. Better to be married secretly, and break the news to him at some later and more favorable minute.

And so the deed was done, and Ursula Bourne became Ursula Paton. Ralph had declared that he meant to pay off his debts, find a job, and then, when he was in a position to support her, and independent of his adopted father, they would break the news to him.

But to people like Ralph Paton, turning over a new leaf is easier in theory than in practice. He hoped that his stepfather, whilst still in ignorance of the marriage, might be persuaded to pay his debts and put him on his feet again. But the revelation of the amount of Ralph's liabilities merely enraged Roger Ackroyd, and he refused to do anything at all. Some months passed, and then Ralph was bidden once more to Fernly. Roger Ackroyd did not beat about the bush. It was the desire of his heart that Ralph should marry Flora, and he put the matter plainly before the young man.

And here it was that the innate weakness of Ralph Paton showed itself. As always, he grasped at the easy, the immediate solution. As far as I could make out, neither Flora nor Ralph made any pretence of love. It was, on both sides, a business arrangement. Roger Ackroyd dictated his wishes—they agreed to them. Flora accepted a chance of liberty, money, and an enlarged horizon; Ralph, of course, was playing a different game. But he was in a very awkward hole financially. He seized at the chance. His debts would be paid. He could start again with a clean sheet. His was not a nature to envisage the future, but I gather that he saw vaguely the engagement with Flora being broken off after a decent interval had elapsed. Both Flora and he stipulated that it should be kept a secret for the present. He was anxious to conceal it from Ursula. He felt instinctively that her nature, strong and resolute, with an inherent distaste for duplicity, was not one to welcome such a course.

Then came the crucial moment when Roger Ackroyd, always high-handed, decided to announce the engagement. He said no word of his intention to Ralph—only to Flora, and Flora, apathetic, raised no objection. On Ursula, the news fell like a bombshell. Summoned by her, Ralph came hurriedly down from town. They met in the wood, where part of their conversation was overheard by my sister. Ralph implored her to keep silent for a little while longer, Ursula was equally determined to have done with concealments. She would tell Mr. Ackroyd the truth without any further delay. Husband and wife parted acrimoniously.

Ursula, steadfast in her purpose, sought an interview with Roger Ackroyd that very afternoon, and revealed the truth to him. Their interview was a stormy one—it might have been even more stormy had not Roger Ackroyd been already obsessed with his own troubles. It was bad enough, however. Ackroyd was not the kind of man to forgive the deceit that had been practiced upon him. His rancor was mainly directed to Ralph, but Ursula came in for her share, since he regarded her as a girl who had deliberately tried to "entrap" the adopted son of a very wealthy man. Unforgivable things were said on both sides.

That same evening Ursula met Ralph by appointment in the small summer-house, stealing out from the house by the side door in order to do so. Their interview was made up of reproaches on both sides. Ralph charged Ursula with having irretrievably ruined his prospects by her ill-timed revelation. Ursula reproached Ralph with his duplicity.

They parted at last. A little over half an hour later came the discovery of Roger Ackroyd's body. Since that night Ursula had neither seen nor heard from Ralph.

As the story unfolded itself, I realized more and more what a damning series of facts it was. Alive, Ackroyd could hardly have failed to alter his will—I knew him well enough to realize that to do so would be his first thought. His death came in the nick of time for Ralph and Ursula Paton. Small wonder the girl had held her tongue, and played her part so consistently.

My meditations were interrupted. It was Poirot's voice speaking, and I knew from the gravity of his tone that he, too, was fully alive to the implications of the position.

"Mademoiselle, I must ask you one question, and you must answer it truthfully, for on it everything may hang: What time was it when you parted from Captain Ralph Paton in the summer-house? Now, take a little minute so that your answer may be very exact."

The girl gave a half laugh, bitter enough in all conscience.

"Do you think I haven't gone over that again and again in my own mind? It was just half-past nine when I went out to meet him. Major Blunt was walking up and down the terrace, so I had to go round through the bushes to avoid him. It must have been about twenty-seven minutes to ten when I reached the summer-house. Ralph was waiting for me. I was with him ten minutes—not longer, for it was just a quarter to ten when I got back to the house."

I saw now the insistence of her question the other day. If only Ackroyd could have been proved to have been killed before a quarter to ten, and not after.

I saw the reflection of that thought in Poirot's next question.

"Who left the summer-house first?"

"I did."

"Leaving Ralph Paton in the summer-house?"

"Yes—but you don't think——"

"Mademoiselle, it is of no importance what I think. What did you do when you got back to the house?"

"I went up to my room."

"And stayed there until when?"

"Until about ten o'clock."

"Is there any one who can prove that?"

"Prove? That I was in my room, you mean? Oh! no. But surely—oh! I see, they might think—they might think——"

I saw the dawning horror in her eyes.

Poirot finished the sentence for her.

"That it was *you* who entered by the window and stabbed Mr. Ackroyd as he sat in his chair? Yes, they might think just that."

"Nobody but a fool would think any such thing," said Caroline indignantly. She patted Ursula on the shoulder.

The girl had her face hidden in her hands.

"Horrible," she was murmuring. "Horrible."

Caroline gave her a friendly shake.

"Don't worry, my dear," she said. "M. Poirot doesn't think that really. As for that husband of yours, I don't think much of him, and I tell you so candidly. Running away and leaving you to face the music."

But Ursula shook her head energetically.

"Oh, no," she cried. "It wasn't like that at all. Ralph would not run away on his own account. I see now. If he heard of his stepfather's murder, he might think himself that I had done it."

"He wouldn't think any such thing," said Caroline.

"I was so cruel to him that night—so hard and bitter. I wouldn't listen to what he was trying to say—wouldn't believe that he really cared. I just stood there telling him what I thought of him, and saying the coldest, cruelest things that came into my mind—trying my best to hurt him."

"Do him no harm," said Caroline. "Never worry about what you say to a man. They're so conceited that they never believe you mean it if it's un-flattering."

Ursula went on, nervously twisting and untwisting her hands.

"When the murder was discovered and he didn't come forward, I was terribly upset. Just for a moment I wondered—but then I knew he couldn't—he couldn't. . . . But I wished he would come forward and say openly that he'd had nothing to do with it. I knew that he was very fond of Dr. Sheppard, and I fancied that perhaps Dr. Sheppard might know where he was hiding."

She turned to me.

"That's why I said what I did to you that day. I thought, if you knew where he was, you might pass on the message to him."

"I?" I exclaimed.

"Why should James know where he was?" demanded Caroline sharply.

"It was very unlikely, I know," admitted Ursula, "but Ralph had often spoken of Dr. Sheppard, and I knew that he would be likely to consider him as his best friend in King's Abbot."

"My dear child," I said, "I have not the least idea where Ralph Paton is at the present moment."

"That is true enough," said Poirot.

"But——" Ursula held out the newspaper cutting in a puzzled fashion.

"Ah! that," said Poirot, slightly embarrassed; "a *bagatelle*, mademoiselle. A *rien du tout*. Not for a moment do I believe that Ralph Paton has been arrested."

"But then——" began the girl slowly.

Poirot went on quickly:—

"There is one thing I should like to know—did Captain Paton wear shoes or boots that night?"

Ursula shook her head.

"I can't remember."

"A pity! But how should you? Now, madame," he smiled at her, his head on one side, his forefinger wagging eloquently, "no questions. And do not torment yourself. Be of good courage, and place your faith in Hercule Poirot."

XXIII. POIROT'S LITTLE REUNION

"And now," said Caroline, rising, "that child is coming upstairs to lie down. Don't you worry, my dear. M. Poirot will do everything he can for you —be sure of that."

"I ought to go back to Fernly," said Ursula uncertainly.

But Caroline silenced her protests with a firm hand.

"Nonsense. You're in my hands for the time being. You'll stay here for the present, anyway—eh, M. Poirot?"

"It will be the best plan," agreed the little Belgian. "This evening I shall want mademoiselle—I beg her pardon, madame—to attend my little reunion. Nine o'clock at my house. It is most necessary that she should be there."

Caroline nodded, and went with Ursula out of the room. The door shut behind them. Poirot dropped down into a chair again.

"So far, so good," he said. "Things are straightening themselves out."

"They're getting to look blacker and blacker against Ralph Paton," I observed gloomily.

Poirot nodded.

"Yes, that is so. But it was to be expected, was it not?"

I looked at him, slightly puzzled by the remark. He was leaning back in the chair, his eyes half closed, the tips of his fingers just touching each other. Suddenly he sighed and shook his head.

"What is it?" I asked.

"It is that there are moments when a great longing for my friend Hastings comes over me. That is the friend of whom I spoke to you—the one who resides now in the Argentine. Always, when I have had a big case, he has been by my side. And he has helped me—yes, often he has helped me. For he had a knack, that one, of stumbling over the truth unawares—without noticing it himself, *bien entendu*. At times he has said something particularly foolish, and behold that foolish remark has revealed the truth to me! And then, too, it was his practice to keep a written record of the cases that proved interesting."

I gave a slight embarrassed cough.

"As far as that goes," I began, and then stopped.

Poirot sat upright in his chair. His eyes sparkled.

"But yes? What is it that you would say?"

"Well, as a matter of fact, I've read some of Captain Hastings's narratives, and I thought, why not try my hand at something of the same kind? Seemed a pity not to—unique opportunity—probably the only time I'll be mixed up with anything of this kind."

I felt myself getting hotter and hotter, and more and more incoherent, as I floundered through the above speech.

Poirot sprang from his chair. I had a moment's terror that he was going to embrace me French fashion, but mercifully he refrained.

"But this is magnificent—you have then written down your impressions of the case as you went along?"

I nodded.

"*Epatant!*" cried Poirot. "Let me see them—this instant."

I was not quite prepared for such a sudden demand. I racked my brains to remember certain details.

"I hope you won't mind," I stammered. "I may have been a little—er—*personal* now and then."

"Oh! I comprehend perfectly; you have referred to me as comic—as, perhaps, ridiculous now and then? It matters not at all. Hastings, he also was not always polite. Me, I have the mind above such trivialities."

Still somewhat doubtful, I rummaged in the drawers of my desk and produced an untidy pile of manuscript which I handed over to him. With an eye on possible publication in the future, I had divided the work into chapters, and the night before I had brought it up to date with an account of Miss Russell's visit. Poirot had therefore twenty chapters.

I left him with them.

I was obliged to go out to a case at some distance away, and it was past eight o'clock when I got back, to be greeted with a plate of hot dinner on a tray, and the announcement that Poirot and my sister had supped together at half-past seven, and that the former had then gone to my workshop to finish his reading of the manuscript.

"I hope, James," said my sister, "that you've been careful in what you say about me in it?"

My jaw dropped. I had not been careful at all.

"Not that it matters very much," said Caroline, reading my expression correctly. "M. Poirot will know what to think. He understands me much better than you do."

I went into the workshop. Poirot was sitting by the window. The manuscript lay neatly piled on a chair beside him. He laid his hand on it and spoke.

"*Eh bien*," he said, "I congratulate you—on your modesty!"

"Oh!" I said, rather taken aback.

"And on your reticence," he added.

I said "Oh!" again.

"Not so did Hastings write," continued my friend. "On every page, many, many times was the word 'I.' What *he* thought—what *he* did. But you—you have kept your personality in the background; only once or twice does it obtrude—in scenes of home life, shall we say?"

I blushed a little before the twinkle in his eye.

"What do you really think of the stuff?" I asked nervously.

"You want my candid opinion?"

"Yes."

Poirot laid his jesting manner aside.

"A very meticulous and accurate account," he said kindly. "You have recorded all the facts faithfully and exactly—though you have shown yourself becomingly reticent as to your own share in them."

"And it has helped you?"

"Yes. I may say that it has helped me considerably. Come, we must go over to my house and set the stage for my little performance."

Caroline was in the hall. I think she hoped that she might be invited to accompany us. Poirot dealt with the situation tactfully.

"I should much like to have had you present, mademoiselle," he said regretfully, "but at this juncture it would not be wise. See you, all these people to-night are suspects. Amongst them, I shall find the person who killed Mr. Ackroyd."

"You really believe that?" I said incredulously.

"I see that you do not," said Poirot dryly. "Not yet do you appreciate Hercule Poirot at his true worth."

At that minute Ursula came down the staircase.

"You are ready, my child?" said Poirot. "That is good. We will go to my house together. Mademoiselle Caroline, believe me, I do everything possible to render you service. Good-evening."

We went out, leaving Caroline, rather like a dog who has been refused a walk, standing on the front door step gazing after us.

The sitting-room at The Larches had been got ready. On the table were various *sirops* and glasses. Also a plate of biscuits. Several chairs had been brought in from the other room.

Poirot ran to and fro rearranging things. Pulling out a chair here, altering the position of a lamp there, occasionally stooping to straighten one of the mats that covered the floor. He was specially fussy over the lighting. The lamps were arranged in such a way as to throw a clear light on the side of the room where the chairs were grouped, at the same time leaving the other end of the room, where I presumed Poirot himself would sit, in a dim twilight.

Ursula and I watched him. Presently a bell was heard.

"They arrive," said Poirot. "Good, all is in readiness."

The door opened and the party from Fernly filed in. Poirot went forward and greeted Mrs. Ackroyd and Flora.

"It is most good of you to come," he said. "And Major Blunt and Mr. Raymond."

The secretary was debonair as ever.

"What's the great idea?" he said, laughing. "Some scientific machine? Do we have bands round our wrists which register guilty heart-beats? There is such an invention, isn't there?"

"I have read of it, yes," admitted Poirot. "But me, I am old-fashioned. I use the old methods. I work only with the little gray cells. Now let us begin—but first I have an announcement to make to you all."

He took Ursula's hand and drew her forward.

"This lady is Mrs. Ralph Paton. She was married to Captain Paton last March."

A little shriek burst from Mrs. Ackroyd.

"Ralph! Married! Last March! Oh! but it's absurd. How could he be?" She stared at Ursula as though she had never seen her before.

"Married to Bourne?" she said. "Really, M. Poirot, I don't believe you." Ursula flushed and began to speak, but Flora forestalled her.

Going quickly to the other girl's side, she passed her hand through her arm.

"You must not mind our being surprised," she said. "You see, we had no idea of such a thing. You and Ralph have kept your secret very well. I am—very glad about it."

"You are very kind, Miss Ackroyd," said Ursula in a low voice, "and you have every right to be exceedingly angry. Ralph behaved very badly—especially to you."

"You needn't worry about that," said Flora, giving her arm a consoling little pat. "Ralph was in a corner and took the only way out. I should probably have done the same in his place. I do think he might have trusted me with the secret, though. I wouldn't have let him down."

Poirot rapped gently on a table and cleared his throat significantly.

"The board meeting's going to begin," said Flora. "M. Poirot hints that we mustn't talk. But just tell me one thing. Where is Ralph? You must know if any one does."

"But I don't," cried Ursula, almost in a wail. "That's just it, I don't."

"Isn't he detained at Liverpool?" asked Raymond. "It said so in the paper."

"He is not at Liverpool," said Poirot shortly.

"In fact," I remarked, "no one knows where he is."

"Excepting Hercule Poirot, eh?" said Raymond.

Poirot replied seriously to the other's banter.

"Me, I know everything. Remember that."

Geoffrey Raymond lifted his eyebrows.

"Everything?" He whistled. "Whew! that's a tall order."

"Do you mean to say you can really guess where Ralph Paton is hiding?" I asked incredulously.

"You call it guessing. I call it knowing, my friend."

"In Cranchester?" I hazarded.

"No," replied Poirot gravely, "not in Cranchester."

He said no more, but at a gesture from him the assembled party took their seats. As they did so, the door opened once more and two other people came in and sat down near the door. They were Parker and the housekeeper.

"The number is complete," said Poirot. "Every one is here."

There was a ring of satisfaction in his tone. And with the sound of it I saw a ripple of something like uneasiness pass over all those faces grouped at the other end of the room. There was a suggestion in all this as of a trap—a trap that had closed.

Poirot read from a list in an important manner.

"Mrs. Ackroyd, Miss Flora Ackroyd, Major Blunt, Mr. Geoffrey Raymond, Mrs. Ralph Paton, John Parker, Elizabeth Russell."

He laid the paper down on the table.

"What's the meaning of all this?" began Raymond.

"The list I have just read," said Poirot, "is a list of suspected persons. Every one of you present had the opportunity to kill Mr. Ackroyd——"

With a cry Mrs. Ackroyd sprang up, her throat working.

"I don't like it," she wailed. "I don't like it. I would much prefer to go home."

"You cannot go home, madame," said Poirot sternly, "until you have heard what I have to say."

He paused a moment, then cleared his throat.

"I will start at the beginning. When Miss Ackroyd asked me to investigate the case, I went up to Fernly Park with the good Dr. Sheppard. I walked with him along the terrace, where I was shown the footprints on the window-sill. From there Inspector Raglan took me along the path which leads to the drive. My eye was caught by a little summer-house, and I searched it thoroughly. I found two things—a scrap of starched cambric and an empty goose quill. The scrap of cambric immediately suggested to me a maid's apron. When Inspector Raglan showed me his list of the people in the house, I noticed at once that one of the maids—Ursula Bourne, the parlormaid—had no real alibi. According to her own story, she was in her bedroom from nine-thirty until ten. But supposing that instead she was in the summer-house? If so, she must have gone there to meet some one. Now we know from Dr. Sheppard that some one from outside *did* come to the house that night—the stranger whom he met just by the gate. At a first glance it would seem that our problem was solved, and that the stranger went to the summer-house to meet Ursula Bourne. It was fairly certain that he *did* go to the summer-house because of the goose quill. That suggested at once to my mind a taker of drugs—and one who had acquired the habit on the other side of the Atlantic where sniffing 'snow' is more common than in this country. The man whom Dr. Sheppard met had an American accent, which fitted in with that supposition.

"But I was held up by one point. *The times did not fit.* Ursula Bourne could certainly not have gone to the summer-house before nine-thirty, whereas the man must have got there by a few minutes past nine. I could, of course, assume that he waited there for half an hour. The only alternative supposition was that there had been two separate meetings in the summer-house that night. *Eh bien,* as soon as I went into that alternative I found several significant facts. I discovered that Miss Russell, the housekeeper, had visited Dr. Sheppard that morning, and had displayed a good deal of interest in cures for victims of the drug habit. Taking that in conjunction with the goose quill, I assumed that the man in question came to Fernly to meet the housekeeper, and not Ursula Bourne. Who, then, did Ursula Bourne come to the rendezvous to meet? I was not long in doubt. First I found a ring—a wedding ring—with 'From R.' and a date inside it. Then I learnt that Ralph Paton had been seen coming up the path which led to the summer-house at twenty-five minutes past nine, and I also heard of a certain conversation which had taken place in the wood near the village that very afternoon—a conversation between Ralph Paton and some unknown girl. So I had my facts succeeding each other in a neat and orderly manner. A secret marriage, an engagement announced on the day of the tragedy, the stormy interview in the wood, and the meeting arranged for the summer-house that night.

"Incidentally this proved to me one thing, that both Ralph Paton and Ursula Bourne (or Paton) had the strongest motives for wishing Mr. Ackroyd out of the way. And it also made one other point unexpectedly clear. It could not have been Ralph Paton who was with Mr. Ackroyd in the study at nine-thirty.

"So we come to another and most interesting aspect of the crime. Who was it in the room with Mr. Ackroyd at nine-thirty? Not Ralph Paton, who was in the summer-house with his wife. Not Charles Kent, who had already left. Who, then? I posed my cleverest—my most audacious question: *Was any one with him?*"

Poirot leaned forward and shot the last words triumphantly at us, drawing back afterwards with the air of one who has made a decided hit.

Raymond, however, did not seem impressed, and lodged a mild protest.

"I don't know if you're trying to make me out a liar, M. Poirot, but the matter does not rest on my evidence alone—except perhaps as to the exact words used. Remember, Major Blunt also heard Mr. Ackroyd talking to some one. He was on the terrace outside, and couldn't catch the words clearly, but he distinctly heard the voices."

Poirot nodded.

"I have not forgotten," he said quietly. "But Major Blunt was under the impression that it was *you* to whom Mr. Ackroyd was speaking."

For a moment Raymond seemed taken aback. Then he recovered himself.

"Blunt knows now that he was mistaken," he said.

"Exactly," agreed the other man.

"Yet there must have been some reason for his thinking so," mused Poirot. "Oh! no," he held up his hand in protest, "I know the reason you will give— but it is not enough. We must seek elsewhere. I will put it this way. From the beginning of the case I have been struck by one thing—the nature of those words which Mr. Raymond overheard. It has been amazing to me that no one has commented on them—has seen anything odd about them."

He paused a minute, and then quoted softly:—

" '. . . *The calls on my purse have been so frequent of late that I fear it is impossible for me to accede to your request.*' Does nothing strike you as odd about that?"

"I don't think so," said Raymond. "He has frequently dictated letters to me, using almost exactly those same words."

"Exactly," cried Poirot. "That is what I seek to arrive at. Would any man use such a phrase in *talking* to another? Impossible that that should be part of a real conversation. Now, if he had been dictating a letter——"

"You mean he was reading a letter aloud," said Raymond slowly. "Even so, he must have been reading to some one."

"But why? We have no evidence that there was any one else in the room. No other voice but Mr. Ackroyd's was heard, remember."

"Surely a man wouldn't read letters of that type aloud to himself—not unless he was—well—going balmy."

"You have all forgotten one thing," said Poirot softly: "the stranger who called at the house the preceding Wednesday."

They all stared at him.

"But yes," said Poirot, nodding encouragingly, "on Wednesday. The young man was not of himself important. But the firm he represented interested me very much."

"The Dictaphone Company," gasped Raymond. "I see it now. A dicta-phone. That's what you think?"

Poirot nodded.

"Mr. Ackroyd had promised to invest in a dictaphone, you remember. Me, I had the curiosity to inquire of the company in question. Their reply is that Mr. Ackroyd *did* purchase a dictaphone from their representative. Why he concealed the matter from you, I do not know."

"He must have meant to surprise me with it," murmured Raymond. "He had quite a childish love of surprising people. Meant to keep it up his sleeve for a day or so. Probably was playing with it like a new toy. Yes, it fits in. You're quite right—no one would use quite those words in casual conversation."

"It explains, too," said Poirot, "why Major Blunt thought it was you who were in the study. Such scraps as came to him were fragments of dictation, and so his subconscious mind deduced that you were with him. His conscious mind was occupied with something quite different—the white figure he had caught a glimpse of. He fancied it was Miss Ackroyd. Really, of course, it was Ursula Bourne's white apron he saw as she was stealing down to the summer-house."

Raymond had recovered from his first surprise.

"All the same," he remarked, "this discovery of yours, brilliant though it is (I'm quite sure I should never have thought of it), leaves the essential position unchanged. Mr. Ackroyd was alive at nine-thirty, since he was speaking into the dictaphone. It seems clear that the man Charles Kent was really off the premises by then. As to Ralph Paton——?"

He hesitated, glancing at Ursula.

Her color flared up, but she answered steadily enough.

"Ralph and I parted just before a quarter to ten. He never went near the house, I am sure of that. He had no intention of doing so. The last thing on earth he wanted was to face his stepfather. He would have funked it badly."

"It isn't that I doubt your story for a moment," explained Raymond. "I've always been quite sure Captain Paton was innocent. But one has to think of a court of law—and the questions that would be asked. He is in a most unfortunate position, but if he were to come forward——"

Poirot interrupted.

"That is your advice, yes? That he should come forward?"

"Certainly. If you know where he is——"

"I perceive that you do not believe that I do know. And yet I have told you just now that I know everything. The truth of the telephone call, of the footprints on the window-sill, of the hiding-place of Ralph Paton——"

"Where is he?" said Blunt sharply.

"Not very far away," said Poirot, smiling.

"In Cranchester?" I asked.

Poirot turned towards me.

"Always you ask me that. The idea of Cranchester it is with you an *idée fixe*. No, he is not in Cranchester. He is—*there!*"

He pointed a dramatic forefinger. Every one's head turned.

Ralph Paton was standing in the doorway.

XXIV. RALPH PATON'S STORY

It was a very uncomfortable minute for *me*. I hardly took in what happened next, but there were exclamations and cries of surprise! When I was sufficiently master of myself to be able to realize what was going on, Ralph Paton was standing by his wife, her hand in his, and he was smiling across the room at me.

Poirot, too, was smiling, and at the same time shaking an eloquent finger at me.

"Have I not told you at least thirty-six times that it is useless to conceal things from Hercule Poirot?" he demanded. "That in such a case he finds out?"

He turned to the others.

"One day, you remember, we held a little séance about a table—just the six of us. I accused the other five persons present of concealing something from me. Four of them gave up their secret. Dr. Sheppard did not give up his. But all along I have had my suspicions. Dr. Sheppard went to the Three Boars that night hoping to find Ralph. He did not find him there; but supposing, I said to myself, that he met him in the street on his way home? Dr. Sheppard was a friend of Captain Paton's, and he had come straight from the scene of the crime. He must know that things looked very black against him. Perhaps he knew more than the general public did——"

"I did," I said ruefully. "I suppose I might as well make a clean breast of things now. I went to see Ralph that afternoon. At first he refused to take me into his confidence, but later he told me about his marriage, and the hole he was in. As soon as the murder was discovered, I realized that once the facts were known, suspicion could not fail to attach to Ralph—or, if not to him, to the girl he loved. That night I put the facts plainly before him. The thought of having possibly to give evidence which might incriminate his wife made him resolve at all costs to—to——"

I hesitated, and Ralph filled up the gap.

"To do a bunk," he said graphically. "You see, Ursula left me to go back to the house. I thought it possible that she might have attempted to have another interview with my stepfather. He had already been very rude to her that afternoon. It occurred to me that he might have so insulted her—in such an unforgivable manner—that without knowing what she was doing——"

He stopped. Ursula released her hand from his, and stepped back.

"You thought that, Ralph! You actually thought that I might have done it?"

"Let us get back to the culpable conduct of Dr. Sheppard," said Poirot dryly. "Dr. Sheppard consented to do what he could to help him. He was successful in hiding Captain Paton from the police."

"Where?" asked Raymond. "In his own house?"

"Ah, no, indeed," said Poirot. "You should ask yourself the question that

I did. If the good doctor is concealing the young man, what place would he choose? It must necessarily be somewhere near at hand. I think of Cranchester. A hotel? No. Lodgings? Even more emphatically, no. Where, then? Ah! I have it. A nursing home. A home for the mentally unfit. I test my theory. I invent a nephew with mental trouble. I consult Mademoiselle Sheppard as to suitable homes. She gives me the names of two near Cranchester to which her brother has sent patients. I make inquiries. Yes, at one of them a patient was brought there by the doctor himself early on Saturday morning. That patient, though known by another name, I had no difficulty in identifying as Captain Paton. After certain necessary formalities, I was allowed to bring him away. He arrived at my house in the early hours of yesterday morning."

I looked at him ruefully.

"Caroline's Home Office expert," I murmured. "And to think I never guessed!"

"You see now why I drew attention to the reticence of your manuscript," murmured Poirot. "It was strictly truthful as far as it went—but it did not go very far, eh, my friend?"

I was too abashed to argue.

"Dr. Sheppard has been very loyal," said Ralph. "He has stood by me through thick and thin. He did what he thought was the best. I see now, from what M. Poirot has told me, that it was not really the best. I should have come forward and faced the music. You see, in the home, we never saw a newspaper. I knew nothing of what was going on."

"Dr. Sheppard has been a model of discretion," said Poirot dryly. "But me, I discover all the little secrets. It is my business."

"Now we can have your story of what happened that night," said Raymond impatiently.

"You know it already," said Ralph. "There's very little for me to add. I left the summer-house about nine-forty-five, and tramped about the lanes, trying to make up my mind as to what to do next—what line to take. I'm bound to admit that I've not the shadow of an alibi, but I give you my solemn word that I never went to the study, that I never saw my stepfather alive—or dead. Whatever the world thinks, I'd like all of you to believe me."

"No alibi," murmured Raymond. "That's bad. I believe you, of course, but—it's a bad business."

"It makes things very simple, though," said Poirot, in a cheerful voice. "Very simple indeed."

We all stared at him.

"You see what I mean? No? Just this—to save Captain Paton the real criminal must confess."

He beamed round at us all.

"But yes—I mean what I say. See now, I did not invite Inspector Raglan to be present. That was for a reason. I did not want to tell him all that I knew—at least I did not want to tell him to-night."

He leaned forward, and suddenly his voice and his whole personality changed. He suddenly became dangerous.

"I who speak to you—I know the murderer of Mr. Ackroyd is in this room now. It is to the murderer I speak. *To-morrow the truth goes to Inspector Raglan.* You understand?"

There was a tense silence. Into the midst of it came the old Breton woman with a telegram on a salver. Poirot tore it open.

Blunt's voice rose abrupt and resonant.

"The murderer is amongst us, you say? You know—which?"

Poirot had read the message. He crumpled it up in his hand.

"I know—now."

He tapped the crumpled ball of paper.

"What is that?" said Raymond sharply.

"A wireless message—from a steamer now on her way to the United States."

There was a dead silence. Poirot rose to his feet bowing.

"Messieurs et Mesdames, this reunion of mine is at an end. Remember—*the truth goes to Inspector Raglan in the morning.*"

XXV. THE WHOLE TRUTH

A slight gesture from Poirot enjoined me to stay behind the rest. I obeyed, going over to the fire and thoughtfully stirring the big logs on it with the toe of my boot.

I was puzzled. For the first time I was absolutely at sea as to Poirot's meaning. For a moment I was inclined to think that the scene I had just witnessed was a gigantic piece of bombast—that he had been what he called "playing the comedy" with a view to making himself interesting and important. But, in spite of myself, I was forced to believe in an underlying reality. There had been real menace in his words—a certain indisputable sincerity. But I still believed him to be on entirely the wrong tack.

When the door shut behind the last of the party he came over to the fire.

"Well, my friend," he said quietly, "and what do you think of it all?"

"I don't know what to think," I said frankly. "What was the point? Why not go straight to Inspector Raglan with the truth instead of giving the guilty person this elaborate warning?"

Poirot sat down and drew out his case of tiny Russian cigarettes. He smoked for a minute or two in silence. Then:—

"Use your little gray cells," he said. "There is always a reason behind my actions."

I hesitated for a moment, and then I said slowly:

"The first one that occurs to me is that you yourself do not know who the guilty person is, but that you are sure that he is to be found amongst the people here to-night. Therefore your words were intended to force a confession from the unknown murderer?"

Poirot nodded approvingly.

"A clever idea, but not the truth."

"I thought, perhaps, that by making him believe you knew, you might force him out into the open—not necessarily by confession. He might try to silence you as he formerly silenced Mr. Ackroyd—before you could act to-morrow morning."

"A trap with myself as the bait! *Merci, mon ami,* but I am not sufficiently heroic for that."

"Then I fail to understand you. Surely you are running the risk of letting the murderer escape by thus putting him on his guard?"

Poirot shook his head.

"He cannot escape," he said gravely. "There is only one way out—and that way does not lead to freedom."

"You really believe that one of those people here to-night committed the murder?" I asked incredulously.

"Yes, my friend."

"Which one?"

There was a silence for some minutes. Then Poirot tossed the stump of his cigarette into the grate and began to speak in a quiet, reflective tone.

"I will take you the way that I have traveled myself. Step by step you shall accompany me, and see for yourself that all the facts point indisputably to one person. Now, to begin with, there were two facts and one little discrepancy in time which especially attracted my attention. The first fact was the telephone call. If Ralph Paton were indeed the murderer, the telephone call became meaningless and absurd. Therefore, I said to myself, Ralph Paton is not the murderer.

"I satisfied myself that the call could not have been sent by any one in the house, yet I was convinced that it was amongst those present on the fatal evening that I had to look for my criminal. Therefore I concluded that the telephone call must have been sent by an accomplice. I was not quite pleased with that deduction, but I let it stand for the minute.

"I next examined the *motive* for the call. That was difficult. I could only get at it by judging its *result*. Which was—that the murder was discovered that night instead of—in all probability—the following morning. You agree with that?"

"Ye-es," I admitted. "Yes. As you say, Mr. Ackroyd, having given orders that he was not to be disturbed, nobody would have been likely to go to the study that night."

"*Tres bien.* The affair marches, does it not? But matters were still obscure. What was the advantage of having the crime discovered that night in preference to the following morning? The only idea I could get hold of was that the murderer, knowing the crime was to be discovered at a certain time, could make sure of being present when the door was broken in—or at any rate immediately afterwards. And now we come to the second fact—the chair pulled out from the wall. Inspector Raglan dismissed that as of no importance. I, on the contrary, have always regarded it as of supreme importance.

"In your manuscript you have drawn a neat little plan of the study. If you had it with you this minute you would see that—the chair being drawn out in the position indicated by Parker—it would stand in a direct line between the door and the window."

"The window!" I said quickly.

"You, too, have my first idea. I imagined that the chair was drawn out so that something connected with the window should not be seen by any one entering through the door. But I soon abandoned that supposition, for though the chair was a grandfather with a high back, it obscured very little of the window—only the part between the sash and the ground. No, *mon ami* —but remember that just in front of the window there stood a table with books and magazines upon it. Now that table *was* completely hidden by the drawn-out chair—and immediately I had my first shadowy suspicion of the truth.

"Supposing that there had been something on that table not intended to be seen? Something placed there by the murderer? As yet I had no inkling of what that something might be. But I knew certain very interesting facts about it. For instance, it was something that the murderer had not been able to take away with him at the time that he committed the crime. At the same time it was vital that it should be removed as soon as possible after the crime had been discovered. And so—the telephone message, and the opportunity for the murderer to be on the spot when the body was discovered.

"Now four people were on the scene before the police arrived. Yourself, Parker, Major Blunt, and Mr. Raymond. Parker I eliminated at once, since at whatever time the crime was discovered, he was the one person certain to be on the spot. Also it was he who told me of the pulled-out chair. Parker, then, was cleared (of the murder, that is. I still thought it possible that he had been blackmailing Mrs. Ferrars). Raymond and Blunt, however, remained under suspicion since, if the crime had been discovered in the early hours of the morning, it was quite possible that they might have arrived on the scene too late to prevent the object on the round table being discovered.

"Now what was that object? You heard my arguments to-night in reference to the scrap of conversation overheard? As soon as I learned that a representative of a dictaphone company had called, the idea of a dictaphone took root in my mind. You heard what I said in this room not half an hour ago? They all agreed with my theory—but one vital fact seems to have escaped them. Granted that a dictaphone was being used by Mr. Ackroyd that night—why was no dictaphone found?"

"I never thought of that," I said.

"We know that a dictaphone was supplied to Mr. Ackroyd. But no dictaphone has been found amongst his effects. So, if something was taken from that table—why should not that something be the dictaphone? But there were certain difficulties in the way. The attention of every one was, of course, focused on the murdered man. I think any one could have gone to the table unnoticed by the other people in the room. But a dictaphone has a certain bulk—it cannot be slipped casually into a pocket. There must have been a receptacle of some kind capable of holding it.

"You see where I am arriving? The figure of the murderer is taking shape. A person who was on the scene straightway, but who might not have been if the crime had been discovered the following morning. A person carrying a receptacle into which the dictaphone might be fitted——"

I interrupted.

"But why remove the dictaphone? What was the point?"

"You are like Mr. Raymond. You take it for granted that what was heard at nine-thirty was Mr. Ackroyd's voice speaking into a dictaphone. But consider this useful invention for a little minute. You dictate into it, do you not? And at some later time a secretary or a typist turns it on, and the voice speaks again."

"You mean——" I gasped.

Poirot nodded.

"Yes, I mean that. *At nine-thirty Mr. Ackroyd was already dead.* It was the dictaphone speaking—not the man."

"And the murderer switched it on. Then he must have been in the room at that minute?"

"Possibly. But we must not exclude the likelihood of some mechanical device having been applied—something after the nature of a time lock, or even of a simple alarm clock. But in that case we must add two qualifications to our imaginary portrait of the murderer. It must be some one who knew of Mr. Ackroyd's purchase of the dictaphone and also some one with the necessary mechanical knowledge.

"I had got thus far in my own mind when we came to the footprints on the window ledge. Here there were three conclusions open to me. (1) They might really have been made by Ralph Paton. He had been at Fernly that night, and might have climbed into the study and found his uncle dead there. That was one hypothesis. (2) There was the possibility that the footmarks might have been made by somebody else who happened to have the same kind of studs in his shoes. But the inmates of the house had shoes soled with crepe rubber, and I declined to believe in the coincidence of some one from outside having the same kind of shoes as Ralph Paton wore. Charles Kent, as we know from the barmaid of the Dog and Whistle, had on a pair of boots 'clean dropping off him.' (3) Those prints were made by some one deliberately trying to throw suspicion on Ralph Paton. To test this last conclusion, it was necessary to ascertain certain facts. One pair of Ralph's shoes had been obtained from the Three Boars by the police. Neither Ralph nor any one else could have worn them that evening, since they were downstairs being cleaned. According to the police theory, Ralph was wearing another pair of the same kind, and I found out that it was true that he had two pairs. Now for my theory to be proved correct it was necessary for the murderer to have worn Ralph's shoes that evening—in which case Ralph must have been wearing yet a *third* pair of footwear of some kind. I could hardly suppose that he would bring three pairs of shoes all alike—the third pair of footwear were more likely to be boots. I got your sister to make inquiries on this point—laying some stress on the color, in order—I admit it frankly—to obscure the real reason for my asking.

"You know the result of her investigations. Ralph Paton *had* had a pair of boots with him. The first question I asked him when he came to my house yesterday morning was what he was wearing on his feet on the fatal night. He replied at once that he had worn *boots*—he was still wearing them, in fact—having nothing else to put on.

"So we get a step further in our description of the murderer—a person who had the opportunity to take these shoes of Ralph Paton's from the Three Boars that day."

He paused, and then said, with a slightly raised voice:—

"There is one further point. The murderer must have been a person who had the opportunity to purloin that dagger from the silver table. You might argue that any one in the house might have done so, but I will recall to you that Miss Ackroyd was very positive that the dagger was not there when she examined the silver table."

He paused again.

"Let us recapitulate—now that all is clear. A person who was at the Three Boars earlier that day, a person who knew Ackroyd well enough to know that he had purchased a dictaphone, a person who was of a mechanical turn of mind, who had the opportunity to take the dagger from the silver table before Miss Flora arrived, who had with him a receptacle suitable for hiding the dictaphone—such as a black bag, and who had the study to himself for a few minutes after the crime was discovered while Parker was telephoning for the police. In fact—*Dr. Sheppard!*"

XXVI. AND NOTHING BUT THE TRUTH

There was a dead silence for a minute and a half.

Then I laughed.

"You're mad," I said.

"No," said Poirot placidly. "I am not mad. It was the little discrepancy in time that first drew my attention to you—right at the beginning."

"Discrepancy in time?" I queried, puzzled.

"But yes. You will remember that every one agreed—you yourself included—that it took five minutes to walk from the lodge to the house—less if you took the short cut to the terrace. But you left the house at ten minutes to nine—both by your own statement and that of Parker, and yet it was nine o'clock as you passed through the lodge gates. It was a chilly night—not an evening a man would be inclined to dawdle; why had you taken ten minutes to do a five-minutes' walk? All along I realized that we had only your statement for it that the study window was ever fastened. Ackroyd asked you if you had done so—he never looked to see. Supposing, then, that the study window was unfastened? Would there be time in that ten minutes for you to run round the outside of the house, change your shoes, climb in through the window, kill Ackroyd, and get to the gate by nine o'clock? I decided against that theory since in all probability a man as nervous as Ackroyd was that night would hear you climbing in, and then there would have been a struggle. But supposing that you killed Ackroyd *before* you left—as you were standing beside his chair? Then you go out of the front door, run round to the summer-house, take Ralph Paton's shoes out of the bag you brought up with you that night, slip them on, walk through the mud in them, and leave prints on the window ledge, you climb in, lock the study door on the inside, run back to the summer-house, change back into your own shoes, and race down to the gate. (I went through similar actions the other day, when you were with Mrs. Ackroyd—it took ten minutes exactly.) Then home—and an alibi—since you had timed the dictaphone for half-past nine."

"My dear Poirot," I said in a voice that sounded strange and forced to my own ears, "you've been brooding over this case too long. What on earth had I to gain by murdering Ackroyd?"

"Safety. It was you who blackmailed Mrs. Ferrars. Who could have had a better knowledge of what killed Mr. Ferrars than the doctor who was attending him? When you spoke to me that first day in the garden, you mentioned a legacy received about a year ago. I have been unable to discover any trace of a legacy. You had to invent some way of accounting for Mrs. Ferrars's twenty thousand pounds. It has not done you much good. You lost most of it in speculation—then you put the screw on too hard, and Mrs. Ferrars took a way out that you had not expected. If Ackroyd had learnt the truth he would have had no mercy on you—you were ruined for ever."

"And the telephone call?" I asked, trying to rally. "You have a plausible explanation of that also, I suppose?"

"I will confess to you that it was my greatest stumbling block when I found that a call had actually been put through to you from King's Abbot station. I at first believed that you had simply invented the story. It was a very clever touch, that. You must have some excuse for arriving at Fernly, finding the body, and so getting the chance to remove the dictaphone on which your alibi depended. I had a very vague notion of how it was worked when I came to see your sister that first day and inquired as to what patients you had seen on Friday morning. I had no thought of Miss Russell in my mind at that time. Her visit was a lucky coincidence, since it distracted your mind from the real object of my questions. I found what I was looking for. Among your patients that morning was the steward of an American liner. Who more suitable than he to be leaving for Liverpool by the train that evening? And afterwards he would be on the high seas, well out of the way. I noted that the *Orion* sailed on Saturday, and having obtained the name of the steward I sent him a wireless message asking a certain question. This is his reply you saw me receive just now."

He held out the message to me. It ran as follows:—

"Quite correct. Dr. Sheppard asked me to leave a note at a patient's house. I was to ring him up from the station with the reply. Reply was 'No answer.'"

"It was a clever idea," said Poirot. "The call was genuine. Your sister saw you take it. But there was only one man's word as to what was actually said —your own!"

I yawned.

"All this," I said, "is very interesting—but hardly in the sphere of practical politics."

"You think not? Remember what I said—the truth goes to Inspector Raglan in the morning. But, for the sake of your good sister, I am willing to give you the chance of another way out. There might be, for instance, an overdose of a sleeping draught. You comprehend me? But Captain Ralph Paton must be cleared—*ça va sans dire*. I should suggest that you finish that very interesting manuscript of yours—but abandoning your former reticence."

"You seem to be very prolific of suggestions," I remarked. "Are you sure you've quite finished."

"Now that you remind me of the fact, it is true that there is one thing more. It would be most unwise on your part to attempt to silence me as you silenced M. Ackroyd. That kind of business does not succeed against Hercule Poirot, you understand."

"My dear Poirot," I said, smiling a little, "whatever else I may be, I am not a fool."

I rose to my feet.

"Well, well," I said, with a slight yawn, "I must be off home. Thank you for a most interesting and instructive evening."

Poirot also rose and bowed with his accustomed politeness as I passed out of the room.

XXVII. APOLOGIA

Five A.M. I am very tired—but I have finished my task. My arm aches from writing.

A strange end to my manuscript. I meant it to be published some day as the history of one of Poirot's failures! Odd, how things pan out.

All along I've had a premonition of disaster, from the moment I saw Ralph Paton and Mrs. Ferrars with their heads together. I thought then that she was confiding in him; as it happened I was quite wrong there, but the idea persisted even after I went into the study with Ackroyd that night, until he told me the truth.

Poor old Ackroyd. I'm always glad that I gave him a chance. I urged him to read that letter before it was too late. Or let me be honest—didn't I subconsciously realize that with a pig-headed chap like him, it was my best chance of getting him *not* to read it? His nervousness that night was interesting psychologically. He knew danger was close at hand. And yet he never suspected *me*.

The dagger was an afterthought. I'd brought up a very handy little weapon of my own, but when I saw the dagger lying in the silver table, it occurred to me at once how much better it would be to use a weapon that couldn't be traced to me.

I suppose I must have meant to murder him all along. As soon as I heard of Mrs. Ferrars's death, I felt convinced that she would have told him everything before she died. When I met him and he seemed so agitated, I thought that perhaps he knew the truth, but that he couldn't bring himself to believe it, and was going to give me the chance of refuting it.

So I went home and took my precautions. If the trouble were after all only something to do with Ralph—well, no harm would have been done. The dictaphone he had given me two days before to adjust. Something had gone a little wrong with it, and I persuaded him to let me have a go at it, instead of sending it back. I did what I wanted to it, and took it up with me in my bag that evening.

I am rather pleased with myself as a writer. What could be neater, for instance, than the following:—

"The letters were brought in at twenty minutes to nine. It was just on ten minutes to nine when I left him, the letter still unread. I hesitated with my hand on the door handle, looking back and wondering if there was anything I had left undone."

All true, you see. But suppose I had put a row of stars after the first sentence! Would somebody then have wondered what exactly happened in that blank ten minutes?

When I looked round the room from the door, I was quite satisfied. Nothing had been left undone. The dictaphone was on the table by the window, timed to go off at nine-thirty (the mechanism of that little device was rather clever—based on the principle of an alarm clock), and the arm-chair was pulled out so as to hide it from the door.

I must admit that it gave me rather a shock to run into Parker just outside the door. I have faithfully recorded that fact.

Then later, when the body was discovered, and I had sent Parker to telephone for the police, what a judicious use of words: *"I did what little had to be done!"* It was quite little—just to shove the dictaphone into my bag and push back the chair against the wall in its proper place. I never dreamed that Parker would have noticed that chair. Logically, he ought to have been so agog over the body as to be blind to everything else. But I hadn't reckoned with the trained-servant complex.

I wish I could have known beforehand that Flora was going to say she'd seen her uncle alive at a quarter to ten. That puzzled me more than I can say. In fact, all through the case there have been things that puzzled me hopelessly. Every one seems to have taken a hand.

My greatest fear all through has been Caroline. I have fancied she might guess. Curious the way she spoke that day of my "strain of weakness."

Well, she will never know the truth. There is, as Poirot said, one way out. . . .

I can trust him. He and Inspector Raglan will manage it between them.

I should not like Caroline to know. She is fond of me, and then, too, she is proud. . . . My death will be a grief to her, but grief passes. . . .

When I have finished writing, I shall enclose this whole manuscript in an envelope and address it to Poirot.

And then—what shall it be? Veronal? There would be a kind of poetic justice. Not that I take any responsibility for Mrs. Ferrars's death. It was the direct consequence of her own actions. I feel no pity for her.

I have no pity for myself either.

So let it be veronal.

But I wish Hercule Poirot had never retired from work and come here to grow vegetable marrows.